THE
STORM
DESCENDS

FIRE AND STEEL

VOLUME TWO

—— THE ——

STORM

DESCENDS

GERALD N. LUND

DESERET
BOOK

SALT LAKE CITY, UTAH

© 2015 GNL Enterprises, LP

Library of Congress Cataloging-in-Publication Data

Lund, Gerald N., author.

   The storm descends / Gerald N. Lund.

      pages cm — (Fire and steel ; volume 2)

   ISBN 978-1-62972-106-4 (hardbound : alk. paper)

    1. Families—Germany—Fiction. 2. Families—Utah—Fiction. 3. Mormon families—Fiction. 4. Germany, setting. 5. Utah, setting. 6. Christian fiction. I. Title. II. Series: Lund, Gerald N. Fire and steel ; v. 2.

   PS3562.U485S76 2015

   813'.54—dc23   2015028563

Printed in the United States of America
Publishers Printing, Salt Lake City, UT

10   9   8   7   6   5   4   3   2   1

Steel is tempered through three dynamic forces:
The fire of the forge.
The hammer and the anvil.
Being thrust into the fire and then plunged into cold water.

—PREFACE, *A GENERATION RISING*, XI–XII

Let them beware . . .
[lest they] stumble and fall when the storms descend,
and the winds blow, and the rains descend,
and beat upon their house.

—DOCTRINE AND COVENANTS 90:5

Yea, they shall not be beaten down by the storm at the last day;
yea, neither shall they be harrowed up by the whirlwinds;
but when the storm cometh
they shall be gathered together in their place,
that the storm cannot penetrate to them;
yea, neither shall they be driven with fierce winds.

—ALMA 26:6

INTRODUCTION

This section is not part of the novel. It is an introduction to the novel. Readers may be tempted to skip over it, but I would encourage you not to because I believe it will greatly enrich your reading experience. It will help you better appreciate the setting and circumstances in which the characters of the novel find themselves.

The end of World War I was a time of great instability, political upheaval, social disintegration, and personal privation. The impact on individuals and families was profound and prolonged. I don't know how many times over the years I have heard people ask, "How could a man like Hitler ever come to power in a state as civilized and advanced as Germany?"

I believe context is the key to understanding. If we better understand the historical and cultural context of that day, it will no longer surprise us that an unknown Austrian corporal with a funny little mustache was able to step onto the stage of history greeted by the thunderous applause of a desperate and grateful people.

While there were many underlying causes for Germany's difficulties, three converging forces came together as World War I ended.

They created a perfect storm of political, social, and cultural crises that would plunge Germany and her people into chaos.

The October Revolution in Russia, 1917

Karl Marx wrote his *Communist Manifesto* in 1848. In terms of its impact on history, it was and is a pivotal document. His call for the revolution of the proletariat (the working classes) against the bourgeoisie (the middle and upper classes and their materialistic values) struck a responsive chord in nations where the various monarchies and noble families of Europe flaunted their wealth on every side and maintained their power and wealth through crushing exploitation of the poor. Filled with corruption, inefficiency, and lavish extravagances, various royal families had gradually turned their worshipful subjects into serfs seething with anger and resentment.

This spawned a new political and economic ideology called socialism. Socialism advocated that the institutions of production, distribution, and exchange of goods should be owned, controlled, and regulated by the community as a whole; in short, by the people. And usually, that term meant the working classes.

In Russia, the Romanov Dynasty, which had ruled for 300 years, had become particularly corrupt and was therefore especially vulnerable to this rising resentment. Talk of overthrow and devastating defeats and catastrophic losses to the Germans in World War I so demoralized the people that revolution became commonplace. In October 1917, it became reality.

That month, Vladimir Lenin and his Bolshevik political party overthrew the monarchy and nationalized all land, businesses, and property. Eventually, he had the last of the Romanovs assassinated.

The revolution created a shock wave that reverberated through Europe like a massive tsunami, particularly in countries under the sphere and influence of Mother Russia. People's and workers' parties began springing up everywhere, finding particular success among the labor unions and other working poor. Russia secretly offered financial aid to these revolutions and sent in their agents to train, motivate, and radicalize local socialist movements.

Three things made Germany a particularly ripe target. First, they were now one of Europe's leading national powers. Second, Germany was only 200 miles away from Russia's borders. Third, and most important, as World War I finally came to an end, Germany was reeling. What had been the most powerful and feared military power on the continent was in shambles. The German people were dazed and disillusioned, blaming their government for the debacle and the loss of about two million of their youngest and finest men. The harsh terms imposed upon them by the Allied forces were humiliating, and they seethed with resentment.

Barely a year had passed since Lenin had triggered the Russian tsunami in Moscow, but Germany's defenses were down. And a flood of revolution smashed its way across the Fatherland. In a matter of weeks, royal dynasties all across Europe began falling like ninepins. Fourteen of the twenty-five states in the German Empire, including all four kingdoms, were already securely in the hands of revolutionaries by December of 1918. Red flags waved over numerous royal palaces. Soldier and worker "councils" ruled many cities.

Hunger and cold stalked the land. The old, the young, and the poor—as always—were the ones hardest hit by food and fuel shortages. Starvation stalked the land. People were freezing to death in their own homes. There was social upheaval on every side, and cultural chaos was the order of the day.

And there was no end in sight.

World War I and the Armistice of Compiègne

By late summer of 1918, it was becoming increasingly obvious that Germany was going to lose the war they had started in 1914. They agreed to an armistice with the Allied Forces that led to a cessation of hostilities without having to accept a full surrender.

The victorious Allies, determined to make the Second Reich pay for their military aggressions, were in no mood for negotiation. When the German delegation arrived at Compiègne, France, to sign the newly drafted armistice, harsh terms were handed to them and they were given little choice but to sign.

There were thirty-five conditions laid down, including the occupation of significant areas of German territory; the surrender of vast amounts of military equipment; the surrender of large amounts of Germany's railway stock; and huge war reparation bills. One American economist predicted it would take Germany more than sixty years to pay them off. One of the most painful of the conditions was that hundreds of thousands of German prisoners-of-war being held by the Allies would not be returned until a formal peace treaty was signed. That did not happen until the signing of the Treaty of Versailles in the summer of 1919.

In addition, the military and civilian bureaucrats responsible for the implementation of the armistice often imposed additional restrictions on the people. For example, in addition to the food shortages and rationing caused by the war, a new "hunger blockade" descended on Germany. The confiscation of large amounts of German railway equipment under the guise of reducing Germany's power to wage war meant that even where food was available, there was not the means to transport it to cities.

German fishermen were forbidden to fish in their own territorial waters, further reducing the availability of meat to a starving people. Even with ration coupons, the people could only get fish once every three or four weeks.

To add further insult to injury, vast stores of German food and other goods still in France were either destroyed or sold to locals at greatly reduced prices instead of being shipped back to Germany where they were so badly needed (191).

This all came as a devastating blow to the German people, who had been led to believe that their willingness to stop fighting would lead to significant concessions from the Allies. In a matter of weeks, the whole country was suffering from physical, mental, moral, and spiritual shock and exhaustion. As one historian noted, "A wave of stupefied indignation and resentment followed the publication of its [the Armistice's] terms, and this feeling was increased by the general realization of Germany's helplessness" (189).

In the long view, the harshness of the Allied conditions would come back to haunt them. The combination of socialist revolution sweeping across Europe and utter demoralization of the German people created a perfect tinderbox for those waiting in the wings. Even Socialists, Communists, Bolsheviks, and anarchists had trouble believing the opportunity that had been dropped in their laps. Joyously, they rushed in to fill the vacuum.

Die Neue Freiheit

As Socialists and Communists toppled one government after another—in municipalities, towns, cities, states, and even nations—their rallying cry became, "*Die neue Freiheit*" (the New Freedom). Throw off the shackles of the bourgeoisie's laws and institutions of authority; experience the liberating freedom of the new order—that was the cry. And hundreds of thousands embraced it with wild enthusiasm. The results were devastating.

Leftist-leaning sailors mutinied and seized a government building in Berlin. In the army, while most frontline soldiers remained steadfast in the final days of the war, many rear echelon units, which were filled with men sympathetic to the socialist cause, threw order and discipline to the wind. They deserted their posts, leaving huge stores and munitions behind. They looted, raped, and terrified the villages where they were posted and then straggled back to the homeland to be welcomed as heroes by the revolutionists (194). They seized palaces and castles and government buildings and then looted them of their treasures and urinated on whatever was left.

Army deserters took whatever motor vehicles were at hand and

raced through the city streets at breakneck speed, deliberately breaking the speed limits, with the helpless police unable to stop them. In
Berlin, cabmen drove unwashed and unshaven hooligans up the wrong
side of major thoroughfares to show just how free they had become.
Gambling sprang up on street corners. Other army deserters set up im-
provised booths and sold cigarettes, soap, and other materials they had
looted from army storehouses (196).

Logic and common sense went out the window as insanity swept
in. Any hope that the new order would bring stability quickly faded
as the new "freedom" became the new reality. Peoples' Revolutionary
Councils and Soldiers' Revolutionary Councils stormed the halls of
government, occupied railway stations and telegraph offices, and commandeered centers of distribution. In most cases the populace let them
seize power without bloodshed and in some cases even cheered them
on, desperate for anything that might change their wretched circumstances. But the euphoria was quickly dashed.

The new rulers paid themselves exorbitant salaries even though
their incompetence was breathtaking. They squandered public funds
at a rate that would have shocked even the most corrupt of previous
governments. Public services ground to a halt. As kings and princes
and kaisers and governors and chancellors fled for their safety, the new
"rulers" took their place. A man who was an avowed atheist and who
could neither read nor write was appointed director of schools and
master of churches in Berlin (209). The new Republic of Brunswick
appointed a tailor's assistant as their president, and he chose a house-
hold servant who scrubbed floors as his secretary of education (222).

Inspired by the philosophy of the "Brotherhood of Man," many of
the new socialist governments opened the doors of the jails and pris-
ons and flooded the country with criminals.

The working classes unquestionably had many legitimate reasons
for hating the so-called "guardians of law and order" in previous governments. But their solution was to disarm and throw out the police

and replace them with those who belonged to the new order, including some of the recently released criminals. Few of these new "officers of the law" were motivated to enforce law and order. But even if they had the inclination, they had no idea how to do it. Crime became rampant and, as usually happens, the poor were the most frequent victims. The result of this "liberated" philosophy was utter chaos (185).

To a nation already reeling from loss of loved ones, near economic collapse, widespread unemployment, food and fuel shortages, violence in the streets, and constant political upheaval, the revolution became one more burden to bear, one more crisis to deal with. As Bouton puts it, "The people, starving, their physical, mental and moral powers of resistance gone, were ready to follow the demagogue who made the most glowing promises" (184).

Chapter Note

Most of this information comes from S. Miles Bouton, *And the Kaiser Abdicates: The German Revolution, November, 1918–August, 1919*, Yale University Press, 1921. The page citations above all refer to this book.

PART
1

CHAPTER 1

*December 1, 1918, 12:57 a.m.—Pasewalk Military Hospital,
northeast of Berlin, Germany*

Emilee Fromme stood by the window of the trauma ward, staring out into the near darkness. Though the war had officially ended over two weeks ago, the Pasewalk city fathers were still in the process of restoring power to the city's street lamps. But there was enough light reflected off the low overcast that she could see that it was snowing quite heavily now.

She wrinkled her nose at the thought of walking home in just her nurse's shoes and thin cotton stockings. It served her right.

Earlier she had checked the forecast in the newspaper. It predicted snow the next afternoon, but just overcast skies until then. But the forecasts were usually slower than the actual storms.

Turning around, Emilee leaned back against the windowsill and let her eyes move over to bed number nine, which was directly across the aisle from where she stood. Only two small lights in the ward were left on at night, one at each end. But in the dim light she could still see that patient #42350 was sleeping fitfully, one leg twitching spasmodically.

Normally at this time on her night shift, Sergeant Hans Otto Eckhardt was awake, waiting for her to come and read to him as she did every night after her one o'clock rounds. So it was surprising to see him still sleeping. It was disappointing in a way. She looked forward to their time nearly as much as he did. But she was relieved in a way, too, because this night was going to be different than usual.

The first difference was going to be that she had not brought the *Berlin Morning Post* with her tonight. That was the morning news-paper that came by train from Berlin each day. When she had first started reading to Hans, he hadn't wanted to hear anything that reminded him of the war. Their first project had been Jane Austen's *Pride and Prejudice*. And for a while, they had stuck to novels. But on November 10th, she had brought the *Berlin Morning Post* with her and showed him the blazing headlines announcing the abdication of Kaiser Wilhelm II and the creation of a new German Republic. She read the other major article on the collapse of the Second German Reich, or German Empire. That was followed the next night with the details of the signing of the Armistice Agreement in France, which formally ended the Great War. It was that night she had begun to wonder if this was such a good idea. He was so incensed that the new government had given way to the Allies that he was still awake and fuming when she came by on her rounds an hour later. They had then had a long and passionate discussion about what this meant for the Fatherland in general and for their own lives and families in particular. It had been pretty depressing to them both.

And that had become their pattern thereafter. He no longer wanted light reading. Hans was obsessed with what was happening to their country. Emilee would bring the paper each time and share with him the turmoil and upheaval going on all around them. The articles about political and social unrest interested him the most. He made her read every word of every pertinent article and then, in some cases, read them again. It was ironic, actually. She had told her supervising nurses that she read to him because he couldn't sleep. But now, he would vacillate between frustrated rage and sorrow so deep it almost left him weeping, and sleep was forgotten.

As for Emilee, normally when she went off shift and went to bed she would be asleep in minutes. But now she too would lie awake, brooding on what this meant for her, for her family, and for the future. What kind of a world were they facing? What would be left of their beloved Fatherland for the next generation?

In 1914, the German people had sent their men off to war with grand and joyous celebrations. There were speeches and parades, rallies and hundred-gun salutes. Martial music filled the air and citizens lined the streets, waving flags and throwing flower petals as the men marched past. Women draped floral wreaths on the tanks and trucks and heavy cannons as they rumbled by.

Four years of war had changed all that. Two million of their young men were either dead or missing in action. Hundreds of thousands more were in Allied prison camps and wouldn't be released until Germany signed a formal peace treaty. It was a rare German family that hadn't lost someone. The economy was reeling from the enormous costs of the war and reparations. Add to that the food and fuel shortages. Add to that the fact that at the same time millions of young men were returning home to look for work, the war industries were laying off hundreds of thousands of workers. The unemployment rate was rapidly approaching half of the employable population.

The jubilation was gone. Now, the same people who had thrown flowers and waved flags seethed with rage. The result was almost universal disillusionment, discouragement, despondency, and growing desperation.

Emilee sighed. It was happening again, and she hated it. She hated the pall of impending disaster that hung over them. So, let Hans be annoyed that she had not brought a newspaper tonight. There were more pressing things they needed to discuss. He might not agree with that, but in her mind, the two of them were approaching a crossroad that couldn't be ignored any longer.

When she had come on shift at 10:30 last night, there was a note attached to Hans's patient chart. "Sergeant Hans Otto Eckhardt, patient #42350, has been approved for discharge from the hospital. Please see that he is at the hospital administrator's office at 9:00 a.m., Monday, 2 December, 1918."

She had known it had to happen sooner or later, but to actually see it in writing had hit her pretty hard. Just like that, Sergeant Hans Otto Eckhardt was going to walk out of her life. Unless she did something about it tonight. Monday morning was less than thirty hours away, and she didn't work Sunday nights. Her next shift started Monday night at 10:30 p.m. By that point Hans could be halfway across Germany.

Emilee kept telling herself that maybe that was for the best, but "herself" refused to listen. She had to know. Maybe he would still walk away, but if she didn't make some effort to clarify their relationship, not knowing what might have been would haunt her for a long time.

From the first day she had started nursing school at age seventeen, her instructors had hammered the neophyte nurses about the dangers of hospital romances. One professor had thundered at them, "You may actually do irreparable harm to the patient, and you will almost certainly find yourself looking for new employment." Two of Emilee's friends had proven him right. One friend broke things off with her patient when he began pressing her to marry him. When she refused, he attempted suicide. The other friend, who had also worked the midnight shift, had given herself to a sailor one night when they slipped into an empty room for privacy. They became "engaged" as the affair continued. A month later, when he received news of his discharge, he slipped away without saying good-bye and she never heard from him again.

Those had been vivid lessons for her, and she had kept her relationships cordial but distant, warm but professional.

Until Sergeant Eckhardt arrived.

He was not the most horribly injured or disfigured patient she had dealt with. Though he carried over a hundred shrapnel wounds in his body—including one that had nearly blinded him—they were nothing compared to the man whose legs had been blown off by a land mine, or the soldier whose lungs were so badly seared by mustard gas that every breath was agony for him.

Emilee had been on duty one night when a new trainload of patients, including Sergeant Eckhardt, had arrived from France. She had been tasked with cleaning him and preparing him for surgery. His clothes were filthy and caked with mud. He had no boots on, only filthy, woolen socks. His hair and whiskers were matted with blood.

But as the man beneath the dirt and grime and blood gradually emerged, she discovered that he was quite good-looking. His hair and week-old whiskers were a light blond, the kind of blond hair that many women would give a month's salary to possess for themselves. His facial features were stark, even gaunt, but beneath the ravages of war she thought she discerned intelligence and strength of character. His body was as lean as a greyhound's, but his shoulders were broad and his torso like steel cords. When the doctor had pried one eye open to check for signs of concussion, she had been startled by their color. They were a light blue, like a robin's egg or a summer sky in the morning.

Remembering the counsel about hospital romances, she had pushed him out of her mind. Then one night as she was doing her rounds, he asked her to read to him. He was having recurring nightmares, he said. He couldn't go back to sleep, he said. She agreed, and it quickly became her nightly routine.

As the nights came and went, Emilee learned that her initial impression had been correct. Hans was intelligent, funny, and often deeply profound. This drew her to him in ways that surprised her. On the other hand, there was another side of him that greatly annoyed her. He was unashamedly self-centered, often moody and petulant. His

7

intensity was almost frightening sometimes. If she disagreed with him on a topic and was able to best him in arguing her point, he would withdraw and sulk like a little boy.

One memory of him that still cut deeply every time she thought of it was from the day his bandages were removed and the doctors told him he wasn't blind. She had been finished with her shift by then but asked the eye surgeon if she might stay for the unveiling. The surgeon's nurse, Magda Rhinehart, who was a good friend of Emilee's, was a statuesque brunette who turned men's heads wherever she went. She was standing near Hans when he opened his eyes. Emilee would never forget what she saw in his eyes when they focused on Magda—first surprise, then pleasure, then amazement. Emilee had been standing back in the corner watching. Magda got that reaction from men on a regular basis.

Then, as everyone else left, Emilee came forward. Hans stuck out his hand and introduced himself. Though they had talked for hours together by that point, he, of course, had never seen her. But the moment she spoke, he knew who she was. And she had been watching closely for his reaction. This time it went from surprise to open disappointment before finally turning into a warm smile.

His disappointment at seeing her was in sharp contrast to his amazement at seeing Magda. Not that it surprised her. She knew what she was. Her hair was a mousy brown and usually pulled back in a bun when she was at work. Her eyes were all right, a little darker shade of blue than his, but her nose looked like it had been stuck on as an afterthought. And she tended to be a little plump, even though she was careful about what she ate. She was honest enough to acknowledge that people liked her, but no one called her beautiful. In fact, her mother, with the typical bluntness of many German parents, summed it up with two words. "You're plain, my *Liebchen,* and there's nothing to be done about it." Before his passing, her father, who had idolized her, tried to soften it by saying, "But you have character, Emmy. A good man will recognize that in you." This only told her that he agreed with her mother's assessment.

Emilee took a quick breath. Tonight she would try to find out just how important her physical beauty—or lack of it—was to Sergeant Eckhardt. It was time, and while it excited her to perhaps get a clearer idea of what his feelings for her were, she could not shake the idea that this might be their last time together.

She sighed, this time with a deep weariness. Reaching into her apron pocket, she fingered the three letters there. These were not going to help in her quest. In fact, they might prove to be pivotal in ending it once and for all. But she had to know. How Hans reacted to these letters might be pivotal for her too, for she was deeply disturbed by what had happened the night before.

The previous night, Hans had dozed off while Emilee was sitting by his bedside reading to him. She decided to wait for a moment to see whether he would wake up again or their time together was over for the night. As she sat there, she noticed something in the small waste bin beside his bed. Curious, she leaned in closer. To her surprise, there were three envelopes there with his name on them. However, they were addressed to the Ministry of War in Berlin and had been forwarded on to Pasewalk. The return address was a village in Bavaria. That and the fact that they showed a woman's handwriting led Emilee to assume these were letters from Hans's mother, or perhaps a sister. But what puzzled her was that none of the three had been opened.

When Hans awoke a few minutes later she asked him about them, thinking perhaps they had been knocked into the waste bin by mistake. To her total surprise, he angrily snatched them out of her hand and stuffed them back in the waste bin. "I put them there," he snapped. "That's where they belong."

Only later did the whole episode begin to bother her. Why the War Ministry? Why not send them directly to the hospital? The answer hit her hard. Because his family didn't know he was here. Could that be? He had been here almost a month—surely he would have written to his parents by that point. The more she thought about it, the more it disturbed her. Maybe there was some logical explanation, but for the life of her she couldn't see what it might be. So on her rounds two hours later, seeing that he was sleeping deeply again, she had retrieved the letters. Tonight, she was going to find out what was going on.

And with that thought, she turned, took a deep breath, and walked swiftly over to bed number nine. Bending down, she peered into his face. There was no question about it. His eyes were closed and his face was in calm repose. His chest rose and fell rhythmically. Disappointed, she reached out a hand to wake him and then pulled it back. One of the policies her night supervisor held to very strictly was that no patient should be woken unless it was for medications, treatment, or some other emergency.

With a sigh, she backed away. Maybe on the two o'clock rounds.

Chapter Note

In *A Generation Rising,* volume one of this series, I identified Pasewalk Military Hospital as being located in Berlin (see, for example, page 245). That was because one of my American sources listed the town as being "near" Berlin. But further research reveals that Pasewalk is actually a small town about eighty miles northeast of Berlin. Though someone from the United States might say that Pasewalk was near Berlin, residents of the city would probably not.

CHAPTER
2

December 1, 1918, 2:05 a.m.—Pasewalk Military Hospital

Emilee entered the ward an hour later, stopping for a moment to let her eyes adjust to the dim light. Then she moved forward, her soft soles making no sound on the linoleum, until she stopped at the foot of bed number nine. As she did so, she noticed that Sergeant Eckhardt's right foot was jerking a little under the covers. Then she heard a soft moan. Moving up to stand beside him, she was startled to see that his eyes were wide open, staring up at the ceiling.

"Hans?"

He didn't respond, so she bent down and laid a hand on his arm. "Hans, it's Emilee." She shook his arm a little to get his attention.

He came awake like an exploding volcano, arms flailing, fists clenched, eyes wild. Yet he made not a sound. She fell back a step and then leaned in again. "Hans, it's me. Wake up."

He struck out at her, and his fist struck her hard on her upper arm. With a cry, she jerked away before he could strike her again. But the chair beside his bed was right behind her. She tripped over it and fell backward. Her elbow smashed into the bed post and sent stabbing flames of fire up her arm. She threw her upper body across the lower part of his bed and managed to pin down his legs. He went berserk, grunting softly, kicking and writhing like a madman. One foot caught Emilee full in the face, knocking her back.

Fortunately, Hans was barefooted. If he had been wearing his boots, he would have smashed her cheekbone. As it was, lights flashed across her vision, and she was momentarily blinded. But instinctively, she again threw her full weight across the thrashing legs. "Hans!" she hissed. "It's me. It's Emilee."

He was rolling back and forth, flailing at her with his fists, trying to get free of her. She could hear him grunting, but that was all. Desperately, she buried her face against his legs and held on. "It's Emilee, Hans. It's all right."

Finally reality registered and the thrashing slowed. Hans fell back against his pillow, gasping for breath. His eyes were still wild as he looked around. In the dimness of the night lights of the hospital ward, there wasn't much to see. Finally he raised his head. "Emilee?"

She pushed herself up, fighting the impulse to clutch at her cheek, which impossibly was both completely numb and registering flashes of blinding pain. She reached out for his hand, found it, and hung on. "Yes, Hans. I'm here."

He fell back, swearing softly under his breath. "I thought you were. . . ." He couldn't finish it. After a moment he pulled himself up on one elbow, staring at her, his eyes glowing spots of light in the near darkness. He blew out his breath in a long, painful sigh. She sensed his body starting to relax. "What are you doing here?" he finally gasped.

She got slowly to her feet, peering at the beds on either side of her. No one seemed to be awake.

She moved quickly to stand beside him. "It's just after two a.m., Hans," she whispered. "I came to read to you. You were asleep at one o'clock."

He was still gasping for breath, but she could see sanity starting to return. She took his hand. "I'm sorry I startled you. I thought you were awake."

He squeezed her hand. "I was awake. I . . . I must have dozed off." Then suddenly he sat up, peering at her. "Was that you I just kicked?" he asked, horrified. "Are you hurt?"

"No." She managed a shaky laugh. "Well, just my cheek." Then she forced herself to chuckle. "And my right arm. And my knee. But other than that, I'm all right."

"Oh, Emilee, I'm so sorry."

She pulled up a chair, sat down beside him, and took both of his hands. "It's all right. I shouldn't have come up to you without warning like that."

He turned his head and looked at her. "Which cheek?" he asked. She pulled away and gingerly felt her left cheek with her fingertips. "This one." He reached up to touch it, but she shrank back. The numbness was leaving now and it hurt like fury. "It's all right."

"Ah, Emilee," he exclaimed. "I'll bet you'll have a black eye by morning. And then what are you going to tell people?"

"I'll tell them I had a little accident," she said with a thin smile. "Like maybe I tripped and fell out of the fourth-story window or something."

He didn't laugh. He closed his eyes as if he were the one in pain. For a moment she thought of the envelopes, but then she decided this was definitely not the time. But his eruption had reminded her of something else she wanted to talk to him about.

"Hans, can I ask you a question? As your nurse, not just as a friend?"

"What?" That approach had clearly taken him aback.

"'Are you still seeing that associate of yours? Hitler, I think his name is?"

"Adolf? Yes. We talk often. What of it?"

"Did you see him yesterday?"

"Yes. We spent about an hour talking about what's happening in the country right now." It was said with deep bitterness. "He finds it as appalling and upsetting as I do. Why do you ask?" This time there was an edge to his voice.

She sat in her chair debating whether she dared say this or not. Finally, she took both of his hands. "Hans, again, I'm talking as your nurse now. I'm wondering if seeing him is a good idea." She rushed on as his eyebrows lowered. "A friend of mine works on that ward. She told me that you were there and—"

"And she told you that he's a madman?" he sneered.

That surprised her. "Not at all. Actually, she thinks he's brilliant. Mesmerizing is another word she uses."

He relaxed a little. "He is brilliant. His grasp of what is happening in the Fatherland right now is amazing. Visionary!"

"It's just that . . ." A quick sigh, then she plunged. "My friend said you were both quite agitated when you finished talking. Very upset. Maybe that is what's causing your nightmares. Getting all worked up can do that."

"Of course I'm upset," he snapped. "The November Criminals are destroying all that we fought for. Germany is crumbling all around us, and no one is doing anything."

That was a blatant overstatement, but she let it pass. "I know, Hans. I know. And I believe Adolf's right. The state of our country upsets me a great deal too."

"Then why does it bother you if I see him? He's a brave man. Did you know that he has been awarded two Iron Crosses? Two!"

"I didn't know that. But I wasn't questioning his bravery, Hans. And it doesn't bother *me* if you see him. But I'm wondering if it not's bothering *you*. When you first came to the hospital, you had nightmares almost every night. Then gradually, they started to go away. But I've noticed that on the days when you talk with him, the bad dreams seem to come back."

That mollified Hans a little, but he still seemed irritated. "Well, you don't have to worry about it. He was discharged this morning. By now, he's back in Munich. That's where he was going."

"Oh." *And tomorrow morning you're going to be released, and you'll go back to Bavaria. Which does worry me.* But she caught herself and only asked, "So you liked him?"

"Very much." Then, to her surprise, a smile spread slowly across his face. "Except for that ridiculous mustache of his."

She had to laugh. "He seemed very proud of it. My friend said he combed it several times each day to make sure the handlebars on each side were in perfect balance." She suppressed a giggle. "Anyway, not having your discussions anymore may help you sleep better."

Hans's smile instantly vanished. "Why do you insist on blaming him for my nightmares?" Before she could respond, he rushed on. "Do you know who Friedrich Nietzsche is?"

"No, Hans," she shot back, "I don't know who the most famous of all German philosophers is."

He ignored her sarcasm. "Nietzsche once said: 'Whoever fights monsters should see to it that in the process he does not become himself a monster.'"

"Yes, I know that quote."

"Well, maybe that's where my nightmares are coming from, Emilee. Not Adolf Hitler, but from the monster the army has created in me over the last four years." He lay back. "Give that some thought as my nurse, why don't you."

Stung by the sharpness in him, she stood up. "I'm sorry, Hans. I didn't mean it that way." But then her own irritation flared up. "But Nietzsche also said something like, 'Out of chaos are born the stars that dance in the night.'"

His eyes widened a little. "Actually, the quote is, 'One must have chaos in oneself to be able to give birth to a dancing star.'" He flashed a thin smile at her. "And what's a girl like you doing quoting Friedrich Nietzsche?"

"A girl like me?" she repeated, her voice cool. "You mean the little working-class girl who got a nursing degree so she could read books to patients who got their education at"—her voice was suddenly mocking—"the Von Kruger Academy of Academic Excellence?"

"Hey," he said, instantly contrite. "I was just trying to be funny."

"No you weren't."

That rocked him back a little, but then he nodded. "No, I wasn't. I felt like you were treating me like a little kid, and so. . . ."

"You wanted to make me feel like a little kid," she finished for him.

"Yeah, I guess I did. I'm sorry. Okay? Sorry to be so grumpy tonight."

"And I am sorry as well." She sat down again. They were silent for a long moment. She knew there was no way she could talk about the letters right now. And yet she felt that thirty-hour clock ticking away behind her. So she had another thought. It took her a little by surprise—even shocked her some. But it was another way to maybe find out what she needed to know.

She took a quick breath. *Okay. Here we go.* "I know that the war was unbelievably horrible for you. And I think that after working in a military hospital for the last two years, I have some small glimpse of that chaos you're talking about. Will you tell me about it?"

He stared at her, not seeming to comprehend.

"I know this is going to sound strange. But in a way I'm envious of what you have learned from it all. I have often asked myself, 'Would I have the courage to go into battle? Would I give my life for a cause greater than myself?' I don't know the answer to that. But you do. I didn't know you before, but I believe that you are a changed man, Hans. A better man, a stronger and more courageous man for it. And maybe that's the dancing star that's being created from the chaos of war."

He swore. "Don't be naive, Emilee. You have no idea what you're talking about."

She said nothing, a sudden bleakness coming over her. "You're right, Hans," she murmured. "I'm sorry." She got to her feet. "I'd better go now. It's time to start my rounds." She spun on her heel and started away. She only got three steps before she whirled back around. "Here's another quote of Nietzsche's from the quaint little girl from Pasewalk. 'To live is to suffer. To *survive* is to find some meaning in the suffering.' Good-bye, Hans." And she started away again.

"I had a best friend named Franck Zolger," he said as she walked away. His voice was low, almost a whisper.

She stopped and slowly turned to face him again.

"We were in basic training together, and then we were assigned to the same transportation unit and drove trucks together for a couple of years. We were even closer than some brothers."

Emilee returned to her chair and sat down, folding her hands in her lap and staring at them, afraid that if she looked at him he would stop.

"We were delivering a load of supplies to the front line in Verdun. This was after the battle had been raging for months. The morning we were getting ready to return to our unit and load up again, this major came up to us. He was a real aristocrat. Acted like he was the son of a count or something. Anyway, he commandeered me and Franck."

"Commandeered? What does that mean?"

"He made us leave the keys to the truck on the front seat, told us to grab our rifles, and marched us off to the front lines. He said they needed every man up there to turn back the French."

"But what about your other unit? What did your commanding officer there say?"

He shrugged. "He was fifteen miles away. Nobody asked him." Hans hooted in disgust. "He probably thinks Franck and I deserted, for all I know."

"So you went into the trenches?"

Hans nodded. After a moment, he went on. "A day or two

17

later—or maybe it was a week or a month or a century—we were sent out on a recon patrol. A reconnaissance mission. Oh, how we hated that word! Recon. Some fat old sergeant would call us in and say, 'We need to recon where the enemy is.' Which meant, 'Go out and get the French and the British to shoot at you so we know where they are.' So we did.

"We left that night at about twenty-two hundred hours—ten o'clock. It was January. January 6, 1917, to be exact. The night was pitch black, and there were four or five inches of snow on the ground. So we wandered around all night, freezing our tails off, and found absolutely nothing. We knew if we went back too early, our platoon sergeant would kick us from there to the south of France, but we were so numb with cold we couldn't go on anymore. So we sat down to kill some time until we dared to report back in to the sergeant."

He closed his eyes and looked away.

"Tell me, Hans," she whispered. "Please."

"We were seated on this little rise where we could watch the forest below—forest, ha! Most of the trees had been blown to smithereens by that time. But we were still in enemy territory and fully alert. I was sitting next to Franck, maybe a foot or two away from him. I remember watching my breath explode in puffs of mist and then hang there in the frosty air for what seemed like forever. It was so bizarre. Such delicate beauty in a world of shattered trees and shell holes and the ever-present stench of death. Well, anyway, we were sitting there griping about life in the army and arrogant majors and fat platoon sergeants and . . ."

His chest was rising and falling visibly now. "There was the crack of a rifle shot. It was fifty, maybe a hundred yards away. From that distance it sounds like someone smacking a piece of wood against a tree stump. I yelled and dove face first into the snow just as a second shot snapped over my head. "Franck!" I yelled. "Get down! Get down!"

Hans's voice broke, and his shoulders began to shake. "But he was already down. He was lying on his back, staring up at the sky, his eyes. . . ." He shook his head. "I can't get the image of his eyes out of my head. There was no pain in them at all. Just . . . surprise. Like someone had snuck up behind him and poked him with a stick. For a moment I thought he was just being his goofy self, and then I saw the hole in his chest and . . . and the blood. His whole tunic was this mass of dark red."

Emilee wanted to reach out and take his hand or touch his cheek, but she sensed that if she did he would stop talking. So she sat there, feeling sicker and sicker to her stomach.

"One moment we were joking and griping, and then . . ." He turned and looked at her, flicked at the air with the back of his hand, as if shooing away a fly. "Poof! Just like that, he was gone." It was so casual, and such an utterly chilling way to describe a man's death.

Hans closed his eyes and laid back on his pillow. Emilee reached out and laid a hand on his. For two or three minutes they sat like that, him silent, her blinking back tears.

"I was so angry," he finally went on, "that I could barely mourn for him."

"Angry at God?" she whispered.

"Yes. And at the world. At the sniper who shot him. At the sergeant who sent us out there. At that imperious major who ripped us from the safety of our trucks. But yes, mostly at God. Why didn't He warn me we were walking into a trap? Why did He let that French sniper take the first shot at Franck? I was the squad leader. He had to have seen me in the lead." Hans looked over at Emilee. "I know this is an awful thing to say, because all of my squad members were good men, but I would have traded any one of them for Franck without a second thought."

"I am so sorry, Hans." It sounded ridiculous, but what could one say to adequately respond to such random and meaningless horror?

"I never got to see him buried. Don't even know where they took him. Maybe they never did bury him. When I dropped his body off at the field hospital, they sent me right back into the line to stop the attacking French. Maybe he's still out there. His frozen body lying behind a tent."

Not knowing what to say, Emilee said nothing. She just clung to his hand, and he to hers, for a long, long moment.

And then he took a deep breath and continued. "As the months went on, I found myself changing. Oh, I was still angry with whatever God there may be in the heavens, but it wasn't because Franck had been killed anymore. It was because Franck had been killed, and I *hadn't*. I even found myself resenting Franck. How come he had been the lucky one? He got his discharge two years before the war ended. Probably never felt a thing. And I was the one left behind."

He turned and looked at Emilee. His mouth was twisted into a smile, but it was cold and bitter. "Is that the chaos that you're hoping will create my dancing star?" he asked.

"Hans, I. . . ."

"I can't tell you how many times I lay out there in the cold and the muck, bullets snapping overhead and mustard gas rolling down the hill at us like some living monster, and cursed God for taking Franck and not me."

Hans's head was turned so that the lamplight fell on his face and softly illuminated it. Now Emilee could see that his eyes—normally so blue that they reminded her of the morning sky—were dark and brooding and the color of glacial ice. Finally, he looked up at her. "I remember enduring an endless artillery bombardment that went on for ninety-six hours. Ninety-six hours! Think of it. That's four straight days without letup! Shells going off every thirty to forty seconds. We were all going slowly mad. Suddenly, I leaped out of my foxhole, threw back my arms, and bared my face to the sky. Shells were screeching overhead. Explosions shook the ground. Shrapnel was flying around me as if someone had kicked over a hornets' nest. I stood there for a moment, and then I shook my fist at the sky and screamed at God. 'Take *me*! I dare you. I'm here. Take me now!'"

"Were you hit by any of the shrapnel?"

"Not a scratch. I must have stood out there for two or three minutes—screaming, ranting, cursing. And nothing. And then it came to me. I realized why nothing was happening. Because God wasn't there. I was screaming into a void."

"And my thought was just the opposite," she said quietly.

"What?" He turned, blinking at her.

"You went through an artillery barrage without a scratch. Maybe God was protecting you."

"Ha!" he cried. "If He was, why didn't He protect me when we were being shelled by our own artillery and I ran for help? Answer that one, if you can."

She hesitated and then decided his question demanded an answer. "You came out of it alive," she said. "You didn't lose a leg or an arm. You came within a fraction of an inch of having your optic nerve severed, but it was spared."

He was staring at her, shocked that she would dare to question his anger, his agony. "It was just pure luck," he muttered. "God had nothing to do with it."

"Why is it that we always curse God when bad things happen to us, but when good things happen, it's good luck or a happy coincidence? Maybe—" She felt her face go instantly hot and hoped the light was dim enough that he couldn't see it. "Just maybe the Lord let you get wounded that day so that you would be brought to a military hospital in the far north of Germany, hundreds of miles away from your home. Maybe there was someone there you were supposed to meet."

"I. . . ." He clamped his mouth shut again.

Emilee managed an embarrassed smile. "I see that my boldness has left you speechless."

"I. . . ." Then, to her surprise, he laughed. "You're kind of feisty, aren't you?"

"Far too feisty, according to my mother." She got to her feet. "Now,

Hans, I really do have to do my next rounds or my supervisor is going to come hunting for me."

Before he could protest, she hurried on. "But I need to tell you something really quickly." And she told him about the note that was in his chart.

That shocked him into silence. "So tomorrow morning?" He finally asked.

"Yes. Isn't that wonderful?"

"Will you be there? Can you stay after you get off your shift?" He gave her a sly look. "Because the moment I am released as a patient here, you have no excuse for not giving me your address and phone number."

"Today is my day off, so I don't work tonight. But, yes, if I can, I'll come back on Monday. However, my mother is coming to visit me today. To celebrate the beginning of Advent."

That caught him by surprise. "Advent? Is it Advent already?"

"Yes, it is. It begins the fourth Sunday before Christmas, and that's today. I'm not sure yet how long she will be staying, probably through Wednesday or Thursday, but I think I can slip away long enough to be here to congratulate you on your discharge."

"And give me your address and phone number?"

She smiled coyly. "Yes."

He fell back on the pillow, genuinely pleased. "And when I walk out of the administrator's office, I won't be a patient here anymore, will I?"

"No," she said slowly, feeling her pulse quicken a little. "Why do you ask?"

"Because the minute we step out of those doors, I'm going to ask you if you would consider letting me take you out to dinner or—"

"Yes, I would." Now it felt as if her face were glowing in the dark. Her forwardness was taking her breath away.

His eyes widened. "And if I were to ask if I might come and meet your—"

"Yes, you can."

He was ecstatic. "Really?"

She laughed softly. "Yes, really. And now, Sergeant Eckhardt," she said in an officious tone, "no more questions. I have to do my rounds and you need to sleep."

He wiggled deeper under his covers, grinning up at her. "I am tired. Will you stop and see me when you're off shift?"

As he asked that question, Emilee started to put her hands in her pocket. As she did so, her hand touched the envelopes again. She actually started, remembering her determination to get to the bottom of this. And then came a flash of inspiration. "Hans, I have a better idea. There is one other thing that I would like to talk to you about." She was blushing yet again. She couldn't believe how brazen she was being. "Breakfast isn't served until eight. What if I met you in the solarium at ten after seven, after I'm off? There's usually no one there that early. It will only take a few minutes."

His grin was like an electric torch in the darkness. "Nurse Fromme," he said with great solemnity, "you tell me when and where, and I don't care how far it is or how hard it is to get there, I *will* be there. *Verstehen?*"

She laughed. "Yes, I understand." She touched his hand briefly and then hurried away.

Chapter Notes

Almost everyone is familiar with Adolf Hitler's iconic mustache that he wore throughout his years as supreme leader of the Third Reich. But archivists have found pictures of him in the army. And his mustache at that point was jet black and what we call a handlebar mustache, which was quite a popular style at that time.

After his rise to power, some of Adolf Hitler's enemies accused him of having been a coward in combat. The evidence suggests just the opposite. After the first battle of Ypres, he was awarded the Iron Cross, Second Class, for bravery. Just three months before the end of the war, he was given the Iron Cross, First Class, a decoration that was rarely given to a common soldier in the old Imperial Army. A member of his unit later said this was awarded after he singlehandedly captured fifteen enemy soldiers (see *Third Reich,* 29–30).

The quotes from Friedrich Nietzsche come from http://www.brainyquote .com/quotes/authors/f/friedrich_nietzsche.html#dqDrgB2Ikz6CwpKU.99

CHAPTER 3

December 1, 1918, 7:15 a.m.—Pasewalk Military
Hospital solarium

The swinging door to the solarium had a round porthole window so people could see who was coming through from either direction. It did not surprise Emilee when she looked through the window and saw that Hans was already inside. He was still in his pajamas and a bathrobe, pacing back and forth. She looked around, then, seeing he was alone, she pushed the door open and went in. Hans was instantly across the room and taking her hand. "I was afraid after last night you wouldn't—" he stopped, gaping at her face. "Oh, Emilee. I did that to you?"

One finger came up and she gingerly explored the purplish-brown half circle around her eye, which was now half shut. "You didn't mean to." Then she smiled. "But, the staff didn't buy my fourth-story explanation. I'll need to think of another excuse. Did you sleep?" she added.

"I did. I slept hard. It felt good."

"No more nightmares?"

"No."

"I'm glad." She pointed to two overstuffed chairs in front of the large window that looked out over the south lawn. "Let's sit. I don't have a lot of time. As I mentioned, my mother is coming in from Königsberg later today. I have to get things ready for her."

As they sat down facing each other he asked, "You're from East Prussia?"

"That's where I was born, yes. My father was a smelter worker at a steel plant there. When the war broke out, a family friend suggested I become a nurse, which I did. And I came down here to work at the hospital. I've been here not quite two years now. My mother and two brothers still live in East Prussia."

"You don't sound like you're from East Prussia. I hear they've got a distinct accent."

She smiled. "No, it's the rest of the country that has the accent."

Laughing, he nodded. "I guess that's how we Bavarians feel, too."

She hesitated for a moment, looking for a way to ease into this, and then decided there wasn't time to finesse it. Reaching into her pocket, Emilee gripped the letters in her fingers. "Hans, I have something I need to give you."

He brightened. "Is it your address and phone number?"

"You are hopeless," she said, shaking her head. "No, it is not. Not until you are no longer a patient here."

She pulled the letters out and laid them on her lap. Hans's eyes widened slightly as he saw what they were. "What are those?"

"You know what they are."

"You took them out of the waste bin?"

"I did."

"You had no right to do that," he said, scowling at her darkly.

"I know. And you had no right to throw your mother's letters away without even opening them."

He didn't answer. Neither did he take them from her.

"Are they from your mother?" she asked.

Still he wouldn't answer.

"I'll take that as a yes."

"Did you read them?" he snapped

The sudden coldness startled her. "Of course not." She thrust them out further. He still didn't take them, so she tossed them onto his lap and stood up. "I have to go, Hans."

That finally got through to him. He picked up the letters. "No, Emilee. Don't go. Not yet." Then, shocking her deeply, he lifted the three letters and tore them in half. Then he got up and tossed them in a nearby rubbish bin. "Please sit down," he pleaded.

She was too shocked to respond.

"Emilee. Please."

She glared at him. "*Are* they from your mother?"

"Yes, but—"

"And you tore them up? Why?"

His mouth pinched into a tight line. "That's what I'm trying to tell you, if you'll just let me."

"I'm waiting."

He motioned to the chair, and after a moment she sat down. Then he sat down next to her. He turned and looked out the windows at the pristine snow that now covered everything. And then he began to talk, speaking quickly and almost in a monotone. He told her quickly about how his father had engineered his early education with Herr Holzer in Oberammergau, even though it was beyond the family's means. He explained how that had led to his acceptance at the Von Kruger Academy. Emilee was struck by how open he was about his superior achievements, about the awards he had won and the honors he had received.

"Halfway through my fourth and final year, I was accepted into the engineering program at the University of Berlin, with a full scholarship, including books, housing, and living expenses."

That got through to her. "The University of Berlin? That's incredible."

There was a diffident shrug. "The whole academy was envious of me. Me. Hans Otto Eckhardt. The son of a dairyman from Graswang."

Emilee said nothing, just watched as his fingers began to pluck at unseen threads on his robe and his voice grew more and more subdued. Finally, his eyes lifted. In them she saw shame, anger, defiance, humiliation.

"I graduated on the 28th day of May, 1914," he said. "Exactly one month later, Archduke Ferdinand and his wife were assassinated in Sarajevo. Exactly two months after that, on July 28th, Austria declared war on Serbia. Three days later, Germany declared war on Russia, and three days after that, on France. On that day, I quit my job, went to the nearest army recruiting station, and enlisted."

He stopped, and silence filled the room. Finally, Emilee leaned forward. "Did you tell your parents what you were going to do?"

He didn't answer.

"Hans?"

His head came up, and she nearly burst into tears at the anguish she saw in his eyes. His jaw was set like stone, but his lower lip was twitching slightly now. "Once it was official and I was given my uniform, I took the train from Munich down to Graswang. I hadn't said anything about it to my parents. I wanted to surprise them." He hooted softly in self-disgust. "Which I did."

"What did they say?" She waited for several seconds. Nothing. "What did they say, Hans?"

"*Vati* wasn't home when I got there," he whispered. "Only *Mutti.*"

"And what did she say?"

His fists clenched so tightly, his knuckles were white. "She buried her face in her hands and began to sob. 'Oh, Hans,' she cried." His shoulders began to tremble as he fought for control. "'What have you done?' she said. 'Oh, what have you done?'"

Emilee was close to tears now too. "Have you not seen them since then?"

"I've seen them twice. I had a week's leave after basic training. And I got a four-day pass when they discovered my father had cancer."

She understood now, but her emotions were in such a whirl that she could hardly speak. Finally, a thought came. "Hans?"

He looked up.

"Those letters were written to the War Ministry, who forwarded them here."

When he looked up, there was a touch of defiance in the set of his mouth. "So?"

"You've been here for over a month now. Have you not written to your parents and let them know where you are? Do they even know that you were wounded?"

"That's none of your affair."

She just stared at him.

Finally, he held out his hands and showed her how they were trembling. "I can't let them see me like this, Emilee. I can't. I'm in a fury one moment and crying like a baby the next. I wake up screaming in the night. I can barely keep my food down sometimes." He shot her an imploring look. "It would destroy my mother."

"Not any more than thinking you are dead!" she cried. "Hans! What are you thinking? You *have* to write them. The war's ended. They'll be desperate to know where you are. You have to let them know that you're alive and well."

"I'm not well!" he shouted. "I'm nothing but a shattered hulk of what I once was." He shoved his hands beneath his legs to stop them from shaking. "And I cannot—*I will not!*—see them until I am better."

Emilee wanted to jump up, drag Hans out of his chair, and shake him like a little boy. He must have seen that in her eyes because he meekly added, "If I write, *Mutti* will come up here and find me. I think my father is still too sick to travel, so she would have to come alone. She's never been farther than Munich, which is only thirty miles from home."

"Then ask her not to come!" she exploded. "Tell her you're too sick to see anyone. Lie to her about it if you must. But let her know you are alive, Hans. You owe your parents that much. That's the very least you can do." The horror in her was making her voice shrill.

But then she remembered the note in his chart. "But, I guess if you're being released tomorrow, you'll be home before a letter can reach them."

"I'm not going home."

She leaped to her feet again. "*What?*"

"You heard me. And you heard why."

"Where are you going?"

He managed a sickly smile. "I'm not going anywhere. I was hoping to spend some time with a nurse I've met at the hospital."

"Then you will write them today. Now! Or better yet, call them. The main receptionist can connect you to the telephone exchange in Pasewalk."

His head turned away to stare out the window again.

"Hans?"

"There's no telephone exchange in Graswang. Not yet. Oberammergau is five miles away."

"Fine. Then write them. Get it in the morning post."

Suddenly Hans went from anguish to anger. "I have explained to you that I do not have the emotional resilience to face my parents at this point, Emilee. I thought you, of all people, would understand. It saddens me deeply that you do not."

"*Emotional resilience?*" she cried incredulously. "You won the Iron Cross for carrying your best friend to safety under fire, even though he was dead. And you're afraid to face your mother? You can do this, Hans. You *must* do this."

He was staring at the floor, his face sullen, his body rigid. But she was having none of his passive defiance. "Remember what Nietzsche said: 'To live is to suffer. To survive is to find some meaning in the suffering.' My heart breaks for what you are suffering, Hans, but don't let there be no redemption in your suffering."

"What would you know about suffering?" he asked quietly. Then, seeing her reaction to that, he quickly capitulated. "Never mind. All right. I will write them. But you have to let me work this out in my own way. And in my own time."

"Do I?" she cried. She strode back to the waste bin. A moment later she had all six pieces of the letters and shoved them in her pocket.

He was to her in a second. "What are you doing?"

"What you should have done three weeks ago."

"No," he cried. "You will *not* write my mother. I will do it." He held out his hand.

"When?"

"Stop it, woman!" he shouted. "I'll do it when I'm ready and not before."

She shook her head, laughing incredulously. "You still believe it, don't you?"

He blinked. "Believe what?"

"That you're the victim here. That you're caught in your own little tragedy with no way out." His hand shot up, and one finger touched the scar beside his eye.

"*Little* tragedy?" he roared. "I was nearly blinded. I can feel pieces of shrapnel inside my body whenever I move. What do you know about tragedy? You, in your shiny white uniform, all starched and prim? Walking your rounds like some angel from heaven, dispensing loving cheer as if you were serving up Bavarian torte and ice cream."

"Good-bye, Hans." Pushing past him, Emilee started for the door.

"Emilee, stop!" He lunged for her, one hand grabbing for the letters. She slapped his hand away with a vicious swipe of her other hand. He came at her with a roar. Her reaction was instinctive. She slapped his face with every ounce of strength she had. The sound rang out in the empty room like a gunshot.

Hans fell back, so shocked that when he tried to respond, nothing came out of his mouth. Emilee stepped around him and plunged out the door. He started after her but pulled up short when the door slammed open again and she stormed back in.

She stepped up to him, eyes blazing, chest heaving, face white, nostrils flaring. "What do *I* know about tragedy?" she cried. "I have three brothers, one older, two younger. As I told you before, my oldest brother is a bachelor. He was engaged once to a lovely girl from Pasewalk. But when my mother went back to Königsberg, she begged him to go with her, so he broke off the engagement and went with Mama. The girl was so angry, she found someone else and married a few months later. He was heartbroken. I don't think he'll ever marry now."

Hans tried to say something; Emilee rode over him. "My youngest brother is mentally deficient. He has the mental capacity of a ten-year-old. He lives with me because he cannot take care of himself. My other brother, who was three years younger than I am, was drafted into the army at age fourteen. They gave him one week's training with a rifle and sent him off to the Russian front. We have not seen or heard from him since. That was two years ago."

"Emilee, I—"

"My father had to retire from the steel mill four years ago because he had emphysema from all of the smoke and chemicals in the air. And from smoking too many cigarettes. Two years ago, the government conscripted him and put him back in the mills. He was dead less than six months later."

Her words pummeled Hans like machine gun fire. Stricken, his head dropped to his chest. "I . . . I didn't know, Emilee. I'm sorry. I'm sorry. I'm sorry." He started for her, hands out, imploring her for forgiveness.

She jerked away. "There are thousands out there—no, millions!—who are facing their own private hell. My family is just one of them. So forgive me for not falling on my knees and begging your forgiveness for not showing you the sympathy you think you deserve."

Her face was a mottled pink, and her chest was heaving as she stopped for breath. "And while we're quoting the great philosophers, here's another one from Johannes Goethe." Her voice mocked him now. "My, my. Will wonders never cease? Emilee Fromme quoting Nietzsche *and* Goethe, and both in the same day."

"I never...."

She ignored him. "Goethe said, 'It is easier to die than it is to endure a harrowing life with fortitude.' I'm sorry that your life fell apart on you, Hans. I weep when I think of the horrors you have endured. But that's life, Hans. Especially now in Germany. Take it or leave it. Like it or hate it, but at least acknowledge that you are not alone in your suffering."

Beaten, Hans turned and walked back to his seat and slumped into it. "You're right. It's not your burden. I'm sorry that I'm not stronger for you."

"Stop it!" she snapped. "I didn't ask you to be strong. All I asked was that you do the right thing and let your parents know you are still alive. And if you had agreed, then...."

She bit her lower lip and looked away.

He was up again in an instant. "And if I had agreed, then what?"

"I ... I had hopes that somehow you and I could—" She stopped, her cheeks flaming, and quickly looked away.

His eyes widened. "Could what?" he cried.

There was one quick, angry shake of her head. "Life is a gift of infinite worth, Hans. It is not something to thrust aside in some fit of childish angst because it doesn't meet your every expectation. When you come to understand what I'm trying to tell you, then come and find me."

And with that, she turned, yanked open the door, and disappeared. Hans stood there, staring at the door as it swung shut again. The slap-slap of the soft soles of her shoes sounded faintly and then died away as she strode down the corridor and out the main entrance.

CHAPTER 4

December 2, 1918, 9:00 a.m.—Pasewalk Military Hospital administrator's office

F ull name, *bitte*?"

"Hans Otto Eckhardt."

"Spell the last name, please."

He did.

"Date of birth?"

"Twentieth of February, 1896."

"Place of birth including district and state?"

"Village of Graswang, District of Garmisch-Partenkirchen, Bavaria."

"Spell the district for me, *bitte*."

He did, growing irritated. Hans watched the man in the white doctor's coat sitting across the desk check the spelling against the form in front of him. The name plate on his desk read Dr. Artur Schnebling, Hospital Director.

"Military serial number?"

Hans rattled it off automatically. "Six-zero-one-one-four-nine-seven-five-three."

Annoyed, the doctor looked up at him. "Again, only more slowly this time."

He repeated it, emphasizing each number. The pencil moved down to the next line. "Highest rank achieved?"

"Really?" Hans snapped. "You called me Sergeant Eckhardt when I came in. I have not received a promotion since then."

The doctor ignored him. "Number of months of active duty?"

Hans folded his arms and set his jaw, staring out the window.

That finally brought Dr. Schnebling's head up. His green eyes were flecked with brown, and at the moment, they did not look particularly pleased. "I know this is tedious, Sergeant, but when you go to the War Ministry to apply for benefits, you will need this form. If there is anything out of order—one word misspelled, or one line left empty—they will send you back here to correct it. Berlin is eighty miles from Pasewalk. If the thought of a round trip of a hundred and sixty miles doesn't bother you, then, yes, I will review it no further. Your choice."

"Sorry," Hans mumbled. "I enlisted in the summer of 1914 but didn't start boot camp until September. So four months in 1914. Then twelve months in each of 1915, 1916, and 1917. And eleven months so far this year."

"*Danke.*" The doctor calculated quickly. "So we'll put fifty-two months total. It will take you two or three weeks to get your paperwork processed, so we'll count next month."

Fifty-two months! For some reason, putting it into months took Hans by surprise. *Fifty-two!* More than enough time to have completed his engineering degree at the university. Enough to now be designing diesel engines somewhere at a very comfortable salary. Even enough to have found someone to marry, perhaps even to have had a child or two. The thought was depressing. Hans's hand subconsciously came up and rubbed at his cheek where Emilee had slapped him yesterday.

Dr. Schnebling picked up the form and re-read it all the way through one more time. Satisfied, he reached over and took a quill pen from an inkwell and signed the form at the bottom with an exaggerated flourish.

As the doctor blew on the signature to help dry it, Hans realized that this man reminded him of the major who had sent him and Franck into combat. His hair was cropped short in the military style. His face was lean, narrow in shape. The chin looked like it had been chiseled out of rock. And the eyes. The doctor's held that same aloof, detached indifference that Hans had seen that day in the war. That was typical of the nobility. Heartless. Bloodless.

Totally oblivious to Hans's scrutiny, the administrator laid the form on the desk, carefully folded it into thirds, and placed it in an envelope. With one quick lick he sealed it and handed it across to Hans. "All of your papers appear to be in order, Sergeant. Be sure you don't lose that."

"I won't. Thank you, sir."

Schnebling spun his chair around and retrieved a bulging file folder from the small table behind him. He turned back to face Hans as he opened the file. "We have petitioned the War Department to let us process our patients' discharge papers, but with their usual infinite capacity for inefficiency, they have allowed us to do only a few things." He waved a sheet of paper at Hans. "Here are directions to the railway station. This also has the times for the trains to Berlin. From here, trains go only to the Berlin East Railway Station, and not the main railway station. It's a good walk from there to the War Ministry, but there are trolleys. It's too complicated to write out directions, but the address of the Ministry is there. Ask at the train station for directions."

Watching the doctor closely, Hans was changing his mind about this rather officious head of the hospital. Cool? Yes. Aloof? Yes, that too. But this was really useful information he was giving Hans, and it was clear that he was trying to be helpful.

He withdrew the next item from the folder and held it up. It was a laminated card a little larger than a playing card. "Here is your new identity card."

"New?"

Schnebling handed it across to him. "Yes. Didn't they tell you that they couldn't find yours when you were brought here?"

Hans shook his head. "I have no memory of being brought here. I was either unconscious or sedated at the time."

"It's of no matter. This will do in its stead."

Hans took it and then groaned when he saw the small photograph. "I think you've given me the wrong identity card."

The doctor's head came up, but his face was inscrutable. "Oh?"

Hans held it up for him to see. "This can't be me."

"You're right," came the solemn answer. "If it was, you would be too sick to be discharged." Hans shot him a hard look. *Was that a joke?*

Schnebling went on in that same dispassionate voice. "Now you know why there are no mirrors in the toilets on the various wards. That was my idea. They caused too much trauma for our patients."

Hans stifled a laugh. Of course there were mirrors in the bathrooms. It *was* his little joke. "Or maybe they'd think I was already dead," he suggested.

The doctor leaned in for a closer look. "You were pretty sedated when the photographer took the picture. Thus the droopy eyes and the lack of any sign of intelligence in your face. But it takes two to three weeks to get a new card, so we didn't dare wait for a better pose."

Again, Hans was tempted to laugh, but then he decided to play along. "Maybe when the War Ministry sees it, they'll authorize some death benefits for me as well."

That won him a flicker of a smile, which was gone again almost instantly. "I think you overestimate the level of intelligence at the Ministry," Schnebling said gravely. Then before Hans could answer, the doctor picked up the next item, a long, thin packet of paper stapled together on one end. "Here is your military food ration book, good for one month or until you are discharged."

"*Danke.*"

Schnebling picked up one last item, a stiff piece of paper about the

size of a playing card. He examined it for a moment. "We are authorized to issue you a chit for the train ride to Berlin," he mused, "but I
see that you are from Bavaria."

"Yes, sir."

"It would seem only reasonable that they would also authorize
train travel to your home, but again. . . ." He shrugged in disgust.
Without looking at it, he was turning the card in his hand over and
over, absently, as if he were still trying to decide what to do with it.
Finally, he turned businesslike again. "So, considering that you are
about four hundred miles from home, that you have very limited financial resources, *and* that you won the Iron Cross and have given
fifty-two months of your young life for your country, I have taken it
upon myself to provide slightly different arrangements." He laid the
card on the desk, face down, and pushed it across to Hans.

Puzzled, Hans picked it up and sat back. The first thing he saw was
that at the top of the card, there were two large capital letters written
with fancy scrolling: DR. Printed directly below this were two words:
Deutsche Reichsbahn. Hans instantly knew what this was. It was a card
issued by the German State Railroad. Directly below those words
were three lines with his name, rank, and serial number neatly typed
on them. In the lower left corner the card had been stamped with the
image of the imperial German eagle, indicating that this was officially
authorized by the government.

But it was the lower right corner that caught his attention and
rocked him back as he realized what he was looking at. The first line
was labeled "Valid for" and the second, "Authorized by." "Valid for"
was followed by, "No restrictions. Expires 01 APR 1919." "Authorized
by" was followed by a bold but indecipherable scrawl of a signature.

Hans peered at it for several seconds and then slowly looked up.
"Is this . . . ?"

Schnebling nodded curtly. "It is a railway pass good for four
months of unrestricted, unlimited travel anywhere in Germany. I'm

told it would also be accepted in Austria, but I cannot guarantee that. So, if I were you, I would not risk having my card confiscated."

"But. . . ." Hans still wasn't sure he was hearing this right.

"I would appreciate it if you did not show that around, except at railway ticket offices. And it would be better for me if you did not tell anyone how it came into your possession."

"So is this your signature?"

A faint but clearly ironic smile softened the doctor's mouth. "No, it is not *my* signature."

Meaning, you signed it so that no one could recognize it. Hans was struck with wonder. He had badly misjudged this kind and decent man. If he was a military doctor, which Hans guessed he was, he could be court-martialed for this.

Hans slipped the card in his inside pocket beside the envelope. "I understand, sir."

Dr. Schnebling removed his glasses and began to polish them with the corner of his white doctor's coat. "Be aware that train travel is not without its problems right now."

"I don't understand."

"One of the Allied Forces' conditions for the cessation of hostilities was that in addition to turning over our weapons of war—tanks, cannon, vehicles, etc.—we are also required to give up nearly one-fifth of our railway rolling stock. One-fifth! Can you believe that?"

Hans's jaw dropped. "Why would we agree to do that?"

"We agreed to do that," Schnebling replied bitterly, "because otherwise, the Allies threatened to invade Germany and turn us into an occupied country. Instead, they have demanded five thousand of our locomotives and one hundred and fifty thousand freight cars."

Hans was aghast. The figures were so astounding that he could scarcely take them in. Hans began to massage his temples. "But we have millions of men to bring back home."

"That's just the half of it," Schnebling exploded. "Do you think this might have anything to do with the fact that food shortages are becoming worse, even though the war is over? There's food out there, but there are no trains to transport it from the farms to the cities. And fuel. Our people are freezing to death here while mountains of coal in the Ruhr Valley wait for trains to transport it."

Dr. Schnebling sighed, shaking his head. "I apologize, Sergeant. I get so angry. How can we as a country ignore such gross injustice?"

Before Hans could answer, the doctor waved a hand. "Sorry. I just felt that I needed to warn you. When you plan to travel by train, allow plenty of extra time." He reached in the pocket of his coat and withdrew a small ring of keys. "One last thing," he went on, "and then we're done." Selecting one key, he inserted it into the top drawer of his desk and opened it. Reaching in, he withdrew a black billfold that was about six inches long and three wide. Hans's eyes were fixed on it as he shut and re-locked the drawer. To Hans's surprise, Dr. Schnebling's cool and detached manner was gone. There was genuine sorrow in his eyes now.

"As you know, when you are discharged from the army, you will be given a sum of money to compensate you for your service."

Hans didn't know that. He perked up. "How much? Do you know?"

"It varies, depending on years of service, rank achieved, months of combat duty, and also on whether or not you received any medals or citations." His eyes flashed with anger. "It will not be anywhere near what you deserve."

Hans laughed bitterly. "It's the army. That says it all."

"It's grossly unfair." Schnebling's voice dropped sharply in volume. "No, actually it's criminal. After all you boys have gone through, they toss you out on the streets with a pittance." He opened the wallet and drew out a thin sheaf of Deutsche marks. When he spoke again, he raised his voice and spoke loudly and clearly. "The amount I am allowed to give you is set by the government. And it is just enough to get you through until you are officially discharged."

"How much do they allow?"

"Fifty marks."

"Fifty?" Hans exploded. "Fifty marks? That's it?"

"I'm sorry." He put it back in the wallet, and slid it across to Hans. "Count it, please. I need you to sign for it."

Hans counted quickly and then jerked up. "Sir, there's been a—"

Dr. Schnebling leaned forward quickly. "Keep your voice down!" he hissed.

"But, sir," Hans whispered. "There are one hundred marks here."

The doctor sat back. "Are you saying that I made a mistake?" he asked loudly.

"I. . . ." Hans was reeling. This was twice what he was allowed.

"I don't make mistakes, soldier," he exclaimed. "Count it again."

Hans didn't. He got it now. He waited a moment and then said in an equally loud voice, "Sorry, sir. You are right. Exactly fifty marks."

Pushing a book across at him, Schnebling said, "Just sign for it, Sergeant. Then we're done here."

Hans scribbled his signature and stood up. "I won't forget this, sir," he said very quietly.

The doctor stood up and extended his hand across the desk. "Yes, you will," he said gravely. "The minute you step out that door, you *will* forget it." He squeezed Hans's hand hard. "Understood?"

"Yes, sir. What about my uniform and other things?"

"When you leave my office, turn left. All the way down on the right you will find the hospital quartermaster's office. He has your uniform, which has been cleaned and pressed. Your other personal belongings are in your rucksack, and he has that as well. The hospital has also provided you with some basic toilet items—a shaving kit, toothbrush, tooth powder, two changes of underwear and socks." He shrugged. "Well, you get the point."

Dr. Schnebling came around the desk and opened the door. Hans snapped to a sharp salute. "Thank you, sir!"

The doctor returned the salute and then extended his hand. "*Viel Glück*," he said softly as they shook hands.

"*Danke schön*," Hans replied. "But I fear I need more than good luck. I'm looking for a whole new life."

A droll smile played around the doctor's green eyes. "You're going to the War Ministry," he drawled. "You are going to need a very large dose of good luck."

10:10 a.m.

Half an hour later, Hans came out of the quartermaster's offices dressed in his uniform and carrying his rucksack and went straight back to the reception desk. A rather large and matronly looking nurse was entering information into what looked like a ledger of some kind. A second, younger nurse was at a file cabinet, putting files away. The first looked up as Hans came up to the counter. "May I help you?"

"Actually, yes. Do you happen to know a nurse by the name of Emilee Fromme?"

"Yes. Not really well, but yes, I know her."

"Have you seen her here this morning?"

"No. I think she works the night shift on the trauma ward."

"Yes, she does. But she said she might stop by this morning."

"If she works night shift, she will have left at seven."

Hans took a quick breath, biting back a sharp retort. "Actually, yesterday was her day off, but she said she might come in to say good-bye. I'm being discharged."

"Sorry. I haven't seen her."

Though he wasn't surprised, the disappointment was sharper than he had imagined. Then came another idea. "Would you happen to have a sheet of paper and an envelope? I'm leaving for Berlin in a couple of hours and would like to leave her a message."

She looked him up and down, her eyes warming a little. "I think I could manage that, Sergeant." Opening a drawer, she drew out a sheet of hospital stationery, an envelope with the hospital's logo and return address, and a pencil.

"Uh . . . would it be possible to get a couple of extra sheets?"

She smiled and gave him several more.

"*Danke*." Hans looked around, not wanting to do this right in front of her.

"There's a table over there," she suggested, pointing. He nodded and gave her a warm smile. "You make a very good receptionist," he said.

Her cheeks colored as he moved away.

After Hans walked away, the younger nurse turned to her companion. "So Emilee asked you not to give him her address or phone number?"

"She did," the older nurse replied. "She made that very clear. But she didn't say that I couldn't give him some paper and a pencil."

Over at the table, Hans sat down and spread the paper out before him. He thought for a few moments and then started.

Dear Emilee,

I'm sorry! I'm sorry! I'm sorry. Please forgive me.

I desperately hoped to see you this morning so I could apologize, but I fully understand why you are not here. Which makes me regret all the more what happened yesterday—

He stopped, frowning at the paper. *Don't grovel.* Hans crumpled that sheet and dropped it in the small waste bin beside the table.

Emilee,

Hello from the hospital's newest "non-patient." Wish you were here to walk me out the door as promised. But I fully understand why you are not. My fault entirely and—

He stopped again. He was back in the solarium, reliving those last horrible moments. Why had he gone after her like that? It was as if she had flipped some switch inside him and unleashed four years of frustration and resentment. But with that memory came a flash of anger, too. *It wasn't her affair. What goes on between me and my mother is my business.*

Absently, he reached up and rubbed his fingers across his cheek where she had slapped him. He still marveled at the swiftness and the violence of her reaction. Now he realized that slapping his face had shocked her almost as much as it had shocked him. Why was that? Was there something more going on with her besides her anger at him for not writing his parents? She had responded so positively when he had suggested that they go to dinner and that he meet her family. Was that part of her anger? And what had she meant when she had started to say that she had hopes they somehow could—? Could what? Get together? Take their relationship to new heights? Get married?

Then the irritation was back. *Who did she think she was? No one in my entire life has ever spoken to me like that. Not Mama, even as sharp as she has been with me occasionally. Certainly not Papa.* Hans gave a low hoot. Well, maybe his drill instructor back in basic training. *Sergeant . . . Ah, what was his name? Sergeant . . . Jessel! Yeah, old Sergeant Jessel. The personification of hell itself. That's who Emilee had been like yesterday. Sergeant Jessel.*

Another burst of disgust exploded softly from his mouth. *Just what I need. Another Sergeant Jessel in my life.* Hans snatched up the sheet and crumpled it as well and started a third time.

Emilee—

Am now discharged from the hospital. Leaving for Berlin shortly. Wish me luck as I do battle with the Ministry of War.

Will send contact information to you in care of the hospital when I get settled. Would enjoy hearing from you. I deeply regret my actions in the solarium. Would like to make amends.

Many thanks for pushing the nightmares out of my head.
Hans Otto
(Also known as der Trottel)

He laid the pencil down and slowly re-read what he had written. He had nearly signed it as *der Dummkopf,* but *der Trottel* carried so many more nuances of meaning—the clod, the blockhead, the dope, moron, sap, jerk, idiot, nincompoop. He hoped she would understand that it was his way of apologizing to her.

For a moment, he considered adding a postscript promising her that he would write his mother once he got to Berlin, but he knew that wasn't going to happen. Not yet. The last thing he needed was his mother coming up and getting lost in the city. So he folded the letter and slipped it into the envelope.

As he lifted it to his mouth and licked the gummed strip, a movement out of the corner of his eye caught his attention. He turned to the window. Through it he could see the sidewalk that led from the main entrance of the hospital out to the street. A woman was coming toward him through the snow. A flash of white skirt showed below the bottom of her overcoat. She was a nurse. Hans leaped to his feet and wiped quickly at the moisture on the glass and peered out. Then he saw that it wasn't Emilee. He slumped back down into his seat.

He watched the nurse come inside, wave jauntily to the receptionist, and then turn left and disappear down the hall. As she did so, disappointment turned to annoyance and then to a deep frustration. Then his frustration quickly morphed into self-disgust. *You are a stupid fool, Hans Otto Eckhardt.* He shook his head. *Der Trottel. Yes. Perfect. You are the village idiot.*

He strode back to the table and tore up his third attempt at a letter. Putting his rucksack over one shoulder, he returned the pencil and the sheets of blank paper to the reception desk. "*Danke schön.*"

Her eyes lifted. "No letter?"

"No, just tell her I'll write sometime."

Hans spun on his heel and started for the door. The young nurse moved up beside the older one, her eyes fixed on the soldier. "What was that all about?"

The older woman just shook her head.

"Well," the young one said dreamily, watching him walk away, "you can have my address and phone number anytime you want, Sergeant. Anytime at all."

Chapter Notes

The Pasewalk Military Hospital was an actual military hospital during World War I. That the hospital played an active role in preparing a soldier for his discharge from the army is wholly my own creation.

One of the conditions of the armistice agreement was the surrender of billions of marks' worth of railway equipment to the Allies as part of their reparation for the costs of the war that the German Empire had started. The figures given here by the doctor are accurate. "The result was a severe overburdening of the German railways. What this meant for Germany's economic life and for the people generally became apparent in many ways during the winter, and in none more striking than a fuel shortage which brought much suffering to inhabitants of the larger cities. . . . The coalfields of the Ruhr district required twenty-five thousand cars daily to transport even their diminishing production, but the number dropped below ten thousand" (*German Revolution,* 190). Similar problems happened with the transportation of food.

The United States vigorously protested the harshness of the terms but was basically told to butt out because the war hadn't been fought on their lands and they had entered the war late, not entering until 1917. As pointed out in an endnote in *A Generation Rising* (volume one of this series), "The victors are rarely either generous or humble. America, through President Woodrow Wilson, tried to convince the Allies not to impose terms on Germany that were so harsh that they would not allow wounds to heal. But Germany and France had been bitter enemies for centuries, and the French, jubilant with victory, were not about to lose their opportunity to 'stick it' to their long-time rivals" (265).

CHAPTER
5

December 2, 1918, 2:38 p.m.—East Railway Station,
Friedrichshain-Kreuzberg District, Berlin

When Hans stepped off the train at the East Railway Station in Berlin, his legs felt like frozen sticks. He moved out of the way of the disembarking crowds and hopped back and forth from foot to foot to restore a little of the feeling into them. The trip from Pasewalk to Berlin had been scheduled for two hours and forty-seven minutes. It had taken more than double that. Three different times they had been shunted onto a siding while troop trains transporting military personnel back from the front rumbled past them on the main line. Eight hours to go eighty miles—a man could go almost that fast on a horse.

But that was the least of Hans's frustrations. To add misery to his inconvenience, the four passenger cars on their train were not heated. They were old and dilapidated to the point that one could hardly make out the name of the railway painted on the sides of the cars. There was a place at the end of each car where a stove had once sat, but those had long ago been turned into scrap metal for the war effort. One of the windows in Hans's car had one pane that was completely gone. Someone had taped a thin piece of cardboard across it, but even that had partly shredded. In the toilet, you could look through open cracks in the floor and watch the railroad ties rolling by beneath you.

Thoroughly frustrated, he started looking for someone to give him directions.

3:20 p.m.—Ministry of War, Mitte District, Berlin

As he approached the building that the man had said was the Ministry of War, Hans stopped and gaped at the sight before him. It was ornate, massive, sprawling. Hans had seen large government buildings, of course, in Munich, but this one dwarfed anything he had seen before. It seemed to occupy a full city block and was four stories high.

Movement at the base of the building caught his eyes. He snorted in disgust when he realized what it was. Men. In uniform. They were two and three deep, some leaning against the building, many more of them seated on the sidewalk and using the building as a backrest. All of them were in uniform, though of various colors and styles. With a groan, Hans realized two things at once. First, he was in the right place. Second, there was no way he was going to get his business done here today.

Swearing under his breath, he hiked his rucksack higher on his shoulder, waited for the traffic to clear, and ran across the square and moved toward the end of the line. It snaked around the corner and went another hundred feet down the side of the building.

The men had gathered into small groups to talk. Most were smoking, and the air was blue over their heads. Many were leaning against the building, their eyes closed. Two or three had stretched full out on the sidewalk. Hans counted six men with rifles by their sides as he went by and two with German Lugers strapped to their waists. Deserters, he thought, who had taken their weapons with them.

He started forward slowly, not sure what was going on. Heads turned to examine him as he started down the line. No one smiled. No one acknowledged him. "Is this the line for getting discharge benefits?" he asked a grizzled-looking man with the stripes of a master sergeant on his arm.

"*Ja,*" he grunted. He let loose a stream of tobacco juice that hit the sidewalk not far from Hans's feet.

"*Danke.*" He started on.

"Ain't no use going that way," the man growled.

Turning back, Hans retraced his steps. "Isn't that the end of the line?"

"It is." Others were listening now, amused with the interchange for some reason.

But Hans wasn't a novice to the military culture and the soldier's ways. "You're telling me I need to go somewhere else first?"

"*Ja.*" The man reached into the breast pocket of his uniform and pulled out a faded, worn card. On it was the number 237. He waved it at Hans.

"I need one of those?"

"*Ja.*"

Hans decided to play the game. "You interested in selling that one?"

"*Nein.*" The man grinned, revealing a mouth full of tobacco-stained teeth.

"Wanna roll dice for it?"

The man shook his head again, openly chuckling now.

"Arm wrestle?"

The man finally laughed softly and pointed to his right. "There's a private at the front entrance. He's giving out the numbers. Can't get in line without a number."

A man about ten down the line from where Hans was standing leaped to his feet and started cursing the men around him. "Why didn't you guys tell me that before?"

No one bothered to answer.

"Much obliged," Hans said to the master sergeant.

The man touched his forehead with one fingertip and settled back against the building.

As Hans walked away, he was shaking his head. There had to be 250 men in line, and it was after three o'clock. Knowing the speed at which the military functioned, there was no way he was getting finished there tonight. Not unless the Ministry stayed open until midnight.

As he rounded the corner, a young private looked up and smiled at him. "Just arriving?" he asked.

"*Ja*. How long you been here?"

The kid laughed. "I got here August 21, 1914. Changed my mind about enlisting and got in line here the next day. I figure another month or two and I'll be done."

Hans acknowledge the irony with a smile and then lowered his head and walked swiftly down the line, keeping his eyes to the front.

The guard was sitting on the lowest step, rifle across his knees, smoking a cigarette and looking very bored. When he saw that Hans was coming toward him, he lumbered to his feet.

"I understand I need a number so I can get in line."

"Not today you don't."

"Oh." Hans was confused. He jerked a thumb in the direction of the men. "They said I have to have a number."

"You do, but not today. The line's already too long. Numbers are not issued after three o'clock. You're almost half an hour past time. Come back tomorrow." The man started to sit down again.

"Wait!" Hans looked around. Anger welled up, but Hans knew that getting angry at the army was like spitting into a stiff wind. It had a way of coming back and hitting you in the face. "What time does the Ministry open tomorrow?" he asked the guard.

"Eight o'clock. But the line will start forming at least an hour before then."

"Do you happen to know where I could find a cheap room for the night? And a hot meal?"

The guard took a long drag on his cigarette and then flipped it away. "Nope." He turned and walked away.

A short, stocky man near the top of the steps had been watching the interchange. He came down the stairs. "You familiar with Berlin at all?"

"No."

"Do you know where the Brandenburg Gate is?"

"*Ja*, I saw a sign as I came in."

"Got a pencil?"

"No. But a good memory."

He nodded and gave Hans quick directions to a hotel. "Don't expect much, but you can get a room for two marks a night. It's about a twenty-minute walk from here."

"*Danke schön.* Do they serve food?"

"No, but if you watch, there's a guy near the Brandenburg Gate who has a frankfurter and sauerkraut cart. Fifty *Pfennige* to fill your stomach. But he packs up at sundown, so don't dawdle. On the way to the hotel you'll also pass some cafés and restaurants. Not fancy stuff, but good food."

"Got it. Thanks." As Hans crossed back over the street, Schnebling's words echoed in his head. *If you're going to the War Ministry, you're going to need some luck.*

As the first snowflakes came fluttering down from the sky, Hans pulled his collar up around his neck and started back the way he had come.

December 3, 1918, 6:13 a.m.—Ministry of War, Mitte District, Berlin

Though his stomach twisted into hard knots as he smelled the aroma of food, Hans walked swiftly past the few cafés and small restaurants that were open for breakfast as he headed back for the square.

One was particularly tempting. He was surprised that he hadn't noticed it the night before. Too busy munching on his frankfurters and sauerkraut, he supposed. Now, the neon sign in the window glowed a bright pink and read *Bayerischer Biergarten*. Hans slowed his pace as he approached. A Bavarian beer garden? Here? Bavaria was four hundred miles away.

He saw quickly that this was a poor imitation of the genuine thing, however. But Hans wasn't in a place to be too choosy. The smells enticed his nostrils as he walked quickly by. Through the window, he could see the traditional breakfast buffet laid out on a round table that allowed customers to easily access it. Compared to beer gardens in Bavaria, the offering here was pretty limited, but then Hans concluded that was probably due more to the food shortages and rationing from the war than the fact that this was northern Germany. It was still enough to make him slow his step. There were no signs of ham, salami, or other salted meats that would have been standard before, and no fish—definitely due to the food shortages. But he saw round loaves of pumpernickel along with other varieties of bread and rolls; little cups of jams, jellies, and honey; boiled eggs; several different cheeses in pie-shaped wedges or small, flat rounds. There was one bowl of what looked like green beans and pots of both coffee and tea with steam coming from their spouts. And all for two marks, a sign in the window announced.

Only the memory of long lines of men circling halfway around the block drove him on.

6:34 a.m.

As Hans hurried across the square toward the looming mass of the Ministry building, he was feeling good. He was almost half an hour earlier than the guard had suggested. But as he came into full view of the building, he swore. There was already a small clot of men near the front entrance, huddled together in the darkness. In front of them was the same sullen guard. If he recognized Hans, he gave no sign. Without a word, he handed Hans a card and pointed to the line. Hans held it up to the light. Number twenty-one. He swore again. An hour and a half early, and there were still twenty people ahead of him. Hugging himself against the bitter cold, he made his way to the back of the line and settled down to wait.

10:22 a.m.

Hans glanced up at the clock to his left and then fought back the urge to throw back his head and scream. Or pick up a bench and throw it through the windows.

They hadn't actually opened the doors at eight o'clock as promised. Though the building was fully lit and the soldiers could see people moving around inside, the men were kept out until nearly eight-twenty. After being outside that long in the early morning darkness, Hans had decided the cold was as bitter as anything he had experienced in the trenches.

Once inside the building, they were directed to a room with a sign that read "Discharge and Retirement Benefits." It was a room large enough to seat about twenty-five people, which meant Hans was in with the first group. Behind him, he heard a woman telling the rest of the men they had to wait in the lobby.

When he saw that there were six clerk stations with small barred windows along the rear wall, his hopes rose a little. Six clerks would help. But a couple of minutes later when the clerks finally came in and perched on their high stools, there were only two of them. A pretty young blonde took the second window, setting up her name plate—Fräulein Katya Freylitsch—and spreading out pencils and some papers. The second was much older, a crone with a face that reminded Hans of the gargoyles carved into the parapets of great cathedrals. As she set up her name plate—Frau Libussa Hessler—she glared at the assembled men as if they had invaded her home and threatened to rob her.

Hundreds of men to process and only two clerks? That was the army for you.

But at least he was inside and warm. Maybe a little too warm. Hans removed his overcoat and then his outer tunic. This helped, but he could still feel sweat prickling on his forehead, in his armpits, and near the small of his back.

The one thing that was driving Hans mad was that the itching had returned. It had started even before he got out of bed. By the time he was shaving in front of the tiny, cracked mirror in the bathroom shared by all the residents of the second floor of the hotel, he realized that he had several small, circular red welts on his chest and arms. He knew what they were due to long experience in the trenches. Bedbugs. That's what you got for two marks a night.

"Number fourteen," Miss Freylitsch called out. The sailor three seats down from Hans got up and went to the window. Only seven more people to go.

Hans glanced at the clock, then did a quick calculation. They had started at 8:20. So fourteen people in two hours, an average of seventeen minutes per man for each clerk! Three men per hour for each clerk. The incompetence was mind-boggling. Hans was way past the point of screaming now. He was wondering where he could lay his hands on one of those big railway-mounted battleship guns, the ones the Allied forces called "Big Berthas." If he could find one, he'd back it up to the main entrance, lower the barrel, lever in a shell, and blast the building with its masses of mindless civil servants into nonexistence.

11:28 a.m.

A soldier walked away from the blonde's window. She consulted the stack of cards with the numbers on them and then looked up. "Number twenty-one."

Finally! Hans got up, taking his form out of his folder, and went to the window. He handed the woman his card.

"*Guten Tag,*" she said, glancing at him for only a moment as she took it. Hans was strongly tempted to vent his frustrations on her, but he quickly resisted. Instead, he turned on the charm. "*Guten Tag*, Fräulein. And how are you on this cold winter's morning?"

She looked up in surprise. "I . . . uh . . . I am well, thank you. And you?"

Ready to throttle you and Frau Hessler. But he only smiled all the more. "Probably better than you."

She cocked her head to one side. "Oh? And why is that?"

"I get to leave as soon as we're done. I'm guessing you'll be here all day."

"Why . . . yes. Yes, we're here until six."

"So ten hours every day? Wow, Katya. That must be hard."

His use of her first name made her blush slightly. "It does get tedious," she admitted.

Out of the corner of his eye, Hans saw Frau Hessler turn and glare at them, but he pretended not to have seen it. As Katya began her examination of his application, he studied her. Nice face, pleasant light brown eyes, a shapely form beneath her bulky dress. Early twenties, he guessed. Not strikingly beautiful, but one of those faces you just liked. Her fingers were long and slender, and she had a simple band on her right hand, but nothing on her wedding finger. Hans was tempted to flirt a little more but decided not to push his luck.

At last her head came up. "Your papers are in order, Sergeant. *Einen moment* while I go find your personnel file." He nodded, glancing up at the clock as she left, noting the time.

Eight minutes later she still hadn't returned, but his irritation had. He looked at Frau Hessler. "What do you people do back there? Take a coffee break while you're in the file room?"

She didn't look up or acknowledge in any way that he had spoken. But when she finished with her applicant, she didn't call out a new number. Glancing over at him, she growled, "I'll see if there is a problem." As she left without calling the next man up, someone behind him groaned. "What did you say to her?" Hans didn't turn around.

Less than a minute later, Katya came back. Her hands were empty. She had neither his application form nor his file folder. "Frau Hessler is looking for your file," she said, clearly embarrassed. "Please step to the next window and she will help you." She quickly lowered her voice. "I'm sorry." Then she called up number twenty-two. Cursing himself for his stupidity, Hans moved over to the next window. He had a pretty good idea what had happened back there.

Frau Hessler was gone for another three minutes. When she returned she had a large brown mug in one hand and his application in the other, but no file folder. Hans smelled the coffee before she reached him. "You've got to be joking," he muttered.

She walked up, took a leisurely sip of coffee, totally ignoring him, and set the cup down. She pushed his application toward him. Then, and only then, did she finally look up at him. "I regret to inform you that we could not find your personnel records, Sergeant Eckhardt."

"*What?*"

"We receive a shipment of personnel files each morning from the army. With luck, yours will come tomorrow." Her voice was bored, but there was no hiding the glint of triumph in her eyes. "But it takes at least a day to sort through them," she went on. "Please check back on Thursday."

"You can't do that!" he hissed as he leaned closer. "I know what you're doing."

Frau Hessler took another deliberate and leisurely sip from the mug. "Or perhaps Friday would be better. Just to be sure."

Hans wanted to reach over the counter and strangle her, but he understood the situation perfectly. This was a contest, and she had all the marbles. He took a deep breath and managed a thin smile, which to her probably looked more like a grimace. "Thank you, Frau Hessler. I appreciate your efforts on my behalf. Can you tell me how much my discharge compensation will be?"

"No. We need your records before we can calculate that." She gave a little flick of her hand. "Come back Friday."

Another quick breath. *Keep calm. The more you fight her the worse it's going to be.* "And if my records are here on Friday, do I then receive a check that day?"

She looked at him as if he were daft. "Oh, no." She was genuinely relishing this now. "If all is in order, we send a requisition to the Disbursement Office. I would allow a minimum of ten days to two weeks to get your payment."

"Two weeks?" he gasped. "But. . . ."

She looked past him, quite smug now. "Yes. Maybe longer. Thank you, Sergeant." Then she sang out, "Number twenty-three, please." As he started to turn away, she added. "Oh, and by the way. I have your paperwork now, so make sure you see me and not Fräulein Freylitsch." *Of course.* He glanced at Katya. "I'm sorry," she mouthed again, and then she quickly turned away as the crone's head snapped around to glare at her.

12:09 p.m.

Fuming, Hans went back out to the main foyer. He stopped and put on his tunic and overcoat as he tried to decide what to do. As he did so, he noticed a desk across the lobby near the stairs. An overhead sign said "Information." A man in a soldier's uniform, who looked to be at least fifty, sat behind it reading a book.

He walked over to the desk. The man looked up and smiled. "*Guten Tag.*"

"Hello," Hans answered.

"May I help you?"

"I . . . I'm not sure. I'm not from here, and it looks like it's going to take a few days for them to process my discharge papers, and I. . . ." He stopped, feeling a little foolish.

The man smiled. "And you're looking for information, *ja*?"

"*Ja.*"

He turned around and retrieved something from a medium-sized cardboard box behind him. When he turned back, he handed Hans a map that had "Berlin City" printed in large letters across the top. His smile broadened. "How may I help you, Sergeant?"

"The hotel I'm staying at has bedbugs." Hans pulled up his sleeve and showed the man two of the bites. "I think there's some kind of treatment that kills them, but where would I buy some of that?"

"Ah, I would guess that an ironmonger's shop would carry that."

Hans snapped his fingers. "Of course. I hadn't thought of an ironmonger. Is there one anywhere close?"

The man thought a moment and then nodded. "There's one on *Unter den Linden.* That's only a few blocks from here. Go out of the building, turn left, then left again at the corner. Go about four blocks. When you reach *Unter den Linden,* turn left again, and it's two blocks down on your left."

"That sounds easy enough. What about an apothecary? I also need some calamine lotion or whatever the pharmacist recommends to stop this itching. It's driving me crazy."

"That's easy. You'll pass one on the way to the ironmonger. It will be on your right."

"*Danke.* You have been most helpful."

"*Bitte.* I try to be. Anything else?"

"One last question. I'm told I'm going to have to wait two weeks for my check."

"At least," he cut in.

"Yeah. Any idea where I might find some temporary work? It won't take long to go through my funds."

His face fell. "Ah," he sighed. "I'm afraid I cannot help you there. As you know, with the end of the war, over a million men are suddenly without employment. Every advertisement for jobs in the paper draws hundreds of applicants, even for the most menial of work. Merchants don't have to put up signs because men are always stopping and asking if they have work."

Hans sighed. This was not a surprise, but it was still a blow. "I understand."

The man leaned in closer and lowered his voice. "One more thing. Be careful out on the streets, especially at night. If you have read the papers, you know that we are in great turmoil here in Berlin. We have deserters from the army by the thousands, many still with their guns. They're a bunch of hooligans. At night, gangs of thugs roam the streets. Even some normally law-abiding citizens are so desperate for food that they will try to steal your ration book. Oh, and if you happen to run into any kind of street demonstration, stay clear of it. We've got Communists, radical Socialists, anarchists, and every other kind of -ist determined to overthrow the government. What appears to be a harmless street demonstration can turn ugly in a hurry."

"That's good to know. So they're pretty common?"

His eyes twinkled. "The British say, 'When an Englishman is upset with something his government is doing, he'll sit down, write a prim and proper letter, and send it to the *London Times*. But when a German is upset with his government, he organizes a parade and marches through the city streets carrying signs and banners, shouting hurrah for those he supports or down with his enemies.'"

Hans was laughing by the time he finished. "And then, just for fun, they call for a general strike and set up a new government."

"*Ja, ja*," the man agreed. "That's our way." Then his smile faded. "And it is only going to get worse," he murmured.

Hans nodded. *Maybe so, but by that time, I'm going to be long gone from this place.*

CHAPTER 6

December 3, 1918, 1:15 p.m.—Prenzlauer Berg District, Berlin

The apothecary did recommend calamine lotion for Hans's bites, and they allowed him to use their toilet to apply it. So by the time he went to Buchwalder & Sons Ironmongers and bought some concoction absolutely guaranteed to kill bed bugs, the itching had subsided to the point that he could think about quieting his rumbling stomach. After what he had seen this morning, he had already decided he was going to splurge and eat at the *Bayerischer Biergarten* on his way back to the hotel. But as he walked along, he read the directions on the bottle of chemical oils. One phrase caught his eye. "Let treatment dry thoroughly (10–12 hours) before allowing human contact."

Ugh. If he stopped to eat on the way, he wouldn't get to his hotel until well after 2:30. Ten hours after that would be past midnight. After one miserable night on a lumpy mattress in a room with only minimum heat and bedbugs feasting on his blood all night, he did not need another late night. So he strode past the *Biergarten,* trying not to draw in the smells too deeply.

It took him just over two hours hour to apply the oil everywhere as directed, wash his hands, and get back to the restaurant. By that time, there were only one or two other customers there.

By Bavarian standards, the cuisine was less than stellar, but after four years of army food and a month of hospital food, it didn't matter. It was heaven, even with the limitations that widespread food shortages were putting on restaurants.

Hans started with *Eintopf* in the largest bowl they had to offer. The word literally meant "one pot," which referred to how it was cooked, not what it was served in. Vegetables, diced potatoes, legumes, and chunks of pork. Although, after looking closely at the spoonfuls he was dishing into his mouth, Hans decided that if there was any pork here it all, it had been waved once or twice over the mixture and then taken elsewhere. But the broth was thick and savory.

He had asked for three large bratwurst sausages but was allowed only one. And they only gave him half a loaf of pumpernickel. Fortunately, beer and wine were not on the restricted list, and so he ordered a large stein of a pale lager. He polished that off and ordered another lager but was refused a second bowl of the stew.

Hans was hoping for apple strudel for dessert, but the waiter said that was available only on Friday nights. Besides, his bill was already up to three marks and had also cost him two rationing coupons, so he pushed back from the table.

Now he was headed back for the city center, and he had the first inklings of a possible plan for getting around Frau Gargoyle. That was his number-one priority. He was willing to bet a hundred marks that his personnel records were there and that she was just stonewalling him. If his plan worked, he wouldn't have to hang around Berlin until Friday and wait in the line again to complete his application process.

If that worked, his second priority was to get back up to Pasewalk and try to mend fences with Emilee. He had come to that decision on the long train ride down. Even though he still fumed about her intrusion into his private life, he was now regretting tearing up his note to her.

When he had walked out of the hospital, he had told himself he was done with her. But as the hours passed, he found himself unable to get her out of his head, which puzzled him somewhat. She was pleasant-looking, but not beautiful. Intelligent and bright, but hardly the equal of a dozen of the girls he had known at the academy. He enjoyed her company immensely, but she had this habit of confronting him in ways that made him squirm a little.

One minute Hans was so vexed with her that he'd tell himself he didn't care if he ever saw her again. Then two minutes later he would find himself brooding about her again. And it still warmed him when he remembered how she had said yes about going to dinner and meeting her family before he could even finish his sentences.

So on his walk back to the hotel he had made a decision. He had an unlimited railway pass, and he had time on his hands until he got his discharge pay, so he was going back to Pasewalk to see what developed. *If*, that is, he didn't have to hang around here until Friday.

4:25 p.m.—*Ministry of War, Mitte District, Berlin*

The line of men sitting on the steps glared at Hans as he walked past them toward the entrance. "Hey, *Dummkopf*," a guy with a heavy beard shouted. "Get in line like the rest of us. The end is around the block."

He ignored him.

The guard who gave out the tickets also tried to stop him. Making sure he could clearly see his sergeant's strips, Hans barked at him. "Cool your heels, *Private*. I was here this morning. I just need some more information." The man stepped aside, glaring at him.

Inside, Hans was pleased to see that the old man was still at the information desk. When he saw Hans coming, he smiled. "Were you successful?" he said.

"Yes, your information was extremely helpful. Thank you again. But now I need to find a shop that sells stationery."

The man frowned, thinking. "Can't think of one right off. . . ." Then his eyes lit up. "Is it just letter-writing materials you're looking for?"

"*Ja.*"

"Then the post office has small packets of letters and envelopes for sale. Turn the other way on *Unter den Linden*. It's not far from there."

"*Danke.* As before, you've been most helpful."

He started to turn away, as though that was all. Then he snapped his fingers and turned back. "Oh, that reminds me. Frau Hessler, the clerk that waited on me this morning, needed one more piece of information from me. I promised I'd meet her at the end of her shift rather than try to cut in line. But I forgot to ask her where. Do the employees come out through the lobby here?"

The man nodded, not the least bit suspicious. "*Ja.* Starting about five minutes past six. But you'll have to meet her outside. They won't let you into the building without a pass."

"I understand," Hans said easily. "That's what we talked about. I'll be back here around six. Thanks again." And with that he waved and started off.

"Sergeant?"

He turned back around. "Yes?"

"If you need to contact someone, there's a telephone exchange right next to the post office. That might be faster than writing a letter."

"Ah, *ja,*" he said. "*Danke.*"

Hans waved and headed for the door without the slightest intention of calling his parents. Maybe in a few days, after they had received his letter. There was no question about him writing them now. That would be one of the first things Emilee would ask him when he saw her. But no phone calls. Not yet.

At the post office Hans purchased a small packet of stationery and one stamp. The clerk let him borrow a pencil, and he went over to one of the tables and sat down. He thought for a moment before writing rapidly for two or three minutes:

Dear Mama and Papa,

I hope this letter finds you well. Your letters finally caught up to me. It was so good to hear from you. I am well. I am very sorry that I have not written for so long. I am sure that you have worried much about me. Let me explain. I have been in a military hospital in Pasewalk, which is about eighty miles north of Berlin. I was wounded when an artillery shell hit just a few feet away from me. When they brought me in, I was unconscious, but even when I regained consciousness, they kept me heavily sedated much of the time, so I was not able to write.

Hans frowned. *Let's hope Mama never asks exactly how much "much of the time" was.* He decided he'd better justify it a little.

I was nearly blinded in one eye, but an operation removed the shrapnel and all is well now. I feel terrible that you didn't know whether I was alive. I assure you I am. I was released from hospital yesterday.

Wish I could tell you I am on my way to Graswang, but I had to come to Berlin to be discharged from the army. Extremely slow and frustrating process. I learned today it may take two weeks or more, but I have no choice but to stay until all is resolved. Would love to see you both, but no point in you coming here. Train fare will be too expensive, and as yet I have no address or phone number. I am staying in inexpensive hotels on a day-by-day basis. For now I am all right for money. I will come as soon as the army gives me my discharge papers and severance pay.

Love to the rest of the family. Especially give kisses to my nieces and nephews. Can't wait to see you all. Will let you know my whereabouts and schedule as soon as I find out what they are.

All my love,
Hans Otto

He read it again and then put it in the envelope, sealed it, and attached the stamp. He walked over to the drop box and hesitated for a moment, but then, picturing Emilee scowling at him, he dropped it through the slot.

5:30 p.m.

Back on *Leipziger Strasse,* Hans stayed on the sidewalk across the street from the Ministry, half hidden behind a parked car. He settled down to wait, going through his plan over and over in his mind. The line of soldiers outside was gone now, but he could see a few of them inside the lobby, waiting their turn to enter the room where Frau Gargoyle lurked behind her iron-barred window.

As the minutes ticked by with maddening slowness, night settled in fully on the city. The traffic along *Leipziger Strasse* was heavier now as taxis mixed with horse-drawn carriages and heavy wagons loaded with kegs of beer lumbered past. The cold was beginning to penetrate Hans's clothing and boots. He cursed himself for not thinking to buy a pair of gloves. The only upside to the cold was that as his flesh chilled, the itching from his bites seemed to diminish.

6:09 p.m.

As the first employee—a middle-aged woman—came down some stairs and entered the lobby, Hans moved so he was looking over the hood of the car and had a clear view of the building entrance. A uniformed officer—not the snotty-nosed private—unlocked one of the front doors for her and then closed it behind her as she pulled up the collar of her overcoat and hurried off down the street. Moments later others appeared, first in ones and twos, then in clusters, and finally in a steady stream.

The Gargoyle came out at 6:12, pulling on gloves and then wrapping a scarf around her face. Hans quickly dropped to one knee, pretending to tie his boot, but she turned to the right and hurried away. He got slowly back to his feet.

Fräulein Katya Freylitsch followed about two minutes later. When Hans recognized her, he groaned aloud. She was with two other young women about her age, and they were laughing gaily as they waved good-bye to the guard and came out into the plaza in front of the building.

What if they were flatmates? Katya was single. It was not likely that she lived alone. That possibility turned him cold. Gloomily, he watched as the three of them descended the steps and crossed the small plaza in front of the building. But then, to his relief, one of them waved and turned off to the right. Katya and the other one moved to the curb and stopped. He had another anxious moment as he wondered if they were going to hail a taxi, but then as traffic cleared, they ran lightly across the street, angling away from him in the opposite direction. When they reached the sidewalk, they linked arms and moved away, talking animatedly to each other. He let them get about fifty yards ahead of him, then rose and fell in behind them.

Hans glumly followed. It hadn't occurred to him that her flatmate might also be a coworker at the Ministry.

But that problem solved itself about five minutes later, when her friend let go of her arm, called out something, and then waved as she turned off onto a side street. Hans looked around, making sure there was no one else from the Ministry nearby, and increased his pace. By now the sidewalks were emptying and there were few people about. When she heard footsteps behind her, she glanced over her shoulder. He didn't turn away. While there were gas lamps along both sides of

Leipziger Strasse, they weren't bright enough for her to recognize him this far away.

But when she looked back again a moment later, she increased her pace. Hans was definitely spotted and making her nervous. He remembered the old soldier's warning about being out at night in Berlin. If he knew that, then Katya did too, and he didn't want to spook her.

He cupped a hand. "Katya! Katya Freylitsch."

She slowed and turned. He waved to her. "It's Hans Eckhardt."

"I'm sorry." She started to walk again. "I don't believe I know you."

"Sergeant Eckhardt. From this morning. Number twenty-one."

This finally registered and she stopped completely. He hurried and caught up to her. "Sergeant Eckhardt? What are you doing here?"

"I was just passing the Ministry and—" He stopped, realizing that this only alarmed her all the more.

"That's not true. Actually, I've been waiting for you to get off work. I was hoping I could speak with you for a moment or two."

Her smile was genuine, but fleeting. Her first impulse was to be flattered, which is what he had hoped for, but almost instantly her eyes narrowed suspiciously. "What about?"

He looked around. "I have a proposition for you. Is there anywhere near here where we might have a cup of—"

In the light of the lamp, he saw her stiffen. Her cheeks went tight; her eyes narrowed suspiciously. "Sergeant Eckhardt!" she exclaimed, "I am not *that* kind of a girl."

He gaped at her for a moment, stunned by the intensity of her reaction. When it hit him, he felt his face go red. He started fumbling all over himself. "Oh, no, Fräulein. I didn't mean that. I meant a business proposition. Oh, dear. I am so sorry for putting it that way."

His obvious embarrassment helped. She visibly relaxed. He went on, more slowly now, choosing his words carefully. "I have a situation. An emergency situation, actually. I was hoping you could help me. I . . . I don't have much money," he went on. He reached inside his overcoat and withdrew the ration book, then held it out to her. "But this is yours if you will help me."

She stared at it for a moment and then recognized it for what it was.

"It's yours. All of it. I've only used a couple of coupons out of it." He handed it to her. "Look at it. You'll see that I haven't signed it yet. So you can put your name on it."

She opened it, studied it for a moment, and handed it back to him. "And what is this emergency?"

He felt a rush of relief. She was at least going to listen him. That was huge, and he knew it. He looked around. "Is there a café or anywhere near here where we could get out of the cold, maybe have a cup of coffee?" Another idea came. "In fact, I'll buy you dinner if you'll just listen to my proposals. Do you know of a place that's open?"

"I'm not sure. . . ." But she didn't finish her sentence. Hans took that as a good sign.

"Come on. It's cold and I'm hungry. And you have to have dinner sometime tonight, right? And we'll be somewhere with lots of light and lots of people so you know you're safe."

Finally there came a genuine smile. "It is cold and I *am* hungry. All right. There's a little bistro about a block ahead. They'll probably only have breads and cheeses. And wine. But that actually sounds pretty good to me right now."

"That sounds wonderful to me, too. Thank you so much for at least listening to me."

CHAPTER
7

December 3, 1918, 6:53 p.m.—Leipziger Strasse Bistro,
Tiergarten District, Berlin

He watched her as she finished the last of her strudel, getting the last few crumbs by mashing them onto her fork. Finally, she sat back. "*Danke schön*, Sergeant Eckhardt."

"Please. Call me Hans."

She nodded. "And you may call me Katya. Or Katie, if you wish. That's what my family calls me."

"I like Katya," he said, sensing that Katie might seem a little too familiar to her, in spite of her inviting it.

"So anyway, that's my story. I was released from the hospital in Pasewalk on Monday. I went right to the Ministry from the train station and learned that you had to have a number to even wait in line. By that point, it was too late to get one, so I came early this morning."

"And got number twenty-one."

"Yes. And then, stupid me, I made the mistake of angering Frau Gar—" He caught himself just in time. "Uh . . . Frau . . . ?"

"Hessler."

"Oh, yes, Frau Hessler. Anyway, because I was kept sedated for so long, I never wrote to my parents. When I finally came out of it, they

69

told me I might be blind. I know I should have written my parents then, but I wanted to be sure I wasn't."

She was looking closely at him. Then she reached up and touched her temple just above her right eye, exactly in the place where his scar was. "You are very lucky," she whispered. "It is so close."

"I know."

"Is that when you won the Iron Cross?"

He reared back.

"I . . . I read it in your file."

"No, this was from an artillery shell. One of our own, as it turned out. The Iron Cross was for—wait! You read my file?"

"Yes."

"So it *was* there this morning?"

"Yes." Then she gave him a puzzled look. "What did you say to Frau Hessler? When she came into the file room, she was boiling mad. I had just found your file, but she made me give it to her and told me she would take over." She reached out and laid a hand on his for a brief moment.

It startled him a little, but it pleased him, too. She was no longer afraid of him.

"I'm so sorry for what she did," she was saying. "But she's that way. She's been a widow for many years, and she's pretty set in her ways."

"I'll say." He smiled. "She made me feel like I was under enemy fire there for a minute or two."

Katya laughed. "Oh, she's not that bad. Just kind of grumpy sometimes."

Kind of? But he let it pass. He took a quick breath. "Katya?"

"Yes."

"That's what I want to talk to you about."

Her eyes lowered, showing dark lashes. "I'm sorry, Serg—uh . . . Hans. But she was right about that. We can't do anything to speed up the refund process. Until we get the discharge papers, we can't order your check."

"I understand, but that's not what I need."

"Oh? Then what?"

"You heard her. She's not going to give me my file until Friday morning. I was hoping to leave by train tomorrow morning and go home and see my family. You know, surprise my parents by coming in person rather than writing a letter. But knowing her, I could be there all day before I get that file."

Her eyes were growing larger as she realized where this was going.

"I have to start looking for work Monday. It's a ten-hour train ride to Bavaria each way. If I have to wait until Saturday to leave, there's no sense in even going. I'd only have a couple of hours with my family."

Picking up her fork, Katya started poking at her empty plate. "What are you saying?" she asked without looking up.

"Let me ask you a question first. Once you get our files from the file room, how long does it take you to finish the processing?"

"Not long. We check the file information against your application. If it matches, then we stamp it approved and forward it on to disbursement."

"Do I need to sign anything else?"

"No. You've already signed the application."

He felt his heart soar. This was what he thought he had observed from watching the process earlier in the day. "So, since you do have my personnel file there, all you have to do is check it against—" He reached inside his coat and withdrew his application. "—against this. Right?"

"Yes. But Frau Hessler kept your file, remember? She put it in her drawer."

"I saw that. Are those drawers locked?"

She stared at him for a long moment and then looked down at this application before finally shaking her head. She started to say something more, but Hans held up a finger. He took out his ration book and slid it across the table. Katya barely glanced at it.

"I can't do anything illegal. I could go to jail."

"I would never ask that of you, Katya. What I'm asking is not illegal. I'm not asking you to change the process in any way."

"Then what are you asking?" As she asked it, she looked at the ration book with obvious longing. But she didn't take it. Not yet. Hans took a quick breath and plunged.

"Here's what I've been thinking. You take my application with you now. Then, what if you go to work early tomorrow? Before Frau Hessler gets there. You find my file, do whatever it is that you usually do, then stamp it approved."

Katya was shaking her head before he finished. "No."

He stared at her for a moment, his stomach dropping. Finally, he looked up and forced a smile. "I understand."

"No, you don't. It won't work that way."

"Why not?"

"Because we put the applications into the personnel file and then deposit the file in a box marked for delivery to disbursement. When Frau Hessler arrives, she'll immediately find that your file is not in her drawer. She'll start looking for it, and even if I put it at the bottom of the box, she'll find it. Then we'll both be in big trouble."

The disappointment was like a stab in the chest. "I understand, Katya. And I don't want you to get in trouble. I really mean that."

She picked up his application, but instead of handing it back to him, she carefully folded it and put it into her purse. "I'll do it," she said softly.

"But—"

"Not because of the ration book." She pushed it back across the table. "You keep it. You need it."

"Then why?"

"Because of the Iron Cross. I've heard about the Iron Cross my whole life, but I've never actually met someone who won it." A shy smile stole across her face. "So, I have a better idea. If you promise to walk me back to the Ministry and wait for me, I'll go in and do it now. They don't pick up the disbursement box until around nine."

His mouth fell open a little. "You can get in there now?"

"Of course. I sometimes work late. The guards all know me."

"You have my word. I'll walk back with you. I'll wait outside for you. And I'm going to walk you home, too. I understand the streets can be dangerous at night."

"They are. Thank you. I was hoping you would volunteer."

She stood up. He stood up to face her. "But how will you do it?"

"When she comes in tomorrow, I'll tell her I worked late and got it done. Fortunately, she left before I did tonight, so she won't know the difference. Your file will be gone by morning. She might be irritated, but it'll be all right. She just can't know that you had any part in this."

"I don't know what to say, Katya."

"Then don't say anything," she laughed. "We'll have plenty of time to talk on the way home. It's a long way."

9:12 p.m.—Tiergarten District, Berlin

It *was* a long way, and they were both shivering by the time they reached the small apartment building. The light on the second floor was on. "My flatmate is home," Katya said. "Good." She turned to face Hans. Her eyes were wide and luminous as she looked up at him. "I wish I could be there when your mother first sees you. That will be a wonderful moment."

"Well, you've made it more wonderful. Now that I don't have to come back to the Ministry on Friday, I can spend more time with them. Maybe even the whole two weeks that I'm waiting for my disbursement." He made a face. "The hospital gave me a little money, but I can't afford to stay in a hotel all that time. So this is a perfect solution." *Except for the fact that I'm not going to Graswang.* But Hans pushed that thought aside. He was feeling guilty about lying to her after what she had done for him, but it wasn't a lie that would hurt her in any way.

He stepped close to her, bent down, and kissed her on one cheek. "I'll be back in a couple of weeks. Perhaps we can have dinner again then."

"I would like that very much," she murmured. Then she stepped back, her face lighting up.

"Oh, by the way. I took a moment and calculated your severance pay. Would you like to know what it will be?"

"Would you like a punch in the nose?" he cried. "Why didn't you tell me that before?"

"I forgot."

"So how much will it be?"

She was suddenly playing with him. "You have to kiss me again to find that out." Chuckling, Hans bent down to kiss her on the other cheek, but as he went to do so, she suddenly turned her head to face him. One hand came up and held his face as she kissed him softly on the lips. When she pulled away, she was smiling. "Three thousand marks," she said. Then she turned and ran lightly up the steps. "*Gute Nacht!*" she called back over her shoulder.

Hans waved, still a little taken aback. When Katya opened the door and went inside, he turned and started back the way he had come, marveling at how well things had turned out.

Katya stepped into her apartment to find her flatmate standing at the window looking out at the street, her winter coat still wrapped tightly around her. Katya walked over and stood beside her, trying to ignore how cold it was in the flat tonight. Their landlady must not have received her delivery of coal.

"*Who* was that?"

"A soldier from the office. I worked late helping him get his application processed, so he offered to walk me home."

"Some walk," she said, giving Katya one of those looks.

Katya laughed. "I thought so, too."

Then as she stepped back, she felt something inside her coat pocket. She reached in and pulled it out.

Her friend was watching her closely. "What's that?"

Katya stared at the ration book for a moment and then put it away again. She stepped to the window and pulled the curtain back, but there was no sign of Hans in the darkness. She let the curtain drop again. "It's a thank-you note," she said, without turning around.

December 4, 1918, 7:12 a.m.—East Railway Station, Friedrichshain-Kreuzberg District, Berlin

Hans was still in a good mood the next morning as he approached the train station. And why not? His plan had worked out perfectly. Even better than he had hoped, thanks to Katya. And it had been fun, too. If for some reason this whole thing with Emilee fell apart, maybe he would see where things might go with her. To his surprise, he felt a little stab of guilt at that thought, but he brushed it aside and strode into the train station, unwilling to let anything spoil his mood.

The train station was busy but not overly crowded, so he walked to the ticket window with the shortest line and let his thoughts turn to Emilee. As Hans worked out in his mind how to approach her, it suddenly occurred to him that it would probably be a good idea to let her know he was coming—let her start thinking about how to heal things between them too. Besides, with train travel being what it was right now, it wasn't a bad idea to make sure she was going to be there. He turned away and went looking for the telephone exchange.

When he reached the window, there was no one there. A woman in her early thirties smiled at him as he approached. "May I help you, sir?"

"Yes. I would like to make a phone call to Pasewalk. To the military hospital there."

"And do you have the number?"

"No, but I'm sure they'll know it at the exchange there. And I need to talk to the hospital administrator there."

"Do you have his name?"

"Yes. Dr. Artur Schnebling. Tell him that it is Sergeant Hans Otto Eckhardt calling, please."

She wrote it all down and then pointed to one of the booths. "Take number one there. I'll let you know when it's ready and how much it will be."

7:15 a.m.

Dr. Schnebling's voice was pleasant but wary. "This is a surprise, Sergeant. Is there a problem?"

"No, sir." Hans told him quickly about his visit to the War Ministry. "They're saying I should have my disbursement in two to three weeks."

"*Gut.* I'm pleased to hear that. And how may I help you?"

"Uh . . . since I've got some time on my hands, I thought I might come up to Pasewalk and see Emil—Nurse Fromme."

A pause, then slowly, "I see. And just what exactly is your relationship with Nurse Fromme?"

"Right now, it's just nurse/patient," Hans said. The question was not unexpected. "She was a great help to me. I had bad nightmares for several weeks after I got there. She would read to me in between her rounds."

"I see," Dr. Schnebling said again. Which from the skepticism in his voice translated into, "And what are you *not* telling me?"

Hans smiled briefly. "To be honest, I'm hoping to change that status now that I've been discharged. She actually told me that once I was no longer a patient, she could give me her address and phone number. In fact, she had planned to meet me at the hospital on Monday when I finished my interview with you."

"I am aware of that."

"But she never showed up. Her mother was supposed to be coming to town that day. Maybe that's why."

"Ah, yes. Actually, that is why. It turned out that Nurse Fromme's oldest brother, whose name is Ernst, came down with their mother from East Prussia."

"He's the one who's the bachelor?" Hans wanted the doctor to know that Emilee had shared personal information with him so he would understand this was more than a lovesick patient with a crush on one of his nurses.

"Yes. And, unfortunately, he brought bad news. Their mother has been diagnosed with congestive heart failure."

"No. Is that bad?"

"It's not immediately life threatening, but it's very serious. It means that her heart muscles are not strong enough to pump oxygen-rich blood throughout her body. But that wasn't all. Conditions in East Prussia are terrible. The Bolsheviks are trying to seize the city government there. Gangs of unemployed ruffians, many recently released from the military, are prowling the streets at night and robbing anyone who comes along. They're even breaking into homes and robbing people at gunpoint."

"Sounds like about half of Germany," Hans muttered.

Dr. Schnebling went on. "Because of that, they have decided to move the mother and the older brother down here to live with Emilee and her younger brother."

"Does Emilee have room for them?"

"No. She rents a small cottage with two bedrooms. Currently she sleeps in one and her younger brother sleeps in the other."

"She told me he's mentally deficient."

"We prefer to call it a disability, but yes. His name is Heinz-Albert. Now Emilee and her mother will share one room, and the two brothers the other. They'll be quite cramped." The phone went silent again. "In case you're wondering, I know all of this because I've been a long-time friend of the family. In fact, I am Emilee's godfather."

"Oh!" That did surprise him. "She never said anything about that to me."

"She wouldn't. She doesn't want people thinking she's in a privileged position with me. But anyway, Emilee called me about an hour after you were in my office, hoping you were still around. But, of course, you weren't. She and Ernst decided to go back to Königsberg to get the house ready to sell. Ernst will give notice at his work that he is leaving."

Hans leaned forward, staring at the floor, and began slowly massaging his eyes. This was not what he had been expecting. "So they're gone now?"

"Yes. They left Monday afternoon by train."

"Do you know how long she'll be gone?"

"Not for sure. She has two weeks of leave coming."

"Two weeks?" Hans cried in dismay.

"Yes. She doesn't have to come back to work until the sixteenth. Or she may be back as early as this Sunday. She just didn't know how long it would take. Were you thinking of coming up to see her?"

"Yes. Actually, that was why I was calling. I was hoping you could give me a phone number to reach her. I . . . I need to apologize to her for some things I said."

"I see."

Do you? What has Emilee told you about us?

"When she called me on Monday," Schnebling continued, "she asked me to give you a message if I heard from you."

"Really?"

"She said to tell you that she's sorry for some of the things she said to you the last time you were together."

In spite of himself, Hans had to laugh. "Just *some* of the things?"

"That what she said, yes."

"Dr. Schnebling, I don't know if she told you this, but Emilee's plan was to give me her address and phone number once I was discharged as a patient. I need to talk to her. Could you please give me a phone number where I could reach her?"

"Sorry, Sergeant. The policy is very strict. I cannot do that without her specific permission."

"But she was going to give it to me. I'm not making that up."

"I believe you. But unless she tells me in person, I can't do it."

Hans felt like shouting at the phone. "Will you at least ask her the next time you talk to her?"

"I will."

"Any idea when that will be?"

"No more than what I've told you." Then Hans thought he heard a little chuckle. "She did say that she would be very pleased if there was a letter waiting for her when she gets back. A letter that included your contact information."

That lifted Hans's spirits a little. "I'll do that." Then another idea popped into his head. He had two weeks before his check would come. Maybe three. "Will you tell her something for me?"

"Of course."

"Tell her I'm at the train station in Berlin right now. Tell her that I've got a ticket for Bavaria."

"Bavaria?"

"Yes. Tell her I'm going home to see my parents. She'll want to know that."

"Yes, she will," the doctor said, the chuckle back in his voice. "She will indeed."

"And that I will write to her."

CHAPTER
8

December 5, 1918, 4:43 p.m.—Oberammergau Railway Station, Bavaria

Next stop, Oberammergau. Ten minutes to Oberammergau." With a groan, Hans hauled himself up to a sitting position. *Finally!* What a nightmare. It had been about thirty hours since he had left Berlin. Thirty hours to go a little over four hundred miles. Under fifteen miles an hour.

Hans sat back, closing his eyes, a sense of dread settling in on him. The thought of meeting his family and having to explain why he hadn't written to them did nothing to improve his mood. Every muscle in his body ached. He had body odor, bad breath, two days of stubble on his chin, greasy, matted hair, and a growling stomach. He decided to find a cheap room in Oberammergau for the night. He would rest, bathe, find a hot meal, get a good night's sleep. Then he would make the five-mile walk to Graswang and surprise his family.

Five minutes later, the train began to slow and the conductor came through again. "Oberammergau. End of the line. Everyone must exit the train." Grumbling to himself under his breath, Hans got to his feet, shouldered his rucksack, and stepped into the aisle.

As he stepped onto the platform and looked around, a rush of nostalgia hit him with unexpected force. After Berlin and Pasewalk, Oberammergau was stunningly beautiful. Fresh snow covered the streets and lay on the roofs of the colorful chalets like frosting on a Bavarian cream cake. It covered the pine-clad mountains in a blanket of white. Everywhere the eye turned, there was something to dazzle the senses.

Hans drew in a deep breath, letting the beauty of it soak into his soul. And he felt a glimmer of hope. In this setting, perhaps even he might find some healing peace.

"Hans!" a voice called from behind him. "Hans Otto!"

He spun around and then stiffened as his mouth fell open. "*Mutti?*"

Fifty feet down the platform, near the last of the passenger cars, a clot of people was coming rapidly toward him. They were waving and hollering, laughing and crying. But the one in front was his short, plump little mama. And his father was right behind her. Tears were running down his mother's cheeks as she rushed toward him, joyously calling his name.

And then she reached him and he swept her up in his arms, crushing her to him, whirling her around and around and around. When he stopped, his father moved in, encircling them both in his large arms, weeping as unashamedly as his wife. The rest of the crowd gathered in around them, crying and laughing all at the same time.

Finally, Hans let go of his father and turned back to his mother, Inga. "*Mutti,* what are you doing here? How did you know I was coming?"

That made her laugh. "First, Hans, come, greet your family. You have some children who did not sleep last night because they were so excited to have you home again."

"Last night? But. . . ."

A sturdy woman in her mid-thirties broke from the group and

81

started toward them. A man followed right behind her, with two girls in their early teens in tow.

"Ilse?" Hans exclaimed as he saw who it was.

With a sob of joy, his oldest sister embraced him, burying her head against his shoulder. "Oh, Hans. Welcome home."

Hans looked over her shoulder at his brother-in-law. "Hello, Karl."

"Good to you see, Hans," he said, his voice heavy, also choked with emotion. "We're so glad to have you home again." Then he reached out and pushed the two girls with him forward a little. "Do you remember our Annaliese and Kristen?"

Letting go of Ilse, Hans stepped forward. "No!" He shook his head in astonishment. "It can't be."

Annaliese did a quick curtsy. "*Guten Tag, Onkel* Hans."

Hans turned to his sister. "My gosh, Ilse, she's a young woman. And beautiful. When did that happen?"

Annaliese blushed right down to the roots of her hair. "I'm almost fourteen now, *Onkel* Hans."

"And you are lovely." He turned to the younger one. "And Kristen? You're twelve now?"

She nodded. "I turned twelve last month."

He reached out and touched her cheek. "And look at you. I can't believe it, Ilse. She looks just like you when you were younger." Then to Karl, "Are you sure you're the father?"

"*Hans!*" Ilse blurted. Behind him, he heard his mother's sharp intake of breath as well.

"Well, look at him," he laughed. "He's almost as ugly as I am. How did he get two such lovely daughters as these?"

And that redeemed him. Everyone laughed in delight as the two nieces turned a brilliant red but beamed back at their uncle in pure adoration.

Next came Heidi, the sister just younger than Ilse. She was with her husband, Klaus, two younger boys, a girl about three or four, and a baby she held in her arms. Hans reared back. "You've had another one?"

"Yes." She pulled the blanket back, revealing a cherubic face with fat little cheeks and a skiff of dark black hair. "This is Inga Helene. She's eight months old now."

Hans glanced at his mother and then back to Heidi. "Another child," he said softly. "Good for you. And you too, Klaus."

"I wrote you about her," Heidi replied. "Didn't you get my letter?"

He shook his head. "The last year of the war was so awful, we rarely got mail."

Then he turned to the two boys who were patiently waiting to be recognized. "And you are?" he said to the older of the two, who looked to be about ten. Before the boy could answer, Hans slapped him on the shoulder. "No! You can't be Klaus Jr."

"Yes I am," he said proudly.

"But you only came up to my knee the last time I saw you."

"It's me," he said, pleased that his uncle hadn't forgotten him.

"And you," he said to the younger one, "you've got to be. . . ." He waggled a finger at him. "Don't tell me. Don't tell me." Then he snapped his fingers. "Are you Gerhardt? Naw! You can't be Gerhardt. He was no bigger than a squirrel the last time I saw him."

"Well, I'm big now," he said proudly. "I am almost eight."

There was a sudden tug on his coat sleeve. "I'm Miki," a tiny voice said. Hans turned and looked down. He thought his heart was going to melt as he saw a little wisp of a thing with enormous brown eyes and dark hair and the most winsome smile he had ever seen. He dropped to one knee and stuck out his hand. "I am honored to meet you, Miki." They shook hands with great solemnity. "And how old are you?"

"I'm four," she answered, holding up three fingers.

Heidi laughed. "Yes, she's four now." Then she spoke to her daughter. "Miki, do you have a hug for your *Onkel* Hans?"

Without the slightest hesitation Miki threw her arms around his neck and planted a wet kiss on his cheek. That did it. He stifled a cry as his eyes instantly filled with tears. He gently kissed her cheek and then stood up, wiping quickly at his eyes in embarrassment.

To cover himself he turned to the last of his sisters and held out his arms. "Your turn, Anna."

Anna was just five years older than Hans, and he had been the closest to her as they grew up. She, like their father, had always been one of Hans's most consistent supporters. Unlike their father, she clearly saw his flaws and blemishes, but it didn't matter to her. He was her champion, and she was his. And she had wept the most bitterly when he went off to war.

"Stop crying," she whispered. "I was doing just fine until you started to cry."

Hans laughed through his tears. "I'm not crying. It's just the cold air. It's making my eyes sting."

"Of course," she said. Then, taking his hand, she pulled him forward. "Hans, I want you to meet my husband." A slender man with thinning hair but a pleasant smile stepped forward, extending his hand. "This is Rudi Lemke, from Hohenschwangau."

Hans shook Rudi's hand firmly. "It is a pleasure to meet you, Rudi. I am sorry that I wasn't able to attend your wedding. Didn't even get the announcement until two months later." He saw Anna's hand drop to her stomach, which had a noticeable swell to it. She blushed. "And we have another announcement, too."

"Ah," Hans said with genuine pleasure. "So you have one in the oven?"

She slapped at him playfully. "Yes. Finally." She went up and kissed her brother on the cheek. "And if it's a boy, we're going to name him Hans, for his grandfather and his uncle."

They held each other for a moment. Hans felt another tug on his sleeve. It was Miki again. He dropped to one knee a second time. "Yes, Miki?"

"St. Nicholas?" she asked.

"St. Nicholas?" he repeated, giving her mother a questioning look.

"It's St. Nicholas Day tomorrow. Don't tell me you have forgotten that. That's why the children are so excited. You'll be here for St. Nicholas Day."

Hans turned back to Miki and took both of her hands. "Yes, Miki, I did remember St. Nicholas." Only because he had happened to see a sign in the railway station in Berlin. "In fact, I met someone on the train who knows St. Nicholas personally."

Her eyes grew big. "Who?"

"Knecht Ruprecht."

Puzzled, she turned to look up at her mother. But Klaus Jr. bent down and answered for her. "Remember, Miki? Knecht Ruprecht is St. Nicholas's helper. He's the one that carries the bag filled with toys."

When Miki turned back to Hans, her eyes were enormous saucers. "Really?"

"Yes, really. And he gave me some presents for someone named Miki Borham. Do you know anyone by that name?"

She jabbed her thumb against her chest. "That's me, *Onkel* Hans."

"Really?" Then he bent in closer. "And guess what else he gave me?"

"What?"

"Three switches."

She looked blank. Annaliese bent down beside her now. "Remember, Miki, if children have been good and said their prayers, then St. Nicholas has Ruprecht give them gifts."

Gerhardt couldn't stand it. "But if they've been bad, they get a switch instead of gifts, because they need to be punished."

"Either that," Hans said gravely, "or Ruprecht carries him off in his sack."

That seemed pretty fantastic to her, so she looked to her mother for confirmation. "That's right, Miki, so you have to be a good girl."

"Do you know someone who's been naughty?" Hans asked her.

Without a moment's pause, she pointed at Gerhardt.

"Have not!" he cried.

"He broke Oma's dish," she said.

Hans got to his feet, shaking his head. "Well, Gerhardt, that doesn't bode well for you."

Kristen spoke up then. "Did Ruprecht really give you gifts for us, *Onkel* Hans?"

Reaching down, he picked up his rucksack, which was bulging now and weighed a good ten pounds more than it had when he left Pasewalk. "He did. The trains are running so far behind schedule right now that St. Nicholas didn't want to take a chance on being late to Graswang. So he had Ruprecht give me your presents." He nudged Gerhardt. "And some switches."

Gerhardt was shaking his head. "St. Nicholas doesn't ride on trains, *Onkel* Hans. He has a magic sleigh." He turned to his mother. "Doesn't he, *Mutti*?"

Heidi just smiled. "St. Nicholas and Ruprecht can ride in anything they like."

Hans Sr. came forward then, smiling broadly. "Well, whatever it is, we need to get home in time to make sure your shoes are all clean before you put them out tonight by the fireplace for St. Nicholas. He won't put any gifts in dirty shoes." Then he briefly touched Hans Otto on the shoulder. "We have arranged for a dinner at Herr Kleindienst's restaurant to celebrate your coming home, son." He pulled a watch from his vest pocket. "He will be ready to serve us in ten minutes. So we'd better start."

"Great," Hans said, "after train food, that sounds wonderful, *Vati*."

"But I need to warn you about two things, son. It won't be a meal like the old days. Even here in our peaceful valley, there is not enough food."

"I'm used to that, *Vati*. That's not a concern."

"The second thing is that a lot of people wanted to come with us to the train station, but we said no. We felt this was a time for only the family. But don't be surprised if you have a whole welcoming party waiting for us at Kleindienst's."

As Hans looked around at his family, and especially his nieces and nephews, he shook his head. "That's fine, as long as I have my family there, too."

The kids scampered ahead, with Annaliese and Kristen taking charge of them. The rest of the family followed along at a more leisurely pace, and Hans Otto and his mother brought up the rear. As soon as the others were engaged in conversation, Hans looked at his mother.

"All right, *Mutti.* How did you know I was going to be on that train?'

"We didn't."

"But—"

She smiled up at him. "From what we were told, you could have arrived as early as yesterday afternoon. So we have met every train since then. Today was our third time, so we were especially glad to see you."

That floored him. "You mean . . . you've come from Graswang three different times?"

"*Ja,*" she said. "We didn't want to miss you."

"And you walked here and back three times?"

"No," she laughed. "Your father bought a new milk cart last year and it's large enough to hold all of us."

Hans nodded but wasn't about to be deflected. "No one knew I was coming. I didn't even know when I was leaving until just a few minutes before I left."

"Oh?" his mother said with a twinkle in her eye. "No one?"

He started to shake his head, and then it hit him. "Emilee?"

"Ah," she said, half musing, "so it's not Nurse Fromme, now, it's Emilee?"

"Emilee called you?"

"Yes. Does that shock you?"

"How? You don't have a phone."

"We do now." His father said, turning around. "First telephone in Graswang," he said proudly. "Now there are four or five others, but we were the first."

"I told you that in my letter," his mother explained. "Didn't you get it? I gave specific instructions on how to make the connection."

"Uh . . . no, I didn't get it." He was reeling. He lowered his voice even more and spoke to his mother. "When did Nurse Fromme call you?"

"Yesterday morning. About nine-thirty. Maybe ten."

"From Pasewalk?"

"No. She said she was in Königsberg, helping her mother." She slowed her step, peering up at him. "She didn't tell you?"

He shook his head.

"Well, well," Inga said archly, "and I thought it was your idea. I just assumed that you wanted us to meet you at the station. You know, it being Christmastime and all."

Hans winced but decided there was nothing he could safely say to that. "So, how long did you two talk?"

"Why do you ask?"

"Because I'm curious, *Mutti*. Did you talk very long?"

"Not very."

Inga had turned her attention forward. Heidi had slowed as Miki broke off from the other children and came back to join her mother. She pulled her mother down and whispered in her ear. Heidi smiled and turned around. "Hans, Miki wants to know if she can walk with you and Oma. She wants to hold your hand."

"Of course," he called. "I'd be delighted." Then to his mother: "So how long did you talk?"

"Umm, I don't know. Maybe twenty minutes."

"*Twenty minutes!* What in the world did you talk about?"

She ignored that and spoke to Miki. "Would you like to hold *Onkel* Hans's hand, *Liebchen?*"

Miki nodded vigorously and stuck out her hand. Hans glared at his mother as he took it. "This conversation isn't over," he muttered.

"It is for now," she said happily.

And so he turned his focus to Miki. "Would you like to ride on *Onkel* Hans's shoulders?"

She shook her head gravely.

"You just want to hold my hand?"

That brought an enthusiastic nod. Smiling, Hans took her by the hand and they set off again. "Isn't she a sweetheart?" Inga whispered.

Hans nodded absently. His mind was racing, and he felt his irritation start to rise again. *Had Emilee been afraid he might back out on the whole thing?*

But as he felt Miki squeeze his hand, shame drove those feelings away. What had happened just now with his family had been wonderful. If Emilee hadn't called, he'd be looking for a room right now. And probably someone in the village would see him and race off to tell his mother that he was home. That would not have been good.

Did Emilee understand all of that? Was this what she had been hoping for?

And with that, he forgave her, for it had been perfect. Absolutely perfect. Hans squeezed the tiny hand in his gently, realizing that he was happier at this moment than he had been in over four years. His thoughts raced out across the miles. *Thank you. Thank you, dear Emilee, for seeing clearly what I could not see at all.*

Chapter Notes

Saint Nicholas was a Catholic saint who lived about 300 years after Christ. He is said to have been a protector of children and often gave them gifts. Though this may have come later, in most pictures he is shown in a red robe and has a full head of hair, a thick mustache, and a full beard, all of pure white. He was born into a wealthy family but decided to follow Christ's admonition to "sell all that you have and give to the poor." This was how his name came to be associated with gift-giving and blessing those in need.

Nicholas died on December 6, 343. Many years later, also on December 6, he was sainted by the Catholic Church. Since then, December 6 was always celebrated as St. Nicholas Day. It is still observed as such throughout much of Europe. It has long been a custom in Germany and other European countries for children to clean their shoes on December 5 and place them beside their doors that evening. While the children are sleeping, Nicholas fills their shoes with nuts, gingerbread, chocolate, candies, and fruits. If they have been naughty, he leaves a switch with their parents. Even today, it is still traditional to have St. Nicholas, accompanied by Ruprecht (dressed in plain brown robes), visit family Christmas parties and deliver gifts.

CHAPTER 9

December 11, 1918, 3:45 p.m.—Eckhardt dairy farm, Graswang, Bavaria

M*utti?"*

"I'm in the back bedroom, dear," a voice called.

Hans walked through the kitchen, up the half-flight of stairs, and into the bedroom where his parents had slept for the last thirty-nine years and where his grandparents had slept for that long before them. His mother was seated on the padded stool in front of the small dressing table and mirror, hunched over and picking the loose threads from the hem of a skirt. Probably Annaleise's, judging from its size.

She looked up and smiled. "Was that the mailman I just heard?"

"It was. How long has Fritz had a bell on his bicycle?"

"About two years now. It came with the new bicycle the Postal Department bought for him."

"Wow. Really coming up in the world, eh?"

"Don't be snippy, dear. It doesn't become you."

Hans ignored that, not wanting to get sidetracked. "I have a question for you, *Mutti*."

"All right. What is it?"

"Has Emilee called you on the phone lately?"

Her hands went still, but she didn't look up. "Why do you ask?"

"Thank you for not asking, 'Emilee who?'" He walked over and dropped a letter on the skirt.

She leaned closer and then shook her head. "I can't read it without my glasses."

He didn't believe that. Emilee wrote in fairly large script. "Where are they?"

"Oh, just read it to me, Hans. They're downstairs somewhere."

He sighed and took it back. "It's dated three days ago."

Sunday, December 8th

Dear Hans,

Returned from Königsberg late last night. Much accomplished, but much more to be done. Ernst and I leave again first thing tomorrow. Hope to finish up in a week. Mother is adjusting well to Pasewalk and a smaller house. It is especially good for Mother to be away from there. Königsberg is not a safe place to be. I was very glad to have Ernst with me at all times. Heinz-Albert provides company for Mother all day long, and vice versa.

Heard you arrived safely in Bavaria.

Hans stopped and gave his mother a sharp look. She pretended not to see it.

Hoping all with your family is well and that you are enjoying getting reacquainted with your nieces and nephews.

                    With warm wishes,
                    Emilee

He lowered the paper. "How does she know all that, Mama?"

"Because she asked."

"So you did call her?"

"No. Actually, she called me."

He mouth fell open a little. "Since I've been here?"

"The day after you arrived."

"And you didn't let me talk to her?"

"She didn't ask to talk to you."

He threw up his hands. "What is this, some kind of conspiracy?"

Inga finally looked up, and her eyes were glinted with a touch of merriment. "Yes."

Hans snorted in disgust. "I can't believe you didn't tell me."

"Is there anything else in her letter?" his mother asked.

"She gave me her address and a phone number to reach her."

"Ah."

"What's that supposed to mean?"

"Just, ah." Inga's amusement deepened. "The phone is downstairs in the kitchen."

"What makes you think I'm going to call her?"

She just rolled her eyes and went back to work on the skirt. "Or," she said, not looking up, "if you'd rather call from the exchange in Oberammergau, that would be fine, too."

Hans spun around and started away but then turned back. "Maybe I will. That would be better than having the operators and everyone else on the party line here in Graswang listening to my conversation."

"Then go, dear. If it bothers you that much, just go."

He stalked out and started down the steps. His mother called after him, "Put on a warm jacket, dear. It's supposed to snow later."

"I'm not going," he called back.

"Oh? And why is that?"

"Because right now I'm pretty upset with Fräulein Fromme, as well as my mother."

"I understand, dear. And the fact that she's gone back to Königsberg has nothing to do with that?" Her voice was filled with sweet innocence.

Hans made some nasty comment as he stomped down the stairs. Inga ignored it. "Why don't you go see Miki, then? She'll cheer you up."

December 21, 1918, 6:05 p.m.

"*Onkel* Hans. *Onkel* Hans. *Onkel* Hans."

The children clapped their hands in rhythm as they chanted the words. Little Miki clapped right along with the others. Hans Otto, laughing at how earnest she was, looked at her father. "Sorry, Klaus."

Klaus Borham, who was seated on a three-legged milking stool in the stall next to him, pulled a face and turned to his wife. "Heidi," he called with pretended offense, "why am I not hearing anyone chanting, 'Papa Klaus. Papa Klaus. Papa Klaus'?"

His wife, trying hard not to smile, bent down to her daughter. "Miki. You need to cheer for *Vati.*"

She kept right on clapping. "No, *Mutti.* I want *Onkel* Hans to win."

"Why?"

"Because I love *Onkel* Hans the most," she responded, surprised that her mother had to ask.

Inga and Hans Sr. burst out laughing. They loved all of their grandchildren dearly, but this little one was a pure delight. "Well, Klaus," Hans Sr. called, "there you have it. But don't worry, Oma and I will cheer for you."

Touched by the simplicity of Miki's words, Hans Otto turned to his brother-in-law and said in a low voice, "You know, of course, that you have to let me win so that I don't break Miki's heart."

"Ha!" Klaus cried. Then he turned to his father-in-law. "We're ready, Opa. Give the signal."

Actually, Hans's jaunty confidence was somewhat forced. Until he had returned home about ten days earlier, he hadn't milked a cow in a very long time.

On the other hand, Klaus and his other two brothers-in-law now ran the Eckhardt dairy farm, and between them they milked thirty-two cows night and morning.

The irony of that had hit Hans more than once since his return.

94

He, who was the designated heir, would someday own the farm, the house, the three cottages that now housed his sisters and their families, and fifteen acres of rich meadowland. But he, by his own choice, had enlisted in the army. Because of the amount of milk, cheese, and butter the farm produced for the war effort, all three of his brothers-in-law had been given agricultural exemptions from conscription into military service. So the heir went through hell while the workers enjoyed four years of relative peace. And had, on average, about twice the amount of food that families in the cities had.

On such small hinges did the gates of fate swing.

When he had arrived home two weeks ago, Hans had offered to help with the milking. His father had been shocked at the thought. Not after all he had been through, his father harrumphed. Hans's three sisters, who had doted on him through his growing-up years, concurred. He hadn't come all the way from Berlin to milk cows. But then his mother had intervened. "I think it would be good for you, Hans," she said quietly. And so he had started the next morning. He was back into it again, but enough to beat Klaus? He doubted that.

The chanting stopped, and a hush fell over the children as their grandfather stepped forward. "All right," he called. "You know the rules. Each man milks three cows. And that means fully milked, including the strippings. Just as we do every night and morning. First man done wins."

"And gets the biggest piece of Oma's chocolate cake," Inga sang out.

Karl, who was a more methodical milker, had decided to let Klaus represent the brothers-in-law. Rudi, who had not been raised on a farm and who had moved here only about a year ago, also bowed out. Anna teased him about it, but not very vigorously.

Hans took the first stall; Klaus was in the second. Both scooted their stools in a little closer to the cows and leaned forward, pressing their foreheads into the cows' flanks.

Hans's father raised one hand. "Ready? *Eins. Zwei. Drei.* GO!"

Their hands shot forward, grabbed the swollen teats, and went to work. The children erupted, cheering, clapping, shouting, and jumping up and down. Hans found himself laughing as he worked his hands feverishly back and forth. Klaus did this night and morning and had done it for years now. For all Hans's big talk, he knew he was in for a contest.

Done! Leaving the nearly full pail of milk for his sisters to move out of the way, Hans grabbed his stool and leaped past Klaus to the next stall. Klaus was still seated, his hands moving more slowly as he stripped the last of the milk from his cow. The kids went wild, and Hans was delighted to see that even his mother was rooting for him, in spite of his father's promise to cheer for Klaus. But for some reason, the second cow was not in a good mood. She kicked back at Hans as he sat down, and he had to jerk to one side to avoid being knocked down. By the time Hans finished with her, Klaus was on to his third animal and had a twenty-second lead on him.

As his sisters set the four milk pails aside, the children were in a frenzy, yelling and screeching. But whether it was for him or for Klaus, Hans could no longer tell. Never had Hans's fingers flown so fast. The streams of milk were coming so fast that the surface of the milk was covered with two inches of foam. He concentrated, forcing his hands to go faster and faster. He could feel the muscles in his forearms starting to seize up on him, but he ignored them. He was barely aware of the children. Sweating, he drove himself on with furious intensity.

A minute later, he leaped to his feet and kicked the stool away. His arms shot into the air. "Done!" he cried.

"No!" Klaus also jumped to his feet and raised his hands, but he was about three seconds too late. Hans started doing a little dance of triumph, and then he saw Miki hurtling at him. With a roar of delight, he swept her up in his arms, swinging her around and around as she squealed happily. "You won, *Onkel* Hans! You won!"

He kissed her soundly on the cheek. "No, Miki. *We* won. If you hadn't been cheering and clapping for me, I could never have done it."

She beamed. "I know." She turned to her father and gave him a pitying look. "Sorry, Papa."

"Yeah," he growled. "I can see that."

8:30 p.m.

Hans looked around the table. By firm decree of his mother, the supper dishes were left stacked in the sink, soaking in soapy water. This was Hans's last night, and they weren't going to spend it doing dishes.

Miki was on his lap eating the rest of his double-sized piece of German chocolate cake. Frustrated that he kept stopping to talk, she had finally turned toward him. She took his face in both of her hands and pulled him down until she was looking directly into his eyes. "I do it myself," she declared in disgust. From then on, she held the fork. About every fifth bite she would turn and put some into his mouth, but if he wasn't paying attention, she'd pop him one on the chest.

Miki's feisty determination tickled Hans so much that it was all he could do not to encircle her in his arms and squeeze her until she cried out in protest. With every passing minute, he was realizing just how much he was going to miss this little girl and her total devotion to him. But it wasn't just her. He turned to watch his mother, who was talking to Gerhardt, Miki's older brother. Something she said brought a huge smile to his face, and he reached out and touched her hand. It was a tender moment, and it hit Hans hard.

He had been eight years without his family. *Eight!* Only now did he realize what he had missed. The birth of two grandchildren, including Miki, with another on the way. Anna's marriage. The deaths of his grandparents. Now the wrinkles in his mother's face were deepening almost daily. Her hands were somewhat gnarled as her arthritis grew worse. But there was a serenity in her that was . . . what? He couldn't even think of the right word. Beautiful? Yes, but . . . content. That was it. She was thoroughly content with life now that she had her son back.

Hans looked at his father, who was half asleep in his chair. He had aged the most of all. The doctors said he was still clean of cancer, but Hans could see the toll it had taken on him. His skin had a sallow look to it. His hair had noticeably thinned, and he had lost enough weight that his clothes hung on his frame. The biggest change, though, was in his energy. He had not only let his sons-in-law take over the farm chores, but he no longer rode in with them to Oberammergau to deliver their product to their customers.

Hans's musings were interrupted when Heidi stood up and clapped her hands. "All right, children. Time for bed." There were groans and cries of disappointment, but when Klaus got up, they immediately stopped complaining.

"You don't have to say good-bye to Uncle Hans now," Ilse said. "We're all going to the train station tomorrow to see him off. So just tell him good night now."

Heidi was nodding. "And, Miki, no more cake."

"But *Mutti*, I'm helping *Onkel* Hans. He can't eat it all."

"That's right, Heidi," Hans said with a grin. "I need help."

Heidi snorted softly. Anna shook her head. "You are not helping these mothers very much here, Hans."

Inga couldn't help but laugh. "I think *Onkel* Hans will be fine, Miki."

Her eyes grew wide. "No, Oma. He needs me."

Her father came over. "Kiss him good night, Miki."

Pouting, she did so, but when Hans set her down and gave her an affectionate swat on the bottom, she promptly went to the back of the line of grandchildren. As Klaus scooped her up, she let out a howl, extending her arms in Hans's direction. "Save me, *Onkel* Hans. Save me!"

How could he resist something like that? He started to get to his feet, but Heidi warned him off with her eyes. "No, Hans. We've got to be up early. She needs to get to bed."

"But that is what uncles are supposed to do," he protested. "Save children from their ogre parents."

As Hans took his other nieces and nephews into his arms one by one and bid them good night, he found it harder and harder to speak. How soon would he see them again? He had missed so much. Annaleise was now attending Herr Holzer's school. Kristen had helped her mother and grandmother cook supper tonight. Klaus Jr. and Gerhardt were already helping with the milking.

He turned to watch Anna, standing beside Rudi. They were holding hands. The roundness in her stomach was noticeably larger than when he had arrived two weeks before. Would he be back when the baby was born? He had not the slightest idea.

As the last of the family shut the door behind them, Hans's father slowly got to his feet and turned to Inga. "I'm quite tired too, *Schatzi.* I think I'll go up to bed."

Hans's mother went over and kissed Hans Sr. on the cheek. "I'll be up in a few minutes, dear."

"*Gute Nacht,* Papa. I'll see you in the morning."

He waved a hand and shuffled off. Inga watched him go up the stairs, not moving until she heard their door open and shut. Then she came over and sat down beside her son.

"He's not doing well, is he, Mama?" Hans asked.

"As well as can be expected, I suppose." Her face, however, revealed more than her words.

Hans decided to change the subject. "Isn't our little Miki a package?" he said. "She is such a little imp but so absolutely adorable."

"Well, she adores her *Onkel* Hans. She's going to miss you a lot."

"Not as much as I'll miss her and the rest of the kids."

"Do you really have to go?" But then she shook her head quickly. "Never mind. I promised myself I wouldn't ask that."

"I do, *Mutti.* I need to be at the War Ministry first thing Monday morning. My two weeks are up then."

"I know all of that," she replied, her mood downcast, "it's just. . . ."

"What?"

"Do you have enough money, Hans? Be honest with me."

"I do, *Mutti*. I've still got about seventy marks."

She reached into her apron pocket, withdrew a thin sheaf of bills, and held them out to him.

"No. I'm fine. Really."

"It's from *Vati*, too," she said. "He said to tell you we will not take no for an answer."

Hans nodded. "*Danke*. It will help if the Ministry is its usual inefficient self and my check isn't ready yet. Now, what were you going to say?"

She was suddenly studying her hands. "I was hoping that we all might go to church tomorrow before you leave. It *is* the last Sunday of Advent."

"I know, but . . . I have to be at the Ministry first thing Monday. And with the train schedules so unreliable, I can't wait for a later train."

"And what if your check isn't there on Monday? Do you think you could make it back here in time for Christmas Eve? It makes me sad to think of you being alone on Christmas."

He had to look away. "I don't think so, *Mutti*. "It's. . . . The trip takes so long. And I have to start looking for a job. I . . . I just don't see how I can."

Guilt washed over him like a wave, so he looked away. How could he tell her that Emilee had invited him to spend Christmas with her and her family?

Deciding it was time to change the subject, he suddenly had an idea. "Wait. Papa's going to church? That'll be the day."

Her eyes never left his. "He goes every Sunday now. We all do."

"Really?" Then the implication of that hit him. He leaned forward. "Have they. . . ."

She shook her head. "No. In fact, when we saw the doctor in

Munich in mid-November, he said there's no sign that the tumor has returned."

"But you don't believe it." He didn't make it a question.

Tears welled up in her eyes. "I don't know," she whispered. "I just know that. . . ." She looked away. "I'm worried about him, Hans."

"So am I. I've been surprised how little energy he has. And his color isn't good."

There was a quick bob of her head. "But you being home has been so good for him, Hans. So good. He's happier than he's been in months. Years."

"As am I, *Mutti.*"

"And you have no idea when you'll be back?"

He shook his head. "I hope soon, but I have to get my discharge pay. Then I've got to find work. And I also want to go the University of Berlin and see if I can get my scholarship restored."

"Oh, good, Hans. That makes me so happy. But you won't start there until the fall, will you?"

"I . . . I just don't know, Mama. I've thought about coming down to Munich to look for work. I know that unemployment is bad everywhere, but Berlin seems to be hit particularly hard."

"Munich would be wonderful."

They both fell silent. After a moment, Hans had another thought. "Which church do you go to?"

"The parish church, of course. Papa doesn't have the energy to go to Oberammergau any longer."

"You mean our church? The Catholic Church?"

"Yes."

"But . . ." He stopped, not sure what to say.

"But what?"

"I thought you were a Mormon."

"Ah," she said, smiling. "Yes, I'm still a member of The Church of Jesus Christ of Latter-day Saints, or the Mormon Church, as people call us. But the nearest branch of our Church is in Munich. So I attend mass here with Papa on most Sundays. When I go up to visit with Paula and Wolfie, Paula and I go together to the little branch there."

"And your God doesn't care that you attend a Catholic church?"

She laughed merrily. "No, I think *my* God, as you call Him, is not easily offended. Actually, I think we may both have the same God."

Then Hans had another thought. "I heard that the missionaries had to leave when war broke out."

"Yes. They all returned to America, except for a few that were native Germans. But I got a letter from Elder Reissner a few months ago. I sent it on to you. Did you not get that, either?"

Hans shook his head, disappointed.

"He's married now, but he said he was going to come back to Germany after the war. He specifically said that he wants to see you again."

"I would like that."

"The branch president in Munich—that would be the equivalent of a parish priest—and his wife come down and visit me every month or two."

"Really? From Munich?"

"Yes. We in our Church believe that we have an obligation to watch over one another and help people in need. They often bring me food."

He cocked his head. "And you take it?"

"Of course. It would be rude of me not to." She smiled, almost shyly. "But we're doing well here on the farm. Better than a lot of others. So I always send them back with something for the other members of the branch. A brick of cheese or some butter. In the summer, fresh vegetables or fruit."

To Hans's surprise, this made him want to cry. It came out so simply, without any sense of it being a sacrifice. "And I'll bet," he finally managed, "that typically they go back with more than they brought, right?"

She didn't answer, which was his answer. Hans got to his feet. "Well, dearest Mama, I need to pack. And you need to get some sleep too."

Inga stood up and came to him, putting her arms around him and holding him close. "Thank you, Hans. Thank you for coming home."

"No, Mama, it is I who needs to thank you. This has been wonderful. I'm sorry that I didn't answer you letters sooner. Really sorry."

"I guess there is no way you could be back for Christmas?"

"I would love to, but it all depends on the War Ministry." He was glad her head was pressed against his chest so she couldn't see his face. The moment he had his check, he was on a train to Pasewalk. "Uh . . . if I can, I'll come. But don't count on it."

"And will you bring Emilee with you?"

He jerked up, staring at her.

"Do you really think I am that naive?" Inga clucked, shaking her head. "I assume that it was Emilee that you called from the telephone exchange in Oberammergau."

"Mama, I—"

She laughed at his expression. "You're in Graswang now, son. Not in Berlin. Here, everyone knows what's going on in your life."

She went up on her toes and kissed his cheek. "I'd better go see to Papa. Good night, Hans. We'll have a good breakfast before you go."

As she reached the stairs, he could see the weariness in her gait, and the guilt became too much for him. "Mama?"

She turned.

"My train doesn't leave until noon. What time is church?"

Her eyes widened and suddenly filled with tears. "Nine o'clock."

"We'll have to go straight to Oberammergau afterward."

A hand came up to her mouth. "Would you do that for Papa?" she whispered.

"And for you, Mama. And for you."

CHAPTER
10

December 23, 1918, 6:35 a.m.—Ministry of War,
Mitte District, Berlin

Hans was in a foul mood as he approached the dark shape of the War Ministry once again. His train hadn't made it to Berlin until after 3:00 a.m. After washing up in the toilet, Hans had found an empty bench in the train station and offered to pay the only porter on duty five *Pfennige* if he would wake him precisely at 5:40.

And now, here he was once again, staring at the building he was coming to loathe almost as much as he did the army itself. He stopped dead as he approached. There was no line outside. No guard handing out tickets. The sidewalks around the Ministry of War were completely empty. There was not a soul anywhere in sight.

He stood there for a moment, uncomprehending. Behind him, up the street about a block away, a milk cart rattled loudly as it made its rounds. Here and there in the apartment buildings and businesses, lights were on and smoke was coming from chimneys, but the Ministry was dark, silent, and utterly deserted.

Had he somehow gotten his days mixed up? Could it still be Sunday? But that was ridiculous. He had been in church yesterday morning with his family. This had to be Monday. Thoroughly baffled,

Hans moved forward, trying to make sense of it. And that was when he saw a large placard taped to the inside of the main door.

NOTICE:
All offices of the Ministry of War are closed for the holidays.
Offices will reopen after New Year's at 8:00 a.m.
Sorry for any inconvenience this may cause.
Merry Christmas and a happy New Year.

Hans groaned and swore as he read it again. Then he smacked the door hard with his gloved fist. The glass rattled back at him. Nothing else changed.

Cursing his luck, cursing the army, cursing Frau Hessler—she probably did this just to spite him—cursing whatever gods there might be in the heavens, he spun around and started on the half-hour walk back to the train station.

7:08 a.m.—East Railway Station, Friedrichshain-Kreuzberg District, Berlin

As Hans walked through the main doors of the station, pushing his way through the outgoing rush of people coming into the city center for work, he suddenly stopped right in the middle of the rush as a thought hit him. People shot him dirty looks as they jostled their way around him. "Get out of the way, *Hohlkopf*," an older man in a business suit snarled at him.

"Blockhead yourself," Hans tossed back over his shoulder as he started forward again. That sent him straight into a woman about Emilee's age, nearly knocking her off her feet. She gave him a venomous look and muttered something under her breath. "And Merry Christmas to you too," he snapped. But he did start angling his way off to the side to get out of the press. Once he was clear, he stepped behind one of the pillars and stopped to collect his thoughts.

On the walk back from the Ministry, he had fumed and cursed

and railed against this newest development. Now, as he looked up at the schedule board and the large clock above it, he realized that he had another problem. There was a northbound train at ten, so he was in luck.

When he had called Emilee, he had warned her that the government bureaucracy might bog him down for the better part of the day. So he had told her not to expect him in Pasewalk until that night. Now, with a ten o'clock train, he would be there by one thirty or two o'clock. But Christmas was only two days away. The chances of Emilee being home at midday were small. She would be out buying food or doing some last-minute shopping for presents. Hans didn't find the idea of sitting in the house trying to make conversation with Heinz-Albert for several hours highly attractive. So he headed for the telephone exchange. He hoped it was still early enough that she would be home.

Fishing her letter from his inside jacket, he found her number and walked over to the small telephone exchange in the far corner of the station.

It took about four minutes before the phone in his booth rang. The operator's voice told him she was putting his call through.

For a few moments, Hans was afraid no one was going to answer. But on the sixth ring, a male voice answered. "*Hallo!*"

"Uh . . . *hallo.* Is Fräulein Emilee Fromme there, please?"

A long pause, then, "Who is calling, *bitte?*" It was Heinz-Albert, the younger brother.

"This is Sergeant Eckhardt. Sergeant Hans Eckhardt."

A soft grunt, then, "*Einen Moment.*"

He heard a door open, and then the voice called out, "Emmy. *Telefon.*"

Footsteps, then her voice come on. "Hans? Is that you?"

"*Guten Morgen,* Emilee. How are you?"

"Oh, Hans. I am so glad you called."

"Well, it's good to talk to you too, Emilee. Uh . . . I've had a slight change of plans and—"

She rushed on, not hearing him. "I was afraid that you wouldn't call before I had to leave."

"Leave?"

"Yes. Things are so mixed up here. I'm sorry, but we won't be able to do Christmas dinner." His shoulders sagged. "Oh." *What did I do wrong now?*

"Ernst and I are leaving for Königsberg in about twenty minutes."

"*What?* Again?"

"Yes. I am so sorry. I didn't know how to reach you. I called your family in Graswang, but they said you left yesterday."

That brought him up straight in a hurry. "You talked to my family?"

"Yes, to your mother. I left them a message for you in case you called them."

There was a sinking feeling in the pit of his stomach. "What kind of a message?"

That took her aback a little. "That we couldn't do Christmas dinner."

Putting his hand up to his eyes, he let out a slow breath. *So now, Mama knows that I lied to her. Wonderful!*

"Hans?"

"Yeah. I'm here. I'm . . . I understand. I'm disappointed, of course, but you do what you have to do."

"We tried to put it off until after Christmas, but. . . . Well, let me explain. You know how Ernst and I went up to Königsberg to get my mother's home ready to sell?"

"*Ja*, I remember."

"Well yesterday our land agent called to say he's found an interested buyer who has made a solid offer on the house. This is wonderful news, but they want to take possession immediately. No later than

January 2nd. Earlier if possible. So that means we've got to go back and get all of Mama's stuff out before the first of the year."

"I see." Yet another setback.

"We arranged for a truck, but then it fell through." She hesitated a moment. "That would have been perfect. I was even thinking that if you didn't have to go right back, I might impose on you to come to Königsberg with us and help us load the truck."

"Really? I could do that. I would love to do that."

"I knew you would say that. Then, late last night, Ernst got a call from a friend of his who lives not far from Pasewalk. He runs a wholesale butcher shop and owns his own truck. Ernst had asked him earlier if we might borrow his truck for a few days. He said no, of course, because he uses it every day. But last night, he called to say that since he's pretty well sold out of all the meat he had for the holiday, he's going to close shop and visit his family in Hanover this week. So the truck is available until Sunday . . ." she paused for a moment for effect, "and he has sufficient gasoline ration to get us there and back. We'll have to pay him, of course, but. . . ."

"That's wonderful, Emilee. What a lucky break for you."

"It's a little miracle, actually."

"And I've got good news too. The Ministry is closed until after New Year's Day, so I'm at the train station. My train leaves in an hour and half. I can be there by two or three. Then I can go with you."

There was a long silence, then, very softly, "That only makes it worse."

"What?"

"No, I didn't mean it that way. The bad news is that Ernst's friend is going to be here to pick us up in fifteen minutes."

"Can you have him wait a few hours?"

There was no answer for a moment. Then she came back on. "Sorry, I was just telling Ernst what you said. How soon does your train leave Berlin?"

"At ten. So I could hopefully be there by two o'clock at the latest." *Unless, of course, there are major delays. Which was almost a given these days.*

"*Einen Moment.*" He could hear the murmur of her voice and that of a man's. From what little he could hear, Ernst didn't sound too enthusiastic.

"Hans?" Her voice was heavy with disappointment.

"*Ja?*"

"Unfortunately, his friend is going to show us how to drive the truck and then we have to take him back to his family, which is about twenty miles northeast of Pasewalk. It's on the way to Königsberg. As much as we would love the extra help, Ernst thinks we have no choice but to leave now."

"I understand, Emilee."

"But I was so looking forward to seeing you again." There was brief moment of hesitation. "And to talking through things."

"Me too."

He quickly told her about the War Ministry being closed.

"What will you do?" she asked after a moment

"Uh . . . to be honest, I don't know. I've got to find a job. And sometime I need go visit the University of Berlin and find out what my status there is."

"Excellent!"

"But with the holidays, they'll be closed too, I'm sure. And who's going to be worrying about hiring people two days before Christmas?"

"So you'll go back to Bavaria?"

"Much as I hate to say it, I guess so."

"Hans!" The disappointment in her voice was sharp.

"Oh, I don't mean it that way. It's been great with the family. But that train ride? Going down took me forever."

"I'm so sorry, Hans. I've really made a mess of things for you."

"It's not your fault," he said. "But I am disappointed."

"I would be very disappointed if you weren't disappointed."

He heard a man's voice in the background calling out something. Emilee broke in quickly. "The truck's here, Hans. I've got to go. Not sure when we'll be back, but I'll call you if I can."

"Okay. Have a good trip. Tell Ernst to drive carefully."

"Why do you assume it's Ernst who's driving?" Then, laughing, she said, "*Auf Wiedersehen*, Hans."

December 28, 1918, 8:30 a.m. —Eckhardt dairy farm, Graswang, Bavaria

As Ilse picked up her bowl and started to get up from the breakfast table, Hans waved her back down again. "*Einen Moment,* Ilse. I have something that I would like to say."

Everyone turned to look at him. The children, who were seated at the other table, all turned as well. Except for Miki, who was sneaking another piece of her grandmother's cinnamon toast.

"I would like to make a proposal. Today is Saturday. And as you all know, I am leaving tomorrow to return to Berlin."

There was an instant chorus of groans and protests. "I have to. I need to be at the Ministry of War first thing in the morning on the day after New Year's."

Annaliese, who was fourteen, cried out. "But that's not for five days, *Onkel* Hans. Are you going up to see Emilee first?"

Hans gave her a dirty look. "How do you know about Emilee?"

"Because I told her," her mother said.

"And I told Ilse," Inga added. She smiled at him. "We all took a vote, and we're all agreed. Emilee is a family matter and we want full disclosure from now on."

"Yes!" Annaliese and Kristen shouted it out together. "When do we get to meet her?"

"Not until after we're married," Hans retorted.

That had the desired effect. His father's head came up with a snap. His mother's mouth dropped open. His sisters were all gaping at him.

Laughing, he shook his head. "I'm playing with you. We haven't even gone out on a date yet, for heaven's sake."

"But you are going to see her?" Annaliese persisted.

"Yes. Emilee has invited me to have dinner with her family for New Year's Day." He glanced quickly at his mother. "I was going to go up to her house for Christmas, but then she had to go to Königsberg. Uh . . . she asked me to go with them to Königsberg, but I told her I needed to spend Christmas here."

Heidi spoke up. "Will you bring her down here after you get your reimbursement check?"

"An excellent idea," Inga said.

Hans just shook his head, trying not to laugh. "Are you kidding? And have you guys pounce on her like a hungry Doberman on a piece of meat?"

Miki took one last bite of toast and then come over to stand by him. "I'll be nice to her, *Onkel* Hans."

Putting an arm around her, Hans pulled her in close. "I know you would, Miki. And do you know what I think?"

"What?"

"I think maybe I'll take you with me to Pasewalk."

"Why?"

"Because once she meets you, she'll marry me just so she can see you all the time."

Anna leaned forward, her eyes holding his. "Did I just hear my little brother use the word *marriage* a second time in two minutes? I think maybe there's more going on here than you're letting on."

"I'm teasing you. We're a long ways from even talking about marriage."

Anna raised her fingers. "That's three times!"

"All right, all right. Can I say what I was going to say now? You people are like bloodhounds."

"Yes," his father said sternly, obviously not pleased with this talk of marriage. "Let's hear what Hans has to say."

"Thank you, *Vati*." Hans looked around the table. "I don't know if you've looked outside yet, but we had about six inches of fresh snow last night."

Klaus Sr. hooted. "Looked outside? While you were sleeping in, Rudi, Karl, and I were milking thirty-two cows."

"Nice try, Klaus, but actually, I wasn't sleeping in. I was out in the woodshed loading the milk cart up with firewood."

"Firewood?" Gerhardt echoed. "What for?"

Hans got to his feet and looked around at the their faces, letting the suspense build a little. "Because we are going to have a snow party."

Cheers erupted from the children. The adults looked a little taken aback. He laughed at their expressions. "That's right. We're going to build a big bonfire. We'll take lunch. We'll make snow angels and take the sleds up to the sledding hill and—"

"Can we play Fox and Geese?" Klaus Jr. cried.

"Why not?"

Several hands shot up. "I get to be the fox first," Kristen said.

Her male cousins booed that down, but Hans cut them off with a sharp wave of his hand. "Sorry, but I've heard tell that because today is a special day, the first person who plays the fox has to be someone who spells her name M-I-K-I."

Before he had finished spelling her name, Miki was jumping up and down and waving wildly at him. "That's how I spell my name, *Onkel* Hans."

He cocked his head to one side. "Are you sure?"

For a moment, that panicked her. She whirled around. "How do I spell my name, *Mutti*?"

Heidi kept a straight face. "M-I-K-I."

As she swung back around, dancing with excitement, Hans swept her up into his arms. "Then this is your lucky day, little one."

Gerhardt was waving a hand. "Can we make a snow fort and have a snowball fight?"

"Yes," Kristen cried. "Boys against girls."

Inga's hand came up slowly. For a moment no one noticed, but she held it up until everyone fell silent. "I have too much work to do today. Dishes. Laundry. Ironing. So I'll stay—"

"Oh, no, you don't," Hans retorted. He looked around at his family. "All who think Oma should stay here and do housework, raise your hand."

There was not a flicker of movement.

"And all who want to see Oma participate in—" Every hand in the room was up and waving enthusiastically. Ignoring Inga's dirty look, Hans said to the others, "I think that was unanimous."

"You can be on our side, Oma," Annaliese said.

Hans gave Miki a kiss on the cheek and then set her down. "Let's go have a party."

8:45 p.m.

Heidi came through the back door, stomping the snow from her galoshes. Then she reached down, slipped them off, and came over to sit beside her husband.

"Is the baby asleep?" he asked.

"Yes. And all the others are out too. Miki has been so wound up all day I was afraid she'd never sleep, but she conked out in about two minutes."

"They all played so hard," Inga said, smiling.

"Yes," Hans agreed. "They *all* did. If someone had told me I'd get to watch my mother having a snowball fight with her grandchildren, I would never have believed him."

"And win," she said, her eyes twinkling.

"Yes," Anna said. "Did you hear what Klaus Jr. said? After catching one of yours in the back, he turned to his father and said, 'Watch out for Oma. She's got a wicked arm.'"

Inga just beamed.

They settled back, savoring the memories as they sipped cups of warm milk and ate the last of the *Vanillekipferln,* crescent-shaped Christmas cookies that were a long-time Christmas tradition in their family.

After a few minutes, Hans leaned forward. "Well, as much as I hate to say it, I've got to pack."

"Yes," Rudi said. "And Anna needs to get some rest too."

"Not yet."

All of them turned in surprise to look as Hans Sr. started to get up. Instantly, Inga was on her feet helping him. "Are you ready for bed, *Schatzi*?"

He straightened and then shook his head emphatically. "No. I have something to say."

The family shot questioning looks at Inga, but she was as taken aback by this as they were. She sat down beside him, reaching out to hold his hand.

He stood there for a moment, swaying back and forth a little as he looked around at his family. Then, with a nod, he began, looking at Hans when he spoke.

"Thank you, son," he whispered. "Thank you for being here with us for Christmas."

"You're welcome, Papa. But I'm the one who should be thanking all of you. It's been a wonderful time for me."

His father seemed not to hear that. He looked around at the others. "As you know, Hans is leaving us tomorrow. We don't know when he will be back. So there is something I must say before he goes."

The only sound now was the crackling of the fire. Every eye was on Hans Sr. He took a breath, and then a deeper one, and then looked down at his wife. And he immediately teared up. "It was twenty-three years ago in February that my beloved Inga delivered a strapping baby boy into our family. And she asked me if we could name him after me."

"I remember that night perfectly," she whispered. "You sat for hours rocking him in the rocking chair, just staring at him."

"I did. Because now, we had not only a son, we had an heir. And I no longer had to worry about the farm. For more than six generations, the Eckhardt name has belonged to this house and to this land. And I was worried that might no longer be so. But then, my Inga gave us an heir."

Out of the corner of his eye, Hans saw Ilse and Heidi exchange nervous glances. And he saw that his mother saw it too—and was concerned.

His father turned so that he was directly facing his son. "Hans Otto, it is of that which I wish to speak tonight."

"All right, Father. I am listening."

"I wish to know if you have found gainful employment since your discharge from the army."

Taken aback by the forcefulness with which his father spoke, Hans shook his head. "I have not."

"And is it true what I read in the news, that nearly fifty percent of men your age are still unemployed in the Fatherland?"

"I believe that is true, yes," Hans agreed.

"Then," he said, his eyes boring into his son's, "then I declare that you shall stay here with us and take your rightful place as heir of this farm and all that goes with it—the land, the livestock, the outbuildings."

His three sisters and their husbands were staring at each other in open dismay now. His father saw that and turned to them. "My dear daughters," he said, "how I love each of you. How faithful you have been to me and your mother. And to your husbands, I say thank you. You have kept the farm going through the war years, and I shall ever be grateful to you for that."

His shoulders lifted and fell, as if he had just thrown off a great burden.

Hans was stunned. He felt his face burning with embarrassment.

He knew his father was expecting some kind of response, but he was speechless. Then he saw Ilse reach out to take Karl's hand. He jerked it away, staring at the floor. She looked at Hans and then at her father. "Papa, I. . . ."

Now Hans Sr. spoke to his sons-in-law. "Karl, Klaus, Rudi, I wish to thank you from the bottom of my heart. You have been faithful helpers. You have been good husbands to your wives and good fathers to your children. I love you as I would if you were my own sons."

Hans winced as he saw Heidi, head down, shake her head back and forth, angered by his last words. Anna, looking as if she were going to be sick, got up and walked out of the room. And at that moment, Hans knew he had to say something, and he had to say it now.

He got slowly to his feet and turned to face his father. "No, Papa," he said softly.

His father blinked, and blinked again. He seemed confused. "Hans Otto, do you have something you would like to say?"

"I do, Papa. I have something I *must* say." He moved over to stand beside his father. He put his arm around his shoulders, inwardly wincing as he realized how old and vulnerable his father had become. He pulled him closer for a moment and then let his arm drop and turned to face the anguish that was so clearly evident on the faces of these people he loved so much. Hans took a quick breath and began. He spoke slowly and clearly so that his father could not misunderstand.

"Father, I am deeply honored that you would make such an offer as this, and I shall ever be grateful to you for it. But I cannot accept it."

Hans felt his father stiffen beside him and saw his sisters' heads come up. He rushed on. "Father, I know not where life shall take me, but of this much I am sure. My path is not going to bring me back to Graswang. As much as I love this place, and you who live in it, I—"

"But you are the heir." It was a cry of pain.

"Yes, I am, Father. But I am not worthy of that title. Not yet, anyway. I hope to change that, but . . ." He wasn't sure how to finish that, so he took another quick breath. "Also, Papa, I want to say this: these three men who sit here before us are your sons now, Papa. They are as fine and loyal to you as any sons a man could ever have. And their wives—my sisters—"

He had to stop because his throat had suddenly pinched off. "*They* are your heirs too. This is *their* farm, *their* cattle, *their* home."

Hans had to stop as he looked around. Ilse had started cry. He saw Karl's Adam's apple bob up and down twice as he swallowed hard. Heidi was gripping Klaus's hand so tightly that her knuckles were white, tears streaming down her cheeks as well. Then a movement caught Hans's eye. Anna was standing at the door, one hand to her mouth, the other resting on the swell of her stomach. She started to say something to him but couldn't get it out. That did it. A great convulsion rose in his own throat and he could say no more.

Suddenly his mother was beside him, stepping in between Hans and his father. She took both of their hands. Though her eyes were shining, she had not given way to tears yet. She looked up at her husband, who looked like a bewildered little boy. "It's all right, *Schatzi*," she murmured. "It's all right. Hans is right. You have other sons now, and Hans has other places to go, other things to do. But the farm is in good hands."

He turned to Hans. "Is that true?"

The hurt in his father's eyes tore through Hans like a knife, but he nodded. "Yes, Papa. If Mother approves, I hereby formally and publically renounce my right to this land once you are gone. And I shall sign whatever paperwork is required to declare that my sisters, Ilse, Heidi, and Anna, and their husbands, are to be joint heirs of this land and all property upon it."

Every head turned toward Inga. She glanced up once more at her husband and nodded. "I fully concur," she whispered. Laying a hand on his cheek, she went up on tiptoes and kissed him softly. "Come, *Schatzi*. It's been a very long day. Let's go up to bed."

CHAPTER
11

December 29, 1918, 7:50 a.m.—Eckhardt dairy farm,
Graswang, Bavaria

This farewell was far more tearful than when Hans had left before Christmas, because everyone knew that it would likely be a long time before they were reunited again. He went through his sisters and brothers-in-law, and tears flowed freely as they whispered their thanks and gratitude to him. Through all the nieces and nephews he managed to keep a pretty tight rein on his emotions, until Miki stepped up and threw her arms around him, weeping as though her little heart was shattered. It was too much for him, and he began to sob. Along with everyone else in the room.

Barely had he gotten that under control when he had to face his father. Neither said a word. They just clung to each other for a long, long time. Did his father remember last night? Had he accepted it now? Hans couldn't be sure. "Good-bye, *Vati.* I'll call often. And I'll come home as soon as I can."

When he finally turned to his mother, Hans felt utterly spent. So he just opened his arms and stepped toward her. To his surprise, she reached out and took him by the hand and pulled him toward the kitchen. "I have something I need to say," she said in a low voice.

Once in the kitchen, she shut the door softly behind her before she turned to him.

"My goodness, *Mutti*," Hans said, curious now. "I didn't expect something quite this dramatic." Inga came over to face him but stopped two paces away. She shoved her hands into her apron pockets and stared past him for a moment. Her face was suddenly so grave that he thought she was going to tell him that his father had cancer again. He grasped her hands. "What, *Mutti*? What's wrong? Is Papa all right?"

She nodded. "Papa is fine. I think he even understands what you did last night and why. He seemed at peace this morning."

She motioned for Hans to sit down and then sat across the table from him. "Hans, I need to say something to you before you go. I don't expect an answer. In fact, I'd like you to just listen."

"All right." He sat back.

"What you did last night—for your sisters, for your brothers-in-law, for your nieces and nephews—it was magnificent. I have never been more proud of you."

"Thank you, *Mutti*."

Inga took a deep breath. "And because of that, I am reluctant to say what I'm going to say now. But I feel that I must."

Hans felt a little tingle of warning. The pride in his mother's eyes had gone as swiftly as it had come. "Go on."

"Why is it, Hans, that you feel that you have to lie to me?"

He knew instantly what she meant but feigned ignorance. "Lie to you? About what?"

Inga sighed. "Even now? Emilee told me when she called that she and her brother were leaving right away to go north. You were still in Berlin. Why would she invite you to go when there was no way you could get there in time?"

Hans felt his face burning but didn't look at his mother. What was there to say? Finally all he could think of was, "It was a stupid thing to do."

"Yes it was," she said. "So why did you do it?"

"Mama, I—I'm sorry. I mean it."

"Shush," she snapped. "Your apology means nothing, Hans. Not now. That's what grieves me the most, Hans. How easily the lies fall from your lips."

"*Mutti*, I just didn't want to make you feel bad."

"How noble of you."

"I. . . ."

"Do you remember the story about the Dutch boy and the dike?"

"What?" *Where had that come from?*

"This happened in Holland. A young boy, whose name was Peter, was on his way to school when he noticed a small leak in the dike that held back the North Sea from the lowlands of Holland. Even though he was late for school, he decided that if something wasn't done, the dike might eventually collapse and the lowlands would be flooded. So he stuck his finger in the hole to plug the leak. Even though it was cold, he stayed there all night until someone came along and found him. Men were called, the leak was plugged, and the lowland villages were saved."

"I know the story, *Mutti*. We studied it in my literature class at the Von Kruger Academy. Did you know that it never really happened? It's a myth. It actually comes from the famous children's book called *Hans Brinker and the Silver Skates*. And here's an irony for you. The book was written by an American author who had never been to Holland. And Hans Brinker, the hero of the story, was not the boy who put his finger in the dike. It was story within a story. And the author made it up. Oh, and by the way, the boy's name wasn't Peter. He wasn't named at all in the original book. Someone gave him that name later."

She watched him steadily as he spoke. When he finished, she

asked, "Are you finished now, Mr. Valedictorian of the Von Kruger Academy?"

"I. . . ." Stung, Hans struck back. "I just thought you ought to know that it is not a true story."

Her eyes bored in on him. "Does it really matter whether it is a true story or not? That was not my point."

"I'm sorry, Mama. I didn't mean to sound condescending."

She harrumphed softly. "Well you did, whether you meant to or not."

He flinched but said nothing. Trying to reason with her was only making it worse.

"You are an engineer," she said thoughtfully. "Let's suppose for a moment that it was a true story. What would have happened if the boy hadn't put his finger in the dike?"

"Well," he said, a little surprised by the question. "Theoretically, the leak is caused by some weakness in the dike structure, a crack of some kind. Engineers would say that its structural integrity had been compromised."

Her head came up. "Structural integrity? They actually use those words?"

"Yes. But the leak itself is caused by the tremendous water pressure behind the dike."

"So, answer my question. What happens if the boy doesn't put his finger in the dike?"

"Well, that's part of the problem. It's doubtful that a boy's thumb could have held back any kind of serious leak."

She sighed wearily. "I said that we're supposing the story was true. What happens if the boy doesn't put his finger in the dike?"

He thought he saw where this was going but saw no way around it. "If something isn't done about it, what is at first only seepage through the dike would become a trickle. A trickle might then widen the crack enough that you have a tiny spray of water, and then a gushing leak, and . . . eventually the whole dam would rupture if it weren't stopped."

"But all of this is just theoretical, right?" she asked quietly.

Hans was silent. There was nothing to say. It was an elegant metaphor, perfectly describing his growing tendency to bend the truth to his own convenience.

"Right?" she pressed.

"All right, *Mutti*, I get it. It was stupid of me to lie to you. But it was only—"

She cut in quickly. "Only a little trickle of a lie, right?"

Hans shrugged, knowing that there was nothing to do but to let her get it out.

They sat there for a moment, listening to the sounds of the family through the door. Hans finally looked at her. "I need to go, Mama."

She nodded but didn't move. After a moment, she reached across the table and laid her hand on his. "You have greatness in you, Hans. I saw a glimpse of that last night, and I wept. But there are places where I worry that your structural integrity is being compromised. Isn't that how you said it?"

"Yes, Mama."

Tears squeezed up from beneath her lower eyelids. "Oh, my son," she said in a tiny, tremulous voice, "I cannot begin to imagine what these last four years did to you. Who am I to judge you?"

He took her hand in both of his, near tears himself. "You're my *Mutti*. That's who."

"Then stick your finger in those holes, Hans. Before they get so big that you can't stop them anymore. Remember Peter."

Hans smiled sadly. "His name wasn't Peter, *Mutti*."

"You don't know that. Peter's a pretty common name in Holland, you know."

"Yes, Mama." Hans got to his feet, came around the table, and pulled his mother up to face him. He went to put his arms around her, but she reared back. "Before we get all mushy here, I've got one more thing to say to you."

Hans feigned a groan. How he loved this mother of his. "I'm listening."

"About Emilee."

"Yes," he said slowly. "What about her?"

Inga raised a finger and shook it at him. "Don't you mess things up with her, boy. If you do, your father and I are going to take a cheese paddle to your bare backside. I don't care how big you are. Got it?"

"Yes, *Mutti*," Hans said meekly. "I understand."

8:55 a.m. — Telephone exchange, Oberammergau Railway Station

Hans sat alone at a small metal table in the train station café, which was really little more than a hole in the wall near the far corner of the terminal with three rusting tables out front. They served stale cheese, stale *Kaisersemmel,* a hard roll named for Kaiser Franz Josef of Austria, wilted red cabbage, and stale coffee.

Hans didn't care. It felt good to be alone with his thoughts for a few minutes before he started on yet another interminable trip to Berlin. And his thoughts were on his family. How long would it be before he got back here? Would his dear Anna be a mother by then? Would Miki still be that impish, impudent little tornado that he so adored? He swallowed quickly. Would he ever see his father alive again?

The phone beside him rang. He picked up the handset. "Yes?"

"I'm ringing your number now, Herr Eckhardt."

"*Gut. Danke.*"

Almost immediately the phone began to ring. Once. Twice. Three times.

"Come on, Emilee," he muttered.

Four times. Then five. A sudden sinking feeling hit him. But then, a moment later, there was a click and a male voice spoke. "*Hallo.*"

It was Heinz-Albert's voice. "Is Fräulein Emilee Fromme there?"

A long pause.

Finally Hans spoke again. *"Hallo?"*

"Who is it?"

"It's Hans Eckhardt. Is Emilee there?"

"No."

"When will she be home?"

"Dunno." He sounded half asleep.

"Is she back from Königsberg yet?"

"No."

"Have you heard from them?"

"No."

"Were they able to get gasoline?"

"Dunno."

Growing exasperated, Hans wondered why Emilee's mother never answered the phone. "Can I leave a message for her?"

"No."

"Why not?"

"Don't have a pencil."

"Isn't there one in the house somewhere?"

"Dunno."

That was when he began to understand why Heinz-Albert, who was nearly twenty now, still lived with his mother and sister. Now he better understood. And how could he be angry with him for that?

"Is this Heinz-Albert?"

Another long pause, then, "Yes. Who are you?"

"My name is Hans. I am a friend of Emilee, your sister."

"Yes, she's my sister."

"Can you tell her that I called?"

"Who are you?"

"My name is Hans. Please tell Emilee that—"

"Do you like my sister?"

He smiled. "Yes, Heinz-Albert, I actually do."

"Me too." And then he abruptly hung up.

Hans was ready to tear his hair out. Now what? Surely Heinz-Albert was wrong about her not being back in Königsberg by now. They had left almost a week ago. Maybe she was asleep. She said she always went to bed as soon as she finished her shift at the hospital. After a moment, he shook his head. Heinz-Albert wasn't that deficient. Hans let out a long, slow breath. Why did everything have to be so miserably complicated? Should he buy a ticket for Berlin or all the way to Pasewalk? Then, with a start, he realized there was a simple answer to that.

Turning on his heel, he headed toward the opposite end of the terminal, where another window had a sign over it: "Telegraph Office."

Five minutes later, he reread what he had printed out on the blank template.

EMILEE STOP TRIED TO CALL STOP ARRIVE BERLIN
TONIGHT 7:14 STOP WILL CALL AGAIN STOP
CAN LEAVE MESSAGE FOR ME AT TELEPHONE
EXCHANGE BERLIN OSTBAHNHOF STOP. HANS.

Satisfied, he returned to the window and pushed it under the mesh screen. The man read it quickly, nodded, and counted the words. "That'll be one mark twenty."

Ouch! But there was no choice. He paid the man and walked back to the ticket window. He recognized the man in uniform there. "A one-way ticket to Berlin, *bitte*," he said.

The man took his card, looked at it briefly, and then looked at him. "You're really burning up the rails, aren't you, Sergeant Eckhardt?"

That made him chuckle. "I have a hard time sleeping without hearing the clickety-clack of steel on steel," he said dryly.

"Right." The man wrote the ticket, stamped it, and handed it to Hans. "Sleep tight," he drawled.

January 2, 1919, 6:27 a.m.—Ministry of War,
Mitte District, Berlin

He didn't have to wait until he reached the building to know the news was not good. The only things in the plaza in front of the ugly old Ministry building were the two lamps that threw small circles of light across the cement. The building was dark. The streets were nearly deserted. And there was no one waiting outside the main doors. Not a soul.

"You can't be serious!" he muttered as he walked across the plaza to the doors. But they were. The same sign was still up.

NOTICE:
All offices of the Ministry of War are closed for the Holidays.
Offices will reopen after New Year's at 8:00 a.m.
Sorry for any inconvenience this may cause.
Merry Christmas and a happy New Year.

"The holidays are over, you idiots," he exclaimed. "It's January 2nd."

But as he read the notice over again, he saw that it said only that they would open *after* New Year's. It didn't say how long after, right? And this was the government, right? Any other business would be open today to see if they couldn't make a few marks. But, in the thinking of a civil servant, why would you open for only two days and then close again for the weekend, when you could just wait until Monday to open? So what if a few thousand people were inconvenienced? They had already said they were sorry for the inconvenience.

Muttering all kinds of disparaging things about some of his fellow men and women, Hans sat down on the steps to figure out what to do next. There had been no message from Emilee left at the station. When he tried her phone again, there was no answer at all. He even called his parents under the guise that he was letting them know he had arrived safely in Berlin. His mother saw through that in an instant. No, she hadn't heard anything from Emilee.

No Emilee. No Ministry. No check. No hotel room. Just what did he do now?

Hans sat there in the plaza for five more minutes, brooding over it, before an idea came to him. When it did, he reared back and then grunted in satisfaction. *Why not? It was something, at least.*

He picked up his rucksack, pulled his overcoat more tightly around him, and started walking—not to the east toward the train station, but toward the west. Toward the Tiergarten District.

Chapter Note

Hans Brinker, alternately titled *The Silver Skates: A Story of Life in Holland,* was written by American author Mary Mapes Dodge and was first published in 1864. She had never been to Holland before she wrote the book. It became an instant bestseller and is still in print. It is considered a children's classic to this day. It was so popular that it is credited with introducing speed skating to America. The boy who put his finger in the dike was not named.

January 2, 1919, 11:38 a.m. —Tiergarten District, Berlin

Katya Freylitsch turned around in surprise when she heard the tinkle of the bell in the downstairs lobby. Puzzled, she laid her book on the lamp table beside her. Then gathering up her cat, *Kleines Kätzchen,* in her arms, she kissed him on the top of his head and set him on the floor. His look of pure astonishment at this travesty made her smile. Had she really just unceremoniously dumped him without warning? Smiling, she reached down and stroked the cat. She went to the door, opened it just enough to slip through into the hallway, and closed it again before her cat could follow.

As she ran lightly down the stairs, the bell tinkled again. It was definitely her bell. Her landlady's bell had a much deeper tone. Through the opaque glass of the front door, she saw a large, dark shape. Clearly a man, she thought. Maybe the postman had a package.

When she opened the door she stopped dead, her eyes growing wide.

"Uh . . . oh, hullo."

He swayed back and forth as he stared stupidly at her. She caught a strong whiff of schnapps. "Sergeant Eckhardt?" Katya gasped.

"At your service." He swept off his army hat and attempted a deep bow. She leaped forward and caught his arm before he toppled backward down the steps.

"Beggin' your pardon, Fräulein," he mumbled. Then he burped loudly. One hand came up and clamped itself over his mouth and stifled a peal of giggles. "Sorry, sorry." Then he put his finger to his lips. He leaned in closer and shushed her in a conspiratorial manner. The smell of the liquor was so strong she turned her head away.

Looking quickly up and down the street to see if anyone had seen them, she tightened her grip on his arm and pulled him inside the tiny entryway and then shut the door behind him. *Thank you, Frau Schmidt, for not being here right now.*

Twice Hans started to teeter backward, so Katya quickly got around behind him and pushed him forward toward the steps.

"We need to go upstairs, Sergeant," she said. "Lift your foot. That's right. One at a time."

"Pleeshe. Call me Hans."

"Yes, Hans. Keep moving. Take another step. That's it."

She propped him against the wall on the landing and opened her door. KK shot past her and down the stairs. Hans jumped a foot. "What was that?" he yelped.

"My cat. Come back here, KK," Katya snapped. The cat ignored her, so she grabbed Hans's arm, wrapped it around her shoulder, and steered him through the door. "Welcome to my humble home, Hans."

He pulled free of her, looking around in surprise. "Where am I?"

"This is my flat, Hans. This is where I live. Where did you want to be?"

"Oh." He did a wobbly half circle. "It . . . it . . . it . . . it's very nice."

"Thank you." She moved around him and removed his overcoat and then led him by the elbow to the sofa by the window. "Sit down, Hans. I'm going to make us some coffee."

"I like coffee."

She smiled. "Actually, you *need* coffee. Sit down and I'll go make a fresh pot."

Hans didn't move, and she finally gave him a gentle shove. He crashed down so heavily that the floor trembled a little. She winced and again was grateful that her landlady was gone for the day. That kind of a crash would have brought her running.

And thank heavens Angelika is gone too.

With a sigh, she took his coat and hung it up on the coat rack. Angelika, Katya's flatmate, was also a civil servant. She worked for the Finance Ministry. But unlike Katya, who had come back to Berlin early because the craziness at home had finally gotten to her, Angelika wouldn't be back until Sunday night. Katya started for the tiny kitchen and then changed her mind and moved over to stand in front of Hans. "What are you doing here, Hans Eckhardt?"

He looked up, squinting at her with that same foolish smirk on his face. "What?"

"Why are you here?"

"Needed to shee you."

"Why?"

Nothing. He was looking around again, still confused. There was a meow and a soft scratching at the door. Katya got up and let KK back in. "I told you," she chided the cat. "You can't go out without me." The cat ignored that, took one look at Hans, and disappeared into Katya's bedroom. She turned back to her guest. "Hans? Please tell me why you came to see me."

But he was gone. His eyes were shut and his head lolled back at a crazy angle. Shaking her head, she went into her bedroom and got a pillow and a blanket. She managed to get him lying down without too much effort, but he was too tall for the sofa and she had to bend his knees to get him to fit. After putting the blanket on him, she tucked it in around his legs so they wouldn't slip out. Finally, she lifted his head and slid the pillow beneath it.

She stood there for several moments, trying to figure out what this was all about. It had definitely rekindled her hope. When she hadn't heard from him again after that night he had walked her home, she assumed he was another one of those men who slipped in and out of her life so casually. That had been almost a month ago now. But here he was again, popping into her life with absolutely no warning, just as he had before.

She went back to her chair, sat down, and picked up her book. KK immediately reappeared and hopped back up on her lap. He settled in and began to purr. Absently, she reached down and stroked the cat's head. But her eyes were on the sleeping figure across the room.

"And just exactly what is it you need me for?" she murmured after a moment or two.

4:17 p.m.

Katya came awake with a start as the book slipped from her hands. It clunked KK on the head before it hit the floor. With a yowl, he leaped off her lap and slunk away in a feline pout. Stifling a yawn, Katya reached down and picked up the book. When she straightened she saw that Hans's eyes were open—and clear—and that he was watching her.

Katya gave a little cry. "Oh! I didn't know you were awake."

Hans yawned and then burrowed more deeply into the pillow. "I'm not. This is an illusion."

"I would say so," she laughed. "I still can't believe that you're lying on my sofa."

His face twisted in pain as he tried to roll more on his side again. "Ow!" His hands shot up and began to massage his temples.

"Headache?"

"I think the word is head explosion."

"Do you always drink that much in the morning?" she teased, getting to her feet. She didn't wait for his answer. "I've got some Bayer. Would you like a couple?"

"Bayer?"

"Yes. Aspirin. For your headache. Would you like some lukewarm coffee with that?"

Hans groaned and shut his eyes again. "Please." As Katya stood up and started for the bathroom, he called after her. "I was pretty drunk, *ja*?"

She turned and smiled. "I thought I was going to have to carry you up the stairs."

"I'm sorry." He pulled himself up, biting his lip so as not to yell out. "Can you make it four aspirin?"

She came back with the pills in one hand and a cup of coffee in the other. She dumped the pills in his hand and he popped all four of them in his mouth at once. But when she handed him the cup, he held up one hand to hold her off and then started chewing. Instantly his face twisted into a horrible grimace.

"You're chewing them?" she exclaimed. "Ew!"

He grabbed the cup, took a big swig, and swished it around in his mouth before he swallowed. Then he downed the rest of the cup. Still pulling a horrible face, he said, "A trick an old army doctor taught me. If you chew them, they don't have to dissolve in your stomach. Speeds up the pain relief by almost half." His whole body did a little shudder as he pulled another face. "Which, incidentally, I do not recommend as a common practice." He handed her the cup.

"Would you like another?"

"Yes!"

When she brought it to him, he downed that as well and handed back the cup. Then he sat back and closed his eyes again. "How long was I asleep?"

"A little more than four hours."

"Really? Four hours. Man, I was blotto."

"Pretty much."

One eye cracked open. "I was hoping for some disagreement."

Just then KK came strolling back out of the bedroom. He stopped, eyeing Hans suspiciously, and then with an imperious sniff he turned and went back into the bedroom.

"What was that?" he asked.

"That's KK. My cat."

"KK?"

"Yeah." Katya laughed. "For *Kleines Kätzchen*."

Hans scoffed at her. "*Little* kitten? That thing's as big as a horse."

She nodded. "Eats like one, too. But he's good company."

He took a quick breath. "All right. I'm sure you've got a ton of questions."

"Actually, no. I have just one."

"Fire away." He gave her a lopsided grin. "But softly, please."

"All right. I don't know if you remember, but just before you passed out, I was—"

"I didn't pass out. I just went to sleep very quickly."

"I see. Anyway, I was asking you what you were doing here."

"And what did I say?"

"You said you needed to see me. I want to know why."

He nodded and then grimaced and started massaging his temples again. "Two reasons. First, if you will remember, I promised to buy you dinner sometime to say thanks for what you did for me the last time I was here."

"I like that idea. And second?"

"Do you know if my discharge money came through?" Before Katya could answer, Hans explained how he had come back before Christmas and found the sign saying the Ministry was closed. "So I came in from Munich last night—actually, early this morning—assuming that now that the holidays were over, I could finally collect my check."

"And you found that same sign on the door."

"Yeah. What do you people do, take the whole month of

December off?" Then he waved that question off. "Never mind. Do you know if Disbursement sent my check yet?"

Katya leaned forward, her mouth pulling down. "As of Friday, December 20th, no. I checked the very last thing before I left that day. And, as you know, the Ministry has been closed since then. I'm sorry."

Hans muttered something under his breath.

"What?"

He pulled a face. "Never mind. Not fit for mixed company. And the Ministry won't be open until next Monday, right?"

"Yes."

Straightening, he looked at his hands for a long moment. "Katya, I…"

"No, Hans."

"No what?"

"No, I can't go to the office and see if your check has arrived."

"Oh." He lowered his head and rested it in his hands. "I understand."

"No, you don't understand," she said. She got up and went over and sat down beside him. Taking one hand in hers, she interlocked their fingers. "Normally, I could do that. And I would. But before we left that last Friday, our supervisor called us all together and announced that because the army was going to be working on a special project during the holidays, none of us would be allowed into the building until the holidays were over. And then they announced that we got the two extra days after New Year's Day as a special bonus."

"Oh?"

"None of us complained, of course. Two full weeks of holiday? With pay? Who cares if they told us not to come to the office during that time?"

Hans turned to face her fully. To her joy, he didn't remove his hand from hers. "So they're not open at all until Monday?"

"No, they're not. Isn't that what the sign said?"

"It said after the holidays. Well, today, the holidays are over. At least for the rest of us common folk," he grumped.

Katya stood up. "That reminds me. I have your rationing coupons. As a government employee, we get a more liberal rationing allowance." She turned and went down the hall, returning a moment later with his book in hand. As she handed it to him, her eyes lowered a little. "I did use five coupons to help my mother get a goose for Christmas dinner. But's that's all I've used."

He took the book and slid it into his pocket without comment. "So why are you back here if you don't have to work until Monday?"

Katya waved a hand airily. "Four days with my mother and step-father was plenty for me. So now," she said softly, "we both have four days to kill."

Hans caught her meaning instantly but pretended he didn't. "Actually, I've got to go back to Pasewalk and . . . uh . . . get my eye checked one last time."

"I see." Disappointment was evident in her eyes.

"But it's too late to do that today. So, Fräulein Katya Freylitsch, how would you like to go to dinner with me?"

Her eyes lit up. "Now?"

"Yes. And no cheap little bistro. We both know that some restaurants do better getting around the food shortages, so you pick one out. My parents supplemented my funds somewhat, so let's make the most of it. Go find your prettiest dress. Put on some makeup. Get out some dancing shoes."

"Really?" She jumped up. "You really mean that?"

"I do." Hans started to pull himself up and then groaned and fell back, putting a hand to his head. He lay back down and closed his eyes. "But, Katya?"

"Yes?" Her face fell as she held her breath.

"Don't feel like you have to be in a hurry to get dressed," he said. He cracked one eye open. "If you know what I mean."

Her laughter was like the tinkling of a bell. "And just how much time would you like me to take, Sergeant Eckhardt?"

He was pleased that she understood. "I don't know much about girl stuff, but I'm guessing it would take you at least half an hour to get ready. Right?"

"Right. A half an hour at the very least."

"Good. But don't feel like you have to rush. I'll just wait right here."

8:05 p.m.—*Ristorante Italiano, Tiergarten District, Berlin*

The *Tiergarten,* or "Animal Park," was both a large park and a municipal locality in the borough of Mitte. Once a hunting park for royalty, it was now Berlin's most famous park, and Hans guessed that in the summertime it would be packed with people. But even now, through the large front window of the restaurant, Hans could see heavily bundled-up couples walking hand in hand. Some carried ice skates.

"Are you from here, Katya?"

She smiled. "Please, Hans. Won't you call me Katie?"

"Yes. Of course. So are you from around here, Katie?"

"No. I was born and grew up in Lichtenberg, which is a borough over in the east part of the city. I only came here when I got a job at the War Ministry."

"Is your family still there?"

"Yes. My mother and stepfather still live there. I was the only child when my mother divorced my father. I was eight. My natural father remarried and had children with his second wife and lives in Köln. I see him every now and again, but. . . ."

Hans was studying her as she spoke, and suddenly he said, "Actually, *you* are quite lovely, Katie."

She instantly blushed and ducked her head. "Why, thank you, Hans."

He meant it. Her face was round and petite. The blue eyes were set close together and gave one the impression that she was always on the verge of saying something funny. Her honey blonde hair, he was glad to see, did not come from a bottle of peroxide, and her skin was fair and without blemish. She did have one tooth that was slightly crooked and showed when she smiled, but it seemed to fit the rest of her somehow.

"Please," she said, blushing more deeply. "It embarrasses me when you study me like that."

He laughed but didn't look away.

She was thoroughly flustered now and laid down her fork. "I'm done. We can go anytime you like."

"Oh, no, you don't. Considering what we just paid for a very mediocre dinner, you can't leave your dessert on your plate. I'm in no hurry."

"All right." She picked up her fork again.

The wine had been better than he had expected, and it had left him basking in a warm glow. "You were supposed to say, 'Oh, Hans, I am so full. I can't possibly finish my dessert. Why don't you eat it for me?'"

To his surprise, she pulled the plate closer to herself. "Oh, no, you don't. You already took the bigger piece. You're not having mine, too."

He burst out laughing, causing people to turn and look at them. Her wit was so quick, and he liked her spunky independence. Most girls would have given it to him without protest. Katya took a large piece, put it in her mouth, and then, half closing her eyes in pleasure, added, "Besides, if I said I was full, you would know I was lying."

"That's true. A piece of pork loin not much bigger than a postage stamp, two starchy potatoes, watery gravy, and a spoonful of canned beans. Before the war they would have been ashamed to call that an appetizer, let alone a dinner."

"I'm sorry. This used to be one of the finest restaurants in the Tiergarten."

"It's not your fault. It's this way all over the Fatherland." Hans picked up his wine glass and raised it like a toast. "But the wine was good. And the company is wonderful."

"It is," she murmured. "So, I'll finish my dessert, and then we can go."

"Would you like to walk back through the Tiergarten?" Hans asked. "Or is it too cold for you?"

"Unlike you Bavarians, I was raised up north. It is not too cold for me." Then her smile faded. "But. . . ."

"What?"

"I read that they've had some of the deserters from the army making trouble in the park."

Hans's lips pressed together. "What kind of trouble?"

"Oh, you know. Drunk and loud and obnoxious. Acting like the pigs they are. Accosting people. Demanding money."

"Do they frighten you?"

"A little," she admitted. "I never walk through there alone anymore. Not even in the daytime. Don't they frighten you?"

"No," Hans said in disgust. "They're cowards. Trash. Garbage. Most of them are from rear echelon bases, supposedly assigned to come up and relieve those of us who had been on the front lines for a long time or to keep us supplied. But there at the end, they turned and ran like the cowards they are. I'd like to meet some of them. Rearrange their teeth for them."

Katya was staring at him. "My goodness, I think I hit a nerve there."

Hans stared at her for a moment, almost surprised that she was there, and then he forced himself to relax. "We'll go home another way, but maybe after I drop you off, I'll come back through the park. Teach those bums a thing or two."

That genuinely alarmed her. "No, Hans. The papers are saying that there are thousands of them in the city now. And they're mean. They beat up one old man because they thought he was a Jew. They run in gangs. "

"Packs, you mean. Like the dogs they are."

She laid a hand on his arm. "Promise me you won't do that, Hans. I mean it. Promise me."

He took a deep breath, then another, surprised by the anger she had stirred up in him. "Okay. I promise. Not tonight."

Relieved, she turned back to her dessert. Leaning back in his chair, Hans turned away so that he wasn't looking directly at her but could still study her. And his thoughts turned to Emilee. How different these two were, in appearance and personality. Katya was blonde with light blue eyes; Emilee had dark hair and dark blue eyes. Katya was slender and shapely; Emilee was a little plump. Though Emilee had a smile that could make him a little dizzy, she was more sober by nature and took life pretty seriously. Katya's smile was dazzling, and laughter seemed to be part of her nature. She had a gift for making him feel totally at ease with her, even after he had showed up on her doorstep roaring drunk. Emilee, on the other hand, had this way of forever keeping him off balance.

"A *Pfennig* for your thoughts," Katya teased, putting her fork down on her empty plate.

"They're not worth that much," he said, reaching out and touching her hand. Then he raised his other hand and caught the attention of the waiter. "Check, please."

8:55 p.m.—*Tiergarten District, Berlin*

Katya's luck held. When they arrived in front of her apartment, Frau Schmidt's lights were off—which meant she was not home from her holiday travels yet.

Katya stopped at the bottom of the steps and turned to Hans. "Thank you for a perfectly delightful evening, Hans. It was wonderful."

"Well," he mused regretfully, "I did owe you that much after turning up like a sotted old bum off the streets."

"Perhaps," she said, smiling up at him. "But that doesn't make it any less wonderful."

139

He reached out and took both of her hands. "Oh. Your hands are cold."

She pulled free and laid both hands on his cheeks. "Yes, they are. So what are you going to do about it?"

He took her in his arms and leaned in. Then at the last minute, he hesitated. *Oh, no, you don't.* She moved her hands so they were around his neck and pulled him in closer, tipping her head back and closing her eyes. The kiss was soft and sweet and lingering. When they stepped back from each other, Hans cocked his head and gave her a quizzical look. "That's how you get your hands warm?" he teased.

"You'd be surprised at how well it works." And this time, she didn't wait for him. She threw her arms around his neck and kissed him hard. For a moment he was surprised, but then he kissed her back. When they stepped back this time, they were both a little taken aback. Katya took Hans by the hand, suddenly shy. "Would you like to come up for a nightcap?"

His eyes were almost black and unreadable in the near darkness, but she sensed his hesitation. "It's all right," she whispered. "My roommate is gone until Sunday." She laughed, trying not to sound too eager. "And my nosey old landlady isn't home yet either."

"Uh . . ." His shoulders lifted and fell. "Ah, Katie, I. . . ."

She moved in again, putting her arms around his waist and laying her head against his chest. "I think I'm falling for you, Sergeant Hans Eckhardt." She gave a diffident laugh. "How's that for a surprise?"

One hand came up, and with his finger he lifted her chin so she was looking up at him. "Oh, Katya, I cannot express how tempting that is right now. You are beautiful. You are incredibly funny and charming and. . . ."

She stepped back slowly. "But?"

The sigh was long and deep. "But I have to catch the first train in the morning and go up to Pasewalk."

"How early?" she said, fighting back the hurt.

"Early. And all my stuff is back at the hotel. I. . . ."

"Is there someone else, Hans? Another woman?"

"No," he blurted. Then, like a flash he heard his mother's voice in his head. *Lies come so easily to you, Hans.* So he shook his head. "Not yet. Probably not." He finally met her gaze. "But I have to find out."

"I understand."

"I'm sorry."

"Is that the only reason? Be honest with me, Hans. You owe me that much."

"Yes, Katya. Yes! I swear."

"Then, believe it or not, I'm glad. I'm glad you're that kind of a man, Hans." Then, before he could see the tears in her eyes, she turned away, getting out her key. At the top of the steps, she stopped, not turning. "Will you let me know?"

"Yes, of course."

"Either way?"

"Yes. I promise."

"Good night, Hans. And thank you again for a wonderful evening."

CHAPTER
13

January 3, 1919, 11:22 a.m.—Pasewalk Military Hospital

D r. Schnebling?"
The man coming toward him down the hallway looked
up in surprise. "Sergeant Eckhardt?"

"Yes, good morning." He walked up swiftly and shook his hand.

"You're back *again?*"

"Yes, sir. I just came by train. I know you're busy, sir. But could I have just two minutes?"

"How long have you been waiting?"

"About an hour and a half. The receptionist said you were in surgery."

"Yes, and I have another appointment waiting, and—"

"Two minutes, I swear. Then I won't be coming back again."

The older man searched Hans's face for a long moment and then gestured toward a small alcove off the hallway.

"Okay, two minutes."

Hans didn't wait for them to get seated. He quickly summarized what had happened since they had last talked almost a month ago. "I tried to call Nurse Fromme on Monday, but her brother said she was still in Königsberg. Is that possible? When I arrived here about three hours ago, I tried to phone Emilee. No answer. I went to the house. It looked deserted."

Dr. Schnebling nodded. "Yes, Emilee and Ernst are still in Königsberg. At least, I assume they are. They've disconnected the phone there and I haven't talked to her. But her mother and Heinz-Albert have moved in with my family temporarily while they're gone."

Hans rocked back. "No wonder I can't reach them."

A shadow passed across the doctor's face. "Elfriede—Emilee's mother—is not doing well. The cold and the limited rations are taking a heavy toll on her."

"Then why doesn't Emilee come back?" Hans exclaimed. "Can't selling the house wait?"

Schnebling studied him for a moment, clearly angered by his outburst. "Because they weren't able to get enough gasoline to return home until yesterday. Because now their truck won't start. Because gangs of hooligans are stopping cars and trucks and looting them of anything of value. That's why. So maybe you shouldn't be so quick to judge."

"The truck? Did Ernst say what it was?"

"He doesn't know what it is," he snapped. "They've tried to get a mechanic to come look at it, but with it still being the holidays, they can't get anyone there before Monday. They're desperate. If Ernst doesn't have it back by Sunday night, his friend in the butcher business won't be able to make his deliveries and could be ruined. So, Sergeant," he said coldly, "as I said. You shouldn't be so quick to judge."

Seeing his mistake, Hans quickly apologized. "You're right. I'm sorry for sounding angry with them. It's not their fault. I know that. But that's why I'm here, Doctor. I've been worried because I couldn't contact Emilee. I've come to see if I can help."

"Well, you can't," the doctor muttered, obviously not mollified by Hans's apology.

"Tell me where she is. Tell me how to find them in Königsberg."

"No!"

"Why not?"

"What can you do? Go up and hold her hand? Tell her you've missed her? I hate to be blunt, Sergeant Eckhardt, but you are just one more complication in Emilee's life right now."

Hans wanted to grab him and shake him, but instead he took a deep breath and let it out slowly. "What can I do? I'll tell you." He fished in his breast pocket and retrieved his railway pass. "In the first place, thanks to a kind and generous hospital administrator I once knew, I have this." He waved it in front of the doctor's face. "Which means I can be Königsberg by tonight."

That startled Schnebling for a moment, but then he started to shake his head again. Hans rushed on. "And, sir, as you may remember from my personnel file, I spent the first two years of my army service in the transportation corps driving trucks. And to qualify as a truck driver you also have to know how to repair engines of all kinds."

Dr. Schnebling was staring at him. "So you think you might be able to fix the truck?"

"Not might, sir. I can fix it. From what you've said, I think I already know what the problem is."

"You're not just saying that?"

"Come on, Doctor. I checked the train schedule when I got in. There's a train going north in just under an hour. We can sit here and debate my credentials, or I can be on that train. What'll it be?"

Schnebling's eyes probed Hans's for several seconds. Then he reached in his pocket and withdrew a small pad.

A prescription? Hans was incredulous. *He's going to write me a prescription?*

Schnebling ripped off the top sheet, retrieved a pen from his pocket, and stepped to the wall. He turned the prescription paper over and quickly scribbled something on the back and handed it to Hans. He had written "Küblerstrasse 17, Königsberg, East Prussia." "I'm sorry I doubted you, Sergeant. Go! And tell Emilee to call me tonight and let me know what is happening."

Taking the paper, Hans snapped off a salute, spun on his heel, and took off down the hallway. By noon, he was on a train headed north.

January 3, 1919, 8:43 p.m.—Küblerstrasse 17, Königsberg

As soon as he saw the truck, he knew he'd found the right address. It was parked out front of a small framed home with a slat fence and large iron gate. What gave it away was that the hood was propped open—a definite sign that something was *kaputt*. Crossing the street, he stopped and peered at the engine. Diesel or regular engine? That was the first question.

He wasn't surprised to see that there were spark plug wires. So it wasn't a diesel. He had guessed that. Diesels were not yet common in trucks, especially the bigger ones.

"Hey! Get away from that truck."

Hans jerked up, cracking his head on the underside of the hood. A tall, very solidly built man in shirtsleeves was coming out of the gate in long strides. Judging from the look on his face in the light of the street lamp, he wasn't coming out to introduce himself. Hans quickly stepped away from the vehicle, raising his hands in the air so the man could see that he wasn't armed in any way. Then he remembered what Schnebling had said about the social chaos spreading across Königsberg, and he realized he had just made a very foolish mistake.

He raised his hands even higher. "It's all right," he cried. "I was just looking." The man swore at him, and as he got closer, Hans saw that he was carrying a short length of shovel handle. "I heard you needed a mechanic," he blurted, backing up three or four more steps.

That finally slowed the man, and he came to a stop on the sidewalk. "Who told you that?"

"Dr. Artur Schnebling."

The man blinked and then blinked again. "You're from Pasewalk?"

"Most recently, but I'm from the south of Germany originally." He

145

was glad to see the shovel handle drop into a vertical position and rest against his pant leg. Hans slowly lowered his hands. "My name is Hans Otto Eckhardt. I'm a friend of Emilee's."

The man blinked yet again, as if this was a little more than his brain could take in at one time. Then finally he spoke. "What are you doing here?"

Hans smiled. "You must be Ernst, am I right?" When he nodded, Hans continued, "Well, Ernst, like I said, I heard that you were in need of a mechanic."

Ernst's eyes narrowed slightly. "Emilee never said anything about you being a mechanic."

"We didn't talk about it much," he said easily, relaxing now. "But I was with the Fourth Transport Brigade, Third Division, Fifth Army. Two years driving trucks and that much fixing them."

Hans fell back as Ernst came at him, right hand extended, and smiling like a man who had just won a gold medal in the Olympics. "Ernst Fromme," he boomed. He pumped Hans's hand so hard that Hans felt his teeth click together. Then, just as abruptly, he spun around, cupped one hand to his mouth, and bellowed, "Emilee! Emilee! Come out here."

They heard the front door open. "Who is it, Ernst?"

Now it was Hans who was grinning.

"Come and see."

A moment later, a figure appeared at the front gate. She stopped, peering out through the wrought iron. Then, with a squeal, she flung open the gate and came flying at him. "Hans?"

He laughed as she threw herself at him, nearly bowling him over. He swung her up, twirling her around and around. When he finally set her down, she stepped back, breathless with excitement. "Is it really you? I can't believe my eyes."

He glanced at Ernst to see how he had taken such an enthusiastic welcome, but he was beaming almost as much as she was. "*Guten*

Abend, Nurse Fromme," he chuckled. "Yes, it's me, and I'm here to fix your truck. And. . . ." He stepped back. "Look at you. You look wonderful."

She did a half twirl. "I'm on a new diet. It's all the rage in Germany now, I understand. It is called the food-rationing diet. Very effective, don't you think?"

Ernst wasn't amused with this banter. "Can you fix it or not?" he said.

"Of course," Hans said. "That's why I came."

Emilee stopped dead. "Do you really think you can? Oh, Hans. That would be wonderful."

"*Think* I can," he scoffed. "I beg your pardon, Fräulein. I *know* I can. Do you happen to have some rubbing alcohol?"

11:08 p.m. —Outskirts of Königsberg

"Hans?"

"Yeah, I see it, Ernst. Have you still got that shovel handle?"

"I do." He reached down and then held it up.

Emilee's hand shot out. She grabbed Hans's arm, her fingers digging into his flesh even through his uniform sleeve.

"It's all right, Emilee," he said softly. "Stay calm."

"But there are five of them. And one has a rifle."

"Yes, I see that." He let off the gas and shifted down one gear. The vehicle slowed dramatically.

The five men were in uniform, just as Hans was. One was waving his arms. The one with the rifle raised it and pointed it directly at them. They were standing beneath a street lamp, behind a low barricade of what looked like wooden apple and cabbage boxes that blocked the road. Hans glanced in the side mirror. There were no lights behind them. And no lights ahead of them. The road was deserted. As he shifted down again, he felt Emilee's fingers tighten even more.

He reached across with his other hand and patted it. "Steady. Steady."

"What are we going to do?" Ernst asked in a strained voice.

"We're going to stop, of course."

"No, Hans. They'll steal the truck and everything in it."

"No one is going to steal anything. Just listen. When I say 'down,' you both duck down as low as you can, all right?"

"Hans?"

"It's all right, Emilee. These guys are a bunch of pigs and dumber than a pile of rocks. Like an apple box is going to stop a one-ton truck? So, again, when I say 'down,' you get down." He looked at Ernst. "You shield Emilee as much as possible with your body. Okay?"

Ernst gave a curt nod, and Hans was pleased to see that the tightness in his face was more from anger than fear.

Hans shifted into the lowest gear and rolled down his side window. They were now just thirty or forty feet away from the barricade and moving at only about two miles an hour. The one man was still waving at them to stop. The one with the rifle stepped into the middle of the road, the muzzle of his weapon trained on Hans. Sticking his head out the window, Hans called, "Is there a problem?"

"*Ja, ja,*" the man called back. "*Halten Sie! Halten Sie!*"

Lifting his foot off the gas pedal, Hans let the truck slow to a crawl. His right hand was on the knob of the gear shift. "Ready?" he whispered, glancing at Emilee.

Her face what white in the glow of the street lamp, but her head bobbed up and down once.

"Then here . . . we . . . go." They were now just twenty feet from the first soldier. "Down!" he shouted. As Emilee and Ernst ducked down, Hans jammed his foot down on the gas pedal and jerked the wheel sharply to the left. For an instant the man's eyes were startled, but then with a yell he dove to one side. Barely missing him, Hans jerked the wheel hard to the right. The truck careened wildly, but now it was bearing down on the rifleman. The man snapped off a shot, but it was high and wide. Then he too threw himself to one side as the truck hurtled past him. The other three men gaped in astonishment as the truck smashed through two of the wooden crates, blasting them into smithereens.

"Stay down!" Hans yelled as he rammed the gear shift into second gear and punched the gas pedal to the floor. Behind them the rifle cracked again. And once more. Then the rapidly diminishing band of thugs disappeared into the darkness.

Hans reached out and laid a hand on Emilee's back. "It's all right. You can get up now."

Emilee and Ernst straightened. Ernst looked into his side view mirror. "Do you think they hit anything?" he said.

Hans grinned. "You may have a bullet hole in your sofa." He reached out and found Emilee's hand. "But now you've got something to tell your grandchildren."

She managed a shaky smile as she gripped his hand tightly, but she said nothing. She was trembling too hard to speak.

January 4, 1918, 3:45 a.m.—Königsberg/Berlin Highway

"Ernst," Hans asked in a low tone, "are you asleep?"

Emilee turned her head to look at her brother too, but the only discernible sound above the steady drumming of the engine was a low, sonorous rumble that sounded very much like someone snoring. Emilee turned back, smiling at Hans. "I think the answer is yes."

"You're sure?"

She reached over and poked his shoulder. "Ernst?"

He didn't stir.

With two fairly large men, the cab of the truck was pretty full, and Emilee was squeezed in between Hans and her brother. But as she turned back, she slid even closer to Hans. When he looked at her in surprise, she ducked her head. "I think he needs a little more room." And she slid another inch toward him.

"Totally agree," Hans said. "He's a big man."

"Yes, he is."

Hans chuckled. "In fact, when the engine finally kicked into life, I thought he was going to crush me. I'm six feet two inches, and he picked me up like I was a child."

Emilee nodded soberly. "I'm not sure of this, because he would never admit it to me, but I think he actually threw up when the truck wouldn't start. He was so sick with worry about not getting it back in time."

"I understand. Ernst seems to be the kind of a man who keeps his word."

"With great exactness. And when you said that it was a simple thing to fix the engine, that all you needed was some rubbing alcohol, he pretty well decided you were some kind of a crank, or just plain loony."

"And was I right?"

"Yes, but you were pretty cocky about it up front, which didn't do much for his confidence. To be honest, I had my doubts about your sanity too there for a minute. I mean, really? Rubbing alcohol? That you keep in the medicine cabinet?"

"So you were a skeptic too?"

She ignored his question. "So when it actually worked, Ernst was so elated, so relieved, of course he picked you up and nearly crushed you. I nearly did the same thing."

"Now that I would have welcomed."

She slugged him. "Be serious."

"I was being serious."

She slugged him again. "So how did you know that water in the gasoline was the problem? And how did you know that rubbing alcohol would help? Did they teach you that in the army?"

"About the water part, yes. Using isopropyl, or rubbing, alcohol, no. That's an old truck driver's trick that some of the old-timers taught us. So the diagnosis part was easy. Dr. Schnebling happened to mention that you had bought some gasoline. When I asked you and Ernst what was happening to the engine before it died, do you remember what you told me?"

"Yes. The engine was vibrating noticeably. There was a definite loss of power, an occasional backfire."

"Idling roughly?"

"Yes. All of that. And then it just died."

"Well, as soon as you said that, I knew that condensation was the most likely suspect. It's a common problem, especially in the winter time, and especially near large bodies of water where there is a lot of humidity in the air."

"Oh? Well, we qualify there. It's December and we are in a port city."

"Exactly. What happens is, water doesn't mix with gasoline at all, and since it's heavier than the fuel, if there is any condensation present, the water sinks to the bottom and gets into the fuel lines. And since, as you might guess, water doesn't burn very well, the engine starts to malfunction. It doesn't take much to give you problems. But rubbing alcohol *does* mix with water."

"And alcohol is flammable."

"Yes, it is. So you pour a bottle of rubbing alcohol in the tank. It mixes with the water enough so that it will burn it off. It's not particularly good for the engine, and we don't recommend it as a standard procedure, but we always carried a bottle of it with us during the war. Actually, it's also a simple way to defrost your windshield. Very handy stuff to have around."

Emilee turned and looked at her brother again. "Well, you can see how enormously relieved he is. I think this is the first he's really slept in three days."

"To be honest, I was pretty relieved when it actually worked too."

Emilee laid a hand on Hans's arm. "Your coming up here means more to us—to me—than I can possibly express, Hans. I was sick with worry about Mama and Heinz-Albert. Ernst was getting ulcers about

151

his friend. And all the time I was not able to connect with you and tell you what was going on. It was awful. And then, all of a sudden, like a miracle from heaven, there you were, standing on our doorstep. And ten minutes later the engine is fixed and we're loading up and ready to go."

"Wow. That's the first time I've ever been called a miracle. And, actually, it was only about seven minutes, not ten."

She slugged him a third time on the arm, only this time hard. "Stop it. I'm trying to be serious here."

"Right. Serious."

Now her voice was heavy with emotion. "And then, you running that road block. I. . . ."

"Don't, Emilee. Don't think about it. Let's talk about something else."

"Yes!" It was said with great fervency.

The headlights from a passing vehicle illuminated the cab long enough for her to see his somewhat goofy, lopsided smile. "What?" she asked, poking him.

"I'm ready to present you my bill for service rendered!"

"Which is?"

"Dinner with your family on Sunday. I mean, you surely wouldn't send a poor starving boy back to Berlin without him first meeting your mother and your other brother, would you?"

She ducked her head, suddenly shy. "The bill is already paid. Not because you asked, but because I already promised Mama that I would introduce you to her and Heinz-Albert at the first opportunity that came up."

"You did?" Hans was grinning that grin again.

"I did." And with that she slipped her arm through his and laid her head against his shoulder. "And now, I think I'll try to get some sleep. You must be exhausted too. Can you last an hour before I spell you off?"

"I can last until dawn. You sleep as long as you can." Then Hans gave Emilee a quizzical look. "You really can drive this?"

"Yes." She shot him a dirty look. "Why do you find that so hard to believe?"

"Because you're too short to see over the wheel."

This time she smacked him on the knee.

"Ow! Man, how are you going to explain all of these bruises to your mother?" Then before she could answer, he poked her with his elbow. "So can you see over the wheel?"

She laughed, and it was a sound that delighted him. "To be perfectly honest, Ernst brought a pillow for me to sit on that puts me high enough."

"Ah, I thought so."

"I knew that Ernst couldn't drive all the way to Königsberg and back without stopping, so I made him teach me how to drive." Again she leaned her head against him, and this time she closed her eyes. "Promise me that you'll wake me in an hour."

"No. But I will promise that I'll wake you if I get sleepy. Deal?"

"Deal," she murmured. And two minutes later, she was gone.

4:35 a.m.

Emilee woke with a start and looked around in confusion. Then she remembered where she was and sat up. She stared out the windshield for a moment, absently running her fingers through her hair, and finally turned to Hans. "How far have we come?"

"We passed through Walcz about ten minutes ago. I figure we're a little more than halfway."

She groaned. "Is that all? How long was I asleep?"

"Not quite an hour. I hoped you'd sleep longer."

"How are you doing? Aren't you exhausted?"

"I'm ready to get out and stretch my legs," he admitted. "But no. During the war, we often drove all night so as not to be seen by the Frenchies in their airplanes. I'm used to it."

Emilee turned her head the other way. "Has Ernst stirred at all?"

"No. You may want to check his pulse."

She laughed. "I'm glad. He was so tired." She leaned against Hans again. After another minute, he nudged her. "What are you thinking?"

"About Sunday."

"And?"

"Do you really have to leave right after we have dinner?"

"Yes. It's been a month since I was released from the hospital, and here I am, no closer to getting my discharge money than I was when I left the hospital. I have got to get back to the Ministry and get that check so I can get on with my life. I'm going to be first in line."

"And do what? What are you thinking you'll do?"

"Well, I'm seriously considering blowing up the Ministry of War. Then, if I have any explosives left, maybe I'll go after the Parliament Building. See if I can knock off at least part of that gang of November criminals."

Emilee didn't laugh. "I hope you don't joke about that in public."

"Who's joking?" Then Hans sighed. "I don't know, Emilee. Three thousand marks isn't going to last very long if I don't get a job soon. Then, I guess I've got to figure out what I want to do with my life."

"What about the University of Berlin?"

He shrugged. "I'll check it out, but I don't have much hope. I assume it reopens on Monday too."

"And you'll go there as soon as you're done with the Ministry?"

Hans chuckled. "You're like a bulldog, did you know that? You never give up, do you?"

"Not on you, I don't," was her soft reply.

He gave her a sharp look but let it pass. "But don't get your hopes up, Emilee. Remember, I'm the one who walked away from that scholarship. I never even wrote them to explain why. I was a *Dummkopf,* an eighteen-year-old kid who turned his back on the opportunity of a lifetime so I could join the army and save the Fatherland." He hooted bitterly. "How's that for a laugh?"

"But that doesn't mean you lost the opportunity."

"It's been four years." Irritation made his voice sharper. "Of course I've lost it."

"I don't think so. There was an article in the paper here a week or so ago saying that soldiers who were attending universities before the war were eligible to return without having to take all of the exams again."

"Yes. My mother showed that to me too."

"So?"

"'I wasn't attending the university, Emilee. I was only accepted, not enrolled."

Sensing his mood, she said nothing more.

"Look, I appreciate your concern, and I know that you're trying to help, but—"

"But what?" she asked quietly.

He said nothing.

"But what, Hans?"

"Well, I'm sort of a 'stand-on-your-own' kind of a guy. So," he shrugged, "I appreciate your concern, but I don't need you to plan out my life for me."

"I see."

The way she said it made him turn to look at her. "You see what?"

She folded her arms, laid her head back, and closed her eyes. He let another two or three miles pass, waiting for her to answer, but she didn't. When the occasional car would approach from the other direction and light up her face momentarily, he saw the pinch around her mouth and knew that she was still awake. And not happy.

"Go ahead," he grumbled. "Say it. I'm a jerk. I know that."

Emilee sat up again. Careful not to awaken Ernst, she turned as much as she could so she faced Hans. "Let me ask you a question, Mr. Stand-Alone-Guy." Her voice was clipped and cool. "Just exactly what are your intentions here?"

"Intentions? I'm not sure what you mean."

"Yes you are. This is your third trip to Pasewalk since your release.

Now you've come almost four hundred miles out of your way to help us." Her voice went soft. "For which I shall be forever grateful. I really mean that. What you did was. . . ."

"I'm glad that it worked out as it did."

"But, I assume you're not job hunting in Pasewalk. So, just what are your intentions?"

"With you, you mean?"

"No," she scoffed. "With Nurse Rhinehart."

"Who?"

"Never mind. I'm assuming all of these visits, and all of your efforts to get my address and phone number, were not driven by some deep longing to meet my mother and brothers."

Her dry sarcasm irked him. He clamped his mouth shut and said nothing.

Emilee suddenly shook her head. "You know what? Never mind. You don't have to answer that."

"No, I want to. I was just—"

She took a quick breath. "I'm not angry, Hans. I just realized that having this conversation at this particular moment is crazy. It's almost five o'clock in the morning. We've been up all night. And that's after two very long and frustrating weeks. Longer than that for you. So let's just shelf it for now."

"All right."

"Why don't we stop for breakfast at the next town? I think we all need a break from this."

"From the driving or from me?" he shot back, trying to make it sound like he was teasing her, though he was not.

"You know what? I will say one more thing."

"Go ahead." Hans forced a smile. "Do I need to hunker down for this one?"

"This is not funny, Hans. Not in any way."

"Sorry. I'm just . . . never mind. Go ahead. Say it."

Emilee threw up her hands. "You're right. Never mind." And she closed her eyes again.

Silence prevailed for another two or three minutes. By that point, Hans had worked out what he wanted to say. No, *needed* to say. For Emilee as well as for himself. So he started without preamble.

"My plan is to go to Berlin and get my severance pay. I hope that takes me no more than an hour or so. Then I'm going to the University of Berlin to see where I stand with them."

Emilee sat up straighter, watching him closely.

"And then, I am coming back to Pasewalk. And I plan to spend however long it takes to see if there is any possible chance that Sergeant Hans Otto Eckhardt and Nurse Emilee Fromme can work out their differences, stop sparring with one another, and. . . ."

"And what?" She was staring at him, her eyes wide.

"And see if this . . . this . . . this inability to get you out of my head means what I think it means."

"It's Nurse Emilee *Greta* Fromme," she whispered.

He stared at her, not understanding.

Her eyes were soft in the first light of the morning. "Well," she retorted, "I just thought that if you know my full name, it will be even harder to get me out of your head."

"Ah."

"And that's all you've got to say? Just, 'ah'?"

"That kind of says it all."

She smiled and took his hand, interlocking her fingers with his. "Yes, I think it does too."

Chapter Note

Even today, isopropyl alcohol is touted as a quick, though not necessarily recommended, solution for water in gasoline (see https://www.youtube .com/watch?v=N01DgXEboD4).

CHAPTER

14

*January 6, 1919, 6:00 a.m.—Ministry of War,
Mitte District, Berlin*

Hans wasn't too alarmed when the long, dark shape of the Ministry loomed up out of the fog and no one seemed to be there. It was only 6:00 a.m. He had come this early determined to get card #1 and then get in and out as if he were on a guerrilla raid. He hoped he would be back at the train station and on his way to Pasewalk by ten o'clock.

But of one thing Hans was sure: if he had to work with Frau Hessler, he would grit his teeth, paste on a big smile, and grovel at her feet if she required it. He would check his pride and his temper at the door and get out of there as quickly as possible.

Hans glanced at the main doors as he approached. There wasn't much light, but yes, he could see that the paper announcing the closure for the holidays was still there, taped to the glass. He angled to the right and chose a spot up against the building just a few steps away from the entrance, where the first man in line had been positioned both times he had come here before.

Even though the temperature had softened a little, the fog had come in last night and was really heavy now. That always made it feel colder than it was. Knowing that he would have at least a two-hour wait, Hans had prepared himself much better than he had before.

Yesterday, when he arrived at the train station, he went into the gift shop and bought himself a fur hat with two large ear flaps and a thermos bottle. And when he left the hotel this morning, he hid one of his two blankets under his overcoat. There was a sign in the hotel lobby saying that residents were forbidden to take towels, washcloths, or blankets from the hotel. But it wasn't like they ever made up his room. And besides, the night clerk was a little scarecrow of a kid who barely dared look at Hans. As a last precaution, Hans had stopped at a tiny, hole-in-the-wall coffee shop and had them fill his jug with the strongest coffee they had.

So now he settled in to wait. He uncapped the thermos, removed the cork, and took a tentative sip.

Ouch! It was hot! Amazing! The coffee shop was nearly half an hour's walk from here, but the coffee was still hot enough to burn his mouth. No wonder thermos bottles were in such high demand. Some engineer was making a fortune off of the simple idea to put an insulated bottle inside a bottle.

Hans settled back and closed his eyes, thinking through the rest of the day, and his thoughts turned to Katya. The last time he had been with her, he had promised her that he would let her know whether things worked out with Emilee. After he had left Katya that night, he decided that the dinner was not the smartest thing he had ever done. And now he'd promised her that he would let her know about Emilee one way or the other. Trying not to think about his mother's comments about holes in the dike and structural integrity, he decided that was not a promise he was going keep. At this point, things with Emilee were looking good. Not without their problems, but looking good. Which meant that Katya was out of his life, and seeing her wasn't going to do much good for either one of them.

Suddenly, he smacked his forehead with the heel of his hand. He *was* going to see her again. In about two hours. She would be behind her window waiting for him, trying not to smile too warmly at him. Oh well. There was nothing to be done about it. Maybe he could slip her a note and tell her that the "other woman" was working out for him.

But then another thought came. Emilee was looking good, but it was not a done deal. Not by a long shot. So maybe it was a little premature to cut things off with Katya. *Keep your options open,* he thought, *just in case.* He did find her to be a very attractive woman, and he really enjoyed being with her. The thought of seeing her again made him feel good. And part of that, he realized, was because Katya really liked him. Whether he went to the university or not. Whether he was employed or not. Whether he went south to see his family or not.

Hans must have dozed off, because he came awake with a start as a motor car trundled past him, belching smoke and waking up the neighborhood. He looked around. Still no one. What time was it? With the fog he couldn't be sure, but it felt like maybe ten or fifteen minutes had passed. Shifting his weight into a more comfortable position, he realized that he was cold. The frigid air had seeped through the blanket, through his overcoat, and through his uniform. He reached for the thermos, removed the cap, pulled out the cork, and filled the lid. He could feel the warmth as it went through his chest and into his stomach.

Hans stiffened. The coffee was warm, but not hot enough to burn his tongue, as it had before. He took another sip and then swore softly as he looked around. Judging from the coffee, it had been more than ten or fifteen minutes since he'd fallen asleep. More like thirty. And still, no guard with numbered tickets. No lights on in the building. No soldiers joining him in the line. Finishing the rest of the coffee, he recapped the thermos, threw off his blanket, and lumbered to his feet. He walked to the nearest window and peered into the lobby of the Ministry. There was only one light on inside, but it was enough to show him that no one was there yet. And . . . he did a double take.

The clock on the wall behind the information desk showed that it was 6:47. Could that be right? Had he slept for more than forty minutes?

With a growing sense of bewilderment, Hans started back to see if the sign was still on the door. He stopped before he reached it. It was. So he headed back for his place, thoroughly puzzled now. So why wasn't anyone else here by now? There should be a two-week back-log of men applying for their severance pay. Suddenly he stopped and whirled around as he realized that the sign hadn't looked quite the same as before.

In three strides he was to it. It was no longer posted on the door itself but on the large glass pane beside it. Before Hans even reached it, he saw that it was *not* the same notice. This one was half again as big as the other sign and covered with heavy black print. He moved in closer.

Suddenly it felt as if he had just stepped on a land mine.

ACHTUNG!

As of January 1, 1919, the War Ministry of the State of Germany is disbanded and no longer exists. This is in accordance with the surrender terms set by the Allied Forces. There are no plans to reopen the Ministry in the foreseeable future. This building is now permanently closed.

Due to extensive war reparations required by the Allied Forces, the German government will no longer be able to fund military pensions, provide discharge compensation, or pay outstanding bills or obligations. We regret this inconvenience.

Hans swore softly, but bitterly. *Inconvenience?* The loss of three thousand marks was an *inconvenience?* Shaking his head, he kept on reading.

SPECIAL NOTICE TO
MINISTRY OF WAR EMPLOYEES

We regret to inform all Ministry of War employees that with the closing of the Ministry, your services are no longer needed. Employment is terminated as of January 1, 1919.

Your final paycheck will be mailed to your home. We regret this inconvenience.

Hans read the whole notice again, his brain too stunned to accept what he was seeing. Could they do this? He had already been approved for discharge compensation. He read through it a third time, slowly, saying each word aloud, as if that might help. And finally he had to accept it. Not just the words, but the enormity of what they meant.

Rage exploded inside him. He hit the glass of the entrance door with the heels of both of his hands. It was thick enough that it barely rattled.

"YOU CAN'T DO THIS!" he shouted at the silent building. He grabbed the handles of both doors and shook them violently. They barely budged. Cursing, raging, blind with anger, he kicked at the glass with all his might. A six-inch crack blossomed in the glass. He kicked it again. But it held. He looked up to the second floor to see if there were any lights on. He considered circling the building to see if there might be an employee's entrance.

Then he remembered Katya's words. Their supervisor had called them in and told them that they had the whole holiday period off. That a team of men were going to be working in the building during that time. That none of them would be allowed into the building for any reason during that period.

It had nothing to do with an audit. The two weeks of time off was not a holiday bonus. It was termination. Only no one bothered to tell the employees.

A sob of raw fury ripped from his throat. *Three thousand marks! Four years of hell, and I get nothing?*

In a daze, he turned and started away, half stumbling. Just off to his right was a large, round, metal trash bin. It was about three feet high and made of heavy-gauge steel. With a cry, Hans bent down and picked it up. Paper and bottles rained down on him as he lifted it high above his head. With a roar, he lunged forward and hurled it at the glass doors. They shattered with a tremendous crash, sending shards of glass spraying into the lobby.

"*Halten Sie!*"

The shout spun Hans around. About thirty yards away, a figure was emerging from the fog. The man broke into a trot. Though he could only see a silhouette, Hans could make out the conical shape of a policeman's hat. He didn't wait to see whether the man had a gun. He dropped the blanket, grabbed his rucksack, and, crouching low, zigzagged back and forth as if a French machine gunner had him in his sights.

"*Stoppen Sie! Polizei. Halten Sie! Halten Sie!*"

Hans lowered his head, increased his speed, and disappeared into the fog.

10:35 a.m.—University of Berlin campus, Mitte District, Berlin

"Excuse me?"

The elderly man who looked like a professor pulled up and peered at Hans.

"Could you tell me where I go to talk to someone about enrollment at the university?"

"Ah, *ja*," the man said with a smile. He turned half around and pointed to the southwest. "Just beyond that large red brick building you can see a smaller building made of white stone. That's the registrar's office. They can help you there."

Hans set off again, wending his way through the throngs of students that filled the quad. School was definitely back in session. He deliberately kept his eyes down so that he didn't have to look into their faces and see the excitement there. But he still heard the laughter, the snatches of conversation, the couples murmuring to each other. His mood grew more and more bleak, and he increased his pace to move through them quickly.

Hans tried to shake off the thoughts, but they were pummeling him now, and he was reeling.

After his flight from the Ministry, he had wandered about the central part of Berlin aimlessly for almost two hours, trying to make some sense out of what had just happened. This whole day was turning out to be one long, maddening nightmare.

Inside the white stone building, the first door he saw had *Registrar* painted on the glass windows. Taking off his hat and putting it in the pocket of his overcoat, Hans smoothed his hair down, took a deep breath, and entered.

It was a pleasant office, with several leather chairs along the walls, warm walnut paneling, and a counter that filled one corner of the room. There was room for three or four clerks, but at the moment there was only one there. Hans looked around. He was the only visitor in the office. *How refreshing is that?* He liked the place already.

"*Guten Morgen,*" the clerk said. "May I help you?"

She was in her late thirties, he guessed. She had a round face and a pleasant smile. She wore her hair pulled back into a bun, and he saw a simple wedding band on her ring finger.

Hans stepped up, giving her an answering smile. "Yes. I am Hans Otto Eckhardt."

"How do you do, Herr Eckhardt?"

"As you might suppose, I am just out of the army, and. . . ."

"It is so good to have you boys home again," the clerk said, her eyes suddenly glistening. "My own Franz is home safely now too, and thanks be to God for that."

"I'm very glad to hear that," Hans replied, and he meant every word of it. He continued, "I was accepted to the university in the spring of 1914 with a full-tuition scholarship and a modest stipend for living expenses."

She nodded, watching him closely.

"Then—no surprise—I ended up in the army that summer." He didn't feel she needed to know that he had volunteered. He would have been conscripted anyway.

"And you would like to reapply?"

"I would like to do whatever it takes to start what I should have started four years ago."

"I understand. Uh . . ." She sighed but then seemed to change her mind about what she was going to say. She reached in a drawer and drew out a slip of blank paper. She took a pencil from a pewter cup and slid it and the paper across the counter to Hans. "Give me your full name, when you applied, what school you graduated from, and your home address."

He wrote quickly and slid the paper back to her.

"Have a seat, Sergeant Eckhardt. This could take a while since you will no longer be in our active files."

"No problem," he said. "I'm in no hurry."

Not exactly true, he thought as he sat down. "I'm not going anywhere" would have been a better way to put it.

She was gone twenty minutes. By then, three other students had come in, two girls and a young man. Hans explained to them what was happening and they too settled in to wait. Gratefully, none of them felt compelled to start a conversation.

When the clerk returned she had a file folder in her hand. Hans got up and went to the window. One look at her face told him it wasn't going to be good news.

She took a quick breath. "I took some time to speak with the dean of students, Sergeant. I wanted to confirm exactly what your options are."

"Go on," he said slowly, feeling the familiar despair starting to knot his stomach.

She managed a quick smile. "Your grades and your recommendations are excellent, and it is clear why you were accepted before."

"But?"

"But university policy does not accept test scores more than two years old. So I am afraid that before you can reapply, you will have to retake the entrance exams. The easiest way to do that would be to work with the Von Kruger Academy."

"But it's been almost five years since I took the exams. It would take me months to prepare for them again." He bit back the anger. "And what about the scholarship?"

"The dean says you will have to reapply for that, too. But . . . with the government in a financial crisis . . . well, there's virtually no money right now." She let it trail off. "I'm so sorry."

Then she leaned in and lowered her voice. "I'm not supposed to tell you this, but the president of the university is trying to get an exception on retaking the exams for those who served in the war, but the soonest we will get a decision will be in the summer. You can check back with us then."

Hans wanted to look around and see if there was another trash bin nearby to throw. But he knew none of this was the woman's fault. He could see the sorrow in her eyes.

"*Danke schön,*" he said. He started to turn away but then turned back. "How is your son doing?"

Tears instantly welled up in her eyes. "He's like a lost little boy," she whispered.

1:15 p.m.—*Tiergarten District, Berlin*

When Katya came down the stairs and opened the door, her pupils were bloodshot and the skin around her eyes was puffy and red. She sniffed back tears and wiped at her runny nose with a crumpled, damp handkerchief.

She didn't seem surprised to see Hans. He thought he had seen her at the window when he was still coming up the street.

She sniffed again. "You went to the War Ministry this morning?"

Hans scoffed bitterly. "What War Ministry?" Studying her face, he asked, "And when did they let you know you no longer had a job?"

"When I read the sign in the window."

The anger rose up again. "So no warning whatsoever?"

"None. A guard was there to make sure none of us went in. Someone had smashed out the front entrance. They were sweeping up the glass."

He grinned. "That was me."

"Good for you," she said fiercely. "I wish you had set it afire, too."

"Any severance pay?"

"None."

"What are you going to do?"

Her face crumpled. "I don't know, Hans. I don't know."

He reached out and took both of her hands. "Run upstairs. Fix yourself up as best you can. I saw that your landlady's home, so I'll wait here."

"But. . . ."

He reached up and wiped at her wet cheek with his thumb. "Katya, if you look in the mirror you'll see what I mean. Trust me. You'll feel better if you wash your face before we go."

"Go where? What are we going to do?"

"We are going to get very, very drunk. Smashed. Blotto. Blitzed. Crocked. Hosed. Plastered. And that's just a start."

She was laughing through her tears. "Give me one minute."

"It'll take more than that," he teased.

She slapped him on the shoulder. "Two minutes, then."

Chapter Notes

As part of the Armistice agreement, the German Ministry of War officially ceased to exist on January 1, 1919. When the Weimar Republic was formed as part of the Treaty of Versailles later that year, the War Ministry was incorporated into the German Ministry of the *Reichswehr* (from *Reich*, "empire" and *wehren*, "to defend"), a much weaker and diluted organization.

No details are given on how exactly that closure was carried out. The cessation of payments, the termination of employees, and the closing of the building are my inventions, though they seem to be logical given the chaos in the German government at that time.

CHAPTER
15

January 7, 1919, 2:10 a.m.—Tiergarten District, Berlin

Hans groaned as pain stabbed at his head. He lay perfectly motionless, hoping that might help a little. It did not. Wincing and biting his lip to keep from crying out, he pulled himself up into a sitting position. Instantly the stabbing sensation gave way to waves of pain that left him nauseous and dizzy. He leaned forward, elbows on his knees, eyes closed, and pressed his fingertips against his temples. It helped a little, so he began to slowly massage the flesh, pressing hard against the bone as his fingers made circular motions.

The pain didn't go away, but it subsided somewhat, and his stomach began to settle a little. Finally, he opened his eyes and looked around.

Where am I?

The room was mostly dark, but he could make out the couch he was on, a table and two wooden chairs across the room, and a lamp on a small round table.

Ah, yes.

It was the lamp that did it. He recognized it from when he had been here before, when he had slept on this same couch. He was at

Katya's apartment. That brought his head up with a snap. He gave a low cry as the pain exploded in his head again. He ignored it.

I'm in Katya's flat. But . . .

He closed his eyes again and started massaging his head. He remembered coming here from the university, looking for company, looking for a drinking partner. They had walked across the Tiergarten, hand in hand, feeling a little like two naughty children. She had led them to another street lined with *Bier Hallen,* taverns, ale houses, brasseries, and bistros. There were several restaurants—a couple of them shuttered—but it was obvious that food was not the primary reason people came here. Hans and Katya had chosen a brasserie with a French name where they served a limited menu of light foods—sandwiches, hard Kaiser rolls, various cheeses, and lots of beer and ale and other liqueurs to wash them down. Before they left the place, Hans's brooding bitterness had begun to lift. After that . . .

He was thinking hard now. He remembered an alehouse and downing two large steins of lager. Then there was a large and very noisy *Bier Halle* with a live band. Katya had asked him to dance, but he'd refused. She took him by the hand and dragged him out on the floor. Something about dancing with her made her suddenly seem incredibly attractive, and they had stopped to passionately kiss. The dance floor was crowded and another couple crashed into them. They went down in a tumble. He remembered laughing uproariously.

But from there on, things were a blur. There was another smaller place. More beer. More kissing. And . . .

His head came up. Was he dressed? He felt quickly in the darkness. Yes. He still had on his uniform. Good. And where was Katya? Suddenly, unbidden, the image of Emilee's face floated into his consciousness. He almost heard her voice saying, "Yes, Hans. Where is Katya?"

With a low moan he hauled himself up. The room began to spin again, but he grabbed for the lamp table. He closed his eyes, and after a moment it passed. Moving cautiously now, making sure his stocking feet made no sound, he crossed the room. He noticed a blur of white on the kitchen table. It looked like a piece of paper, but it was too dark to tell for sure. Moving past the table, he entered the hallway and then stopped, trying to remember which side of the hall the bathroom was on. He had only been in it once. He could make out a door on the right, which seemed familiar, and he assumed that was it. But he moved past it to the door across the hall. It was slightly ajar. He pushed it open very slowly.

Curtains covered a small window, but they were thin and let in enough light from the street that he saw that Katya was in bed, lying on her side, her face away from the door. A movement made him jump, and then he saw that it was the cat with the ridiculous name. The cat stared at him steadily, eyes glowing in the partial light, unblinking and aloof. Hans stepped closer. He could make out Katya's blonde hair splayed across her pillow and saw the gentle rise and fall of her shoulder. She had a blanket over her, but it didn't come all the way over her shoulder, and he saw that she still wore her coat.

"*Gut*," he murmured to himself. "*Das ist gut.*"

Hans couldn't shake the feeling that Emilee was following right behind him, looking over his shoulder, seeing everything he was seeing. He backed out of the bedroom and pulled the door shut behind him, turning the knob carefully until it clicked. With that, he made a quick stop at the bathroom and then went back into the main living area and turned on the lamp. He looked around. His overcoat was on the floor beside the couch. One boot was nearby, but he couldn't see the other one. He vaguely remembered kicking them off in the night. The clock above the electric fireplace showed it was 2:16 a.m.

The light was causing jabs of pain somewhere behind his eyes, so he tiptoed back to the bathroom and pulled the chain to turn on the light. In a small medicine cabinet above the sink he found some aspirin, tossed four pills in his mouth, and chewed them quickly, nearly gagging on the bitterness.

Leaving the bathroom light on and the hallway door open, he came back into the kitchen. His eyes turned to the paper on the table. He could see now that it was a note with a pencil beside it. Careful not to make a noise, he went over and saw several lines of Katya's handwriting on it. He picked it up.

Dearest Hans,

Thank you for a most wonderful evening. I can't tell you how much I needed that. You were my life saver. I was about to drown in self-pity, and you found the perfect cure.

Never thought I could out-drink a soldier, but what can I say? You passed out before I did, so I think I win the prize.

I took three marks from your wallet to pay for a taxi and to tip the driver for helping me get you upstairs without waking the landlady.

If you wake up before I do, I'm in the bedroom. I'm always cold at night. Come in and warm me up.

K.

Hans read it again and then sat back, staring at the wall, his thoughts far away, a frown furrowing his brow. He was thinking about that first night when he had asked Emilee if she could read to him.

After almost a full minute, he picked up the pencil, turned the paper over, and started writing.

Katya,

I can't believe that you've had to deal with this drunken bum twice now. I've always prided myself on being able to hold my liquor. If there are thanks in order, they should be coming from me to you, not the other way round. Thanks for holding my hand when I was too sotted to keep going. You are wonderful.

When I woke up, I realized that all my stuff—my civilian clothes, my toilet items, etc.—are still back at the hotel where I'm staying. It's a cheap flophouse that I have to pay for day

171

by day. I fear that if I don't come home before dawn, the clerk will toss my stuff into the street.

That wasn't quite true. The hotel did allow payment night by night, but when he'd come in from Pasewalk the previous night, he'd paid for two nights just in case it took longer than he hoped to get his check.

It's at least an hour away from here, so I think that when I get there, I'll probably grab some more sleep and then take a bath and shave.

Don't look for me before noon. Maybe later.

Hold that thought on being cold.

Love, H.

Hans stopped and stared at his note for a long moment, a little shocked at how brazen it sounded. Frowning even more deeply, he flipped the pencil over and erased the last three lines, careful to leave no trace of what he had written.

He sat back, blowing out his breath in exasperation. This whole thing was getting more and more complicated. What did he do now?

He laid down the pencil and reached inside his jacket pocket. Withdrawing his wallet, he extracted the bills from it and laid them on the table. Then he patted his pants pockets. Nothing in one, something in the other. He fished for a moment and brought out a five-mark note, three one-mark coins, and a handful of *Pfennige*. Wincing as the throbbing in his head exploded again, he counted out what lay before him.

When he finished, he swore softly. Thirteen marks and a few *Pfennige*. Hans was stunned. The money he had received from Dr. Schnebling, along with the money his parents had given him—gone? He counted it again, unable to believe what he was seeing.

He hadn't been too concerned about keeping track of his funds before, because he had three thousand marks coming in. He did a quick calculation. His hotel was two marks per night, and he was spending

172

about that same amount on food each day. At four marks a day, he had until Saturday before he ran out of money. Three days!

That can't be right. His eyes suddenly narrowed. He read Katya's letter again, focusing on her comment about taking money out of his wallet. Had she . . . ? Then he shook the idea off, ashamed for even thinking it.

Someone turned the vice in his head a notch tighter.

Hans got up. He needed to get out of here before Katya woke up. She was as intoxicating as the liquor in a way, and he needed to sort things out in his head before he did something foolish.

Reaching out, he picked up the pencil, pulled her letter closer to him, and began to write again.

Not sure when I will get back next. May have to return to the dairy farm for a time while I sort out my life. Sounds ghastly, but I'm running out of options. I know it is the same for you. I hope you can find work with another government ministry, but if you are forced to move, please leave a forwarding address with your landlady.

I promised I would tell you about that "other person," the one in Pasewalk, when I found out if it was going to work. No decision yet, but not entirely hopeful. If it doesn't work out, I will be back. You can count on that.

He reread the addition and then wrote one more line.

With warmest affection, H.

He laid the letter and pencil on the table and stood up. A minute later, he had his boots and overcoat on and was out the door, being careful not to make any sound as he slowly shut it behind him.

7:35 a.m.—Hotel Lindenberg, Prenzlauer Berg District, Berlin

Hans smoked steadily as daylight gradually lightened his room, revealing the water stains on the ceiling and the patches of missing wallpaper. He had slept only fitfully. As usual, the radiators cracked and popped all night but produced very little heat. But his thoughts were not on the dismal room, nor the dismal day. They were on his dismal life. *Three days, and the money would be gone?* How did he tell Emilee that? And that there would be no severance pay? And no university? And no job? Nothing. He brought absolutely nothing to the table.

On the way back to the hotel his headache had gradually subsided and his thoughts had cleared. He knew that what he wanted—what he *needed*—was Emilee Fromme. Thoughts of her constantly filled his mind—the sound of her footsteps on the tile floor, the faint smell of flowers in her perfume, the softness of her touch, his first sight of her sweet smile and upturned nose when they had removed his bandages, the lilt of her voice as she had read *Pride and Prejudice* to him. Katya was exciting, enchanting, intoxicating—but she didn't fill his thoughts like this.

Which only added to his sense of hopelessness. Emilee already had three people she was caring for—herself, her mother, and Heinz-Albert. He couldn't go back to her with nothing but a few marks in his wallet.

He stubbed out his cigarette and sat up. Well, there was Graswang and milking cows. But the thought of going back home with the same bleak news was even more depressing than the thought of seeing Emilee.

Putting on his boots, Hans went out in the hall and down to the toilet. He wet his hands and ran them through his hair, combing it back into some kind of order. He rubbed at the stubble on his chin but decided he didn't want to take the time to shave. An idea was starting to form in his mind, and he decided to act on it immediately.

Back in his room, he rejected the temptation to change into his civilian clothes. The government might be throwing their men to the wolves, but the people knew what the soldiers had gone through—almost everyone had lost someone in the war. He hoped the uniform would get him at least a foot in the door.

Downstairs, he paid the pimpled clerk with fuzz on his cheeks for two additional nights. That took a chunk of his remaining funds, but at least he had a roof over his head for a couple of nights and didn't have to carry his rucksack with him everywhere.

8:20 a.m.—Bayerischer Biergarten, Prenzlauer Berg District, Berlin

The Bavarian beer garden was much more crowded than when he had stopped here before. He paused for a moment before crossing the street, checking things out. The last time he had been here it was still dark, but now, in full daylight, he could see the restaurant better. It was a two-story building, the main floor being the restaurant itself and the upper floor being the residence of the owner, judging from the curtains and flower pot with red geraniums visible in one window. Now he could also see the garden part of the *Biergarten*. He had guessed right. It was tiny, barely large enough to fit four tables.

Turning his attention to the windows, Hans watched the small crowd for a moment. Mostly working class. That was evident. Several old men drinking coffee at one table. He crossed the street and moved to where he had a clear view of the hall leading to the kitchen in the rear. About a minute later, he saw the man with the white chef's hat and huge beer belly that he had seen the first time he was here. He brought out a tray of cheeses, bowls of diced red cabbage, and a few cold cuts of meat. He spread them out on the long serving table next to several round loaves of bread. There was no one else waiting tables, Hans noted. The cook was doing it all. That was good.

He waited until the cook was out of sight and slipped inside. By this point he was ravenous, but he held himself to one mark thirty, which bought him half a loaf of bread, four slices of cheese, and a small carafe of water at no extra charge. All together it took only one of his ration cards.

The crowd was thinning when he finally stood up. He looked

around, making sure the cook was nowhere in sight, and then began clearing the dishes off his table. He moved to the next one and added those to his stack before heading for the back.

The cook came out with another tray of food just as Hans set the dishes in the sink. He stopped, taken aback, and then his face instantly darkened. "What are you doing?"

"I just want to help," Hans said.

The man swore. "Get outta here. This ain't no charity hall." He started to push past him, but Hans blocked his way. The cook was powerfully built, but it had gone mostly to flab, and he was three or four inches shorter than Hans.

"I'm not asking for a salary," Hans said earnestly. "Just one meal a day, and for that I'll bus your tables, do dishes, scrub out pots and pans. Whatever you need."

He swore again. "Move it!" he snarled.

Hans stood his ground. "Look," he said, trying to sound as meek as he could. "Have you heard about the closing of the War Ministry?"

"Yeah. What of it?"

"I've got three thousands marks in severance pay from the Army coming, but with the Ministry closing, it's going to take me a few days to get it. Please. Just breakfast. That's all I ask, and I'll work three hours every day."

For a long moment they locked eyes, and then the cook thrust the tray at him. "Put these on the serving table, then we talk."

10:47 a.m.

"Hey, Fritzie," Hans called, sticking his head into the kitchen. "Things are slowing down now. Mind if I take a smoke break?"

"Five minutes," the cook growled, without looking up from the grill.

"*Danke.*" Hans headed for the back door but stopped just before he reached it. Quickly checking to make sure no one could see him, he reached behind a barrel of flour and took out the sack he had hidden there earlier. Holding it in front of him so it couldn't be seen, he opened the door and stepped out into the alley. It had started to snow, but he barely noticed.

Again checking quickly to make sure he wasn't being observed, he reached in the sack and brought out the scraps he had salvaged from three different tables—three or four crusts of bread, a two-inch length of bratwurst, and a cup of raisins that had barely been touched. Those last two were godsends. In these times, finding anything left on someone's plate was unusual.

He wolfed them down and then reached over and scooped a handful of snow off of one of the garbage cans, put it in his mouth, and let it wash it down his "second breakfast."

Refusing to even acknowledge the shame gnawing at his gut, he quickly lit a cigarette, took three long, deep puffs on it, and then stubbed it out and put the butt in his pocket. As he went back in, he paused momentarily at the opening to the kitchen. "Three minutes," he called.

"Who's counting?" Fritzie snapped. "Take these eggs out." But as Hans took the kettle of boiled eggs, he saw that there was a touch of grudging acceptance in the cook's eyes.

4:09 p.m.—Post office and telephone exchange, Mitte District, Berlin

"Emilee?"

"Hans!" Her voice was filled with joy. "Is that you?"

"Yes. Hello. How are you?"

"I'm fine. But how are you? I've been so worried. I thought you were going to call yesterday."

"Did I wake you up?"

"*Nein, nein.* I only sleep until three. I'm preparing supper at the moment."

Hans winced. Funny how the mere mention of food could hit you so hard. "*Gut. Gut.* How are things there?"

"Things here are fine, Hans. But what about with you? How did things go at the War Ministry?"

He didn't answer.

"Hans?"

There was no getting around it, so he told her. When he finished, her voice was tight with shock. "Oh, Hans, no."

"Yes, Emilee. There's no money. The whole Ministry is shut down."

A long silence, then, "What are you going to do?"

"Look for work. I did manage to find a part-time job this morning, but I'm still looking. It's not very hopeful. There are a few jobs listed in the paper, but by the time I find where they are, they're either filled or there are huge lines waiting for them."

"*Ja, ja.* They say the unemployment rate is approaching thirty percent. Nearly fifty percent for men of your age."

Earlier that morning Hans had asked himself what else could go wrong. Now he had his answer.

There was another pause, and Hans could sense Emilee's hesitancy. "Did you go—"

He cut in quickly. "Yes. I spent about an hour at the University of Berlin yesterday."

"And?"

He told her.

"Then you must begin studying to retake the tests," she said.

His voice was bitter when he answered. "Emilee, I think I'll probably concentrate on finding employment first."

She was instantly sorry. "Of course, Hans. I'm sorry. It's just that I feel so bad for you." Another pause. "Do you need money, Hans? I've got a little saved."

"No!" Then more softly. "I'm fine. I've still got some left from what Dr. Schnebling and my parents gave me. I'm okay. Really."

"Promise you'll tell me if you need it?"

"Promise. Are things any better in Pasewalk?"

"For jobs, you mean?"

"*Ja.*"

"No, worse actually. A large clothing factory in a nearby town, which was making uniforms for the navy, just closed. The military canceled their contract, of course, and they finally shut their doors just before Christmas. Four hundred workers are now looking for work here."

Neither of them spoke for several seconds. When Emilee finally did, her voice was soft and filled with concern. "Hans?"

"Yes?"

"You may have to go home for a—"

"No, Emilee. I'm not to that point yet."

"Have you called them?"

"No." He almost said, "I don't have enough money," but he let it pass. "But I did write them today." *Or, I will later.*

"*Gut.*"

"Emilee? Just . . . just don't give up on me, all right?"

"Give up on you? Hans, I pray for you every night and morning."

"Oh, your prayers are a big help, I'm sure."

He had tried to say it lightly, but from her soft intake of breath, he knew he had hurt her. "Look, Emilee, my time's almost up. I'll call you again when I hear something. But it might be a while."

"Hans, I would like to say one last thing."

He braced himself. "All right. What?"

He could sense her sudden embarrassment. "I hope you don't think this changes things with me. I don't plan on giving up on you— not so long as you don't give up on yourself. You're not giving up on yourself, are you?"

He didn't answer. It had caught him totally off guard.

"Hans?"

"No, Emilee. I am not giving up."

"Then I'm afraid you're stuck with me. Call me as soon as you can." And she cut the connection.

CHAPTER

16

January 9, 1919, 9:10 p.m.—Bayerischer Biergarten,
Prenzlauer Berg District, Berlin

T hat's it," Fritz Kharkov called as the last couple exited the
restaurant. "You lock doors, put up closed sign, turn out
lights. Then come. We have nightcap before I start on books."

"And before I put up the chairs and sweep out the place."

Fritz waved a hand. "Do that in morning."

Hans shook his head. "I'd rather do it tonight and sleep in a little
longer."

"Cooks don't have such privilege. I am here always two hours before you."

"You should talk to the owner about that," Hans said as he locked
the door.

"I am owner."

"I know. And you have an ogre for a boss."

"*Ja, ja.*" Fritz laughed. "I try to talk to him, but he won't listen."

Hans grunted and joined his boss at the table, where he had a
bottle of schnapps and two cups waiting. This was Hans's third day
since he had weaseled his way into Kharkov's good graces. At the end
of that first day, Fritzie had grudgingly offered him two meals a day for

six hours of work. It was a good deal for him—no cash laid out—but Hans jumped at it. It wasn't just getting two full meals a day, which was significant, but Hans had sensed that if he worked hard and well, it might turn into something more. And he had been right. By the end of the second day—yesterday—Hans had a full-time job for ten marks a week and all the food he could eat.

And he and Fritz Kharkov had become friends. It had surprised Hans last night when Fritz had asked him to join him for a schnapps and conversation. He had also invited Hans to call him Fritzie, as everyone else did, including his wife.

As Hans returned to join his employer, he saw there was something else. There was a newspaper on the table beside the glasses. Fritzie poured two generous portions, and then they touched cups together—a salute to the day. Neither spoke until both cups were empty. Then Fritzie tapped the paper. "You are Bavarian, no?"

"Yes. From a little village near Oberammergau, which is south of Munich."

"Ah, *ja.* I know this Oberammergau." Kharkov sobered. "You know about the troubles in Bavaria?"

"Troubles?"

"*Ja, ja.* Have you not seen?" Kharkov turned the paper over and shoved it at him. It was the *Munich Observer,* and Hans saw that it was dated two days before. That surprised him.

"You subscribe to a Munich newspaper?" Hans asked.

"But of course. Many customers from the south of Germany. They like to read local news." He reached out and opened the first page, spreading it out before Hans.

POLITICAL UPHEAVAL IN BAVARIA

Hans rocked back as he read the headline
"Read it," Fritzie commanded. "I go tell Liliya I work late tonight."

And with that, he slipped away and went upstairs. Hans pulled the paper over and began to read.

> Kurt Eisner, Prime Minister of Bavaria, is facing increasing pressure from both right-wing and extremist left-wing parties to step down. It is unlikely that his "People's Republic," created on November 7 of last year, will survive the general elections set for later in the month. Political pundits predict upheaval and chaos to follow if that occurs.
>
> Eisner, 51 years old, was born in Berlin to Jewish parents.
>
> On November 7, Eisner led a bloodless coup that finally toppled the Wittenberg monarchy after nearly eight centuries of rule. This was just one more example of socialist and soviet republics that spontaneously arose all across the Fatherland at war's end. It is a trend that threatens the very existence of our nation, and events in Munich suggest that it is not over yet.

The paper went on with a discussion of other cities and states that were struggling, but Hans wasn't interested in that. He sat back, frowning. Would political upheaval in Munich affect his family down in the Garmisch-Partenkirchen District? Hopefully not, but Uncle Wolfie, who was more like a brother to Hans than an uncle, was a civil servant in Munich. How would that affect him? Hans decided he had better write his mother and ask her those questions. Then another headline caught his attention.

PARIS PEACE CONFERENCE ANNOUNCED— GERMANY AND AUSTRIA EXCLUDED

> Negotiations for a permanent peace treaty between the Allied Powers and the Central Powers will begin in Versailles, near Paris, on January 18. Sadly, the German/Austrian Alliance will not be allowed to send delegates to the conference to represent their national interests. In a word, only the victors will be allowed at the table to divide up the spoils.

The conference will be led by two delegates each from France, Great Britain, the United States, Italy, and Japan—the so-called "Big Five." Their purpose will be to draft a treaty that will form a new government in Germany and set the conditions for demilitarization of Germany and war reparations. It is widely expected that France will demand that Germany repay all the costs of the war incurred by the Allied Forces, including losses and damages to civilian population. That is a staggering figure, which some estimate to be 134 billion marks.

Germany and Austria are already reeling from the effects and costs of the war, and their economies are in chaos. We can only pray that reason will prevail; otherwise, Germany and Austria may face complete bankruptcy. These are dark days for our country.

Hans pushed the paper aside, staring at nothing. Then he got quickly to his feet and walked to the back stairs. He cupped his hand and called up. "Fritzie?"

A moment later his boss appeared at the head of the stairs. "*Ja?*"

"I would like to call my family. If I pay you for the call, can I use the phone here?"

"*Ja, ja.* It is bad, no?"

"I think my family is fine. They're in a little backwater village thirty miles away from Munich. But I have an aunt and uncle who live in Munich. They have two children. He's a civil servant in the Bavarian Ministry of Public Works."

"This is not good."

"No, it's not. Not at all good."

"You make call. Don't worry about pay." There was a short bark of laughter. "I just make you work more, *ja?*"

Laughing, Hans waved and moved over behind the bar.

9:17 p.m.

"*Hallo.*"

"Mama, is that you?"

There was a gasp and then a cry. "Hans?"

"Yes, Mama. It's me."

"Is everything all right?"

"Yes, *Mutti.* But I'm calling because I just read an article about the government in Bavaria. The paper is predicting that it will fall after the general elections."

"It will?"

This was good. In their little village, they hadn't heard any of this. And it probably would have very little effect on them.

"Never mind, *Mutti.* How are you and Papa doing?"

"We're good. Life is good to us, Hans. With our farm, we rarely go hungry."

"Yes, I know. That's wonderful. Uh . . . how are *Tante* Paula and *Onkel* Wolfie?"

Inga seemed surprised by the question. "They are good too. Wolfie is up for a promotion. Paula is very proud."

"*Gut.*"

There was a pause, then, "Hans, Emilee called me a few days ago. She told me what you did for her up in Königsberg. That's wonderful, Hans. She was in tears when she told me."

"Things turned out well," he said. He wondered if Emilee had talked about the road block.

"She also told me what happened at the War Ministry. I am so sorry, Hans." Another pause. "Would you like to come home? There is always a bed for you."

"No, Mama. Thank you. But I have a job now."

"Emilee said you're exchanging work for food. That's something, Hans."

"Since I spoke to her last, it has become a full-time job, Mama. It's not much. Ten marks a day. But that's something."

"That's wonderful. Do you need money?"

"No, Mama. Not now. I'll let you know if I do."

"Promise?"

"I promise. Well, this is my boss's phone. I'd better say good-bye."

"Bye, Hans. Take care of yourself."

10:05 p.m.

"Thank God your family is safe, Hans," Fritzie said.

Hans sighed. "*Danke.* I can't believe my home state is now in such trouble."

"Everywhere now," Fritzie said. "Some think we have soviet republic in Berlin too very soon."

That brought Hans's head up. "And do you support such a thing?"

Fritz's answer was a snort of disgust followed by a bitter laugh. "You not serious? Never. Worst thing that could happen." Fritzie seemed puzzled, then suddenly understood. "Ah, you think I am a Bolshie, no?"

"I . . ." Hans managed a noncommittal shrug. "No, I just. . . ."

He laughed. "You did. You think I am Bolshevik because my name is Kharkov and I speak with Russian accent?"

"Well, I . . . you don't talk like one, but. . . ." He shrugged again.

"My family not Russian. We come from Belarus. In Belarus, not many Red Communists. We are White Russians."

"White Russians?"

"Yes. Different from Reds. Reds are communist. We fight against Communist revolution."

"Oh." Hans was relieved to hear that. He had wondered about the name and the accent, but he had been so pleased to get food and a small salary that he had kept his mouth shut. And besides that, he liked Kharkov. He was gruff and barked a lot, but he had treated Hans fairly. "So, when did you and your family come to Germany?" he asked.

"In 1905, during first revolutions by Lenin and Marxists. My father want no part of it. He had brother living here in Berlin for ten years. My uncle Anatoly. So he tell us to come. He take us in. Together he and my Papa, they start small restaurant. When I marry my Liliya, I become apprentice cook." He waved a hand at the expansive room in which they were sitting. "Now we have all this."

Hans had met Fritzie's uncle Anatoly on his first day. "I see. And are your parents still living?"

Frtiz looked away. "Mama and Papa die in Spanish flu epidemic last year. So only me and Anatoly now."

They were both silent for a moment, and then Kharkov leaned in toward him. "I want to talk about Uncle Anatoly. That why I give you newspaper."

Surprised, Hans nodded. "All right."

"How you like to work for me?"

Startled, Hans stared at him. "I thought I was working for you."

"*Ja, ja*. You like?"

"I do. Very much. I like having good food, too."

Fritzie reached across the table and poked Hans but then winked at him. "Better than sneaking food out back and eating garbage, no?"

Hans felt his face go red. "Yes. Much better."

"*Gut*. You are good worker. I trust you."

"Thank you."

"Wish you could stay with Fritzie, but with wife and children, no room."

"That's not a problem," Hans assured him. "The Hotel Lindenberg is only five or six blocks from here, and if I pay in advance for a whole month, then it is only one mark per night."

"*Gut*. I give you advance pay, so you pay by month now. Save you money."

"I . . . That would be wonderful, Fritzie. Thank you."

"No thank me yet," he said. "I ask more."

"What?"

He leaned forward, his craggy face filled with concern now. "I ask you questions first."

"Okay."

"You like to make twenty marks each week, *ja?*"

Hans rocked back. "Twenty? I'll say I would."

"Is true that you were driver in Great War?"

That was not a question he expected. "*Ja*, I drove trucks for two years."

"Were you in war too?"

"Do you mean, did I ever see combat?"

"*Ja*, combat."

Surprised at this sudden line of questioning, Hans nodded. "I was in the infantry for two more years," he said quietly. "On the front lines. Eventually I ended up as a platoon sergeant."

Fritzie rubbed at the dark stubble on his chin. "Before you say yes to offer of more money, I explain. You may think not a good idea."

"For twenty marks a week, I'm willing to do just about anything, Fritzie, so what is it that you want me to do?"

"Ride shotgun."

"I beg your pardon?"

Grinning, he explained. "You have seen American cowboy movies, no? When stagecoach is out in country, they have two drivers, no?"

"Yes," Hans said slowly, beginning to sense where this might be going.

"One is driver of the horses, and the other one is . . . ?" He made it into a question.

Hans understood him perfectly. "And the other driver carries a shotgun to protect the passengers and whatever the stagecoach is carrying."

"*Ja, ja!* Riding shotgun." He took a quick breath. "Uncle Anatoly is old now. We celebrate seventy-two birthdays last month."

"Okay." The sudden change of subject threw Hans off a little.

"*Ja.* Anatoly drive truck to markets, buy food, bring back."

"I see. Go on." Hans was actually elated. He would take driving a truck over scrubbing pots and pans anytime.

Fritzie leaned in and lowered his voice, even though they were alone. "You know about the *Freikorps*, no?"

"Of course. Soldiers who either should have been or have been discharged from the army. Freed from their army service. Demobilized and unemployed."

"And they have guns."

"Yes, some of them have guns."

"*Ja, ja.* That's why I need you."

"Has Anatoly had problems with the *Freikorps*?" Hans asked.

"*Ja.* Yesterday."

Hans started at that.

"He is home with broken wrist."

"*What?* How did that happen? Did he fall?"

"No. He was pushed. Then man who push him, stomp on wrist and kick him in ribs. But Anatoly curl up by then. Ribs bruised but not broken."

Hans rocked back. "Where did this happen?"

"At butcher shop at *Zentralmarkthalle*, on *Friedrichstrasse*."

Hans fell back, a little shocked. That was pretty brazen.

Fritzie went on grimly. "We lucky they not steal truck too. But we lose two hundred twenty marks' worth of meat. But worse than money. Meat is very hard to get."

"And they'll sell it for two or three times what you paid for it."

Fritzie went on quickly. "Last Wednesday, at *Markthalle* XI in the Kreuzberg district, Anatoly also stopped by bad men. We lose eight cases wine, six cases ale and lager, and five cases whiskey. Costing us three hundred marks more."

Hans was shaking his head in astonishment. Over five hundred marks in three days?

Fritzie got to his feet and went around behind the bar. When he came back to join Hans, he had a German Luger in his hand. He waved it at him, with the barrel pointing at the ceiling. "Last night, after you go home, I am getting ready for bed. I hear shouting out from street. I look out and see four, maybe five hooligans. Screaming and shaking fists at me. I run down the stairs and grab this." He waved the pistol. "When I step outside, I see one has big rock in hand. I shoot in the air and they run off."

His hands were trembling with rage as he relived it. "You know what they scream at me?"

"What?"

"'Go back to Russia, Bolshie! Death to Soviet pig.'"

Hans understood instantly. "They think you are a Bolshevik. That's not good. Not with what's happening all around us right now."

"*Ja, ja.* They are too stupid to know difference between Russian and Belarusian."

"And you want me to help you protect yourself."

"*Ja.* And go with Anatoly. Must stop this or I am not in business. It is bad enough with no food to buy, but. . . ." He looked heavenward and shook his head.

Hans nodded without hesitation. He was thinking of the five men at the road block. "When do you want me to start?"

"Today is Thursday. Anatoly next go to market Saturday morning."

"Then I'll be with him on Saturday."

Kharkov pushed the Luger across the table. "You take this."

Hans pushed it back. "No. You keep it here in case they come back. Are you willing to put up a little money?"

"For what you need money?"

"If I'm riding shotgun, I'm going to need a shotgun."

CHAPTER 17

*January 10, 1919, 8:30 a.m.—Bayerischer Biergarten,
Prenzlauer Berg District, Berlin*

With the morning rush over, the tables cleared, the floor swept, and the dishes washed and set out to dry, Hans went into the kitchen. Fritzie Kharkov was working over the grill, greasing it with lard. He looked up and nodded. "You go now?"

"If that's all right."

"*Ja, ja.* It is good time. How much money you need?"

"How many bullets do you have for that Luger?"

"Six."

"That's all?"

"*Ja*, six."

"You're going to need more than that, so I'll buy a box of nine millimeter shells for you."

"*Gut.*"

"And you're all right if I buy another pistol?"

"I thought you want shotgun."

"That was just a figure of speech. I'm looking for something easy to keep concealed but with pretty good stopping power. A rifle or a shotgun will be too big."

"But not Luger?"

"Actually, the *Pistole 8,* which is the official name of your weapon, has a high muzzle velocity, but it's a smaller caliber bullet, so it doesn't have as much stopping power."

Fritzie went back to greasing the grill. "I have no idea what you just say. But I trust you. How much you need?"

"I'm not sure. While I was waiting in line at the Ministry of War, some of the guys were saying that a lot of soldiers who deserted before the end of the war simply walked away with their weapons. Now they're selling them on the cheap."

"Like to a pawnshop?"

"*Ja,* exactly. They pawn them off because they need the cash. I'm hoping we can find a decent pistol for about ten marks. Do you know of any pawnshops nearby?"

"No nearby, but one on the corner of *Unter den Linden* and *Friedrichstrasse.* You want me to call Anatoly to drive you?"

"No, no. It's not that far. And besides, I need to go to the telephone exchange, anyway."

"You are free to use telephone here."

"Thanks, but once is enough. I don't want to wear out my welcome here. I will be back in time for the noon rush."

"*Gut.*" Fritz reached in his back pocket and brought out his billfold. He extracted two twenty-mark notes. "You think this be enough?"

"Probably more than enough, but I'll bring the rest back."

"And you pay hotel clerk for full month rent this morning?"

"I did. Thank you for that advance, Fritzie. That's a great relief to me."

"*Gut.*"

Kharkov was thoughtful now. "I have Anatoly pick you up tomorrow. Five thirty in morning?"

"That's fine." Hans pocketed the money, waved a hand, and headed out of the restaurant.

10:20 a.m.—Corner of Unter den Linden and Friedrichstrasse, Mitte District, Berlin

The clerk at the pawnshop didn't bat an eye when Hans asked to look at pistols. To Hans's surprise, among the large selection was an American-made Colt Service Revolver, chambered for a forty-five-caliber shell. The clerk claimed the soldier who brought it in had captured it from an American army captain. It was three marks more than any of the other guns, and six more than the Lugers, of which he had almost a dozen. But Hans wanted the heavier caliber and bought it for the asking price. He also bought three boxes of forty-five shells and a box of shells for the Luger. Total cost, twenty-two marks.

10:50 a.m.—Post office and telephone exchange, Mitte District, Berlin

"*Hallo!*"

"Heinz-Albert?"

"*Ja.*"

"This is Hans. Hans Eckhardt. Do you remember me?"

"*Ja.*"

"*Gut.* May I speak with Emilee, please?"

"Emee is sleeping."

"Oh." He stifled a curse. He should have thought of that. She would have worked last night. "Could you wake her up for me, Heinz-Albert? It's very important."

"No. She's sleeping."

Hans gritted his teeth. This was Heinz-Albert—simple logic, simple responses, and fierce loyalty to his older sister. Getting angry at him wouldn't accomplish one thing. Then he heard the murmur of a woman's voice. Good. Maybe Heinz-Albert's mother would intervene. But it was Emilee's voice that came on the line. "Hans?"

"Emilee. Yes, it's me. I'm sorry to wake you up."

"I wasn't asleep yet. I was just in my bedroom reading. When I heard the phone, I was hoping it would be you. How are you? I've been so worried about you."

"I'm good. How are you?"

"Are you really, Hans? Be honest. Ever since you told me about the Ministry closing, I've been sick about it. I can't stop thinking of you. Tell me what's happening."

"I have a job. A full-time job."

"Really?" she exclaimed. "What is it?"

Suddenly he realized that a bus boy and dish washer might be considerably less than what she was expecting. "Uh . . . I'm working at a restaurant. I told you about my part-time job. Well, now it's full time. It's actually a Bavarian restaurant, if you can believe it."

"Wonderful!" And it was said with genuine enthusiasm.

"Right now I just help wait on tables and clean up around the kitchen, but Fritzie—that's my boss—says he's going to train me as a cook." He wasn't about to tell her the other part of his job description. "He's paying me twenty marks per week, with all meals included."

"Oh, Hans," she said. "I can't tell you how happy that makes me."

"Really? It's not much. Not for someone who should have been an engineer by this point. But even though the food is limited, I don't have to use my ration cards, so that is a huge blessing."

"But Hans, there are tens of thousands of men who can't find any work at all right now. So this is wonderful news. A salary and meals. It's an important start."

That made him feel good. She was genuinely pleased for him.

"How is the food situation up there, Emilee? Are you and your family getting by?"

"Yes. Things are difficult here too, but not like they are in the big cities. Ernst has been making trips to the little villages out away from town and can occasionally find eggs, butter, cheese, and even flour from time to time. Oh, I forgot I haven't told you. Ernst has a job too."

"Really? Doing what?"

"Driving for his friend that lent us the truck. He's getting enough business now that he wants Ernst to do all the deliveries so he can spend all of his time in the butcher shop. And occasionally, he lets him bring home some of the better meat scraps. It makes a wonderful stew."

"Good for him. He's a good man."

"I think so too. How is your family doing?"

"They live on a dairy farm. They're better off than most."

Then she sobered. "Have you heard what is happening in Bavaria right now?"

"*Ja.* I called my mother the minute I read about it in the newspaper."

"Really? Oh, I'm so glad you did, Hans."

"Everyone's all right," he assured her.

"Well, thank the Lord for that."

"Really? You're thanking God for all these wonderful blessings we're having right now?"

"Did I just detect a sour note in your voice?" she asked dryly.

"Guilty as charged."

"That's too bad."

"Why's that?"

"Because in my prayers tonight, I'm going to thank the Lord that you found this job. Obviously you're not going to."

Hans said nothing for a moment. He knew they were bantering back and forth, and he enjoyed that about her. She had a quick mind and stood right up to him. But . . . "Do you pray every night, Emilee?"

"I do. And morning."

"Seriously?"

"Does that bother you?"

"No, not really. I just think the whole idea is ridiculous."

"Do you want me to stop?"

That took him by surprise. "It's not my affair what you do."

"It could be," she shot right back at him. "If things keep going as well as they are now." She gave an awkward little laugh. "Does that shock you that I'm so brazen?"

"I don't think of you as brazen."

"All right, forward."

He thought about that for a moment. "Actually, I like it when you're forward. Keeps me on my toes."

Emilee was quiet for a time, but after a moment, she cleared her throat. "Can I ask you a forward question, then?"

"Sure."

"If we were ever to get married, would you ask me to stop praying?"

"Whoa! Where did that come from?"

"I'm serious. I'd like to know. If it bothers you, would you want me to stop?"

He thought about it for a moment, sensing that this was not a playful question. Finally, he shook his head. "No. What you do is your business."

"Good."

"Would you try to make me pray with you?"

"Of course not. I believe that prayer is a very personal thing."

He glanced out of the booth at the clock on the wall. "Well, I've only got another minute of time. I'd better say good-bye."

"All right, but I just thought of another question I have."

"Go ahead."

"What's a Mormon?"

"What?"

"Your mother said something about her and your Aunt Paula being Mormons."

"Oh, yeah. Why? Does that matter to you?"

"No, I was just curious. I'd never heard that word before."

"Okay. Down to thirty seconds. So can I ask you one last question?"

"Sure."

"How often do you call my mother?"

She actually giggled. "Oh! That was not what I expected!"

"So?"

"Every three or four days. I'll call her today when we're done. And she calls me after you've talked to her. That way we catch each other up on what we've heard from you. Does that bother you?"

He forced a light chuckle, glad that she couldn't see his face. "I'm getting used to it."

"I love to talk with her, Hans. She's a wonderful woman. I can't wait to meet her sometime."

"I know. Well, gotta go. I'll call again in a few days."

There was a moment's pause. "Hans?"

"Yes?"

"I miss you."

He felt a little thrill shoot through him. There was longing and fervor in her voice.

"And I miss you, Emilee. I think about you all the time."

Just then, he saw the exchange woman coming over, wagging her finger at him. "Hold on a sec." He retrieved a one-mark note and handed it out to her. "I'll come get the change in a moment."

She nodded and retreated. He picked up the receiver again. "Okay, I'm back."

"Say again what you just said. I wasn't sure if I heard you right."

He hooted softly. "You heard me very well."

"Say it again anyway. I want to hear you say it again."

He spoke slowly and distinctly. "I miss you, Emilee Greta Fromme. I think about you all the time."

She sighed. "I think of you all the time, too. Especially every day at one a.m., when I'm doing my rounds. I . . . I think I'm beginning to really care for you, Hans," she added, her voice low and hesitant.

"Ah, then," he teased, "with that lead-in, I have something I want to say too."

"I'm listening."

"I am doing a special job for my boss tomorrow. It's something really important to him. If I do it right, I'm going to ask him if I can have this Saturday and Sunday off. My railway pass is good for a few more weeks, so maybe I could come up and see you. Would that be all right?"

"*All right?*" she squealed. "Do you have to ask?"

"Good. I'll call you and confirm for sure what time I'm coming."

"Wonderful. Write me in the meantime! *Auf Wiedersehen*, Hans."

"*Auf Wiedersehen*, Emilee. Oh, and one more thing."

"What?" He could tell she was holding her breath.

"I think I'm beginning to care for you a lot, too."

"I'm sorry, Sergeant. I didn't quite hear that. Would you mind repeating it for me?"

He laughed aloud. "Good-bye, Emilee. I hope I'll see you on Saturday."

CHAPTER 18

January 11, 1919, 6:12 a.m.—Zentralmarkthalle,
Alexanderplatz, Kaiser-Wilhelm-Strasse, Berlin

Anatoly Kharkov let up on the gas pedal as they approached a well-lit intersection about half a block from the massive black hulk of the central market hall. He pointed through the windshield. "There's the market."

"My word. That's huge."

"It is very big. This street where we are turning leads to the back loading docks. It is a one-way street. We go in here; we come out the other end. That's where they were waiting for me when I came out of the alley."

With a light mist catching the light from the street lamps, it was hard to see very far. "Pull over to the side here for a minute. I have some questions for you."

Anatoly did so, leaving the engine idling but turning off the lights.

"All right. First question. In both cases, it sounds like they waited until after you had gotten the food and were on your way out again. Is that right?"

"*Ja.* Both."

"Do you carry cash on you?"

"*Nein.* No more than five or six marks. Everyone knows that it's not safe on the streets anymore, so all of us have a line of credit set up with the markets."

"So what they're after is the food. Not surprising. With rationing and food shortages, the black market must be very lucrative right now."

There was a weary sigh as Anatoly nodded. "When the city started building these central market halls in the late 1880s and early 1890s—I think they eventually built fourteen in all—they put a police station close to every one of them so people would feel safe. What a laugh that is."

Hans's eyebrows lifted. "A police station? Tell me more."

"It's at the other end of the market, just before we come out of the alley."

That surprised him. "And that's where they attacked you?"

Subconsciously, Anatoly began rubbing the cast on his left wrist. "Yes. Maybe a block or two away from the station."

"Did you see any policemen that morning?"

Another nod. "Two were standing on the sidewalk watching me as I went by."

"How far was that from where the gang stopped you?"

Anatoly's voice was bitter now. "No more than two blocks."

This was making more and more sense to Hans. "And the police did nothing when you were stopped?"

"That was my first thought," Anatoly said. "That they would help me. But when I saw the men up ahead of me, I looked in the mirror and the policemen were no longer there."

Hans nodded thoughtfully. "That changes things."

"How so?"

"If the police are in on it, that's not good. The thieves are probably giving them a case of wine or a hind quarter of pork to look the other way. What else? You say the alley doesn't open out directly on *Kaiser-Wilhelm-Strasse*? There's this other street?"

"That's right." Then Anatoly cocked his head, thinking hard. "But

I remember seeing another truck pulling away from the docks after I did. I could see his lights coming behind me."

That piqued Hans's attention. "Was he right behind you?"

"*Nein*. More like thirty or fifty yards back."

"So what did he do when you were stopped?"

Anatoly rubbed his chin. "Well, that's the other strange thing. Just before those thugs stopped me, I looked in my mirror again, checking to see if the other truck was still following me. But he was gone. I don't know what happened to him. Maybe another group held him up."

"No," Hans said. "That doesn't make sense." Then he snapped his fingers. "Is it possible that the police could have stopped him? Held him back?"

He gave Hans a strange look but then began to nod. "That could be. Once the thugs had me out of the cab and were unloading my stuff, I saw two or three trucks come out of the alley, but they turned the other way, which is strange. That's not the shortest way to *Kaiser-Wilhelm-Strasse*."

"Okay, okay." Hans's mind was racing. This was making more sense. "So the police stop anyone else behind you, hold them back until you are completely alone, and then turn them in a different direction. It's really quite brilliant, actually. Smarter than I was giving these goons credit for."

"But why choose me? Why not one of the other vehicles?"

"Good question." Hans thought a moment. "It may be purely random." His brows furrowed. "Or they've got one of the guys in the market in their pocket. He tells them which loads are the most valuable. That would make sense."

"So what do we do?"

Hans smiled grimly. "We beat them at their own game."

6:48 a.m.—Loading docks, Zentralmarkthalle Allee

It took them only about twenty minutes to help the dock workers load in several tubs of beef, pork, various sausages, and other cold cuts, all packed in ice. They hadn't filled all the tubs they had brought, but

Kharkov was delighted that they had been able to find as much as they did.

With the cargo secured, they climbed back into the cab of the truck. Anatoly inserted the key, but Hans reached out and stopped him. "Hold on. I have more questions."

Kharkov sat back, watching him nervously.

Hans was looking at the activity all around them. There were a dozen trucks lined up at the loading docks. Men were swarming around them like ants in an anthill, carrying boxes, and rolling slabs of meat on hand dollies.

"I should have paid attention, but you don't have your name or the name of the restaurant painted on the truck, do you?"

"No." Anatoly squinted at Hans. "What are you thinking?"

"The inside man probably describes the target vehicle to the gangs using color, size, and the fact that we have a canvas cover, not a metal one. So whoever is selling them the information—and they're probably selling it directly to the police—are not saying, 'Watch for the Kharkov truck,' or 'Watch for the truck that belongs to the *Bayerischer Biergarten* restaurant.' It would be, 'Watch for the one-ton truck with a yellow cab and black canvas cover.'"

"And why does that matter?"

"Because," Hans said, his face grim, "if we pull this off this morning, we don't want them knowing who we were or where we came from. Because they're gonna be out for blood. Our blood. But with no names, we're just one of thousands of other trucks in the city."

Anatoly got it, and he clearly didn't like it. "Why would they come after us if they don't get anything from us? Won't they just pick another truck?"

Hans patted him on the shoulder. "To answer that, let me ask you one more question. When these guys jumped you the other day, how long did it take them to pull you over and unload the truck?"

"Hmm. Probably eight or nine minutes."

"That's right. And how can they dare to take that long? Because the police are making sure no one disturbs them."

"*Ja.* Exactly."

"Which means that we're going to have eight or nine minutes with these slime balls too."

That puzzled Anatoly for a moment, but then suddenly his eyes went wide. "What are you planning to do?"

"I'm planning to put these bloodsucking parasites out of business once and for all."

"You mean you're going to . . ." His voice was filled with horror.

"No, Anatoly. No one's going to get killed this morning. But when we're done with them, they're gonna think seriously about changing occupations."

That didn't reduce Anatoly's anxiety. "What if something goes wrong?"

"My job is to see that nothing goes wrong. That's why I'm riding shotgun. Okay?"

There was a long sigh, and his face was troubled. "You're sure?"

"Yes. Just give me one minute, and then we're out of here."

Without waiting for a response, Hans slipped out of the truck and moved around to where the truck mostly shielded him from the view of the dockworkers. Bending down, he found a patch of mud that hadn't been packed down by the trucks and scooped up a handful.

Anatoly watched in wonder as Hans looked around again. Then, with one quick swipe of his hand, he smeared the front registration plate with mud. A moment later he'd done the same to the back plate. After quickly wiping his hand off in a patch of wet grass, he came back to the truck. He withdrew the two scarves he'd bought yesterday at a men's haberdashery store and handed one to Anatoly. "Cover your face. Tie it tight so it doesn't slip. We want nothing but our eyes showing."

As Anatoly tried to put it on, Hans saw that with the cast on his wrist and thumb, he couldn't tie it. His hands were also shaking, which made it worse. So Hans quickly reached over and tied it for him. Then he did the same for himself.

"You ready?" he asked softly.

The older man swallowed hard and then nodded.

"Okay. I'm going to get in the back of the truck. Let's hope that the fact that you just bought over two hundred marks' worth of fresh meat makes us their number-one target this morning."

Managing a wan smile, Anatoly nodded again.

7:00 a.m.

As they turned out of the alley onto the narrow, dimly lit street that led to *Kaiser-Wilhelm-Strasse*, Anatoly opened the small, sliding window between the cab and the truck's cargo area. "Can you hear me all right?"

"Yes. That's good. But when you see them, Anatoly, don't turn around. They've got to think you're alone."

He waved his cast at Hans. "And what if they decide to beat me up again?"

"Then someone is going to end up with a forty-five-caliber slug in his gut. But that's not going to happen. Not if you keep cool. Act scared, but whatever you do, don't turn around like you're looking for someone, all right?"

"Yes."

A moment later, the Belarusian turned his head slightly. "Coming up on the street. There are two policemen waiting at the stop sign. They're waving me through. What do I do?"

"Whatever they say," Hans called back.

Hans reached out and made sure the two canvas flaps that covered the back of the truck were closed so there was only a narrow slit between them. As the truck slowed and then accelerated again as it turned the corner, Hans looked out through the slit in time to see them roll past two uniformed officers. And—no surprise—the moment the truck rolled past them, they stepped into the head of the alley. Both had their hands up, waving for the next truck to stop.

Brilliant, Hans thought. Stop them. Talk to them until Anatoly is out of sight. Then turn them the other way. It was actually smarter than he had expected. Slick as a child's slippery slide. No fuss. No fanfare. And now, Anatoly's was the only vehicle on the deserted street. "All right, Anatoly," Hans said in a low voice. "It's happening."

"*Ja.* I can see them in the mirror."

"Easy does it."

Yeah, Eckhardt, easy does it. So why is your heart pounding like a kettle drum and your mouth as dry as a piece of leather?

"Remember. No matter what. Don't fight back. Act scared."

There was a soft, sarcastic grunt. "I'll try." That was followed by a quick intake of breath. "There they are. Up ahead. Just like before. And the same truck is parked behind them." Anatoly let off the gas pedal, and the truck began to slow.

"How many?"

"Five. Three of them are armed. Two rifles. One pistol."

"In uniform?"

"Yes."

Hans felt the anger surge up inside him. Men like these absolutely disgusted him.

"Here we go," Anatoly hissed as the truck came to a stop.

"*Halten Sie!*" a gruff voice barked. "Out of the truck. Now! Now!"

Anatoly set the brake and shut off the engine. "Don't shoot! Don't shoot!" he cried. It was a pretty good imitation of someone scared out of his wits.

"Out! Out!" another voice barked.

Hans felt the vehicle rock a little as Anatoly climbed out and shut the door behind him.

The first voice growled again. "Kaspar, if that guy so much as blinks, shoot him."

There was a harsh hoot of laughter. "With pleasure, boss."

Heavy boots scraped briefly on pavement and then stopped. Through the window, Hans saw a man come up to Kharkov, a rifle pointed at his gut. Then the boss started barking orders. "Werner, go down the street a ways. Make sure those stupid cops don't let anyone turn this way. Horst, you do the same up ahead of us." As footsteps sounded, Hans watched through the slit in the canvas. A moment later a uniformed man sauntered past carrying a rifle. Werner, he guessed. Hans tensed as he heard the sound of boots on pavement coming closer to him.

"Let's see what our fat little friend has for us today," the boss said. He gave a raspy laugh.

Perfect! Hans had hoped the leader would be the one to come back and check out their haul. He pressed himself into the corner and raised the pistol. A moment later, the canvas was jerked back and the man stuck his head in. He didn't look up but bent over the nearest tub and pulled it toward him. Grunting in satisfaction, he transferred the pistol to his left hand and leaned on the floor of the truck as he reached in with his right hand to push aside the ice that covered the meat. "Fresh pork, boys," he called out. "And plenty of it."

Hans did two things simultaneously. He stomped down hard on the man's left hand, knocking the pistol from his grasp. At the same instant, he jammed his own pistol into the man's cheek bone and ground it down hard. The man yelped and tried to jerk away. Hans pressed harder with the pistol. "Don't move!" he cried.

"Karl?" It was another man's voice. Karl tried to jerk free but could only scream as Hans dug the heel of his boot into the man's forearm and leaned even harder into the pistol. "Tell them to stay back, maggot, or I'll blow *your* brains out."

"Karl?" Footsteps started moving toward them.

Quick as a cat, Hans swooped down and grabbed Karl's Luger and then leaned over him. "I've got a forty-five caliber Colt revolver pointed at your brain, you piece of garbage, so I suggest you tell your men to stand back, drop their weapons, and put their hands up."

From the faint light of the nearest street lamp Hans could see the man's jaw set and his eyes were calculating his odds. He twisted the muzzle of the pistol back and forth against the man's flesh hard enough that the gunsight on the barrel drew blood. "Now!" Hans screamed into his ear. "Do it now."

"Drop your weapons! Drop your weapons!" Karl shrieked, his eyes bulging out like marbles.

Hans heard a rifle clatter to the pavement.

"Step back!" Anatoly shouted. "Step back from your weapons."

Hans risked a quick glance down the street. Werner had heard the commotion and was sprinting toward them, his rifle up. Like lightning, Hans jumped down from the truck, spun Karl around to form a shield in front of him, and transferred the forty-five from Karl's face to the nape of his neck. "Tell Werner to drop his rifle. *Now!*"

Their leader screamed the order. Werner stopped short, wavering, and then laid his rifle on the sidewalk.

"Tell everyone to get over there on the sidewalk where I can see them." Then he raised his voice. "Get their weapons, driver."

"You heard him," Karl shouted at them. When they just stared at him, he screamed at them. "*Idiots!* Over on the sidewalk. Now! Don't try anything." He reached up with the back of his hand and wiped at his cheek, leaving an ugly red smear across the flesh.

Nudging him a little, Hans leaned in. "That's better, Karl. We don't want anyone hurt today, now do we?"

He called to Anatoly again. "Put the weapons in the back of the truck."

As Karl started to move forward toward his men, Hans grabbed his arm. "Oh, no. Not so fast, maggot."

"I've got them," Anatoly called as he appeared with a rifle. Hans handed him Karl's pistol. After he put them in the truck, Hans nodded toward Werner's rifle. "That one, too."

Karl half turned, trying to see their faces. "Masks, even? You think that's going to stop us from coming after you?" he hissed.

Hans flipped the forty-five from his right hand to his left, doubled up his fist, and drove it into the man's side, aiming for the right kidney. Karl screamed with pain and dropped to his knees. Hans leaned down and spoke in his ear. "You talk when I tell you to talk, swine! Other than that, keep your mouth shut."

Anatoly's eyes were wide as he came trotting up with the other rifle. "Keep the others covered," Hans told him. Then he moved around to face Karl, who was still bent over, groaning with pain. Holding the pistol's muzzle just inches from his face, Hans spoke quietly. "Empty your pockets."

Glowering at him, eyes glittering with hatred, Karl complied. Out came his identity card, a ration book, a wallet with a few bills in it. From another pocket he brought out a handful of coins and half a dozen bullets for the Luger. And a set of keys. Hans scooped up the wallet, the bullets, and the keys.

"No," Karl blurted. "Not the truck."

Hans lifted the pistol high, butt first, and Karl shrank back but didn't look away. "It's an army truck," he said.

"Not anymore," Anatoly chortled.

Karl ignored that, still looking at Hans.

"You take that vehicle and they'll hunt you down. If you're a soldier, you know that's true."

There was no question that it was a military vehicle. After a moment, Hans pocketed the keys, deciding that stealing an army truck was probably not a good idea. "All right," he said. "We're turning right on *Kaiser-Wilhelm-Strasse*. I'll leave the keys behind the first fire hydrant we find on our side of the street." Then he turned to the other men. "Take your boots off!"

"In this cold?" Karl yelped. But he quickly started unlacing his army boots before Hans could hit him again. The others, muttering and swearing under their breath, did the same. "Driver," Hans said to Anatoly, "collect their boots and put them in the back of the truck. We're going to make a donation to the old soldiers' home tomorrow."

Then, without warning, Hans reached down and patted the breast pocket of Karl's tunic, which had a noticeable bulge in it. "I meant all of your pockets, *Dummkopf.*"

"No!"

Hans shook his head and pulled the hammer of the forty-five back until it clicked. Then he touched the muzzle against the tip of Karl's nose. "What did you say?"

Fumbling clumsily, hands shaking violently, Karl finally got the top button of his tunic undone and reached inside. He withdrew a sheaf of bills. As he handed it up, Hans nearly gasped aloud. The top bill was a hundred-mark note. Without a word he pocketed it and then grabbed Karl's arm and dragged him to his feet, kicking his boots to one side. "Get out of here, scum," he snarled. "And take that pack of curs with you."

As they stumbled away, Hans called out. "Not that way." They were headed for the police station. "The other way."

They whirled and broke into a stumbling run. He watched them until they were about a hundred feet away, and then Hans spoke to Anatoly. "Get the rest of the boots and start the engine. I'll be right there." He walked swiftly over to the other truck and pulled the canvas back. A moment later he came back with his arms loaded. "Okay, let's get out of here."

Anatoly, as gleeful as a child at Christmas, turned to him. "Incredible, Hans. Absolutely incredible."

Hans, suddenly struggling to calm the tremors running up and down his body, threw back his head and laughed. "You think that's incredible? Look at this!"

He held up the sheaf of bills and waved it under his nose.

CHAPTER
19

January 11, 1919, 10:29 a.m.—Bayerischer Biergarten,
Prenzlauer Berg District, Berlin

F ritz Kharkov lifted his stein of ale high in the air. The foam head and some of the golden liquid sloshed over the rim and spilled down his arm. He gave it no mind. "To Hans!"

"To Hans!" everyone in the restaurant roared back. Then they all drank deeply. Hans smiled. Only part of their merriment was for him. Most of it was because Fritzie was buying a second round of beer for everyone.

"To *der Donner and der Blitz Mann*," Uncle Anatoly yelled, wiping his mouth with his hand.

"To the Thunder and Lightning Man," everyone shouted back, tipping their mugs to Hans before taking another deep swig.

"Enough!" Hans called "Let's drink to Uncle Anatoly, who set the trap with perfect calm."

Fritzie Kharkov set his stein down and threw his arms around Anatoly in a crushing bear hug. "To *Onkel* Anatoly. Our brave driver." Though his stein was drained by a third now, he still sloshed it over the top as he grabbed it up again and jerked it to his lips.

The toasting went on like that for another several minutes, but when it became clear that Fritzie wasn't going to offer any more steins of free beer, the celebration quickly died and the customers soon filed out. In five minutes, it was just Uncle Anatoly, Fritzie, Fritzie's wife, Liliya, and Hans. Fortunately, their three children were all at school. Fritzie looked at his wife. "*Schatzi,* pull blinds down and put up closed sign. I want to hear it all again, and I don't want interruptions."

"But, Fritzie, it will be time for the lunch crowd soon."

"Do it," he said with an affectionate nudge. "We open again in few minutes, but I want to hear it again. This is a day of celebration." He pointed to a table and they all sat down.

"Okay," he said, slapping the wood sharply in his enthusiasm. "From beginning."

Hans and Anatoly took turns going through it all again. When they finished, Fritzie turned to Hans. "And tell me again what you got from them."

Hans pointed to the corner, where two rifles were leaning against the wall. "Well, we now have two army-issue rifles and about a hundred rounds of ammunition for them. Also, our friend Karl contributed another pistol, and we found a box of shells for that."

"Contributed," Liliya smiled. "I like that word." She was a small woman with light brown hair and dark brown eyes. She was about the size of Hans's mother, but next to Fritzie's bearish mass she seemed like a child.

"And one of them is yours, Hans," Fritzie exclaimed. "Which one you like? You like rifle?"

"No rifle. I can't be lugging one of those around." Hans reached in his pocket and withdrew the Colt revolver, waving it back and forth. "And I'm happy with this, if you'll let me keep it."

"Of course, of course," Fritzie roared. "What else you get?"

Hans deferred to Anatoly with a nod, who gleefully responded.

"We have five pairs of army boots, several cartons of cigarettes, and . . ." He slapped the table with his good hand. "And just under"—he paused for effect—"forty-five hundred marks!" He took a little bow. "Yes, ladies and gentlemen. You heard me right. *Forty-five hundred!*"

Even though they already knew the amount, they exploded with applause, shouting and stomping their feet on the floor.

Raising his stein of beer, Hans acknowledged the praise. "For a moment, I thought about making them take off their socks, too, but then I decided that the smell might spoil the meat."

Everyone roared.

Fritzie snatched up his stein again. "To the boots."

"To the boots!" came the response.

Hans sat back, feeling a little lightheaded. It was obvious that they were all a bit drunk. Across from him, Fritzie sobered. "Four thousand five hundred marks. Can you believe?"

Fritzie reached in his shirt pocket and pulled out a thick wad of bills. He counted out several of them and slid them across the table to Hans. "And, dear Hans, rider of shotgun, two thousand of marks are yours."

Rocking back, Hans stared at the money. Finally, he looked up. "No, Fritzie. That's way too much. I was just doing my job."

Liliya, who was sitting next to Hans, poked him. "Take it quickly. You will not see such generosity from this husband of mine again."

"Amen," Anatoly cried.

Fritzie was laughing too. "Be thankful I am drunk." Then he went very serious. "It's yours, Hans. We have great debt of gratitude. And this only small token." He raised his stein again. "And I am raising wages to twenty-five marks per week. We call it 'riding shotgun wages.'"

Hans bowed solemnly. "*Danke.* Thank you very much."

Hans took the money and put it in the pocket of his overcoat along with his pistol. "Fritzie, we need to talk about the consequences of what happened this morning."

"Like what?" Liliya asked.

Hans took a deep breath and let it out slowly. "We outwitted five violent and lawless men this morning. We sent them home on a cold winter's morning, without their boots, without their weapons, without their cigarettes, and without their money. A whole lot of money! But most of all, we absolutely humiliated them. Rubbed their noses in the mud. They're not going to forget that."

Fritzie blinked twice, looking confused. "What you saying?"

"I'm saying that we have to be prepared for retaliation." He quickly held up his hand. "I think there's very little chance of that. They have no idea who we were. And there are hundreds of trucks in Berlin. Thousands. And I really doubt they'll want to tackle us a second time. But...."

The mood around the table had quickly soured. Anatoly murmered, "*Ja, ja*. Hans is right."

A stab of guilt hit Hans as he saw a dark shadow pass across Liliya's face. She turned and looked at her husband, her eyes questioning. After a moment, he nodded. "*Ja*, I agree. We must be ready. Fight if we must. I am ready. What you think we do, Hans?"

"Well, first, we stay away from the *Zentralmarkthalle* for a few weeks. It won't be as close, but we'll use the other markets for a while. Second, we'll put one of the rifles in the truck. I'll go with Anatoly on every run for a while. And Anatoly, I want you to keep one of the pistols with you at all times. Fritzie, you keep the other one where it's in easy reach at all times."

"I keep it behind the bar," Fritzie said.

"*Gut*. And leave one of the rifles out in plain sight." Hans looked around the table. "Word is going to spread rapidly among your regular customers about what happened today. And that's good. Talk it up. Exaggerate the story a little. Let people know that the Kharkovs are armed and ready for any trouble. Having the rifle in plain sight will help."

Another thought came. "Are you still all right with me going up to Pasewalk tomorrow?"

"*Ja, ja*, Sunday is always a slow day. We are fine."

"Thank you. When I get back, maybe I'll sleep in the wine cellar for a few days so we can keep a guard posted at night."

Liliya reached out and touched Hans's arm. "I could go to my mother's for a time. Take the children out of school."

Hans nodded. "I think that's a good idea, Liliya. We're probably being overly cautious, but we don't want to take any chances with the children." He gave Fritzie a questioning look. "What do you think of that?"

"*Ja*. Is good idea."

Liliya was visibly relieved. She stood up. "I'll start packing." Bending down, she kissed Hans on the cheek. "*Danke*," she whispered. Then she left them.

Hans waited until she started up the stairs before speaking again. "If you think it is better that I don't go to Pasewalk, I can postpone that for a week."

Anatoly was shaking his head. "If they do find out who did it, it is you that they'll be after. Maybe they will think you skipped town."

"I drink to that," Fritzie Kharkov said quietly, raising his mug. Hans and Anatoly raised their mugs. Leaning in, they touched their rims together with a soft clink and then drank deeply.

When they finished, Fritzie looked at the two of them. "All right. It's time to open up for lunch."

"If you can do without me," Hans said, "I'm going to go set up some trip wires around the grounds. Make sure the locks on the doors are in good condition. Then, if it's all right, I think I will go pack my stuff and head for Pasewalk this afternoon. Make a weekend of it."

Fritizie waved him away. "You are free to do whatever you want this weekend, my friend. Anatoly and I owe you very much."

Anatoly tipped his glass to him. "Amen," he said again. "Amen to that."

CHAPTER 20

January 12, 1919, 6:50 p.m.—Fromme home, Pasewalk

Hans got to his feet as Emilee came down the stairs, crossed the entryway, and entered the small drawing room, where he was waiting for her.

"Is she asleep?"

Emilee smiled briefly. "Oh, no. It's too early still. She'll read for a while. Probably drop off about eight o'clock or so."

"And then what time does she wake up?"

"Usually not until seven o'clock or so. Sometimes even eight."

That took him aback. "She sleeps for eleven or twelve hours? Is that every night?"

There were sudden tears. "Yes. Dr. Schnebling says that she's gradually getting worse. Part of that is being aggravated by poor diet and not enough food."

He took her hand. "Oh, Emilee. I'm so sorry."

She wiped quickly at her eyes. "It's hard, watching her going down and down. For most patients with congestive heart failure, no cure exists. So we just try to maintain her quality of life and keep her comfortable." She squeezed his hand. "I am just so thankful that we got her out of Königsberg and down here. She has her family with her now, and she's happier than she's been in years. We owe you a lot for making that happen."

"I'm glad I have gotten to know her. She's a strong woman. Like my mother."

Emilee pulled her hand free from his and clasped her hands together in her lap. "My mother is fifty-nine years old. Fifty-nine, and she looks seventy-five. And do you know why? Because my father was handsome and charming and my mother loved him with all her heart. She stayed with him through all the years of chasing rainbows that were just over the next hill. She stayed with him through the women, the drinking, the gambling, through the countless jobs."

Her hands were in her lap now, but he could see they were trembling. "When I was a teenager, I came to hate my father, because I saw what he was doing to my mother. And one day, being the snotty person that teenagers can be, I asked her what had ever possessed her to marry a man like that. Oh, I was so bitter."

"And what did your mother say?"

Emilee didn't look up. Her voice was very low. "At first, she didn't say anything. I could tell I had hurt her very deeply. I started to get up and leave, but then she began to speak. I had to come back and sit beside her, she was speaking so softly."

"And what did she say?"

Her shoulders lifted and fell. "One sentence. That was all. She looked at me in a way that I shall never forget and said, 'Life doesn't often conform to our expectations.'"

"Wow," he murmured. "That says a lot, doesn't it?"

Emilee barely heard him. "We sat there for several minutes, neither of us saying anything. And then finally she spoke again. It was strange, actually. It was as if I weren't there, as if she were speaking to . . . I don't know. It was almost like she was a teacher talking to her class, like she wanted me to understand something. It was really odd."

Hans said nothing, watching Emilee carefully, sensing that this was very hard for her and wondering why she felt compelled to tell him.

"When they were first married, Papa got a job as a dock worker in Königsberg. The pay wasn't good, but she said they were very happy. Having children didn't come easily for Mama. Ernst didn't come until four years after they were married. I came two years after that. When I was four, Papa got a job in a new steel factory that was opening up there. The pay was about the same, but the work wasn't nearly as hard.

"And that was when the pattern first began. That's what Mama called it—a pattern. And she said it was a pattern repeated among the families of the poor countless times."

"What kind of a pattern?"

She went on as if Hans hadn't spoken. "My younger brother was two when Papa started at the factory. A year later, Heinz-Albert was born. It wasn't just Papa and Mama anymore. Now there were six mouths to feed. And one of their children was mentally handicapped. So things were really tight for them. On payday, which was every Saturday, they would sit down together and budget their money. Most of it went for food, of course. And that was when the pattern began.

"They would buy what food they could afford, which was never enough. And gradually, as the week went by, there was a little less food each day, even though they tried to spread it out evenly across the week. I remember that there were some weeks where we had nothing in the house on the day before payday. We went to bed hungry.

"Mama talked about the guilt they felt, listening to their children whimpering in their beds on those nights. But on payday it was wonderful. We had food again. And Mama said that they couldn't help themselves. Even though they knew what it would mean by the end of the week, they didn't have the heart to limit how much food we ate that first day or two."

Hans nodded. His thoughts were on his childhood, and he

realized that he could not remember ever in his life going to bed hungry. There was always bread and milk, if nothing else. Sometimes he made himself whipped cream sandwiches. He'd take the cream they skimmed off the buckets of milk and beat it into a fluffy texture, add sugar, and spread in on his mother's warm bread. Pure heaven. What a far cry from what Emilee was talking about.

"Then Mama asked me a question," Emilee went on. "She asked me how I thought it made my father feel hearing his children crying because there was no food, knowing that he wasn't making enough money to give them what they needed. 'Ashamed, I guess,' I said, angry that she was trying to excuse him. Then one day, when I was six or seven, Papa came home about an hour late. He was very happy. He'd bought little gifts for each of us."

"He got a raise?"

"No." Her mouth turned down. "He had stopped by the beer hall 'to lift a pint' with some of his working buddies. Between the beer and the gifts, he had spent half of the food money. Soon, mother started going to the factory on Saturday afternoon and taking the paycheck from him. She did it in front of his fellow workers, hoping to shame him into being more responsible."

"Which didn't work," Hans guessed.

"No. They cut a hole through the back fence of the factory yard and slipped away to town. Often he would be out all night and come home with nothing but a few *Pfennige* left. By the time I was twelve, Mama was the breadwinner in our home, and Ernst had joined Papa at the factory. It was an interesting division of labor. Ernst worked in the factory. Mama took in washing and ironing or walked into town and cleaned other people's houses. And I. . . ."

She bit her lip and looked away.

"And you what?" Hans asked softly.

She finally looked up, and he saw that she was crying. "It was my job to go to the pubs or the beer halls or into some flophouse hotel.

And I'd kick aside the empty bottles and breathe through my mouth so that I didn't have to smell the stale beer and the vomit and his pants where he had wet himself, and I'd drag my father home."

She was staring out the windows, far away from him now. "I wanted so much to love my father," she whispered, "and I couldn't. Not when I saw what he had become. Not when I saw my mother aging before my eyes every day. When she gave me my little lecture that day, it seemed like she was excusing him for what he did, trying to help me understand why he did it."

"And did it work?"

"Oh, I understood, all right. I understood his pride and his shame and his weakness. But . . ." She looked over at Hans. "But now my mother is dying of congestive heart failure. At the age of fifty-nine. How can I ever forgive him for that?"

Hans said nothing. Why had she felt compelled to tell him all of this? Was there some kind of unspoken message she was trying to give him? He finally shook his head. He didn't think so. It was just something that she needed to share with someone.

Hans got to his feet and went over and pulled Emilee up. He encircled her in his arms and held her closely, softly rubbing her back as the tears came more freely. After a minute, she looked up at him. "I'm sorry," she murmured. "I don't know what came over me. I—"

He took her face in his hands and kissed her. For a moment she stiffened with surprise, but then she put her arms around him and kissed him back.

"I'm glad you told me. I had no idea."

She brushed at the tears and gave a short, bitter laugh. "It's terrible to say, but it wasn't until after my father died that our lives gradually began to improve. I do miss him. He was always a loving father to me. But I'm still glad that he's gone."

Hans just held her, stroking her hair.

Finally she pulled free and looked at the clock. "Oh, dear. We have to leave for the train station in a few minutes." She reached up and laid her hand on his cheek. "I don't want you to go."

"And I don't want to. This has been a wonderful weekend for me."

"Really? We live a pretty boring life in the Fromme home."

He laughed. "Actually, that was kind of what I expected it would be."

She punched him softly. "Thanks."

"But it wasn't, Emilee. It's been wonderful for me. Most of that is being with you, of course, but I've enjoyed getting to know your family, too. Actually, as you probably sensed, I was a little wound up when I got here. It's been a crazy week for me. And being here has been like . . . I don't know. Like ointment on a burn, I guess."

There was genuine pleasure in her eyes as she looked up at him in wonder. "It makes me so happy to hear you say that, Hans." Then a smile stole across Emilee's mouth. "When you fell asleep mid-sentence yesterday, I wondered."

Hans laughed. Shortly after his arrival, they had been seated in the living room with her family. He had felt his eyes getting droopy and tried to fight it. He lost—which said something about how exhausted he was. When he awakened, he was on the divan with a blanket over him and was told that he had slept for two hours.

He nudged her. "You're not going to let me forget that, are you?"

She smiled sweetly. "Well, it does make a girl wonder if she's losing her charm."

"Hardly! I . . . I've been meaning to talk to you about something, but we haven't had much time alone."

Emilee's eyes widened a little. "I know. I'm sorry."

"No, no. I'm not complaining." He glanced at the clock on the mantle.

She looked at it too and then said, "I plan to walk you to the train station. Do you want to talk about whatever it is while we walk?"

Hans almost said yes. There would be no chance of being

disturbed. But then he shook his head. "No, this is good. It's quiet now."

Emilee sat back again. "All right, Herr Eckhardt, I'm ready."

Suddenly he was fumbling for words. "I . . . uh . . . how old are you?"

Emilee laughed gaily. "Really? That's what you want to talk about?"

"No. I just remembered that I've been wanting to ask you that for quite a while. I especially want to know when your birthday is."

"I was born on July 23, 1896. So I am—"

"Twenty-three years old. Just like me."

"You are too? When is your birthday?"

"February 20."

"So, old man," she teased, "you are five whole months older than I am. Why do you ask?"

"I just wanted to know. Plan on something nice for your birthday." He gave her a lopsided grin. "Not expensive, but nice."

"I shall hold you to that."

"Which brings me to what I want to talk to you about."

"My birthday?" Emilee asked in surprise.

"No." In the light of the overhead bulb, her blue eyes looked darker, larger, more beautiful. "Did I ever tell you that I love your nose?" he blurted, losing his nerve again.

She cocked her head. "Are you serious?"

Laughing, he nodded. "I do. I love how it turns up ever so slightly on the end."

"Hans Eckhardt," Emilee chided. "First it's my birthday. Now it's my nose. What is going on?"

"Okay, okay." He took a deep breath. "Here goes. I . . . I had some unexpected good fortune a few days ago."

She cocked her head to one side. "Oh?"

He dug in his pocket and pulled out the wad of banknotes Fritzie had given him, glad that he had brought the money with him. He wanted to impress her.

"My goodness, what is this?"

"I am now two thousand marks richer than I was when I last saw you."

"*Two thousand. . . .* What did you do? Rob a bank?"

That almost caused Hans to choke, but he recovered quickly. "No, actually, I got an unexpected letter from the War Ministry on Monday and. . . ."

She clapped her hands in delight. "They changed their minds about your severance pay?"

Just as he was about to nod, he thought of his last conversation with his mother. So instead, he shook his head. "I wish. No, I'm pretty sure I'll never see that money. Actually, an unexpected opportunity came up at work. Uh . . ."

She leaned forward. "Go on, I'm listening."

"Well, as I told you, I got a part-time job at that Bavarian restaurant by kind of forcing myself upon them, cleaning off tables and doing the dishes and so on. The owner almost threw me out, but when he saw I was a good worker, he let me stay—one free meal each day for two to three hours of work. Then he hired me on full time."

"And now he's paid you two thousand marks?"

"No. Well, kind of, but not for nothing. The other day he happened to mention this guy—a supplier of his—who owed him a lot of money but was refusing to pay. He told me that if I could get it back, I could have half."

Emilee was watching him closely. "That's a pretty hefty reward."

"Yeah, well, the guy was somewhat intimidating. He was making threats against my boss." Hans shrugged, "So I went and talked to him."

Her eyes narrowed. "And he paid your boss back? Just like that?"

"Uh . . . no . . . not just like that."

"Did you hit him?"

He shook his head. "Not exactly."

She gave him a sharp look. "What does that mean?"

"I had a pistol, and that seemed to persuade him. He gave me the money—the full amount—which was over four thousand marks. The boss was so grateful that he paid me half of that. And he says he has other debts he may need my help on."

"That's astonishing," Emilee said, finally accepting his story.

"Yeah," Hans grinned. "I thought so too."

Emilee's face lit up and she leaned forward and slapped Hans playfully. "And you waited all this time to tell me this? What am I going to do with you?"

"Well, actually, that's what I want to talk to you about. What *are* you going to do with me?"

Her eyes instantly fixed on his. "I'm listening."

"I've been thinking a lot about my life this week. Things have been pretty grim since I got out of the hospital, but they're finally looking up. So, I've been thinking about the future."

"As have I," she murmured.

"So . . ." Hans was grinning again. "Here's what I've been thinking. I want to go to the university eventually. But there may not be money for scholarships anymore, so I may have to work full time while I go to the university. So, with this sudden windfall, I have been thinking about another possibility, and I'd like your opinion on it."

"Go on."

"Aside from the time commitments, I'm not sure I'm cut out to work in a restaurant. Not even as a cook. Don't get me wrong. I was very lucky to find work, and my boss is great. But it sounds awful, actually." He grinned. "And besides, I'd probably get all fat and paunchy."

Emilee chuckled. "I find that hard to picture. So what *will* you do?"

"Guess," he said impishly.

"I . . . I have no idea."

"Yes, you do. Actually, it's you who gave me the idea."

"Me?"

"Yes. You and Ernst. In Königsberg."

"Königsberg?" She was thoroughly baffled now.

"Yes. I'll give you hint. On my twelfth birthday, my father gave me my own tool set. Not a kid's tool set. A full adult tool set. And over the next few years I added to it substantially, because I've always loved mechanical things." He reached out and took her hands. "And those tools are still there. Out in the barn. Wrapped in oilskin to keep them from rusting."

Emilee's eyes grew suddenly wide. "Are you thinking that . . . ?" The thought was so astonishing she had to stop.

"*Ja.* What if I became an auto and truck mechanic?"

"*Yes!*" she cried. "Oh, Hans. That's a marvelous idea."

"Do you really think so?"

"I do. I really do. Ernst and I were so amazed at how quickly you fixed the engine in Königsberg. And . . . and . . ." She had to stop again.

"And what?"

"You'd be doing something you love. And that way you'd have more control over your hours. And it would be in the same field that you want to study at the university. It's a wonderful idea."

Hans was immensely pleased with her reaction. "I agree. It feels right, Emilee. I'll put this money in the bank and use it as my seed money. Then maybe I'll try to find a second job. I'm going to have to rent a garage to begin with. I know it will take a lot of work to get started, but I could study for my exams and. . . ."

"Yes, Hans!" she exclaimed. "You don't have to sell me on the idea. I think it's brilliant."

"Really?" he exulted, thrilled at her reaction. "I was afraid you'd think I was being stupid."

"No! Just the opposite."

"Really?" He could scarcely believe it.

"Yes, really."

"Okay, then." He took a quick breath. "Then there's one more thing I want to ask you."

"Yes," she said.

"Good. I . . ." Then he stopped. "Yes? Yes what?"

"Yes, I would like to get engaged."

Hans gaped at her, so completely stunned that he didn't know what to say. And suddenly Emilee was a brilliant red. "Wasn't that what you were going to ask me?" she stammered.

"Yes, but how. . . ."

"Then ask me."

Hans was still reeling. Emilee got to her feet and pulled him up to face her. "Just say it!"

"Emilee Greta Fromme, will you marry me?"

"Yes."

"It won't be for a while. I'll have to go back home and get my tools, and—"

Her look stopped him. "What?"

Emilee stepped closer and took his face in her hands. "Do I have to teach you everything?" she said, her face radiant. "I said yes. So just kiss me. That's all I need for right now."

CHAPTER
21

January 12, 1919, 11:40 p.m.—Hotel Lindenberg,
Prenzlauer Berg District, Berlin

They were waiting for him in the lobby of the hotel.

When he came through the door, exhausted from the four-hour train ride and the half-hour walk from the train station, he had only two things on his mind: a warm bed and dreams of Emilee. So while he was a little surprised to see three uniformed men in the lobby at such a late hour, he shrugged it off. Then two things hit him simultaneously. The first was that the night clerk behind the desk was rigid with fear, his face white as a sheet. One of the soldiers was standing right beside him. The second was that Hans recognized the other two men. They were Werner and Horst, from the outing the other morning.

Before Hans could react, a figure who had been pressed against the wall next to the front entrance stepped up behind him and put an arm around his shoulder. At the same instant, Hans felt a gun barrel jammed hard into the small of his back. "Hans, old friend," Karl exclaimed with oily smoothness. "How are you? We were starting to think you weren't coming."

Hans saw the ugly scab on the man's cheek, which was grey and yellow with bruises.

Werner and Horst came forward, pulling their overcoats open to reveal pistols in their belts. It wasn't necessary. Hans had assumed they were armed. There were only four of them tonight. Not five, as there had been on Wednesday. Not that it made any difference. Four was quite enough. Hans licked his lips and swallowed quickly.

Karl yanked the rucksack out of his hand and tossed it to Werner. "Come," he said, obviously enjoying himself. "We can't stay long. But we'll have a drink for old times' sake. *Ja?*"

Hans started forward, saying nothing. He had kept the forty-five on him on the way to Pasewalk, just in case, but for the return journey, he had put it in his rucksack. Karl pushed his pistol harder against Hans's back and ground it back and forth, just as Hans had done when he had put the pistol against Karl's cheek. "I asked you a question," Karl snarled.

"*Ja.*"

As they moved toward the stairs, Karl jerked his head at the man next to the clerk. "Günther, you stay down here and keep this young lad company," he said. Then to the clerk, as he waved the pistol at him, "Wouldn't want you getting worried and calling the police or anything like that."

The kid's face was a sickly grey. "Yes, sir. I understand."

Karl gave Hans a hard shove. "Up to your room, and don't try anything. Let's see," he mused, "how did you say it? 'Don't move, maggot, or I'll blow your brains out'?"

Hans nodded, knowing with awful clarity that there was not one thing he could do. His only hope now was to not resist. Then maybe they wouldn't kill him. He started for the stairs. Once inside the room, the men stood Hans up against the far wall with his hands up and Karl took his post at the door. The pistol pointed at Hans never wavered. Karl jerked his head at his two companions. "Horst, search the room. Werner, you search him. And don't miss anything. You know what we're looking for."

The two men moved into action. Horst looked under the bed and then went to the small wardrobe and jerked it open. Since Hans had worn his uniform so that he could use his rail pass, the only things in the wardrobe were two shirts, two pairs of pants, and his only other pair of shoes.

Werner walked over to the rucksack, unzipped it, and dumped the contents on the bed. He grunted in satisfaction when he saw the pistol. "Hey, Karl," he said. "I think you might recognize this." He lobbed the gun to him.

Karl caught the forty-five one-handed, checked quickly to see whether it was loaded, and then pocketed his own pistol. "*Gut*," was all he said. Next, Werner dumped out his shaving kit and pawed through the dirty clothes. "That's all," he said to Karl. Then to Hans: "Where are our boots?"

Hans shrugged. "I told you. We gave them to the old soldiers' home. Besides, it looks like you've already found new ones."

In two steps, Karl was behind him. Hans screamed as the toe of Karl's boot kicked him in the back of his shin. He dropped to one knee, grabbing for his leg. Karl put one boot against his shoulder and sent him sprawling onto the floor.

"Search him," Karl barked at Werner. Then to Hans, "And you'd better have what we're looking for, stupid swine, or it's going to be a very long night for you."

"It's here," Hans said, motioning with one hand at his tunic pocket.

Werner moved to stand in front of Hans. "Off with the overcoat. Toss it on the bed."

Getting to his feet, Hans did as he was told.

"Okay, now the tunic. And empty your pants pockets. Real slow."

Hans complied, careful not to make any jerky moves. He dropped his tunic on the bed beside the overcoat, and then from his pants pockets he took out his billfold, his hotel room key, and a few coins and dropped them on the bed.

"Are you army?" Karl suddenly asked.

"Not anymore. I was discharged, same as you." Then he cocked his head to one side. "Oh, that's right," Hans shot back. "We're not the same. I didn't desert my post."

Hans leaped back, but not quickly enough to dodge Karl's boot. This time he stomped on his foot and then smacked him in the chest with the butt of the pistol. Hans crashed back against the wall and sank to the floor.

"What did you say, maggot?"

Hans didn't answer, nor did he try to get up again. Waves of pain were radiating outward from his chest. Karl eyed him. His mouth was twisted with anger. "Get up."

Moving slowly, Hans got to his feet.

Werner handed the stuff from Hans's pockets to his boss. Karl pocketed everything but the railway pass. "What's this?"

One part of Hans was shouting at him to not provoke him any further, but another part was seething to the point that he didn't hear. "What? You can't read? It's a railway pass."

Karl's eyes narrowed dangerously, but he continued to examine the pass. "Who gave you this? This isn't a normal pass."

"Don't remember his name. His signature's on the card."

Karl stepped closer, raising the pistol butt. "You're a real smart-mouth, aren't you?"

"It was the administrator of the hospital where I finished out the war. It was part of my discharge papers."

"Don't lie to me!" he shrieked, causing both of his men to jump. "This is not a normal railway pass. Were you an officer?"

"No. I was a platoon sergeant in a combat infantry unit. The administrator knew I was from the very south of Germany and had very little money. So he took pity on me."

Surprisingly, Karl seemed satisfied with that and pocketed the card. Just then, Horst finished a more careful search of the armoire. "Hey, Karl. Look at this."

They all turned, and Hans felt his heart drop. Horst was holding up his Iron Cross. Horst walked over and handed it to his boss.

"Where did you get this?" Karl hissed.

"From my battalion commander."

"For what?" he sneered.

"I cleaned latrines better than anyone in the battalion," Hans drawled, tensing for another blow.

Surprisingly, Karl ignored that. "Where's our money?"

"Like I said. It's in my inside tunic pocket." Werner immediately stepped forward and retrieved it. He handed the sheaf of bills to Karl, but Karl didn't take it. "Count it," he said.

A moment later, Werner looked up. "Two thousand marks."

"My boss took the rest," Hans volunteered. "Part of that was to recoup what you guys took from him. He gave me two thousand and kept twenty-five hundred for himself."

Again Karl surprised Hans when he merely grunted at that. "And that was your cut for 'riding shotgun?' Is that how you say it?"

A chill shot through Hans. "How did you know it was us?" he whispered.

"And you think *I'm* stupid? We chose the Kharkovs three weeks ago because everybody at the markets knows that they have the money to buy the best meat available. We've been watching them for a fortnight."

Karl nodded to his two men. Werner leaped in and grabbed Hans's arm from the back, pinning him against his own body. When he had him fast, Horst came up beside Hans and grabbed his head with both hands, holding it in place. Karl moved forward again, his face just inches from Hans's. He gently tapped the scab on his cheek with the tip of his forefinger. "See this little gift you left me, swine? The doctor thinks it may scar."

Then he reached out and touched Hans's cheek in the exact same spot. His voice dropped to a whisper. "But yours, *Dummkopf*? Yours is definitely going to scar."

Karl's right hand came up, the fist balled up to reveal a grey metal ring with the insignia of an army unit on it. Then it drew back. Hans fought like a tiger, but he could barely move. The fist flashed past his vision and a searing pain shot through his cheek. As he gasped, Karl leaned in, peering at the gash he had opened up on Hans's upper cheekbone. Then the fist flashed again.

Hans's knees startled to buckle. Karl stepped back, pleased with his work. "Boys, he's all yours."

Hans screamed as he went down hard. The last thing he saw as he threw his arms up over his head and curled into a ball was Werner and Horst moving in with wolfish grins, delighted for the opportunity to participate in the kill.

Mercifully, it only took a few seconds before all went black.

January 13, 1919, 6:38 a.m.

The first thing that came into Hans's consciousness was a wave of nauseating pain. He lay there for a moment, trying desperately to remember where he was and why he hurt so much. Was he back in France? His eyes fluttered open after a moment. In the faint light from the window, he saw a dark mass looming over him. He started but then realized it was his bed. He was on the floor beside his bed. Then it all came flooding back. Karl. The others. The beating.

He rolled over, moving very slowly, but pain still shot through every part of his body. Panting, he tried to get his bearings. He was lying on his right side near the foot of his bed, his right arm pinned beneath his body. He listened intently for a moment. Nothing. He was alone.

The relief was almost as intense as the pain. They were gone. How long had he been lying here? There was no way of knowing. He lay there, taking deep breaths, wincing as pain speared into his left side. Probably a cracked rib. Or ribs.

Groaning, Hans reached out with his left hand and tried to push himself up. A scream was ripped from his throat as fire shot through his arm and he collapsed again. He rolled onto his back. With his right fingers, he gingerly explored his arm, deciding that while the pain was fierce, it was not broken. Then he became aware that his left cheek was a circle of fire. He reached and explored the double gash on his cheek and the dried blood on his face. Cursing the pain, cursing his stupidity, cursing his inability to move, he finally pulled himself up into a sitting position. Waves of dizziness washed over him.

He froze as he heard footsteps out in the hallway. *No! Please! No more!* But he remained sitting, because lying down again would have been unbearable. A moment later a figure appeared in the doorway. "Herr Eckhardt?" The voice was strained with fear and very soft. "It's me. Georg. The night clerk." He took a step closer and Hans closed his eyes, sobbing with relief. "Can I help you?"

"Have they gone?" Hans asked through clenched teeth.

"Yes, hours ago. I came up earlier but you were unconscious."

"Did you call the police?"

"No, I . . . They threatened to come back and kill me if I did."

"No police." Hans was having a hard time keeping his mind from slipping away. "Do you have any aspirin or something else for pain?"

"Yes. We have aspirin. I'll be right back."

"And water," he called after him. Pain ripped through his left rib cage.

Two minutes later, the boy was back. He knelt beside Hans, a glass of water in one hand, a small bottle in the other. "Give me four," he whispered. "Put them in my mouth."

When he did so, Hans bit down on them and began to chew, shaking his head at the bitterness of the taste. "Now the water," he croaked. Georg held it up to his lips, and he drank deeply.

"Thank you. Help me up. On the bed." Every word was sending more pain through his body.

Hans nearly passed out again as Georg got behind him and put his hands under his armpits. But in a moment he was on the bed. He closed his eyes.

"What can I do?" Georg asked anxiously.

"Get a doctor," Hans managed, and then the blackness rolled in again.

8:15 a.m.

Hans winced as the doctor put the last strip of tape on the large bandage wrapped around his chest. He sat back and gave Hans a hard look. "Is that shot not working for you yet?"

"It is," he said. "The pain is at least bearable now."

The doctor grunted, stood up, and began putting his things back in his medical bag. "You're not going to be driving, are you?"

Hans shook his head, fighting not to laugh at such a ridiculous question.

"Good, that morphine can make you pretty drowsy."

"I hope so."

"Try not to get those stitches in your cheek wet for at least a week. Then come back and see me, and I'll take them out. And it's critical that you stay as still as possible for the next few days. That will help keep the pain in your ribs down."

"I will," Hans lied.

"Animals," the doctor muttered darkly. "The whole city is overrun with mad dogs. In my opinion, they ought to shoot them on sight."

"Dr. Ballstrum? I'm sorry I can't pay you right now. As you know, they took all my—"

The doctor waved that away. "I understand," he said. "Pay me when you can."

"*Danke schön.* I am very grateful."

Dr. Ballstrum nodded curtly and started for the door. "If the pain gets too bad, come to the office and I'll give you another shot. The clerk has the address."

"Thank you. I might do that."

As the doctor waved and disappeared down the hall, Hans laid his head back on the pillow and closed his eyes. He waited two minutes until he was sure that the doctor was gone, and then, holding his arm firmly across his left rib cage to cushion the pain, he pulled himself up to a sitting position, jaw clenched so that he didn't cry out.

Please. Don't let them have searched the room after I passed out. He swung his legs over the edge of the bed and hunched down, taking quick, shallow breaths. The room began to spin around him and he clamped his eyes shut tightly. Gradually, things settled.

Grunting with every effort, Hans stood up and moved down to the foot of the bed. Using only his right hand, he carefully felt under the mattress. *Ah, yes!* He pulled out the envelope and dumped its contents on the bed. He had put this here after his third day of work, not wanting to risk being robbed on the streets. And then he had forgotten about it until now. There were two ten-mark notes, a five-mark note, and three one-mark notes. Twenty-eight marks. It wasn't much, but it was something. His hotel was paid in advance, so he had a place to stay.

Hans sighed. A glimmer of hope flickered inside him. It wasn't much, but at least he had something. He turned and, pressing his left elbow against his rib cage to reduce the movement, he cupped his right and called out. "Georg?"

"Yes, Herr Eckhardt?" The voice floated up to him.

"Can you get me a taxi, *bitte*?"

"Yes, Herr Eckhardt. Immediately?"

"Yes, as soon as possible."

8:55 a.m.—Bayerischer Biergarten, Prenzlauer Berg District, Berlin

Hans gingerly leaned forward. "Take a right at the next corner. The restaurant is just a block down from there."

"Yes, sir," the cabbie said.

Hans had his window partially down and was breathing in the cold air deeply. The snow had stopped now, but the overcast was low and threatening. "That's it up ahead," he said as they rounded the corner. "Where the people are." A small crowd was milling about on the sidewalk up ahead of them. "You can let me out here. How much do I owe you?"

"Seventy-eight *Pfennige*."

Hans reached in his pocket, careful not to move too quickly, but then had another idea. "Can you wait for me? I'll only be a few minutes."

"*Ja, ja*. But I have to charge you."

"That's fine. Just wait here."

Hans opened the door, gingerly slid out, and then shut it again and hobbled away. The aspirin and the shot the doctor had given him had reduced his pain from staggering levels to blinding levels, so he forced himself to keep moving.

After three steps he slowed again. Three large fir trees lining the sidewalk ahead blocked his view of the restaurant, but the smell of smoke was heavy in the air, along with the acrid smell of wet wood. *No! No!* He broke into a shuffling run, holding his left side as tightly as he could.

He nearly dropped to his knees and began to sob when he saw what was left of the *Bayerischer Biergarten*. All but one back corner of the roof had collapsed into heaps of smoking rubble. The two-story stone walls were still intact but blackened and scorched. The rest was a grim skeleton of what had once been. There were no flames now, but smoke rose in billowing clouds from the ruins. Hans had to stop and close his eyes as his head started to spin. He wasn't sure if he was going to faint or throw up or both.

"Hans!"

He looked up as a figure broke away from the small group of

onlookers and hurried toward him. He groped for the stone wall that enclosed the garden and leaned back against it as Anatoly Kharkov came running up to him. "Hans. Oh, no! They found you." His eyes kept shifting between the stitches and bruising on Hans's face to the bruises that covered both of his arms. Anatoly sat down beside him, his face torn with grief, rocking back and forth.

"Where's Fritzie?" Hans croaked.

The old man bent forward and buried his face in his hands. "He's in the hospital. He's in pretty bad shape. They made him tell them where the money was. Not just their money. All that Fritzie had saved, too." He choked back a sob. "He held out for a long time. Wouldn't give them your name or where you were. But then the leader, the bad one, told him they would find Liliya and the children, and he . . ." His voice trailed off as his shoulders began to shake. He buried his face in his hands. "I'm sorry, Hans. I'm so sorry."

"It's all right, Anatoly. They would have killed Fritzie if he hadn't told them. What about Liliya and the children?"

"They weren't here. Liliya talked about coming back yesterday, but Fritzie said no. And thank the good Lord for that." He looked away. "I had gone to my granddaughter's house in the Charlottenburg district for Sunday dinner, so I wasn't at my home. But they broke in and completely trashed my apartment."

"Good thing for you. Don't go back there. Not until we're sure this is over."

Anatoly turned to the smoking hulk behind them. His face twisted with grief. "Look at it, Hans. Our life's work. Gone."

"Is it insured?"

"Yes, but in these days, who knows what we'll get out of it?"

"You're alive," Hans said grimly. "There's that, at least."

Finally, the old man's head lifted. "I have to get back to hospital. They think Fritzie's got a ruptured spleen. They're operating on him now. I just came back to make sure the fire was out. The fire brigade left just a few minutes ago." Then he had another thought. "Can I give you a ride back to the hotel?"

Hans pointed without looking. "I have a taxi."

"Do you have money?" He pulled out a few bills and thrust them at Hans.

"No, Anatoly. I have a little."

"Take it, please. Fritzie would want you to have it."

He did, seeing at least two more twenty-mark notes. "Thank you, Anatoly."

"Go pay the taxi. I'll take you back."

"No. You get back to the hospital. I'll try to come see Fritzie. Maybe tomorrow."

"He would like that. He's at the *Charité* Hospital on the campus of the University of Berlin."

Hans nodded. He was tiring fast. "I know where that is. Tell the family how sorry I am."

Anatoly was peering at him. "Are you all right?"

"Yes. Go. I'm leaving now too. I've seen quite enough."

As Hans slid into the taxi and shut the door, his ribs seized up and he had to grind his teeth together to stop himself from screaming out. "Back to the hotel, please," he said to the cabbie.

"Yes, sir."

Then he had an idea. He had to get something more for the pain. "Is there an *Apotheke* nearby?" Then quickly, "Never mind," he said. Aspirin was like spitting on a forest fire. "What about a liquor store?"

"There's one about three blocks from here, sir."

He fished in his pocket and pulled out all the bills he had and handed them up across the seat. "Take out your fare and a tip, and then I need you to go in and spend the rest on whatever you think will dull the pain the most."

"Bourbon works well for me, sir."

"Bourbon it is, then. Just hurry."

PART
2

January 14, 1919, 7:15 a.m.—Fromme home, Pasewalk

Emilee Fromme carefully shut the door behind her and listened for a moment. The house was completely quiet. She removed her coat, scarf, and nurse's cap and hung them on hooks behind the door, slipped off her shoes, and then tiptoed down the hallway. To her surprise, there was light coming out from beneath the kitchen door. And she smelled eggs cooking. And something else that took her by surprise—there was a rich smell of bacon in the air.

Easing the door open, she slipped in and closed it softly behind her. "*Guten Morgen, Mutti.*"

Elfriede Fromme turned in surprise and then smiled warmly. "*Guten Morgen,* Emmy."

Moving over to her mother, Emilee leaned in and kissed her on the cheek. "You shouldn't be up so early, *Mutti.* You need your sleep."

"And you need to eat, Emmy. Besides, I can never sleep past six or six-thirty anymore."

Emilee moved around so she was standing beside her mother. There were two frying pans on the stove. In the first, she was scrambling eggs. In the other, half a dozen strips of bacon were crackling pleasantly.

Emilee picked up the fork that was beside the mixing bowl and speared the piece of bacon that looked the most done. "Bacon, Mama? Really?" She held it up, blew on it for a moment, and gingerly put it into her mouth. Her eyes closed in pure pleasure. "Oh, Mama. That tastes so good. Where in the world did you find bacon?"

She reached for another piece, but her mother slapped playfully at her hand. "Sit down. It will be ready in a moment."

Emilee did as she was told, sitting at the table where three places were set. "Really, *Mutti*. Where did you get bacon? We haven't seen that for weeks and weeks."

Elfriede glanced over her shoulder. "Ernst brought it home last night."

"Oh? So he's back, finally."

"He got back about half an hour after you left for work. There is a new restaurant opening in Neubrandenburg this weekend. He went with Christoff to deliver whatever meat he was able to beg and borrow, stopping at a couple of farms on the way. One of the farmers gave them three pounds of bacon." She turned again, smiling now. "After debating about it about five or ten seconds, they decided that the restaurant's needs were less than our needs. So Christoff took half, and Ernst got the other half in payment for helping him."

"Wonderful. Hurry, please. The smell is driving me quite mad."

"That's not all. Christoff asked Ernst if he wanted to work with him full time."

Emilee clapped her hands. "In truth, *Mutti*? That's great news."

"Yes. Ernst was so elated. He couldn't stop talking about it."

"I'll go up and congratulate him." She started to get up, but her mother shook her head. "Ernst left more than an hour ago. Christoff has found another farmer out in the village of Trebenow who is offering to sell them a hog, a heifer, and two sheep. Christoff didn't want to take a chance that another buyer would come along with a better offer before they got there."

"My goodness. That is a find."

"*Ja, ja*! It is wonderful. When they get the animals back to Pasewalk, Ernst will help Christoff butcher them. He's going to start him on kind of an apprenticeship. See how he does with it."

"Ernst a butcher? He could do a lot worse than that."

Her mother moved the two frying pans off the stove and brought one over to the table. She dished a healthy serving of eggs onto Emilee's plate.

"I'll get the bacon," Emilee said, getting up. "Wouldn't want it to get cold." She then looked toward the hallway. "Do you want me to get Heinz-Albert?"

"I'm not sure he's up yet," her mother answered. "He'll come out when he's ready." She waited for Emilee to finish and sit down and then folded her hands together. "I'll say grace."

Emilee bowed her head as she clasped her hands together and closed her eyes.

"Holy Father, full of grace," her mother began. "We thank you for the bounties that are set before us this day. We thank you for the beauties of the earth and for your goodness unto your children. We thank you for this new employment that Ernst has found and pray that you will watch over him and Christoff as they are out on these snowy roads. Bless the Fatherland, O Father, in this time of upheaval and strife, that we may find our way to peace."

She was silent for a moment and then added, "We also ask you, Father, to watch over Hans Eckhardt and his family. May they too receive of your grace and mercy. In Jesus' name, amen."

"Amen." Emilee nodded at her mother. "Thank you, *Mutti*. I suppose he didn't call last night?"

Her mother slowly shook her head. "But, Emmy, it's only been three days since he was here."

"I know," she said, picking up her fork. "But he told me he would call. Will you wake me up precisely at three, Mama? I want to get to the telephone exchange before it closes."

Her mother nodded, not pointing out that the telephone exchange was open until nine. "I'm sure he's fine, Emmy, but I will wake you." Then she smiled. "Would it be all right if Heinz-Albert went with you? He loves to go on walks with you."

"Of course, Mama," Emilee said, trying to keep the worry out of her voice.

4:30 p.m.

Her mother was watching for them out the front window and held the door open as Heinz-Albert darted inside, gave his mother a quick kiss, tossed his coat in a corner, and went upstairs to his room. Elfriede, or Friede, as everyone called her, picked up her son's coat and hung it up, watching her daughter out of the corner of her eye.

Seeing that, Emilee shook her head. "No luck."

"He wasn't at the hotel?"

"I don't know. The number he gave me isn't working." When she finished hanging her things up, they went into the kitchen together and sat down at the table. "He also gave me the phone number at the restaurant where he works. He asked me not to call it except in the case of an emergency because he didn't want to get in trouble with his boss, but . . ." She was chewing nervously on her lower lip. "But I did anyway."

"And what happened?" her mother asked.

"Nothing. The operator said that number was not available either." Emilee was staring at her hands.

"So what are you going to do?"

"What can I do?" she cried. "I called his parents. They've heard nothing either. His mother is sick with worry. I have this bad feeling, *Mutti*. Like something is wrong. Where could he be?"

"I don't know, Emmy, but—"

Emilee pushed her chair back and abruptly stood up. "I'm going to go talk to *Onkel* Artur."

Her mother reared back a little. "Really? What can he do?"

Emilee bent down and kissed her mother on the forehead. "I don't know, but if I leave now, I can catch him before he's off work."

5:10 p.m.—Pasewalk Military Hospital, Pasewalk

Dr. Artur Schnebling was not really Emilee's uncle. She had just always called him that. Actually he was her mother's cousin, though they had been more like brother and sister growing up. When Emilee was born, Friede had asked Artur if he would be Emilee's godfather. When Emilee's father died, Artur had taken over some of his roles, watching over the whole family as well as Emilee. From the day of her birth, he had been there for every birthday, bringing a gift that she always treasured. When she got married, he would be the one to give her away.

Now, as she waited in the reception room outside his office, she had to smile. Many in the hospital thought of him as this stern, unbending administrator, strict in his adherence to rules and standards. New staff, especially nurses, were often terrified of him, fearing they might lose their jobs if they didn't meet his exacting standards.

Only a few of her closest friends knew that their hospital administrator was Emilee's godfather and was actually such a softy that she could get him to do just about anything she really wanted. But, as her mother often reminded her, that was a special trust, not to be abused. Now, one knee bouncing nervously as she waited, she wondered if she was about to violate that trust.

"Nurse Fromme?"

She looked up as his receptionist appeared. "Yes?"

"Dr. Schnebling will see you now."

Once seated, she waited for him to speak first. He studied her for a moment and then sat back and asked, "What is it, Emilee?"

It poured out in a rush of words. She told him about Hans's visit over the weekend and how they had ended becoming informally engaged.

"*Das ist gut*. Good news for you." Then he added with a smile. "And better news for him."

"Thank you, *Onkel,* but . . ." She rushed on, telling him about her attempts to call Hans. "I know that there might be some simple explanation, but I can't shake this awful feeling. I really think something is wrong."

Schnebling sat back, making a steeple with his fingers—a typical pose when he was thinking. "And what do you propose to do?"

"I want to go down to Berlin," she said. "I want to try and find him."

His eyelids narrowed a little. "Have you read the papers?"

"Yes," she whispered.

"Things are in great turmoil in the capital right now, Emmy. They've called for a general strike. The newly formed Communist Party of Germany is vowing to back the workers. They're predicting there will be hundreds of thousands of people in the streets. They say that the leftist parties have already seized some government facilities. I'm guessing they've got the main telephone exchange and that's why the phones aren't working."

"But that's downtown. They said the main rally will be in the plaza around the Brandenburg Gate and around the government buildings. Hans's hotel is out away from that. He told me it's not that far from the *Ostbahnhof*."

He exhaled slowly. That was a point worth noting. The East Train Station, where the trains from Pasewalk came in, was some distance from the city center. "I still don't like it."

"Please, *Onkel* Artur. I'm not just being emotional. Something's wrong. I can feel it."

He was looking past her now at some blank spot on the wall. She knew that she had said enough. Now he had to work it out in his mind. But since her hands were in her lap where he couldn't see them, she crossed her fingers on both hands.

After a time, his eyes raised to meet hers. "Does your mother know that you're here?"

"Yes."

"Does she know what you're planning?"

"Uh . . . I think she's guessed why I'm here with you."

He gave a barely perceptible nod. "You have to tell her everything, Emmy. And if she doesn't agree, then you have to give me your word that you'll accept it."

"I will." Hans had really charmed her mother, spending quite a bit of time with her while he was in Pasewalk. She liked him a lot. And knowing how excited her mother was about the engagement, Emilee was pretty sure she could bring her around to about anything.

"Then. . . ." Dr. Schnebling sat forward, still deep in thought. Emilee waited, half holding her breath.

Finally he began to speak, and his first words took her aback. "I want you to wear your uniform."

"My uniform? Why?"

"Because you are a nurse in the Imperial German Army. And you were a primary caregiver for Sergeant Hans Otto Eckhardt while he was convalescing here. I will write a letter attesting to that fact. We don't want the officials wondering why a single nurse is wandering around Berlin."

"Yes. That's good."

The doctor reached down to a bottom drawer, opened it, and retrieved a small, pocket-sized card. He placed it on the desk in front of him, took out his pen, and signed it with a grand flourish. Then he pushed it across to her.

"A railway pass?" she asked as she looked at it.

"Yes. As a military nurse, you are entitled to that." He retrieved another one and prepared to sign that as well. "And one more thing."

"What?"

"I want Ernst to go with you."

Her face fell.

Seeing that, his mouth pressed into a tight line. "I mean it, Emmy. I don't want you going there alone. Especially not now. I'll pay for his ticket."

Her head was down, and she couldn't bear to look at him. "Ernst got a job yesterday with that butcher who let us borrow his truck. He left early this morning to go out and get some livestock from a farmer."

Schnebling grunted, frowning deeply. Emilee wanted to jump up, lean over the desk, grab him, and shake him. But she did none of that. She knew him too well. If he didn't come to this on his own, it was not going to work.

He sat back again, took in another breath, and then sighed. "Do I have your word that if you mother doesn't approve, you won't go?"

"Yes, *Onkel* Artur."

"And that you'll stay away from anything that looks like it could be dangerous?"

"Yes, *Onkel* Artur."

"And that if there is even a hint of danger, you'll come back immediately? And that you'll call me every night and report in?"

"Yes, but . . ." She should have said this earlier. "It means I'll have to miss my shifts for a few nights."

He brushed that aside with the wave of his hand. "With the war over, we're way down in our patient count anyway. I'll tell everyone that you've taken a leave without pay."

Another long sigh. "And, Emmy, I don't want you going tonight."

"But *Onkel* Artur, I—"

His look cut her off. "It's in the morning or not at all. You can take the first train."

She got to her feet. "I will. Oh, thank you, *Onkel* Artur. Thank you."

He got up too and then reached into his back pocket and withdrew his wallet.

"No. I don't need your money. Just saying I can go is all I need."

He came around the desk, handed her several bills, and then took her in his arms and kissed her on the forehead. "You always need money, my dear. Take my word for it. Go with God, Emmy. And remember. Every night you call me. You hear me?"

CHAPTER 23

January 14, 1919, 10:10 p.m. —Hotel Lindenberg,
Prenzlauer Berg District, Berlin

About the only thing that Hans remembered as his eyes fluttered open was not to move.

He wasn't sure where he was, except that he sensed he was in a bed.

He wasn't sure what time it was, but he could tell that the light coming through the window was lamplight, not daylight.

And he wasn't sure why his head felt like it was four times bigger than normal and like someone inside it was using his brain as a bass drum.

But he was keenly aware that if he moved even a fraction of an inch, it hurt. A lot.

So he closed his eyes again and listened, taking slow, deep breaths. He heard a wagon rattle by in the street below, and far away he heard a train whistle. He could tell it was not from one of the main railway locomotives. Probably a local city line.

And with that he remembered he was still in Berlin.

At his hotel.

As remembrance flooded back, he jerked bolt upright. He screamed in agony as the whole left side of his body exploded in pain.

There was a sudden hammering on the wall. "Hey, *Dummkopf*!" a man's voice shouted. "Shut that hole in your face, or I'll come shut it for you."

Hans barely heard it, because images were filling his mind with such rapidity that he could barely take them in. The men waiting for him in the hotel lobby. Karl's ring slicing his cheek open. Dropping to the floor and curling up in a ball. Boots kicking out at him. The smoldering ruins of the *Bayerischer Biergarten*.

Moving slowly, Hans raised his right hand and touched his cheek, carefully exploring the seven stitches the doctor had put in the first jagged cut and then the six in the lower one. Even that little movement caused him to groan in pain, but he ignored it. As his hand moved away, it brushed across the stubble on his cheek. He absently scratched at it, a little surprised that it was as thick as it was.

How long had he been unconscious? Had he been out since Karl and the others had left? He turned his head to confirm it was still night outside. So five, maybe six hours? Judging from the sparse traffic outside, it was late at night or maybe early in the morning. For some reason it seemed he had been out even longer than that, but he wasn't sure why.

Gradually other things began to register. The metallic clanking of the radiator let him know the heat in the hotel was working, not that it was enough to really warm the room. He had a blanket over him, and he was wearing his army shirt and the heavy wool tunic that served as a jacket, but no trousers, nor boots, though he still had on his socks. His body from the waist down was quite cold, and his feet were like blocks of ice.

Raising his head, Hans realized that he had been half holding his breath because of a heavy stench that filled the room. It took him a moment before he registered what it was. In addition to the hotel's usual smells of dust and mildew and mold and bed bug oil, the air literally reeked of three other things: liquor, urine, and vomit.

The liquor he understood. He remembered now having the taxi driver buy him two bottles of bourbon. But . . .

Hans swore under his breath as he grunted with pain and rolled over onto to his right side. Waiting for the waves of dizziness to pass, Hans pulled himself into a sitting position, gasping audibly as spears of pain radiated through his rib cage. Ignoring them, he looked around, trying to work out what had happened.

Taking a deep breath, Hans stood up. Suddenly, the drummer in his head really put his heart into it, and it felt as though his head might be knocked right off of his shoulders. He closed his eyes, drawing in deep breaths and willing himself to hold on. When the throbbing finally passed, he hobbled over to the door and found the light switch.

The light blinded him at first, so he kept his eyes closed for a few moments. When he finally opened them and looked around the room, he was appalled at what he saw. The few clothes in his wardrobe were scattered on the floor, and it looked like someone had tromped back and forth across them. The contents of his rucksack, which Karl's men had emptied on the bed, were now scattered across the room. His trousers were wadded up in a ball at the end of the bed.

Shivering violently now, he quickly grabbed them and pulled them on. Then he got his boots and put them on as well. Only then did he continue looking around. Liquor bottles were scattered here and there across the floor. He saw that two of them were the bottles of bourbon. But there were also three other much larger bottles. He hobbled over and stared down at the closest one, recognizing what it was before he could read the label. It was a wine bottle. He was hardly a connoisseur, but he was pretty sure this was one of the cheaper labels. Maybe even watered down somewhat. The other bottle was identical.

Now the stench pressed into his thoughts again. He moved over to the window, and while holding his ribs with one arm, he managed to open it a few inches with his other hand. He stood there for a moment, drawing in the cold, wintry air in deep, hungry gulps. Then he turned back to survey the room. Immediately, he identified the source of odor. In getting out of bed, he had thrown his blanket off to one side. Now the dark stains on the mattress were clearly visible. At almost that same instant, he looked down and saw that the whole front of his tunic was stained from where he had thrown up on it.

The shame coursed through him with sharpening intensity. Had he been so sotted that somewhere along the way he had emptied his bladder without bothering to get up and go down the hall to the toilet? And gotten sick all over the bed and all over himself?

He whirled around, heedless of the stabbing pain, and moved to the door. He yanked it open and stuck his head out. "Georg! Are you down there?"

The same man's voice sounded almost instantly. "You stupid oaf. Shut up and go to bed."

Hans ignored him. "*Georg!*"

After a moment, he heard a chair scrape across the floor, followed by footsteps. Hans opened the door wider and stepped out into the hall. From there he could look down the stairs. A moment later, the young clerk appeared. "*Ja*, Herr Eckhardt?"

"I need you. *Now!*"

Hans moved back into his room, leaving the door open. The pimply-faced boy entered the room and shut the door behind him, without being told. Hans saw his nose wrinkle in disgust; then, as he looked around the room, his eyes grew very large.

"Georg! What's been going on here?" Hans asked.

"What?" He was suddenly nervous.

"Did those men come back? The ones who beat me up?"

"No, sir."

"Who's been in my room?"

"Uh . . . I was this morning. You asked me to come see you when I got off shift."

"Wait. After the doctor left, you called me a taxi, remember?"

"That wasn't this morning, Herr Eckhardt. That was yesterday morning."

Hans's jaw dropped. "What?"

"It was two nights ago that you were beat up, Sergeant."

"I've been here for *two* days?" Hans was incredulous.

"Yes." He was clearly relieved to see that Hans was finally accepting what he was saying.

"But . . ."

Georg came a step closer. "I was off shift by the time you came back, but I sleep here at the hotel. My family owns it. When you came back in the taxi, you were real upset, Sergeant. I mean, real, real upset. You kept mumbling something about a fire. Me and the taxi driver had to get you up to your room. We tried to get you to lie down, but you started cursing and swearing at us. You had already started drinking some of the liquor you had with you. So my father said we were to just leave you alone."

Rubbing at his eyes with the heels of his hands, Hans nodded. "Go on."

"Then early this morning, you called down to me again. When I came up here, you told me to take all the money left in your billfold and go buy as much wine as I could get with it." He looked down at his hands. "You said I could take one mark as a tip for helping you."

The mention of his billfold triggered a reaction. He had noticed it earlier on the small night table beside the bed. He walked over and got it, opening it as he came back to join Georg. When he saw what was inside, his eyes narrowed. "There's only one mark here."

George fell back a step. "Yes, sir, Sergeant Eckhardt. You gave me all the money you had, which was seven marks. I bought three bottles of wine. They cost me five marks."

Hans was nodding slowly. Things in his head were very hazy, but that rang true to him. He remembered wanting something more to drink. And there were empty wine bottles in the room. Three full jugs of wine explained a lot—the pounding in his head, throwing up, wetting the bed. He had to look away, unable to bear the pity on Georg's face.

"So," Georg was saying, "I took one mark as my tip, like you said, and put the other mark back in your billfold. Honest, Sergeant. I wouldn't steal from you. Especially after what happened to you the other night."

Hans was nodding. "I know, Georg. And I am in your debt." He thought quickly. "Georg. Would you like to earn some more money?"

"Uh . . . yeah."

"I know that I've only got one more mark left, but I'll get more tomorrow." *Oh, really? And how is that?* He brushed the thought aside.

"What do you want me to do?"

"Well, right now, I need you to strip the blanket and sheets off the bed and get me fresh bedding. You may have to replace the mattress cover, too."

"*Ja, ja.* I do the beds as part of our service at the hotel. I was going to do it when I came on shift tonight, but I saw you were sleeping, so I didn't want to wake you up."

"That's all right. And can you clean up the room for me? Get rid of the bottles. Hang up my clothes. I'm going to shave and take a bath. Clean myself up a little."

"Uh. . . ." Georg was crestfallen. "I'm not allowed to do that."

"Do what?"

"Clean the rooms for guests. We only change the bedding. Papa is very strict about that."

"Fine," Hans growled. "I understand." He blew out his breath, trying to get his brain working again. "Can you at least get me some more aspirin? My head is killing me."

Georg started to turn away, eager to please. "*Ja,* I can do that."

"Wait. I'm famished. I obviously haven't eaten anything for two days, and—"

"We don't keep any food in the hotel," Georg cut in. "I'm sorry."

"I know that," he snapped. "I was going to ask if there are any restaurants close by."

"*Ja*. There are several over on *Danziger Strasse*, which is only about four or five blocks from here. But. . . ." He was suddenly embarrassed.

"But what?"

"Well, begging your pardon, Sergeant Eckhardt, but you don't have any money." He fished in his pocket. "Do you want your mark back?"

"No. Don't worry about it. I'll work something out." He glanced at his tunic on the bed and then lowered his voice to a conspiratorial whisper. "But I've got a problem, Georg."

"What?" He was immediately wary again.

"When I was sick, I threw up all over my tunic." He retrieved his wallet again and removed the one-mark note. "Is there any way you could get the worst of it off for me while I bathe?" He held out the note. "This will be strictly between you and me. Your father doesn't have to know."

Georg was clearly interested, but still hesitant.

"You can do it while I bathe and shave off some of this stubble. As soon as I get some money, I'll give you two more marks. I'm good for it, you know that."

Finally, the boy nodded. "Uh . . . I will do it."

"Great. Thanks, Georg. You are a real friend." And he meant that. "I know your father turns off the hot water at nine o'clock, so the bathwater is going to be cold—"

"Uh . . . but, Sergeant?"

Hans wanted to throw his hands in the air. The kid was eager to help, but so methodical in his thinking. "But what, Georg?"

"Uh . . . it's ten past ten right now," he said. "A couple of the larger restaurants stay open until midnight, but they don't take new customers after eleven. The smaller cafés and bistros mostly close by ten."

"Oh." Hans felt like screaming at the ceiling. Couldn't anything go right for him? But he bit it back and nodded. "All right. No soaking. And I'll wait until morning to shave. But can you still get the jacket done for me? It doesn't have to be perfect."

"Yes, sir." Georg walked swiftly to the bed and picked it up with two fingers, holding it out away from him, his nose wrinkling.

"*Gut.* I'll start the bath. Bring the aspirin to the bathroom, okay?"

"*Ja.*" He was out the door and starting down the hall when Hans called after him.

"I am paid up through the end of the month for my room, right?"

"Yes."

Well, Hans. The bitterness was like bile in his mouth. *At least you did one thing right.*

10:45 p.m.—*Danziger Strasse, Prenzlauer Berg District, Berlin*

As Hans turned left onto *Danziger Strasse,* moving as rapidly as the pain in his side would allow, he saw that Georg had been right. There were cafés, cantinas, bistros, beer halls, and restaurants scattered along both sides of the wide thoroughfare, but most of them were now dark.

He was shivering pretty badly in spite of his exertions. The overhead sky was clear, and the temperature was well below freezing now. To make things worse, the whole front of Hans's woolen tunic was still damp, and that made his shirt and undershirt damp as well. Even with his hands jammed into his trouser pockets, he could feel the cold seeping into his bones—which did not numb the pain but only exacerbated it.

He passed up two restaurants with French names and settled on a smaller place named Schnitzel and Strudel and walked over to the door. Through the main window he could see that the café was nearly empty. Two couples were at one table. A single man was at another. Hesitating for only a moment, Hans pushed the door open and went inside. He stopped and drew in a deep breath. The blast of warm air was filled with the most delicious smells he could imagine.

A middle-aged waitress in a simple grey dress came over. "One, sir?"

"Uh . . . yeah. But . . . is the owner here?"

She shrugged, jerking a thumb over her shoulder. "That's him behind the bar." She eyed Hans up and down, her eyes narrowing as they focused on the yellow and brown bruises surrounding the ugly gashes on his cheek and the stitches that protruded from it like the legs of a caterpillar. Her nose wrinkled in disgust as she sniffed the air, which confirmed Hans's feeling that while Georg had done a good job in getting the encrusted residue of vomit off of his coat, it was going to take a lot more than that to get the smell out of it. When the odor hit the waitress, she pointed to the door. "Out!"

Face burning with embarrassment, Hans slunk out as everyone turned to look at him.

11:40 p.m.

Retracing his steps, Hans tried the two French restaurants. The results were the same. The first one gave him a flat no. The second one saw him coming and hurriedly locked the door just as he reached it. By that time, few places were still open. Those that were open refused to even talk to him.

The utter bleakness of life settled down on Hans as he watched the lights in the last of the eating establishments on *Danziger Strasse* go out. He was cold, wet, hungry, aching with pain, and utterly exhausted. He had a few *Pfennige* in his pocket, but other than that he had no money, no identity card, no ration book, no railway pass.

Even if he put aside his pride and went to either Emilee or his family for help—which he was not yet ready to do yet—he had no way of contacting them to let them know he was in trouble. He didn't have enough for a phone call. And even if he did, it was beyond his capacity to walk to the nearest telephone exchange.

Too weary to continue, he sat down on the curb and put his head in his hands. *How quickly things can turn.* Sunday night, he was waving two thousand marks under Emilee's nose. Now he was a battered drunk who wet his pants and threw up on himself.

But the hunger in him was too desperate to allow him wallow in his self-pity for very long. He had to have food. The combination of bitter cold, prolonged pain, and no food was sapping the last of his strength rapidly. Did he even have the stamina to hold off until morning, until he could find another Fritzie Kharkov who would let him clear tables and turn his back when he pilfered the scraps from the plates?

His head came up slowly at that last thought. He had once done exactly that. Scavenged the leftovers from others' plates and then sneaked into the back alley to eat them before he was discovered. Biting back the pain, he got to his feet and began looking around. Maybe he hadn't hit rock bottom quite yet.

11:48 p.m. —Wedermeyer Gasse, near Danziger Strasse, Berlin

With his strength ebbing fast, Hans moved pretty slowly, but eventually he saw an unmarked passageway between two buildings. He turned into it, barely daring to hope. Fifty feet further in, it came to a T. Peering up at the street sign, he was gratified to read "Wedermeyer Gasse." In the near darkness, it looked like one side of the alley was lined with apartment houses that butted right up against the street. But the other side? Hans actually smiled. He could see the small loading dock of the nearest building. Barely visible was a sign painted on the bricks: Danziger Café. He shuffled forward, jaw set in a tight line.

He knew he would be lucky to find anything. Food rationing was still in effect, and food shortages were virtually everywhere. Fewer people were eating in commercial establishments, and those that did were less likely to leave anything on their plates. But human nature being what it was, he hoped that his search would not be entirely unsuccessful. He headed for the loading dock.

There was one street lamp near the far end of the alley, but it didn't give much light this far away. So, careful to not make any noise, Hans spread newspapers and pieces of cardboard on the ground and then dumped the trash out a little at a time. He would paw through it slowly. What few edibles he did find were cold—in some cases even frozen—and were typically mixed with the scrapings from the plates. Twice as he bit into what he found he nearly gagged because the food was spoiled. In those cases he threw it aside, not daring to risk food poisoning.

It didn't matter how bad it was. It was food. Disciplining himself, he ate slowly, fighting the urge to wolf it down. And all the while he forced himself to ignore the fact that instead of cold, greasy gravy or soggy bread or slivers of gristle and fat off of a discarded ham bone, he could be eating his mother's Bavarian *Leberkäse*—liver meatloaf—or her *Weisswurst*—veal and pork sausage flavored with onions and fresh parsley. And then he would top it all off with torte and fresh whipped cream.

He thrust the thoughts aside. Graswang was an option that was looking more and more attractive, but tonight, his focus was twofold. Get enough food to fill his stomach, and watch out for such things as half-eaten apples or discarded rolls that he could put in the pockets of his greatcoat to take back with him to the hotel. Then he had to get back to the hotel so he could collapse in exhaustion.

It was a few minutes after he had heard a far-off church bell tolling two o'clock, while he was working through the garbage cans of his fourth or fifth restaurant, that he heard a sound that froze him in his tracks. He was bent over, pawing through a half-filled can, when a low growl sounded right behind him.

Moving very slowly, Hans straightened and turned around. In the faint light, he saw a large, dark shape and two glowing eyes. As he peered more closely, he made out that it was a full-grown Doberman Pinscher. Its lips were curled back, revealing very big and very sharp teeth. Its ears were laid flat, and the hair along the back of its neck was standing straight up. Hans fell back a step, snatching up the garbage can and holding it out in front of him.

"Get out of here!" Hans hissed, jabbing the can at the animal. The Doberman jumped back but then instantly darted in, snarling and snapping. Knowing that if the dog came after him he wouldn't be able to fight it off, Hans unceremoniously dumped the can on its head. It yelped, backed away for a moment, and then immediately fell upon the papers, rooting through them for any food.

When the dog came up with what looked like a half-eaten pork chop, rage exploded in Hans. He looked around and saw a push broom on the dock. Careful not to trigger an attack, he edged over to the dock until he could reach the broom. Knowing that what he was about to do would hurt like fury, Hans gripped the broom with both hands, gritted his teeth, and inched toward the dog. "Good dog," he murmured. The animal's head came up, and another low growl emanated from deep within its body. The hackles were straight up again.

With a yell, Hans lunged, swinging the broom with all his strength. He cried out as his whole left side erupted in pain, but it didn't stop him. He had the broom positioned so that the bristles were up and the wooden base was down. It caught the dog right on the snout. It dropped the pork chop with a sharp howl and leaped backwards. Hans went after it, cursing and shouting and waving the broom. The animal moved backwards several feet and then stopped, growling and snarling and crouched down as if to spring. Hans quickly snatched up the meat. He was right. It was a half-eaten pork chop that was still partially warm. For a moment he was sorely tempted to wipe it off and put it in his pocket, but then he flipped it toward the dog. If that dog charged him, there was no way he could fight it off. The animal caught the meat in mid-air and, still growling, backed away.

Hans threw the broom at the dog, and with a yelp the animal slunk away, growling as it left. A light in the second floor of the restaurant came on, filling the alley with light. Hans heard a window open.

Moving as quickly as he could to sidle up against the building, he waited until the person was satisfied and shut the window again.

Half an hour later, so racked with pain that he could barely shuffle along, Hans found what he was looking for. In another alley, next to a four-story apartment house just off of *Danziger Strasse*, he saw steam rising from the ground. When he moved closer, he was elated. It was a large exhaust grate for the boiler room that heated the building beside it. Wishing he had thought to find a piece of cardboard to lie on, he stretched out upon it, pulled his overcoat more tightly around him, and fell into an exhausted sleep.

CHAPTER 24

January 15, 1919, 6:30 a.m. — Pasewalk Railway Station

I don't like it. Not one bit, Emilee."

"I know, Ernst. I don't like it either. But what choice do we have?"

"I'm going to explain the situation to Christoff and tell him I'll be back as soon as I can."

"But you said he has three full days of work lined up. If you don't help, what will he do?"

Ernst looked away. "He'll have to find someone else."

"You can't let that happen, Ernst. It could be months before you find another opportunity like this." She went to him and took his hand. "These are hard times, Ernst. And hard times make for hard decisions. But I'll be all right. I'll be really careful."

"What time does your train get into Berlin?"

"Supposedly about eight-thirty or nine. The ticket master said that this first train typically doesn't get shunted off on side tracks as much as the later ones."

"If you see any kinds of crowds starting to gather, you run the other way, Emmy. Promise me!"

"I promise. Now go. Or you're going to be late."

Ernst bent down and gave his sister a peck on the cheek. "You'll call tonight. Promise?"

"Yes, Ernst." Smiling, Emilee gave him a gentle shove.

Emilee watched him go and then turned and looked at the clock on the far wall. Just after five-thirty. Which meant she still had about twenty-five minutes until the train arrived. Turning, she walked quickly over to the telephone exchange.

The sleepy-eyed clerk stifled a yawn and straightened in her seat. Emilee saw that it wasn't the same one that had been on duty yesterday afternoon when she and Heinz-Albert had come here.

"Are you open now?" Emilee asked.

"Just barely." Another yawn. "How can I help you?"

Reaching in her pocket, Emilee extracted a piece of paper from her purse. "I'd like to place a call to this number, please."

The clerk peered at the paper and then looked up. "Where is Graswang?"

"In Bavaria. It's connected to the Oberammergau/Garmische-Partenkirchen exchange."

"And how much time will you need?"

"Two minutes. No more." Then she had a thought. "If I need more time, can I signal you?"

"Of course. Wait in the first booth, and I'll let you know when it goes through."

It took almost two minutes for the girl to work it out, but finally the phone in the booth rang. Emilee snatched up the mouthpiece. *"Hallo!"*

"Did you hear from him?"

Relieved that it was Hans's mother who had answered, she spoke quickly. "No, Frau Eckhardt. I haven't heard anything more."

There was no answer, and Emilee could sense Inga's head dropping and tears coming. "Frau Eckhardt, I—"

"Please. Call me Inga, and I shall call you Emilee, if that's all right."

"Of course. I would like that . . . Inga." Emilee took a quick breath. "I just wanted you to know that I am at the train station here in Pasewalk. I am catching the train for Berlin in about twenty minutes. I am going to go look for Hans."

She heard a soft intake of breath, and then without another moment's hesitation, "Then I shall come too."

"*No!*" Emilee cried. "That's not a good idea, Frau Eck—Inga. It is too far. It would take you all day to get there."

"I want to help find my son."

"I know. I understand." Emilee should have foreseen this. Of course Hans's mother would want to come. She almost told Inga about the general strike but quickly changed her mind. It would only worry her more. "I . . . I just wanted to make sure that you hadn't heard from him."

"No, nothing."

"All right. I shall call you tonight and let you know what is happening."

"Even if you don't find him?"

"Yes."

"*Danke*. You are very kind to think of me."

"Inga, Hans is very independent."

"*Ja*, and not very good about letting his *Mutti* know where he is."

"Or me, either," Emilee said with a smile. "As you've probably read in the papers, the government in Berlin is having some problems. I think some of the phone service is down. But Hans was with my family on Sunday. And everything was fine then."

"How fine?" came the reply. It was not a question Emilee had expected, but with what little she knew of Hans's mother, she knew that she wasn't asking about Hans's physical well-being. She found herself blushing a little.

"Um . . . before he left to go back to Berlin, we became engaged. That is, unofficially. We just talked about it and agreed that—"

263

"*Wunderbar!*"

"Really? You're not upset?"

Inga laughed, and Emilee heard something of Hans in it. "Upset? Did he not tell you the last thing I said to him when he left here to go back to Berlin?"

"No, I—"

Just then there was a sharp rap on the glass. The clerk had two fingers up and was pointing at the clock on the wall.

"Hold on a minute, Inga." She opened the door. "Can I have one more minute?"

The clerk didn't like it, but she finally nodded. "If you come and pay me the moment you ring off."

"I will." Emilee shut the door again. "What did you say to him?"

"I told him that if he messed things up with that girl named Emilee Fromme, his father and I were going to take a cheese paddle to his bare bottom."

Emilee clapped her hand over her mouth to stop from hooting aloud. "Really?"

"*Ja*, and I meant it, too. I know you have to go, Emilee. You will be in my prayers today."

"I'm going to need them. *Auf Wiedersehen.* I'll call you tonight if the phones are working."

6:39 a.m.—Wedermeyer Gasse, near Danziger Strasse, Berlin

The blast of an air horn ripped Hans from his fitful sleep. The horn blasted again. Then a man was shouting at him. "Hey, *Dummkopf*! Get out of the way."

In a blind panic, not sure what was happening, Hans threw one arm up to block out the brilliant lights that were bearing down on him. The roar of a heavy engine gearing down also registered in his head. With a yell, he rolled frantically to one side, coming to a stop up against the brick wall of the apartment house.

The roar of the engine deepened as the truck accelerated and shot past him. He caught a glimpse of a figure leaning out the window of the cab. "Your mother is an idiot!" the man yelled as he went by.

Heart pounding, Hans got to his feet, cupping his hands around his mouth. "And what was your mother?" Breathing heavily, he watched as the taillights turned a corner and disappeared. After a moment, Hans looked up at the sky. It was lightening, and he could see that low clouds had rolled in during the night. What time was it?

Then he realized that out on *Danziger Strasse*, there were vehicles passing by. Not a lot yet, some cars but mostly trucks, like the one that had nearly run him down. Which meant that morning had come. He guessed it was somewhere between five-thirty and six.

Only then did the cold impress itself on his mind. He was shivering from head to toe, which was not helping the pain in his ribs. Sitting down on the grate again and keeping an eye on the alley in both directions, Hans fished the food he had scavenged from his pocket and did a quick inventory. A nice, large apple with one bite taken out of it. Two plums, both of which had probably been discarded because there were parts of them that were soft and mushy. Spoiled? He tentatively bit into the first one. There was a slightly moldy taste to it, but not enough to worry him. He ate it quickly, sucking off every bit of the pulp from the pit before eating the second one. In his other pocket he found a hard roll that was somewhat soggy and mashed. With it was another roll, half eaten, with a slice of cheese and ham still in it. He ate the plain one first and then slowly nibbled on the second. He had to brush some dirt off of the ham, but its savory flavor was divine.

Hans licked his fingertips and thumbs to get the last hint of any flavor, realizing that about all these scraps had managed to do was enhance his ravenous appetite. When the same truck appeared coming back up the alley, Hans made a decision. He had spent the night looking for a solution and had come up with nothing. He had frozen his tail off, been insulted, spurned, rejected, and nearly run over. This was obviously not an answer.

He would go back to his hotel and sleep for a few hours to see if he could recover some of his strength. Then, though it shamed him to do so, he would try to find Anatoly. Or maybe even go visit Fritzie in the hospital. He would ask them for a short-term loan to see him through until he found another job. If that failed, he would call his parents. Maybe they would wire him enough money to get him home. But that was a last resort.

As the truck approached, still driving too fast for the narrow alley, Hans pressed himself up against the wall. As the truck rumbled by, he shouted, "Your mother eats with the pigs!" An even more serious insult than the driver's original offense.

When Hans saw the driver shake his fist at him, he actually grinned. It wasn't much of a victory, but on this day, it was something. He started off, dreading what would normally be a ten-minute walk but would now take him closer to an hour.

7:35 a.m.—Volkspark Friedrichshain, Berlin

Hans came to a stop as he saw that he was approaching a large park. Confused for a moment, he stopped to get his bearings. He hadn't come through a park last night on his way to *Danziger Strasse*. He was sure of that. He started ahead again, more slowly now, trying to figure out where he was. There was still snow on the ground, and the park was deserted. Then he saw a sign announcing that this was the People's Park for the neighborhood of Friedrichshain, which shared a common border with the Prenzlauer Berg District. He had come across it once before when he was lost, and that was enough to give Hans his bearings. He decided cutting through the park was his shortest route now.

Though he kept his head down and didn't look at anyone, every time someone passed him, he could feel their eyes on him. They openly gaped at this hunched-over, lumbering hulk of a man with the horrible gashes on his cheek and bruises discoloring most of his face. A few looked away so as not to appear rude. But most of them slowed their pace and gaped at him as they passed. He wasn't sure which he detested the most—the looks of horror and revulsion or the pitying shaking of the heads and clucking of the tongues. One older woman, walking with what looked like her daughter, even blurted, "Oh, look at that poor old man," as they hurried by.

Hans waited for a taxi and a couple of motor cars to pass and then crossed over and entered the park, relieved that he could set a slower pace now. He was rapidly nearing the end of his endurance and realized now that it was a mistake to think that he could walk this far with his ribs in the shape they were in.

He was not quite halfway across the park's open spaces when he stopped at a bench along the walkway. After gingerly brushing off the snow, he sat down, willing his muscles to relax for a few moments. His thoughts immediately turned to Emilee. She was probably wondering why she hadn't heard back from him yet. He pulled a face. *Probably?* But even if he had money, he wasn't ready to make that call yet.

He could hear their conversation now. "Hi, Emilee. Just wanted you to know that I got back safely. That is until I reached the hotel. Remember that guy I told you about that owed Fritzie some money? Well, he wanted it back. He was a little upset by the whole thing. So even though I willingly agreed to give it back, he still beat me to a pulp. Oh yeah, then he burned down Fritzie's restaurant and my job with it. So, I'm out looking for work again today. What's that? What have I been doing the last two days? Nothing much to speak of. Sorting through trash cans looking for food. Fighting a dog over a pork chop. You know, that kind of stuff."

A movement out of the corner of his eye cut off his thoughts. To his surprise, a lone woman was coming along the walkway toward him from the opposite direction. She was tall, slender, and obviously well-to-do. She looked to be in her mid-forties. She wore a full-length leather overcoat with matching black leather boots that came to her knees. Her hat was made of some kind of fur and had ear flaps that were down. But somehow it all still managed to look very chic, as the French would say. She had a rather large handbag, also black leather, with the strap hung over her shoulder. Elegance. Money. Class. She reeked of it. Hans knew it well. That was what he had lived with those four years at the Von Kruger Academy.

He saw her head come up with a start as she suddenly caught sight of him. Though the sky was grey and overcast, it was light enough for her to easily see him now. Her step slowed, and she started edging over to the far side of the walkway so that when she passed by him, she would be as far away as possible. Hans saw that her lips were curled in disdain and that she had determined to move past him swiftly lest she be contaminated by such a wretch as this.

Anger began to rise in him. Her contempt was the same as he had seen on the face of the waitress last night and at every other place he had stopped. Suddenly Hans was on his feet and turned to face the woman. He moved over to block her way. She turned to go around him. He moved again and she came to a stop, watching him warily. She licked her lips and turned her head quickly to see if there was anyone else around. There wasn't, and when she turned back to Hans he saw something else in her eyes. Fear.

That's right. You show me the respect I deserve from the likes of you.

Hans lifted his head so his face was fully in the light. When she saw it, she recoiled in disgust and horror. Who was this horrible monster approaching her? This only irritated Hans more. But he kept his voice level and calm. "Frau, may I speak with you *für einen Moment?*"

There was a quick, almost imperceptible shake of her head, but she made no answer. Her lips were pinched into a tight line. He saw that she was clutching her handbag, her knuckles white.

He kept moving, but slowly. If she bolted and ran, there was no way he was going to keep up with her. "Frau, I'm not going to hurt you. I was just wondering if you might spare a few marks for a soldier in distress."

She shrank back a step.

"I know I look a fright, ma'am. But two days ago, I was robbed and beaten by four vicious thugs. They stole all my money and left me like this." He motioned toward his face. "I haven't eaten for two days. Even ten marks would be a blessing. So I can get some breakfast." He had another thought. "And call my mother and tell her that I am safe."

He saw that her eyes, now large and frightened, were almost as black as her hair. And as beautiful. Her lower lip was visibly trembling. "No. Go away. Please, just go away."

Go away? He felt his jaws clench. That's what he had said to that stupid dog last night.

Both of his hands were in his overcoat pocket, so without even thinking about it, he formed his right hand into a make-believe pistol and pointed it at her. "Frau, I have a pistol pointed at your heart." He pushed it forward so she could clearly see the bulge in his overcoat. "Please don't move."

There was an audible gasp, and instantly her face drained of color.

He walked up to her and stuck out his other hand. "Your handbag, please."

She fell back another step. "No! Please. I have only a very little money."

"Yeah, I can see that," he said.

She understood his meaning exactly. "No, you don't understand. I am not rich."

"Lady," he said, "just give me the handbag."

"Please." She was pleading now.

He raised his hand so the bulge in the overcoat was pointing directly at her waist. "If you don't give me the handbag, I'm going to rip it off your shoulder."

That did it. She reached up, removed the handbag and handed it across to him. Then her face crumpled and she buried her face in her hands and began to sob.

He stepped back, unmoved by the tears. Keeping one eye on her, he opened the handbag. It was filled with the normal things you saw in a woman's handbag—a compact, a brush, a comb, lipstick, two letters, some keys. Ah! And a small woman's wallet. It was as elegant and expensive as the purse.

"Well, well," he said, handing the purse back to her, "and what do we have here?"

"Please. It's not what you think."

He ignored her, and using his left hand he opened the wallet. And there it was. A whole fistful of marks. He felt a spurt of elation. He thumbed through them and saw that at least four of them were hundred-mark notes. *Fantastic!* He shot her a hard look. "You should have settled for the ten marks, lady."

She said nothing, but her eyes were smoldering now through the tears. There was fear there, too, but anger and defiance along with it. Hans ignored her. He felt like doing a little jig. Only the very wealthy would consider this kind of money to be pocket change. Any guilt he was feeling totally evaporated. This was her definition of having no money? Poor thing.

Withdrawing his right hand from his pocket, he quickly removed the bills, stuffed them in his pocket, and tossed the wallet back to her. She made no effort to catch it, nor did she look at it when it dropped to the ground.

Her head came up and her eyes met his. "My husband is dead."

That knocked Hans back a little. He leaned in, his eyes boring into hers. "I'm sorry to hear that. So you're a rich widow. I'm sorry for your loss." He turned and pointed. "Here's what we're going to do. You're gonna go sit on that park bench where I was sitting. I'm going to walk away. But know this. I am a crack shot with a pistol. If you move before I disappear into those trees over there . . . Well, let's just say, it won't be pretty."

"You don't understand," she cried, taking a step forward, her fists clenched. "That is not my money. It's the mortgage payment for my home. I . . . My husband was a captain in the war. He was killed last August in the Battle of the Somme."

Eyes narrowing, Hans searched her face. The Battle of the Somme, so named because it was fought near the Somme River in France, was considered to be one of the bloodiest and most costly battles of the war.

She rushed on. "I haven't been able to get his pension yet from the government. I finally borrowed enough money from my father-in-law to pay our house payment. It's all I have." She buried her face in her hands. "Please. I'll lose my home."

Hans was torn, but then a thought hit him. "Wait. Your house payment is six or seven hundred marks a month? What kind of castle do you live in?"

His question took her aback. "I . . . I'm trying to sell it. But if I don't make this payment now, my children and I will be thrown out on the streets. Please. Take your ten marks. Take twenty. Fifty. But leave me the rest."

For a long moment, Hans stood there, studying her. One part of him was awash in guilt, but another part of him was sizing her up—the elegance of her clothes, the substantial diamond ring on her finger, the gold necklace at her throat. And the arrogance. Even in her desperation, she kept looking at him with utter disdain.

It was the diamond ring that made up his mind. "Why don't you sell some of your jewelry? That will pay your house payment."

Anger flared in her. "How dare you tell me what to do? My husband gave me this ring. I could never part with it."

Hans shook his head in amazement. "I'm touched. And to show you I'm not totally heartless, I'll let you keep the ring. And the gold chain. And the fancy purse. And the elegant dress that probably cost you a hundred marks. Do with your life whatever you like, but as I said, you should have given me the ten marks. Now go sit down before I hurt you."

Without a word, her face tight with indignation, she picked up her wallet and purse and stepped past him. A moment later she was seated on the bench. She didn't look at him again, just stared out across the snow-covered lawns. Wary now, not sure if she was going to try something, Hans watched her for several moments. Ignoring the tumult of feelings going on inside him, he called to her again. "Don't try to run on me. You sit right where you are until I'm past those trees over there. If you move before then, I'll shoot you down. You hear me?"

There was no answer, no flicker of movement.

Swearing to himself—*at* himself—Hans pushed back the thoughts of Emilee and his mother and the Dutch boy and the dike and structural integrity and took off in his shuffling walk for the stand of trees up ahead of him. He kept glancing over his shoulder, but she never moved. It was as if she had turned to stone.

The line of trees—maples or lindens or something like that—was about fifty yards from the park bench. He realized that he was still at risk here. If she got up and bolted for the next street, she could have the police looking for him in five or ten minutes.

Though stricken with guilt, he was nevertheless elated. "Sorry, Mama," he said as he moved into the trees. "It's not been a good day."

7:52 a.m.

He had to stop about thirty yards into the trees. There was a slight rise of ground and it was too much for him. Turning, he looked back, peering through the trees at the park bench. He couldn't tell if the woman was looking his way or not, but he was pleased to see that she was still taking him at his word. She hadn't moved.

He hunched over, pressing his left arm and elbow against the ribs to help ease the fiery pain there. And it was right then that he heard the voice speak. Not heard. More like *felt* it speak.

"Peter."

He jerked up. The hair on the back of his neck was standing straight up and chills were coursing through his body. No one was anywhere in sight. He wasn't even sure if he had heard it at all. It was like it was in his head. No, not in his head. It was just *there.*

"Peter!" More emphatic this time.

He realized that it wasn't a woman's voice. Nor a man's either. It was just an eerie, chilling voice speaking at him.

"*Peter!*" Louder. More demanding. More urgent.

"What?" he cried in exasperation. "I'm not Peter. Who are you? What do you want?"

He was answered by silence. His whole body was tingling—like when someone jumps out at you unexpectedly in the darkness. But there was nothing.

Thoroughly spooked, Hans pulled his overcoat around him and started forward again. "I'm not Peter," he muttered again, looking up through the bare branches of the trees.

Then, out of the blue, he understood. It was the DTs. *Delerium tremens.* Latin for "shaking frenzy." A violent but very real physiological reaction involving bodily tremors or seizures, mental confusion, and vivid hallucinations. Caused when one drinks too much alcohol in a short period of time, especially on an empty stomach. He and Franck had learned that from an army doctor after going on a binge during a weekend leave early on in their friendship.

The relief was so immense that he threw back his head and laughed up at the sky. "Good one. You nearly had me," he cried.

Hans straightened, glancing back at Lady Glitz one last time to make sure she hadn't moved—she hadn't—and then started forward again. He got another ten steps before it hit him. In one flash of perfect clarity, he knew who Peter was. His words to his mother on that last morning in Graswang hit like a physical blow. "His name wasn't Peter, *Mutti.*" At which she had shot right back, "Peter's a pretty common name in Holland, you know."

Hans stood there for what seemed like several minutes, and then he turned around and painfully started back down the hill toward the bench.

CHAPTER
25

January 15, 1919, 7:55 a.m.—Volkspark Friedrichshain, Berlin

When the woman saw Hans coming out of the trees again, she got slowly to her feet. As he got closer, he saw that she was rigid with fright. Afraid that she might bolt, Hans called out to her. "It's all right, Frau." He pulled both hands out of his pockets and held them up. "I don't really have a pistol. I'm not going to hurt you. I'm going to give your money back to you."

Skittish as a baby fawn, she poised there looking around nervously. There were pedestrians passing by on the street that bordered the park, and that seemed to bolster her courage, even though they were fifty or sixty yards away. Finally, she turned slowly to face him.

As Hans shuffled up to her, he pulled the wad of bills from his pocket and handed it to her.

She didn't move to take it. "I don't understand."

"Believe it or not, I'm not a thief and a robber."

She stared at him in utter disbelief, still not taking the money. Then he saw her nose wrinkle a little and she pulled back. He suspected that she had just caught a whiff of his tunic and the residue of his two-day binge.

Anxious to be out of her presence, he reached out and tucked the money in her coat pocket. "I deeply regret my actions. I was desperate and lost my head." He stared at the ground. "And if my mother were here right now, she would be crimson with shame."

He started to back up and turn away.

"Wait!" she cried. She was clearly having trouble believing this was actually happening.

He turned back. Withdrawing the money from her pocket, she peeled off one of the bills. "Don't," he said. "That's not why I came back."

It was a twenty-mark note—which looked like a small fortune to him at the moment. "I wish I could give you more, but . . . The bank, you know."

Too desperate to let his pride speak for him, Hans took the money from her and shoved it into his overcoat pocket. "That is very generous of you, Frau. . . ."

"Von Schiller," she said.

Of course, he thought. He should have known that her name would have a "von" in it. It was the designator of noble, wealthy, and powerful families.

"*Countess* Monika von Schiller," she said, seemingly amused by his reaction.

His jaw went slack. He had just committed armed robbery on a countess?

"Of the Leipzig von Schillers," she went on, pulling a face. "Who have recently fallen on hard times."

"I . . ." Hans was awed in spite of himself. "I dated a countess once."

The woman was instantly skeptical. "Truthfully?"

"Yes. Lady Magdalena Margitte Maria von Kruger."

Her mouth fell open a little. "Of the Munich von Krugers?"

"Yes. I was a student at the Von Kruger Academy."

"Tell me your name."

"My name is Sergeant Hans Otto Eckhardt. I am from Bavaria."

"What family in Bavaria?" There was new respect in her voice.

He laughed. "I doubt that you would know them. My father is a *milchbauer*."

She visibly recoiled.

"Yes. And like you, I too have fallen on hard times." When the woman said nothing, Hans straightened, suddenly feeling the vastness of the social gap between them. "I'll be going now. And, again, please forgive me for the wrong I have done you."

She turned her head, looking toward the street. A long, black car had pulled up to the curb. A man in a uniform got out. He shouted and started waving. The countess gave a little cry of joy.

"What?" Hans cried.

"My . . . uh . . . neighbor has taken pity on me," she said. "That is his chauffeur."

"Well then, I shall bid you farewell."

She swung back around and to his utter surprise grabbed his hand. "No, wait. You are having difficulty walking. We will take you home."

Hans was stunned. "No, I. . . ."

"Please. Since I cannot give you more money, let me do this for you."

Another man had gotten out of the car, and he and the chauffeur were walking swiftly toward them. Hans started as he realized the second man was in the uniform of an Imperial Army officer. "Uh . . ." He started to back away. Tempting as it was to have a ride to the hotel, he wasn't about to get into that car and let an officer see—and smell—the state he was in.

She grabbed his elbow and hung on. "Please, Sergeant. I feel so awful for treating you so badly. Don't go. That's our neighbor and good friend, Captain Wilhelm Ballif. He is a good man. He will gladly take you anywhere you want."

By this point the two men had broken into a trot and were approaching rapidly. Had it not been for Hans's battered body, he might have turned and sprinted for the trees. Instead, he accepted what he could not change. With a sigh, he nodded and turned to face the approaching men.

The officer was in the lead now. He was solidly built, with a square face and strikingly handsome features. He did not have his cap on, and Hans noted that his dark hair was streaked with grey. He looked to be in his early forties. Then he noticed something odd. The insignias on the man's greatcoat were not those of a captain, but of a colonel.

The man rushed up to her and reached out, grabbed her hands, and pulled her close. "Darling, are you all right?"

Darling?

The countess laid a hand on his arm. "Yes, Stefan, I am fine."

Wait. *Stefan?* But she had just called him Wilhelm.

"I can't believe you decided to walk," he said, sternly now.

She gave a little toss of her head. "It's all right, *Schatzi.*" She went up and kissed him, not on the cheek but on the lips.

Before Hans could process that, she turned to face him. He was shocked to see that those flawless features were now an ugly mask of fury. "Stefan, this beast, this hateful man, tried to rob me at gunpoint."

"*What?!*" Even as the colonel cried out, he snatched the Luger from the holster in his belt. Hans lunged to one side, but the chauffeur was on him and drove him to his knees. A millisecond later he felt the cold steel of the Luger's muzzle grinding into the flesh just behind his ear.

"Move and you die," a voice hissed in his ear. Then a moment later, "Alfred, go find a policeman."

10:55 a.m.—*Hotel Lindenberg, Prenzlauer Berg District, Berlin*

"Is this it, Fräulein?"

Emilee looked out the window of the taxi at the three-story building with the dilapidated sign over the entrance. "Just a moment." She opened her purse and extracted the paper. "Yes. The Hotel Lindenberg. This is it. How much is the fare?"

"Seventy-eight *Pfennige.*"

Emilee took a one-mark note from her purse and handed it up to the driver. "Keep the change."

"*Danke.*" He half turned in his seat. "Don't know what your plans are, Fräulein, but it's best if you don't go into the central part of the city today."

She smiled. "That's what everyone keeps telling me. I know about the general strike."

"Good. There have already been clashes between the Socialists and the government."

That raised a question in Emilee's mind. "But taxi drivers are not joining the general strike?"

The driver frowned. "Many are, but some, such as myself, do not stand with them."

As the taxi drove away, Emilee stood there for a moment, eyeing the building across the street. Hans had called it a "flophouse." She saw now that it was a pretty accurate description. The building had to be eighty years old. The bricks were dark with accumulated soot and smoke. Several of the windows had visible cracks in them. Two or three sported cardboard patches over broken-out segments.

Emilee took a quick breath, clutched her purse tightly to her side, and darted across the street. A moment later, she was inside the lobby. She took a moment to let her eyes adjust to the dimmer light and then turned as a movement in the far corner caught her eye. A man in dark pants and a white undershirt was getting up from a large overstuffed chair. From the expression on his face, she guessed that she had awakened him from a nap.

"Yes? May I help you?"

He was an older man with a day's growth of whiskers, a bald head, and tufts of black hair on his chest poking out from beneath his undershirt. His eyes were small and close-set, giving him a bit of a feral look.

They were staring at her with unabashed interest. Then he spoke again. "If you're looking for a room, this is a men-only hotel."

"I'm not."

He walked across the lobby and went through a half door that put him behind the main desk. She saw him glance at her hands, checking for a ring. "Then how can I help you, Fräulein?"

"I am looking for one of your tenants. At least, I was told that he is staying here."

"I see. And what is his name, *bitte*?"

"Hans Otto Eckhardt. Sergeant Hans Otto Eckhardt."

His eyebrows lifted momentarily, as if he found that hard to believe. "And are you a relative of his?"

"You might say that. We are engaged to be married."

That clearly startled him. "I . . . I don't believe he's in at the moment."

"Do you know where he is?"

He shook his head. "My son works the night shift. He said Sergeant Eckhardt left at about ten thirty. According to Georg, he was just going to find something to eat."

"At that time of night?" Emilee asked skeptically.

He shrugged, irritated at her directness. "Hope he wasn't going to some fancy restaurant. He's got three days of whiskers, smells like an outhouse, and could barely put one foot in front of the other when I last saw him."

This only irked her more. "May I speak with your son?"

"He's in school until three."

"Is there a possibility that Herr Eckhardt might have come in when. . . ." She deliberately let her eyes move to the overstuffed chair. "While you were distracted?" His eyes narrowed, and she realized it was foolish to provoke him. "Would it be possible for me to go up to his room and check?" she asked, forcing a smile.

The man considered that for a moment and then shrugged. He

took down a key from the rack behind him and laid it on the counter. "Suit yourself. It's room 214."

"Thank you." As Emilee started for the stairs, she had another idea. "Sir, I know this is a little presumptuous"—she flashed him a warmer smile—"but if he's not there, would you mind if I waited for him in the room? I've come down from Pasewalk on the train this morning. I was up at four. I'll just maybe take a little rest while I wait."

For some reason he found that amusing. "From Pasewalk, you say?"

"Yes. Do you know where that is?"

He ignored that. "What's your name?"

"Emilee Fromme."

He grunted. "He left standing instructions that if a Nurse Fromme from Pasewalk should call, I was to get him anytime day or night."

"That's me. I tried to call last night, but they said your phone was not working."

"The telephone workers are on strike."

Of course. That would explain the restaurant not answering too. "So, may I wait in his room?"

Again there was a sense that he found something very funny in her request. But then his next question took her aback. "Are you sure you want to do that?"

Emilee bristled a little. "I'm sure."

He pushed the key toward her. "If you leave before he comes back, please bring the key back." She took the stairs two at a time, disappearing out of his sight.

The second floor hallway was deserted. As Emilee reached the door marked 214, she stopped and listened. There was no discernible sound—not from the room, not from anywhere in the hotel. She knocked once. Then again. Nothing. Bracing herself, she unlocked the door and pushed it open.

With a soft cry she fell back a step, throwing her arm across her mouth and nose. The smell was like a blow to the face. Bewildered, she looked at the key again, and then at the room number. Yes, this was room 214. Emilee took a deep breath, pushed the door all the way open, and stepped inside. She groped for the light and flipped the switch up.

For several long seconds she just stood there, her eyes taking it all in, her mind refusing to accept what she was seeing. Then, with a low cry, she turned the light off again, backed out quickly, and locked the door again. Now she understood the man's condescending smiles.

He was seated forward in his chair when she came back down again and laid the key on the desk. "Decided not to wait?" he drawled.

"You think that's funny?" she snapped. "When did you last clean that room?"

"We don't clean the rooms," he sneered. "Not for two marks a night. We give 'em fresh bedding once a week. That's all."

Furious at the man, sickened by what she had seen, and disgusted to think that Hans was responsible for it, she asked one last question. "What time does your son come on tonight?"

The man thought about that for a moment and then shrugged. "Normally, ten o'clock or thereabouts. But the Frau and I have an engagement this evening, so he'll come on shift about seven tonight."

"I'll be back then." Emilee had another thought. "Is there an inexpensive hotel nearby?"

He chuckled aloud, relishing the fact that she was asking for his help. "You're welcome to stay in Sergeant Eckhardt's room. We'll make an exception to our males-only policy for you, Fräulein Fromme. Just two marks a night."

Emilee whirled and plunged out the door.

January 15, 1919, 3:25 p.m.—Imperial German Army Barracks, Finckensteinallee, Berlin

There was a brief knock on the door, and then it opened immediately. The corporal who had brought the food tray in earlier was back. He glanced at the empty tray, smiled, and looked at Hans. "Could I bring you anything else, Sergeant?"

Watching him suspiciously, Hans shook his head.

"You sure? I've been instructed to give you anything that we have in the mess hall."

Those words brought Hans's head up. "Mess hall? Where am I?"

The answer was immediately regretful. "Sorry, Sergeant, I'm not allowed to say."

"Is this a jail?"

The corporal smiled but shook his head. "Someone will be in to talk to you very soon. Are you sure there's nothing else I can get you?"

More than anything, it was the politeness and the respect that were confusing him. Hans had never been in a prison or jail before, but he had talked to men who had, and they hadn't been treated with anything other than the utmost contempt. "Uh . . . could I get some more aspirin?"

"Yes. In fact, the medical officer said you can have something stronger if you'd like."

Medical officer? A full meal with second helpings? Mess hall? A corporal in army uniform? What was this place? The door to his room was locked from the outside, but there were no bars on the window. No uniformed prison guards.

Pushing all of that away, Hans shook his head. Tempting as it was to get something stronger, he didn't want anything drugging his mind. Not yet. "Aspirin will be fine."

With a curt nod, the young man left the room. Five minutes later he was back with aspirin and a glass of water.

When he left, Hans sat back, trying to sort it out. He gave up trying to figure out where he was or what was going on. But as his thoughts turned to the "voice" in the trees, he went back to the idea of the DTs. That made sense. No, that was the *only* thing that made sense. He simply refused to accept that it was some kind of spiritual prompting from his mother. Or, on the other hand, maybe it was God yanking him around. And yanking it was. One minute Hans had six or seven hundred marks in hand. The next, he was lying face down on the sidewalk with a pistol grinding into his cheekbone. One of the men in his unit back in France had once called God "the Divine Trickster." There might be something to that.

Hans lay back on the cot and closed his eyes, too tired to care anymore. Just as he was drifting off to sleep again, he heard a key turn in the lock. He pulled himself up to a sitting position, wincing as the pain shot through his whole upper body. But when he saw who had stepped into the room, Hans leaped to his feet, stifling a cry. Then he saluted. Colonel von Schiller was standing before him, a sardonic smile on his face. The corporal was right behind him, hands extended in front of him. Laid across them was a set of army fatigues, folded and neatly pressed, including fresh underwear and socks. A file folder rested on top of the pile.

The corporal laid the uniform on the foot of the bed and then handed von Schiller the folder. He stepped out of the room and reappeared a moment later carrying a wooden, military-issue chair. He set it down beside the colonel. "Anything else, sir?"

"Yes, Jürgens. As soon as I'm finished, I want you to take Sergeant Eckhardt to the bathroom and let him take a shower. Find him a razor and shaving soap. A hairbrush, too." The colonel turned to Hans. "You don't have to shave, but I'm guessing you prefer to be clean shaven."

"I . . . Yes, I do." *How would he have guessed that?*

"Good. So do I. Thank you, Corporal. I'll call you if I need you."

As Jürgens left, the colonel turned back to Hans and nodded curtly. "At ease, Sergeant."

Hans was too stunned to respond. He gaped at the man, feeling as though the earth had just been yanked out from beneath his feet. He wondered if this was why he was not in jail. The colonel wanted to even the score for what Hans had done to his wife.

An amused smile curled around the officer's mouth. "At ease, Sergeant Eckhardt," he said more forcefully, gesturing with his hand. "Please, sit down."

Hans spread his feet apart and clasped his hands behind him in the classic at-ease posture. "I prefer to stand, sir," he said.

The colonel glanced at the uniform. "I hope that's the right size. But I suppose it'll have to do until we can get your other one cleaned."

Hans said nothing. His brain was in such a whirl, he didn't dare open his mouth.

The officer moved the chair so it faced Hans directly and then sat down. "You may as well sit, soldier. No one's going to shoot you. At least, not yet." He seemed to find that idea amusing.

Hans slowly sank down onto the cot.

Crossing his legs and revealing highly polished, knee-high boots, von Schiller watched Hans steadily for several seconds. Hans forced himself to submit to the scrutiny. Finally, the officer shook his head. "Monika said that you were beat up by some other soldiers. *Freikorps*?"

"I didn't ask, but probably. They wore army uniforms and had army-issued weapons."

"Uh-huh. When I first saw you, I thought you might have been run over by a tank."

"It felt like it, sir. There were four of them. They were waiting for me at my hotel."

"And what had you done that brought them to your hotel?" Then even as the colonel finished the question, he waved his hand as if brushing it aside. "Never mind. We'll get to that soon enough. All right now, Sergeant. We have a lot to talk about, but let's start with how you came to rob my wife and what made you change your mind and give the money back to her." His eyes suddenly went very cold. "And I would encourage you to be completely forthright in your answers. If I catch you lying. . . ." He gave an enigmatic shrug. "Well, you'll wish that I turned you over to your *Freikorps* comrades. *Verstehen*?"

"Yes, sir."

"I'm guessing this story begins before you and Monika met in the park. So why don't you start wherever you think will be most helpful to me?"

Talk about sensory overload. Hans was having a hard time keeping up with this man. He was career army. He had a rod of steel down his back. There was no question about that. But for a man whose wife had been robbed at gunpoint by the person sitting before him, the colonel seemed amazingly unperturbed.

Hans hesitated. Where should he start? How far back should he go?

As all of that was going through his mind, he kept glancing at the folder on the colonel's lap. He had to assume that it was his army personnel folder. If so, von Schiller knew a lot about Hans already. He decided not to hold much back.

So he began to speak softly but without rushing, beginning when he had been caught in the artillery shelling of their own forces and was severely wounded. "When I woke up," he concluded, "I was in the Army Hospital in Pasewalk."

"Was that when you won the Iron Cross?"

So the colonel had read his file. "No. That came from the Battle of Verdun."

"They say you carried a fellow soldier out of harm's way, even though he was dead."

"I couldn't be sure he was dead, sir. I did what anyone would have done."

Von Schiller grunted something, opened the file again, and scanned it quickly. "Two battle ribbons. Verdun and the final defense of the Siegfried Line, *ja?*"

"Yes, sir."

"I see that's also where you earned a letter of commendation from your battalion commander."

"Yes, sir."

"So it was on the Siegfried line where you were earned the *Verwundetenabzeichen,* the Medal for the Wounded?"

"Yes, sir."

"How badly were you hit?"

Hans touched the scar next to his eye. "They thought for a time that I might be blind. A few days after I woke up, the war was over."

Von Schiller closed the folder and dropped it on the floor. His eyes were locked with Hans's. Hans wasn't sure what was going on here, but for the first time he had the tiniest glimmer of hope. He thought what he saw in the colonel's eyes was respect. He went on with his story. He told the colonel about the closure of the Ministry of War and the loss of his severance pay. Von Schiller nodded from time to time but said nothing. Hans told him about the job at *Bayerischer Biergarten,*

Fritzie's offer to have him "ride shotgun," and their confrontation with Karl and his men.

"How much did you take from them?"

"All of it," Hans said quietly. "About forty-five hundred marks."

Von Schiller gave a low whistle. "No wonder they came looking for you."

"We thought we had covered ourselves. I convinced my partner that there was no way they could identify us. But I was wrong." He reached up and touched his cheek. "As you can see."

"What about your partners?"

"One's in the hospital, and the restaurant was torched."

Von Schiller seemed satisfied. "All right. That brings us up to this morning. Go on."

For a moment, Hans was tempted to skip the part about scavenging for food, but suddenly he wanted the colonel to know. He wanted him to know how utterly desperate he was. That he was not the kind of man who accosted vulnerable women and stole from them. So he described it all—even the dog—in flat, unemotional tones. To his surprise, von Schiller only nodded.

"And," he concluded, "I know there's no excuse for what I did, but when your wife looked at me and wrinkled her nose up as if she'd just stepped in something disgusting, it was the last straw." He reached up and rubbed at his eyes. "But I still can't believe I robbed a countess."

The colonel jerked forward. "She told you she was a countess?" He was incredulous.

"Yes," Hans said slowly, "the Countess von Schiller, of the Leipzig von Schillers."

Von Schiller was shaking his head, half in wonder, half in amusement.

"She also told me she was a widow."

"Yeah, she told me that. What else did she tell you about me? About her?"

Hans was staring at him as he went on slowly. "She said that you were killed in the Battle of the Somme. That the money was your house payment for the bank. She said they were going to foreclose on your house if she didn't get it paid today."

And then, to Hans's utter amazement, the colonel threw back his head and laughed. "Ah, Monika, Monika, Monika." It was said with amazement, affection, and . . . yes, even pride.

Hans just stared at him.

Then von Schiller sobered, and there was a hint of anger in those cold, grey eyes. "So, she told you she was a starving war widow, trying to stall off a foreclosure on our house, and yet you still robbed her. If you're the innocent victim of circumstance, as you say, robbing her sounds like a pretty cold and calculating thing to do."

Hans shook his head. "It's hard to explain."

"Well, I suggest you try, because you, my friend, are teetering on a very thin wire at this moment. Why did you rob her if you believed her story?"

Hans sat back. That was a very good question. He took a quick breath and began. "In the first place, I had no intention of stealing anything from her. I asked her if she could spare me ten marks so I could get something to eat. She refused, saying that she wasn't rich. That she had very little money. And then, I . . . I happened to mention I was the son of a *milchbauer*, and she actually recoiled, like she was afraid I might touch her or something. She told me to go away. But it was the way she said it." His eyes couldn't meet the colonel's. "That was exactly what I had said to the dog. And with that same kind of contemptuous tone. That did it. That was when I decided I would take ten or twenty marks from her whether she liked it or not."

"It must have been a jolt when you found more than seven hundred marks."

"I couldn't believe it. Then I realized she had been lying to me. But when I confronted her on it, she started on that whole thing about you being dead and needing to take the money to the bank. But as I looked at her, I realized that something didn't add up. Her clothes, her purse, her boots, the gold necklace. The diamond ring. Everything about her reeked of money. Any trace of feeling sorry for her went out the window. Even if she was a widow. Even if it was true about the mortgage payment. I just snapped."

The colonel stood up. "So what made you come back? You were away clean. She really believed that you had a pistol and would shoot her if she moved. She was terrified."

Hans wasn't about to tell him about the voice, but he sensed that this was an important point to the colonel. He studied his hands as he spoke. "Sir, I was raised in a good family, believe it or not. My parents are simple farmers, but they are honest folk. As I was walking away from her, it hit me just how far I had fallen. Taking money from a war widow. At least, that's what I believed."

"Go on."

Hans raised his head. "May I speak freely, sir?" The colonel gave him a curt nod. "Your wife is a beautiful woman, and even though things didn't add up, she was still utterly convincing." Hans gave a short, bitter laugh. "Hey, if I had happened to have any money on me, I probably would have ended up giving it to *her*. I mean, something was obviously wrong with her life. Why else would a woman like that be walking alone in the park at that hour of the morning?"

For a moment, Hans thought he had crossed the line. Anger flashed across the colonel's face, but then he sighed. "The money was not to pay the bank," he said. "We own clear title to our home. Actually, it was to pay for a new dress."

"A dress! For seven hundred marks?" Hans cried, dumbfounded.

"That and a few other things. Our regiment commander is retiring, and there's a big banquet for him next week. Monika found this dress, but they had to do some alterations. She was to pick it up today. I promised her that Alfred would take her to get it this morning."

He stopped, looking at Hans closely. "You're not a native Berliner, are you?"

"No, I'm from Bavaria."

"Are you aware of what is going on in the city right now?"

"A little. I've heard there's a general strike going on. And a lot of gangs running around."

"The Communists are planning to seize the government tomorrow."

"*What?!*"

Von Schiller nodded grimly. "Yes, but more on that in a minute. So anyway, I was called to an early meeting this morning. I had Alfred bring me in. Monika was furious. She said she needed the car. But I didn't want her going out today, especially not downtown. I told her I needed to keep Alfred with me so she would have to wait until things calmed a little. Well, as you have learned, Monika is used to having her own way. She was quite irritated with me. What was a general strike compared to getting her dress? So she tried to call a taxi to come get her. No taxis. The drivers are part of the strike. So then she went down to the trolley stop." He smiled thinly. "Which is quite unbelievable. Monika on a trolley?"

"And the trolleys were not running either," Hans guessed.

"That's right. By that time she was so furious, she took off walking. My Monika? Walking? Alone? Unbelievable."

"How did you find out?"

"The nanny called me as soon as Monika left. So Alfred and I went looking for her. And I found her with you. And that's another question I have. When you saw us, why didn't you take off running?"

Hans laid one hand on his injured ribs. "Well, in the first place, I can't run right now. In the second place, she grabbed my arm and begged me to stay."

He shot Hans a skeptical look. "And you stayed?"

"She told me you were her neighbor. And that she was so grateful that I had brought her money back, you would give me a ride to my hotel. With my ribs, that sounded pretty good to me."

Von Schiller was shaking his head. "There was no way she was going to let you get away after you humiliated her the way you did."

"I humiliated *her*?"

The colonel laughed. Then he quickly sobered. "Just be grateful that you changed your mind and brought the money back to her. Otherwise I would have hunted you down and. . . ." He shrugged. The gesture was so casual that it sent a little chill up the back of Hans's neck.

"So, if I may ask, sir. What *is* going to happen to me?"

Von Schiller abruptly stood up. "The first thing is to get you bathed and in a clean uniform." He waved a hand back and forth in front of his nose. "You are right. You do smell like a latrine. I have another meeting, but I'll be back here at about five. Then we'll talk some more."

CHAPTER 27

*January 15, 1919, 3:55 p.m.—East Railway Station,
Friedrichshain-Kreuzberg District, Berlin*

E milee?"

"Yes, *Onkel* Artur. It's me."

"Thank heavens. Are you all right? Where are you?"

"I'm still in Berlin. I'm sorry to call you during work hours, but I'm back at the train station. I tried to call you earlier, but this is the only telephone exchange still working."

"I know, I've been reading about the strike. Have you found Hans yet?"

Emilee leaned her head back against the wall of the telephone box, fighting back tears. "Not yet. I've been to his hotel and. . . ." She shuddered. "Not yet. He's gone out somewhere."

"Then leave it, Emilee. I want you on the next train to Pasewalk."

"Not yet, *Onkel*. I'm seeing someone at seven tonight. I think he'll know where Hans is."

There was a long pause, and then, "Emilee, listen to me very carefully. I've checked the schedule. The last train out of Berlin coming north is at 8:30 tonight. And the stationmaster here said that may be canceled. The strike is quickly spreading to the railway workers."

"I have to find out where he is, *Onkel* Artur. Something's wrong. Terribly wrong."

"The next-to-the-last train leaves at 6:45, Emmy. Promise me you'll be on it."

"*Onkel* Artur, please. I have to find him." He started to answer, but she rushed on. "If I can't find him by tonight, then I'll come home. But I have to try. I'll be careful, *Onkel*. I promise. I'm not down in the center of the city where all the people are. I don't have to go there."

Dr. Schnebling's voice suddenly dropped to a whisper. "Emmy, listen to me. I shouldn't be telling you this, but we got a telegram from the War Office this afternoon. Every military hospital within a hundred miles of Berlin is being put on standby."

"Standby?"

"Yes!" he hissed. "We are to have two surgeons and five nurses with as much surgical equipment and medicine as we can spare ready to leave within two hours' notice."

Emilee felt her knees go weak. She didn't have to ask why. It was rumored there were half a million workers in the city right now. Half a million! If violence erupted on that vast of scale . . . It was a horrific thing to contemplate.

"All right, *Onkel* Artur. I'll be on the 6:45 train."

"Promise!"

"*Ja*, I promise."

She went back to the exchange operator and had her place a call to Graswang. She had to know if Hans had gone back home again or if he had contacted his family in any way. She quickly regretted it. He had not. Inga had not heard from her son for nearly a week and was frantic with worry. Emilee promised to call her if she learned anything. But it still took all the power of persuasion Emilee possessed to convince Inga that getting on a train and coming to Berlin was dangerous.

For several minutes, Emilee sat there, going over all of the possibilities in her mind and feeling her anger starting to rise. *Where are you,*

Hans? Sleeping it off on some park bench? In the drunk tank in one of the jails? Out buying more liquor?

Finally she grabbed her purse and walked swiftly down to the area of the train station where there were a few small shops. In a stationery shop she bought a fountain pen, a pad of stationery, and a small packet of envelopes. Then she went to the combination bookstore and apothecary and bought a few personal items. Satisfied, she headed for the door.

A wave of relief washed over her as she saw the same taxi driver as before parked at the curb. She increased her pace, waving and calling to him.

His face broke out in a grin at the sight of her. "Fräulein, it's you again."

"Yes. Can you take me back to that same hotel? And wait for me?"

"*Ja, ja*, I can do it. Get in."

4:12 p.m.—Hotel Lindenberg, Prenzlauer Berg District, Berlin

"Am I right in assuming that Herr Eckhardt has not returned?" she asked, her voice cool.

The owner of the hotel gave her a long, insolent look and then nodded. "Yes."

"Then may I have his key, please? I have to return to Pasewalk, and I would like to leave a note."

The man reached for the key and handed it to her without a word. Emilee went to the stairs and ascended without looking back.

She stopped outside the door and knocked again, just to be sure Hans hadn't slipped past him. Then, taking a deep breath, she opened the door and stepped inside.

Breathing through her mouth so as to knock the worst edge off of the smell, she turned on the light and looked around. For a moment she was tempted to clean up the worst of his mess. At least put some of his personal belongings back in his rucksack, maybe hang up his clothes. She thrust that thought aside. After all his promises, all his fine talk, he had done this? And she was thinking of cleaning up after him? Disgusted, Emilee pulled the single wooden chair over to the small lamp table, took out her writing materials, and wrote quickly.

Dear Hans,

I came here this afternoon hoping to find you. I am sorry that I could not call you in advance. I tried, but the phone exchanges are down. I have been worried sick since I have not heard from you since Sunday. I called your family but learned that you have made no contact with them, either. I decided to come to Berlin, thinking that in the chaos going on down here, something had happened to you. What you said to me Sunday night before your departure lifted to me to such happiness, and I hoped that we might talk more about it.

Now, as I look about your room, I can see that you were engaged in other things. I don't know what brought on this sudden urge for "celebration"—perhaps your recent financial windfall—but were you really too busy to call or write?

I love you. I know that now. But I guess for me, love alone is not enough. Right now, I have enough people in my life who need me to care for them. I am too weary in spirit to take on another.

I am sorry that I am not stronger for you, but as I look around this room, I have to acknowledge the fact that I am not. And that makes me want to weep. Good-bye, Hans. May you someday find in life what you are so desperately looking for.

Emilee F.

She read through it once, resisted the urge to add a post script, folded it, and put it in the envelope. Stepping over one of the wine bottles, she laid it on the bed where it would be easily seen and quickly left the room.

5:25 p.m.—Imperial German Army Barracks, Finckensteinallee, Berlin

Colonel von Schiller seemed more agitated when he came back into the room, which set Hans's teeth on edge. But when he sat down on the chair again, he seemed to push whatever it was that was bothering him aside and focus on Hans. He looked him up and down and then smiled. He sniffed the air with exaggerated care. "That's a definite improvement." His smiled broadened. "And did the doctor come and look at your stitches?"

"He did. There's no infection. They should come out in another few days."

"You'll carry those two scars for life. I suppose he told you that."

"He did. In fact, he said"—he lowered his voice to mimic the physician's pompous pronouncement—"'You are now part of the great brotherhood of Teutonic warriors who carry the scars of battle on their visage for all the world to see.'"

The colonel laughed. "Dr. Bochert is a student of the classics and especially loves the history of Germany's role in the Crusades."

Hans nodded. "Well, I very much appreciate you sending him in. He also taped up my ribs. They seem a little more bearable now."

"*Gut.*"

"*Danke schön.* I am deeply in your debt."

"Yes, you are," came the reply. "I'm glad that you see that." Von Schiller sat back in his chair, studying Hans thoughtfully. "Surely you have questions about what is going on here."

"Just one. Why?"

"Why?" There was short bark of laughter. "That's not one question. That's ten or more. Why are you here? Why aren't you in jail? Why didn't I shoot you on the spot? Why am I feeding you and clothing you and . . . Well, you get the point."

"Yeah, all of those. So, why is a man of considerable authority playing the part of the Good Samaritan for a man who tried to rob his wife at gunpoint? To be honest, sir, you don't seem like the Good Samaritan type."

Von Schiller hooted at that. "You know what, Sergeant. I like you. I like your style."

"Begging your pardon, sir, but that's not an answer."

He sobered immediately. "No, it's not. And no, I'm not a Good Samaritan. I assure you that my motives are in no way altruistic or noble. They are purely selfish and self-serving."

"Good. I can understand that. The rest totally baffles me."

"So, before I answer your question, let me ask you two questions. One practical, one theoretical."

Hans nodded and sat back on the cot.

"Question one. Tell me more about those men who attacked you. You said they were in uniform and had army-issue weapons. Did they have any unit patches on their uniforms?"

"Not that I saw."

"Name tags?"

"No, but I did hear them call each other by their names. The leader was named Karl. One was Horst. One was Werner."

Von Schiller nodded, but obviously the names meant nothing to him.

"Next question. Tell me your feelings about our current government."

Hans snorted in disgust. "Utter contempt. They're nothing but thieves and criminals."

"Ah, yes. The 'November Criminals.'"

"*Ja.* Exactly. They betrayed the Fatherland and stabbed the army in the back when they sold us out on November 11. All that we worked for, all that we fought for, all that we died for—they gave it away with the stroke of a pen at Compiègne." Hans had to stop. His chest was heaving. "I think they need to be taken and out and shot," he concluded.

"You have a lot of company in those feelings, Eckhardt." A long pause. "Including myself." Another pause, all the time his eyes never leaving Hans's. Then the colonel leaned in, very earnest now. "And what would you say if you were asked to defend them, to fight for them?"

The question stunned him. "Begging your pardon, sir?"

"You heard me. Are there any circumstances that would lead you to defend our government?"

"None! Absolutely none."

"Including a firing squad?"

Hans rocked back. *Was that a threat?* He said nothing.

Again, that seemed to please von Schiller rather than anger him. "*Gut, gut!*" he said. "No false bravado. None of this, 'I'd rather die than support them in any way.' Only fools talk like that, and I didn't take you for a fool."

"Is that what this is all about, Colonel? *Are* you asking me to defend the government?"

"That is precisely what I'm going to ask you to do, Sergeant."

Hans had to look away. It was happening again. Exhilaration, despair. Jubilation, misery. Hope, hopelessness. The Divine Trickster. It was like this was becoming the pattern of his life.

"And do you know why I am going to ask that of you?" von Schiller exclaimed. "Because that is what I am asking of myself." There was a short, bitter laugh. "Yes, that's right, Sergeant. I detest our government. They are a bunch of spineless idiots, little boys playing at politics. I'll grant you, they are making a valiant effort to govern, but they have no backbone, no courage to stand up to the forces that are threatening our very existence."

"What forces?"

"I'll get to that in a minute. I could give you a dozen examples, but I'll just give you one. Two days ago, one of the so-called 'People's Councils' sent representatives to Parliament to present their demands.

Care to guess who those representatives were? Teens. Yeah, that's right. Juveniles. Fifteen-, sixteen-, and seventeen-year-olds. They came in and made demands of the National Parliament. And they let them speak. Treated them like they were visiting royalty. It's idiocy!" he exclaimed. "Pure madness. It's like they're senile. Our country is collapsing around our heads, and they call in children!"

"So," Hans persisted, "again I ask, why fight to defend them? To keep them in power?"

"Because," von Schiller said grimly, staring right through Hans, "it is better to be governed by weaklings than by madmen."

Chapter Notes

The conditions described here by von Schiller accurately portray the situation in the government at this juncture. With the fall of the Empire and the abdication of Kaiser Wilhelm II, the elected members of Parliament were mostly replaced by representatives from numerous state and local governments that had come to power in the Socialist revolution of October through December 1918. The primary governing body in Parliament became what they called the *Vollzugrat*, or "Volunteer Board or Council." Many of these were poor and uneducated civilians with no experience in government whatsoever. "People's Councils" and "Soldiers' Councils" formed in local areas during that revolution were given a voice as well. Even small political parties with only a few members had representation (see *And the Kaiser Abdicates: The German Revolution November 1918–August 1919*, digitized edition, chapters 12–119, pp. 176–292).

The army, particularly the career officer corps, detested the government, but they detested the leftist groups even more. They were practical enough to see that if they did not support and shore up the government, Germany could easily be turned into another Soviet Republic.

Political chaos is not too strong of a word to describe the situation in Germany at this time.

CHAPTER
28

*January 15, 1919, 5:40 p.m.—Telegraph Office, East Railway
Station, Friedrichshain-Kreuzberg District, Berlin*

P lease check your message carefully," the clerk said, handing a
sheet to Emilee.

She took it and read it slowly.

ARTUR SCHNEBLING PASEWALK MILITARY
    HOSPITAL
NOT COMING TONIGHT STOP VERY SORRY STOP
SOMETHING I MUST DO STOP BE ON FIRST TRAIN
TOMORROW STOP WILL FIND HOTEL NEAR
OSTBAHNHOF TONIGHT STOP FORGIVE ME
EMILEE

She handed it back. "Yes, that's correct."

"That will be one mark fifteen."

She got it from her purse and paid him. "How soon will it be
delivered?"

"Within the hour, assuming he is at the address you've given me."

"Thank you." She turned and hurried out the main doors. Her taxi
driver wasn't there, but there were others. She went to the nearest one,
gave him the address, and climbed inside.

*5:42 p.m.—Imperial German Army Barracks,
Finckensteinallee, Berlin*

With a long, weary sigh, Colonel von Schiller got to his feet and began pacing back and forth. "So, let me briefly summarize what has been going on here for the past few weeks." He frowned at Hans. "Frankly, I'm a little surprised that you haven't read all of this in the newspapers."

Hans shrugged. "I had a lot of bad nightmares from what the doctors call 'shell shock' or 'combat fatigue.' I found that reading the news tended to make them worse. So while I was back home in Bavaria with my parents, I deliberately asked them not to talk about what was going on or show me the newspapers."

"Well then, I'm sorry if what I say now makes them worse again, because this is a living nightmare that we're in."

"I'm doing much better now."

"*Gut.*" Von Schiller took a quick breath. "As it became clear that Germany had lost the war, the effect on the German people was devastating. It wasn't just the loss of millions of our young men and the humiliation of losing the war; it was the realization that the sacrifices had all been for nothing. Rationing, food shortages, suppressed wages, loss of some of our richest lands—all of these were demoralizing to the people. And they demanded that those responsible be held accountable. Kaiser Wilhelm fled the country in disgrace, and overnight, the Social Democrats seized power, promising to restore order, dignity, and stability to the Fatherland.

"But at the same time there were other voices clamoring to be heard, voices that accused the new government of being too weak and morally bankrupt. The Socialist and Communist parties—which held only small minorities in the *Reichstag* at that point—rushed in to fill the political vacuum. In a matter of days—literally days!—local, city, and state governments all across Germany were overthrown, and the leftists were raising the red flag of revolution over the Fatherland. And the Spartacans were the worst."

"Who?"

"The Spartacans. They take their name from Spartacus of ancient Rome. He was the slave and gladiator who led the slaves in a revolt against the emperor. Get it? The slaves rising up against their masters? It's actually a brilliant name, if you're part of the enslaved working classes. But these Spartacans are really radical. They believe in revolution for revolution's sake. Tear down the old order so the proletariat—the working classes—may rise up and take their rightful place. That's why they call themselves Red Communists. In their eyes, the reordering of society requires bloodshed."

"But we've always had these groups in our midst. Why all of a sudden are they in power?"

"Because events have come together in ways we have not seen before. The monarchies are collapsing of their own corruption and decadence. The poor, who have been exploited for centuries, are now told they can become part of a new dictatorship, the so-called 'dictatorship of the proletariat.' In other words, the new ruling class will be the working poor. Imagine how exciting that must sound to them. Centuries of smoldering resentment has exploded into a consuming fire."

The colonel stopped, peering down at Hans. "Is it any wonder that the people are so utterly exhausted, so desperate for some escape from this terrible tragedy, that they are willing to listen to any wild-eyed demagogue who comes along and promises them something better? Think about it: states like Bavaria, Saxony, and Brunswick; great cities like Hamburg and Hannover and dozens of others are now flying red flags."

"And now Berlin?" Hans asked slowly, shocked deeply. "Is that what this strike is about? Are they trying to overthrow the government here as well?"

"*Trying?*" von Schiller exploded. "They're succeeding, Sergeant. This city is in a crisis. For example, right after the Armistice, there was a large demonstration by the leftist groups at the main police station here in Berlin. They were demanding that the president of the police step aside and one of their own number be put in charge. Then this man called Emil Eichhorn, a swine of the lowest order, pushed his way through the crowd, walked into the station, and announced that he had been appointed by the people to be the police president. He told the current president that he and his officers would be given safe escort through the mob if they surrendered without a struggle. *And they did!* They walked out and turned one of the most pivotal centers of power over to the radicals without a single man resisting them."

"And the government didn't respond to that?"

He snorted in disgust. "Of course they did. In the same way they did to everything else. They wrung their hands. Thumped the pulpits. Made impassioned speeches and then authorized Eichhorn to be paid and given full control of the police."

Von Schiller was raging now as he paced back and forth. "And do you want to know what this 'people's grand leader' has done for the poor since coming to power? Well, he now pays himself a monthly salary of eighteen hundred marks. His wife is now a highly paid clerk in his office, though she has no clerical skills. His young daughter receives a salary for greeting visitors who come to headquarters. He opened the jails and freed over fifty hard-core criminals. He's also using the police budget to finance new *Freikorps* units, made up mostly of deserters and other lowlifes. In other words, he's engaging in open treason. He's even handing out weapons to teenage hooligans and women if they promise to support 'the cause.' And what does the government do? Like Chicken Little, they run about crying, 'The sky is falling, the sky is falling. Whatever shall we do?'"

As the colonel paused for breath, Hans nodded at him. "Yes," he said evenly.

Von Schiller pulled back a little. "Yes what?"

"Yes, I am willing to defend the very government I so bitterly despise."

The colonel's eyes narrowed as he studied Hans's face. "And why is that, Sergeant Eckhardt?"

"Because," Hans said, "it is better to be governed by the weak than to be ruled by the mad."

Von Schiller's eyes were dancing with pleasure. "I knew it. I knew you were the kind of man I've been looking for."

"What do you want me to do?"

"Well, here's the deal. I am happy to say that the government has finally recognized that we are on the brink of civil war. About a month ago, as you may have heard, nine regular army divisions returned from the Western Front. They are loyal to the government and ready to fight for our freedoms. But it's going to take some time to get them ready and mobilized. So in the meantime, our ministers have authorized us to form *Freikorps* units of our own from the numerous men like yourself who have been discharged from the army but have no employment. The pay is generous, and the government will provide arms from government armories."

"How generous?" Hans asked, trying not to sound too eager.

"Fifty marks a week, with a hundred-mark bonus payable on enlistment."

Hans whistled softly. *Fifty marks?* His pay as a platoon sergeant had been only ten marks a week.

Von Schiller went on, "My commanding officer is authorized to organize several *Freikorps* battalions loyal to the government to stand against the revolutionists until the regular army can join us. I have been given command of one of those battalions."

"But those men are scattered all over the country. It will take weeks to assemble them."

"Actually, no. There are thousands of them here in Berlin. Due to the generous pay incentives authorized by the government, we have been able to organize three battalions thus far. All of them are rapidly approaching full strength, and all of them are mostly armed.

"Three battalions?" Hans was stunned. At full strength, a battalion was over a thousand men.

"Now do you see why I am interested in you?"

"Yes, I. . . ." Hans shook his head. This was all so astonishing.

"So, I am looking for men who meet the following four conditions: One, they are totally loyal to me. Two, they are combat veterans. Three, they will not hesitate to do battle with the Communists or anyone else opposing the government, even if they are fellow German citizens. And four, they are able to start service immediately."

"Define immediately."

"Tonight," came the answer. "It looks like we are going to march on central Berlin tomorrow morning. So?"

"I'm definitely interested, sir. But I have two or three questions."

"Go ahead."

"I had my identity card, railway pass, and ration book stolen when I was attacked."

"Yes, I noticed that when I searched you. When I found no papers, I took you for a deserter. We have an estimated sixty thousand deserters in Berlin, and they're scum. They have violated their oath of allegiance to the Empire and turned their backs on their own brothers-in-arms. They are contemptible. I really was considering shooting you and saying you tried to get away. But when my wife told me that you had come back and returned her money, that . . ." He shrugged.

"But anyway, in answer to your question, Corporal Jürgens is already on working on getting you new papers. He thinks he can have them by tonight."

More astonishment. "Including a railway pass?"

"Yes, good for your time of service with the *Freikorps*, if you accept our offer."

"That's a huge relief for me, Colonel. Second, I need to go to my hotel and get the rest of my things. It should only take a minute, but as you can see, I'm not up to walking very—"

"I've also asked Jürgens to arrange a driver for you as soon as we're done here."

"Thank you. Third, as you have seen, with my cracked ribs, I'm pretty beat up, sir. That's going to limit what I can do physically for a few days. If you're picturing me charging down the street in hot pursuit of these Spartacans, then I'm not your man."

"I understand. What else?"

"Would I keep the same rank I have now?"

"No. I'm very short on officers. Haven't found one to lead Third Company yet. So I've asked my commanding officer if I can make you a master sergeant and give you command of the company. That would make you senior in rank to the other platoon sergeants and, for all intents and purposes, would put you in command of Third Company. You'll be a lieutenant in every way but name, pay, and grade."

Hans's head was swirling. Was this some incredibly wonderful dream? It was unbelievable. All he could think of to say was, "That's typical for a master sergeant, sir."

Von Schiller laughed. "True, master sergeants keep the army moving. Oh, and that gives you ten marks more per week and an additional hundred marks in your signing bonus. Is that satisfactory to you?"

Hans smiled lazily. "Considering I came within a hair's breadth of being shot this morning, yes, sir! That is quite satisfactory."

"Anything else?"

Hans thought for a moment and started to shake his head, but then he had another thought that he couldn't resist. "Does your wife know you are making me this offer, sir?"

The colonel slapped his leg and roared. "Not on your life. I would rather face a hundred Communists than her wrath if she finds out. I think I will tell her that I took you out and had you shot. I'm not positive, but that might possibly satisfy her."

"Then count me in, sir."

Chapter Notes

The idea that outlying military hospitals were put on standby to help deal with massive casualties during the January uprising is a device of the author and not based on any known historical records.

Though Colonel Stefan von Schiller is a fictional character, his representation of events is accurate, including the weakness of the government, the seizing of police headquarters, and the forming and calling up of *Freikorps* units to help the regular army put down the uprising.

CHAPTER
29

January 15, 1919, 5:48 p.m.—Hotel Lindenberg,
Prenzlauer Berg District, Berlin

Private," Hans said, leaning forward. "If you see a postbox, pull over. I need to mail a letter."

"Yes, sir."

"Don't call me sir," he snapped, fighting back a smile as he remembered Sergeant Jessel, his old drill sergeant from basic training. "I am not a commissioned officer. I work for my pay."

The private laughed. "Yes, Sergeant."

Hans reached in his tunic pocket and withdrew the envelope. He took out the letter, written on plain army stationery, and opened it and read slowly.

Dearest Mama and Papa,

I am sorry that you have not heard from me before this. Can't explain now, but three days ago, things kind of fell apart for me. Pretty badly, actually. Wasn't sure I would pull out. But things are good now. In fact, very good. I would have called, but Berlin is in turmoil and telephone exchanges are not working. Will call or write as soon as possible, but rushing off now to accept a new full-time job.

Mama, thank you for your prayers. Something in me finds it very difficult to believe in God anymore, but I know that you believe in Him, and perhaps that is enough for the both of us. You know I don't believe in miracles, but today miraculous things happened that are far too remarkable to be mere coincidence. I credit that to your prayers and Emilee's. No other explanation seems sufficient. So don't stop.

It may be several more days yet until I can call. I wasn't able to contact Emilee, and there's no time to write her now. If she calls, please tell her I am okay and not to give up on me.

All my love, Hans

"There's a mailbox up ahead, Sergeant Major."

"I see it." Hans folded the letter and put it back in the envelope and then quickly sealed the flap. He checked to make sure the stamp was firmly attached and handed it to the driver.

Once the driver was back in the car, Hans leaned forward again. "The hotel is about a block off of *Unter den Linden*, about three blocks ahead on the right. I'll show you where to turn."

"Yes, Sergeant Major."

Hans grinned. He had his own driver who said 'Yes, Sergeant Major' or 'No, Sergeant Major' about every ten seconds. He could get used to this.

But as the driver pulled up in front of the hotel, Hans had another idea. "On second thought, Private, let's go around the block. There's an alley behind the hotel."

The driver gave him a puzzled look but shrugged and accelerated again.

"The owner of the place is a sour old man who's always claiming I owe him more money, even though I'm paid up through the end of the month. There's a back stairway."

"Yes, Sergeant Major. Whatever you say."

Five minutes later, Hans walked slowly to the car, opened the door, and tossed his rucksack into the backseat. He turned and looked up at the back of the hotel for a long moment, and then mumbling something under his breath, he climbed in. The driver turned around. "Where to now, Sergeant Major?"

"Back to the barracks."

As the car started forward, Hans opened the white envelope, took out the letter, and read it through again slowly. Finished, he stared out the window, feeling the anger starting to rise. He understood her bitterness. Emilee had no way of knowing why he had disappeared, why he hadn't called or written. But surely she knew about the turmoil in Berlin. Was she serious about calling off the engagement? Without even talking to him?

Hans read her words again, his eyes stopping on one line in particular. *Right now, I have enough people in my life who require me to care for them. I am too weary in spirit to take on another.*

He hadn't asked her to help him. Even though the thought had come to him, he had rejected it. Even in the desperate situation he was in, he hadn't asked her for anything. So what was she talking about? Hans blew out a long breath. *Then go! I don't need you to care for me.*

He folded the letter again and returned it to its envelope and then stared at the window. *Hey, Mama! Forget what I said about your prayers. I think I'm getting about all the miracles I can handle right now.* He laughed softly and bitterly. The pattern was back. The Divine Trickster was at it again. Exhilaration, despair. Jubilation, misery. Hope, hopelessness.

He took the letter in both hands, prepared to rip it in half and chuck it out the window. It was then that his use of the word *pattern* hit him. It was the same word Emilee had used that night she told him about her father. That was the word her mother had used to describe her father's fall into alcoholism.

It was my job to go to the pubs or into the beer halls or into some flophouse hotel. And I'd kick aside the empty bottles and breathe through my mouth so that I didn't have to smell the stale beer and the vomit and his pants where he had wet himself, and I'd drag my father home.

Hans put the envelope back in his pocket and then lay back and closed his eyes, sick at heart as he realized just how utterly, colossally stupid he had been.

6:55 p.m.

Emilee instructed the taxi driver to park across the street from the hotel. Then she settled down to wait, peering through the open window at the front entrance. Five minutes later, her patience was rewarded. The hotel owner, now dressed in a suit and overcoat and wearing a Homburg hat, came out of the hotel accompanied by a woman of approximately the same age. They turned right and disappeared down the street.

Emilee leaned over the seat and touched the driver on the shoulder. "Wait here. I shouldn't be long."

"Yes, Fräulein."

She was immensely relieved to see that it was a boy of about sixteen or seventeen behind the front desk. She pushed the door open and strode across the lobby. As soon as he saw her, he flashed her a warm smile. "Good evening, Fräulein."

"*Guten Abend.* I'm Fräulein Fromme. I—"

"Yes, my father said you might be coming. My name is Georg."

"Has Sergeant Eckhardt returned yet, Georg?"

He frowned. "*Nein*, Fräulein. To be honest, I am worried about him."

"There is one thing I needed to do for him," she said. "Could I get his room key, please?"

Before handing it to her, he hesitated. "The room is pretty bad, Fräulein."

"I know. It's all right."

He handed the key to her. Emilee took the stairs two at a time, praying that Georg was right, that Hans hadn't been there. It was fully dark now, and she had to grope for the light switch. When it came on she saw two things simultaneously. His rucksack was gone, and the clothes and other personal items previously scattered around the floor were gone with it. Then her stomach lurched when she saw the bed. The letter was gone, but the personal toilet items she had bought for Hans were still where she had left them.

Barely mindful of the smell, she searched the room quickly, desperately. Nothing.

Cursing herself for being so quick to react, she felt her eyes start to burn, and this time it wasn't from the smell.

"Is there anything I can do to help you, Fräulein?" Georg asked anxiously as Emilee stumbled past him, half blinded by tears.

She turned back. "Can you tell me anything more?"

There was a slow shake of his head. "*Ja*. He said he was famished. But . . . I'm not sure what he was going to do; he didn't have any money."

Her head jerked up. "Wait. He didn't have any money? That's not true. He had lots of money."

Georg looked down, staring at his hands. "When did you last talk to him, Fräulein?"

"On Sunday."

There was a deep sigh, filled with pain. "You are engaged to Sergeant Eckhardt, no?"

"Yes." *At least I was.*

He came out from behind the desk and pointed to the lounge area. "You'd better sit down."

When he finished his account several minutes later, Emilee's eyes were wide with horror. "How badly was he injured?"

"The doctor said he probably had two or three cracked ribs. The leader of the gang hit him in the face with his ring. Twice. Each cut required six or seven stitches." He went on, but she didn't hear him.

She buried her face in her hands and began to sob. "Oh, Hans," she cried over and over. "What have I done? What have I done?"

7:25 p.m.—East Railway Station, Friedrichshain-Kreuzberg District, Berlin

Emilee's eyes were still red and puffy when she walked up to the ticket counter. She guessed that was why the ticket agent was staring at her. She ignored it. "Could you tell me if the last train to Pasewalk tonight has been canceled?"

He shook his head. "*Nein*, but we are expecting word any moment that it will be."

She sighed. "Do you know of a hotel near here where I might get a room for the night?"

"But, Fräulein, the 7:30 train has not departed yet. Would you like to purchase a ticket for that one?"

"It's still here?"

"Yes, Fräulein. Would you like a ticket?"

"Yes, I would. I need to go home."

CHAPTER
30

January 15, 1919, 7:30 p.m.—Imperial German Army Barracks,
Finckensteinallee, Berlin

Colonel von Schiller had described Gustav Noske as a humorless man without many social graces. And yet, von Schiller's voice had been tinged with respect and admiration. Seeing the puzzled look Hans gave him, he had explained it this way. "I would probably never invite a man like Noske to dine with us." He chuckled. "Monika would be horrified. But if I have to go to war, this is the man I would choose to follow."

As Hans watched Noske walk to the podium at the front of the assembly hall, he better understood why. He was not overly tall—barely six feet, if that—with closely cropped dark hair, large ears, thick, bushy eyebrows, a prominent nose, and a thick handlebar mustache. There was not any trace of a smile, either present or past, around that mouth. In some ways he looked like a prison guard on watch—alert, grim, determined, implacable—a man with no tolerance for sympathy, weakness, incompetence, or stupidity. Just the kind of man you wanted to lead you into battle.

He had not been in the army per se, according to the colonel, but he was a member of Parliament during the war and became an expert

314

on military matters. A strong right-wing Socialist, he had negotiated through the sailors' mutiny with such skill that the sailors had elected him chairman of their Soldiers' Council. But when the sailors accepted deserters, leftists, radicals, and freeloaders and turned against the government, Noske was called. When he learned what was happening, his answer was simple. "What you need here is a bloodhound. And I will be it." In under twenty-four hours, he had driven the sailors out of the palace, had them in full retreat, and had earned for himself the nickname *der Bluthund*, "The Bloodhound."

As the political crisis continued to escalate, the ministers of the government announced that Noske had been appointed as Minister of the Military. *Der Bluthund* had been called on once again. And he had full authority to put down the revolt.

The officers and non-coms of the newly formed First Battalion quickly quieted as Noske stood at the podium. They watched their commander-in-chief with curiosity and anticipation. *Der Bluthund* tapped the microphone with one finger, causing it to screech loudly. A faint smile came and went. "It works," he noted. Laughter rippled through the crowd. Then he leaned forward. "All of those here who are associated with the nine regular army divisions that recently returned to Berlin, please stand."

Hans, who was about halfway back from the front, turned and looked around. He was not surprised that there were only about twenty men standing. Von Schiller had told him that the army divisions were still being brought up to strength but wouldn't be ready for another day or two.

"General," Noske said to a man seated on the stand behind him, "how soon can we expect to see the first of your regular army troops?"

A man in full uniform with two stars on each shoulder stood up. "Give me two days, sir, and I'll have three thousand pairs of boots marching through the Brandenburg Gate. On the third day I'll give you three thousand more, and that many more each day thereafter until you have all 20,000 men at your back."

Noske grunted in satisfaction. "Thank you, General." He turned back to the men. "Now there's a soldier's response for you, men. What a day that was when the general's nine divisions marched into Berlin last month. I was there, and I have never been prouder. It was like 1914 all over again. I watched them march through the Brandenburg Gate in perfect cadence like the veterans they are. Every rank, every column was as straight as the shaft of an arrow. Their uniforms were clean and pressed. Their boots looked like black glass. Their rifle barrels gleamed."

He half closed his eyes, as if seeing them again now. "And the people. Ah, the people. The Communists would have you believe that the people despise the army. But that day, the people lined the streets, shouting and waving handkerchiefs, scarves, and flags. Women ran forward and festooned their rifles with flowers. Children put garlands around their necks. Men, weeping as unashamedly as the women, hung wreaths over the cannons that rolled behind them.

"And now we are being called on again," Noske continued. "To do what?" He slammed his fist down against the podium, and the sound was like a gunshot. "I'll tell you what," he roared. "To save our Fatherland from becoming"—now he emphasized every word with another blow to the podium—"ONE . . . MORE . . . MINDLESS . . . GODLESS . . . PUPPET . . . RUSSIAN . . . BOLSHEVIK . . . STATE."

The response was thunderous. The rafters shook. Had there been a Communist in the room, Hans had no question that he would have been torn to pieces. No wonder they called this guy the Bloodhound. Every man in the room was baying for the blood of their enemies.

Noske let it roll for over a minute before he raised his hands. Everyone sat down again. Hans was grateful, for the yelling had set his ribs afire.

"Now, you *Freikorps* units. You stand in the breach until the regular army can close ranks with us. But you are no less brave, no less prepared, no less loyal than are they. Would you like to know how the Communists feel about the army? Well, I'll tell you. Liebknecht and his Spartacans recently formed a new *Freikorps* unit. Would you like to know what they chose as their name?"

Several voices cried out yes.

"Their official name is 'The People's Council of Deserters, Stragglers, and Furloughed Soldiers.'"

Laughter and hoots of disbelief rang out. Hans wondered if this was some kind of joke.

"You think I made that up, don't you?" Noske went on. "Well, I did not. That's how much respect these men have for themselves. The Spartacans have gathered the dregs of the military. These are the men who left their posts, who threw down their weapons and ran like frightened dogs. They are scum. Vermin. Rats slinking through the sewers of the city." He scoffed in disgust. "Know what we do to deserters in times of war? We shoot them down like the dogs they are."

Thunderous applause. Noske let it go on for a moment, and then again signaled for silence.

"The Spartacans are telling these men of theirs that you won't fire on them, that you are brothers-in-arms, fellow soldiers, part of the Brotherhood. And how do you feel about that?"

The response was deafening. Men were stomping on the floor, pounding their hands together, shouting in anger. And Hans was one of them. *This is the real brotherhood*, he thought. Courageous men in war. There was nothing like it, and it sent his blood singing.

Noske held up his hands again, and gradually the noise subsided and the men took their seats. "Now, my brethren," he said when it was quiet again. "There is one thing I need to say to you. Not all of the people you are going to see tomorrow are Bolsheviks and revolutionists. Many of those who will be there tomorrow are the people of the Fatherland—the poor, the workers, the farmers, the unionists, the old and the infirm. Are they the enemy?"

"No!" the group shouted back at him.

"No? And what if they have rifles in their hands? What do you do to them?"

Noske leaned forward. "How can you tell the difference between those poor wretches who are innocent pawns and those who are hard-core leftists ready to die for their cause?"

Finally, an officer near the front raised his hand. Noske pointed at him. "Yes, Captain."

"If they pick up a rifle?"

"Exactly!" he shouted. "Or if they pick up a stone or a bottle. If they are setting fire to a building. Then they are the enemy and they must be stopped. That is why we are here. If we do not stop them, all is lost. But if they are simply standing by, watching events unfold, you do not—you must not!—fire on them, for these are the people that we fight *for*, not against."

Noske raised one hand and briefly rubbed at his eyes. "Almost certainly, innocents will die tomorrow. Not long ago, as we put down the sailors' mutiny, I found a sixteen-year-old girl lying in a pool of blood, breathing her last breath."

The hush in the room was total now. "Was it our fire or theirs that struck this innocent down? We shall never know. What I do know is that the picture of that girl shall always be in my mind."

"But," he raised a fist and shook it at them as his voice roared out again. "But had I known in advance that an innocent girl might die, would I have let those mutinous traitors slink away to fight again another day? NO! I would not. I cannot! The collective good of the Fatherland is greater than the good of any one individual."

Just then a colonel entered the room and went quickly to the podium. He had a sheet of paper in one hand. He handed it to Noske, who read it quickly, looked up at the colonel, and said something the microphone didn't catch. The colonel nodded.

Noske nodded back, and the colonel moved away. The

Bloodhound's face was grave as he turned back to the microphone. "My brothers," he said softly, "we have a new development. As you know, the government has demanded that Emil Eichhorn, that pig of a man who claims to be our legitimate president of the metropolitan police, step down. Today, his supporters called for a massive rally to protest his removal from office. Hundreds of thousands are expected to respond tomorrow. But there is something new in this. Even as we meet here, Karl Liebknecht and Rosa Luxemburg, those two traitorous leaders of the Spartacus movement, are urging their followers to rise up and take immediate action to overthrow the government. And their people have responded. They have attacked and seized"—he raised the paper and read from it—"the *Vorwärts* offices and printing plant."

Gasps and cries of shock exploded all around Hans. *Vorwärts* was the central organ of the Social Democratic Party of Germany and a leading newspaper in Berlin.

Noske went on grimly. "We have reports that they have already changed the name of the paper to *The Reds Forward* and will print an edition tomorrow morning telling Berlin that the 'real revolutionists have seized power' and that 'no power on earth can take it from them.'"

"In addition," Noske went on grimly, "they have also successfully stormed and taken the newspaper plants of the *Tageblatt* newspaper and the Ullstein Company plant, which prints the *Berlin Morning Post* and *Zeitung am Mittag.*"

Hans swore softly under his breath. He was not a Berliner and didn't recognize those names, but from the shock going on around him, he assumed these were not small losses.

Noske thumped the pulpit once to get their attention again. "I am not finished," he said. When they quieted he went on, not reading now. "There have also been bloody clashes tonight at Wilhelm Plaza, Potsdamer Plaza, and along *Unter den Linden* near the Brandenburg Gate."

He lifted the paper again. "There is one small light in this dim and dark tunnel," he said, waving the paper back and forth. "The government, who, if I do say so, has been as weak as water in their response to these criminals, is finally mobilizing. We are not going to stand by and let it happen. All four battalions will start deploying at oh-seven-hundred hours tomorrow."

Every man in the room leaped to his feet, shouting and whistling and stomping. Noske actually smiled and then raised a hand, shouted something back, and turned and left the room.

8:08 p.m.

Hans walked swiftly up to where Colonel von Schiller was standing. He stayed back a few yards, seeing that two captains—probably two of his company commanders—were talking with him. As soon as they finished, the colonel waved Hans forward. "All right, Eckhardt. What is it?"

"I don't mean to be presumptuous, sir, and I'm sure you've already thought about this, but I'd like to recommend we do some recon before we deploy tomorrow."

"Reconnaissance?"

Hans took a quick breath. This was sensitive. His colonel had no battlefield experience, but colonels didn't always take warmly to a master sergeant giving advice.

"Well, sir, in a normal battlefield situation, we'd typically send out a full platoon. But here, I think that would be too much. Too obvious. It could trigger a reaction we don't want."

"I agree. Go on."

"I've been thinking about what Noske said. About civilians. About the innocent. That was brilliant. He's right. That's going to be a major challenge for us. So, what if I were to slip into the city tomorrow morning while the units are getting in place?"

"Just you? They'll cut your throat."

"Not if I go in dressed as a laborer, sir. Not if they think I'm one of them." Hans pulled a face. "Actually, I am one of them. I'm a *milchbauer*, remember?" Then he touched a fingertip to the stitches on his cheek and the bruises around his eyes. "And you might say that these are my bona fides. People will ask what happened to me. I'll tell them I was beaten up by government thugs."

Colonel von Schiller was too smart not to see the value of what Hans was offering, so Hans rushed on. "What I'd be looking for tomorrow would be how many civilians there are—are they organized? How many are carrying arms? Have their leaders given them strategic objectives? Sir, we're taking in machine guns and a couple of light cannons. I agree that some innocents may end up dying in this conflict, and I realize that every battle has collateral damage, but if we were to open fire on a crowd of unarmed civilians, we'd be playing right into the hands of the enemy."

Eyes somber and thoughtful, von Schiller studied Hans for several seconds. "And how do you plan to 'slip in,' as you say it? I saw you wincing every time you got up and down tonight. We're three or four miles from our assigned area. Don't tell me you can just walk in."

"If I could have that same driver, I'd go in early, sir. Then I'd join up with you as soon as you arrive."

"What about your four platoons?"

"I'll meet with my four sergeants tonight. They'll know what to do. I'll be there when they arrive, and I'll take command."

Von Schiller chewed on his lower lip thoughtfully, obviously intrigued. "It's a huge risk."

"Sir, combat is always about risk. It's how you manage it that makes the difference."

That seemed to make up his mind. "Well put, Eckhardt. All right. Tell your sergeants what's going on, and then see Corporal Jürgens to help you get whatever you need. Our battalion is to assemble just west of the Brandenburg Gate. I want you there when we arrive. No excuses."

"Sir, I can do that. But the crowds will probably still be gathering by then. I'm guessing the parade or formal demonstrations won't start until eleven. If I leave too early, I'll miss a lot, sir."

The colonel harrumphed something but then nodded. "All right, but if anything at all starts to unravel, I want you back here on the double. I don't care if your ribs hurt or not. You double-time it back to our battalion. I need you to lead your company. Got it?"

"Yes, sir. Thank you, sir." Hans saluted and walked away.

Chapter Notes

What is called the January Revolution in Berlin started on January 5, 1919, with a massive rally in support of Emil Eichhorn, the man who had taken over as commander of the Berlin police. It quickly escalated into a full-scale battle between the government and the revolutionary forces. It lasted for ten days before it was finally put down.

In the novel, I have the revolution starting about ten days later than it actually did and the events compressed into a shorter time period to cover all of the key elements.

Gustav Noske is a real person who was given charge by the government to put down the rebellion. One source mentioned him addressing the troops but gave no specific details on time or place. So his words here are mine, though they are based on what we know about him and about the situation at the time.

Other events as described here are factual. For example, nine regular army divisions returned to Berlin on December 10, 1918. They were greeted by the people with great celebration (see *German Revolution,* 210).

In the government's battle with the rebellious People's Marine Division, a teenage girl was hit and killed by a stray bullet while riding on a trolley. Noske led that assault on the sailors (see *German Revolution* 219–20; *Bloodhounds,* 3).

As ridiculous as it seems to us, Karl Liebknecht, leader of the Spartacans, did actually ask the government for permission to form a unit called the "Council of Deserters, Stragglers, and Furloughed Soldiers." Permission was refused, but he formed it anyway and armed many of them. They became a major factor in what followed (see *German Revolution,* 187).

The Spartacans and the other radical leftist groups seized several of the major newspaper offices and printing plants as described above (see *German Revolution,* 226–27).

January 16, 1919, 1:30 a.m.—Fromme Home, Pasewalk

Weary beyond belief, Emilee walked with her head down as she approached the door of their home. But as she turned up the walk, she stopped. The sitting room lamp was on. A lurch of panic shot through her, and she hurried up the walk and burst through the door.

It was Ernst who rose from his chair to greet her. He gave her a hug and kissed her on both cheeks. "How was the train ride?" he asked gently.

"Long. Cold. Slow. What are you doing up?"

"I have something for you." He walked over to the lamp table where an envelope was visible. She felt her heart leap for joy.

"From Hans?" she cried, quickly joining him.

"*Nein.* I'm sorry. It's from *Onkel* Artur." He handed it to her.

To Emilee's surprise, it was a telegram. "Is this the one I sent to him?" she asked.

He shook his head. "Read it," was all he said.

She opened it quickly, stepped closer to the lamp, and held it up.

EMILEE STOP LEARNED FROM TICKET AGENT YOU
ARE IN PASEWALK STOP MUCH RELIEVED STOP
HOSPITAL UNIT ACTIVATED STOP SETTING UP
AID STATION IN BERLIN TOMORROW MORNING
STOP THINGS HERE NOT GOOD STOP SO GLAD
YOU ARE SAFE STOP UNDER NO CIRCUMSTANCES
ARE YOU TO RETURN STOP HOSPITAL NEEDS YOU
THERE STOP WILL UNDERTAKE INQUIRY INTO
LOCATION OF HANS IF POSSIBLE STOP WILL KEEP
YOU ADVISED STOP LOVE ARTUR

Emilee looked up, stricken. "He's in Berlin?"

Ernst nodded. "Yes. They left right after noon." He took his sister by the elbow. "He means it, Emilee. He was very firm with me before he left. You are not to go back there."

"I have to, Ernst."

"Emilee," Ernst said gravely, "*Onkel* Artur said that if you disobey his instructions, you will no longer be employed at the hospital."

"*What?*" she gasped.

"He's serious about this, Emmy. He doesn't want you in Berlin. Is that clear enough?"

7:12 a.m.—Eckhardt dairy farm, Graswang, Bavaria

Inga Eckhardt nearly jumped out of her nightdress when the telephone rang just above her head. She was kneeling at one of the chairs beside the kitchen table, earnestly praying. She scrambled to her feet and snatched the receiver off its hook.

"*Hallo,*" she said in a low voice into the mouthpiece, her heart pounding loudly in her ears.

"*Hallo.* Inga?"

Her hopes plummeted like a rock. It was not Hans.

"*Ja,* is this Emilee?" She was looking up the stairs and listening with her other ear to see if the phone had awakened Hans Sr.

"Yes, Inga. It's me. I'm so sorry to call you so early but—"

"Oh, my dear," Inga said with a chuckle, "seven o'clock in the morning is not early for dairy farmers. The boys have all the cows milked already and the day is well underway."

"*Gut*. I was afraid I would wake you up."

"Have you heard from Hans?" Inga asked eagerly.

Emilee's answer was a strangled sob followed by uncontrollable weeping.

Feeling her knees go weak, Inga blindly grabbed for a chair and leaned against it. She listened as Emilee fought to get control of herself until she could stand it no longer.

"Emilee!" she said sharply. "Tell me what is wrong. Has something happened to Hans?"

"Yes!"

Inga gasped and went limp.

"No, no!" Emilee cried. "I didn't mean it that way. He's not dead. At least I don't think so."

Inga's eyes closed.

"Oh, Inga," Emilee sobbed, "I've done a terrible thing."

"Emilee," Inga said quietly. "Calm yourself. Tell me what's wrong. What happened?"

It took several more seconds, but finally Emilee got control of herself and began to talk. And it all came out. She told Inga again how Hans had asked her to marry him on Sunday night before leaving. That, of course, brought a demand that Emilee share all the details. Inga was so thrilled that Emilee almost just hung up then. How could she dash a mother's hopes with such cruel news? But she took a quick breath and forged on.

"Inga, I don't have a lot of time. As you know, I went to Berlin to find Hans."

"And did you find him?"

"Yes. Well, no, not really. I went to the hotel. He had given me

325

the address. And I. . . . And I. . . ." She lost control again. "I can't say it, Inga. I don't want to hurt you."

"Emilee. He's my son. I need to know."

So, in halting sentences, mingled with a lot of tears, it all came out. The hotel. The filthy room. The empty wine and bourbon bottles. The unbearable smell.

Inga had to sit down. It felt as though someone were sucking the breath out of her. *Oh, Hans. Will you never learn?* But all she said was, "What happened next?"

"The more I thought about it," Emilee said, in a bare whisper now, "the angrier I got. This is what I went through with my father. If anything went wrong, even the tiniest setback, he turned to the bottle. It didn't matter that he was drinking our food money. Or if Mama was sick. I—"

"I understand, Emilee, but tell me what happened."

"I wrote Hans a letter and left it in his room."

Inga gave a long, pained sigh. "And you told him that you didn't want to marry him anymore."

"Yes," Emilee whispered. "I basically said that I never wanted to see him again. Oh, Inga!" she burst out. "I'm so sorry."

"If you're sorry, then go back and get the letter, Emilee. Before he returns. He doesn't have to know that you were there. You can give it to him later, when you can talk."

"I can't, Inga," Emilee wailed. "I went back to get it, but Hans had already come and got it." And then she lost control and began to sob again. "It wasn't there. The letter was gone."

That took Inga completely aback. "I don't understand."

"The boy at the hotel thinks Hans came to his room through the back entrance. All of his personal things were gone too."

"So he *is* alive."

"Yes." It was barely audible. "And he has my letter." Emilee continued to cry as she told Inga what Georg, the hotel clerk, had told her about the beating.

For a moment, Inga thought she was going to throw up.

"Inga?" Emilee's voice rang out clearly through the earpiece. Inga stood up again so she could speak into the mouthpiece.

"Yes? I'm here."

"Can I ask you a question?"

"You want to know if you should marry my son?"

"Yes!" Emilee burst out. "That's assuming I can find him. Or that he will ever speak to me again. I know that he went through a terrible experience, Inga. I understand that, but is this what it's going to be like every time something goes wrong? If so, I don't think I can stand it."

"Only you can answer that, Emilee," Inga said after a long moment of silence.

"But what do you think?" she cried. "You know him better than anyone."

Inga was silent again for a turn, and then she spoke. "This is not an answer to your question, my dear girl. But I need to say it."

"What?"

"I think you are the only one who can save him."

"But. . . ."

"I know, Emilee. And if that is going to be too much pain for you, then that is your answer."

There was no response, so Inga went on.

Tears were streaking Inga's cheeks now. "But if you can help him find the man that is somewhere deep inside him, then he will make you happy for the rest of your life. Of that, I am sure."

For a long, long moment, there was no sound from the telephone. Inga waited. Finally, Emilee spoke. "Thank you, Mama Eckhardt. Will you keep praying for us?"

Inga laughed softly. "I was on my knees when the telephone rang, Emilee."

CHAPTER
32

January 16, 1919, 7:35 a.m.—Pariser Plaza,
near the Brandenburg Gate, Berlin

It reminded Hans of a sluggish river after a heavy rain. The overall impression was that there was no color at all. On closer look, there were a few splashes of color here and there, but mostly everything was a greyish-brown current pouring through the Brandenburg Gate. Then it began to fan out as the people entered Pariser Plaza, like water on a river delta. They flowed past him almost soundlessly. No one spoke. Their heads were down, their eyes fixed on the ground. Hands were thrust in their pockets or clenched at their sides.

The sky was covered with a thin overcast that allowed some sunlight to filter through, warming the air enough to blunt the bitter cold of the previous few days. Which was fortunate, for very few had coats or jackets that were equal to the chill in the air.

Hans was pleased that the clothes Corporal Jürgens had procured for him carried the same drabness that he saw all around him. The only problem was that with his uniform on under his clothes, he looked fat and well fed, which no one else is this crowd did.

Three things had surprised him since his arrival. The first was that with his change of clothes, he had assumed he would blend in nicely. But as soon as they started arriving, he realized that he was still a distinct cut above these people. And it was more than just the clothes. He hadn't even thought about his hands. They were callused from carrying a rifle for four years, but his fingernails were clean, and the lines in his palm were not permanently darkened by grime that would never wash off. When he realized how starkly different his hands looked, he slipped over to one of the flowerbeds near the Brandenburg Gate and rubbed his hands in the dirt, making sure that every fingernail had dirt beneath it. He also wiped his hands on his coveralls so they didn't look like they had been freshly laundered.

The second thing that left him almost flabbergasted was how many of the men smoked. There was no breeze at all this morning, and clouds of blue-grey smoke hung over the moving mass of people. Probably two-thirds of the men and boys were smoking cigarettes. Hans had smoked off and on throughout his army career, but since getting out of the hospital, he had only smoked once or twice. Mostly that was financially driven. A pack of cigarettes cost twenty *Pfennige*. Where did they get the money? The answer came almost immediately, and it made Hans angry. They took it out of the mouths of their wives and children.

The third surprise for him was how many members of the crowd pouring into Pariser Plaza were women. They ranged in age from young girls in their early teens to *Grossmütter* with gnarled hands and faces lined deeply with wrinkles. And they were even more shabbily dressed than the men. Many wore shoes with one or both of the soles partly missing or loose. Their plain dresses hung limply from their near-skeletal frames. Thin scarves covered greasy, stringy hair. Many of the women had only light jackets over their flimsy dresses.

Last night Hans had confidently told Colonel von Schiller that he was one of the working class, that he would fit in. But now he knew he was wrong. These poor wretches were born, raised, and died in a poverty so total, so relentless, that it showed on their faces, in the thinness of their bodies, in their lifeless eyes and their broken spirits.

Whipped cream sandwiches? That was so far above what these people had ever known. And, to Hans's surprise, this realization moved him profoundly.

Just then a young girl, probably twelve or thirteen, who was passing by with her parents, glanced at Hans. She stopped dead, staring at him with a horrified look on her face. For a moment it startled him. Then he realized why she was looking at him like that. It was his face.

He smiled at her, but she was transfixed. Her parents went another few steps before they realized she had stopped, and then the mother turned to see why her daughter wasn't moving. "Nattie," she called softly. "Come, *Liebchen*. We must keep walking."

The girl seemed not to hear. She was a frail thing, with a thin face and cheeks that were hollow. Her hair was a light brown and her eyes—wide-set beneath almost blonde eyebrows and eyelashes—were a pale emerald. There were quite lovely.

The girl took a step closer, pain twisting her expression. Hans smiled. "*Guten Morgen*, Fräulein."

"*Nattie!*" Her father spoke more sharply.

The girl glanced his way but immediately focused on Hans again. Another step closer. "Does that hurt awfully bad?" she asked. Her accent was definitely Berliner, but her voice was as light as a feather. She looked like she was on the verge of tears.

"*Nein*," Hans answered softly. "Not much anymore."

Her mother grabbed Nattie's arm, greatly embarrassed. "I'm sorry, she's just a child."

"It's all right," Hans said. As her father came striding back, he held up a hand toward him. "Really, sir, it is all right." Then to the daughter: "Would you like to take a closer look?"

She was still staring at him, and her eyes seemed enormous now. "What are them black things? Bugs?"

Hans chuckled. "No, Nattie. They are stitches. Tiny threads used to sew up my cuts. They'll come out in a few days."

She came up to him, peering more closely. He turned his face slightly so she could see better. One hand came up tentatively, starting to reach out.

"Nattie! No!" her father barked. Her hand jerked back.

Turning to the father, Hans said, "Sir, she is just curious. I am not offended in any way." Then to her: "Would you like to touch them, Nattie?"

She glanced nervously at her father. After a moment, he nodded. Gingerly her hand came up. Her touch was so light that had it not been for her cold fingers, Hans might not have felt it. There was a soft gasp of wonder.

"Be gentle, Nattie," her mother warned.

"It doesn't hurt," Hans said a second time.

So she touched it again. Other people slowed to see what was happening. Hans smiled at them too.

She ran her fingertips lightly across the stitches, and then even more gently, she touched his actual wounds, eyes wide with wonder. "Was you hurt in an accident?" she asked.

He shook his head. "No."

"Who did such a terrible thing to you?" the mother asked.

"A gang of *Freikorps* thugs. I made the mistake of calling one of them a thief."

"Government *Freikorps*?" her father asked in disgust.

"*Ja, ja.* Swine, every one of them." Hans stepped forward and extended his hand. "I am Herr Hans Eckhardt."

The man hesitated but then took his hand. It was as if Hans had put his hand in a vice. As Hans looked down he saw that the man's thumbnail was black from a blow of some kind. The fingernails were ragged, and each had thick dirt beneath it. But what caught his eye were the veins on the man's hand. They stood out like cords of bluish steel. They reminded Hans of his father's hands. These were the hands of a man who had spent his life in hard manual harbor.

"I am Herr Jakob Litzser," he said in the same thick Berliner accent. "This is my wife, Anna, and my daughter, Natalee."

Hans shook both of their hands formally. "It is good to meet you all." Then he turned back to Jakob. "Are you going to the gathering over there?" He pointed across the square.

They could clearly see a large crowd gathering. There were two or three army trucks beyond the crowd and two or three platoons of soldiers standing around them. There was also a small farm truck with an open back with people standing in the back, which suggested this was going to be their speaking platform.

The soldiers were undoubtedly *Freikorps*, and probably part of "The People's Council of Deserters, Stragglers, and something-or-other." They looked the part. They were not in any kind of formation. They stood around, smoking and laughing, rifles slung casually over their shoulders. Even from this distance, Hans could see that their uniforms were slovenly and unkempt. Hans felt a wave of disgust. Colonel von Schiller had called them vermin. It was a good description.

"*Ja*," Jakob answered. "We're going there. Would you join us?"

"I would like that very much." Hans smiled at Anna and Nattie. "That is, if the ladies don't object."

Anna blushed deeply, probably at the thought of being called a lady. Nattie was delighted. She clapped her hands. "Good. Good," she cried.

Touching his left side briefly, he spoke to Jakob again. "My 'friends' also left me with three cracked ribs, so I have to stop and rest now and then. I move slowly, but I hope I will not slow you down too much."

"We are not in a hurry," Anna said softly.

"I hear that Herr Eichhorn is speaking today," Hans said. "Our beloved police president."

Jakob shrugged. "We were told that it was to be Herr Liebknecht."

"Ah, the leader of the Spartacan Party."

"*Ja*."

Anna spoke up. "They also say that Frau Luxemburg may speak too. She too is a leader of the Spartacans. She is a strong and powerful woman." The way she said it made Hans look at her more closely, but he couldn't tell if it had been said in admiration or fear—or maybe both.

"*Gut.* I have heard of her. I am glad I am here, then." Hans realized that his way of speaking was much more educated and refined than theirs, and decided he had to be more careful. Not with this family, but with others he might talk with. He fell into step beside Nattie, and they rejoined the flowing river of humanity.

8:15 a.m.

As they moved slowly across the square—partly to accommodate Hans's needs and partly from the sheer press of the crowd—they got to know each other, with Nattie eagerly peppering Hans with questions. He told them of his growing up on a dairy farm in Bavaria and that he had recently been released from four years of army service, both as a truck driver and a combat platoon sergeant. He explained that he was now looking for work in a city where the unemployment rate was at almost fifty percent. They clucked their sympathy softly.

Embarrassed by Nattie's openness, her parents kept trying to fend off her questions, but Hans, who was quite enchanted with her, kept assuring them it was all right.

Jakob worked on the furnace floor of a foundry just outside the city, and had been there since the age of seventeen. He was a member of the union—of course—and hoped to make shop steward in the next few years. They desperately needed the pay raise that would come with it.

As they talked, Hans studied Jakob's face, wondering if he was one of those who fit the pattern of Emilee's father, but he saw no signs of it. His eyes were clear, his nose was not pink and bulbous—a typical sign of a heavy drinker—and his hands were steady. He did have a persistent cough, which he said was from the effects of working in the smoke and dust around the furnaces, but he clearly was not a drinker. Nor did he smoke, it seemed.

This was a revelation to Hans. Emilee and her mother had been wrong. Yes, there was a pattern among the poor working-class men that led them down the path to alcoholism, but it was not a given. It wasn't inevitable or inescapable. They still had a choice. Hans made a note of that in his mind. He wanted to discuss it with Emilee.

To his surprise, Hans found himself being drawn more and more to these simple people. When Anna spoke of her family, her whole countenance changed. Jakob and Anna had five other children— Nattie being the oldest. The others were home with their *Oma*, Anna's mother, who also lived with them. And again Hans marveled.

He had seen workers' tenements before. Usually they filled a whole street, sometimes whole blocks. They were typically two stories high, but only one room wide and two rooms deep—so four rooms to a flat. The buildings were inevitably black with the soot and ashes of the factories that sustained them. Row after row of outhouses lined the narrow alleys behind each street, and raw sewage ran down the middle of them.

So, if there were nine people in the Litzser family, counting *Oma*, that meant they slept three to a bedroom. Hans guessed they had only one bed, or maybe two, between the nine of them. And he could not fathom how they could purchase enough food for nine people on Jakob's salary. Maybe, like so many women of the working class, Anna took in washing or did housecleaning.

"So, did your foreman let you have the day off to come in for the rally?" he asked Jakob.

Jakob and Anna exchanged quick glances, and Anna uttered a soft "Ha!"

He shot her a look but then decided it required an explanation. "We were told to come."

"Told to come? I don't understand."

"By the union." Jakob seemed surprised that Hans didn't

understand this. "The new Communist Party of Germany, formerly called the Spartacans, sent word to all the union shops around Berlin. Everyone who could be spared by their employers was encouraged to come in to hear Liebknecht."

"Not encouraged," Anna muttered. "Commanded."

"Anna," her husband warned softly.

"Well, it's true." She looked at Hans. "If you refuse to come, you are not paid, even if you work that day. And Jakob would probably have lost his job."

Hans gaped at her. "And how do the factory owners feel about that?"

"They don't dare say anything," Jakob said. "Not now, especially."

"Why not now?"

"Because the unions and the workers are seizing factories and plants all across the country. Even the big industrialists don't dare stand up to them."

Hans was astounded. "How many from your plant were told to be here today?"

Jakob shrugged. "I don't know. Hundreds maybe."

"We had to leave at six o'clock this morning," Anna explained. "If we return before six tonight, the union will withhold our pay for the day."

Hans was outraged. "How can they do that?"

Jakob gave him an incredulous look.

"In my brother's factory," Anna said, "a soap factory not far from us—"

"Anna!" Her husband showed genuine alarm. Anna glanced at Hans and shrugged.

Hans lowered his voice. "Look, I'm all for change, and our government hasn't done much for people like you and me, but sometimes I think the Socialists go too far. I . . ." He lowered his voice even more, looking around furtively. "I even wonder if sometimes, in spite of all

335

their glowing promises, they're not more concerned about taking power for themselves than helping people like us."

"Indeed," Jakob muttered, clearly embittered.

Hans looked at Anna. "So what happened to your brother?"

She looked at her husband. After a moment, he nodded.

She moved in closer and spoke in a low voice. "He told his shop foreman that he had already been here all day yesterday for the Eichhorn march. So he said he wasn't coming today. The man was furious. He told him that he'd lose a day's pay." She smiled briefly. "My brother's got a hot temper, so he told him he didn't care." She stopped, her eyes angry.

"And what did the foreman do?" Hans asked softly.

"He put a pistol to his head and gave him two choices. Go or die."

9:35 a.m. Pariser Plaza

As they joined the main crowd, Hans saw that he was right. This would be where the speakers harangued them. There were three folding chairs and a microphone in the back of the small farm truck, and three or four dozen soldiers were loitering nearby. A cloth banner had been raised over the cab of the truck. Large red letters on a white background trumpeted the words *DIE REVOLUTION IST HIER: GENOSSEN VEREINEN!*

Hans felt a touch on his shoulder and turned to see Anna looking at him. She pointed. "What does that sign say?" she asked in a timid voice.

So she couldn't read, Hans thought. Probably not Jakob either.

Nattie moved up. "It says, 'The revolution is here.' Then something about 'unite.'"

"The word is *Genossen,*" Hans explained, pleased to know that Nattie was getting some schooling. "It means comrades, friends, brothers."

"I don't understand," Anna said.

Jakob answered, lowering his voice and leaning in closer. "It refers to the brotherhood of the people. The Socialists say that all of us are brothers, and that means we must stand together."

"Ah." And that seemed to satisfy her.

Hans continued looking around. Now he saw that other men carrying rifles or pistols were also working their way through the crowd. The party goons, he decided. They were men with hulking bodies and faces that you didn't want to meet up with in a dark alley. Hans was a little curious and watched for a moment. In their wake, people were suddenly lifting posters, placards, and an occasional small banner. Things like DOWN WITH EBERT AND SCHEIDEMANN. They were the two chief ministers of the government.

STOP THE BLOODHOUND! Hans assumed that referred to Gustav Noske.

LONG LIVE THE *GENOSSEN*!

CHEERS FOR EICHHORN, OUR BELOVED POLICE PRESIDENT!

BURY THOSE WHO WOULD BURY THE REVOLUTION!

UP WITH THE PROLETARIAT! DOWN WITH THE BOURGEOISIE! That one was just a few feet away from them.

This time Nattie tapped Hans on the shoulder. "What does that mean?" she asked, pointing.

Anna and Jakob both moved closer to hear his answer. "The proletariat is just a fancy word for the working classes, for the poor of the world. People like—" He almost said "like you," but caught himself. "People like us."

"Oh." Nattie seemed genuinely surprised by that, almost pleased.

"And the *bur-zhwa-zee*"—he pronounced it slowly for them— "just means the middle classes, like merchants and bankers, business and factory owners, doctors, lawyers."

Jakob was listening too, and they all nodded. "And are they bad people?" Nattie asked.

It was an innocent question, but he saw now that several of the people around them were listening to their conversation. One man was staring at Hans with open hostility.

"Well," he said, choosing his words carefully, "the problem is that the bourgeoisie tend to be very materialistic. Uh . . . that means they care more about things than they do about people."

"They're the ones who keep us poor people locked in poverty," the man snarled. "Until the bourgeoisie are put down, the proletariat cannot and will not rise."

Hans could feel the hairs on the back of his neck prickle. This was more attention than he wanted. "And the proletariat," he said, giving the man a curt nod, "have certainly suffered long enough." Taking Nattie by the arm, he moved away, with Jakob and Anna following.

How ironic! Hans thought. The Socialists were encouraging the people to revolt with language they didn't even understand. He glanced over at the speaker's platform. Take the two leaders there. The colonel had told the men a little about them last night. Karl Liebknecht and Rosa Luxemburg were both handsome people, very impressive. But Liebknecht wore a Sunday suit, white shirt, and bowtie and an overcoat of thick wool. Tens of thousands of his listeners were shivering in the cold, and he wore an expensive overcoat.

Luxemburg was not richly dressed, but she was miles away from looking like the women who had come to hear her. She wore shoes with thick soles and heels and also had on a warm winter coat. A hat was perched on her head, probably held in place by hat pins. Did Anna own a hat of any kind? Did she even know what a hat pin was? Both of them held doctorates from prestigious universities. No wonder they used words like *proletariat* and *bourgeoisie* and *Genossen*. The irony was so heavy that it made Hans sick to his stomach.

Remembering why he was there, he glanced up at the sky and then turned to his new friends. "Jakob, I need to go. My chest is really hurting me, and I need to find a place to sit down."

Instantly concerned, Jakob looked around. "I'll go with you."

"No. Stay here with your family. I'll try to catch up with you when they start to march." As he said it, Hans felt a stab of guilt. He wasn't going to march with them. He was headed off to link up with his battalion. What would Natalee say if she knew that he was the enemy?

"Do you have to go?" Natalee asked. The look on her face nearly broke his heart. Hans laid a hand on her shoulder. "I do, Nattie. *Auf Wiedersehen*. It was my pleasure meeting you." He leaned in closer. "You have a grand curiosity about life," he whispered. "Never lose that."

"I won't," she exclaimed, both blushing and beaming at the same time.

Anna came up and briefly touched his hand. "We'll watch for you."

And with those words came an idea that startled him. He turned. "Jakob, would you be offended if I asked you for your address?"

His jaw dropped a little.

Hans rushed on. "I would very much like to meet you again. I . . . I am hoping to get married when all of this is over. I would like to bring my fiancée to meet your family."

"Of course," Jakob said, clearly honored by the request. Then his face fell. "But I have nothing to write with."

"I have a paper, *Vati*," Nattie sang out. She took a small, soiled piece of paper from her dress pocket. Then her face fell as well. "But nothing to write with."

Feeling in his jacket, Hans withdrew a pencil. "I do." He started to hand it to Jakob, but Jakob quickly motioned to his daughter. "Nattie, I will tell you, and you write it down for him."

Kicking himself for not remembering Jakob and Anna very likely could neither read nor write, Hans handed the pencil to Nattie. Dictating slowly, Jakob gave her the information. Finished, Nattie proudly handed the paper and pencil back to Hans. He took the paper, folded it up, and put it in his pocket, but refused to take the pencil. "It's yours, Nattie."

Wide-eyed, she gazed at him for a moment, and then turned to her father. "May I, *Vati*?"

He nodded. Hans turned to him. "I have only been in Berlin a few days, so I have no permanent address yet. But I promise that as soon as I get one, I shall write to you. And. . . ."

He turned to Anna. "There is much turmoil and upheaval in the Fatherland right now, so I can't say when it will be, but someday, somehow, I promise I will come and meet the rest of your family, if you will have me."

Tears sprang to her eyes, and then, to his surprise, she stepped forward, went up on tiptoes, and kissed him softly on the cheek. "We would be honored."

Barely able to speak, Hans nodded, impulsively kissed Nattie on the cheek, and then lumbered away, blinking rapidly as he pushed his way through the crowd.

9:45 a.m.—Brandenburg Gate

As he cleared the last of the crowd and limped across the plaza toward the Brandenburg Gate, Hans was in emotional turmoil. His so-called "recon patrol" had turned out to be an experience that had affected him deeply. Now he realized that the picture Noske had painted for them last night was not as simple as he had made it sound. The Litzsers were not just innocents, they were victims. Pawns in the power play between the left and the right. They weren't here because they were on fire with ideological fervor. They were here because their jobs—and therefore their very existence—depended on it.

So what if they were moved by the fiery sermons of Liebknecht and Luxemburg to the point that they picked up a club or a stone or a bottle of petrol with a lighted wick? They were poor, hapless, miserable, suffering human beings looking for any glimmer of light in a world of endless hopelessness.

The guilt tore at Hans like a knife. Which was irrational, in a way. He knew that. He wasn't to blame for their plight. Nor was he sympathetic to the government that was oppressing them. But that didn't make the guilt go away.

Hans was suddenly struck with a sense of wonder. Last night, he was supposed to have received his first salary payment from the *Freikorps* disbursement officer. Two hundred marks for his signing bonus and sixty marks for his first week's pay. He hadn't gotten it. By the time he got back from the hotel, the paymaster's window was closed. And he had left too early this morning. But he suddenly realized that if he had gotten it, that money would now be in Jakob Litzser's pocket. He knew that. He wouldn't have hesitated for one moment to give it all to the family.

Ironically, it only made him feel worse. What would that money do for them? Feed them for a week, maybe? There wouldn't be enough for a new dress for Nattie, or a warmer coat for Anna. Even if he were a millionaire and gave all his fortune to the poor, what difference would that make? It would be one tiny drop in a vast ocean of suffering.

CHAPTER

33

January 16, 1919, 10:40 a.m.—Near the Brandenburg Gate, Berlin

C olonel von Schiller raised one hand and called out. "All right men, gather round."

Immediately the thirty or so men loitering around the command center started moving in. These were the officers and non-coms of the First Battalion, all of whom were under the colonel's command. Hans, who had been trying to give his ribs a rest by leaning against the radio wagon—a horse-drawn cart that carried the battalion's heavy radio equipment—stood up and moved in as well. Colonel von Schiller's battalion staff consisted of about eight men. The four companies that made up the battalion had a sprinkling of about five or six officers or sergeants in each. Hans had been worried that the other sergeants would resent being led by a master sergeant instead of a commissioned officer, but he should have known better. Amongst themselves they were saying that their company would be the only one led by someone with any real intelligence. That was typical of the "love" enlisted men had for commissioned officers.

"All right," von Schiller snapped, cutting off the chatter. "We're waiting for final orders from Brigade, but we expect to move out no

342

later than 1100 hours. So listen up." He turned and motioned Hans to come forward. "Last night, I ordered Master Sergeant Eckhardt here to undertake a reconnaissance mission for the battalion."

Hans kept a straight face, not about to contradict him about whose idea it was.

"Sergeant, give us your report."

"Thank you, sir." Hans moved up beside him. "I arrived here about six o'clock this morning and have been here ever since. I have watched most of the people come in for the Liebknecht-Luxemburg rally and parade."

One of the captains raised a hand. "Liebknecht's men are bragging that he's brought in a hundred and fifty thousand people. Is that true?"

Hans shook his head. "You have to remember that the men that Liebknecht and Rosa Luxemburg have recruited haven't passed a mathematics class since kindergarten."

That brought a burst of laughter, and Hans was pleased to hear von Schiller join in.

"Actually," he went on. "It's hard to get an accurate count, but I was right down among the crowd for over an hour. I did a rough count going in and coming out. I'm pretty confident that there are no more than twenty thousand there, maybe less."

Major Rolf Ott, a graduate of the University of Berlin and von Schiller's adjutant, scoffed openly. "Are you sure of that, Sergeant? From here it looks like a huge crowd to me."

"Twenty thousand is a huge crowd, sir. But it's not a hundred and fifty thousand. But I assure you, there are plenty enough to be worried about."

"How many of those are armed?" another officer called out.

"That's harder to tell," Hans said. "Some of the civilians may have small arms under their coats, but that's not true of the vast majority of the workers. But I did see at least one full company of the Courageous Deserters' council near the speaker's stand, and they are armed."

There were smiles at his sarcasm.

"Also, there are probably at least a hundred of Liebknecht's followers—civilians who are armed, mostly with pistols—circulating among the crowd. And I think we have to assume that Liebknecht is holding some of his forces back, probably out of sight, that he can call in as needed. Make no mistake about it. His men will fight. They look like rejects from the Sicilian mafia. They're mean, they're foul-tempered, and they're spoiling for battle. They're definitely not the kind of men you want your sisters dating."

More laughter.

"Tell them the rest, Eckhardt," von Schiller said.

"This was a real surprise to me, but it's important for all of us to understand. I am convinced that the vast majority of that crowd over there is not here to fight. They do not want to fight, and they will not fight unless we back them into a corner and give them no choice."

That brought another skeptical look from the adjutant, which Hans ignored. "I talked with them. These are not radicals. These are not soldiers. They're workmen. And what shocked me the most? When you get closer, you'll see that more than a third of the crowd is made up of women—ranging in age from grandmothers to teenage girls."

That brought a lot of heads up sharply.

"That's right. Their union bosses told them that if they didn't all come, they'd be out of a job. One man I learned about had a gun put to his head and was told to come or he would be shot."

Someone swore under his breath. "I ain't gonna be shooting no women and children."

Hans raised his voice. "This is what the Spartacans want. They want us to open fire on innocent people so they can put their pictures in the newspapers, show their blood washing down the cobblestones. They want people so outraged at the government that they will join the revolution en masse."

That sobered even Major Ott. "So what do you suggest, Sergeant?" he asked in a low voice.

"We have to protect ourselves, we know that," Hans answered, speaking to everyone. "If the people actually join in with the soldiers and the radicals, we may have no choice but to fire on them. But we have rifles. We have to take aim at someone before we can shoot him. So let's do what Herr Noske suggested last night. Don't shoot anyone unless you're sure he's a threat to us. The miserable excuses for soldiers down there may use the people as shields, but see if you can draw the *Freikorps* men away from the crowds before you open fire. If you can't, see if you can give warning to the other people to get out of the way."

Hans looked around at the men, pleased to see deep concern on many of their faces. "I say again, most of these people are not here to fight us. They are here because they have no choice. Please, please, do not give them a reason to hate us."

To his surprise, Colonel von Schiller stepped up beside him. "This is good counsel, men. These people are going to be terrified if shooting starts. They're not going to be running toward us. They're going to be running as fast as they can away from us. So don't be shooting anyone in the back."

As Hans watched the faces of the other officers and sergeants, he was relieved to see that they not only accepted that order, they seemed to welcome it.

"All right," von Schiller said. "A couple more things and then we'll move out. First of all, remember that we are not alone out here. There are three other *Freikorps* battalions, each with the same overall objective." He turned to a large map pinned to a board propped up against the side of the truck. Retrieving a long, wooden pointer, he tapped the map near the very center of it. "This is our sector right here." He pointed to a black square. "This is the Brandenburg Gate and Pariser Plaza. For those of you not familiar with Berlin, the gate is the western terminus of *Unter den Linden* boulevard. At the opposite end of the boulevard is the royal palace. Third Battalion is stationed there and has orders to stay in place and protect the palace. We already lost control of the palace once to the People's Marine Division. We don't want that happening again.

"Second and Fourth Battalions are assigned to protect the *Reichstag* and other key government buildings." Von Schiller pointed to the north. "That is just a block or two from where we are. Their headquarters is here on the west side of the *Königsplatz,* directly west of the Parliament building."

The colonel went on when there were no questions. "Our battalion's assignment is the area where we are. As most of you know, the Brandenburg Gate is where most of the major demonstrations and marches start. So our task is to keep them under control, immediately cut off any violent actions on their part, and arrest key leaders if possible. Liebknecht, Luxemburg, and Eichhorn are to be captured unharmed so they can stand trial for treason."

Von Schiller turned and looked at his adjutant. "What else, Major?"

"The medical aid stations."

"Ah, yes. In addition to having access to the city's hospitals, the army is bringing in three aid stations, one for each battalion. They will be staffed around the clock until this is over. Please note this, because it is important. Second Battalion will have a small but fully functioning field hospital at its location. Any soldiers or civilians who are severely or critically wounded should be transferred there as quickly as possible."

"And where is that, sir?" another of the captains asked.

"Right there in Republic Plaza, behind Second Battalion headquarters."

One of the captains raised a hand. Von Schiller nodded at him. "Sir, what about those newspaper plants that were seized last night? Is anyone going after them?"

"One thing at a time, Captain. We've got to secure our positions first, and then we'll start moving against the places the Spartacans have taken, including police headquarters."

"Yes, sir."

"Today our job is to see that this march and demonstration does not get out of hand. So, here's how we'll deploy. Captain Blenheim's Company A will secure the north end of Pariser Plaza so that the crowds can't move north toward the *Reichstag*. You will hold that position unless one of the other companies gets in trouble."

The captain snapped off a salute. "Yes, sir."

"B Company will do the same on the south side of the plaza. Two blocks south of us is Potsdamer Plaza and the War Ministry. Even though that building is closed now, it's still a prime target for the rebels. So, Captain Ruger, you are charged not only with making sure our marchers don't break out and go south, but also with ensuring no rebels come in from the south. As you heard Noske say, Potsdamer Plaza was a hotspot last night."

"Got it, sir."

The Colonel turned to Hans. "Eckhardt, C Company's task is to do shepherd duty around the monument itself. Twenty thousand people are a lot of sheep to worry about. If they do start moving, the only way we want them going is east on *Unter den Linden*, where they'll run smack into Third Battalion. But don't crowd them. You're to stay back unless something starts to unravel. Then move in fast and hard."

"Understood, sir."

Von Schiller turned to the lieutenant that was in charge of D Company, a guy by the name of Sisam, who looked even younger than Hans. "Lieutenant, D Company will hang back here in reserve. You'll also be guarding the aid station and battalion HQ."

Corporal Jürgens, the colonel's aide, had been hovering around all morning. Now he appeared from inside the radio truck waving a small slip of paper. "Wireless message from Minister Noske, Major."

He handed it to the adjutant, who passed it over to von Schiller. The colonel glanced at it quickly and then swore and jerked forward to read it more closely.

When he finished, he started swearing softly and steadily. Everyone stared at him, not sure what this meant. "They've done it again," he finally muttered, speaking to Major Ott.

"Done what, Colonel?" the adjutant asked.

The colonel swore yet again and then lifted the paper and spoke. "This is from the office of the Minister of the Military. Quote: 'Urgent. Government ministers insist that *Freikorps* units not fire on the *Genossen* partisans.'"

There were audible groans from all around.

"The Brotherhood is to be honored and respected while peace negotiations continue at the cabinet level. Units are authorized to respond appropriately if fired upon first, but otherwise, they are to allow peaceful demonstrations and marches to proceed without interference. Signed Friedrich Ebert; Philipp Scheidemann; Gustav Noske."

Von Schiller wadded up the note in his hand and flung it away. "You have your orders," he snapped, looking around. "But our hands are tied yet again."

11:55 a.m.

Hans was searching the faces of the crowd on the off chance that he might spot Jakob, Anna, and Nattie, but even with binoculars, it was impossible to discern many faces in the mass of people. The "parade," if it could be called that, was barely moving. It varied in size from as few as ten or fifteen marchers in a row to as many as fifty or more abreast. He handed the binoculars back to the sergeant, and then leaned on his rifle to ease the pain in his side.

"See anything?" Sergeant Norbert "Bert" Diehls asked. He led the Second Platoon, which Hans had chosen to stay right around him. All of his platoon sergeants were competent, but of the four, Diehls was the best. Hans wanted him close by in case anything broke loose.

348

"A lot of paid goons trying to whip the people into a frenzy, and a lot more people who are trying to ignore them," he answered.

"Why don't the people just turn on them goons?" one of the men asked.

Hans shot him an incredulous look. Had he not heard anything Hans had told them?

"Well, why not? They outnumber them probably a hundred to one."

"Would you go up against armed soldiers if you were unarmed, had no training, and had everything to lose if you failed?"

The man turned away, irritated at being contradicted. A moment later, Diehls spoke again. "Have you been paying attention to that bunch of deserters over by those trucks?"

Turning to look, Hans shook his head. "Not particularly. What's going on?"

"Not sure. For a while I thought they were just bored and messing around with each other, but now I'm almost thinking they're forming up." He handed Hans his binoculars.

Forgetting about his ribs, Hans peered through the glasses. The four army trucks and the smaller farm truck were all moving along very slowly a few yards away from the line of people marching. There were several men walking alongside of them, rifles slung over their shoulders, looking thoroughly bored. "Looks pretty normal to me," he said.

"Look between the third and fourth trucks," Diehls said. "And keep watching."

A moment later, Hans stiffened. The distance between the two trucks widened a bit, and through the gap, Hans saw a dark mass of men. He adjusted the focus a little and swore. It was a row of men, shoulder to shoulder, marching in a loose cadence.

"Look under the last truck. All you can see are the feet, but . . ." Diehls let it hang.

Hans swore again and handed the glasses back. "Looks like half a company. Maybe more."

"Yeah, and we can't see behind the first two vehicles. The angle's not right, but . . ." Again he didn't finish his sentence. "There could be more."

"Alert the men," Hans said. "Keep it quiet. I don't want them gawking over there. But gradually move the other platoons in closer. Not in any kind of formation. Just real easy. And have the radio man bring the radio over here as well."

"Right, Sarge."

"And Diehls?"

"Yes, Sarge?"

"Good eye."

Hans saw the small pushcart that held their portable radio and angled over to get it. Rumors were that electrical engineers were working on field radios small enough that they could be carried by one man, but even if that were true, they didn't have them yet. This was a behemoth, and it took two men to lift it on and off its cart. As he passed a couple of his men who were moving closer as ordered, he called out softly to them. "Hey, keep yourselves between me and those trucks while I use the radio. Okay?"

They waved and slowed their pace.

"Get me Colonel von Schiller," Hans commanded before he even reached the two radio men. Thirty seconds later, the colonel was on the line. "Yes, Eckhardt?"

"Sir, we have at least one *Freikorps* unit forming up behind the trucks."

12:07 p.m.

"Eckhardt? What are they up to now?"

Hans now had his four platoon sergeants at his side. "It's a full rifle company. In formation. They're cutting through the route of the march, headed right for us. Still maybe fifty yards away."

"Steady, then."

"Sir? They've been yelling at us. They're trying to provoke a fight, I think."

The colonel scoffed. "You can handle a few insults, Eckhardt. Just stay loose."

"Sir, don't you want to know what they're yelling at us? In addition to the usual insults?"

There was a long pause, then, "What?"

"They are chanting that we can't fire on them because Ebert and Scheidemann won't let us. That we're their comrades. Brothers-in-arms. That we don't dare shoot back or we'll be court-martialed."

There was no answer for a moment. "Are they still coming toward you?"

"Yes, sir. At about half speed."

Another long silence.

"Sir? I know what the orders are, but if we wait until they're right on us, we could be in a bad situation. And there's something else. It's like the people know what's going on. They're almost in a panic, trying to put distance between them and the soldiers. I don't like it, sir."

"Do you have a recommendation?"

"I do, sir. Near the end of the war, as my company was retreating, we had to pass through a small town in France. Suddenly a sniper started shooting at us from the bell tower of the church. Every time one of us moved, he'd fire again. We shot back, of course, but we could never hit him. It was a real dilemma. The Allies were coming behind us and we had to keep moving, but he had us pinned down. We didn't have the time to send a squad after him, and there was no artillery to call on. And we certainly didn't want to backtrack and go around the town."

"So what did you do?"

"We rang his bell, sir."

"Say again?"

"We discovered that when we shot back at him, we often hit the large bell that was right over his head. The noise was so loud that he had to drop down and put his hands over his ears. So we assigned a man to keep shooting at the bell until we were all through the village."

"I see," von Schiller said. "So what are you saying, Eckhardt?"

"I'd like permission to ring their bells, sir."

"You can't shoot anyone unless they shoot first."

"You have my word, Colonel." And he clicked off before von Schiller could answer.

He turned to his sergeants. "All men are to fix bayonets. First and second platoons, line up your men on both sides of me, platoons in firing formation. First row down on one knee, second row behind them shooting over their heads. Third platoon muster around me, rifles at ready but not up to their shoulders yet. Fourth platoon, you hang back in case we get in trouble."

As they sprang into action, Hans called to them. "Who's the best shot in the company?"

For a moment no one spoke, but then Diehls grinned. "I guess that would be me, Sarge." The others were nodding.

"Good. Then you stay here."

Seeing twenty-four men lined up with fixed bayonets and their rifles pointed directly at them slowed the oncoming soldiers down, but it didn't stop them. Their leaders were still screaming the same drivel at them "It's a bluff. Comrades don't shoot comrades. They're not going to fire."

Crouching down beside Hans and hidden behind two other men, Diehls looked up. "What's my target, Sarge?"

"See that guy in the front holding the banner?"

"The one that says 'Government troops are trash'?"

"That's the one. You good enough to hit the board it's nailed to?"

"No problem."

"Tell me when you're ready."

"I'm ready."

Hans reached out and pushed the two soldiers in front of Diehls apart. The crack of the rifle followed an instant later.

Three things happened instantaneously. The sign went flying. The man who had been holding it yelled and dove for the ground, as did his fellow soldiers. And on the parade line, men and women screamed and scattered like a flock of chickens with a fox in the yard.

"How about the black and yellow sign?" Hans asked.

BLAM! a second sign spun away.

The Deserters' Brigade went to pieces. Men rolled away, shouting and clawing for their weapons.

"All rifles up!" Hans shouted at the top of his lungs. "Prepare to fire!"

Every rifle in every platoon—just under fifty of them—was up and trained on the men now only about thirty yards away. Screaming wildly at his men to follow, the *Freikorps* commander turned and ran. Moments later, the only targets Hans's men had were the backs of the deserters' uniforms.

Hans extended a hand to Diehls and pulled him up. "Well done," he said.

Diehls had a grin a mile wide on his face. "Ringing their bell. I like it."

Chapter Notes

The Spartacans did boast that 150,000 of the working classes had joined the general strike and come to Berlin to demonstrate against the government. But an author who was there during those events estimated it was no more than 20,000. He described the marchers thus: "The great mass of the paraders were ragged, underfed, miserable men and women, [who bore] mute testimony to the sufferings of the war-years" (*German Revolution,* 226).

Though it didn't happen on the same day as the great march in Pariser Plaza, the *Freikorps* unit made up of deserters and other riffraff, marched on government troops chanting that they wouldn't dare fire on them. They fully expected that the government forces would fall back. The government troops stood fast and fired over their heads. The "Deserters, Stragglers, and Furloughed Soldiers" unit turned and fled (*German Revolution,* 206).

CHAPTER 34

January 17, 1919, 7:20 a.m.—Brandenburg Gate, Berlin

Sergeant Diehls took one last bite and then threw the can in the garbage. He pulled a face. "You forget how bad these are," he grumbled. "They taste like dog food."

Smiling, Hans threw his army ration can away. "I can tell you from firsthand experience, dogs do better than this." He lifted his canteen and drunk deeply from the water. Having been out all night, the water was cold and sweet. Reattaching the canteen to his belt, Hans looked around. "All right, let's get these bedrolls put away and police up the area. Platoon sergeants, get your men started and then report for briefing in ten minutes. We move out at oh-eight-hundred."

The 180 men of Third Company got to their feet grumbling. They were griping about how cold it was, how badly they had slept, the food, the weather, the stupidity of the government, the overall injustice of life, and cheap cigarettes. Hans paid them no mind. This had been the way of the foot soldier from time immemorial.

As Hans made his way through his men, several of them called out to him or waved. Yesterday's little exercise with the Deserters' Brigade had been good for morale. All four platoons had erupted in cheering when the Spartacans turned tail and ran. That was good. One of the worst things for morale was the feeling that the men in charge of your life had no idea what they were doing. It was a good feeling, and right now, for Hans, any kind of good feelings were welcome.

7:30 a.m.—Battalion Headquarters Tent, near Brandenburg Gate

"Okay, listen up." Colonel von Schiller clapped his hands once to cut off the noise.

"Let's start with the bad news. In spite of the our clash with the Spartacans yesterday, the ministers still refuse to make it illegal to hold a march or a demonstration in opposition to the government."

That was met by a chorus of boos and groans. "Even though the Bolsheviks have used force to seize those newspaper buildings?" asked Captain Blenheim, the commander of A Company.

"That's right," von Schiller grumbled. "You don't like it. I don't like it. But those are our orders. The good news is that it should be a quiet day today. C Company taught those Bolshie traitors a little respect for us yesterday. They got their tails whipped pretty good."

The men reacted to that with calls of "Yeah!" "Amen!" "They sure did."

Sergeant Diehls, who was standing next to Hans, punched him softly on the shoulder.

"So, same deployment as yesterday. A Company takes the north side of Pariser Plaza again. B Company takes the south, C Company stays in the plaza, and D Company stays back with battalion HQ and the aid station. Your orders are to intercept and stop anyone who is a real threat. But be wise. The government's not bending on this one yet."

A hand in the back came up. "Sir, permission to have my platoon guard the aid station?"

Laughter erupted. It was Lieutenant Sisam, commander of Second Platoon, D Company.

"Nice try, Sisam," von Schiller said dryly, "but the answer is no.

And, while I'm at it, no more reports of men trying to get on the sick leave roster because they have ingrown toenails. I don't care how cute those nurses are, I'll put the whole platoon on latrine duty. You got that?"

Everyone roared as the lieutenant blushed all the way down to his socks. *This was good, too*, Hans thought. Von Schiller was proving to be an effective commander. He could be tough as nails, but the men liked him. The fact that a young lieutenant felt comfortable enough to joke with him was another sign that the battalion was in high spirits.

"Anything else?" the colonel asked.

"Yes, sir," a voice from behind them called out. They turned to see Corporal Jürgens wheeling out a motorbike from behind the radio truck.

"Ah, yes," von Schiller said with a smile. "Bring it forward, Corporal."

He did so, putting down the kickstand and parking the bike. The others gathered in around it.

"As you know," von Schiller said with a straight face, "we have a real whiner in our midst. Not to mention any names, but there's this master sergeant who keeps complaining about how sore his ribs are, and that his face hurts, and that his lips are chapped and that he has a bunion. . . ."

That got him a big laugh. Every man there was either staring or pointing at Hans.

"Well, I'm tired of his bellyaching. So, Sergeant Major Eckhardt, here is some transportation for you. And I don't want to hear any complaints."

The men applauded as a red-faced Hans said, "Sir, I'm fine. I'm getting better every day."

The colonel sobered. "I know that, and my hope is that you won't need it. But if something does start to unravel today, I can't have you hobbling across the square to deal with it. Have you driven a motorbike before?"

"Yes, sir. In France."

"Good. Then that bike stays close to you from now on. Got it?"

"Yes, sir."

"And one other thing, Sergeant Major."

"Sir?"

"If I see you giving any young ladies, especially any of our nurses, a ride on that machine, you'll be joining Lieutenant Sisam on the special duty roster."

Trying hard not to smile, Hans snapped off a salute. "Yes, sir, Colonel, sir."

"All right. Start deploying your men as soon as they're ready. Good luck, gentlemen."

12:21 p.m.—Pariser Plaza

The morning fog had burned off by ten, and now the sky overhead was a clear blue and the temperature was moving into the mid-thirties, which felt wonderful. C Company was stationed about dead center in the square. Fifty yards away, a large number of citizens—eight, maybe ten thousand—were gathered around the Spartacan site, listening to various speakers shouting at them. Hans wondered if Liebknecht and Luxemburg were there, but he doubted it. These speakers were putting the crowd to sleep, not stirring them up to revolution.

Though Hans had his men deployed in a semicircle facing the crowd, they were pretty relaxed. Most were sprawled out on the ground. Many had taken off their overcoats and were seated in small groups talking or smoking. Some were stretched out, catching a few winks. One or two were writing letters to their families or their girlfriends. Hans, who was seated on the pavement beside his motorbike, was kicking himself for not having thought to bring paper of his own. He could have written a long letter to Emilee by this point. On the other hand, what would he say?

Sergeant Diehls was seated on the motorbike studying the crowd through the binoculars again. So far there had been nothing to get him alarmed. All of a sudden, the radio crackled. Hans got to his feet and went over to the radio cart. The radioman saw him, covered the microphone, and said, "It's Captain Ruger of B Company. He wants to talk to you, Sergeant Major."

Hans moved over and picked up the microphone. "This is Eckhardt."

"Eckhardt, this is Ruger. We've got some movement to the south of us. Down by *Leipziger Strasse*."

"What kind of movement?"

"Two or three dozen men, most in uniform. It's a couple of blocks away, so we can't see them really well. But they're definitely armed. They seem to be heading for the War Ministry."

"But the War Ministry's closed."

"Yeah, I know that. Not sure what they're up to. We're going down to check it out. I'm going to leave one platoon here. Can you send one of your platoons over to back them up?"

"Will do. They're on their way. You want some help?"

"Not yet. We'll let you know."

"Yes, sir."

He handed the microphone back and turned. All around him men were getting up, having heard some of what had just happened. "All right," he called. "Listen up. Third Platoon, you're going down to give B Company some backup." Hans pointed to the south. "They're just off the plaza in whatever street that is that heads south to Potsdamer Plaza."

"It's called *Königgrätzer Strasse*," Diehls volunteered. He was a native Berliner.

"Okay. It's probably nothing, but settle in with the B Company and stay alert."

Hans turned to the others. "That goes for the rest of you, too. On your feet. Check your weapons. Stay sharp." He moved over to the motorbike and straddled it. "Diehls, keep an eye on those guys over there. And stay close to the radio. I'm going to take a look."

"Got it, Sarge."

Just as he raised his foot to kick the engine into life, Hans froze. The crackle of distant and sporadic gunfire echoed off the surrounding buildings. Every head turned in that direction. Making sure his rifle was secure on his shoulder, Hans gave the starter a hard kick, and the motorbike exploded into life. He popped it into gear and roared away.

As he left Pariser Plaza he saw that the platoon Ruger had left behind was deployed along *Königgrätzer Strasse* rather than in the square itself. Which was good. Here they had more cover—low walls, hedges, a couple of motorcars parked at the curbs. They waved him through. "Call us if you need us," someone yelled. He waved back and shot past them.

About three blocks down he caught up with the other three platoons that were jogging south down the street. "Where's Captain Ruger?" he shouted.

"Here." In the front line of men, Ruger turned and started back toward him.

Hans dismounted and moved to join him. "What have you got?" he asked.

"Not sure yet. Got a squad on recon now."

Gunshots rang out again, still ahead of them but this time much closer, and everyone dropped down to one knee. "There they are," someone cried.

Hans turned to see several of their men running hard toward them. They were in a crouch and zigzagging as they came. More shots rang out, but the shooting didn't seem to be aimed at their men. He walked over with Ruger as the squad reached them.

"What have we got?" Ruger asked.

"About half a company of Spartacans. Don't know why, but they attacked a group of unarmed government supporters down by the War

Ministry. One man is dead; at least two more are wounded. One of them badly. We need to get a medic over there on the double."

Ruger snapped his fingers, and a man with a red cross on his helmet trotted forward. He turned to the squad leader. "Send your squad back to provide cover for him, but you stay here. Tell me what's going on. Where are the Spartacans?"

The corporal in charge of the squad shook his head slowly. "That's what is weird, sir. They didn't engage us at all. They were running pell-mell in the opposite direction. Then, just past the War Ministry, they turned down some side street. That's where we found the injured and stopped. But it looks like they may be circling back the way they came."

"Wait," Hans exclaimed. "That doesn't make sense."

Someone behind them shouted. "Is there a Sergeant Eckhardt here?"

"Here." Hans walked swiftly over to him. It was the radioman.

"A Sergeant Diehls for you."

"Yeah, Diehls," he said. "What's up?"

"We've got movement here, Sarge. All of a sudden, we've got Spartacans coming out of the woodwork." Suddenly the air exploded with the rattle of gunfire behind them. Hans could hear it coming through the radio, too, nearly drowning out Diehls.

"Under fire! Under fire!" Diehls shouted. "Everybody down!"

"Diehls!" Hans yelled.

"Gotta go, Sarge. We've got what looks two companies coming straight at us. Looks like another one is attacking A Company's position. We're taking heavy fire."

"Fall back to the gate," Hans cried. "Use the pillars as cover. I'm on my way."

"Got it."

Hans turned as Ruger joined him, nodding to let Hans know he'd heard the broadcast. "This is it," he yelled. "No bluffing this time." He grabbed at Hans's arm. "That's why our group is doubling back on us."

"You think they're gonna try to ambush us?"

"No." He reached in his jacket pocket and yanked out a folded map. It was a smaller version of the one the colonel had used in the briefing. Each company commander had one. He quickly unfolded it and spread it out on the pavement. Hans dropped down to one knee beside him.

Ruger stabbed the spot near the center of the map that was labeled *Brandenburger Tor* and *Pariser Platz*. "This isn't some spontaneous eruption, Eckhardt." His finger drew two quick lines on the map. "It looks like it's a coordinated attack, a pincer movement to pin us down. One is going straight up the middle against your company. One is going after Captain Blenheim's company here on the north." He moved his finger down and tapped a spot just below where they were now. "These Spartacans aren't after us. They drew us away from the plaza on purpose, I think." He traced a line into the huge green area on the map labeled *Der Tiergarten*. "If they double back through on the street they're on now, it will take them back into the park. Then"—his finger moved some more—"if they turn north, you tell me. What's the objective?"

Hans gasped. "They're headed for battalion HQ and the aid station." He leaped up, shouting now over the deafening thunder of gunfire. "I've gotta go!"

Ruger shouted back. "We'll cut through the park and see if we can cut them off."

"Agreed," Hans said. He jumped to his feet and turned to the radio operator. "Can you get battalion HQ?"

"No, Sarge. We've been trying, but we've got nothing so far."

"Then get me Sergeant Diehls back. Now!"

A moment later the man handed him the microphone. The sound of gunfire coming through the speakers was almost deafening. "Diehls," Hans shouted. "We think they're going after battalion HQ and the aid station. Coming in from behind. Once you get a defensive line set up at the gate, take a platoon and warn the colonel."

There was the sharp whine of a ricocheting bullet and Hans heard someone scream. "Did you copy that, Diehls?"

"Yeah. Got it. We're already falling back in that direction. I've got five men down. But we're slowing them down. We'll see what we can do."

Ruger took the microphone from Hans. "Diehls, this is Ruger. We're going through the *Tiergarten*, where we'll link up with you at the Brandenburg Gate. Watch for us."

"Yes, sir! Gotta go."

Hans started for his motorbike. "One more second, Eckhardt," Ruger said. He turned to his radioman. "See if you can get Third Battalion. Tell them what's happening. See if they can send two companies down to our battalion HQ on the double. Tell them we're heading there now, coming up from the southeast. We'll try to link up with them at the monument."

As the radio operator began transmitting, Hans climbed on his motorbike. Ruger turned to him. "You take my platoon with you. Tell them you're their commander for now."

"Right."

As Hans kicked the motorbike into life, Ruger touched his arm. "Keep your head down."

12:47 p.m.—Königgrätzer Strasse and Der Tiergarten

As Hans raced northward, hunched low over the motorbike, he wondered if Captain Ruger would use the forest of the *Tiergarten* as cover to get to First Battalion's headquarters site without being seen. If the Spartacans were using the streets that ran through the park as their route, the trees might give Ruger enough of an advantage to get out in front of them.

A rifle cracked sharply. At the same instant, a bullet hit just to Hans's left and about ten feet ahead of his bike. It left a gouge in the pavement and whined away. He instinctively jerked the bike to his right, almost sending it into a spin. He corrected quickly.

Crack! Crack! Two more shots rang out. The roar of the motor-bike was pretty loud, but not enough to drown out gunfire. One shot hit the street just beside Hans's right foot. He thought he felt the other one snap past his ear.

His mind went into high gear as he crouched even lower and started zig-zagging wildly, using the width of the street to full advan-tage. Snipers. At least two. From the trees? No. The angle was too high. From the upper floors of the buildings on his right. Hans looked ahead.

Crack! Crack! Crack! The motor bike jerked hard to one side and nearly took him down. Without thinking, he released the throttle, and the bike immediately started to slow.

The smell of petrol was suddenly burning his nose. Glancing down, he saw liquid gushing out of a hole in the tank next to his right knee. Several thoughts came to him in one instantaneous flash of clarity. He was lucky the snipers didn't have tracer bullets, or he would be a flam-ing torch right now. If any of that petrol sprayed onto the spark plugs of the engine, he would be torched anyway. If he laid the bike down in a long slide, as they had been taught to do, the metal on pavement would send out a stream of sparks and BOOM! He was still toast.

That left Hans one choice. He winced, thinking about what roll-ing off a moving motorbike was going to do to his ribs. But he didn't hesitate.

Straight ahead the street ended and opened into Pariser Plaza. Men in uniforms were jumping up and swarming toward him. He could see the flashes of their rifles and hear the thunder of their shots. Hans felt a rush of relief. They were returning fire at the snipers, hop-ing to drive them back into cover.

He glanced at the speedometer and saw that he had slowed to about twenty-five miles per hour. Still too fast. He let off the accelerator completely and squeezed the brake lever. The bike started to skid to a stop, but now the petrol was no longer blowing backward in the rush of air from the bike. It was spraying directly onto the engine. Hans's time was up.

Without thinking, he cast aside his rifle. Then, in one smooth movement, he scooted back to the edge of the seat and rolled to his right.

He was probably down to under ten miles per hour as he fell, but Hans still shrieked with pain as his body smashed rump first into the pavement and he started sliding with his feet forward, using his elbows as skids.

There was a roar of sound and a flash of brilliant yellow. A blast of heat seared Hans's face. Almost to a stop now, he rolled onto his stomach and covered his face, yelling out as the pain shot through his ribs.

Dazed and half blinded, he sensed men running past him. They were firing their rifles. Then others reached him. Someone grabbed Hans by the collar and dragged him away from the flames. Suddenly a face appeared just in front of his. It was Sergeant Houtz, the platoon sergeant of his own Fourth Platoon. He was grinning like a kid.

"Whoo-ee, Sarge," he hollered. "Colonel von Schiller ain't gonna be happy when he sees what you done to his motorbike!"

2:15 p.m.—Pariser Plaza

The Spartacans had planned well, but they had made one serious mistake. When the Spartacans saw Ruger leaving, they thought all of his troops had gone with him. So they pressed hard against Diehls and C Company. They were trying to close the trap on the battalion HQ, which would have been a real coup for them.

In the meantime, Ruger, as Hans had guessed, had taken his company into the *Tiergarten* woods and reached the aid station just minutes before the Spartacans attacked. Those idiots had not given thought to what Ruger would do and were caught totally by surprise. The firefight was intense, bloody, and hard-fought, but it delayed the

Spartacans long enough for the two companies from Second Battalion to arrive. When they saw the troops coming, the Spartacans threw down their weapons and ran, leaving the ground around the monument littered with the dead and the wounded.

What had been a near victory for the Spartacans became a total rout.

But it was not without its cost. The First Battalion had seventeen dead, including Lieutenant Sisam, who had caught a bullet in the neck as he defended the front entrance to the aid station. There were also more than fifty wounded. One of those was Colonel Stefan von Schiller. He had been shot in the upper leg, and the bullet had half severed his femoral artery. With bullets flying around them, a surgeon and two nurses had rushed in, stanched the bleeding, and rushed the colonel off to the field hospital in Republic Plaza. That had left a pall over the entire battalion. Two hours later he was still in surgery, and the chances of his recovery were questionable.

Sporadic gunfire could still be heard as various platoons moved through the streets looking for snipers. Farther off, they could hear the rumble of light artillery.

Major Ott watched as the doctor put the last strip of tape on Hans. "You gonna be all right?"

"Yes, sir. I think I may have shaved about five pounds off my rear end, and I've got Corporal Jürgens out trying to find me a new uniform. But my ribs are not as bad off as I thought."

The doctor looked up. "Next time, Sergeant, you might try falling on your head. Your men all seem to think it's a lot harder than your tail."

Chapter Notes

In his history of the German Revolution of 1919, Bouton records that on Thursday, January 7, after their seizure of several newspaper publishing buildings the day before, Liebknecht's Spartacans launched numerous attacks around the central part of Berlin. "There was much promiscuous shooting in various parts of the city. Spartacans fired on unarmed government supporters in front of the war ministry building, killing one man and wounding two. There were also bloody clashes at Wilhelm Plaza, Potsdamer Plaza and in Unter den Linden. . . . The Spartacans succeeded in driving the government troops from the *Brandenburger Tor* (Brandenburg Gate), but after a short time were in turn driven out" (*German Revolution,* 227).

No details are given of specific units involved on either side, how the fighting progressed, or the number of casualties suffered, so the details in this chapter are of my own making.

People familiar with Berlin may be puzzled by the mention of a street named *Königgrätzer* in central Berlin. There is no such street there now, but there was in early 1919. The government changed its name to *Budapester Strasse* a short time after the World War I ended. Today it is known as *Ebertstrasse.*

CHAPTER

35

January 17, 1919, 6:55 p.m.—Battalion Headquarters Tent,
near Brandenburg Gate

For reasons that he couldn't explain now, Hans had at first found
Major Rolf Ott, Colonel von Schiller's adjutant, annoying.
He was too arrogant, too pleased with himself, too concerned
about his looks, and a bit disdainful of the battalion's only sergeant
major.

Ott was slender, like a marathon runner, with a sharp tongue that
could flay the flesh of an enlisted man if he did something deemed
stupid in the major's eyes. He was very German in his looks, with light
blond hair that had a gentle wave in it. His eyes were a light blue but
rarely rested on anything for more than a moment or two. He was
from Hamburg, a port on the North Sea, and spoke with a heavy
North German accent.

Now, as Ott began the briefing, Hans realized those feelings were
gone. He was growing more and more impressed with Major Ott in his
role as acting battalion commander as the day wore on.

Major Ott strode into the room, smiling and nodding as the men
snapped to attention. Corporal Jürgens was right behind him, as atten-
tive to Ott as he had been to von Schiller.

"At ease, men," the major called, shucking off his overcoat. Jürgens was instantly there to take it from him. Ott looked around, waiting for the men to get seated, and then he jumped right in. "Good news, men. On several fronts. First, we just came from the field hospital. Colonel von Schiller is out of surgery and out of danger."

The group erupted with applause and cries of pleasure.

"He was still a bit groggy from the anesthesia, but he was alert enough that he wanted a full report of how things went today. And though he was saddened by our losses, he was deeply pleased that we prevailed. He asked me to convey his personal appreciation and commendations to each and every one of you. In his words, 'A job well done.'"

"Any idea of how soon he'll be up and around?" Captain Ruger called out.

"Anxious to get the adjutant back in his rightful place, Captain?" Major Ott asked dryly.

Ruger's face flushed, much to the amusement of his comrades. "No, sir, I just. . . ."

"I know, I know," Ott said, growing more serious. "We're all anxious to have him back, me most of all. But it'll be at least two weeks. Maybe more."

"Any permanent damage?" Sergeant Diehls asked.

"The lead surgeon says the colonel may have a limp, but nothing that will restrict him from continuing to serve."

That got a warm response too.

"But that's not the only reason Corporal Jürgens and I are so happy, eh, Corporal?"

Hans couldn't resist. "I'm not sure I've ever seen Corporal Jürgens actually smile, sir. How do you know for sure that he's happy?"

Jürgens shot Hans a dirty look as everyone, including the major, hooted at that.

Major Ott quickly sobered. "Before I went to see the colonel, all battalion commanders were called to the *Reichstag* to meet with the cabinet ministers, including Gustav Noske, and the generals of the regular army."

Men straightened or leaned forward in their chairs. This was what they were waiting to hear.

"They, of course, knew about what happened here today and were deeply shocked by it. But, it turns out that we actually had one of the lighter encounters."

He went on quickly as the men glared at him. "The battle over in the newspaper district has been fierce. There have also been other major battles throughout the city today. Witnesses say that the grounds in front of the forest were strewn with the wounded and dead. There were pitched battles this afternoon around the *Herrenhous* and *Wertheim's* department stores, with customers huddling under counters and desks for safety.

Ott shot them a grim smile. "However, the good news is that with all that has happened, the cabinet, and even the People's Council, understand that this is not just a political issue anymore."

He stopped for breath, and several hands came up. Major Ott pointed at Ruger. "Yes, Captain."

"What exactly does that mean? Are we going to be allowed to take the gloves off?"

"Yes. The cabinet and People's Council have finally recognized that parades and demonstrations are not expressions of free speech but are used as excuses to incite rebellion. Therefore, as of tonight, all such gatherings are declared illegal, and government forces are charged to inform such gatherings that they are breaking the law."

"And if they just laugh at us?" someone else called.

"If they do not immediately disband, you have a 'shoot-to-kill' order," he said soberly.

The men nodded their approval, and some of them began applauding.

"Second, the government has authorized the use of heavy weapons to put down the rebellion. Even as we speak, artillery pieces are being put on top of the patent office, where they have a clear field of fire against some of the occupied buildings. Seven-centimeter cannons are being placed where they have a clear field of fire at police headquarters and Eichhorn and his goons.

"Third, machine-gun companies are on their way here in armored cars, with a tank accompanying them. Machine guns will be placed atop Brandenburg Gate, as well as all around its base."

The men were stunned, almost too overjoyed to react.

"Fourth, those machine-gun companies will be accompanied by troops carrying flamethrowers. Tomorrow morning, those three hundred Spartacans who are hiding behind the barricades in front of the *Vorwärts* plant will be looking down the barrels of three ten-centimeter field pieces and a mine thrower that can hurl a hundred pounds of explosives over a hundred yards."

The men could be restrained no longer. They shouted and whistled and clapped and cheered. Ott watched, nearly as pleased as they were. Finally, he cut them off. "Question. If you had your choice of where to fight tomorrow—which we don't, this is strictly a hypothetical question—where would you choose?" That caught the men off guard, and they looked at each other. To Hans's surprise, the first hand up was Sergeant Diehls's.

"Yes, Sergeant?"

"Police headquarters."

"And why is that?"

"The others leaders are bad," he said. "There's no question about that. Liebknecht, Luxemburg, and the others. But that pig Eichhorn is still holed up in the building, and he's arming anyone who will carry a gun and come against us—criminals, deserters, teenage hooligans, even young girls. We fought some of them today. I say it's time to put an end to it."

A slow smile stole across the major's face. "Those are almost exactly the same words I used with Noske tonight."

Hans's head came up. "And?" he asked, holding his breath.

"We're moving out at oh-five-hundred hours. We'll link up with Third Battalion. Our assigned objective? Police headquarters and the capture of Emil Eichhorn."

The last sentence was barely heard as the men leaped to their feet again and exploded in a frenzy of celebration.

7:25 p.m.

When the group finally began to break up, Hans joined Diehls and began talking strategy as they moved toward the door of the tent. Major Ott was near the door, shaking hands and accepting congratulations. As Hans approached, Ott broke off his conversation with Captain Ruger. "Eckhardt?"

He stopped. "Sir?"

"A word, please." Then to Ruger: "I'll only be a minute."

Puzzled, Hans nodded and stepped back. "I'll see you in a bit," he said to Diehls.

Hans assumed it was something about tomorrow, so Major Ott's first words knocked Hans completely off balance. "Eckhardt, Colonel von Schiller would like to see you."

"Me, sir? Now?"

He smiled and nodded. "Yes to both. I can have Jürgens get you a driver."

"Uh . . . no. I'm fine. The hospital's only a block or so."

"You sure? Jürgens is working on getting you another bike. You sure your ribs are all right?"

"Sore, but better than expected, sir."

"*Gut*. We need you at full strength tomorrow."

"Yes, sir. Uh . . . Major, do you know what the colonel wants?"

"If I did know, I couldn't tell you. But I don't. And he didn't ask me to have you bring anything. Get back here as soon as you can. We've got a lot to do."

"Yes, sir." Hans saluted and left.

7:33 p.m.—Field hospital, Königsplatz, near the Reichstag building

The colonel's eyes were closed when the nurse escorted Hans to his bedside. Hans shot her a questioning look. She smiled. "He said to wake him."

And with that, the colonel's eyes opened. "Ah, Eckhardt. Thank you for coming."

Hans moved closer. "It's good to see you, sir. You had a lot of us pretty scared today."

Von Schiller dismissed that with a wave of his hand. "Nurse?"

It was as if she had expected him to have a request. "Yes, Colonel?"

"Can you get the surgeon, please?"

"Yes, sir." She spun on the balls of her feet and walked away. The tent, which was fifty or sixty feet long, was filled with beds, and more than half of them were full, but the nurse left the tent through a side door, which led outside.

Von Schiller pointed to a metal folding chair beside the bed. Hans sat down, fighting not to stare at him. His face was as pale as the sheets, and he looked exhausted. His eyes closed for a moment and then opened again. "I understand you abandoned that motorbike, Eckhardt."

"Uh . . . yes, sir. Kind of."

A weak smile came and went, and then the colonel reached down and laid his hand on his left leg. It was elevated with pillows underneath it. "I understand you came pretty close to ending up with one of these too."

"Yes, sir. The one shot missed my leg by about two inches. I was lucky. I'm sorry you weren't."

Von Schiller acknowledged the comment with a barely perceptible nod. "Eckhardt, you interested in a career in the army?"

Hans's mouth fell open, then clamped shut again.

Von Schiller actually laughed softly. "Thought that might get your attention."

"I . . ." Hans didn't know what to say.

"I told Major Ott to draft the paperwork to get you a field commission. I'd like to make you a lieutenant junior grade and officially make you the commanding officer of C Company."

This time Hans's mouth fell open and stayed that way.

"It would be a good start to a successful career."

"Whoa. I didn't expect that, sir. Uh . . . can I think about it?"

"Of course. I heard you've got a girl waiting for you."

Another shocker. How did he know that? Hans had told no one in his unit about Emilee.

The colonel continued. "Why don't you talk to her about it when this is over?"

"I . . ." Hans decided he had to be honest. "To tell you the truth, sir, she's not talking to me right now."

The colonel smiled fully now, actually enjoying Hans's discomfort. "Yep, that's what I heard. Found out about that little drinking binge you went on, did she?"

The only word that Hans seemed to be able to come up with was *uh*. "Uh . . . yeah. Kind of."

"Don't blame her for being disappointed. It was a stupid thing to do. Almost as stupid as trying to rob my wife." Von Schiller lay back and closed his eyes. "Well, some things can be fixed and some can't. Takes a wise man to know the difference."

As he was searching for an answer to that, Hans saw the nurse come back into the tent. A man in a white coat was walking just a few feet behind her. "Sir?"

The colonel opened his eyes.

"The surgeon's here, Colonel," Hans said. "I'd best be going."

Von Schiller laughed, which was barely a whisper of sound. "Oh, he's not here to see me."

Hans jerked around, staring at the two figures coming down the aisle toward them. As they passed under one of the hanging lights, the man's face was fully illuminated. Hans gasped and then leaped to his feet. The man was looking at him, smiling broadly now. He waved a hand.

"Dr. Schnebling! What are you doing here?"

Schnebling laughed in delight. "That's odd. That was exactly the same question I was going to ask you."

Chapter Note

In addition to Houton's excellent history, the *New York Times* published a summary of the final days of the German Revolution, giving additional details such as the placement of artillery and other heavier weapons, the locations of some of the key buildings, and so on (see *German Revolution*, 225–230, and "When Revolution Stalks Streets of Berlin: Tourist Landmarks Converted into Fortresses, and Battered with Heavy Guns, as Spartacides, in Armed Revolt, Attempt the Overthrow of the Ebert Regime," *New York Times,* January 19, 1919).

CHAPTER 36

January 18, 1919, 6:47 a.m.—Police headquarters building, Alexander Plaza, Berlin

As first light gradually stole over the central area of Berlin, it revealed a warren of deserted streets and silent buildings. Unlike the night before, there was no sound of gunfire, no rumble of artillery, no crack of sniper's rifles from the roofs and upper floors of buildings.

Though the First Battalion had decisively put an end to what the men were now calling "The Battle for the Brandenburg Gate," fighting in other parts of the city had raged on well into the night. Spartacans had stormed the government troops holding the Potsdamer and Anhalt railroad stations several times but were driven back. Reports said there were heavy losses on both sides, but the government forces had prevailed.

Now, as dawn broke, First Battalion was on the rooftops of several buildings along the south side of Alexander Plaza, waiting for the final signal to move. Soldiers sat beneath the parapet smoking, drinking weak coffee, and talking quietly.

Major Ott had secured three field pieces along with about three dozen 10.5-centimeter shells—each about three inches in diameter and two feet long. Now the artillery officer was sighting them on the building across the square.

Hans stood off to one side with Captain Ruger and Sergeant Diehls, gripping their canteens filled with hot coffee to keep their hands warm. The sky was clear and the cold was numbing. Their breath hung in the air. While they waited for Major Ott to return, the three of them talked strategy for the coming battle.

The Central Police Headquarters was a huge five-story building that sprawled across the entire front of Alexander Plaza. It, and the jail it contained, filled almost a whole city block. Built of stones and brick, it was more of a fortress than an office building and, in spite of his conviction that they would take it, Hans knew it wasn't going to come easy. The battalion had roughly a thousand men, but the building had somewhere over a hundred rooms, and every one of them was going to have to cleared. This was not going to be a walk in the park.

Ruger took one last draw on his cigarette and then flipped it over the side of the building. "What are the chances that the building has fire escapes on the back side?" he asked.

Hans and Bert Diehls exchanged glances. An intriguing question. Diehls, who knew Berlin better than either of the other two, said, "I think there's a pretty good chance there are. It's required by city code now, but whether it was back when the building was built . . ." He shrugged. "Not sure. I don't remember ever being around the back before."

"What are you thinking?" Hans asked. He liked this captain. He was serious but pleasant. A man probably in his early thirties who wore a simple wedding band on his left hand. He had a quick mind, as he had proven yesterday, and was fearless in battle, as he had also proven yesterday.

Ruger frowned and pulled at his lower lip. "I'm thinking, that's a lot of building to secure. And there are likely several hundred men inside. What if we took both of our companies, made a wide circle so

Eichhorn and his thugs can't see what we're doing, and came around the back? If there are fire escapes, we climb to the top, start on the top floors, and then start working our way down. Drive those Commie scum down and out the front entrance."

"We're going to have to do that sooner or later," Diehls agreed. "I like sooner."

Hans was musing over the idea. He looked at the two of them. "What if we coordinate that attack with the artillery guys? They wait until we're in place, and then the minute they open fire on the front of the building, we go in through the roof."

"Excellent!" Ruger said. "Hit them from both directions. Catch them totally off guard."

The sound of an engine from behind them and below brought their heads around. Coming up *Alexanderstrasse* from the south was a staff car followed by an army truck. "There's the Major now," Ruger said. "Let's pitch it to him."

7:15 a.m.

To the further joy of the battalion, Major Ott had wrangled two machine gun platoons from another battalion and the truck to transport them. A subdued cheer went up from the men when the new men followed Ott onto the roof carrying four MG 08s, water-cooled machine guns on tripods. Hans didn't applaud, but he was grinning happily. This was something he knew and knew well. With a range of almost a mile and the ability to fire about eight rounds per second, one MG 08 was a formidable weapon. Four were phenomenal.

Once the major directed them where to set up the guns, Captain Ruger asked if he had a minute to talk to them. He did, and they moved off to one side. Ruger laid out their proposal, talking quietly but earnestly. Ott was nodding vigorously before he even finished speaking. "I like it. I like it a lot. Approved. Ruger, you're in command. You all right with the plan, Eckhardt?"

"Yes, sir. I think it's a brilliant idea."

"*Gut.* How long will it take you to get into position?" he asked Ruger.

"I'd say about an hour, sir. We'd like to make a wide circle so they don't see us coming. The element of surprise will be important."

"All right. Move out as soon as you're ready."

"Yes, sir!" The three men started away, but Ott called after them. "Eckhardt?"

He turned back. "Yes, sir?"

"I stopped off at the hospital to check in on Colonel von Schiller this morning."

"How's he doing?" Diehls asked.

"Better, actually. He's got some color back in his face. Those blood transfusions are really helping, but he's still pretty weak." He looked at Hans. "But he asked me to remind you that you didn't answer his question last night."

Taken aback, Hans asked, "About whether I would ever consider the army as a career?"

The other two men's heads snapped up, but Hans ignored them. "I thought a lot about it last night. I think the answer is yes, but I need to think about it some more."

"Excellent. I signed the order requesting a battlefield commission for you, Eckhardt. It'll take some time, but see Jürgens. As of now you're an acting lieutenant. Have him find you some bars to stick on your shoulders later today."

Diehls reached out and poked him. "You're going to be a shavetail louie? Does that mean I've got to start treating you with respect now?"

"That'll be the day," Hans growled.

"Okay, go!" Major Ott said. "I'd like to knock on Eichhorn's door as early as possible. Oh, and by the way, we want Eichhorn, that *Schweinbauer*, taken alive. He's going to stand trial."

8:33 a.m.—On the roof of police headquarters

Ruger darted across the roof in a low, running crouch and rejoined the men. "All right, we've got two minutes. Everyone in place. The instant you hear those cannons open fire, we're going through the doors."

Hans looked around. His men were nervous but eager. They wanted this done. "All right," he said. "Remember, C Company is taking everything to the left as you get off the elevators. That's on every floor. B Company takes everything to the right."

Sergeant Diehls spoke. "Be absolutely sure a room is clear. Check closets and toilets. We can't have someone coming up on our backs."

"That's right," Ruger spoke up. "And don't shoot unless they do. Our task is to drive them down and out the front entrance. Then we've got them." He looked at his watch. "Thirty seconds. Eckhardt, you take in C Company first. We'll be right behind you."

Thirty seconds later all hell broke loose as the cannons and machine guns across the plaza opened fire. The constant fire of four machine guns and the bullets slapping into the building was deafening. The concussion from the cannon explosions shook the whole building and rattled the windows. Hans was at the door that led into the building by then. Standing back, he fired one shot, blowing the lock away. Diehls flung the door open, leaped through the doorway, and started pounding down the stairs, his platoon right behind him.

In four years of war, Hans had always fought in the trenches. This was true of most of the men on both sides of the conflict. The lines were typically static, sometimes for months at a time. So he had never done any city fighting. But he had talked to veterans who had, and from their description it seemed a dangerous and hellish way to fight. Every building had a dozen hiding places. In this case, there were hundreds. If the enemy was courageous and determined, he would lie quietly in wait until you opened the door and then fire without warning. One old sergeant had told Hans that he had never had the shakes after a battle until he and his company were charged with sanitizing a French village before the main body of troops passed through.

Fortunately, the entire top floor of the building was empty, but they still had to go room by room, their hearts pounding like a hammer every time they kicked open a door. But when they dropped down to the fourth floor, pandemonium broke out. About half of the offices had clerks in them, mostly women—some young, some surprisingly old. Many of them were hysterical. Some actually seemed relieved and quickly went to the stairwells and started descending, their hands in the air.

Yelling at Ruger to do the same, Hans stationed a soldier in the stairwell to make sure no one went back upstairs and got behind them. As he was leading Third Platoon down to the third floor, gunshots rang out. Taking the stairs three at a time, Hans opened the door cautiously and then stepped into the hall. One of Ruger's men was standing over a writhing body down past the elevators. "Ours or theirs?" Hans called to him.

"Theirs. Watch it. We've got men in there with guns."

Ruger appeared. "Got an idea," he hissed. He cupped his hand to his mouth, waited for a moment for a break in the shelling, then shouted. "You are surrounded. Come out with your hands up and you won't be harmed. If we come in after you, we come in shooting."

To their surprise, doors up and down both sides of the hallway started opening. One woman held out a white handkerchief and waved it, sobbing when she finally came out. An older man in civilian clothes, his face as white as chalk, crawled out on his hands and knees. "Don't shoot! Don't shoot!" Farther down, a door opened and a pistol was tossed out into the hall. A moment later, a man in uniform came out, his hands high in the air.

Hans turned and waved to his men. "Hold on." Then he shouted the same message loudly enough to be heard over the firing outside.

They waited for a moment and were pleased to see about half of the office doors open and people stream out with their hands up.

Then he had another idea. "Teams of two," he shouted. "One stands back, rifle at ready. The other one kicks in the door. Stay out of the line of fire until it's clear."

And thus they started, some racing down to the far end of the hall, others starting where they were.

Hans paired up with a rangy private from Bremen. He was the kicker; Hans was the one who went in. The private stopped at the door, raising a foot. Hans nodded and he kicked it in.

BLAM! Hans felt the bullet whiz past his cheek. He dove to the floor, firing his rifle blindly as he rolled into the office. A man in an officer's uniform screamed and leaped to his feet, emptying his Luger at Hans. Hans, rolling away, fired again. The man slammed back and went down hard.

His partner burst into the room. "You okay, Sarge?"

Hans got to his feet shakily. The private was gaping at the figure on the floor. Not trusting himself to speak, Hans walked over, rifle at the ready, and looked down at the man. He was not moving. Blood was spreading across his chest. Hans bent down and took the Luger from his hand and pocketed it and then searched the man's jacket pockets and found two loaded clips and pocketed those as well. "Make sure there's no one else in here," he said to his man before going back into the hallway, gripping his rifle hard to stop his hands from trembling.

They cleared the third floor more quickly than they had the fourth. Ruger's strategy seemed to be working. Also, though they could hear a lot of rifle fire outside, the heavy shelling and the chatter of the machine guns had stopped. Hans and Ruger met for a moment before descending to the next floor. "You okay?" the captain asked.

"Yeah. You?"

"I'm good. Sounds like the resistance may be collapsing."

"Let's hope so." Hans started for the stairway. "Watch your back," he called.

When he reached the second floor, it was already filled with people with their hands in the air moving down the hallway toward the stairs, none of them meeting his eyes. Sergeant Diehls stopped for a moment as he was passing him. "Heard you had a close one."

He nodded. "A lot closer than I like. Let's get this done."

Even though virtually every office was empty now, they still had to check them. Hans was working with the same private as before. In the fifth or sixth office, they found an older woman cowering under her desk, sobbing hysterically. At the sight of the soldiers, she totally fell apart. "Please don't shoot!" she screamed. Hans slung his rifle over his shoulder, motioned to his partner to do the same, and then bent down so he was looking into her eyes. "Frau," he said softly. "We're not going to hurt you." He gently took her by the hand and pulled her out from under the desk. Her body was shaking so violently that he thought she might collapse. He spoke softly, his voice soothing. "Private Burkhardt here is going to take you down to where it's safe. No one is going to hurt you. We just want to get you to where you're safe."

Hans transferred her hand to Burkhardt's. "Stay with her until you know she's safe."

"Yes, Sarge."

The two of them exited and Hans started after them, but then he stiffened. Something just behind him had scraped softly across the floor. Whirling like a cat, he jerked the Luger out of his pocket, rammed a magazine in the butt, and levered the barrel back to chamber a bullet. He pressed his back against the wall as he looked around.

This was a smaller office, but now he saw that there was another small room near the back corner. A closet? Toilet? He wasn't sure. Pressing himself against the wall, he raised the pistol. "I know you're in there," he called. "I've got a rifle. Come out, and you won't be hurt."

There was not a sound. Wishing he could remove his boots but knowing he couldn't do that without making a lot of noise, he inched forward. The floor beneath him creaked sharply. There was another scraping sound from the corner.

"Come out now, or I'll shoot!" he yelled.

Nothing happened. Dropping into a crouch, Hans scuttled quickly across the room, stopping to one side of the door. Motionless now and trying to suppress his breathing, he listened.

Nothing. Carefully, he reached out and gripped the door knob. Taking a quick breath, he turned the knob, jerked the door open, and spun away.

The muzzle of a rifle appeared in the doorway and a flash of fire shot out of the muzzle. BLAM! Without thinking, Hans brought the Luger down in a vicious arc. The butt of it crashed into the rifle barrel and it clattered to the floor. Sweeping the pistol up so that its muzzle was pointed at the chest of the dark figure inside the tiny room, Hans started to pull the trigger.

Later, he would wonder what had stopped him, and he wouldn't be able to answer that. But he didn't fire. A white-faced young boy with a wild shock of red hair stared out of the darkened room at him. His eyes were huge and filled with terror. After a moment, when he realized that Hans had not fired, he buried his face in his hands and his body began to shake with huge, silent sobs. He sank to his knees, bowing his head, as if he expected Hans to execute him.

Heart pounding, Hans stepped back. It was a small office closet, barely large enough to conceal an adult. The boy was no more than fifteen. Maybe younger. His face was marred by acne scars and there was a wisp of light red whiskers on his upper lip and chin. He wore a uniform three sizes too big for him. And, to Hans's surprise, he wasn't wearing army boots. He wore a pair of rubber-soled shoes with blue canvas tops, which were the common footwear on farms or among poor laborers. They were cheap and sturdy.

"Get up!" Hans barked.

The boy didn't move.

"*Get up!*" He screamed it at him.

Slowly the kid got to his feet, his eyes still fixed on the ground, his body visibly trembling. Hans kicked the rifle away, and then he cuffed the boy hard on the back of his head. "What were you doing, you stupid *Trottel*? You almost killed me."

He heard footsteps running down the hall toward him. A moment later the door flew open and two of his men were there. They stopped dead, staring first at the kid and then at their sergeant. He grabbed the kid by the elbow and pulled him forward. "This *Dummkopf* nearly blew my head off. Get him outta here."

"What shall we do with him?"

"Take him down and put him with the other prisoners. And take his rifle, too."

As they started to lead him out, Hans stepped in front of him, thrusting his face right up next to the boy's. "How old are you? And don't lie to me!"

"Fourteen," the boy said, his eyes never leaving the floor.

As they went out into the hall and disappeared, Hans moved over to the desk and leaned back against it. He was stunned. A fourteen-year-old kid with acne, who hadn't even started shaving yet, had just come within an inch of ending Hans's life. He gripped the edge of the desk hard. Suddenly his hands were shaking so badly he couldn't get them to stop.

CHAPTER 37

The main foyer of police headquarters was a large, cavernous area two stories high. As Hans and Captain Wolfgang Ruger stepped off the elevator, they both stopped short. The air was cold, hovering near freezing. For a moment Hans was puzzled. The upper floors of the building, where they had been for the last hour mopping things up, had been warm. Here the temperature was icy cold. Then he saw why. All of the large plate glass windows across the front of the lobby were gone. The lobby floor was aglitter with broken glass.

Ruger swore softly as his eyes took it in. The scene was one of utter chaos and the noise was deafening. The lobby was filled with two or three hundred people. About half of those were soldiers screaming instructions or obscenities at the other half as they put them into groups.

Just to the left of the grand staircase was a group of about fifty men in various military uniforms—army, navy, and marines. They were under the close guard of *Freikorps* troops with rifles. These were Eichhorn's troops, the Spartacan regulars who had fought so bitterly to hold the building. Though sullen and angry, they were also clearly defeated.

The second group, off to their right in a back corner of the lobby, were the casualties of the last couple of hours. Here there were both soldiers and civilians, women as well as men. Most wore bandages of some kind and were seated or lying on the floor behind the aid station. Some moaned in pain, others seemed barely aware of their surroundings. Some were covered with blankets. Two doctors and four nurses were still working on their last few patients. Hans winced. The next person in line was a woman. She held one hand to her head. Her hair was matted with blood, and Hans saw that some still seeped from between her fingers. The front of her dress was spattered red. She was weeping softly, staring at the ground.

In the far corner was the largest group, and they were surrounded by soldiers as well. But here there were no rifles out, and their guards were more relaxed. All were civilians, and most were females. They were waiting in long lines in front of four tables. *Freikorps* officers sat behind the tables, interviewing each person individually. Some were escorted over to join another group. Most were being allowed to leave when the officer was satisfied they were police headquarters employees.

Hans felt a nudge. "There's Major Ott," Captain Ruger called out over the noise.

Hans had seen him too. He was one of the four officers at the tables. "Come on," Ruger continued. "Let's go report. Then we'll go see if that rumor about there being a mess tent outside is really true."

Scoffing openly, Hans said, "Come on, Captain. How many rumors in the army actually turn out to be true? One in ten thousand?"

Ruger laughed. "That's way too optimistic, Eckhardt. More like one in a million." He punched him on the shoulder. "Let's go find out."

As they crossed the lobby, the crackle of broken glass was loud enough that all four officers looked up at them. Major Ott was instantly on his feet. He told the woman he was interviewing to wait for him and came over and joined them. They both saluted him as he came up.

"The building is secure, sir," Ruger said. "We have completed a second sweep of all floors, and we've posted guards at all entrances, including the one on the roof."

"Excellent. Good work, men."

"Anything else you need at the moment?"

"No. Go get yourselves a hot meal."

Ruger and Hans exchanged looks. "There really is a mess tent outside?" Ruger asked.

Ott grinned. "There is. It's right behind battalion HQ. Go enjoy." The major started to turn away.

"Sir?" Hans asked. "Did they get Eichhorn?"

The major's brow furrowed, and anger flashed across his face. "No. He slipped away. Whether that was before or after we got here, we haven't determined, but he's gone."

Hans and Ruger left, stepping through one of the windows out to the sidewalk. Hans looked up. The first snowflakes were drifting down from a leaden sky. Somehow, that seemed fitting on this day.

Outside, the scene was almost as chaotic. Dozens of soldiers were standing around smoking and talking, relaxed even though they were on guard duty. As the two men headed across Alexander Plaza, Hans looked over his shoulder. "What a shame," he muttered.

Ruger turned and looked too, but he said nothing and walked on. Hans didn't follow.

No one would have called the headquarters building beautiful. It was huge and squat, even though it was five stories high. The outside of it was blackened with smoke and soot from years of pollution, like almost every other government building in the world. Now, it was pockmarked with hundreds of smaller holes from the machine gun bullets. Here and there were larger, gaping wounds where the artillery shells had made a direct hit.

On the mezzanine floor, one group of three large windows caught Hans's eye. The center one was blown completely away, with only shards of glass and splintered wood left. Yet the windows on both sides of it were untouched, their elegant draperies still perfectly in place.

"Pretty amazing what some light cannon can do to soften things up, eh?" Ruger said. He had stopped to see what Hans was looking at.

Unaccountably depressed by the site of the scarred building and the rubble in the streets, Hans grunted something unintelligible and started walking again.

12:35 p.m.—Mess tent, Alexander Plaza

An hour later, Hans, Captain Ruger, Sergeant Diehls, and Corporal Jürgens were still seated in the mess tent, sipping coffee and munching on sugared biscuits. When Jürgens had returned with lieutenant's bars for Hans, Ruger and Diehls had turned it into a minor celebration. After Ruger pinned the silver bars on Hans's shoulders, everyone in the mess tent raised his canteen and sang the first verse of a bawdy song about the stupidity of new second lieutenants. As they finished, Ruger and Diehls snapped off a pantomime of drunken salutes. Then Ruger popped Hans one on the back. "Welcome to the joy of command," he grinned.

Hans grinned back. "Well, at least I don't have to work for a living anymore."

12:47 p.m.

Ten minutes later they were still at the table, with the exception of Jürgens, who had gone off on some other errand. Hans told Sergeant Diehls that he was going to recommend him as Sergeant Major for C Company. Ruger agreed, saying he would write the letter of recommendation.

At that moment, Diehls's hand came up. "Hold it," he said, cocking his head to one side. "Do you hear that?"

They both stopped to listen. Other men in the tent were shushing each other too. From somewhere distant, they heard the sound of singing—men singing!

"What the—?" Ruger exclaimed. Now the sound was mixed with the rumble of drums and many other voices shouting and cheering.

Suddenly the flap on the mess tent was pulled open, and a man stuck his head in. "The army's coming! The army's coming!"

The tent quickly emptied. As the men ran out into the square, Hans looked around the plaza and saw nothing. Every other soldier in the square was craning his neck to see where the sound was coming from. Then Major Ott came striding out of the building, with the other senior officers behind him.

Ruger turned. "They say it's the army coming, sir."

"Yes," Ott replied. "Noske told us that they would be here later today." He grabbed Hans and Ruger by the arms. "Three thousand of them. You know what that means? This is over. The rebellion is finished. So let's go welcome those boys."

Even as they hurried across the plaza toward the place where *Alexanderstrasse* fed into Alexander Plaza, they saw the townspeople streaming toward them, most at a swift walk, others actually running. At first there were dozens, and then hundreds. Men, women, and children. Mothers pushing babies in carriages. Grandfathers with white beards and lined faces. Businessmen, shopkeepers, street sweepers, a man in a railway uniform, a woman with a flour-covered apron. Another woman, heavy with child, held her stomach as she walked along as swiftly as she could. All were exuberant, joyous, running, and cheering and waving hats, handkerchiefs, and scarves.

Hans laughed to himself. So much for the idea that the people were ready for the dictatorship of the proletariat. Here was the real voice of the people, the law-abiding citizens who only wanted an end to the warfare in their streets and peace and stability reestablished.

With a train station, several government buildings, and many shops, Alexander Plaza was one Berlin's busiest areas. Or had been, up until a few days ago as rioting and street battles around the police headquarters made it a dangerous place to be. Now, it was as if the dike had broken, and people were flooding in to welcome the promise of order and stability once again.

Ott, Ruger, Diehls, and Hans stopped about midway across the plaza as the crowds reached them. Due to the press of the people, they still couldn't see very far into *Alexanderstrasse*, but now the roll of drums and the sound of thousands of marching feet were like a low rumble of summer thunder.

And then, there they were. The first group was only two ranks deep, and Hans saw that it was the fife and drum corps. They were led by a drum major with gold braid on both shoulders and a huge brass baton. It flashed up and down as they came, setting the tempo for the drummers.

Just behind them, the first full company of men appeared, coming around the bend of *Alexanderstrasse* into view. Ah, what a sight that was. The crowd thought so too. A mighty roar went up, echoing off the buildings and rattling what windows had not been smashed. Hans felt like his chest was going to burst with pride. Here was the real army. Here was the pride of Germany. They came as troops ought to march, every uniform clean and pressed, eyes locked to the front, their ranks and columns in perfect alignment, rifles with fixed bayonets rigid on their right shoulders.

Their commanding officer, walking just to their right, was calling out the cadence in a loud voice, matching the timing of the drumbeat. "Left. Left. Your left, right, left. Left. Left. Your left, right, left." As they always did in formal parades, the soldiers were keeping their knees stiff in what was called a goose step. It was impressive. Every boot hit the pavement at exactly the same instant.

The piercing sound of a whistle rose above the frenzy of sound in the square. The drum major spun on his heel so that he now faced his men. He raised his baton high. The second rank of fifers brought their tiny instruments up to their mouths. Three slow, measured blasts of the whistle, and the baton came down sharply. The shrill sound of ten fifes split the air. The crowd applauded and cheered even more loudly. Who didn't love martial music at a time like this?

And then the company behind the fife and drum corps began to sing. Hans instantly stiffened as he recognized what song it was. *No!* He had expected something like "Eyes Straight to the Front" or "Tomorrow We Are Marching," two of the most popular of the army's marching songs. Maybe even *"Deutschland über alles,"* the national anthem. But not this. *Please!* Not this. Not *"Mein guter Kamerad."* That's not a marching song.

But as the pain pierced him like a lance, he understood perfectly. Which only made him want to weep all the more. This was the soldiers' ultimate tribute to their brothers-in-arms. And at this moment, they had chosen to honor those who had fallen and were no longer marching with them.

> *I had a comrade, a better one you won't find.*
> *The battle drums were beating, he was by my side,*
> *In even step and stride, in even step and stride.*

Hans spun away, mumbling to those pressed in around him. *"Bitte.* Excuse me. Please excuse me."

Suddenly Diehls was at his side, clutching Hans's arm. "You all right, Sarge?"

"I . . . Yeah. I . . . I've got a splitting headache. I'm going to get something for it at the aid station."

His friend gave him a searching look, but Hans pulled free and plunged into the crowd—a crowd that was now suddenly quiet and subdued as they too realized what the men were singing.

> *A bullet came a-flying, was it meant for me, or you?*
> *It struck down my comrade, he lay at my feet,*
> *Like a part of me. Like a part of me.*

"Oh, Franck," Hans gasped in a hoarse whisper. He was dimly aware of the strange looks he was getting as he shoved his way through the mass of people, crying, "*Bitte*. Excuse me. Let me through, please." As he broke out into the open at last, he began to run. But it was as if the chorus had him surrounded now, as if every man were looking only at him as they sang the last verse in full voice.

> *His hand still reaches out to me while I reload my rifle.*
> *I cannot give you my hand, rest on in life eternal,*
> *Mein guter Kamerad, My good comrade, Mein guter Kamerad.*

2:55 p.m.—Police headquarters building

Hans got slowly to his feet as he saw Major Ott coming across the lobby toward him. From the look on his face, he guessed what was on his mind.

"You all right, Eckhardt?"

"Yeah, I'm fine."

Ott peered at him, clearly not believing him. "Want to tell me what was going on back there?"

Hans didn't, but he felt compelled to explain his bizarre behavior. "It was at Verdun. We were on a recon patrol. I was the platoon sergeant. We sat down to rest for a minute, and . . ." His voice was flat and expressionless. "A sniper opened up. He hit the guy right next to me."

Ott was nodding. "I wondered. Were you close friends?"

Hans nodded his head. "He was a good man."

"I understand." He touched him briefly on the shoulder. "We've been relieved. The trucks should be here for us in about ten minutes. Round up your men. They'll be coming in from *Alexanderstrasse,* so meet them there."

Hans saluted. "Yes, sir."

He waited until the major had gone out again and then got up and moved across the lobby. It was nearly empty now. The prisoners had been taken away in horse-drawn jail wagons. The wounded had been taken off in ambulances. The civilians were all gone. Outside, a team of carpenters were unloading sheets of plywood, preparing to board up the windows. Turning so as to avoid them, Hans stepped through one of the shattered windows and went out into the square.

Evidently, word of their relief was already spreading, because Diehls was already rounding up his platoon. Hans called to him. "*Alexanderstrasse,*" he called. "Ten minutes."

Diehls called something and waved back. Hans angled away from him, not anxious for conversation right now. His head was down as he moved slowly along, stepping around the rubble that littered the sidewalks. As he looked up to watch where he was going, he saw a large truck parked about thirty yards ahead of him. Several men were moving around it, two of them carrying something long and heavy between them. They heaved it up into the back of the truck.

Hans stiffened. It was a human body. Instantly he knew what he was looking at. This was a graves registration detail, the unit that took care of the dead on both sides.

Hans couldn't have turned away if his life depended on it. His eyes were riveted on the men and the rows of dark shapes on the sidewalk behind them—most in uniform, some not. Breathing in quick, shallow breaths, as if he were standing over the bodies and smelling the stench of decomposing flesh itself, Hans finally forced himself to move away. He jerked to his left and started toward the rendezvous point. But he couldn't stop himself from taking one last look. This time they were lifting a uniformed body into the truck. Gratefully, it wasn't one of his. In this skirmish, Hans had had three of his men wounded slightly, but none killed.

But as the men hoisted the body up, Hans gave a strangled cry. "Stop!" He broke into a run. "Hold it!" he screamed at them.

The men turned, puzzled when they saw a lieutenant running toward them frantically waving his arms. They set the body down again and turned to wait. Hans stopped about ten feet away, breathing hard. His hands were trembling as he took a step closer.

The body was turned half on its side, so he could not see the face. But he didn't have to. The splash of red hair was clearly visible, as were the blue canvas, rubber-soled shoes on the boy's feet.

"Never mind," he mumbled, swallowing hard, waving for them to continue. And then Hans turned and stumbled blindly away, heading for one of the alcoves along the street. He ducked inside the welcoming shadows, dropped to his knees, and became violently sick.

Chapter Notes

Emil Eichhorn, self-appointed president of the Berlin metropolitan police, managed to slip away without detection when the government forces took back the headquarters building. Eichhorn went into hiding in the German state of Brunswick, but when things eventually quieted down, he came out of hiding and got back into politics. He was elected as a deputy to the Weimar Constituent Assembly later in 1919 and was elected to the *Reichstag* several more times before he died in Berlin in 1925.

"*Mein guter Kamerad*" was a song popular in the German Army during both World War I and II.

CHAPTER
38

*January 19, 1919, 8:15 a.m.—Field hospital,
Königsplatz, near the Reichstag building*

Colonel von Schiller was sitting up in bed with a breakfast tray on his lap. He was picking at some scrambled eggs and ersatz bacon in between sips of steaming coffee. When he saw Hans coming up the aisle of the hospital tent, he set the coffee cup down and transferred his tray to a small table beside his bed. "Ah, Eckhardt," he cried. "Thank you for coming."

Hans saluted. "Good morning, sir." Hans peered more closely at him. "If I may say so, sir, you are looking much improved today."

"I am feeling much improved, actually."

"I'm glad. I'll tell the men. They're all asking about you."

The colonel gave him a sharp look. "All? I doubt that." He motioned to the chair beside the bed. "Sit down, Eckhardt. Tell me how it went yesterday."

Hans did so, talking for about five minutes.

Von Schiller laid back. "Ah, I wish I could have been there to see the regular army march in."

"Yes, sir. It was a glorious sight. And to watch the people's reaction—that was wonderful."

The colonel cocked his head to one side. "Major Ott told me you were sick."

Hans jerked up a little. Had Ott seen his encounter with the graves registration people? He didn't think so. "I had a severe headache come on all of a sudden. Probably just a reaction to the tension of taking the headquarters building."

"Probably," von Schiller agreed. "So, Major Ott also said that you asked for permission to see me this morning. Is this about the offer I made you?"

"Yes, sir. It is."

"Ott said that you're seriously considering it, Lieutenant. And by the way, the bars look good on you."

"Thank you. And thank you for your trust in me, sir. I am honored."

"But?" von Schiller asked, frowning now.

"But, even though I am sorely tempted, sir, I'm not sure I'm cut out for a career as a soldier."

The colonel cut in. "Don't say no yet. I want you to think about it some more."

"Sir, I . . . ."

"If that's what you decide, I won't stop you, but I think you've got too many other things on your mind right now."

That took Hans aback. "Sir?"

"Dr. Schnebling asked to see you this morning as soon as we're through."

"But . . . Did he say what for?"

"I told him about my offer last night. He seems to think he can help you make up your mind."

Hans sighed. *Of course he does. A career in the army gets Hans Eckhardt very neatly out of the way.* He sighed again. "If it's all the same to you, sir, I don't think there's much point in—"

"It's not all the same to me, Lieutenant," he snapped. "That was an order. Schnebling is in his office. Go out the door on your left, and then go to the second tent on the right. Any questions?"

"No, sir." Hans got up and left without saluting.

Artur Schnebling was waiting for him outside the tent, smoking a cigarette with another doctor. When he saw Hans, he dropped it and ground it into the mud. The other doctor murmured something and moved away. "Ah, Sergeant—or, I see that it's Lieutenant Eckhardt now. Congratulations."

"Thank you. You wanted to see me, sir?"

"Yes." He stepped forward and pulled the flap on his tent back. But as Hans started forward, he gave him a strange look. "Can I ask you a question?"

Hans nodded, wary.

"Are you related to Colonel von Schiller?" Schnebling asked.

Hans's jaw dropped. "Me? Heavens no. What made you think that?"

He shrugged. "Never mind." He pulled the flap back further. "Go in, I'll be right there."

Schnebling dropped the flap and walked away. Still puzzled by the question, Hans straightened. The entrance to the tent was actually a double entrance, with a small dead space of air between openings. It was designed to keep the inside of the tent a little warmer. Hans opened the interior flap and then froze in place. There was a nurse inside. Her back was to him. For a moment, he wondered if he was in the wrong tent and started to back out again. Then she turned around. He fell back a step. "*Emilee?*" he gasped.

There was a fleeting smile. "The face is familiar, but the name escapes me."

Stunned, he stared at her for several seconds, and then he stepped into the tent and let the flap drop. "What are you doing here?"

"I am here to assist Dr. Schnebling. There are five of us, actually."

"But . . ." He was almost too flabbergasted to speak. "Your uncle didn't say anything about you being here when I saw him the night before last."

"I wasn't here then," she replied. "I came down yesterday afternoon after *Onkel* Artur told me he had found you."

"How did he find me? How did he know I was here?"

"When he arrived, he started asking every soldier that came into the hospital if they knew a Sergeant Hans Eckhardt."

"And he asked Colonel von Schiller?"

"Yes. We were elated, of course. So when I got here, I met the colonel and asked him if he might arrange a time when we could talk." Her eyes were suddenly anxious. "So, can we talk, Hans?"

"I . . . Of course. I was going to write you today, but. . . ." He shrugged. Lame. It sounded so lame. "I also tried to call you last night, but the phone exchanges are still not fully operational."

There was a sardonic smile, but nothing else. There were two cots in the room. She motioned to one and then, not waiting for him, sat down on the other. Hans sat down across from her.

"I want to apologize for that letter," she began after a moment. "I . . . uh . . . I actually went back to the hotel to get it, to tear it up. But you had come and gone."

"You came back?" It was one bombshell after another.

She nodded. "When you didn't call or write, I was frantic. And your mother was frantic too. I had to . . . Anyway, I'm sorry. That letter was unfair. Especially considering what Georg told me about what happened to you. When I realized that you had the letter and had probably read it by then, I gave up and went back to Pasewalk."

Wanting very much to reach across and take her hands, Hans shook his head. "It was not unfair. In fact, considering what you saw in my room, I'm surprised you wrote anything."

She started to respond, but he cut her off. "Emilee, I don't have a lot of time. They're moving our battalion up to the Royal Palace this morning, to help with cleanup. So, though I have no right to ask any-thing, can I ask one small thing of you?"

"Of course."

"I would . . ." He shook his head. "I could spend the rest of to-day and the rest of this year apologizing for what happened, but as my mother once pointed out to me, words tend to come cheaply to me. So, let me cut right to the quick of the matter." He took a quick, deep breath and let it out slowly, feeling his pulse start to race. "If I were to ask you once again, right now, if you would consider marrying me, what would you say?"

"I. . . ." That had clearly taken her completely by surprise.

"Be honest. We don't have time to play games, Emilee."

"I would have to say that, as much as I would love to say yes, I can't. I'm not sure anymore that we are good for each other."

He laughed at the irony of her words. "Thank you for being so generous, but I'm sorry. 'We' is not the operative word here. I know that *you* would be the best thing that ever happened to me, Emilee Greta Fromme. I have absolutely no question about that. But I have serious reservations about whether you can say the same of me."

"Hans, I . . . Look, it has been an insane time. I need time to think about it. We need time to think about it."

He forced a smile. "Granted. However much you need, however long you want."

She was watching him closely, as if she might be wondering who this person was. "But," he went on, "I have one request. And it's a big one."

"What?"

"Your godfather needs to be here to hear this. Is he still outside?"

There was a wan smile. "Knowing *Onkel* Artur, I'm guessing he's not too far away."

8:40 a.m.—Artur Schnebling tent

It took Emilee several minutes to find her uncle, and Hans's anxi-ety rose sharply with each passing minute. What if Schnebling refused to even talk to him? Or maybe Emilee was taking the time to fill him in on what Hans had said. Whatever it was, he was a nervous wreck by the time they returned.

Always cool and businesslike, Schnebling's face contained no hint of what was going on in his mind. He sat down on the cot beside Emilee and folded his hands.

"Okay," Hans said slowly. "Here's my proposal. There are two parts to it. First, I have about an hour before I have to report to my unit. I would like to spend most of that time with Emilee. I'm not going to try and talk her into anything, but I have much to explain to her."

"I would think so," Schnebling said dryly.

Hans stopped, looking at Emilee, but she said nothing, so he went on. "Second, I would like to take Emilee with me to meet some people."

Her eyebrows came up. "Your family?"

"Yes. And I know that sounds like I'm assuming something will come of it, but believe it or not, that's not my purpose. You and my mother have established a special bond through all of this. If I tell her it's over, I'll never hear the end of it. If you tell her it's over"—he shook his head ruefully—"she'll probably congratulate you for your good judgment."

"And that's in Bavaria?" Schnebling asked, openly skeptical.

"Yes. I'll pay for her train ticket. And we'll stay with my family. I assure you, Emilee will be well chaperoned by my family. I have three sisters."

Emilee turned to Schnebling, watching him steadily and not saying anything. He was searching her face thoughtfully. "And how do you feel about that?" he asked.

"I would like that very much."

He gave a curt nod. "Emmy has her own railroad pass. A ticket won't be necessary. Is that all?"

"There are also a few people I need to see here in Berlin before

400

we leave. That will only take half a day, and then we'll head south for Graswang." He spoke to Emilee. "It's not critical that you meet them, but I would like you to."

"Why?"

"I . . . I'm not sure."

That caused her brow to pucker. She started to ask another question but then shrugged. "And you'd like them to meet me?"

The way she worded it caught him off guard. "Uh . . . actually, I guess it's more that I want you to meet them."

"So you're not seeking their approval of"—she hesitated for just a moment—"your choice?"

Taken aback, Hans shook his head. "No. It's not like that." He was searching his own mind now. "I want you to meet them because they're a part of my life."

"Then yes, I would like to meet them. When would you like to leave?"

"As soon as Colonel von Schiller releases me. But when can you leave?"

Emilee turned to her godfather. He responded immediately.

"With the army here now," he answered, "I think our work is finishing up here. It'll take us a day or two to pack up, but we can do that without Emmy." He turned to Hans. "Are you going to treat her right?"

"Yes, sir. On that you have my word."

Schnebling turned, took Emilee by the shoulders, and drew her in so he could kiss her on the cheek. "Then go, child. Let's get this settled in your mind."

She threw her arms around him. "Thank you, *Onkel* Artur. I love you."

He stood up. "You two talk. I'll call your mother. In the case of an emergency, I think I can get a telephone call through." Then to Hans: "If you'd like, I'll put a call through to your parents, too."

"I would like that very much. *Danke*."

"And also," Dr. Schnebling added with a droll smile, "I'll bring Emmy a surgical kit, and she can take those stitches out. I'm not sure the Frankenstein look becomes you." Then, half chuckling at his own little joke, he walked out.

They sat quietly for almost a full minute after he left. Emilee was studying Hans closely. He was content to submit to her scrutiny. "Don't listen to him, Hans," she finally said. "You look wonderful. Well, not your face, of course. That's awful. It makes me shudder to think. . . ."

"You should have seen it when it was brown and yellow. But I'm barely aware of it now." He too chuckled. "Except for when the kids run and hide behind their mothers. But it doesn't hurt much anymore."

"And your ribs?"

One eyebrow came up. "How do you know about those?"

"Because Georg told me, remember?" Folding her hands in her lap, Emilee sat back. "All right, I'm listening."

Hans drew in a deep breath. "Feel free to break in and ask questions anytime." And then he plunged.

He started back when he had left Pasewalk and come to Berlin to get his army compensation. Though she knew some of that, he went through it all again. All of it. Including Katya Freylitsch. He had decided he was going to follow his mother's advice. No more lies. If he had any chance of healing this breach between them, he had to convince Emilee there was nothing he was holding back. Now, as he watched her eyes slowly narrow as he talked about Katya, he wondered if that had been a good idea. When he talked about going to her flat after learning that the war ministry was closed and then going on their drunken spree together, he could see the hurt in Emilee's eyes. Glad to be done with it, he stopped and watched her.

She finally looked up. "Did you kiss her?"

"Yes." All right, so he hadn't told her *every* little detail.

"More than once?"

"Yes."

Long silence. "Anything more than that?"

He lifted his chin and met her gaze. "No. There could have been, but. . . ."

"But what?"

"I thought of you, and I got up and left."

"Good answer," she murmured. Then, "Do you plan to see her again?"

He nodded. "If I can find her. Actually, that's one of the people I hope to see, but she lost her job when the War Ministry closed. She may not even be here in Berlin any—"

"Why?"

"Why do I plan to see her? Because when I told her about you, I promised I would come back and tell her what happened, either way. She made me promise."

"Don't," Emilee said flatly.

"But. . . ."

"You think that's just me being jealous, Hans. But it will only hurt her. It's done. Let it stay done. She'll know when you don't come back. Trust me on that."

He considered that and then nodded. "All right."

"Thank you."

From there he told her about Fritz and Anatoly Kharkov, how he had wormed his way into a job, and how he and Fritzie had become friends. He talked about riding shotgun and the events that followed.

She interrupted him as he finished the account of taking down Karl and his *Freikorps* thugs. "Do you remember that night when I told you that I envied your experience in combat?"

"I do."

"That's what I'm talking about. I would have been so terrified of them. I would never have stood up to them. But you took them on.

Just like that night coming back from Königsberg, when you ran the roadblock. I wish I had that kind of courage."

"Or recklessness?" he asked. "Look where it got me."

She wept quietly as he continued, describing in detail the night Karl and the others had come for him. He spoke quietly, dispassionately, as though he had been a spectator watching from the sidelines. But when he got to that night in the alley behind *Danziger Strasse*, the shame was so hot inside him that he had to look away. But he spared no details, describing the scraps he had found and his encounter with the dog.

He stopped and waited. Emilee said nothing.

Hans went on. "At that point, I thought I had hit rock bottom. But I was wrong."

She was leaning forward now, her elbows on her knees, her face buried in her hands.

"It gets worse," he finally said.

"I don't know if I can bear any more, Hans."

"I'll stop if you want."

"No," she said in a bare whisper. "Please go on."

And so he began to tell her about his encounter with Monika von Schiller in the *Volkspark*. He watched Emilee closely as he spoke, wanting to see her reaction, but she kept her eyes fixed on the floor of the tent. When it was finally over, he was too filled with pain to say anything more.

Her head finally lifted. "Thank you, Hans."

"Thank you?" he blurted. "That's all you've got to say? Especially about the last part? I thought you'd be deeply shocked."

"I was. Earlier today."

"What?"

"Monika von Schiller came to see me this morning," she said after a moment.

He nearly leaped to his feet. "*What?!*"

"Her husband told her I was here to see you. That we were suppos- edly engaged to be married."

"And she came to see you? Why?" Hans was completely non- plussed by that revelation.

"Because she wanted to 'save' me from the clutches of someone as evil as you." There was a fleeting smile. "She really doesn't like you, Hans. I mean, she really, *really* doesn't like you."

"Can you blame her?"

"No." She looked up. "But I wondered whether you would tell me about that."

"Well, now you know."

She went on as though he hadn't spoken. "When I went into your hotel room, I was so disgusted by what I found in there. I was furious with you. Fuming mad. Do you know why?"

"Because it reminded you of your father?"

"No. Because I kept saying to myself. 'How could he do this *to me*? After all the words, all the promises. How could he do this *to me*. And that's when I wrote the letter." There was a deep sigh. "But as Frau von Schiller talked, I had a different reaction. I could barely breathe. I thought I was going to be physically sick. And then I said, 'How could he do *this*?' Not just to me. How could the man I thought I knew and loved do such a thing?"

Her eyes were desolate when they came up to meet his. "And that's when I made up my mind that it was over for me. I never wanted to see you again."

"Yet here I am. And here you are. Why?"

"Because she didn't tell me that you brought back the money."

That rocked him back. "She didn't?"

"No. She didn't tell me any of that. The colonel did. He didn't give me all the details either, but he just kept saying over and over, 'He brought the money back. Can you believe that? He brought it all back.'"

405

Emilee faced him, her eyes glistening again. "When you came this morning, I made a decision."

"To give me another chance?"

"No. I haven't decided that yet."

"Oh."

"But I decided that I would listen. See what you had to say. See what excuses you would make. And do you know when I knew you weren't lying to me?"

"When I told you about Monika?"

"No. It was when you told me about Katya."

"Katya? Why Katya?"

"Because no one knew about Katya except you and her. And you knew it was going to hurt me. I could see that in your eyes. But you told me anyway."

They sat quietly for a time, both lost in their own thoughts, their own turmoil of emotions. Then Emilee got to her feet. "Well, time is going fast. Let me go see if I can find that surgical kit and get those stitches out."

Hans stood too. "Emilee?"

"Yes?"

"I didn't tell you all of that to make you feel sorry for me."

"Good. Because if you did, it didn't work. It fact, even now, I still feel like kicking you. Two bottles of bourbon and three bottles of wine? Stealing a poor widow's mortgage payment? What were you thinking, Hans? Where was your head?"

"That's what I'm trying to tell you, Emilee. I'm better now. I came through it, thanks to Colonel von Schiller. But, who knows when that other *Trottel* will show up again?"

Very sadly, Emilee shook her head. "I've asked myself the same question many times." Then after a moment, she turned away. "I'll go get that surgical kit," she said.

January 20, 1919, 8:15 a.m. — Charité Hospital,
University of Berlin, Mitte District, Berlin

Emilee, let me introduce you to this big ugly guy in the bed there. Fritzie, meet Emilee Fromme. Emilee, this is Fritz Kharkov, from Belarus. He's going to tell you that some thugs burned down his restaurant. But in reality, it was the food. He put too much vinegar in the sauerkraut."

Fritzie completely ignored him. "So this is the young lady from Pasewalk?"

Emilee came forward and took the outstretched hand that was twice as big as hers. "Yes, I am. And it's a pleasure to meet you."

"But this cannot be so," he exclaimed. "You are lovely lady." He jerked his thumb at Hans. "He is jughead, no?"

Emilee laughed. "In more ways than one."

Hans ignored them, walking around the bed as Liliya jumped to her feet and came around to meet him. Her smile quickly disappeared as she looked up into Hans's face. Tears instantly sprang to her eyes as she reached up and touched the scars on his cheek. "And this is what they did to you? Oh, Hans."

He gave her a quick hug. "It's all right, Liliya. It's not as bad as a busted spleen." Then he turned her around. "And this is Liliya," he said to Emilee. "Marrying her is the smartest thing Fritzie ever did in his whole life."

"*Ja, ja,*" Fritzie boomed. "This is true. She is light of my life."

Liliya came around to Emilee and they embraced. "Ah, now I understand," she said.

"Understand what?" Emilee asked.

"Why Hans's eyes would light up every time he talked about his Emilee in Pasewalk."

Emilee blushed and looked at Hans. "You never told me that."

He looked at Liliya. "You never told *me* that." Then he changed the subject. "How are the children, Liliya?"

"Driving us all crazy. We are living with my mother until we get things back to normal. But they are down in the hospital playroom at the moment. Would you like to meet them, Emilee?"

"I would love to."

As they left the room, Hans turned to Fritzie. "So, is the insurance going to pay for the restaurant?" he asked quietly.

Fritz exploded in disgust. "*Ach*! Those swine. They are saying that because I left the grill on all night, they will only pay seventy *Pfennige* on the mark."

"Did you leave the grill on?" Hans asked.

"At one in the morning? Of course not." He shrugged. "But Anatoly and I are anxious to rebuild, so we'll probably settle with them."

He reached out and cuffed Hans on the arm. "So, you are setting a date yet? We expect invitation, *ja?*"

"Of course." Hans pulled up a chair. "But nothing's settled yet," he admitted. "But she likes you, and that gives me hope. If she can like a bear like you, maybe she'll get used to me." Again he changed the subject. "How is Anatoly?"

"He is *gut*. Doing well. He will be here in one hour. He will be glad to see you."

"Unfortunately, Emilee and I have a train to catch. But we'll come back."

Fritzie grasped his hand, nearly crushing it in his grip. "If you don't, I break head open, no?"

Hans laughed. "I believe you would, Fritzie."

8:37 a.m.

As Emilee and Hans left the hospital, she reached out and took his hand. He shot her a look, which she ignored. This was the first time she had done so since they had been reunited. "I like them," she said. "I like them a lot."

"They are good people."

"So, you still won't tell me what we're doing next?" Emilee asked.

"We're seeing some friends. I want to say good-bye to them before we leave."

This wasn't much of an answer at all, but she said nothing more on that. "Does Fritzie want you to come back and work for him?"

"*Ja.*"

"Liliya told me that if you do, he and Anatoly will make you a partner."

Hans's eyebrows lifted, but he said nothing.

"Does that interest you?" she asked.

He shrugged. "Not really. As much as I would enjoy working with them."

She nodded. "*Gut.* I don't picture you as a cook."

"Because I would get all fat and lumpy like Fritzie?"

"No, because I think your customers might burn you out too."

She jumped away as he threw a playful punch at her. Then she took his hand. "So, where to?"

9:20 a.m.—Stressenberger Allee 86, Moabit District, Berlin

Hans had been wrong. The tenement buildings here were not two stories high; they were five and six stories high, with four flats to each building. Most of the windows had small clotheslines strung across postage-stamp-sized balconies, and most of these had clothes hanging on them that were frozen stiff in the cold.

He had also been wrong about the outhouses. As near as he could tell, there were no back alleys here, so it was the gutters on both sides of the street that ran with sewage. At the moment there was no hint of a breeze, so the smell was boxed in between the high buildings and even permeated the inside of the taxicab. It was pretty overpowering.

Hans leaned forward and spoke to the taxi driver. "We'll be about half an hour. Can you pick us up again right here?"

"Not sure. I might have another fare."

"There'll be a healthy tip in it for you."

"How healthy?"

"Ten marks if you're here on time."

"I'll be here."

Hans got out and went around and opened the door. For a minute, Emilee didn't move. Her eyes took in the building across the street from where they were parked. Her nosed was wrinkled into a grimace. "And you won't tell me what this is all about?"

"It won't be long now." Hans extended his hand. She got out, and the taxi driver drove away.

"Does this bother you?"

Her head came up slowly. "This is what I grew up with," she said. "Why would it bother me?"

"Because it's been more than a few years, right?"

She nodded grimly. "But some memories never fade."

"Come on. It's number eighty-six."

Emilee looked around and then pointed to a tenement three doors down. "There."

He took her hand. "You've got good eyes."

"So does everyone else," she said quietly.

"Yeah, I noticed." At virtually every window, there were little faces with their noses pressed up against the glass. And behind them, adult faces peered over their heads and shoulders at these strangers who had come to their neighborhood in a taxicab.

9:24 a.m.

On the top floor, in a darkened hallway, Hans lifted his hand but then lowered it again.

"Are they expecting us?"

Hans shook his head. "They don't have phones here."

"You could have sent them a note."

"I just met them three days ago," he said.

Ignoring her surprise, Hans went on. "It's Sunday. And it's cold outside. They'll be home."

In fact, he could hear voices from inside. He rapped sharply on the door. Hans reached out and took Emilee's hand. "Thank you for doing this with me."

"Don't thank me. I have no idea what I'm doing here."

Footsteps approached, and Hans stepped back. When the door opened, it was Anna. For a moment, her eyes couldn't make out who they were. She opened the door a little wider. The light fell on Hans's face, and she gave a little squeal. "Hans!"

"Hello, Anna," he said. "I told you I would come."

Shocked, she just stared at him, and then she whirled. Behind her a little boy, maybe three, with long, tousled, dark hair, came into the hallway. "Jakob!" Anna called over her shoulder.

"Yes," a man's voice called from somewhere in the back. "Who is it?"

She turned back, radiant with joy. "Come and see." And then she grasped both of Hans's hands. "I told him you would come. He didn't believe me, but I told him you would come."

Now other children were poking their heads out, eyes wide and curious. Anna stepped back. "I'm sorry. I'm forgetting my manners. Come in."

Just then a figure came shooting out of one of the side doors, brown hair flying. "Hans! Hans!" She hurtled across the room, and threw herself into his arms. Laughing, Hans caught her in mid-air and twirled her around. "Yes, Nattie. It's me."

He set her down, leaving her somewhat breathless. Suddenly she went up on tiptoes, peering up at his face. Then a tiny smile appeared. "The bugs are gone," she said with great satisfaction. "Yes," Hans laughed, reaching for Emilee's hand. "And guess who took them out."

9:57 a.m.

Before Hans even got into the taxi, Emilee had the other window rolled down and had her head out, waving to the family on the front step of the tenement. "Bye! *Auf Wiedersehen.*"

Hans got in, shut the door, and slid over beside her. "*Auf Wiedersehen,*" he called, moving so he could see them too. Anna and Natalee stood together, clasping hands, tears streaming down their faces. The other children were smiling and shouting their farewells. Jakob had one hand up. In it were a few bills. "God bless you, Hans," he cried. "God bless you."

Hans pulled his head back inside and tapped the driver's shoulder. "Okay. Back to the hotel."

As the cab started forward, Emilee rolled up the window. "How much did you give him?"

"You weren't supposed to see that."

"How much?"

"A hundred marks."

Her eyes widened momentarily, but she said nothing.

"I wish it could have been more. It won't go far."

Emilee started to fiddle with the buttons on her jacket. "I told Anna to use some of it to buy something special for the children."

He reared back. "My goodness. You've really hit it off with these ladies. First Liliya, now Anna."

"The hunger will be back," she said quietly, "but I told her if she bought some tiny trinket, even something utterly useless that the

412

children get to pick out for themselves, I promised her they would never forget it."

Hans was dumbstruck, but then after a moment he nodded. "I wish I had thought of that."

She smiled. "That's why you brought me along." The smile vanished again. "That, and to soften me up, right?"

"I knew you'd think that."

"Well, didn't you?"

"No."

"Not even a little?" she asked skeptically.

"All right, maybe a little. But I would have come without you."

"Tell me about them. How did you meet?"

So he told her of his reconnaissance mission to Pariser Plaza, and how Nattie had stopped and stared at him when she saw the stitches. He shrugged. "We kind of became friends."

"Kind of?" she retorted. "Natalee absolutely adores you."

Hans blushed a little. "She's amazing. She has so much curiosity. Wants to know everything."

Emilee was watching him closely. "So why did you bring me?"

He looked away. "Because . . . I hoped it would help you better understand something."

"All right, what?"

He was staring out the window as he began to speak. "I don't know what it was about them. And not just them. I was in the midst of thousands of others just like them."

She shook her head. "There are thousands like them," she said.

He nodded. "I don't what it was, but it deeply affected me. Profoundly affected me. And I . . . I don't know. I'm not even sure how to say it. First, I realized how lucky I was—to have been born in my family, to have a good life, even though it was a simple one. To have an education." He turned to her. "I don't think either Jakob or Anna can read or write."

"I don't know about Jakob, but Anna can't."

"She told you that?"

"Yes. Natalee went to primary school for a couple of years, but then Anna's mother's health began to fail, and she couldn't care for the children anymore while Anna went out to do laundry and house-cleaning. So Natalee has to stay home with the younger ones now." Her voice caught. "Which breaks Anna's heart."

"And I got to go to the Von Kruger Academy," Hans said. "An arrogant prig like me. Where's the justice in that?" He took a quick breath. "And—I don't know what came over me. Suddenly, I had this overwhelming urge to do something."

"For the Litzsers, you mean?"

"That too, but no. Bigger. To do something more with my life than making a living and making a name for myself. To . . . to . . ." He threw up his hand. "I don't know. To matter, I guess."

Hans stopped, waiting for Emilee to speak, but she just watched him, her eyes unreadable.

"I'm not even sure what that means," Hans continued. "Do I get a university education? Invent some fantastic new device and make a fortune so I can help people like Anna?" He suddenly burst out in exasperation. "I gave Jakob a hundred marks. What will that do for them? Feed them for a week? It's nothing. In fact, it may only make it harder to go back to what they had before. Think if I could pay for Natalee's education. Even send her to the Von Kruger Academy. That wouldn't change the world, but it would matter a great deal to her."

"Yes it would," Emilee murmured.

"Or maybe I just go back to Graswang and become a dairyman. Or take the colonel's offer and make the military my career. That would at least be a steady income while I try to sort it all out."

"No."

That surprised him. "No? Why not?"

"Do you have to ask? When you heard them singing '*Mein guter*

Kamerad' you couldn't bear it and had to leave. And when you saw that that young boy had been killed, you got physically sick. That is not what you want for a career, Hans. The price is too high for you."

"And what about joining my brothers-in-law on the dairy farm?"

"No. That's not for you either."

"Then what is, Emilee? The University of Berlin? I once thought so, but I'm not sure anymore."

"You can do it," she said with great conviction. "And with an education like that, you could really make a difference, Hans."

"I know I could," he exclaimed. "That's not the question. The question is whether that is what I *should* do." He hurried on. "I know how you feel about it. And I understand why. But I'm not sure anymore, Emilee. And until I am, I'm not going to tell you I'll do it just to win you back."

She visibly flinched, but after a moment she pulled a wry face. "Maybe this total honesty phase is not all it's cracked up to be."

That won her a smile from him. Then Hans sighed. "Sorry. I've thought of little else since I met Jakob and Anna and Nattie." Then he cocked his head quizzically. "So, is it working?"

"What?"

"Is all of this softening you up?"

She almost quipped something cute and clever back, but she couldn't do it. "I don't know, Hans. To be honest with you, I don't know what I think right now. I came here expecting to talk to a drunk, a loser, a thief. Not this starry-eyed idealist who suddenly wants to change the world. I'm still trying to process that."

"I understand."

Emilee reached out and took Hans's hand, interlocking her fingers with his. Then she scooted closer to him and laid her head against his shoulder. "But don't stop trying. I kind of like it."

10:45 a.m.—Hotel Lindenberg, Prenzlauer Berg District, Berlin

A knock sounded on the door of room 214. Hans walked over to it and opened it. Georg was standing there. "*Guten Morgen*, Sergeant Eckhardt. It is so good to see you again."

"Thank you, Georg. Come in." As he did so, Hans motioned to Emilee. "I understand you two have met already."

"Yes," Emilee said. "Good morning, Georg."

"*Guten Morgen*, Fräulein. I'm glad you were able to find him." Then he looked to Hans, anxiety twisting his face a little. "My father asked if you want to come settle up," he said.

"No. Tell him I'm not going to ask for the rest of my money back. I wanted to talk to you, Georg. Sit down." He motioned to the bed.

Georg did so, visibly relaxing a little.

Hans reached back, pulled out his billfold, and extracted a ten-mark note and handed it to him. "That's the tip I promised you for helping me."

Georg's eyes grew bigger. "But we settled on two marks. And even that is not necessary, Sergeant. That's not why I did it."

"All the more reason for taking it." He extracted another ten-mark note and extended it. This time Georg fell back a bit. "What's that for?"

Hans got to his feet, stepped in front of Georg, and put a hand on the back of his neck and pulled him up to his feet. "It's for your college."

The kid's mouth fell open. "What?"

"It's not much, but I want you to put it in the bank. That starts your college fund. I want you to save every *Pfennig* you can spare from this moment on and add to that fund."

Georg was speechless. Hans pulled him closer until their faces almost touched. "Georg, listen to me. You're too bright to spend your life behind a hotel desk. Do you understand me?"

His face came alive with a grin that split his face nearly in two. "Yes, Sergeant. I do."

Hans let go of his neck and stepped back. "Good. I've watched how you study at night. You love to learn, Georg. I can see that. So don't quit."

Hans walked over and picked up his rucksack and then turned to Emilee. "You ready?"

She went over to Georg and gave him a hug. "The sergeant has done some really stupid things," she said with a smile. "But that advice he just gave you isn't one of them." Then, without waiting for Georg's response, she turned to Hans. "Yes, I'm ready."

Hans shook hands with Georg. "We're going down the back stairs. The taxi's in the alley. Why don't you wait until we're gone to tell your father?"

10:52 a.m.—Alley behind Hotel Lindenberg

As Hans put their bags in the back of the taxi, he noticed that Emilee was watching him with a bemused expression. He shut the lid of the trunk and turned to her. "What?"

"Are you sure you've got enough money to get us to Bavaria?"

"Of course, why do you ask?"

"I guess I'm not used to watching you spend money like a drunken sailor, and I just wondered."

He frowned. "I . . . ."

She cut in before he could finish his sentence. "That's not a criticism, just an observation."

He relaxed and opened the door for her. "You're jealous because I'm not spending it on you."

"Ha!" she cried as she popped him on the arm. "I'm just worried that it's all going to be gone before we're out of Berlin." She laughed as Hans leaned forward and spoke to the driver. "Berlin Central Station, please."

CHAPTER
40

January 20, 1919, 7:35 p.m.—Near Murnau am
Staffelsee, Bavaria

Emilee came awake with a jerk. Her head snapped up and she looked around wildly. Hans reached out and put his arm around her, pulling her close. "Emilee, I'm right here."

She looked at him, eyes confused for a moment, but then she visibly relaxed. He smiled at her. "*Guten Abend*, Fräulein."

She pulled away and sat up straighter and then turned and looked out the window. It was pitch black outside, and the only thing she could see was a scattering of lights off in the distance. Yawning, she rubbed at her eyes and finally looked at Hans. "Where are we?"

"We'll be to Murnau in about ten minutes."

She pulled a face. "Oh, that's helpful."

He smiled. "We are currently on the Munich to Garmisch-Partenkirchen line, but at Murnau we change trains and take another line to Oberammergau."

She shook her head in disgust. "Even less helpful. Just tell me how long until we're there."

"Well, we'll have half an hour's wait in Murnau, and then Oberammergau is about half an hour after that."

One hand shot up and touched her hair. "Oh, dear. I must be a fright." She started to get up. "I need to comb my hair and freshen up. Oh, and put on my new dress."

"Emilee," Hans said, laying a hand on her arm. "We'll have half an hour in Murnau. The bathrooms in the *Bahnhof* will be much better than the one on the train. You'll have plenty of time to get yourself fixed up."

She pulled an arm away from his touch. "Don't be so smug. Just because all you have to do is run your fingers through your hair." She looked out the window again. "How long was I asleep?"

"About three hours. You slept right through Munich."

She started for a moment but then slapped his arm. "I did not. I remember changing trains there."

"*Gut.* I nearly had to hire a porter to put you on a cart and wheel you onto the train."

Her eyes narrowed. "Let me warn you, Herr Eckhardt," she said tartly, "if something ever does come of this turbulent relationship of ours, you should know that teasing me right after I wake up could put your life in extreme danger."

"Ah, I see," he replied gravely. "And how long does that condition last?"

"About an hour and a half. And that's assuming I get an injection of coffee immediately upon awakening."

He laughed. "Duly noted." Then he grew serious. "You were tired. I'm glad you got some rest. This has been a rough few days for you."

"Not really. Other than wondering every minute if you were dead or alive, drunk or sober, a child who needed spanking or the man I had agreed to marry." She slid in closer to him, smiling softly now. "It was exhausting. Did you sleep at all?"

Hans shook his head as he put his arm around her. "Not really."

"So, what have you been thinking?"

He shrugged. "I don't know. About life, I guess. About us, of course."

"Hans, I. . . ."

"I know, Emilee. I'm not assuming anything. You have every right to wonder whether this is going to work."

"I'm not trying to be difficult, Hans. I just. . . ." Her voice trailed off again and she laid her head against his shoulder, closing her eyes. "But I am very excited to meet your mother. I'm surprised how close we've grown over these past few weeks."

"No surprise. You're both worrying about the same little boy."

Laughing softly, she nodded. "Yes, we are."

They were silent for a while, and then Hans stirred. "Emilee, there's something I need to tell you."

She immediately sat up. "Oh no," she said, only half teasing, "I don't like the sound of that."

"Before I ever knew that you and Dr. Schnebling were in Berlin, I made up my mind that the only way I could make up to you all that I had done was to be completely honest with you about what happened."

"It's a good thing you did, or I wouldn't be here now. Wait! Are you saying there's more?"

Hans nodded.

The corners of her mouth tightened. "And you've waited until now to say it?"

He couldn't help it. "It's nothing bad, but maybe I should get you a cup of coffee first."

"Don't joke about this, Hans. Tell me."

He took a deep breath. "All right. Remember when you asked me why I decided to return the money to Frau von Schiller, and I told you that it was because I felt guilty?" Emilee nodded slowly. "Well, that's true, but it's not the whole story."

"I'm listening."

And so, in a low voice so he wouldn't be overheard by the other

420

passengers, Hans began. He started with the conversation he'd had with his mother about lying and how she had told him the story about the Dutch boy with his finger in the dike. "So," he said when Emilee just nodded, "here's what I didn't tell you. As I was walking away from Frau von Schiller as fast as I could—or hobbling away is a better description—I . . ." He looked away. "I heard a voice."

That brought Emilee's head up with a jerk.

"Well," he hurried on. "I'm not sure that I *heard* it. It was more like I *felt* it."

"And it told you to give the money back?"

"No. It only spoke one word. It said, 'Peter.'"

"Peter? I don't get it. Why Peter?"

"That's exactly what I thought at first. And then it hit me. Mama thought the boy's name in the story was Peter. I told her it wasn't. That it had been added into the story later. That irritated her. She knew what I was doing, which was dodging the point she was trying to make. She was telling me that something little, like a small lie, was like the crack in the dike, and that if I didn't stop now, the whole structural integrity of the 'dike'—meaning my life—would be compromised."

"How ironic," Emilee murmured. "And this was before you came back to Berlin?"

"Yes. Little did I know that the dike was about to bust wide open and I'd be drowning."

"Why didn't you tell me this yesterday?"

"Because, I . . . I don't know. It's just so weird. Hearing voices? At first I thought it might be *delerium tremens*. That's when you—"

She jabbed him with her elbow. "I'm a nurse, Hans. I know what DTs are."

"Oh, yeah, right. Now, I wonder if it wasn't just a combination of the pain, the hunger—"

"Anything but inspiration, right?" she cut in.

"I knew you'd say that. That's why I didn't tell you."

For a long moment her eyes searched his, but then she slowly nodded. "I understand."

"And that's all you've got to say?"

"You didn't tell me," she snapped right back at him, "so I assume that means you didn't want to hear what I would say."

"I don't think it was an answer to prayer, or from God, or some angel or something. Not some grand miracle." He threw up his hands. "To be honest, I don't know what it was."

"Nor do I," she said. "But I do know what it *wasn't*. It wasn't DTs or mental exhaustion or hunger. It was from your mother."

"It wasn't her voice."

"It was from your mother," she said more forcefully. "In answer to her prayers. And mine. I know how you feel about God and all that, but how can you not see it, Hans? If that voice hadn't spoken to you, you would very likely be in prison now."

"Von Schiller said that if I hadn't brought the money back, he would have had me shot."

"So you'd be dead!" she cried. "And instead, you got food, medical treatment, a shower and shave, a job with a bonus, a commission as a lieutenant, and . . . and. . . ."

"And I came within an inch of being shot twice in the police headquarters."

"Call it whatever you want, Hans—good luck, fate, Providence, God, an angel—but at least acknowledge there was some higher power in all of this. That can't all be just pure coincidence."

"I suppose."

"Then thank Him for it."

"What if it's not God?" Hans shot right back. "What if there is another explanation for it?"

"You thanked Dr. Schnebling for all he did for you and me. And you thanked Colonel von Schiller for giving you another chance. And you thanked me for coming and agreeing to listen to you. And I'm guessing you'll thank your mother for not giving up on you. So why do you find it so repugnant to lift your eyes to heaven and say, 'Thank you, God?'"

Hans exhaled slowly. "Don't get me wrong, Emilee. I am very grateful for what has happened to me these past few days. I know that I don't deserve any of it. But I just can't believe that there's someone up there in the heavens manipulating things on my behalf. So, I am thankful. I just don't know who or what to thank."

Emilee said nothing, just stared out the window.

"That's not helping my case, is it?" he asked after a moment.

She didn't answer him.

8:13 p.m.—Murnau am Staffelsee Railway Station, Bavaria

Hans gave a low whistle as Emilee came out into the main hallway again. Then he walked swiftly over to her. "Excuse me, Fräulein, but have we met before?"

She laughed, pleased at his reaction.

"Wow! That dress is lovely." He touched her arm. "And so are you, Emilee. You look exquisite."

She took a little bow. "Exquisite, I can live with." Then she noticed he had something tucked under one arm. "What's that?" she asked, pointing.

"I bought a newspaper while I was waiting."

"Oh?"

"Yeah. They finally caught Liebknecht and Luxemburg."

"Who?"

"The two leaders of the Spartacan revolt, the two who were the most responsible for the last week of violence and murder."

"And they'll put them on trial?"

He shook his head. "Their captors didn't wait for that. They made Liebknecht kneel down and shot him in the back of the head. Rosa Luxemburg's captors beat her with the butt of their rifles, then shot her, and then dumped her body in a canal somewhere in—"

"Don't, Hans!" Emilee exclaimed.

Surprised, he stopped. "What?"

"I don't want that in my head right now," she said.

"Oh. It's just that these were the two that—"

"I know. But not tonight, okay?"

"Sorry." Feeling stupid and embarrassed, Hans stepped over to a trash bin and tossed the paper into it. "They're boarding now," he said glumly. "We can get on if you're ready."

Emilee came over and took his hand. "Go over your family with me again, but slowly this time. Do you think they'll all come to the station? It will be almost nine o'clock by the time we get there."

"Oh, yeah," he said, squeezing her hand. "And definitely all of Graswang with them. And probably half of Oberammergau as well. And they're not coming to see me, that's for sure."

8:55 p.m.—Oberammergau Railway Station, Bavaria

An interesting thing happened at the train station after their arrival. Emilee and Hans hadn't said much on the ride to Oberammergau. She could tell that her reaction to the news story had hurt him. She would talk to him about it later, she decided.

In spite of Hans's predictions, the family members were the only ones there to meet them, though every single member of the family was there. Hans first introduced his parents to her and then stood back with his father as Emilee and his mother clung together for a long time, tears of joy falling freely. Inga had only managed to choke out one sentence. "Thank you for bringing our son home."

First, Inga introduced her daughters and their husbands and children in order from oldest to youngest. Ilse and Karl, Heidi and Klaus, Anna and Rudi. The children's names were mostly lost in a bewildering whirl, but before morning Emilee would review the sheet Hans had written up for her. Only then did Inga give permission to the children to greet their *Onkel* Hans.

Emilee watched in wonder as they swarmed around him. Little

Miki shot out of her father's arms, nearly bowling Hans over. She hugged him tightly as she planted kiss after kiss on his cheeks, chattering away as fast as her little tongue could move. The older ones were no less enthusiastic, talking all at once, asking him questions, telling him about some new event in their lives, asking him how long he was going to stay this time.

Gradually they calmed down, and Hans huddled them up in a circle with his arms around them all. He began to talk to them in a low voice. When they began to giggle and kept stealing glances at her, Emilee realized he was telling them about her. Smiling, she started over to join them, but Hans waved her away. "Sorry," he called, "local Bavarians only. East Prussians not allowed."

Inga and the others came over and stood beside Emilee, watching with affection. "He's one of them," Anna observed. "That's why they love him so much."

And just like that, Emilee knew. Even as the answer came to her, it left a thousand questions tumbling in her head. But that was all right. She had never expected to have all of her questions answered. Just the one.

"Stay here," she whispered to Inga and the others, and then she walked over to the circle.

Miki gave a squeal. "Here she comes!"

"No Pasewalkians allowed," Hans exclaimed, turning to face her.

She walked right up to him and jerked her thumb in the direction of the other adults. "Out!" she growled. Trying not to laugh, Hans meekly bowed his head and backed away.

"Okay, gather in," Emilee commanded the children. She went down on one knee, gathered Miki into her arms, directed Annaliese and Kristen to come in on her left side, and told Klaus Jr. and Gerhardt to stand on her left. She motioned them to bend down, and then she began to talk.

Hans watched, smiling at this sudden conspiratorial togetherness. "She's wonderful, Hans," Ilse said.

"Delightful," Heidi agreed.

"Absolutely," Anna chimed in.

Now the giggles were coming nonstop. Miki was listening, her eyes growing wider and wider, and suddenly Emilee whispered something in her ear and Miki clapped her hand over her mouth and doubled over with peals of giggles.

Finally, Emilee stood up. She stood Miki directly in front of her. Annaliese and Kristen stood on her left, the boys on her right. "We have an announcement," Emilee called. "Come in closer."

The family moved in. Emilee laid a hand on Miki's shoulders. "You first, Miki."

She stepped forward, her hands clasped in front of her, as if she were in church. She glanced back at Emilee, who nodded to her. She turned back, took a deep breath, and said, "I'm the flower girl."

Inga gasped, and her hand shot to her mouth. Hans was dumbstruck. There were cries from the others. Emilee motioned to the two girls. Annaliese was fifteen, Kristen, thirteen. They were holding hands. They looked at each other, nodded, and then in perfect unison said, "And we're the maids of honor."

Hans started forward, and then Emilee waved him back. "Boys?"

"And we're the groomsmen," Gerhardt blurted.

Smiling mischievously, Emilee came forward and took both of Hans's hands. "Sorry to box you into a corner, Herr Eckhardt, but I'm afraid you have no choice now. So down on your knee."

Hans dropped instantly to one knee. He didn't need to be told what to do. "Emilee Greta Fromme, will you—"

She threw back her head and shouted it at the sky. *"Yes!"*

The family burst into applause. Everyone else on the platform turned and looked, and, not sure exactly what was going on, they started to applaud too.

CHAPTER
41

January 25, 1919, 11:10 a.m.—Eckhardt dairy farm,
Graswang, Bavaria

Hans stopped at the door to the kitchen, his face softening. Emilee was at the stove with his mother. She was stirring a pot of pork stew while his mother added a dash of seasoning. They were talking quietly. His mother said something and Emilee laughed. It was a sound of pleasure and contentment, and it made him smile.

Hans was pleased with how the whole family had taken to Emilee, but her relationship with her future mother-in-law was especially satisfying. Inga had already told Hans that she thought of Emilee as one of her own daughters.

His mother leaned in toward Emilee and spoke again, this time loudly enough for Hans to overhear. "Don't look now," she said, "but there's some strange man at the door watching us. Do you think he's here for you or for me?"

Hans laughed and walked into the room. Both women turned around and smiled at him. He went up and took Emilee in his arms and kissed her lightly. "Smells good," he said.

"Yes, your mother makes the best stew ever."

He smiled. "Yes, that smells good too." Emilee blushed as Hans turned to his mother. "Can I steal Emilee for a while? What time is lunch?"

"This needs to simmer for another hour or so. We'll eat at one."

"Good." He turned back to Emilee. "Let's go for a walk."

11:20 a.m. — Graswang Valley

They walked slowly, following the path that wound along the banks of the Lech River. There had been a light snow yesterday, but now there were only some scattered clouds scudding across the sky and the temperature was a little above freezing. Emilee and Hans were holding hands, and their shoulders were touching. She looked up at him. "You really are spoiled, you know."

He shot her a dirty look. "Have you been talking to my mother?"

She laughed. "No, I mean that you're spoiled getting to live in this place." She looked around. Except for a few patches, the snow was gone from the valley, which was framed in on all sides by pine-covered hills. Beyond them, here and there, the towering peaks of the Bavarian and Austrian Alps could be seen. After the bleak flatlands of northern Germany, this was breathtaking to Emilee. "It really is incredibly beautiful, and you just take it for granted," she added.

"Actually, I don't," Hans said over the sound of the gurgling water. "I love this place."

"Thank you for bringing me here. Thank you for letting me meet your family. They really are quite wonderful."

"You say that only because they treat you like visiting royalty," he teased.

"Yes," she shot right back. "But I deserve it, don't you think?"

He nodded soberly. "Yes, your majesty."

They walked on for several more minutes without speaking, and then Hans said, "I'd like to talk to you about our marriage, Emilee."

She stopped dead. "I don't like the sound of that."

He took her elbow, chuckling. "Our marriage ceremony, I mean. Okay?"

She didn't move. "What about it?"

"I want to ask you a question, but I need you to be really honest with me, all right?"

"Of course."

He was suddenly hesitant. "I know that you and your family are Lutheran. And, as you know, we are Catholic, as is most of Bavaria."

She stepped back so she could watch his face. "Go on."

"Papa wants us to be married in the Church of St. Peter and St. Paul in Oberammergau. It is a very beautiful church, almost like a small cathedral. But it is also very Catholic, with statues of saints everywhere, lots of gold leafing, murals, and the like. Is that going to be offensive to you and your family, especially your mother?"

She was nodding as he finished. "Before I answer that, let me ask you a couple of questions. Where would *you* like to be married?"

Hans's shoulders lifted and fell. "You know me. I'm not what anyone would call a devout anything, so it doesn't really matter. But I want you to be happy, Emilee."

She reached out and laid a hand on his arm. "Thank you for that. What about your mother?"

"Mother," he said with soft affection, "is always the peacemaker. She'll do whatever we say, but I know she's worried about offending your family."

"What would she choose if it were completely up to her?"

"Good question. Remember, my mother is a Mormon. She's no longer Catholic."

"Oh, yes, I remember you saying that. So what does that mean? Would she like to have it in a Mormon church?"

"Not necessarily. First of all, they meet in rented halls. In the second place, the nearest congregation is in Munich. If it weren't for that, she'd probably love it if her Mormon pastor, or whatever they call them, performed the wedding. And that's not just because she's a Mormon. From what she says, I understand that the Mormons believe that marriage should be for eternity, not just for time only."

That brought Emilee's head up. "What does that mean?"

"I'm not sure. Mama just says that she hates that part of the wedding ceremony where they say, 'Until death do you part.'"

"I do too. So what do they do differently?"

He shrugged. "You'll have to ask her. But back to your question. I think Mama would prefer it if we had the wedding at our parish church right here in Graswang. It's small. It's quiet. Most of their friends are here. But, what do you want, Emilee?"

She took his arm as they began to walk again. "Actually, Mother is not very happy with our pastor lately."

"Why is that?"

"When we first moved back to Pasewalk, we were welcomed into the local parish quite warmly. Then, as Mama's health declined, we just kind of dropped off his list. He never came to see her. Never inquired after her. She was not used that. Her pastor in Königsberg was very caring and concerned. But she knows that your family is Catholic. I think she just assumes it will be in a Catholic church."

"Is your *Onkel* Artur coming down with your family?"

"Of course. They'll all come together."

"*Gut.* So, let's talk to Mama. If she agrees, I'll tell Papa that we want it in our local church, and that will be that. With you, me, and Mama united, he'll give in."

"Then it's settled."

February 1, 1919, 7:40 p.m. —Der Leuchtender Stern Restaurant, Oberammergau, Bavaria

As Hans watched the waitresses in the Bright Star Restaurant distributing the last of the dessert, he leaned over and put his arm around Emilee. "Well, Frau Eckhardt, are you happy?"

"Do you have to ask?"

"I think the wedding went well. Do you think your mother was pleased?"

"More than pleased, Hans. Afterward she told me how worried she had been about it being a Catholic wedding and how happy she was with how it turned out."

"Good. I'm very glad."

"In the Lutheran church, we believe that a wedding is a religious service and not just a social occasion. The reception is the time for the social aspects, but the wedding ceremony itself should be a worship service that praises God and sanctifies the marital union."

"I'd say that was true of our Catholic service, too."

"Exactly. That is what pleased her. It was reverent, worshipful, and sacred. Actually, I was surprised to see how much alike our two services are—the processional, the prayers, the music, the reading of selected scriptures. We have all of those too." Then she jabbed him with her elbow. "So, newly wedded husband of mine, which scripture was your favorite?"

If she had thought she would catch him by surprise, she was wrong. He answered without hesitation. "Well, I'm hardly a scripture scholar, but I really liked the one from Genesis about Adam and Eve."

"Why?"

"Well, after God created Eve, he said that the two of them should become as one flesh. With you standing right there beside me and knowing that in a few moments we would be husband and wife, the idea that we could become as if we were one person was really profound to me."

"And me as well," Emilee murmured.

Just then there was a sudden clinking of metal on crystal. They turned. Hans's father was on his feet, tapping his glass with his spoon. The room quickly quieted.

"Ladies and gentlemen," he began. "Friends, neighbors, and family. Before we begin the dancing, we would like to present the bride and groom with gifts from their families. We shall begin with a gift from Emilee's family. Then, Hans Otto's sisters shall present them with our family's present. Then, Dr. Schnebling, Emilee's godfather, and I will present our gifts. And finally, we shall have a very special presentation by our grandchildren." He nodded to Emilee's mother. "Frau Fromme, would you like to begin?"

Emilee's mother got slowly to her feet, looking wan and somewhat tired, but joyful, too. "Thank you, Herr Eckhardt. I shall be brief. To Hans we say, welcome to our family. You have filled my daughter's life with joy, and for that I shall be eternally grateful. *Danke schön.*"

She turned to her sons. "Ernst and Heinz-Albert shall present our gift to you."

Hans leaned over to Emilee. "You were behind them in the processional, but I wish you could have seen Heinz-Albert as he marched with the groomsmen and the bridesmaids. He was so proud to be paired up with Annaliese."

Almost instantly tears welled up. "He told me later. He even remembered her name. Thank you for including him, Hans. Mama and I are very grateful."

The gift Emilee's brothers brought over was a large punch bowl made of lead crystal and embellished with an elegant floral design cut into the glass. With its base and ladle it made a beautiful set, and the audience responded with exclamations of wonder.

Next, two of Hans's three sisters got up and headed for the gift table. Anna, who was now in her eighth month of pregnancy, stood and waited where she was. Ilse and Heidi returned carrying a gift that was not wrapped, because it was a large and bulky quilt. Each sister got ahold of one side of the quilt and held it up high, letting it fall out to its full length. Emilee's hands flew up to her cheeks as she gasped in delight. The quilt was for a double bed and was obviously handmade. It was deep, royal blue. In the center was a large red heart with stitching across it.

HANS AND EMILEE
LOVE ETERNAL
FEBRUARY 1, 1919

Emilee got to her feet and came around to join her new sisters-in-law. "It's beautiful!" she exclaimed, close to tears. "Turn it so everyone can see." As they did so and more applause began, Emilee hugged each of them.

"Thank you," Emilee whispered. "Thank you for accepting me into your family."

Ilse choked up. "After seeing what you've done for our little brother, you *are* our family." Hans Sr. was tapping on the glass with his spoon, so everyone quickly sat down again. "All right," he said, not waiting for everyone to get settled. "Dr. Schnebling and I have decided to present our gifts together. Artur?" As the doctor got up, he turned to his left. "And would the happy couple please join us as well?"

Hans's father shook hands with Emilee's godfather, and then together they withdrew envelopes from their jacket pockets. Artur handed his to Emilee. Hans Sr. handed his to his son. "Open them together," he suggested.

When they did so, Emilee and Hans both gasped. "Five hundred marks?" Hans cried. Emilee held hers up too. "Five hundred marks also."

"To get you started in life," Artur said, stepping forward and taking Emilee into his arms. He kissed her on the forehead. "I am so happy for you, Emilee. And so proud."

Hans was staring at his father. "Papa, I . . . I don't know what to say."

Hans Sr. smiled, immensely pleased. "I think *danke schön* is a good start."

By this time, everyone was standing and applauding. Finally, Hans Sr. held up his hands. As the group sat down again, Artur, Emilee, and Hans returned to their seats.

"Thank you, thank you," Hans Sr. called. "Now, as I said, Hans's nieces, nephews, and cousins have a presentation to make." He held out his hand toward a side entrance into the hall. Immediately the children marched in, with Annaliese, the oldest, in the lead. They came in single file, not in order by age, but by height. The girls were glowing with anticipation. The boys looked like they were trying very hard not to giggle. Bruno and Miki, the two youngest, brought up the rear. They formed a line in front of the head table facing the audience. Miki and Bruno came forward in front of the others. Bruno held a roll of butcher paper in his hands. He held it out so that Miki could take the edge of it and they moved apart, unrolling it for all to see. Instantly the crowd erupted with laughter followed by even more enthusiastic applause.

Hans Sr. called out over the noise. "Hans. Emilee. This is all the children's doing. You need to come around and look." Taking Emilee by the hand, Hans led her out and around the children. When they saw what it was they stopped, and then they too clapped their hands and started to laugh.

In the center of the banner was a red heart, identical to the one on the quilt. Inside the heart, painted in white letters, it said ONKEL HANS & TANTE EMILEE. To the left of the heart, in larger black letters, it read PLEASE COME SEE US. To the right, in the same sized letters, the sentence continued. AT LEAST ONCE A WEEK.

Instantly, Emilee was in tears. She started forward to hug the children, but Annaliese waved her back. "Miki has something from all of us to you. Please stand together."

Hans and Emilee did so, facing the crowd now. Miki handed her side of the banner to Bruno and came around in front of the pair. She was very solemn and held her hands together in front of her, as though she were ready to pray. She stood there for a moment and then took two steps forward, stopping in front of Hans. She beckoned for him to bend down. When he did so, she went up on tiptoes and kissed him on both cheeks. "We love you, *Onkel* Hans."

Pretty close to tears himself, he managed a hoarse, "And I love all of you."

Miki moved to face Emilee. Again her finger wiggled. Emilee bent down close, and Miki kissed her on both cheeks with that same solemnity. "We love you, too, *Tante* Emilee."

Tears were streaming down Emilee's cheeks and she couldn't speak. Miki stepped back and started to return to her place. But suddenly, she whirled around and ran back to Emilee, throwing her arms around her. "I love you so much, *Tante* Emilee. I want to be just like you when I grow up."

Except for a lot of sniffles that could be heard, the room was silent as Miki turned and trotted back to rejoin Bruno. Hans Sr. got to his feet, wiping at the corner of his eyes with his handkerchief. Then he cleared his throat and called out. "All right. Let's get these tables and chairs moved back, and let's dance."

8:45 p.m.

Hans Sr. and Inga came over to where Hans and Emilee were talking with Herr Holzer, the schoolmaster who had been such an influence in Hans Otto's life. Holzer and his wife shook hands with the Eckhardts and then said good night and moved away. Hans Sr. and Inga turned the bride and groom around and moved with them over to the corner. "Hans, Emilee," Inga said. "Your father and I have one more thing to give you."

Hans Sr. withdrew another envelope from his jacket and handed it to Hans Otto. He just stared at it. "What's this, Papa?"

"A little more to help you get started."

Hans gave his mother a questioning look. "Open it," she said with a smile.

When he did so, he fell back a step. After a moment, he held the check out so Emilee could read it. One hand flew to her mouth. "Two thousand marks! But you already gave us so much!"

"Shh," her father-in-law said. Then to Hans Otto: "Your mother and I believe that your plan to open up a mechanic's garage to repair trucks is a wonderful idea. If the army had given you your severance pay, you would have had enough to do that. But they didn't."

Hans looked quickly at Emilee and back at his father. "We will take it on one condition. It is a loan, and we shall pay it back as quickly as we are able."

"Yes," Emilee said firmly. "A loan. But how generous of you. I don't know what to say."

Hans Sr. was shaking his head. "On the day your mother and I were married, my father deeded over the dairy farm to us, even though he and Mama lived with us for many years after that. Since you have signed the farm over to your sisters, this is the least we can do for you."

Struggling to keep his voice level, Hans said again, "It's a loan, Papa. And we will pay it back. But this is heaven sent. Thank you, Papa. Thank you, Mama."

Emilee wiped at her tears, laughing softly. "You'd think that I wouldn't have any more tears left today, but. . . ." She stepped to Inga and put her arms around her. "I know your daughters will always be there for you, Inga, but we would be honored if, when the time comes that you need some help, you would come and live with us."

"Thank you, dearest Emilee," Inga said, weeping unashamedly, "but surely you know by now that you are one of my daughters too. It just took me a while to convince Hans of that."

CHAPTER 42

*February 15, 1919, 2:40 p.m. —Herrnstrasse 16,
Obermenzing District, Munich*

Five-year-old Bruno Groll looked up from his stack of blocks. The sound of an engine outside was unmistakable, but normally he didn't take notice of passing cars. But there was a squeak of brakes. When the motor died, he was up like a shot and to the front window. He took one look and then began jumping up and down and hollering at the top of his lungs. "Mama, Mama! Emilee! Come look! It's a taxi. Hans and *Tante* Inga are here!"

Paula Groll came out of the kitchen wiping her hands on her apron. Emilee was beside her.

"Look, Mama. It's *Tante* Inga."

Highly skeptical, Paula looked at Emilee. "That can't be." But Bruno was now shouting through the window and waving wildly.

"Oh my word," Paula cried. She whirled and called up the stairs. "Gretl! Come down quickly. Bruno, pick up the blocks." Then she turned to Emilee. "Did you know Inga was coming?"

"No. Hans called his father yesterday and asked him to ship his toolbox up. He called back last night to say it would be on this afternoon's train. But he said nothing about Inga coming."

Just then, Gretl, who was thirteen, came running down the stairs and joined them at the window. "*Tante* Inga's here?"

"Yes. Hurry. Put the dishes in the sink and the bread dough in the ice box." As she started away, Paula took off her apron and threw it at her. "Here, Gretl. Take this." Then taking a deep breath, she calmly walked into the front hallway, motioning for Emilee to follow her. "Come. Let's go say hello."

2:45 p.m.

"Why didn't you call?" Paula asked.

Inga reached up and removed her hat and set it on the lamp table beside the sofa. "Because I didn't know I was coming until about an hour before we left. My Hans was out in the barn getting young Hans's toolbox ready to take to the train station. I was watching him and saying something about it being two weeks since the wedding and things like that, when Ilse, Heidi, and Anna came in. They had my suitcase all packed." Inga laughed gaily. "At first I started giving them all these reasons why I couldn't go, but then I just stopped and said to myself, why not? And so here I am."

"Well, what a wonderful surprise."

They heard the front door open, followed by a loud clunk. A moment later the door closed again, and they heard the taxi driving away. Finally Hans came into the room, brushing his hands against his pant legs. He came over and sat down beside Emilee. As he took her hands, she pulled them away. "Ooh. Your hands are cold."

He reached out and took hers again. "I know. That's why I want you to warm them up."

"Did the tools make the journey all right?" she asked.

"Not a scratch," he said.

Inga chuckled. "Your father threatened the porter with physical harm if anything happened to them." Hans turned to his aunt. "Paula, is it all right if I leave the toolbox in the hallway for now? I'll move it upstairs later."

"Of course."

"How about my crate of cheese?" Inga asked her son. "Is it all right?"

"It's in good shape too, *Mutti*."

"Crate of cheese?" Paula asked, looking at her sister.

"Yes, six rounds. About a hundred and twenty pounds. One for you and Wolfie. One for Hans and Emilee." She turned to Emilee. "A housewarming present from Graswang."

"Mama," Hans broke in. "We haven't signed the papers on the flat yet. Who are the other four wheels of cheese for?"

"I'm giving them to the branch." She turned to Paula. "I assume we're going to church tomorrow."

Paula nodded, but Emilee was a little irritated that Hans had given her such an abrupt explanation about their new home. So she turned to Inga. "We sign the lease on Thursday," she explained to Inga. "They already have our deposit. And then we move in on Saturday." She turned back to Hans. "Tell her, Hans. Tell here where it is." Then to Inga: "It's a wonderful place for a mechanic's garage."

Though he tried to look annoyed, Hans was actually delighted to be asked about it. "Well, Mama, I know you don't know Munich any better than I do, but Wolfie helped me find it. It's in a district called *Milbertshofen*."

"It's not that far from here," Paula said.

"The building is just one block north of what they call the Frankfurter Ring, which is a main street there. It will be very easy for people to find me and bring their trucks there for repair."

"That sounds wonderful, Hans," his mother said, as pleased with how happy he was as she was that they had found themselves a home.

Hans looked at Emilee. "Tell Mama your news."

"What?" Inga asked.

"I found a job at a hospital. I start on March 1st."

"Really?" Inga exclaimed. "That's wonderful news, Emilee."

Emilee nodded. "It's closer to downtown, but it's just half a block from a trolley stop. And there's a trolley stop on the Frankfurter Ring road, so I don't have to walk far on either end."

"I am very proud of her," Hans said.

Emilee smiled in embarrassment. "It helps to have your godfather, who is a hospital administrator for the army, writing your letter of recommendation."

"Oh," Inga said with a start. "That reminds me. I have a letter for you, Hans. From the army."

"What?"

Inga got to her feet and went over to where she had left her purse. A moment later she returned and handed Hans a letter in a brown envelope. He looked at it closely and said to Emilee, "It's from First Battalion Headquarters."

"From Colonel von Schiller?"

"It doesn't say." Hans ripped the envelope open and extracted a single sheet. Unfolding it, he glanced at the bottom of the page. "Yes, from von Schiller."

Emilee turned to Inga and Paula. "He was his commanding officer up in Berlin."

Hans scanned the letter quickly and then looked up, staring at Emilee.

"What is it?" she exclaimed, not liking the expression on his face. He looked down and started to read:

Lieutenant Eckhardt,

Greetings from the First Battalion. Hope this letter finds you well and happily married. Congratulations to your beautiful Emilee as well.

"That's nice," Emilee said." Hans nodded and went on.

Things here in Berlin are still somewhat chaotic. But I am happy to say that the Army High Command has finally

decided to step in and take whatever action is necessary to stabilize things in the Fatherland.

Which brings me to the purpose of this letter. There is
much concern here with what is happening in Bavaria. The
"People's Republic," set up last November by Kurt Eisner, is
tottering like a house of cards. If it falls, it could take all of
Southern Germany with it. This concerns the Army General
Staff greatly. Therefore, we are being recalled to duty and are
reinstituting the *Freikorps* regiment. More to the point, our
regiment, and possibly one or two others, are preparing to
come south and help stabilize Bavaria.

Hans looked up. The three women were staring at him. "They're
coming here?" Emilee asked. "To do what?"

Hans shook his head and continued.

I know that you are recently married and anxious to
start your mechanic's shop, but this is as serious as what we
saw in January. Therefore, I am asking you to take command
of C Company once again, if only long enough to see us
through this crisis. The pay will be the same, and will be paid
in advance.

If you accept, your first task will be to recruit men for
your company. C Company is down to less than fifty men at
present. I'd like to bring the company up to its full strength of
about two hundred men.

"My goodness," Emilee breathed.

Lieutenant, I am once again extending my invitation to
become a career army officer, but this offer is not contingent
on that. I know you have other career plans, and if you are
committed to them, I do not wish to interfere. But I beg of
you to seriously consider accepting this command. As a native

Bavarian, you must be very concerned about what is happening in Munich.

Please consider this request with the utmost gravity. I value your leadership skills highly. And—though this is unfair of me to say—I would remind you about where you might be today if it weren't for my intervention. You may take a few days to consider it. However, I must know no later than the 25th of this month so I can make other plans if necessary. Please telegram your decision to the address below.

> With warmest regards to you and Emilee,
> Colonel Stefan von Schiller, Commanding Officer,
> First Battalion, Black Eagle Regiment

For almost a minute the room was silent. Hans read over the letter again, nodding or shaking his head as he did so. When he looked up, Emilee gave him a questioning look. "What are you going to do?" she asked.

"What do you think I should do?"

"Well," she said slowly, "he's right about you owing him a debt of gratitude."

"And he's right about Bavaria being in a crisis," Paula added. "Wolfie is gravely concerned."

"And three hundred marks is three hundred marks," Hans added.

"It would be that much more you could put into the garage," Inga said.

Hans gave the three of them a searching look. "I can't believe that the three most important women in my life are encouraging me to re-join the army." His face was dark and gloomy. "I swore with a vengeance that I was done with war, done with combat, done with the army."

"I know," Emilee whispered. "So it's your choice."

Inga spoke up hesitantly. "It's Saturday today, Hans. And Sunday tomorrow. I'd guess that your colonel is not in his office over the weekend. What if you take a few days to think about it?"

Hans glanced at Paula and then at Emilee, who said, "I think that's a wonderful idea, Hans. Take some time. And then, whatever you decide, you know that I'll support you in it."

Gretl and Bruno had sat quietly through all of this, sensing the gravity of the situation. Now Hans motioned to them. "Would you two help me unpack our things?"

Hans stood, thrusting the letter into his pocket. "I don't want to think about this right now."

As they clunked up the stairs, Paula turned to Emilee. "Well, that was not good news."

"No." For a moment, Emilee was tempted to explain what had happened to Hans on that last day of combat in Berlin but then decided she shouldn't be the one to do that. So she changed the subject and spoke to Inga. "Let me tell you about the place we have found."

"*Gut*. I am anxious to see it."

"The landlord is meeting us there at six tonight so we can sign the paperwork."

"Wolfie will be home by then," Paula said. "We planned to go too."

"The flat is upstairs," Emilee went on, "and the shop is on the main floor. It used to be a welding shop, so it's going to take some work to fix it up. But it has large swinging doors that are big enough to bring in even a medium-sized truck. The landlord is letting Hans and Wolfie clean it out before we actually move in."

"I'm anxious to see it," Inga said.

"What about tomorrow?" Paula asked Emilee. "A few days ago you said something about wanting to find a church and attend services. Inga and I are going to our church, but we'd be happy to help you find a Lutheran church. Or, if you wish, you can just stay here. Hans and Wolfie will be working in the shop all day."

"Or," Inga added, "you are welcome to attend the branch with us."

"Yes," Paula said eagerly. "We would love to have you come with us."

"I. . . . Would that be all right? Do they let Lutherans come?"

"Of course," Paula said with a laugh. "Anyone is welcome to attend our church."

"All right. I think I shall go with you. That would be nice."

Paula was elated. She turned to Inga. "Wolfie can drive us there on their way to the shop. We don't want to be carrying eighty pounds of cheese with us that far. The weather is supposed to be good tomorrow, so we can walk home afterward while the men are at the shop."

"Why is your church called 'the branch'?" Emilee asked, somewhat tentatively. "I thought Hans told me you were Mormons."

For a moment both looked startled, but then Inga chuckled. "We are Mormons, though the actual name of our church is The Church of Jesus Christ of Latter-day Saints."

Inga laughed. "Hans teases me about that. He says that's why we don't have more members than we do. The name is so long, people can't remember it."

Paula went on. "We call a local congregation a *ward*, just like some towns or cities have wards, or neighborhoods, in them. For us, a ward is the equivalent of a parish. It is a local congregation."

"Oh," Emilee said slowly, not sure how that answered her question about the branch.

"But," Paula went on, "a congregation that is not large enough to be a ward is called a *branch* of the Church. So instead of the Munich Parish, we attend the Munich Branch."

"Oh, that makes sense." Another moment's hesitation. "Will you tell me what I need to do?"

"Just sit and listen," Paula responded. "We do take the sacrament— like the Eucharist or communion—but you don't have to take it unless you want to."

"Other than that," Inga added, "we just sing hymns and have the branch president or other members talk to us. And have prayers, of course."

Emilee smiled and nodded. "I think I can handle that."

CHAPTER
43

February 16, 1919, 8:50 a.m.—Munich Branch, LDS Church,
Sofallingstrasse 23, Munich

When Wolfie slowed the car and pulled it over to the curb in front of *Die Gelbe Zwiebel,* Hans turned and gaped out the window. "This is it?"

Paula laughed. "Yes, Hans. This is it. The Yellow Onion Restaurant."

Even Emilee was taken aback. "You meet in a restaurant?"

"No," Inga said, not disturbed at all. "We meet in a large room over the restaurant. That's why we meet so early. The business doesn't open until noon on Sundays, and we're finished and gone by then."

As they got out, Emilee could see that the place was closed, but the smell of beer and food was in the air. Gretl and Bruno shot away as soon as they were out of the car, heading for a set of steps that ran up the west side of the building. Paula called after them. "Gretl, stay with Bruno. Don't let him get too rowdy." Gretl waved as they disappeared into the upper hall.

As Wolfie and Hans got the heavy wooden crate out of the trunk, Paula turned to Emilee. "When I first started learning about the Church, we met in the home of one of the members. But as we got more people, they found this room to rent each Sunday."

Inga came up beside them. "The first time I came here with Paula

I had the same thought. 'A restaurant? Really?' But once inside, as I was looking around wrinkling up my nose and being critical, a thought suddenly came into my mind."

Curious because that was exactly what was running through her mind, Emilee turned to her mother-in-law. "What?"

"About when Christ was on earth. On the night before His death, He met with the Twelve in an upper room. And where was that upper room?"

"I . . . I'm not sure that I know."

"That's the point. Jesus sent two of the disciples into the city and told them to watch for a man carrying water—which I suppose would be quite odd, because the women were the ones who got water from the wells. So they followed him to his home and asked if they might come there with Jesus to observe the Passover. So we don't know where they met that night or even whose house it was. But we know where it *wasn't*. They didn't meet in a cathedral, or even a parish church. The cup they drank from and the plates they ate off of were most likely made of wood. When you think about it, most of His sermons were given outdoors."

She smiled at her daughter-in-law. "And as all of that rushed through my mind, I had this thought, 'So this was what it was like in the first days of Christianity? Small numbers, humble surroundings. Probably with children in the congregation, wandering around and interrupting things.'"

Emilee nodded. "Thank you for that, Inga. I had never thought what it must have been like for those first Christians."

Hans and Wolfie were lugging the crate up the stairs now, so the women started after them. As they reached the top landing, a man came out to greet them. He was a tall and slender man in his late fifties or early sixties. He had light blue eyes made wider by the wire-rimmed spectacles he wore. He was balding and clean shaven, and the smile that he wore was genuine, warm, and welcoming. "*Bruder* Groll," he boomed, "and what have we here?"

"About eighty pounds of cheese, *Präsident*," Wolfie answered with a grin.

Hans added, "Feels more like a hundred and eighty. Where would you like it?"

The man was startled, and his eyes turned to Inga. "*Schwester* Eckhardt, is this from you?"

"*Ja, Präsident* Schindler. From our family in Graswang. It is for the branch."

Tears filled his eyes as he motioned for Hans and Wolfie to carry it inside. "Just put it up front in the far corner, where the other donations are." As the men moved inside, he came over and gripped Inga's hand. "It is so good to see you again, *Schwester* Eckhardt. But this—" he motioned toward the disappearing crate. "How can we ever thank you for such a gift?"

"When I told my husband that it was for the members who are in need, I asked him for two rounds. He gave me four. We are blessed to live on a dairy farm, *Präsident*."

"Your husband is a good man. Tell your family how grateful we are."

Wolfie and Hans reappeared at the door. Wolfie said, "*Präsident*, do you remember my nephew, Hans Eckhardt? He stayed with us off and on before the war."

"Ah, *ja*." He stepped forward and shook hands with Hans firmly. "*Guten Morgen*, Hans. It is good to see you again."

Hans smiled and nodded, but from his expression, Emilee guessed he did not remember meeting him before. Wolfie turned. "And this is his bride of about three weeks, Frau Emilee Eckhardt. They are staying at our home while they find a place of their own here in Munich."

The man came over and took Emilee's hand. His grip was firm but not crushing, and his pleasure at meeting her was evident. It was one of those faces that you liked almost instantly. "May I call you *Schwester*

447

Eckhardt? We call ourselves *Bruder* and *Schwester* because we believe we are all children of the same Heavenly Father. But I would not want to offend you."

Emilee was taken quite off guard by his openness. "I . . . No, I don't find it offensive."

"*Gut.*" He gestured toward the door. "Come in, come in. *Will-kommen.*"

"We'll be off," Wolfie explained. He kissed Paula on the cheek and then asked, "Are you sure you want to walk home? I can come and get you."

"I'm sure," she said, glancing up at the sky. "It is going to be a pleasant day. We'll be fine. You and Hans stay as long as you need to. We'll have supper in the oven when you get home."

9:30 a.m.

At the wedding, both Emilee and her family had been surprised at how similar the Catholic service had been to their own Lutheran weddings. But here at the Mormon church, things were dramatically different, and that was putting aside the fact that they were meeting in the upper floor of a business. It was much less formal than she was used to. President Schindler and two other men—Paula said they were his counselors, another odd title—sat behind a small table with a portable wooden lectern on it. And none of them wore clerical collars or robes. The congregation had about thirty-five people, with a surprising number of those being younger children, even down to babies in arms. In their congregation back in Pasewalk, younger children were not forbidden, but neither were parents encouraged to bring them, lest they disrupt the reverence of the service. Here from time to time, children would speak aloud or start to cry, and one of the parents would try to quiet them or take them out.

The next surprise was that when the services began, Gretl and Bruno, who had been excitedly mingling with the other children, came over and joined their mother without being asked and then sat quietly

448

listening to the service. For the rambunctious Bruno, that was quite amazing.

Also, the congregation was far more varied in their dress than Emilee's parish in Pasewalk. There were a few men in suits, white shirts, and ties, and their wives wore nice dresses—nothing particularly fancy, but definitely more than a house dress. There were several women who had no men with them. The group was made up mostly of working-class people. Their clothing was clean but plain and worn. And they had that same gaunt look that she had seen on the faces of Jakob and Anna Litzser and their children, and yet they too seemed happy. She also noticed that there seemed to be no established seating. In most churches, the wealthy contributed sufficient money to have pews named for them and reserved exclusively for them and their families, even if they were not in attendance. It seemed strange in a way, and yet it impressed her, too. There were no visible signs of ranking here.

The most surprising thing to her was that everything was done by the congregation. President Schindler stood up and welcomed the people there and announced the program. Then an older woman came forward. She gave a number in the hymnal, hummed a note, and they sang without accompaniment. But what really shocked Emilee was when two older teen boys offered the prayer on the Eucharist, the emblems of Christ's body and blood given to the congregation. She was even more unsettled when two more boys, barely in their teens, passed those emblems to the people instead of President Schindler. In a way, it seemed almost sacrilegious. How could someone who was not an ordained priest or minister do that? It was quite unsettling to her.

And so it continued. After the sacrament was finished, the president called on two members of the congregation to speak. One was a woman about Emilee's age, a young war widow with two children. The other was a soldier recently returned from the war. The woman spoke of how God had sustained her in her loss. The soldier spoke about the challenges of maintaining his faith in such adverse circumstances and then testified that he was actually stronger now than before he went into the army. Both were quite touching, but Emilee could scarcely take it in. *Members of the congregation giving the sermons?*

However, as the meeting went on, she began to realize that through it all, puzzling and unorthodox as it was, she wasn't offended. It was simple, reverent, and—she searched for a good word. *Uplifting.* Yes, it was uplifting. Somewhat disconcerting, too, but uplifting.

When the soldier finished, President Schindler stood up. After a moment of glancing at some notes on the lectern, he looked up and began to speak. "My dear brothers and sisters, I have assigned myself to be our concluding speaker today, for I have news from our mission president, President Angus Cannon. We also have news from Salt Lake City."

Emilee frowned. She had no idea what so many of their words and phrases meant. Inga must have seen her expression, because she leaned over and whispered in her ear. "Salt Lake City is the headquarters of our Church. It's in America."

Emilee nodded, grateful for these little enlightening explanations.

"I have received a copy of a letter from *Präsident* Cannon addressed to all district and branch presidents in the Swiss-German Mission. Though President Cannon was called and sent here in late 1916, we have not seen him for the past few years because he is an American citizen, and travel to Germany was, of course, not possible for Americans during that time."

Emilee's head came up. "An American?" she whispered to Inga. "I thought they were our enemies."

Inga smiled. "Maybe politically, but not in the Church."

President Schindler was continuing. "*Präsident* Cannon is seeking permission from Berlin to enter Germany and visit all of the branches and districts in the mission so that he can assess for himself how things are with us. So far his request has been denied, but he promises to continue trying to get that permission. He is especially anxious to learn how Salt Lake City can help us. He wishes to commend all members in Germany for their faithfulness through these difficult times."

The president paused and took off his spectacles. He was sober and thoughtful as he seemed to be collecting his thoughts. Then he continued. "Though our Church is thought of as an American church, because its beginnings were in America, we believe that all who join the kingdom of God become members of a brotherhood and sisterhood that transcends national boundaries. Many people in Germany and in America still consider our peoples to be mortal enemies. But we do not. Nor do our brothers and sisters in the gospel who live in America consider us their enemies. Some may find that hard to believe, but it is true."

He picked up a letter from the pulpit and held it up. "I have here the letter from *Präsident* Cannon. As I said, he and his wife have been in Europe since 1916, which I am sure has caused their family back home much anxiety. I should like to read you some of what he says as evidence of the power of the gospel brotherhood and sisterhood we feel in the Church."

He put on his spectacles and began to read. "'We have learned that in many places in Germany the Saints are in urgent need of clothing—shoes, underwear, and suits of all kinds. The Saints in Switzerland give all the help they can, but it is not enough. They too have suffered deprivations because of the war and their means are limited.'"

He lowered the letter for a moment. "I remind you that many of these Saints in Switzerland sided with the Allies and against Germany in the war, even though their country remained neutral. Still, they reach out to us even in their own shortages."

Emilee, wondering if what he had just said could be true, looked at Paula and Inga, but neither of them seemed at all surprised. President Schindler continued.

"'It would be a great blessing if the folks at home could gather up their old things and ship them directly to Hamburg. And I have written to Salt Lake suggesting that the Church formally encourage our members to do that as rapidly as possible. Our Saints here particularly need warm clothing, for they have not been able to purchase much in the last five years. Now, only those with plenty of money can buy new things. A good brother in Germany recently wrote and said that he must now work half a month to earn enough to buy a good pair of shoes. It is so cold in Germany. And it will get colder. I am afraid to think what will happen to our people in another winter if we do not get help. It's terrible that we should have so much at home and they have so little.'"

President Schindler again lowered the letter as he sighed deeply. "*Meine Brüder* and *Schwestern,* these are the words of an American citizen. I ask you: does that sound like the voice of an enemy? Is this a message of hate and retaliation and revenge? *Nein!* Listen to this next part."

"'We are constantly receiving reports from our members in Germany of great suffering and hardship. We are especially concerned when we hear of young children who are desperately sick with tuberculosis, malnutrition, and other afflictions. We weep when we hear of such things, and we feel a great sense of urgency about this matter. Therefore, I am asking that all branch presidents identify those children who are critically ill and send us their names and addresses immediately. We have secured permission from both the Swiss and German governments to bring those children to Basel, where we here in the mission home stand ready to care for them until they are restored to their full health. Salt Lake City has authorized me to use mission funds for this rescue effort and to begin purchasing food for our people who are in most critical need.'"

That brought murmurs of surprise and joy from the congregation. Emilee was stunned, scarcely able to believe what she was hearing. *This from an American? This from their recent enemies? Unbelievable.* But what came next was even more stunning.

"'The Church has learned,'" President Schindler continued, "'that there are tons of food and other commodities purchased for the American army during the war that are now surplus and sitting in dozens of railway cars in France. Salt Lake City is currently negotiating with Washington to purchase those commodities and distribute them to our members in Germany.'"

Emilee gaped at him. *Dozens of railways cars? What will that cost them? Who were these people?*

The president laid the letter down and removed his glasses. His eyes were glistening as he looked around at his congregation. "How gratifying it is to belong to a Church that remembers their own. But, my beloved brothers and sisters, as you heard, this will take time. It may be summer, or even fall, before we see it. So we too must act. We too must follow the example the Church is setting."

He paused, deep in thought. It was clear to Emilee that he was not reading a prepared sermon. Another surprise. "In the book of Acts, the Apostle Peter described the Master with one simple, but deeply profound, statement. He said that Jesus 'went about doing good.' There is our example, *Brüder* and *Schwestern.* That is what we are called to do. Even in the midst of war, even now in the terrible aftermath of war, I believe that God expects us to follow the example of His Son and to do good in any way we can. These do not have to be grand and marvelous deeds. Sometimes it can be as simple as a smile, reaching out to those who sorrow, feeding the hungry, remembering the poor, or visiting those who are afflicted."

He sighed, letting his eyes move from face to face. His gaze was so penetrating that Emilee wanted to look away, but she could not. And she sensed that no one else could either.

"I know that many of us are living in great hardship. Food is scarce. Unemployment is rampant. There is much sickness and suffering among us. Many of us have lost loved ones. Some of you cannot give because you have nothing to give. But that is not true of all.

"So once again, as we have on previous Sundays, I ask of you to sit down as families and counsel together. Examine your circumstances and resources to see if there is anything more you can do to bless those in need. Your response thus far has been both astonishing and humbling to me. Without revealing names, let me give you two examples of what I am talking about." He turned and gestured to the pile of boxes, cans, sacks, and bottles in the corner. "Many of you have brought food and clothing and other necessities to share with our branch members. One of those contributions is eighty pounds of cheese." He went on quickly over the gasps that exploded all around him. "That is enough for about two pounds of cheese for each person here. A tremendous blessing to us all.

"Yet, someone else brought a half of a cup of sugar, which was the last sugar their family had. But they felt that someone here needed it more than they did. That is what I am talking about. We do not expect you to take food from your children's mouths and bring it here. All we ask is that you do what you can. If you have nothing more to give from your pantries or from your closets, then give someone a kind word, a prayer, a helping hand."

Emilee, who to her surprise felt tears trickling down her cheeks, looked quickly at Inga and Paula, who were on either side of her. Both were also crying. Inga, seeing Emilee look over, reached out and took her hand. Paula quickly took the other.

President Schindler picked up a book with a black leather cover. He opened it, looking for a particular place. From its cover, Emilee assumed it was the New Testament. She was wrong.

"Perhaps my favorite of all the scriptures that describe what it means to be true followers of Christ is found in the Book of Mormon. As you will remember, numerous people had come to a prophet named Alma and asked to be baptized of him. He asked them this question:

'Are [you] willing to bear one another's burdens, that they may be light; Yea, and are [you] willing to mourn with those that mourn; yea, and [to] comfort those that stand in need of comfort?'"

He closed the book and leaned forward. "I leave it to each of you to answer that question for yourselves. But I pray that each of us may, as the Savior did, go about doing good. And I ask that in the name of our Beloved Savior, even Jesus Christ, Amen."

11:48 a.m.—Near Herrnstrasse, Obermenzing District, Munich

They were pretty quiet on the walk home. Well, not Gretl and Bruno, of course. They chattered away about their friends at church and about school and a dozen other topics. But Emilee, Paula, and Inga were all pretty subdued. Emilee guessed that she was the topic of their thoughts and that they were dying to ask her what she thought about her experience, but she wasn't ready to talk yet. Now, as they approached the street where Paula and Wolfie lived, she decided it was time.

"Do you always have members of the congregation give the sermons?" Emilee asked.

Paula and Inga exchanged quick glances. Paula deferred to her older sister. "Yes," Inga said. "We are a lay church, which means that we do not have a paid clergy."

"You mean *Präsident* Schindler is not an ordained minister?"

Inga smiled. "Not in the sense you mean. He has authority to preside, much like a priest or a pastor, but he is actually a shoemaker by trade. And all of us have what we term 'callings' in the Church. Some of us teach children, some work with the adult women in what we call our Relief Society, and so on. I don't have a calling that requires me to be here on Sunday, because I cannot come to Munich every week. But the president has asked me to write regularly to the widows in the ward to make sure their needs are being met. It is not a grand calling, but it lets me be of service."

"And do you give sermons?" Emilee asked incredulously. "I would be terrified to do that."

Paula laughed. "I do. Only we don't call them *sermons*, we just call them *talks*. But yes, I've spoken in the branch twice now. And yes, I was terrified."

Inga was shaking her head. "Because I am so far away, I have not been asked yet, but . . ." She looked at Emilee. "But I am terrified too," she said with a smile.

They fell silent again. As they turned onto *Herrnstrasse* and they could see Paula's house up ahead, Inga spoke up. "Do you have any other questions?"

Emilee's lips pursed for a moment. "Actually, I do. I . . . To be honest, I was absolutely astonished by what happened today. Asking people with nothing to do something good for others was . . . I can't even find a word that expresses it. Someone giving his last cup of sugar to someone who is 'really in need'?"

"Actually, it was half a cup," Paula teased.

Emilee barely heard her. "What was that last scripture he read? That was amazing."

To Emilee's surprise, Inga reached in her purse and extracted a book with a black leather cover.

"Is that the same book *Präsident* Schindler had?" Emilee asked.

"Yes. It's called the Book of Mormon." Inga opened it and thumbed quickly through the pages. Then she handed it to Emilee, pointing at a spot that was underlined. "This is what he read."

Emilee took it and read it slowly. There was more underlined than what he had read, but she quickly found the verses he had cited. "I love that concept," she murmured. She read on for a moment, concentrating hard. Finally, she closed the book and handed it back.

"You're welcome to keep it for a while," Inga murmured.

Emilee shook her head. "Thank you, but no. I have quite enough to think about right now."

Chapter Notes

There was a branch of the Church established in Munich as early as 1869 (see *Mormonism in Germany*, 26). According to the general minutes of the Munich Branch in the LDS Church History Library archives (call #LR 5883 11), it was located on Sofallingstrasse until 1919, and Anton Schindler was probably the branch president at that time. He served for thirty years in that position. The first chapels constructed by the Church in Germany seem to have been in the early 1950s (see *Mormonism in Germany*, 156). Existing buildings were probably purchased for meetinghouses before that time, but in the early history of the Church there, branches typically met in rented facilities. There is no information about the building in Munich, so the Yellow Onion Restaurant is my creation.

The talk given here by President Schindler is not based on any known speech. However, we do know that branch presidents throughout Germany at time encouraged their members to help other members in need. The letter he reads from President Cannon is largely based on a letter Cannon wrote to the First Presidency, which was later published in *Der Stern* ("The Star"), the German-language magazine published in Germany for many years (see *Der Stern*, 52:36–38; translated into English and inserted in *Swiss-German Mission Manuscript History*, 1 February 1920). The letter was written a few months later than is shown here.

President Cannon did undertake an effort to bring seriously ill children to Switzerland, where they were treated in the mission home by mission staff. Eventually about a dozen children were rescued through this program (see *Mormons and Germany*, 80–81).

PART
3

CHAPTER
44

February 15, 1919, 1:45 p.m.—EDW Ranch, Monticello,
San Juan County, Utah

Long before she and Mitch were married, Edna Rae Zimmer—
known to everyone as Edie—had worried about her ability to
have children. Her mother had been the only child to live out
of four births. Edie was the oldest of three children and was the only
one who had not died shortly after birth. When she miscarried about
four months after she and Mitch were married, the fears came roaring
back. When she passed the fourth month of her next pregnancy without incident, she was ecstatic. Two months later, through a tragic series
of events that led to a hard fall, she gave birth to a perfectly formed
baby girl who never took a breath.

After a special fast and a priesthood blessing from Mitch, his father, and Bishop Frederick I. Jones, Edie gave birth to a robust boy
they named Mitchell Arthur Westland Jr. Mitch Jr. raised their hopes
that the problem had been solved. However, as Mitch Jr. approached
his second birthday, Edie lost another baby at four months. The following year she carried a little girl to full term and named her Rena,
after her paternal grandmother. A second girl followed three years later
but lived only two days and was buried in the cemetery next to her
unnamed sister.

Finally, things seemed to stabilize for Edie. Franz Arthur Westland was born in 1904 and was given the name of both of his grandfathers. Franz, however, quickly became Frank. Four years after that, Edie gave birth to another little girl on December 26th. She was six weeks premature, but she survived. Since she was born one day after the celebration of Christ's birthday, they named her Christina. Somewhere around her second birthday, she pointed to herself and proudly announced, "I Tina." The name stuck, and only her parents ever called her Christina any more.

No more children came after that, but Edie and Mitch were content. They had four wonderful children—four more than they believed they would have—and they were the light of their lives.

Edie's grandmother, Renate Zimmer, came to live in Monticello just before Mitch and Edie were married. Born in Switzerland and raised in Germany, she and her husband were converted to the Church as young newlyweds and came to America shortly thereafter.

In her patriarchal blessing, *Oma* Zimmer was told that her posterity would take the gospel to her extended family back in Germany. Determined to facilitate that promise, she spoke mostly German in the home until her death in 1910, despite speaking fluent English.

Once she was gone, the family gradually moved away from speaking German every day. But by that time, Mitch and Edie and the children were fluent German speakers.

Then fate put an interesting spin on that "patriarchal promise." As Mitch Jr. approached mission age, three years after *Oma* Zimmer's passing, everyone in Monticello assumed that he would be called to a German-speaking mission. So when a letter from Box B arrived at the ranch in May of 1913 addressed to Mitchell A. Westland, they immediately gave it to Mitch Jr., assuming the "Junior" had inadvertently been left off. They thought it was a little strange, since he wouldn't turn twenty for another month, but the age didn't seem to be a hard and fast rule then. With great elation, Mitch Jr. sent back his mission acceptance letter.

Five days later, Mitch got a call from a confused member of the Missionary Department in Salt Lake City. They had sent a mission call out to a man living in Monticello who was a natural-born American citizen but who spoke nearly flawless German. Though they knew that he was married with several children, the First Presidency decided to extend the call anyway. Now they had received an acceptance letter from an unmarried man.

And so it was that Mitch Westland Jr.'s call was rescinded and Mitch Westland Sr., who was forty-five years of age and had four children, the youngest of whom was five, received a call to serve for four years in the Swiss-German Mission, headquartered in Basel, Switzerland. He was to depart for his field of labor no later than July 1, 1913.

Stunned but ecstatic, Edie didn't flinch for an instant about him going. She decided that *Oma* Zimmer had just gotten tired of waiting and worked things out from the other side. Of course he would go, and they would make do for the years he would be gone. Mitch's parents came up from Bluff and moved in with Edie—Gwen would help Edie with the children and Arthur would help Mitch Jr. run the ranch. Mitch Sr. left on the fifteenth of June.

But fate was not done playing with the Westlands. Much to Mitch's dismay, just over a year later, Archduke Franz Ferdinand and his wife Sophie were assassinated in Bosnia. Within days, the world was engaged in war. All American missionaries were evacuated from war-torn Europe and returned home.

It was a bittersweet reunion for Edie. She was overjoyed to have Mitch back, but saddened that the promise to her grandmother had not been fulfilled. Mitch had never even got close to the Mannheim area where the Zimmers had lived.

Mitch Jr. reached the age to go on his mission shortly thereafter, but by then America had entered the war, and he was drafted into the army. When the military learned of his facility in German, they sent him to France to help with the interrogation of German prisoners of war. A month after the Armistice in Europe, Mitch Jr. returned home to his family.

Finally, it looked as if life were going to settle back into a normal routine for the Westlands. But who ever said that fate doesn't have a sense of humor? Three months after Mitch Sr. returned from Europe, a stunned Edie announced that the doctor had just confirmed that she was pregnant. And then came the next surprise. In May of the next year she gave birth—to a little girl and a little boy, born nine minutes apart. They named them Abigail and Benjamin. They were quickly dubbed "Abby and Benji" by their siblings, and "The Miracle Twins" by the rest of the town.

Edie was thinking about all of this as she sat on the front porch swing of their spacious ranch house. The January thaw had not lessened, and it was an almost spring-like day in southeastern Utah. Mitch was carrying bales of hay from the barn to the corrals, and Edie watched with considerable satisfaction as the twins—now not quite four—trailed after their father like two eager puppies, chattering away at him with every step. It was a sight to warm her heart. What a joy these two were to them at this stage of their lives.

All three wore cowboy hats and cowboy boots. Mitch's belt had a large silver buckle. On a trip to Colorado two years earlier, he had found miniature buckles for the twins, who had worn them virtually every day since. After distributing the hay, Mitch retrieved his lariat and coiled it in one hand. He was headed for the corral to lasso a couple of calves he was going to wean from their mothers. Abby, almost stepping on his heels, carried a smaller rope coiled in her right hand and was tapping it against her leg as she walked, in perfect imitation of her father. Benji had his rope too, but he held it by one end and let it drag out behind him like a snake. That was typical, too. Whatever his "older" sister did, Benji did just the opposite.

This always intrigued Edie. Was it because Abby always made sure that everyone knew she was nine minutes older than her brother? Was it because at four, she was already an inch taller than he was? Edie wasn't sure. What did please her, though, was that in spite of their fierce competitiveness, the twins were almost inseparable.

Just then the screen door slammed open and Tina shot out across the porch. Seconds later, Frank burst out after her. "I called it first, Tina," he shouted angrily.

Tina, who at eleven was as lithe and fast as an antelope, didn't even glance back. Frank, who was built somewhat along the lines of a Hereford bull, realized he had no chance of catching her and turned to his mother for adjudication. "Mom! That's not fair. I saw the mailman first."

Edie got to her feet. "Christina!" she shouted. "Let Frank get the mail." But Tina was already around the curve and halfway out to the road. Edie was pretty sure Tina heard her, but she didn't stop. "Sorry," Edie said. She patted the cushioned seat beside her. "Sit down, Frank."

He didn't. "It's not fair, Mom. She always gets the mail."

"I know. I'll talk to her."

"Yeah, sure," he grumped. Two minutes later Tina reappeared with a handful of mail, smiling at her brother in scornful triumph.

Edie sighed. "Tina, I know you heard me. That load of clothes in the washing machine should be done by now. Put them through the wringer and then hang them up on the line. It's such a nice day, they should dry by sundown."

From the look on her face, you would have thought Tina had just been banished to a nunnery for the rest of her life. "Mama! That's not fair."

"Ha!" Frank said, thrusting his face next to hers. "Told you not to go."

"And Frank, since you seem to need something to do, I want you clean out the ashes in the fireplace, put in fresh wood, and then vacuum the living room. We're having family night here tomorrow evening."

"What!" It was a cry of shock and outrage. "But I didn't do anything, Mama!"

Edie was thoughtful. "Well, your father did say that the chicken coop needed cleaning, so—"

Suddenly she was alone on the porch, and there were no further sounds from the house.

February 16, 1919, 6:15 p.m.

Edie looked around the large room filled with chairs placed in a circle. How she loved this house that had been their home for nearly thirty years now. Most of what was now their living and dining room had originally been the entire cabin that Mitch had built for her in the summer and fall of 1889. Back then, it included their bedroom and a bedroom for *Oma* Zimmer. Over the years, as their family grew, the building had more than doubled in size and become a large ranch house instead of just a cabin. Mitch had built the equivalent of another full cabin on the back of the house, only this time with a loft. That addition contained their kitchen, washroom, and five bedrooms. Their four youngest—the twins, Tina, and Frank—now each had their own bedroom, a corrupting luxury that was ruining them, according to Mitch.

In the ensuing years, Mitch had also brought running water into the house and put in an indoor toilet—the ultimate luxury, especially in the winter. It was a house made for living in and a fit headquarters for a working ranch. And Edie loved every square inch of it.

When they had first come to the Blue Mountains, Mitch was just starting what he was calling the Flying W Ranch, its name taken from his registered cattle brand, which was a W for Westland. The brand had short lines extending from the top of the W to represent simple wings. When Edie agreed to marry Mitch, he was so thrilled that he decided to incorporate her name into the ranch's brand and asked her what she thought. In a little flash of inspiration, she turned the "wings" on either side of the W into a backwards E and a forward D, so that it became the EDW brand, for Edie Westland.

Farther up the lane from where they were, there was another, smaller ranch house. This was where Mitch Jr. and his wife, June, lived with their two children. From the time Mitch Jr. was ten or so, it was obvious to his parents that he was going to be a rancher like his father. Now he was ranch foreman and would take over completely when Mitch and Edie decided to retire.

Rena had married one of the Redd boys, who were also successful ranchers over near La Sal, forty miles southeast of Moab. Mitch had offered them a place on the ranch, but they chose to start their own spread. Rena's husband had started with his own small herd, but more and more he turned to growing alfalfa. Now he was the number-one supplier of hay to many ranches in the area.

All of this was, of course, a great satisfaction to Edie. If she had her way, all of her children would always live within twenty miles of them. She felt a hand on her shoulder. She turned, and Mitch Jr. and his wife, June, were there. "Do you think that's enough chairs, Mom?" Mitch Jr. asked. They each had a thin sheaf of paper and several pencils.

"I think so. It's just the three families besides our own. George and Evelyn Adams, Fred and Mary Jones, and John and Sarah Rogerson."

"Which, with our family, makes almost fifty," June chuckled. "It seems like the Lord knew what He was doing when he called you to come here. You're almost a whole town by yourselves."

A faraway look came into Edie's eyes. "Yes. But so many are gone now, moved away from San Juan or passed on to their reward." She looked around the room. "I wish we could invite more."

At that moment, Mitch Sr. entered the room. "I do too, dear, but there are eight hundred people in Monticello now. I don't think they would all quite fit." Then he turned to Mitch Jr. and June. "So are we ready? There are a couple of families coming up the lane."

"We're ready," they responded.

Mitch bent down and kissed Edie on the cheek. "This should be fun. We'll show these young whippersnappers that we old geezers can show them a thing or two after all."

6:40 p.m.

By the time the last family was in and settled, the Westland living room was bursting at the seams and filled with lots of noise. Each of the families had, like the Westlands, three generations represented—parents, children, and grandchildren. These weren't the only families who had come in that first group to settle Bluff, but every one of them had arrived by the summer of 1889 and had been here ever since. Almost thirty years now.

Edie caught her husband's eye. "I think this is it, Mitch. We can get started."

Mitch got to his feet, and immediately the room quieted. All eyes turned to him. "Welcome to our family night," he said with a smile. "As I look around, I believe it is safe to say that Zion is growing."

There were smiles and chuckles from all of the adults. He went on. "Since we are all old friends here, there is no need for introductions. We have a full program tonight, so let's get started. We've asked Bishop George Adams to open our activity with prayer. George."

When the prayer was finished, Mitch was on his feet again. "I know that President Joseph F. Smith has encouraged our weekly family nights to be gospel centered, and tonight will be no exception to that counsel. But as an introduction to our gospel message, which, incidentally will be given by our former bishop, Frederick Jones, we are going to play a game."

That brought the heads of the young people up in surprise.

"Yes, that's right. A game. And the teams will be made up of families. Every family is to work together as a team. You will need a paper and pencil for each family, and I'll have Mitch and June pass those out while I explain the game."

As Mitch Jr. and June got up, Mitch Sr. began his explanation.

"This game is called 'What's New?' And no, you've never heard of it before, because . . ." He grinned at them. "Because I just made it up this week."

More laughter. There were also a couple of groans from his own children.

Mitch held up a hand. "Okay, as noted, the teams are made up of families. So pull your chairs into a circle as best you can. If your family is too large—such as the Adams family . . . or the Jones family . . . or the Rogersons, or the Westlands . . ." Again he had everyone laughing. "Just do the best you can." All of you Westlands, gather around Grandma."

He moved over beside Edie as the room filled with noise and movement.

"I don't have my glasses," Edie said as her children and grandchildren started to gather in around her. Abby laid a hand on her mother's shoulder. "I'll help you, Mama,"

In a few moments, everyone was settled. Mitch went to the cupboard and withdrew two sheets of paper filled with his handwriting. Every eye was fixed on him. "All right," he began. "From the time of Abraham, if people wanted to get anywhere, they walked, rode donkeys or horses, or rode in carts and wagons. That was true of Jesus, and it was true when I was born, with the exception of the railroads. Now we have trains, automobiles, motorbikes, tractors, trucks, airplanes, and all kinds of other means of transportation."

Dan Perkins, who was married to Cornelia Adams, called out. "Give me a horse any day!"

Mitch laughed with everyone else. "Sorry, old-timer," he said to Dan, who was probably ten years his junior. "We're the old geezers now." Then he sobered. "But it's not just transportation. Just this last year, Monticello got around-the-clock electricity. And it was only a few years ago that we got our first telephones. Now we have indoor plumbing, a sewage system, telephones in almost every home, and cars parked in most yards."

He raised the two sheets of paper he had retrieved. "So here's what we're going to do. As families, you will try to think of things that we now have in our everyday lives and take for granted, but which we didn't have a few years ago. I'll give you one example. I can still clearly remember the first time I ate Aunt Jemima pancakes with Log Cabin syrup."

Many of the older people were smiling and nodding. However, Tina was genuinely puzzled. "Really?" she asked Edie. "So how did you make pancakes before that, Mom?"

Edie laughed and reached out and patted her hand. "Oh, Christina, we actually used real flour, and real eggs, and real milk and did it ourselves."

"Okay," Mitch exclaimed above the laughter. "You get the idea. Think of as many things as you can that we have now but didn't have in 1880. Write them down. You've got fifteen minutes."

Chapter Notes

The introduction of Mitchell and Edna Rae Westland into the Fire and Steel series at this point may come as a bit of a surprise to some readers. They were introduced to readers in *Only the Brave*. But from the beginning, the plan was to have these two families—the Eckhardts from Germany and the Westlands from San Juan County, Utah—eventually come together and have their lives intertwined. From this point on, both families will be part of Fire and Steel.

Though we think of family home evening as being a somewhat modern innovation, its beginnings go back a century ago. President Joseph F. Smith introduced a weekly home evening program in 1915, which was often called "family night" by members. No specific day of the week was set, but the First Presidency called for families to "spend an hour or more together in a devotional way—in the singing of hymns, songs, prayer, reading of the Scriptures and other good books, instrumental music, family topics, and specific instructions on the principles of the Gospel" (Clark, *Messages of the First Presidency*, 5:89).

Aunt Jemima pancake mix was first created in 1889. Log Cabin syrup was first introduced two years earlier.

CHAPTER
45

February 16, 1919, 7:15 p.m.—EDW Ranch,
Monticello, San Juan County, Utah

Mitch got to his feet and waved his arms. "Okay, time's up. Scoring's easy. We'll go by families. Read out what you've got. If it's on my list, you get one point. If you have something I've missed, that's legitimate, you get two points. Okay, let's start with the Adams family."

Mitch was pleased to see how eager the young people were. Several of the younger Adams clan were clamoring to read the list. *Good.* He had hoped that the youth would find this interesting.

What followed next was almost dizzying, because they came with great rapidity. Mitch checked items off as fast as he could and scribbled in the ones he had missed.

Nean, or Cornelia, was the oldest of the Adams children and was chosen to read.

"Okay," she said, taking a quick breath. "We have, first, the electric light bulb."

"Good," Mitch said.

"Time zones in the United States," Nean said. Groans erupted. No one else had thought of that. "Dr. Pepper," she continued, "then later, Coca Cola and Pepsi Cola. Aunt Jemima pancakes."

"You can't count that one!" Sarah Rogerson cried. "Mitch already gave us that one."

Nean crossed it off and went on. "Electric ovens. Electric irons. Electric curling irons for ladies." She hesitated, suddenly blushing. "The elastic brassiere."

Her husband, Dan, jerked forward. *"Cornelia Adams Perkins!"*

She whirled on him. "Well, you may not think that is a great invention, but then, you've never worn a corset."

The men laughed as Dan blushed even more furiously than his wife. The women applauded with great enthusiasm. Nean then quickly finished with, "Hershey's chocolate bars, Kellogg's Corn Flakes, peanut butter, and Tootsie Rolls."

Sarah Jane Rogerson read for her family and added the Statue of Liberty, the Washington Monument, Cracker Jacks, Campbell's soups, and the first national Mother's Day.

The Jones family was next. They had a lot of what had already been read, but they contributed Jell-o, Gillette safety razors, Lincoln Logs, Tinkertoys, and electric washing machines.

As they moved from family to family, new entries became less and less frequent, but when they came to the Westlands, with Frank as their designated reader, Mitch was delighted with how many they had listed—with no help from him—that no one else had thought of: Teddy bears, ice cream cones, Palmolive hand soap, Oreo cookies, the zipper, permanent wave kits for women's hair, Wrigley's chewing gum, Life Savers, pop-up toasters, and the Happy Birthday song.

Sarah Rogerson broke in. "Really? I thought that Adam sang 'Happy Birthday' to Eve in the Garden of Eden."

That brought a burst of laugher, but then her husband quipped, "And it was after hearing him sing that she partook of the fruit." And then everyone roared.

"Any others?" He looked around. When no one raised a hand, he went on. "Here are the last two I thought you'd all get. First, the state of Utah was created in 1896." Groans all around. "And here in Monticello we now have mail service six days a week. Unbelievable! When Edie and I were first courting, we were lucky to see mail once a month."

Mitch looked around, pleased with how much fun they'd had with it. "So, total up your scores. The family scoring the highest gets first place in the pie line."

"That's not fair, Dad," Frank exclaimed, "you old people know a lot more than us."

"Yeah," Bishop Jones sang out, "but we *remember* a heck of a lot less."

7:45 p.m.

Frederick I. Jones was a not a particularly large man, but he was solidly built with square shoulders, a full head of hair, and a full beard and mustache, which included sideburns right up to his ears. Now, at age sixty-nine, his hair and beard were pure white, and he looked like an Old Testament patriarch. His eyes were blue and quick to twinkle. Now they were quite serious as he looked around the group.

He looked over at Edie and Mitch. "Our deepest thanks to Brother Mitch for a delightful activity"—he slapped his stomach—"and to Sister Edie for making my belt much too tight." Everyone applauded. Mitch and Edie smiled and waved in acknowledgment.

Bishop Jones let it die out and then nodded thoughtfully. "We do live in a time of rapid change. I was really quite surprised at how many things we were able to list. And those things have brought us many blessings. New things come in and old things fade away. I predict that someday even stubborn old Dan Perkins will be found driving a car around his pasture."

Dan, who was laughing, raised a hand and conceded that might be the case.

"But here is my question for you young people," Bishop Jones went on. "We have listed many things that have changed in the last forty years, but what things haven't changed?"

For a long moment, the room was silent, and then Tina Westland raised a hand. Bishop Jones nodded at her. "Families," she said softly, looking at her parents.

"Excellent. What else?"

"Truth," one of Nean's daughters said. "Integrity," called someone else. Now the hands were coming up rapidly. "The importance of an education." "Love." "Helping others." "True friends." "Chastity." And then Rena gave the answer that said it all. "God. God has not changed."

"Aye," Bishop Jones said softly, "and as you young people become adults and take our places, always remember that. There is nothing wrong with new inventions, or new foods, or new clothing styles, or even new ideas. But let us not get so caught up in acquiring the things that do change that we let the things that never change slip out of our grasp."

Bishop Jones continued. "Let me illustrate this with a story. A true story, actually."

He clearly had their interest. Even the younger children were listening raptly.

"It has to do with this thing we call the telephone. In 1906, the Moab Telephone Company completed a ground telephone line to Monticello, giving us reliable phone service for the first time. Then they ran a line down to Blanding and Bluff. Finally, in 1910, a line was run down to Mexican Hat from Bluff.

"Well," Bishop Jones continued, "One day, a Navajo brave by the name of Bilgay came in while Will Brooks, who owned a trading post down there, was on the phone with Frank Hyde. Frank ran the trading post in Bluff. After listening to one side of the conversation, Bilgay was puzzled and asked Will what he was doing. 'I'm talking to Nock-I-Eze'—that was Frank's Navajo name. Bilgay, of course, didn't believe him, because he knew Nock-I-Eze was thirty miles away. So Will put

Bilgay on the phone and told him to talk to Frank. Frank, by the way, was fluent in Navajo. So he started talking to Bilgay as if they were in the same room together."

"Well, poor Bilgay, this was too much for him. 'Wait a minute,' he said, and handed the phone back to Will. Then he ran outside and went all the way around the store looking for Frank. When he came back in, Frank told him again that Nock-I-Eze was in Bluff. Bilgay, still finding this impossible to believe, ran out and jumped on his horse and took off for Bluff."

Mitch was chuckling, as was everyone else. The younger ones looked a little skeptical.

"Will said he wished he could have been there to see Bilgay's face when he confirmed that Frank really was in Bluff, but then he quickly forgot about it. The next day, the phone rang. It was Frank. 'Have you got any Navajo in your store right now?' he asked Will. When Will said yes, Frank said, 'Put one of them on the phone.' So Will did, and it was Bilgay on the other end. He started telling his friends that he was in Bluff on this new invention called the telephone. They laughed him to scorn. Talking to someone thirty miles away? Ridiculous. They recognized their friend's voice and understood his words, but they assumed he was hiding somewhere close by."

The story was well received, and people were chuckling or laughing all around the room.

"Now, here's the lesson," the bishop said as it finally quieted. "I surely do not comprehend how a telephone actually works, but that doesn't stop me from using it. Sometimes the Lord does miraculous things for us, things that we don't understand or can't comprehend. He asks things of us that make us uncomfortable. He makes promises that seem too wonderful to be true. By the still, small voice, He warns us in times of danger. But we may shake our heads and say to ourselves, 'That couldn't possibly have been from the Lord.'" He paused for just a moment and then added, "And because we refuse to believe, we may lose those blessings." Another pause, and then he concluded. "Remember," he said, very solemn now, "you don't have to fully understand something in order to believe in it or make use of it in your lives."

Edie was pleased to see Tina turn and whisper something to Frank and then see him nod, looking almost as solemn as Bishop Jones.

The bishop drew a deep breath. "The second story I would like to share with you tonight is a good example of what I'm trying to say. It too is a true story and involves some of the people in this room." He looked around. "In my mind, the lesson we learn from them is the one of the most important—if not *the* most important—lessons of life."

He took a deep breath and quietly began. "It was in the spring of 1888, not quite thirty years ago now. We had come back for our second season in the Blue Mountains after wintering in Bluff. But this time we came determined to get homes built and fences strung and crops planted so that we could stay through the coming winter. The men had come up in March, as soon as the snows had melted enough to make the road passable—if you could call it a road back then."

Bishop Jones had not told Mitch what he was going to say, but by this point, Mitch knew exactly which story he was going to tell. He reached out and took Edie's hand as she looked up at him, and he saw that she understood too.

"Well, there were three women who were anxious to be reunited with their husbands, fathers, and—in one case—her fiancé-to-be. So they decided not to wait for the rest of the families to come north. They started out on their own. One of them had her three-year-old daughter with her."

He turned and looked at Evelyn and Nean. "She was three, right?"

Evelyn nodded. "Not quite, but close."

"The weather in Bluff was warm and beautiful when they set out. They had only been across that road twice before, and both times in good weather, so they were not familiar with what a difference three thousand feet in elevation can make, especially in springtime. As they approached the Blue Mountains, they were caught in a fierce storm. Very quickly they were in snow up to the horses' bellies, and the animals were unable to pull their wagon any farther."

Edie had started to silently weep. Seeing that, Abby moved over and climbed onto her lap. A moment later, Benji did the same. Mitch saw that Evelyn Adams and Nean were also crying now. And it was clear that Bishop Jones was struggling with his own emotions.

"Those of us who were already here had no way of knowing they were coming. We never dreamed that there could be someone out in such a storm." His voice was barely audible now. "The women unhitched the team and rode one horse for a while, taking turns riding and holding the child on their laps. But the snow proved to be too much for the exhausted animal, and he finally collapsed in his tracks. Incredibly, those women struggled on through snow up to their thighs. Wet, cold, on the verge of collapse themselves, they pushed on, all the time carrying a precious child, determined they would die before they let her die."

Many in the room knew this story well, and there more than a few wet cheeks now. There wasn't a breath of sound.

"And then, the Lord took a hand. One of our number—also here this evening—was coming home from the mountains. He was tired and cold and anxious to be home. His team was headed for the barn with eagerness. But as he came to the turn that led homeward, he had an impression. 'Keep going south.' It wasn't a voice. Nothing shouted at him. It was just a feeling. An insane feeling—that was his first reaction. This blizzard was so fierce that even the horses were anxious to find shelter. But he couldn't shake off that feeling. And so he turned south. And he kept going, even when all reason was shouting at him to turn around. And then. . . ."

He had to stop. Sister Jones reached out and briefly touched her husband's hand. His Adam's apple bobbed as he swallowed quickly.

"And then, there they were. Three women and a little girl. Barely visible through the blowing snow."

He turned. "And they are all here now, with the exception of Leona Walton. Would those four people who are here tonight please come up and stand beside me?"

They did. Evelyn and Nean gripped hands as they stood up, as did Mitch and Edie. They lined up beside Bishop Jones.

"Some decisions, though they may seem simple at the time, have enormous consequences for us and others. For Mitch Westland, the decision was whether to turn south or go home. I want to illustrate the importance of learning to hear, recognize, and then follow the still, small voice of the Spirit, even though we may not understand how it works. Would all of you who are present here tonight who would *not* be here if Mitch Westland had not followed that prompting and gone south, please stand?"

For a moment there was total silence, and then people began to get to their feet, holding up the small children as necessary.

Mitch stared in astonishment as people all around them got to their feet. Beside him, Edie clutched blindly at his arm. "Oh, Mitch," she whispered. "Look at that."

He was looking, but he could barely see through his tears.

Bishop Jones had been counting. "If I am right, we have thirty-eight people on their feet right now."

His wife called out. "Don't forget Leona, who isn't here. She and her husband have seven children and six or seven grandchildren. So there's fifteen or sixteen more."

Her husband nodded, adding quickly in his head. "So over fifty."

The bishop nodded for them to sit down. He waited until all were seated and then spoke in a voice heavy with emotion. "Do you see that, you young people? Do you see how important one seemingly insignificant choice can be? Thanks be to God that the Lord whispered to

Mitch Westland to go south that night." His voice caught. "And thanks be to God that Mitch Westland listened."

Chapter Notes

The numerous "new items" listed here come from *The People's Chronology*, 554–732.

The story of the Navajo and the telephone is told in Norma Perkins Young's *Anchored Lariats on the San Juan Frontier*, 197, 149–52.

Dan Perkins stubbornly refused to buy an automobile until 1927, when he and Nean paid $600 for a new Model A Ford (*Anchored Lariats*, 199).

The story of Mitch's rescue in the spring of 1889 is told in more detail in *Only the Brave* (2014), 259–270.

*February 18, 1919, 3:25 p.m. —EDW Ranch, Monticello,
San Juan County, Utah*

Dad!"

Mitch had the ax above his head, so he swung it down-ward, burying the blade deep enough in the piece of cedar wood that it split neatly in two. Then he turned. Frank was coming at a trot from around the front of the house.

"Dad! There's a car turning into our lane."

Mitch turned, but he was far enough around the back of the house that he couldn't see the lane. "Who is it?" he asked.

"Dunno. But Dad! It's a Cadillac."

That brought his father's head around. "You sure?"

"Yup," he exclaimed. "A Model 55 Club Roadster."

Along with all of his buddies, Frank knew every make and model of car on the road. Mitch could hear the sound of an engine now and the crunch of tires on gravel. He buried the ax in the chopping block and moved forward enough that he could see around the house with-out making himself conspicuous. To his surprise, a car with a bright red body and black trim was coming slowly up the driveway.

"Who do you think it is?" Frank asked, gawking like a kid looking at the new girl in town. "No one from Monticello, that's for sure. Maybe they're just turning around," he added.

Frank moved closer. "Ain't she a beaut?" he crowed as the vehicle drew closer.

His father shot him a dirty look. "What did you say?"

"*Isn't* she a beaut?" he crowed. "Wow! That's the first one I've ever seen in real life."

It was something to see, Mitch had to admit. He stepped back as the car turned into the yard. He pulled Frank back as well. "Stay back until we're sure they're stopping."

The crunching sound stopped, and a moment later the engine was shut off. Mitch gave his son a swat across the bottom. "Go tell Mom we may have company. I'll go see who it is."

As Mitch came around the house, brushing his hands off on his Levi's, a man was just getting out of the car. Mitch could see that there was a woman in the front seat, and thought he also saw movement in the back seat. "Howdy," he called.

"Good afternoon." The man wore a dark brown leather bomber jacket over a light-colored shirt and brown twill cotton pants. His trouser legs were tucked into laced boots that came up almost to his knees. It was quite jaunty looking, as if he had come to camp out for a week. Definitely not cowboy dress.

As they shook hands, Mitch took further note of him. He was about three inches shorter than Mitch, with thinning sandy hair and eyebrows and pleasant blue eyes. He was clean shaven, with a strong jawline and a warm and pleasant smile. One thing caught his eye, though—there was a prominent two-inch scar just above his left eyebrow.

"I'm looking for Mitchell A. Westland," he said.

"That's me," Mitch said, "only everyone in these parts calls me Mitch."

"I am delighted to meet you, Mitch. Or perhaps I should call you

Kirchenältester Westland. My name is Jacob Reissner. *Kirchenältester* Jacob Reissner."

Mitch eyes widened. "*Kirchenältester?* I haven't been called that for a long time."

"Since about late summer of 1914, I'm guessing." The visitor was clearly enjoying himself.

"Yes, I. . . ." Then Mitch snapped his fingers. "Reissner? From the Swiss-German Mission?"

"The same," the man said, laughing aloud now. "We've never met, but I saw and heard your name often enough when I worked in the mission office."

Mitch was dumbfounded. "What in the heck are you doing in Monticello?"

He laughed. "Actually, we're on our way to Mesa, Arizona, to spend some time with Adelia's family. So we thought we'd stop and meet you at last." He took Mitch by the elbow and pulled him toward the car. "Come. I want you to meet my wife and daughter."

Inside the house, Edie and Frank stood at the door that led from the kitchen to the living room. From there they could see through the front window to the yard. Edie watched as the husband came around and opened the door for his wife. The woman got out of the car and then helped a little girl out from the back seat. The man's casual dress had barely caught her attention, but the sight of his wife caused her to stare. He might be dressed for the outdoors, but she was dressed for a night at the opera.

She wore a full-length black woolen coat trimmed with fur around the hem, neck, and cuffs, along with expensive-looking snow boots that came to her ankle. A brilliant red scarf covered her head. *To match the car, of course*, Edie thought.

The little girl was equally well dressed. Her coat, also wool, was a deep blue. She wore a knitted stocking cap to match and had both of her hands thrust into a muff of white rabbit's fur. The black galoshes, however, seemed a little out of place with the rest of her outfit.

Tina came up behind them. "Who's that, Mama?"

"I have no idea." She was still studying the three of them, who were now talking with Mitch. But then Mitch motioned toward the house and started forward, which jerked Edie out of her reverie.

"Oh, dear," she cried, reaching back and fumbling to untie her apron. "Dad's bringing them inside. And I'm a fright."

She felt a tug at her back and half turned. Tina was untying the strings or her apron. "Let me take this, Mama. You go meet them."

"No!" She was in a sudden panic. "Frank, you go to the door. I'm going to go brush my hair. Maybe put on another dress."

Obviously pleased with that assignment, Frank started forward, but Tina grabbed at his arm. "No, Frank! Daddy will want Mama to meet them." Then to her mother: "You look okay."

Right. Okay. She looks like a fashion model, but I look okay. But she knew Tina was right. "Frank, go tell Mitch Jr. and June that we have company. Get the twins, too. Oh, and tell June to call Rena and Bill. Tell them we're having company for dinner."

Frank stared at her. "How do you know they're staying for dinner?"

"Because I know your father. Now go."

"But Mom, I want to talk to them about their car."

The look she shot him turned him around in an instant, and he started toward the back door. Edie ran her fingers through her hair and tried to straighten her dress a little. *Her house dress. The one she had worn yesterday, too.*

"All right." Edie was half in a daze. "Clean up the kitchen a little. And start a pot of water boiling." And then she moved into the living room as the front door opened, and she put on the warmest smile she could muster.

4:15 p.m

Careful not to stare, Edie studied Adelia Reissner as Mitch introduced her and her husband to Frank, Tina, the twins, and Mitch Jr.
and June, along with their two kids. With her coat off now, the woman
was even more intimidating than she had been outside. Up close, she
wasn't what you would call a classic beauty, and yet she was a very striking woman. Her hair was part of it. Thick and deep auburn, it fell in
soft curls halfway down her back. Her almond eyes were large and dark
brown, her cheekbones barely visible in the porcelain perfection of her
skin. She was about five feet, four inches tall with a tiny waistline and
slender form. Her hands and long fingers were graceful, and the nails
gleamed with a clear polish.

Elegant. That had been Edie's first impression. And now, there was
no other word Edie could think of to describe her. Her skirt was of a
long and narrow cut, which emphasized her slenderness even more.
It was made of wool with alternating vertical stripes of dark and light
grey. Very fashionable. She wore a long-sleeved silk blouse with a
round neck and no collar. It was a light pink, like that of a morning
sunrise, and had an intricate embroidered pattern around the neckline
and the cuffs. A delicate gold necklace held a locket in the hollow of
her throat.

One thing was for sure, Edie decided. Whatever Jacob Reissner did
for a living, it was profitable. Mitch brought her back to the present
and motioned the twins forward. He had saved them for last. "Abby.
Benji. Come here. I want you to meet someone." The two exchanged
looks, but in a moment both were standing beside their father. Mitch
introduced them first to the parents and then knelt down beside the
girl. "Tell me again how old you are, Liesel?"

"I am almost five," she said bashfully, eyeing the twins from beneath lowered eyelashes.

Liesel was a combination of her father and mother. Her hair was
the same light brown as his, and she had his eyes. But her features were

clearly an inheritance from her mother. Dressed in a white dress with pink ribbons, full-length white stockings and white patent-leather shoes, she was utterly charming.

"Well, this is Abigail," Mitch said, putting a hand on his daughter's shoulder. "We all call her Abby. And this is her twin brother, Benjamin, whom we call Benji. And they will be four in May. These are our miracle babies," he said softly. "A bit of a handful, but a pure delight."

Adelia dropped down into a crouch and extended her hand. "I am very pleased to meet you, Benji and Abby," she said solemnly. "I don't think I've ever met miracle babies before."

Mitch straightened and turned to Christina. "Tina, why don't you take Liesel and the rest of the children to your room? Find something fun to do, all right?"

Reissner shook his head. "Oh, no. We can't stay long. We're trying to get to Blanding tonight. We were told there's a hotel there."

Mitch was shaking his head.

"There's not?" Elder Reissner said.

"There is, but you're not staying there tonight. You're staying here with us."

As Adelia and Jacob exchanged quick glances, Edie came over. "Absolutely. We have plenty of room, and we'll have supper on in about an hour. Hope you like beef. We kind of have a lot of that around here."

Jacob Reissner was still hesitant. "Mitch, we didn't come here to impose on you and—"

Mitch clapped him on the shoulder. "Jacob, here in San Juan County, we don't use the word *impose*. Come on, I'll help you bring your things in."

As they went out the door, Adelia turned to Edie. "This is so nice of you. What can I do to help? Just get me an apron."

Right! I can just see you getting grease on that blouse. But Edie smiled and shook her head. "Why don't you just relax? June, will you show Adelia to the spare bedroom?"

To their surprise, Adelia leaned in closer. "I would like to change," she admitted. "I fear I am a bit overdressed."

That surprised both June and Edie. Adelia laughed softly. "Can I be really honest with you?" As they nodded, she lowered her voice. "Last night in Green River, we were asking people at the hotel if they knew you. It seems like everyone there knew you or at least knew of you."

Adelia was blushing now. "They told us that you not only had the biggest ranch in all of southeastern Utah but that you were one of the richest families in the whole area."

Edie hooted aloud. "They told you that? Heavens no."

"They said you had ten thousand acres and about three thousand cows."

Now Mitch Jr. laughed. "We do run that many cows, but we only own about two thousand acres and have grazing rights for eight thousand more. I wish we owned it all."

Adelia was blushing now. "I'm a city girl, born and raised in the Phoenix area. After listening to these people talk about you, I was picturing us coming down to this grand western-style mansion with servants all around, maybe a butler waiting at the door."

Edie was staring at her. "Really?"

"Yeah," she said sheepishly, "so I told Jacob that I was wearing my best dress today. And we put Liesel in her best clothes." She chuckled ruefully. "I tried to get Jacob to wear a suit, but he just laughed at me." She visibly relaxed, glad to have made her confession. "So, if you don't mind, I think I will get into something more comfortable."

At that moment, Edie decided that she and Adelia Reissner were going to get along just fine. Edie also decided that as soon as Adelia disappeared into the bedroom, she was going into her bedroom and changing into something a little *less* comfortable.

Just then, Frank opened the kitchen door and slipped into the room. "Begging your pardon, Sister Reissner, but can I ask you a question?"

Edie shot him a warning look, but Adelia nodded. "Of course, Frank."

"Is that a Cadillac Model 55 Club Roadster you're driving?"

"Frank!" Edie said in dismay.

Adelia laughed. "Well, Frank. You're asking the wrong person. I know it is a Cadillac, but as for the model. . . ." She shrugged.

"It is. I know it is. That is so neat, Sister Reissner. How fast can it go?"

"Frank," Edie scolded. "You get in there and help with supper."

Adelia ignored her. "I know we went almost forty-five miles an hour coming down from Moab where the road was paved. I don't know if it goes faster than that. Ask Brother Reissner."

Frank rushed on. "The US Army bought Cadillacs for their officers in the Great War. They tested all kinds and models, and the Cadillac proved to be the most rugged and the easiest to maintain."

"Yes," she laughed, "I did know that. You see, this isn't our car. This is my father's car."

Ah. I'm liking this girl more and more every minute. Edie was suddenly glad Frank had come in and uncovered that little piece of information.

"He ordered it from Detroit and then had it shipped to Salt Lake. We're just driving it down to Mesa for him. But my father did know about the army. That's why he bought it."

"Neat! How much did it cost?"

Edie jerked forward. "*Frank Westland!* You don't ask questions like that."

Laughing, Adelia reached out and laid a hand on Edie's arm. "It's all right, Edie. I have a fifteen-year-old brother who loves cars too. I am not offended." Then to Frank: "It cost three thousand seventy-five dollars, plus one hundred and ten dollars to ship it to Salt Lake."

With eyes as big as saucers, Frank gave a low whistle. "Whoo–ee!" he exclaimed. "That's gonna take a lot of saving up to get me one of those."

Laughing in spite of herself, Edie gave him a swat across the arm. "All right now, git! Get into the kitchen and help your sisters. Sister Reissner is going to freshen up."

CHAPTER
47

When supper was over and the dishes done and put away, the six children went back to Tina's bedroom to play, giggling and whispering to each other. Liesel, the Reissners' girl, now seemed as much a part of the family as the others. Edie sent Frank and Tina to supervise, even though Frank had begged to be allowed to stay with the adults. Maybe after the children were asleep, Edie had said.

As they disappeared, Adelia turned to Edie. "You have a wonderful family."

"We think so," she said, taking Mitch's hand. "As do you. Liesel is like a little pixie doll."

"Until she doesn't get her way," Jacob Reissner said. "She's pretty strong-minded."

"Do you have other children?" Edie asked Adelia.

"Yes, Jacob Jr. He's two. We left him home with Jacob's parents."

Adelia was sitting by her husband. She was now dressed in a pale blue skirt and white cotton blouse, both of which were simple but still stylish. She slipped off her shoes—a pair of black flats—and tucked her legs up under her skirt as she leaned in against her husband.

Edie watched her, still fascinated by the contrasts she was seeing. Jacob's clothes were not shoddy, so she guessed he made a pretty good salary, but he was so down to earth. But Adelia had this undefinable air of grace and class about her that hinted of a privileged upbringing. Nevertheless, Edie was coming to like her very much. That she had so openly admitted she had dressed up to the nines for the Westlands had really impressed her.

Adelia looked over at Mitch Jr. and June. "How old is your oldest again? Noah, right?"

"Yes. Noah's four," June responded. "He'll be five this summer."

Adelia turned back to Edie and Mitch. "So you have children who are younger than your and grandchildren? Am I right in that?"

Mitch laughed. "Yes. Noah is a year older than Abby and Benji, who are his uncle and aunt. Edie and I get teased about that a lot, actually."

"Right from the beginning," Edie broke in, "Mitch and I agreed that we would take as many babies as the Lord would send us. However, we quickly learned that you don't get to choose *when* you have children. There were many prayers and many blessings, but after twenty-five years of trying. . . ." She shrugged. "It was hard, but we did get four wonderful children. By then I was nearly forty and we assumed that was all we would have. Then Mitch got his mission call to Germany for four years, and we decided that for sure ended it."

"How did you feel about his call?" Jacob asked.

"Sick, of course. That was my first reaction. We had a ranch to run. A family to support. But then almost immediately I was elated."

"Elated?" Adelia asked in surprise.

"Yes. My maiden name is Zimmer. My grandparents are from Germany. They joined the Church and came to Zion as a young married couple. So we think *Oma* Zimmer engineered a little miracle for us, even though she had died several years before."

"Actually," Mitch cut in, "it was more like four miracles."

"Four?" the Reissners blurted at the same time.

Mitch went on. "I got home from my mission in mid-September of 1914. Miracle one happened on Christmas Day three months later. That night, after everyone was in bed, Edie gave me my Christmas gift. She told me that the doctor had just confirmed that she was with child again."

Adelia's jaw dropped. "Oh my word."

"Then," Mitch continued, "about two months later, miracle two came along. Edie had been to the doctor again. He told us that he was pretty certain she was going to have twins."

"No wonder you call them your miracle babies!" Jacob exclaimed.

Mitch nodded. "Miracle three took place when, after almost thirty-six hours of exhausting labor, Edie gave birth to a boy and a girl, who were born nine minutes apart. They were five weeks premature but were healthy in every way, as was their mother."

"I can't begin to imagine how you must have felt," Adelia whispered.

"Yes," Edie said quietly, "I think you can. Mothers can imagine such things."

Mitch was smiling now. "And miracle number four? In a way, it was the sweetest one of all. Because the twins came five weeks early, they were born on May thirteenth." He leaned forward, his own eyes glistening. "May thirteenth is Edie's birthday. It was her *forty-fifth birthday*!"

"No kidding!" Adelia exclaimed. "You were forty-five?"

"They were born on your birthday?" Jacob cried.

Edie nodded. "To Mitch's surprise, I wanted him to pick names for the twins because I was certain that this blessing had come to us due to his willingness to go on a mission." She smiled mischievously. "Of course, I reserved the right of veto. But he took it very seriously."

"Both names came from the Old Testament," Mitch explained. "Abigail means 'a father's joy,' and Benjamin was the last son of Jacob, born in his old age. And, as you can see," Mitch continued, "they are the joy of our lives."

The room was silent for a long time, and then Jacob looked at Mitch. "So is that where you learned your German? From *Oma* Zimmer?"

"Yes," Mitch said. "She insisted that we speak German a lot in the home."

Jacob looked to Mitch Jr. and June and then to Rena and her husband "So do any of you speak German too?" he asked in German.

Rena smiled as Mitch Jr. answered for them both. "*Ja, ja! Wir sprechen Deutsch.*"

Mitch decided to change the subject. "So, if you don't mind me asking, why Monticello? This is hardly the shortest route between Salt Lake and Mesa."

The couple exchanged glances and Jacob responded. "Good question. Adelia is an Arizona girl, born and raised in Mesa. I was born and raised in Salt Lake, but we met at Brigham Young University. After I graduated, Adelia's father, who owns a bank in Mesa, offered us a job there."

Edie's head came up. *Ah. The daughter of a banker. That explains a lot.*

"Before we could move down, however, her father and some of his partners decided to start a bank in Salt Lake. One of Adelia's older brothers came up to act as president, and they offered me a job as a bank clerk. So we stayed in Utah."

"Now," Adelia said proudly, "Jacob is the senior loan officer in the bank."

Jacob brushed that aside. "So, back to your question. Because of that change of plans, Adelia has not been back home since our marriage. So this year, we decided that once the baby was old enough to stay with Grandma and Grandpa, we'd take Adelia back home for a vacation. Originally we planned to go by train, but when Adelia's father ordered the Cadillac and asked us to drive it down for him, we decided that was too good of an offer to turn down."

"But why by way of Monticello?" Edie asked again.

"Ah yes," Jacob said. "That is the real question. And it gets to the real reason why we are here. Mitch, it may interest you to know that we have quite a few former missionaries from the Swiss-German Mission living in Utah. We get together a few times a year," Jacob went on. "President and Sister Valentine live up in Box Elder County, so we see them from time to time, too."

"Oh, that must be wonderful."

"It is. And so we've decided to have a mission reunion in connection with general conference."

"A reunion?" Edie exclaimed. "What a wonderful idea."

"Yes!" Mitch agreed.

"So, we've been gathering names and addresses. When someone gave us your name, I was going to write to you and see if you would be interested. But when Adelia's father bought the car, we thought, 'Why not take a little longer route and go down and meet the Westlands in person?'"

"We are so glad you did," Edie said. She was actually quite astonished by it all. They had only met this family a few hours ago, and now they seemed like lifelong friends.

"We're preparing invitations now. I was hoping to bring one, but there's a complication."

"Oh?" Mitch said.

"The Church has just announced that they are postponing conference for two months."

The Westlands were surprised by that. "Why?" Rena's husband asked.

"Because of the Spanish Flu."

Rena reared back. "I thought the worst of that was over." Her hand slipped down to the swell of her stomach. She was expecting their second child in just a few weeks.

"It is definitely not as bad as last year," Adelia explained, "but there's talk that it might flare up again on a limited basis."

Jacob went on. "General conference will now be June first through the third. But a lot of our former missionaries are farmers like you, and we decided that holding the reunion in the early spring will be easier for them. Since we're a much smaller group, the Health Department said it wouldn't be a problem. We plan to hold it in Provo instead of Salt Lake."

"That's better for us," Edie said. "A little closer."

"We're trying to get permission to hold it on the BYU campus," Jacob went on, "but that's still being negotiated. As soon as we know, we'll send out the invitations."

"That is wonderful news," Edie said. "Thank you for coming in person to share it with us." Then she started to get up. "Well, I think it's time to call the kids in and have some pie and ice cream."

Mitch pulled her back down. "Two last questions for Jacob, then we'll eat. When we were evacuating from Germany back in 1914, we heard a rumor that two elders in Munich had been attacked in a bank and gotten pretty badly beaten up. I noticed the scar over your eye, Jacob. You wouldn't happen to be one of those elders, would you?"

"*Ja,*" Reissner said soberly. "My companion and I were trying to withdraw enough money to get our elders out of Germany. Someone learned we were Americans, and pow! Instant mob."

Edie was appalled. Mitch had talked about those days, but she hadn't heard there was violence.

"And one more question," Mitch said. "You were in Bavaria for a while, right?"

"Yes."

"Tell me what you know about Oberammergau."

"The Passion Play, you mean?"

"Yes."

Rena leaned forward. "What's a Passion Play?"

Mitch and Jacob exchanged glances, and Jacob nodded for him to answer. "In Latin," Mitch began, "one meaning of the word *passion* is 'sorrow or suffering.' So the Catholics and other churches call the last few days of Christ's life the time of His passion. We would call it an Easter play or pageant. Only the one in Oberammergau is a big deal. It's world famous."

"I've been to Oberammergau several times," Jacob said. "It's this quaint little village with houses like Swiss chalets. They're painted with murals of Alpine scenes or religious themes. There are all these wonderful little nutcracker shops. And it's set in the mountains in a spectacular setting. One of the times we were there, we got to see the place where the play is put on. It's a huge, open-air theater. The seating is covered, but the stage is large enough that they have shepherds drive live sheep and cows through the streets, and the Romans ride on real horses."

"They do it in years ending in zero, right?" Mitch asked. "So the next one should be in 1920? With the war, have you heard if they're going to do it next year?"

"No, they're not. Because of how bad the economic and political situations are in Germany right now, they're planning to postpone it a year. It'll be in the summer of 1921."

Mitch turned to his wife. "I haven't told Edie this yet, but someday, I'm taking her there."

She gasped. "We can't afford to go to Germany. And besides, it's too dangerous."

"I didn't say we were going now. But someday." He turned back to Jacob. "Maybe even 1921. That would give us two years to plan and give Germany time to settle back into normalcy."

Adelia and Jacob exchanged looks, and she whispered something to him. Whatever it was, it took him aback. He stared at her for a moment and then broke out in a huge grin. "Why not?" Then he turned to Mitch. "Would you ever consider—" He stopped, looking suddenly sheepish.

"What?" Mitch asked.

"Adelia and I have been talking about this very thing, about going to the Passion Play sometime. I've promised her that someday I will take her there."

"A promise I'm going to hold him to," she said happily. "So. . . ." She looked at her husband, who nodded. She turned back to Mitch. "So, I know we're just dreaming here, but would you ever consider us traveling together?"

Mitch was caught by surprise, but then he exclaimed, "Yes! That would be delightful."

Edie, on the other hand, was really taken aback. "It sounds wonderful, but. . . ." She looked at Mitch. "We have to be realistic, Mitch. We'll never be able to afford something like that."

He was smiling. "We sold a bunch of cattle to the army during the war. We've got a good part of that left in savings. We'll just have to be careful that we don't spend it on frivolous things. You know, like food, clothing, and shelter."

She slapped at his arm. "I'm serious, Mitch."

He instantly sobered. "So am I, honey. I'm not sure when, but someday it *will* happen."

Reissner snapped his fingers. "I know a family, who lives just four or five miles from Oberammergau. In fact, she was the last convert I baptized in the mission field."

"Really?" Mitch asked in amazement. "I didn't think we had missionaries down there."

"We didn't. But my companion and I had met her son, who was studying at a private school in Munich. We became close friends with the son, even though he had no interest in the Church. But through him, we met his aunt, and through that aunt, his mother. Her name is *Schwester* Inga Eckhardt. On the night that we were fleeing Germany, we had a three-hour stop in Oberammergau. So my companion and I decided to go visit Inga. To our amazement, she asked us to baptize her before we left. She had read the Book of Mormon her sister had given her and was converted by it. It was an astonishing experience, actually."

"Jacob writes to her all the time," Adelia said. "She's the one who told us that the Passion Play was postponed. She's invited us to stay with them whenever we go to Oberammergau. *And* she said that includes anyone traveling with us. That would save us quite a bit of money."

Jacob was delighted. "Well, there you have it. We have a place to stay, good people to travel with, and we've solved all the money questions. So, what say you? Is it a deal?"

Before Mitch or Edie could answer, Rena was waving her hand. "Can Bill and I go with you? We'll pay our own way."

"Count us in, too," Mitch Jr. said with a smile.

Edie was shaking her head. "I can't believe what I'm hearing."

Mitch leaned closer to her. "Sister Westland, the man asked you a question. Is it a deal?"

"Do you promise me it will be safe?"

"Yes, or we won't go. If it were right now, I'd say absolutely not. But in two more years?" He took her hand. "It's possible. You have my word, Edie. I will never put you in danger."

She gazed at him for several seconds, and then a twinkle began to dance in her eyes. "And do I get a say in which frivolous things we cut back on?"

He chuckled. "Of course."

"Then, yes." Edie said firmly, turning to Jacob and Adelia. "It's a deal."

February 28, 1919, 2:37 p.m.

When Edie appeared at the barn door, Mitch was momentarily startled. "Oh, hi."

She came inside, looking around. "Where are Benji and Abby?"

"We're up here, Mama," Abby's voice called out. A moment later, both of them appeared in the hay loft.

"We're making a fort," Benji explained.

"Okay," she said. Then in that automatic way that mothers have, she added, "Be careful."

Edie walked over to where Mitch was filling a bucket, waving a white envelope at him. "Look what just came in the mail."

"Another bill?"

"No, this is from Salt Lake."

With that he turned off the faucet and stood up. "From the Reissners?"

"Yep." She handed it to him.

He looked at it and then looked up. "You opened it already?"

She scoffed at his chiding tone. "If you look on the envelope, you will see that it is addressed to both of us."

He grunted in what she took for an apology, opened the envelope, and withdrew a card. He held it up at arm's length and turned so the light from the door fell on it.

SWISS-GERMAN MISSION REUNION
April 5, 1919
Brigham Young University Campus and
Provo Tabernacle, Provo, Utah

3:00–4:00 p.m. Registration, Karl G. Maeser Building, BYU

4:00–5:00 p.m. General session and welcome, Maeser Building

5:00–6:30 p.m. Picnic and social hour, southwest corner of Campus Drive (in case of inclement weather, BYU Academy Building, North University Avenue)

7:00–8:30 p.m. Devotional with President Hyrum W. Valentine, Provo Tabernacle, corner of Center Street and University Avenue

9:00–11:00 p.m. Dance and social, BYU Academy Campus

Food and accommodations: For attendees who don't have family in the area, housing and meals will be arranged with local members. Please write to this address immediately if you are in need of accommodations.

Families: Due to restrictions set by the Utah Department of Health, this year's reunion will be adults only. We expect that future reunions will include all family members.

RSVP: Please return the enclosed card to Jacob Reissner, 324 C Street, Salt Lake City, Utah, no later than March 20th and let us know how many will be attending, if you need accommodations, or other special needs you may have. We look forward to a wonderful day together.

Mitch lowered the card. "Well, that's wonderful. They're really doing it. We'll go, right?"

"Of course." Edie turned the card over. "There's a handwritten note on the back."

"Read it to me."

"'Dear Mitch and Edie, we are so excited that this is finally happening. Your accommodations and meals are already arranged. No protests, please. San Juan County is not the only place that doesn't like the word *impose*. You will be staying with us. Our trip to Arizona went well, but the highlight was our stop at the EDW. Love, Jacob and Adelia.'"

She lowered the card. "So what do you think of that?"

One finger came up. "Shush!" he said.

Her eyes narrowed. "Did you just tell me to shush?" she asked tartly.

"Shhh. I'm thinking."

"About what?"

"About going a couple of days early, seeing Salt Lake, maybe going to the temple."

A smile stole slowly across Edie's face.

He gave her a curious look. "What?"

"Shhh!" she said. "No interruptions, please."

CHAPTER 48

*February 19, 1919, 8:47 a.m.—Prannerstrasse,
near the Maximilianeum building, Munich, Germany*

It was a cold, wintry morning as Kurt Eisner left the prime minister's palace surrounded by several body guards. The sky was low and the color of slate. There was still some snow on the streets and in the plazas, but he paid it no mind. He was rehearsing his speech for the opening session of the new Parliament, but his mind was going back, remembering.

Could it be only three months ago that political chaos had swept the land like a tidal wave? In some ways it seemed liked decades, in other ways more like it had happened just this morning.

The polls for the general election had closed a few days ago. In the new Bavarian Parliament that was being seated today, Eisner's party got only three percent of the vote. They lost most of the few seats they had held before. And so, today, instead of welcoming the new members of Parliament as their prime minister, he was going to announce his resignation and walk away.

Eisner laughed softly and bitterly. Finally, he was doing something the people would support him in. He sighed, his eyes lifting to stare at the graceful lines of the building ahead of him. And then he quickened his step, suddenly eager to be done with it.

So lost was he in his own thoughts that Eisner did not notice the young army officer trailing behind them. Neither did his guards. Their eyes were fixed to the front, watching the milling crowds around the Parliament building.

Count Anton Graf von Arco auf Valley was the son of one of Munich's noble and influential families. Just twenty-two years old, he had been a lieutenant in the army and fought in France. Though one line of his family tree was Jewish, he was a fanatical anti-Semite. He was also an ardent nationalist who wanted to restore the monarchy and sweep out the "Communist trash."

Seething with rage, he wanted to prove that he was a man of action and not just empty words. And now, he was here. And his target was in sight. The Jew, the Communist, the man who had overthrown the monarchy after eight centuries, was just paces ahead of him.

Anton drew his pistol and increased his pace. He heard a cry somewhere to his left and realized someone had seen his pistol. One of the guards started to turn around. Screaming "Death to the Jew, death to the Communist!" he lunged forward. He fired twice and saw that both bullets hit the back of Eisner's head and sent him crashing to the ground.

A wave of ecstasy coursed through him as he whirled and ran. The blasts from the guards' rifles came almost as one explosion. He felt something hit him in the back with tremendous force. Everything went black before he hit the ground.

4:10 p.m. —Bremer Strasse 122, Milbertshofen District, Munich

Hans was on his knees, using a square and a carpenter's pencil to mark and measure where his main workbench would go. He was concentrating hard, making sure that his measurements were precise. The bench was going to cost him almost seventy-five marks, and there would be no altering it once he put in the order at the mill.

BAM! BAM! BAM!

The hammering on the main door of the shop was like the sound of gunfire. Instinctively Hans crouched down and spun around.

"Hans! Quick! Open up! It's me, Wolfie!"

Wolfie? Hans glanced at his watch. Wolfie had said he couldn't be here until after six.

"Let me in, Hans! Quickly!"

Hans dropped the pencil, got to his feet, and swiftly walked to the small side door. He unlocked it and threw it open. Wolfie shot through, knocking him aside in his haste, and slammed the door behind him. Then he sagged back against the wall. His face was white and his chest was heaving. And then Hans saw the blood. He had a gash on his cheek, and dried blood ran down to his chin.

"Wolfie! What happened?"

"They've killed Eisner." Wolfie's hand shot out and gripped Hans's arm. "They're after me."

"*What!* Who? Why would they be after you?"

"There's rioting in the streets, Hans. The government has collapsed. The Communists and the Bolsheviks and the Spartacans have seized the Parliament building and are declaring that Bavaria is a Soviet Republic."

Hans's jaw dropped. "That can't be."

"A mob came to the public works building about three hours ago. They were armed and demanded that we turn over the building to them, that it was now the People's Public Works Department. When my supervisor tried to reason with them, they shot him."

"They killed him?"

He rubbed at his eyes. His hands were visibly trembling. "I don't know, Hans. I don't know." A sob was torn from his throat. "We have to go. They know where I live."

Hans grabbed him by the shoulders and shook him gently. "Wolfie, calm down. You're not making sense. How would they know where you live?"

"They beat me up. Took my wallet. They have my identification card." He jerked free. "We've got to go, Hans. Paula. The children. Inga. Emilee. We have to go now!"

"Wait. Why would they be in danger?"

"Because they hate us. They hate us because we are the government in their eyes. The man who hit me told me they were coming for all of us."

Hans swore, his mind racing. "Okay, okay. Do you have your car?"

"Yes, it's out front. I waited until they were looting the office, and I ran. Fortunately, the car was still in the parking lot. Now, Hans! We have to go now. I'll drive."

"No!" Hans grabbed him and held him fast. "Anyone with a car will be a prime target." He looked around. "Bring it in here. It'll be safe here."

"No, Hans! I've got to get home to Paula before they do."

Shaking him hard enough to get his attention, Hans leaned in. "We'll take the trolley. It will be safer. Faster too, if they've barricaded off any of the streets. I'll open the main doors. You drive the car inside." When Wolfie just stared at him, Hans gave him a shove. "Now, Wolfie!"

A minute later they had the motorcar inside and the large doors shut, with a heavy beam in place. This was a quiet street, a block away from the main thoroughfare. He doubted anyone would find it.

Wolfie was still pretty shaken and kept saying over and over, "Hurry, Hans. We've got to hurry."

Hans grabbed his jacket and put it on. Then he reached into the drawer of a small cabinet in the corner and retrieved his Luger. Wolfie's eyes widened. "You've got a gun?"

"Yes. But my rifle's back at your house. Let's go!"

5:23 p.m.—Herrnstrasse 16, Obermenzing District, Munich

As they approached the corner of Wolfie's street, Hans grabbed his arm and pulled him to a stop. "Easy," he said in a low voice. Hans moved forward, his head swinging back and forth, scanning for any movement. The street was quiet and totally deserted. He watched for a moment and then nodded. "Okay, it's clear. Let's go." They both broke into a run.

Wolfie was yelling as they burst through the door. "Paula! Paula!"

From the kitchen a voice answered. "Wolfie? Is that you?" A moment later she came through the door, Emilee and Inga following behind her, all of them smiling in greeting. Then Paula saw her husband's face. She gasped, and then her knees nearly buckled as she went white as a sheet. "Wolfgang? What happened to you?"

He ran to her and swept her into his arms. "It's all right," he said. "It's all right. It's just a scratch."

A scratch that would need stitches, Hans thought. He was an expert on that.

Emilee rushed over to them. "What is it? What's happened?"

"Where are the children?" Wolfie asked, gripping Paula's arms to steady her.

"They're—they're upstairs playing."

"Go get them. We have to leave."

Hans took Emilee's hand and pulled her over to his mother. He motioned for Paula to come, too. "The prime minister has been assassinated," he explained. "There is rioting in the streets around the Parliament building." Actually, Wolfie hadn't said where the rioting was, but the Parliament building was a long way from where they were. He didn't want the women panicking. "We've got to go."

"Go?" Paula cried. "Go where?" Inga stared at Hans in horror.

"To Graswang," he said without hesitation. The women gaped at him. That even brought Wolfie around with a jerk. Hans rushed on. "We have to leave, and we have to leave now. There may be men coming here. Pack one suitcase each. Leave everything else. Be sure you have your personal documents and any cash or valuables you need." He squeezed Emilee's hand. "I'm going to change into my uniform. Is my rifle still in the closet?"

"Yes." As Hans started to turn away, Emilee pulled him back. "Is it really that bad?"

"It could be," he said grimly. He put an arm around his mother's shoulders. "Mama, go with Emilee. Pack only what you need. We need to leave quickly."

5:40 p.m.

They gathered back into the living room. Bruno was very scared. Gretl was trembling a little but was trying to comfort him. The women were also pale as they lined up, each with a suitcase or valise. Hans did a quick assessment, his eyes stopping on Wolfie. "Wolf, you've got to wash that blood off your face. We don't want people noticing us."

"I'll help you," Paula said as she followed him to the kitchen sink. Hans knelt down in front of Bruno. "I need you to be brave, Bruno. We men have to help the women, right?"

Bruno sniffed and then nodded. Hans reached up and wiped away his tears with his thumbs. "Good. You and Gretl go over to the window." He looked at Gretl. "Watch the street. Tell me if you see anything moving out there. Anything, okay?" They both nodded.

"Don't pull back the curtain," Hans added. "Just watch through the opening." Then he turned and encircled his mother in his arms. "We'll be all right, Mama. This is all just starting, but we need to get you out of here before it spreads."

Inga looked up at him and managed a smile. "I'm all right. I'm just glad that you are here." Hans kissed her on the forehead. "Me too." He moved to Emilee and hugged her too. "I'm going to take the lead," he whispered. "Will you stay right with Mama?"

"Of course."

"Hans!" Gretl's cry spun him around.

"Someone's coming."

Wolfie rushed over and joined Hans at the window, dabbing at his face with a towel. Up the street to the east, four men had come around the corner onto *Herrnstrasse*. They were not in uniforms, which was good, but one of them had a rifle, which was not good. Hans leaned in closer to his uncle. "Wolfie, take everyone out through the alley. I'm going to try to slow these guys down a little. I'll meet you at the trolley stop. But if I'm not there, don't wait for me. Get to the train station. Get tickets to Oberammergau. If there's time, call Papa and the others. Have them meet us at Oberammergau. I'll catch up with you there if not before."

Wolfie took his children by the hand. "All right, let's go. Out the back. No noise."

Hans went to Emilee. Her eyes were swimming with tears. "I have to do this," he whispered. "But I will catch up with you. I promise."

"I know." She threw her arms around him. "I know."

He kissed her hard. "I love you. I'll see you soon."

5:44 p.m.

Hans watched his family until they left the alley and turned onto the narrow side street that led out of the neighborhood, and then he walked swiftly back into the apartment. He started for the large window in the living room but changed his mind and ran up the stairs. Paula's and Wolfie's bedroom was on the front of the house with a window that overlooked the street. Moving carefully, Hans went to the window and peered out. The men were coming slowly, two on one side of the street, two on the other. They were not stopping at anyone else's door. Their eyes were fixed on the house where Hans was waiting for them. Which meant Wolfie had been right.

He eased the window open without pulling the curtains back and dropped to one knee. With practiced ease, he chambered a round. Closing one eye, he took aim at the man carrying the rifle. Hans took a deep breath, let it half out slowly, moved the barrel slightly to the right, and squeezed the trigger.

The sharp crack of the rifle and the instant ricochet of the bullet bouncing off cement shattered the evening silence. The man probably felt the whip of the bullet past his cheek, for he dove to the ground and rolled away. The other three scrambled like crabs to any kind of cover. Aiming at the closest man, Hans fired again, just to the left of his head. Then he took off. Taking the stairs three at time, Hans stopped long enough to make sure the front door was locked, and then he darted out into the alley. He heard someone yelling but paid it no mind as he took off in a dead run.

6:55 p.m.—Munich Railway Station, Munich

Wolfgang Groll was off in a corner of Munich's central train station. He had bought a children's book from the magazine shop and was reading it to Gretl and Bruno. Emilee saw Bruno toss back his head and laugh. *Oh, for the resilience of children*, she thought with envy. Once they were away safely from their home, the evening had turned into a grand adventure for them. Their greatest joy, however, had come when their parents told them they were going to *Tante* Inga's house and there would be no school for a while.

Behind Emilee, Paula and Inga were seated on a bench with their handbags beside them and the one suitcase they hadn't checked lying at their feet. Emilee saw that her mother-in-law's eyes were closed. She guessed she was praying again, and not sleeping. As was she, though her eyes were not closed. She was searching the faces of the people streaming into the station through the multiple entrances to the main hall. Clearly, the Eckhardts and the Grolls were not the only ones who had decided to get out of the city.

"Hey, you!" a soft voice said behind her.

Emilee whirled and then squealed aloud and threw herself into Hans's outstretched arms. He kissed her soundly. "How did you get in here?" she cried, laughing and crying at the same time. "I've been watching the doors the whole time."

Hans didn't get a chance to answer. Bruno came hurtling at him like a miniature missile. Gretl was calling out, "Hans! Hans!" causing everyone in the station to turn and look.

"Oh, Hans," his mother cried. "Thank the Lord. Are you all right?"

He removed one arm from around Emilee and drew Inga in with them. "Yes, Mama. I'm all right. The trolleys have stopped running. And when I did finally get a taxi to stop, we had to detour around a lot of hot spots."

Paula laid a hand on his cheek. "Thank you, Hans. Thanks to you and Wolfie for acting so quickly." A shudder ran through her body. "When I think about those men coming. . . ."

"Don't, Paula," her husband said. "Don't think about it. We're all safe. I called Opa Eckhardt, and he'll have someone waiting for us when we arrive." He looked at his sister-in-law. "And yes, Inga, we do thank the Lord that we are all here safely."

Hans withdrew a piece of paper from his pocket and then took a ten-mark note from his wallet. "Wolfie, how soon does our train leave?"

"Not for half an hour."

"Will you take this to the telegraph office and send it off?" He looked at Emilee. "I think you need to go with Wolfie and send a telegram to your family and Dr. Schnebling. When the news about what's going on here reaches them, they'll worry."

"Thank you, Hans," she said quietly. "I was thinking the same thing just a few minutes ago." Emilee extended her hand. "Would you mind if I read what you're saying to Colonel von Schiller? I assume that's who your telegram is to."

"Of course not," Hans said as he handed the paper to her. "You may as well read it out loud."

She did so.

To Colonel Stefan von Schiller, Commanding Officer, First Battalion, Black Eagle Regiment, Imperial German Army Barracks, Finckensteinallee, Lichterfelde, Berlin.

Received your letter. Was honored to be so considered. Though my career decisions have not changed, current circumstances in Munich compel me to accept your offer. Have fled the city this very day. Army intervention only real hope. Await further instructions from you. Can be reached at previous address and phone number in Graswang Village, Bavaria.

Lt. Hans Eckhardt.

Emilee handed it back to him. "Do you agree?" he asked.

"Without reservation," she said.

"Amen," Paula said. "Amen to that. Go take back our home."

Chapter Note

The assassination of Kurt Eisner, prime minister of the State of Bavaria, did happen as described here on February 19, 1919, following a devastating loss for Eisner's government in the general elections (see Shirer, *Rise and Fall*, 34). Shirer noted that immediately after the assassination, "the workers set up a soviet republic." Another source states, "This assassination caused unrest and lawlessness in Bavaria, and the news of a soviet revolution in Hungary encouraged communists and anarchists to seize power" (http://www.ww1 -propaganda-cards.com/Munich%201919.html).

April 2, 1919, 10:35 a.m.—Eckhardt dairy farm,
Graswang, Bavaria

O*nkel* Hans?"

Hans opened his eyes, squinting against the bright sunlight. His niece was seated right beside him on the grass. How long had she been there? He started to sit up, but she put a tiny hand on his chest and pushed him back down.

"Are you sleeping?"

He smiled. "Not anymore, Miki. Why?"

"Will you tell me a story?"

Heidi, who was sitting on the porch with Emilee and Inga, spoke up. "Miki, let *Onkel* Hans sleep. He's tired. He can tell you a story later. In fact, why don't you lie down beside him and tell him a story? Maybe he can go back to sleep then."

Hans lifted his head up enough to look at his sister. "I'm not tired; I'm just being lazy."

Heidi just shook her head. Emilee reacted with a hoot. "Right. And that's why your snoring is upsetting the cows out in the barn."

Miki ignored the women, focusing only on Hans. She scooted around so she was facing him directly. One hand came out and touched his face. "Does that hurt, *Onkel* Hans?" Her fingers lightly brushed across the two scars on his upper left cheek.

"Miki!" Heidi cried. "Be soft."

Hans turned onto his side to face her. "She was being soft, Heidi. It's all right." Then to this impish little blonde-haired angel, he said, "No, it doesn't hurt anymore, Miki. It just makes me look all the more handsome, don't you think?"

To his surprise, her mouth pulled down. "No, *Onkel* Hans. It makes me sad."

Hans sat up and gathered her into his arms. "Oh, Miki, you are such a little sweetheart. Come on. Lie down here beside me, and I'll tell you a story."

She instantly complied, pulling him back down too. Then she snuggled up against him.

"All right, then," Hans began. "I want to tell you a story about a little Dutch boy."

"What's a Dutch boy?" she interrupted.

"It's a little boy who lives in Holland, which is a long way from here."

Inga sat forward on her chair. "Oh," she said innocently, "this is one of my favorite stories."

Hans pretended not to hear. "And this little boy's name was. . . ." Then he turned and looked at his mother, waiting for her response.

"Peter," she said, laughing right out loud.

Miki, of course, was already enthralled. "I like that name."

As he continued, Emilee leaned in toward Inga. "Did he tell you how hearing the name *Peter* helped him to decide to give the money back to that woman he was robbing?"

Heidi's mouth dropped open. "What did you say?" she gasped.

Inga reached out and patted her hand. "I'll tell you later." Then to Emilee: "Yes, he did tell me. I told him that was the hand of the Lord."

Emilee smiled. "So did I. Interesting that he would choose to tell Miki this story."

Inga's smile deepened with satisfaction. "It's not just for Miki. It's for me."

Suddenly they heard the phone ring from inside the house. Emilee started to get up, but Heidi was faster. "I'll get it," she said, and she went inside. A moment later she hurried back out. "Hans, it's from Berlin. It's Colonel von Schiller."

Up in an instant, Hans ran inside, leaving Miki looking confused. Emilee got up and followed him in. As he picked up the receiver, he motioned for her to move in closer.

"Yes, this is Lieutenant Eckhardt."

"Ah, *gut*. How are you, Lieutenant? How are those ribs coming along?"

"Barely notice them anymore, sir. Thank you for asking. And how is your leg doing?"

"The same. I'm still limping quite a bit, but I threw the cane away last week."

"Very good, sir."

"Sorry for the long delay, but this is the army, remember. They have three speeds—slow, slower, and dead stop."

Hans chuckled. "Not to mention reverse."

"Right. So, how are you coming along with finding men for C Company?"

"Well, as I mentioned in my last letter, I've been going up to Munich two or three times a week to recruit, and I've found some good men. But I was getting stonewalled by the army here until the anarchists declared that Bavaria is now a Soviet Republic."

"What? When did they do that?"

"Just three days ago. But that finally got these lunkheads off their behinds, and I'm getting full cooperation now. I've identified over a hundred potential men. They're ready to sign and start training the moment you give me authorization to move ahead."

"Excellent, Eckhardt. I knew you'd come through. I think it's time you move up to Munich. If things are deteriorating that rapidly, I want you where you can keep your finger on things."

Hans glanced at Emilee, who pulled a face. "Yes, sir. I need a few days to tie up some loose ends here. If I were there by Friday morning, would that work?"

"Friday's fine. I'll have Corporal Jürgens get you a place in the officer's quarters."

"Very good. Uh . . . any chance Jürgens could requisition another motorbike, Colonel?"

There was no answer.

Hans went on. "It's not like the men I need to talk to are all in one place. And right now, trolley service is really spotty. I spent over two hours the other day just waiting for trolleys."

"All right, but if you get this bike shot out from under you, that'll be it, got it?"

"Yes, sir. Thank you, sir. Uh. . . ."

There was a deep sigh. "What is it, Lieutenant?"

"If he could have that by Friday, that would be wonderful. Some of the men are day laborers. I'll have a better chance of catching them on a weekend."

That was true, but it was only part of the picture. The first time he had gone up to Munich, he had been tempted to go to his shop and borrow Wolfie's car for transportation. It didn't take much to talk himself out of that. Too high of a profile. Too costly in petrol. Too much chance it would be damaged or stolen. But a motorbike? That was a whole different picture. It was cheap. It was highly mobile. And it was fast enough to outrun most pursuers.

"All right," the colonel finally said, "but I want to see results."

"Understood, sir."

"Anything else, Lieutenant?"

"No sir, I don't think so. Thank you for everything. I am in your debt once again."

"Yes you are," von Schiller growled, "so don't you forget it. If you need anything, call Jürgens." And he hung up.

Hans and Emilee stood together for a few moments, not speaking. Finally, Emilee looked up. She was very close to tears.

"I have to go, Emilee," he said. "You know that."

"Yes."

"It's time. We've been here over a month now. I'm glad something is finally happening."

"I know that, too. I've seen how restless you are here. Wolfie too."

He pulled her to him. "I want to get on with our lives." Then he flashed her a boyish grin. "Though I neglected to mention this to Colonel von Schiller, one of the reasons I asked for the motorcycle is so I can come home on the weekends during training."

"Really? Oh, Hans, that would be wonderful. Are you sure?"

"I can also go to the shop at night and do some work."

"You are shameless," she said, managing a smile.

"I have learned to always tell the truth to your commanding officer. And it really will help me recruit more men to have a motorbike. But you don't have to tell him *all* of the truth."

Emilee didn't laugh. Instead, she threw her arms around Hans, clinging to him fiercely. "This is good, Hans. I know that. But I still worry. If Munich becomes another Berlin, then. . . ."

"Remember, there's the extra money, too. Three hundred more marks at the very least."

"It's not worth it," she said flatly.

He put a finger under her chin and tipped her head back until her eyes met his. He kissed her softly on the lips. "You know I'll be careful, Emilee. I have something to live for now."

April 4, 1919, 8:50 a.m.—Mars Camp, Maxvorstadt District,
Munich

Hans lowered his duffel bag and looked around. No surprises here.
It looked like a dozen other army posts he'd seen. Three-story barracks
of white stucco with unit flags flying from their roofs. Large parade
ground. A mess hall. A squarish two-story building with the national,
Bavarian, and regimental flags on three poles in front of it. That would
be post headquarters.

A shout brought Hans around to the left. Two men in uniform
were coming toward him from the nearest building. He raised a hand
and called back, recognizing them immediately. Master Sergeant
Norbert Diehls and the ubiquitous Corporal Jürgens.

"Welcome, sir," Jürgens called out while they were still ten or fifteen paces away.

"Jürgens? What are you doing here?"

"I'm on TDY, sir."

"What kind of temporary duty?"

Jürgens grinned. "The colonel says I am to help you and Sergeant
Diehls get your company up and running before he gets here, or my
behind will be in a sling for the rest of my life."

Now it was Hans who grinned. Wonderful. Hans hated paperwork, and if the men he had found were going to get paid and clothed
and armed, there was a ton of paperwork to be done. That was Jürgens's
forte. "Have you had a chance to—"

"Yes, sir. It's around the back of the officer's quarters." He reached
in his tunic pocket and extracted two keys on a ring. "The tank's full,
sir. It's got a few miles on it, but the quartermaster assures me it's the
best motorbike he has available."

Hans extended his hand. "Good to see you again, Diehls. Glad to
have you at my back."

"The feeling's mutual."

Hans turned to Jürgens. "I'm anxious to get started so we don't have to work all weekend. Show me to my quarters and I'll dump my gear, and then find us a place to work."

"Already did, sir. They've given us an office in the basement of post headquarters."

Hans slapped him on the back. "Jürgens, don't you ever let them make you an officer."

"Why's that, sir?"

"Because you're far too valuable right where you are."

April 13, 1919, 6:28 p.m.—Herrnstrasse 16, Obermenzing District, Munich

As he slowed the bike and rounded the corner onto *Herrnstrasse*, Hans was feeling pretty good. By five o'clock yesterday, they had processed the paperwork for ninety-four men, and Jürgens had managed to contact more than half of them and tell them to report for duty at oh-eight-hundred Monday morning. Leaving Jürgens to contact the rest of them as best he could, Hans and Bert had left shortly after five and taken the motorbike into *Altstadt*—Old Town Munich, a major center for Munich's night life. They had spent the next three hours moving between the bars, bistros, restaurants, cafés, *Rathäuser,* and beer halls, looking for men who either were in uniform or looked like they should be. About a half of those they picked out were already part of one *Freikorps* unit or another, but those men recommended friends, relatives, or former army buddies who might be interested. When they left they had commitments from another seventeen men and forty-two names to check out. It was a good thing, too.

The new "Soviet Republic," which was set up and run by the Independent Social Democrats, lasted exactly six days after the assassination of Eisner. The gross incompetence was much like it had been in Berlin. As just one example, the leadership of the party chose as their foreign minister a man who had been in and out of psychiatric hospitals numerous times. One of his first official acts was to declare war on Switzerland when they wouldn't lend him sixty locomotives. A day or two later, he sent cables to the Pope in Rome and Vladimir Lenin asking them if they knew the whereabouts of his key to the lavatory.

It had been easy pickings for the Communists and Spartacans to step in and take over. They moved swiftly and with ruthless efficiency to enact Communist reforms. When the army tried to intervene and negotiate with them, they spurned them and organized their own army from unemployed workers, who flocked to their banner in large numbers. But Hans was close enough to his quota that he told Jürgens and Diehls they were taking the weekend off. An hour later he was on his way to his shop.

At the shop, Hans was relieved to find the lock undisturbed and Wolfie's car gathering dust. There was also a note tacked to the door saying that the workbench he had ordered was ready for delivery. And with that he left to fulfill his promise to Wolfie and Paula to check on their house and make sure everything was all right, and then he would head back to the barracks to grab some much-needed sleep.

But as Hans approached number 16, the first thing he saw was a curtain blowing softly in the breeze—*outside of the window*! For a moment he wondered if someone had left the window open, but then it hit him. That window didn't open. It was a fixed pane of glass. Hans let off the gas and coasted slowly by the house. The whole window was gone. The front door was kicked in, and across the brickwork, in large black letters, were the words *DEATH TO THE MONARCHISTS.*

Hans's heart was suddenly pounding so hard he could barely breathe. He gently accelerated again, turning his head to the front as if he hadn't noticed anything unusual.

But once he was past that block, he bent low, made a right turn onto a side street and then another turn into the alley that ran behind the Grolls' home. He shut off the engine and the light and let the bike roll to a stop. There were no street lamps in the alley, and only faint light from a few of the windows provided any light. Hans hopped nimbly off the bike and walked it forward, counting the houses as he passed them.

Parking the bike behind the garbage cans, he fished in his pocket for the house keys with one hand while he drew his pistol with the other. A moment later, he was inside the apartment. He came to a halt to let his eyes adjust and his pulse slow a little. The hallway was pretty dark, but with the curtains open, the street lamps provided enough light for him to see into the kitchen, living room, and sitting room pretty well. And what he saw made him nearly retch.

Every kitchen cupboard was open, and the cupboards were empty. As Hans stepped into the room, glass crunched beneath his feet. The floor was littered with broken crockery and glassware. He bent down to see what he at first thought was sand on the floor. It was sugar, made yellow by the lamplight. Coffee, flour, beans, and pasta were mixed in with it and the broken glass. A smear on the wall caught his eye. It looked as though someone had thrown a glass of water at it, only it was not water. Something thicker, with little bits of something sticky in it. Then he saw a can of peaches on the floor. It was split clear open. Someone must have hurled it against the wall.

In the corner, the stove had been tipped on its side. That had pulled the stove pipe out of the wall, and soot drifted up in little black puffs as he stepped forward. Suddenly he heard movement behind him. Hans spun around, jacking a bullet into the chamber of his Luger. A dark shape scurried across the floor. He knew instantly what it was. He had seen them often enough in the trenches. Hans swept up a broken coffee cup and hurled it at the rat, but he missed it by a foot.

In the living room, every cushion of the sofa had been savagely ripped apart. Paula's favorite lamp table had its legs smashed. The lamp had been trampled under someone's boots. More words were painted on Paula's shattered mirror, which had been a treasured gift from her parents on her wedding day. *DOWN WITH BOURGEOISIE PIGS.*

Disgust welled up in him. These weren't looters. Maybe they had taken a few things, but not much. This was wanton destruction, smashing anything that might have any value to its owners. Blind rage simply because Wolfie was a successful civil servant and they were scum.

Hans started up the stairs, but the stench of urine and feces was so strong that he backed down again. If there was anything of value left in his and Emilee's bedroom, he didn't want to touch it. He turned around and checked the deadbolt on the front door to make sure it was in place, even though the bottom panel had been kicked in and it wouldn't take much to squeeze through the hole. He looked for the rat again. He didn't care if the neighbors heard the gunshots. If he saw that sucker again, he was going to empty his entire magazine at it, consequences be damned. But he didn't see it. Nothing moved. An eerie silence hung over the place like a shroud. Swearing, Hans kicked at a shattered chair and then made his way back out to the alley.

He waited until he was a block away before he started the engine and drove slowly toward the telephone exchange. When he reached it, he changed his mind and went by it, even though its lights were on and a sign said that it was still open. He decided he wouldn't call tonight, even though he had promised that he would. He would drive down to Graswang tomorrow instead. He'd surprise Emilee. Surprise everyone.

A deep gloom settled in on him. He would especially surprise Paula and Wolfie.

CHAPTER 50

April 16, 1919, 10:55 p.m.—Headquarters building,
Bayerische Armee, Munich

Wolfgang Groll got off the motorbike and stepped back, his head tipped up so he could read the letters over the door. "Bavarian Army?" he asked without turning.

Hans dismounted, put down the kickstand, and removed the key from the ignition. "Yes, Wolfie. This is it. Relax. The army is just trying to identify the bad guys responsible for the revolution."

"But why me? I'm not in the army."

"You were there when they seized control of the Public Works Building. You saw their faces. You saw what they did. And now you've seen what they did to your home. Not every home on the street, Wolfie. Just yours and Paula's. And that's what these people need to know."

Grumbling, Wolfie fell in step with Hans as they went up the steps and into the building.

11:28 a.m.

Wolfie looked at the clock for the tenth or eleventh time in the last five minutes. "It's been almost half an hour," he grumbled. "Let's go."

Hans sighed. "Wolfie, this is the army. Okay? Nothing moves fast in the army." He looked around. There had been one man ahead of them when they came in. He had not yet come back out.

"So I say we just go. I've got things to do."

"What?" Hans scoffed. "Go back to Graswang and help them milk the cows?"

"No, I say we go over to the apartment and start cleaning it up. I don't want Paula to see it like that. She'll never get that picture out of her head."

"Wolfie," Hans sighed. "You know we can't do that. Not until we get these Bolsheviks out of power. If they learn that you're back, they'll come after you again." He reached up and touched the scars on his cheek. "Believe me. I know what I'm talking about."

His uncle folded his arms and sat back, staring moodily up at the ceiling. Two minutes later, another man in uniform came out through the doors and turned right, headed for the side entrance, but it was not the man who had been with them earlier. Hans leaned forward, peering at the man. There was something familiar about him. He was a little older than Hans and at least six inches shorter. In profile, his nose was straight, but prominent. His hair—jet black and combed straight down toward the ears on both sides of the part—revealed a high forehead and thinnish eyebrows.

Just then, the man half turned and glanced back at something, and Hans saw his mustache, a small patch of black perched precariously beneath his nose. He jumped to his feet. "Stay here," he said to Wolfie, and then he took off, half running and half walking. The man was almost to the entry doors. Hans cupped his hand to his mouth and called, "Adolf? Adolf Hitler?"

Stopping, the man turned around, not sure who had hollered at him. Hans couldn't believe it. It was him! He strode forward, lifting a hand in greeting. "Is that really you?"

He stared at Hans for a moment, looking confused, and then

suddenly his countenance changed. "Hans? Oh my word. Sergeant Hans Eckhardt!"

People stared at them as they came together and embraced in a huge bear hug, slapping each other on the back. Then they stepped back. "What are you doing here?" Adolf asked.

"I'm Bavarian," Hans laughed. "Remember? This is my state. We're being interviewed by the tribunal looking into causes of the revolution. The real question, is, what are you doing here? I thought you were Austrian."

Adolf took him by the elbow and steered him out of the way of the people coming in and out of the building. "I am Austrian. I was born in Braunau am Inn. It's right on the border. My father was a customs agent for the government."

Hans was grinning. "So we could say that you are half Austrian, half Bavarian."

"No," he said irritably. "I am all *German*. I spit on the artificial borders drawn by men. We are not Austrian Germans and Bavarian Germans and Berliner Germans. We are Germans who merely live in those places." Then he laughed and clapped Hans on the shoulder. "But pay me no mind. So, what are you doing here? You told me you were getting out of the army."

"I was. I did. Then I got caught in the Spartacan riots in Berlin and joined a *Freikorps* unit."

Adolf leaned in, suddenly eager. "You were part of what happened in Berlin?"

"*Ja*. My battalion took back the police headquarters building from that swine Eichhorn."

"Ah," Adolf exclaimed. "What I would give to have been part of that proud moment." Then he looked at Hans's uniform. "So then you stayed in? And they made you an officer?"

Shaking his head, Hans chuckled. "Actually, it's a little more complicated than that. When the trouble in Berlin ended, I left and came down here to be with my family."

"Over near Oberammergau, as I remember."

"Your memory is good, Adolf. But the commander of our battalion called me a few weeks ago. The general staff is sending regular army units and more *Freikorps* units here to put down this so-called Soviet Republic."

"Yes!" He nearly shouted it. "I heard that. I am ecstatic. The army is the only force with the courage to take these Communists and Jews head on."

"Well, what about you? It looks like you stayed in the army too."

"Yes, much the same as you did. I came back to Munich, which I consider my adopted home, with the intent of doing something of great significance. I have this consuming passion to do something for our country and our people."

Hans started at that. "As do I. During the conflict with the Spartacans, I had an opportunity to be among the poor and the working class. I determined I wanted to do something to help them."

Adolf's response was immediate and heartfelt. "You helped defeat the Spartacans."

"I know but. . . ." Hans shrugged. "That's why I told my commander I'd come help here."

"Yes. This is the next battleground," Adolf replied. He reached out and gripped Hans's arm. "I have thought much on this. During my schooling, I became interested in history and read voraciously, trying to identify the forces that shape society, the forces that change history."

"And what did you find?"

"One word above all stood out. *Politics.* That is how one person can make the greatest difference. Yet," he grimaced, as if in pain, "as I lay in the hospital after that gas attack, thinking that I might be permanently blinded, I found myself in great despair. What was I to do? I had no job. No friends. No money. I was nameless and unrecognized by even the poorest wretch on the streets. And then—" He was looking past Hans now, seemingly far away. "And then, that pastor spoke to us that day in the hospital. Do you remember that, Hans?"

"As though it were yesterday."

"He inflamed me with a consuming determination to do something. To start somewhere. So I decided to come to Munich. But I hardly recognized it. Chaos was everywhere. That Jew swine Eisner had seized the government and set up the People's Republic. My own battalion had become a 'Soldier's Council' and was totally corrupted with Bolshevik and Communist ideology. I refused to be part of that. But I found another unit, where right-thinking people still held to the belief that Germany and Austria could be healed." There was a brief smile, little more than a flicker. "And I did have to eat. So I joined myself to them."

Hans was nodding soberly. "This tale has a familiar ring to it."

Hitler went right on. "They assigned me to be a guard at Traunstein, a prisoner-of-war camp near the Austrian border. What a muck of a place that was. So when spring came, I left and came back here. And hardly was I back when some of those Communist swine tried to arrest me as a deserter, since I had refused to serve under their 'Soldier's Council.' But I shoved the barrel of a rifle in their faces and they slunk off like the craven cowards they are."

Hans turned and waved to Wolfie to come over. When he did, he introduced him to Hitler. "Wolfie is also a civil servant," he explained.

"Like my father," Adolf said. "What branch of civil service?" he asked Wolfie.

"Public Works. Here in the city." Then, at Hans's urging, Wolfie told Hitler what had happened to him.

"And you are both here to testify before the tribunal too?" Adolf asked Hans. "Good for you. I am as well." He glanced up at the clock. "Oh, dear. I must run. I have an appointment back at the barracks.

But let's get together. We are kindred spirits, you and I. Where are you posted?"

"At Mars Camp Barracks."

"It may take me a day or two," he said, "but I'll find you. And then, my friend, I shall buy you a plate of bratwurst and a pint of ale and together we'll solve the world's problems."

"I would like that, Adolf. Very much."

Hitler shook hands with both of them, and then he turned and was gone.

"Do you think he will look you up again?" Wolfie asked as he disappeared out onto the parade grounds. "He seems a little distracted."

"I think the better word is *intense*. But I hope so. I like him. I like his passion."

Behind them, a woman's voice called out. "Sergeant Hans Eckhardt?"

He turned around, raising his hand. "Here," he called. Then to Wolfie: "Okay, here we go."

April 19, 1919, 8:05 p.m.—Mars Camp barracks, Maxvorstadt District, Munich

There was a sharp rap on the door. Hans looked up from his desk, where he had been poring over the names of his company members. "Come!" he barked.

The door opened and Corporal Jürgens came in. He waved an envelope at Hans. "Mail call."

"At eight o'clock at night?"

Jürgens shrugged. "Hand-delivered at the gate." He laid the letter on the desk and left.

There was nothing written on the envelope except *Lieutenant Hans Eckhardt*. Curious, Hans retrieved a letter opener from the drawer and slit open one end. It was a single sheet with three lines written in a slanting, barely legible scrawl.

Enjoyed our brief meeting enormously.
Dinner tomorrow, 8:30 p.m. Marienplatz. Café Deutschland,
across from the Glockenspiel.
Bratwurst. Ale. More stimulating conversation. A.

Hans stared at it for a moment and then smiled. "And Wolfie thought you'd never show."

CHAPTER 51

*April 20, 1919, 8:35 p.m.—Café Deutschland,
Marienplatz, Munich*

Hitler was waiting for him outside the café, pacing back and forth. "Sorry," Hans said as he hurried up. "Couldn't find a place to park my motorbike."

"It's not a problem," Adolf said, a smile breaking out. "I was afraid you had not received my note. Come. I have a table reserved for us in a back corner where it won't be so noisy." He removed his cap, and Hans did the same.

The room, which was long and narrow, with a bar running the full length of one side, was nearly full. The air was blue with cigarette smoke, and there was a lot of noise. Hans saw an upright piano near the far end of the bar, but gratefully no one was sitting at it. More than half of the men were in uniform of one kind or another, and many of them were officers. Definitely an army hangout. The girls ranged in age from late teens to mid-thirties.

Adolf slowed and let Hans come up beside him. "Have you been here before?"

Hans shook his head. "No, but I haven't been in Munich for that long."

"I like this place. Only German products are sold here."

They were seated, and a moment later a young woman in a brightly colored *Dirndl* brought them menus. As Hans glanced at it, he took off his tunic. It was hot and humid in here. "So what beers do you like best here?"

Adolf barely glanced up. "I don't drink beer. I'm having coffee. But I'm told that the *Alts* are the best."

Hans fought back the urge to stare at him. Was he joking? A German who didn't drink beer? That was like a Frenchman who didn't like food. Or a Brit that smiled. But Hans saw that he wasn't joking. He shrugged it off and looked at the list on the back of the menu.

When the same waitress returned a few minutes later, smiling prettily at Hans, he had already decided what to have. In addition to a stein of beer, he ordered beer-glazed brats with sauerkraut and black bread. Adolf, who had barely glanced at the menu, asked for *Roulade* and red cabbage, with black coffee, no cream or sugar.

When the waitress walked away, Hans asked, "Is the *Roulade* here good?" That was one of his mother's favorite dishes. Chopped bacon, onions, and gherkin pickles were mixed with Dijon mustard and rolled up in large, thin slices of beef, tied with string, and baked in the oven.

"Don't know. Haven't tried it before." At Hans's look of surprise, Adolf laughed. "I don't have much money, but since it's my birthday today, I'm going to splurge."

"It's your birthday? Really?"

"*Ja*. Really. My thirtieth. How old are you, Hans?"

"I turned twenty-three in February."

"And a second lieutenant already? Do you come from a well-to-do family?"

"Me?" Hans laughed. "I'm the son of a *Milchbauer*, as my mother frequently reminds me. I was given a field commission for my part in the Battle of Berlin."

"So a man of the soil. Is that what you will do when Munich is restored to normal?"

"No, my father wanted that, but I signed my inheritance over to my three sisters. The thought of milking cows for the rest of my life was more than I could stomach, so . . . I am planning to start a mechanic's garage here, for trucks, in the Maxvorstadt District."

Hitler slapped the table in delight. "This is marvelous! I did the same."

"You are a mechanic?" Hans said in amazement.

"No, no. I am speaking of going against my father's wishes. He was absolutely determined that I should also become a civil servant like he was, but I refused. We battled for years over it. But I wanted to do something meaningful with my life. At first I decided I wanted to be an artist. A painter." He laughed at Hans's expression. "Does that surprise you?"

"A little."

"I went to art school in Vienna, but I discovered I had more of a talent for architecture, and so I determined that would be my career."

Just then, the waitress returned. She set a large cup of steaming coffee in front Adolf and a foaming stein of beer in front of Hans. "So are you an architect, then?" Hans asked.

"*Nein.* I dabbled in art for a time, mostly to survive." He gave a short bark of derisive laughter. "Mostly I learned what it was like to go without food. Hunger was my faithful bodyguard. It never left me for a moment. Hunger became my constant and pitiless friend."

He stopped as he saw the look on Hans's face. "Have you known hunger like that?"

"I have," Hans replied quietly. "Not for long periods, but enough to know that it can consume your every thought, your every waking moment, your every longing and desire."

Adolf sat back, pleased. "Exactly. But from it, I learned much about myself. It was then—I was sixteen at the time—that I came to realize my real passion lay elsewhere."

"In politics?" Hans guessed. Then he smiled. "At age sixteen? All

I cared about at sixteen was becoming an engineer and chasing a few skirts."

Again, it was as though Hans weren't even there.

"It consumed me. I read everything—history, government, newspapers, political journals. And the more I read, the more I realized that I had a passionate love for Germany and a burning hatred for forces that were destroying her. Under the Hapsburg monarchy, the Austrian-Hungarian Empire had turned its back on the German people and mingled the pure, Aryan blood with all kinds of inferior races and peoples—Poles, Hungarians, Slavs, Serbs, Bosnians." He had to stop for breath. "Jews, Communists, Bosheviks, anarchists."

He sat back, his chest rising and falling. "And that was when I realized that until my dying day, I will be a passionate—yes, even fanatical—German nationalist, who wants to spend his life restoring the Fatherland to its former grandeur and return us to our true Aryan roots."

His eyes were hooded and seemed far away as he brooded over his thoughts. Hans studied him, fascinated by the intensity of the fire that burned in the man. It made him a little envious, he realized. Not because he wanted to be an ardent German nationalist—though he did agree it was a noble ideal—but because this man had found his cause, his dream, his way to change the world. But politics?

Hitler's voice was quiet and thoughtful now. "That time in my life was pivotal in other ways."

"How so?"

"Just before I turned sixteen, I developed a lung ailment and my mother took me out of school and sent me to my aunt's house in a village where the air was good. Oh, what a glorious time that was. No school, no more battles with my mother. My father had died by this point, but she was determined to keep me on the path he had wanted for me. But that year, I was free to go my own way for a while." There was a soft, self-derisive laugh. "In fact, that was the first and last time in my life that I ever got drunk."

"What?" Hans blurted. "You've only been drunk once in your life?"

Embarrassed by his bluntness, Hans started to apologize. "I'm sorry, Adolf. It's not that I'm doubting your word, but I think I was eleven the first time some friends and I stole some of my father's beer and got fall-down drunk."

Hitler seemed stunned that he had revealed that about himself. Then, very slowly and very seriously he said, "If I tell you something, will you swear never to tell anyone else?"

"I . . . Yes, I swear. I didn't mean to sound like I was prying, Adolf."

"It's all right. It was an important turning point in my life. I went to a *Bierhalle* in another village and drank myself silly. The next thing I remember, I was lying facedown on this little country road near some village I didn't even recognize. I had been sick and had puked all over myself."

Hans winced but said nothing.

"I was so drunk, I couldn't even get up. Then, thankfully, a milk-maid from a nearby farm came along. She saw me and took pity on me. She helped me up and took me back to my village. I was so ashamed of myself." He was silent for a long moment before he looked up. "And on that day, I determined that I would become a teetotaler."

It was just one shock after another. "You don't drink *any* liquor?"

"None. Nor do I smoke." He waved his hand in the air, making the cigarette smoke over their heads swirl. "It is a filthy habit. And I am seriously thinking of becoming a vegetarian."

Just then, their waitress returned and placed their dishes before them. As she left again, Adolf looked at his steaming *Rouladen*, picked up his knife and fork, and began to cut into the meat. "But not to-night, Hans. Not tonight."

9:15 p.m.

Hans took his last bite of cake, set his fork down, and pushed back his plate. "I surrender," he said. He took a sip from his second stein of beer, which was almost half empty, and forced himself to stop there because he still had to drive home.

Adolf glanced up and smiled briefly and then went back to eating. Adolf was eating his cake methodically and with the same intensity that he went at everything.

"How does a restaurant manage to get food when the rest of the country is starving?" Hans wondered.

Finishing his last bite, Adolf sat back, wiping his mouth with his napkin. "As you can see, they cater to an army crowd. I'm guessing some of the higher brass have pulled some strings for them."

"Figures," Hans said. "The poor starve; the powerful get fat."

Setting his napkin down, Adolf peered at him. "How did it go for you and your uncle at the board of inquiry the other day?"

"All right. Nothing much. It wasn't like we knew any names of the perpetrators or key leaders. We were only there about fifteen minutes. How about you?"

"A big surprise, actually."

"How so?"

"Not in the interviews. Like you, I didn't have many specifics. But you know me; I couldn't resist putting forth my views on what is happening and the root causes that need to be addressed." He flashed a grin. "With considerable passion, of course."

"And how did they take to that?"

"Oh, they listened politely. But, that afternoon, I had a messenger show up at the barracks. Turns out that someone was impressed enough with what I had said to share it with the higher-ups. That afternoon, I was called in and given a new job." He was beaming now. "I am now assigned to the Press and News Bureau of the Political Department of the Bavarian District command."

"Really! Just like that?"

"*Ja*, just like that. I'll be writing press copy and maybe developing pamphlets."

"I didn't know the army had a Political Department. I thought they kept clear of politics."

"With all the political chaos going on in the country, especially down here in the south, the brass have decided that if they don't do something, we'll end up like Russia. So they created this new department. One of the things they're doing is conducting courses of 'political instruction' for all the troops to make sure they're not swayed by all that left-wing drivel the Socialists are spouting. I'm surprised you haven't heard about it."

"You shouldn't be. Remember, my battalion isn't a local one. They're coming down from Berlin. Rumor is we're going against the Communists by the first of May."

That didn't seem to register. "Would a position in the Political Department interest you? My commanding officer told me to keep my eye out for promising talent."

"Nope," Hans said with a firm shake of his head. "I'm in until we get this Soviet Republic out of here. If we can get it done in a hurry, then I'm opening my garage."

"I understand." Adolf was still watching Hans closely. "So, if that's the case, tell me how you came to be a lieutenant in a Berlin army battalion?"

"It's a long story. Maybe another time. I probably ought to get going. We had more men sign up today, and I need to make sure they're all processed and tucked into bed."

Adolf immediately stood up. "I cannot tell you how much pleasure it gives me, Hans, that we have reconnected and become friends again."

"I feel the same, Adolf. You have given me much to think about."

"We shall meet again," Hitler said. Then he clicked his heels together, gave Hans's hand one curt shake, and turned and walked out, not waiting for Hans to follow. Hans stood there for a moment, smiling. He *was* different, that was for sure. By the time Hans got out to the street, Adolf was gone.

Chapter Note

Much of this reminiscing by Hitler comes from his autobiography, *Mein Kampf*, which he wrote while in prison for trying to overthrow the government in Munich in 1924 (see *Mein Kampf*, 30). Some of the dialogue here is taken from his own words. He told the story about the milkmaid and his first drunken outing much later in life (1942) to a group of Nazi intimates. After that experience he did become a teetotaler for life. He also never smoked, and at some point in his life he became a vegetarian (see Shirer, *Rise and Fall*, 14–15).

CHAPTER 52

April 5, 1919, 6:48 p.m.—Provo Tabernacle, Provo, Utah

When Edie and Mitch arrived at the tabernacle, it quickly became obvious that it wasn't just former missionaries and their wives who were coming in for the devotional. Throngs of older people were pushing their way to the door. It appeared as though the meeting had been opened up to any and all who wanted to come.

When Mitch and Edie saw how rapidly the tabernacle was filling up, they climbed up to the balcony and found a seat near the front that looked almost straight down on the speaker's rostrum. "Is this okay?" Mitch asked his wife as they sat down.

She smiled. "This from the man who comes to church ten minutes early so he can get the back row? Are you sure you're close enough?"

He ignored that, watching the crowd rapidly filling the seats on the main floor. Then he settled back and reached out and took her hand. "Sorry that we couldn't bring the kids?" he asked.

She looked at him astonishment. "Surely, you jest."

He laughed softly. "Don't you miss them? I do."

"So do I, but not enough to have them here. This has been wonderful. To get to go to the Salt Lake Temple for the first time. To see

Salt Lake City. And the university here. I think we ought to see if we can get Frank up here. And Tina too, when the time comes."

"I agree. Frank is so inquisitive. I think he would thrive there."

Down below, a group of official-looking people were entering the hall from the west side. Mitch instantly recognized Jacob Reissner, and he was followed by President and Sister Valentine, who were smiling and waving as they entered. Three men followed them, and Edie recognized them as the three who had been introduced at the picnic as the presidency of the Provo Stake. They all took seats on the stand.

President and Sister Valentine looked up and waved. Mitch and Edie waved back. So did everyone else. She leaned a little closer. "How well did you know President Valentine?"

"Not as well as I would have liked. You have to remember that mission headquarters was in Switzerland, and I served mostly in northern Germany. So we didn't see him for months at a time. But I served as a branch president in Hannover, so we did a lot of correspondence. The other thing to remember is that there were over three hundred missionaries. That's a lot to keep track of."

"Hmm." Edie was studying Sister Valentine now. "She looks younger than I expected."

"Sister Valentine? Oh, yeah. The president is three years younger than I am, and she's probably that much younger than he is."

"She's a lovely woman."

"And the perfect Mission Mother. When we first arrived at the mission home, she fed us warm cinnamon rolls and milk. Oh my, they were wonderful."

The bottom floor was more than half full now, and the balcony was about the same. Only a trickle of people were still coming in. The clock showed 6:59. "Come on, Reissner," Mitch murmured. "Let's start on time."

As if he had heard him, Elder Reissner leaned over to the president, got a nod, and stood up.

The preliminaries went quickly—a warm welcome, a few brief announcements, an opening hymn and prayer. When that was finished, Elder Reissner invited the stake president to say a few words. Wisely, he did just that. He took less than three minutes.

Next, Sister Valentine was invited to speak. She took six or seven minutes and delighted everyone. She was gracious, funny, and articulate as she spoke in English. They had arrived in Switzerland in 1912. When the war broke out, she and her husband stayed on to preside over the mission, even though he could only contact the German Saints by letter. They had remained until late 1916.

The hall went absolutely quiet when she told how the mission home in Basel was located right where the French, German, and Swiss borders came together. So France was right across the river, which meant that the mission home was only a few miles from the front lines. She described how they often could hear the distant rumble of artillery. One day, while out on the balcony, she had heard a sputtering sound and looked up to see an Allied airplane trailing smoke as it limped its way into Switzerland. In her mind's eye, she pictured a very frightened young pilot desperately trying to get his plane to neutral territory so he wouldn't be captured by the Germans. When she concluded with her testimony—given in German and with a generous amount of loving tears—she had a lot of people in the audience tearful as well.

As she sat down, Mitch whispered. "When she first arrived in the mission, she spoke no German at all. Now listen to her. She's wonderful."

President Valentine began almost without preamble, as if he were picking up an interrupted conversation. Gratefully, probably because he knew there were many family members in attendance who didn't speak German, he spoke in English.

"My brothers and sisters, what a wonderful sight you are—you missionaries and your spouses. And all of you other wonderful Saints.

How joyful it is to see so many of our German brothers and sisters here with us tonight. It warms my heart greatly."

And with that, he got right down to business. "I am happy to report to you that Ella and I recently received a long letter from President Angus J. Cannon and his wife. I think that most of you know that the Cannons replaced us as mission presidents when we were released in late 1916. It has been their privilege to remain in Europe until now. President Cannon gave us an updated report on how the missionary work has gone since all of you were so unceremoniously pulled out of Germany and left the faithful Saints there to fare as best they can.

"Some members and leaders of the Church were sure that the work of the kingdom in Germany would wither and die when all of you American missionaries were withdrawn. And the worry was not just about the missionary work itself, but the very existence of the Church, because so many of you held key leadership positions in the districts and branches."

Edie saw several of the brethren nodding, including her own husband.

"Some of those skeptics are here in Utah. Some are in the audience this night." That caused a stir as people looked at each other in dismay. Who was he talking about? He smiled, but it was without humor. "I know that for a certainty, because"—he let it hang for a moment—"because I was one of them."

As smiles appeared through the hall, President Valentine slapped the podium with the flat of his hand, making a sharp crack and startling many. "Well," he suddenly thundered, "*we . . . were . . . wrong! I* was wrong, my brothers and sisters, and I apologize to you, and I apologize to the Saints in Germany and Switzerland for doubting their faith.

"Brothers and Sisters, the Lord knows what He is doing. And sometimes His mission presidents forget that. President Cannon reports that instead of the Church in Switzerland and Germany withering away as many feared, just the opposite is true. Church attendance is up. Our tithing and other offerings have actually increased, in spite of the tremendous hardships the war placed upon the people. Think of that. About five hundred members of the mission were called up for service in the war. But notwithstanding the fact that these bread-winners were taken out of the home, their wives continued to pay their tithes and offerings. That is astonishing. What faith! How could I have doubted them?"

Mitch reached out and took Edie's hand and squeezed it. "Oh, how I wish I could have stayed longer to witness that for myself," he whispered.

"It is incredible," she agreed. "I want you to tell our children that story."

President Valentine paused again, and then in a subdued voice he said, "Many of you have asked when missionaries from Utah can return to Germany and complete their missions. Some of you are hoping that you will be among those first ones to return." Numerous heads came up at that, many of them nodding in agreement. "President Cannon has already sent a letter to Salt Lake asking that US missionaries be sent back as quickly as possible. But it is not likely that will happen soon. President Cannon guesses that will not happen until 1920 at the earliest, and maybe later than that."

That brought a chorus of groans.

"For the last two years, President Cannon has not been allowed to go into Germany. He has been forced to stay in contact by phone, letters, and telegrams. Food shortages are systemic. Unemployment is everywhere. The German mark is weak as measured against foreign cur-rencies. Throughout a long, cold winter, the people have not had suf-ficient fuel. Tuberculosis and other diseases are almost omnipresent."

He stood there with his head bowed for several moments. When he began again it was in a low voice filled with pain. "And yet—" He raised a finger as his voice caught in his throat. "And yet the people remain faithful. They attend church. They pay their tithes. Like the house upon the rock in the parable of Jesus, the rains fell, the storm came, and the winds blew against the house, but the house did not fall, because it was built upon the rock of Jesus Christ."

President Valentine wiped at his eyes. "My brothers and sisters, may we keep these dear friends across the sea in our daily prayers. May we reach out in any way possible to help them. The Church has undertaken and is still undertaking efforts to bless our fellow Saints both temporally and spiritually. So I would ask of you—beg of you!—to follow the Church's example. And I say that in the name of our beloved Savior, Jesus Christ. Amen."

Chapter Notes

I was not able to determine when missionary reunions first became part of the culture of the Church. The earliest documented reference I could find was in 1914. This chapter is not based on any known Swiss-German Mission reunion.

President Hyrum W. Valentine, from Brigham City, Utah, and his wife Rose Ellen (Ella) Bywater Valentine, presided over the Swiss-German Mission from 1912 until 1916. President Valentine was asked to speak in general conference in April 1917 (see CR, April 1917, 146–147). What he said in that setting provided the basis for his words here. The information from President Angus Cannon comes from what he wrote in Church periodicals shortly after the end of the war. Other details come from Anderson (*Mormons and Germany*, 78–81), and Scharffs (*Mormonism in Germany*, 55–59).

About seventy-five men who were members of the Church lost their lives in the war (see *Mormonism in Germany*, 58).

CHAPTER 53

April 25, 1919, 10:05 a.m. —EDW Ranch, Monticello,
San Juan County, Utah

Edna Rae Westland was at the sink, washing out the bowls and
pans she had used to make twelve loaves of bread. Those loaves
were now lined up on the table, where they caught the morning sun. Edie was alone in the house, enjoying a moment of solitude.

Those moments were getting increasingly rare. There were now a
dozen people living on the ranch on a full-time basis, counting Mitch
Jr., June, and their four children, as well as Edie and Mitch and their
own four kids. And though Rena lived in Verdure with their two children, right now her husband was engaged in spring planting, so she
often came up to spend the day. Which Edie loved, but it did get a
little hectic from time to time.

But this morning, Rena had called to say that the baby was a little
fussy so she wasn't coming. And once the older kids left for school,
Mitch Jr. and June had taken the twins and their two youngest for an
all-day trip to Moab to pick up supplies. It was just Edie and Mitch,
and Mitch was out in the barn, putting new straw in the stables. So
Edie decided to steal some time for herself and read a book.

10:43 a.m.

The *brrrrring* of the telephone made Edie jump a little, and she realized she had dozed off for a moment while reading. She looked around, a little confused. The phone rang again. She got up, set down her book, and walked swiftly into the kitchen. The phone rang a third time just as she lifted the receiver off of its hook. "Hello, Westlands."

A man's voice, very official, spoke in her ear. "Is this the Mitchell A. Westland residence?"

Mitchell? No one ever called him that except Edie and his mother, and then only when they were irked at him. "Yes, it is."

"Is he there? May I speak with him, please?"

"He's out in the barn at the moment. It will take me a few minutes to get him. Would you like to hold, or shall I have him call you back?" This was definitely a long-distance call. She could tell that from the soft static in the background. And those were expensive.

"I'll wait, thank you. Could you tell him that this is the Office of the First Presidency calling?"

Edie nearly dropped the phone. She reared back, staring at it in disbelief. Was this someone's idea of a joke? "I . . . all right. I'll go get him."

She closed the screen door softly behind her and took off running. "Mitch! Mitch! Come quickly."

Two minutes later he was back. As he reached for the phone, he absently brushed the flecks of straw from off his pants. "Hello. This is Mitch Westland."

Edie moved closer, standing right next to him so she could hear every word.

"Brother Westland, this is Brother Leroy Mangelsen. I work in the Office of the First Presidency and am making this call in their behalf. Do you have just a few minutes?"

"I . . . Of course." Mitch gave Edie a baffled look. She was still too shocked to respond.

"Brother Westland, I need to ask you some questions. The Presidency is working on a problem of some complexity, and they are looking for individuals with a unique set of qualifications to assist them in this matter. Jacob Reissner suggested you as one who might be considered."

"Okay," he said slowly. "How may I help you?"

"Well, I suppose the first question for you is, are you willing to have your name put forth for consideration for a special project?"

"Uh . . . yeah. I suppose." *Are you sure you've got the right man?* But Mitch didn't say that.

"Good. For now, I just need to get some information from you. If it's all right, I have a list of questions for you."

"I'm ready."

"Your full name is Mitchell Arthur Westland?"

"Yes."

"How old are you?"

"I turned fifty-one on January 31st of this year."

"So your year of birth was. . . ."

"Eighteen sixty-eight."

"And your address is Rural Free Delivery Box 236, Monticello, Utah."

"Actually, it's RFD Box two-*forty*-six."

"Oh, good. Thank you. And your wife's name is Edna Rae Zimmer Westland?"

"Yes, but she goes by Edie."

"And she is of German descent?"

Mitch's eyebrows raised as he looked at her. "Yes, her grandparents on her father's side were from Germany. They immigrated here in 1878. But both of them are now deceased."

There was a moment's pause, and Mitch could hear the faint scratching of a pen.

"We understand that you spoke German in your home while the grandmother lived with you?"

"Yes. My wife and I and some of our children can speak German."

"And how would you describe your fluency in German?"

"Excellent," Edie mouthed.

"Excellent," Mitch said, frowning at her.

"And . . . let's see. You were called to serve in the Swiss-German Mission . . . ah, yes. In June of 1913. And you were released early due to the war." They weren't questions, so the man was obviously reading off of something.

"Yes." Edie, whose face was pale now, moved to the table and sank heavily into a chair.

"How many children do you still have in the home, and what are their ages?"

"We have four. A boy, fifteen; a girl, eleven; and twins who are four, a girl and a boy."

"Is your passport still valid?"

"Yes, I renewed it last year."

"Do you have any plans to travel back to Germany?"

That rocked him back a little. "Uh . . . no, not immediate ones. My wife and I have talked about going to the Passion Play in Oberammergau sometime. But that's still just talk."

"I see. Are you affiliated with any German clubs, groups, or organizations here in America?"

That one took Mitch by surprise. "No."

"Not even some of those groups of Church members here in Utah? We have a large contingent of German-speaking Saints here in Salt Lake."

"No. Monticello is too far away to make that a possibility."

"I see." The man was silent for a moment, as if checking his list. "And please excuse the personal nature of this question, but the First Presidency needs to know this information. If you prefer not to say, they will understand. How would you describe your financial situation?"

On hearing that, Edie dropped her head in her hands and stared at the table. "I would say we are comfortable. I am a cattle rancher, and we've had a few successful years, thanks to the war. So we are debt free and have some savings in the bank."

There was another moment of scratching and the turning of paper, and finally: "All right, I think that's everything I need, Brother Westland. Thank you very much. I may be back in touch if they have further questions. Do you have any questions?"

About a thousand. "No, I don't think so."

"Then good-bye. And thank you again."

Mitch replaced the earpiece in its hook and sat down heavily beside his wife. She didn't look up. "They're going to call you on another mission," she said in utter dejection.

He had thought the same thing but had already rejected that idea. "Edie, I'm fifty-one years old. And you heard what President Valentine said. Germany is not issuing any visas yet."

Edie stiffened. "Do you think they're looking for a new mission president? The Valentines have been there for almost three years now."

For a moment Mitch was speechless. Then he shook his head. "There's no way. Me, a mission president? Besides, our kids are too young. The Church wouldn't send a young family over there."

"Then what?" Edie burst out. "If it's not a mission, what else could it be?"

Mitch searched his wife's face, seeing how many lines the years had added around her eyes and mouth. "All right, let's suppose for the sake of argument that it is a mission. Then what?"

Her head came up slowly. "You know the answer to that."

"Are you sure?"

"You be careful what you say," she scolded. "If *Oma* Zimmer is listening, she'll pop you a good one for even asking that question. And think about your own mother, Mitch. She hated it here. She was terrified of the Indians. When the Brethren offered releases to anyone who wanted to quit, my parents went back to Richfield. Your mother stayed. Why?"

"Because it was a call from the Prophet."

"Yes, Mitch. And whose office were you just talking to?"

His jaw set. "I still don't think this is about a mission call. He called it a special project."

Edie threw up her hands and shot to her feet. "Oooh! You are so stubborn sometimes."

As she stomped out of the kitchen he called after her. "I wonder who I learned that from."

CHAPTER 54

*May 2, 1929, 7:00 a.m.—Mars Camp, Maxvorstadt District,
Munich, Germany*

Colonel Stefan von Schiller strode up to the podium and looked around the large assembly room. Hans noted that he carried no cane, and though his limp was noticeable, it was not pronounced. The hall was about half full with the officers and platoon sergeants of the First Battalion. There was a buzz of excitement in the air. The word was that today they would march on Munich.

Von Schiller cracked the podium with his fist, and instantly the hall quieted. "Gentlemen," he roared. "Welcome back."

The men applauded enthusiastically.

"Are you ready to help solve Munich's problems the same way we did in Berlin?"

Whistles and shouts.

He suddenly went very still and frowned deeply. "Gentlemen, I have a problem. Today, is the second day of May. My wife has scheduled a banquet at our home on Saturday, the tenth of May. That is one week from tomorrow." He looked at Hans for a moment. "Some of you know my wife. She does not view war as an acceptable excuse for postponing a party."

Laughter filled the hall. He leaned forward. "Do you understand what I'm saying? I need to be back in Berlin by next Saturday morning. Do I make myself clear?"

The response was instantaneous. Clapping right along with the rest, Hans marveled. This man was a genius at motivating men. "Or better yet, how about we finish this whole thing up by tea time tomorrow?" von Schiller continued. That won him a thunderous response with much stomping of the feet.

After letting it roll for a few moments, the colonel held up a hand and gradually the room quieted again. "You company commanders and platoon commanders have all been briefed on our objectives and your specific assignments. But I have just learned some things from an intelligence briefing that I think your men should know."

He held up one finger. "Number one. The so-called Soviet Republic's Red Army now consists of about twenty thousand men." The reaction to that was instant dismay, and Hans's reaction was no different. *Twenty thousand!*

"Ah," von Schiller said softly, "I can see that number concerns you. Good. You should be concerned. But you tell your men this: First, very few of those men are soldiers. They are factory workers, railway workers, unionists. Second, they are poorly trained. We estimate about half do not know how to fire a rifle." He smiled. "But then, about half of them have no rifles!"

Laughter erupted at that. "More important, counting our *Freikorps* troops, regular army, and a group that calls itself the 'White Guards of Capitalism,' we now have about *forty thousand* men who are fully armed, combat-trained, and battle-hardened." He grinned. "How do you like them odds?"

The response was thunderous, and the colonel's smile broadened as he watched them celebrate. As the noise died down again, he raised two fingers. "Number two. The Communists are convinced that when this battle commences, the people will rise up and join them. How blind can they be? These Communists are the same ones who turned the middle classes against them by expropriating their apartments and automobiles, looting their homes and businesses, forcing them to sell goods below cost, and brutally executing nearly thirty of Munich's most respected citizens." His eyes were flashing fire. "Do you think the people will rise up and fight for them?"

"No!" the crowd roared. As Hans joined in the cheering, he looked around, and once again his admiration for Colonel von Schiller rose higher. Morale was always a major factor in battle. And Hans had not seen the morale of his men higher.

"So," the colonel said when they were quiet again. "I have only one more question." His voice rose sharply. "What think you? Can Colonel Stefan von Schiller call his wife tonight and tell her to set a place for him at the table next Saturday?"

The answering roar was so loud, the colonel actually laughed. Then, knowing his work was done, he snapped off a salute, turned, and walked out.

10:38 a.m.—New Town Hall, Marienplatz, Old Town, Munich

Hans cocked his head and listened to the rumble of artillery and the distant crack of rifle fire and then motioned his four platoon leaders to move in closer. "All right, listen up. I just received word. The White Guards are waiting for trucks to transport them into the city. Until they arrive, our previous orders are put on hold. First Battalion is to hold St. Mary's Plaza until the White Guards arrive. Companies A and B are covering the roads to the north of us; D Company is to the south. Their task is to cut off any incursions before they reach us." He jerked his thumb over his shoulder at the huge, ornate building behind them. "Our company is to defend New Town Hall and the Glockenspiel and the Marian Column and Mary's statue at all costs."

He saw disappointment on their faces. This morning they were charged up by von Schiller. Now they were going to babysit some huge cuckoo clock with life-size dancing figurines and a statue of the Virgin Mary. No wonder they were frustrated.

Hans had to do something about that. "For those of you who are not from Bavaria, you need to understand the importance of where we are right now. This square has been the heart of Bavaria itself since the 1100s. That statue of Mary was erected in 1638 to celebrate the Bavarian victory in the Thirty Years' War. The Glockenspiel is world-famous. And if something happens to any of this because we were careless or thought it wasn't important, those mobs of people that Colonel von Schiller spoke about this morning are going to come after you and me, and they will tear us to pieces with their bare hands. Do you understand me?"

Everyone nodded. No one spoke.

"So, Sergeant Diehls and First Platoon will be the rovers. I want you moving at all times, watching the side streets, checking out the buildings. We don't want to be surprised. Second, Third, and Fourth Platoons will deploy along the length of the town hall. We have four machine guns, so I want two in front of the main entrance and one at each end. Make sure you have overlapping fields of fire facing to the south. If they're coming, they'll likely come in from the south. As soon as the guns are set up, get the sandbags from the trucks and protect your positions."

"Can I ask what our deployment will be once we're relieved here, sir?" That was from Sergeant Lenz, who led the Second Platoon.

"The moment we see the White Guards, we're to contact battalion headquarters. Depending on who's in the fiercest firefight, we'll either move north to the *Englischer Garten* to join Third Battalion or to the west to defend the train station with Second Battalion."

"Sounds like we'll get action either way," Diehls said to the men.

Hans was only half listening. He was looking to the south, where a smaller street opened into the square. He nudged Diehls. "What's that street there?"

Diehls quickly consulted his map. "*Rossenstrasse.*"

"A dead end?"

"No sir, it joins *Sendlingerstrasse* about a block or so south of here."

"Is D Company deployed there?"

Diehls looked at the map again. Hans walked over and joined him, and they studied it together. "Uh . . . I'm not sure, sir. They said D Company was going to set up here on *Rindermarkt*, in the church-yard here. Looks like they're about two blocks south of us."

Hans muttered angrily under his breath. "Which means the Red Army could come up *Sendlingerstrasse* here"—he traced his finger along the route—"and cut over to *Rossenstrasse* without being seen by D Company."

"That's not good," Diehls grunted.

Hans grunted an assent. "Sergeant Lenz, send a man down to D Company. Tell them to move farther south and block the entrance to *Rosenstrasse*."

"Yes, sir."

Slinging his rifle over his shoulder, Hans looked at Diehls. "Bring your platoon. Let's make sure *Rosenstrasse* is secure until D Company gets in place."

"Yes, sir."

"The rest of you men, deploy as ordered. You are not to leave your posts under any circumstances, even if we run into trouble. The Glockenspiel and Mary. Nobody gets to them." Hans didn't wait for an answer. Diehls's platoon was already forming up. He hitched his rifle higher on his shoulder and went over to the men. "All right, let's move out."

10:43 a.m.—Rosenstrasse, south of Marienplatz,
Old Town, Munich

Rose Street was a relatively narrow avenue with ground-level shops and boutiques with four- and five-story apartments above them. It was the apartments that worried Hans. He deployed half of the platoon with Diehls on the left, and he took the rest with him on the right. "Stay close to the buildings," he called in a low voice. "And watch the upper windows opposite you for snipers. But there may be people who are just curious about what's going on, so don't get trigger happy."

They started forward. There were no vehicles moving and no pedestrians. But that was probably true of much of the city right now. They moved slowly, using the few automobiles parked along the curb as cover. Thirty yards down the street, Hans suddenly stopped. A familiar prickling sensation was tingling in the back of his neck. During the war, he had learned to trust that feeling.

He gave a low whistle and motioned for the men to take cover. Then he crouched down to wait, cocking his head to one side and listening intently. It didn't take long. First it was the sound of footsteps—a lot of them. They weren't loud, but they were unmistakable. Then he heard the murmur of voices—men's voices. Hans shook his head in amazement and disgust. Von Schiller had described the Red Army as undisciplined. But this? Walking into what they had to know was one of the prime targets in all of Munich, and they were talking like a bunch of schoolboys?

The man behind Hans whispered. "Could that be D Company, sir?"

"Not a chance," Hans snapped back. "Not this soon."

A moment later, his question was definitively answered. The street itself was perfectly straight, but where it joined *Sendlingerstrasse*, it curved away to the right. Two men in uniform with their rifles slung over their shoulders were in the lead. Behind them was a ragtag collection of soldiers and civilians. They were not in ranks or any kind of order, just following behind their leaders like a slow-moving mudflow. They were now about fifty yards from the platoon.

Hans signaled to his men. "No one fires until I do—or they do," he hissed. "If things go bad, take out their leaders first, and then go for the ones carrying arms."

He heard the soft metallic clicks of safeties being released. He watched until all of his men were in place, and then he stood up and moved out into the center of the street. As he did so, he fired his rifle in the air. *"Anhalten!"* he shouted as loudly as he could. "Stop where you are!"

It was almost comical, like dropping a fox in the middle of a flock of chickens. There was one second of stunned shock, and then men dove for cover. The leaders were frantically grabbing for their rifles. Hans fired in the air again. "Throw down your weapons, and you won't be hurt."

The taller of the two leaders jerked up his rifle and fired off a round in Hans's direction.

As the bullet snapped overhead, Hans dropped down. At that same moment, his men opened up fire in a deafening barrage. Leaping into a crouch behind one of the cars, Hans peeked out to see the damage. Both leaders were down. Flashes of gunfire were winking like fireflies, and the blasts within the narrow confines of the street were deafening.

"Don't shoot them if they're unarmed!" Hans shouted as he watched men dropping all around their fallen leaders. Diehls's platoon was at full strength at forty-eight men. The Red Army group looked to be about that same number. But that didn't even the odds. First Platoon's superior firepower and accuracy tore through the ranks like a scythe. Half were already down, though whether they were hit or taking cover, Hans couldn't tell. The rest broke and ran.

His men leaped to their feet, firing from the shoulder now. He was tempted to call a cease-fire, but there were still flashes of gunfire from a few of the rebels, and as long as there was resistance, he wouldn't pull his men off. But Hans lowered his own rifle and watched from behind a car. He saw two men, one young, one old—a father and son?—raise their hands high in the air. Neither carried weapons. The older went down in a spray of blood. The younger one took off in a zigzagging run. He got maybe ten yards before a bullet caught him in the back and flung him forward like a rag doll.

In seconds, the only ones firing were Diehls's platoon. "Cease fire! Cease fire!" Hans screamed. He stood up. Just ahead of him, one of his men was taking aim at another unarmed running figure. BLAM! He fired just as Hans kicked him hard in the buttocks. The shot went high, and the figure disappeared into a side street. "I said cease fire!" he raged.

The gunfire gradually died away, and in moments the street was filled with an eerie silence. Hans motioned his men forward, taking out his Luger and leaving his rifle on his shoulder. As they approached the rebels, he wanted to look away. He had seen so much blood, so much carnage in the last four years. Of the approximately fifty men who had been marching up the street just moments before, about thirty were down. A few were moaning and twisting in pain. Most were still. Blood was everywhere.

"No more firing," he called to the men around him. "Check for wounded. Collect any arms." Then to Diehls he said, "Get a corpsman up here."

11:18 a.m.—Marienplatz, Old Town, Munich

Hans was standing off to one side, watching the White Guards unload and start setting up three machine gun nests behind sandbagged revetments. That was good. The Glockenspiel and Marian Column were safe now. How ironic that over in the tower of New Town Hall, the thirty-two life-size figures of the Glockenspiel had just finished marching, jousting, and dancing to the music of the forty-three bells. It was a macabre backdrop for the thirty-three bodies laid out on Rose Street, where two horse-drawn wagons from the graves unit were just pulling up. Fortunately, none of them were *Freikorps* bodies. They had four wounded, but none of them seriously.

Hans looked up as Bert Diehls came up to join him. He was lighting up a cigarette. As he puffed it into life, he held out the package to Hans. "Want a smoke?"

"You know I don't smoke."

"I know. Want one?"

Hans slid a cigarette out from the pack and lit it off the end of Bert's. "Thanks."

"You can quit again tomorrow."

"Yeah."

Blowing out a cloud of smoke, Bert lowered his voice. "My men found three more Commies hiding behind a garbage bin. Do you want to interrogate them before we haul them away with the others?" The rumor was that all prisoners were to be executed, but no one had confirmed that.

"Were they armed?" Hans asked Diehls.

"One had a club, but he dropped it when my men appeared. They're not soldiers."

Hans said nothing for a while but finally nodded. "Yes, I'll interrogate them."

"Second alley on the right down *Rosenstrasse*. Want my men to come with you?"

"No," Hans said quickly. "I'll take care of them," he said. "Any word on where we go next?"

"*Ja*. I guess Third Battalion ran into one of the Red Army's better units as they entered the English Gardens from the north. That's the firing we've been hearing to the north of us. I guess it's a real catfight. Von Schiller's already pulled off A and B Companies from our battalion and sent them north. He's also sent D Company in a long sweep around to come in behind them from the north. The colonel says we are to join them as soon as possible."

"Okay. How soon will the trucks be here to transport us?"

"No trucks," Diehls said in disgust. "They're over at the *Bahnhof* trying to unload supplies from some train cars, but they're taking fire too. So we're on foot. But it's only a couple of miles to the park. Von Schiller wants us on the move no later than 11:45."

"Got it," Hans said. "This won't take me long."

Hans flipped the cigarette away as he entered the alley, even though he had only smoked a third of it. When Diehls's two men saw him coming, they immediately came to attention. Hans came up to them and returned their salute. "You're relieved. Report to Sergeant Diehls on the double."

"Are you sure you'll be all right?" one of them said.

Hans removed the Luger from its holster and chambered a shell. "I'll be fine."

The three men before him, all in work clothes and battered shoes or boots, went an ashen grey when they saw the pistol. One looked like he was seventeen or eighteen; the other two were near their thirties. They had the same beaten look that Hans had seen on the faces of the marchers in Berlin—haggard, worn, crushed by the sheer relentlessness of life. Hans waited until Diehls's men disappeared, and then he turned to the oldest man. "Do you men know each other?"

The man hesitated for a moment, and then his head bobbed.

"Do you come from the same neighborhood?" Hans guessed.

"*Ja*," the youngest one said. "*Bogenhausen.*"

Hans nodded. "How much were you paid to join the Red Army?"

The question obviously surprised them. The older one finally said, "Ten marks per week."

"If I let you go, will you give me your word you won't go back to the army?"

There was incredulity followed by a flicker of hope. "*Ja, ja!*" the oldest man said.

Hans held the pistol above his head and fired off three shots in slow succession. Then he holstered the pistol and pointed to the west, even though *Bogenhausen* was to the east. "There will be fewer troops that way. But stay low. Find a safe place to hide, and wait until dark." He turned and walked away, not looking back to see if they obeyed.

Bert was waiting for him with the two guards that Hans had sent away. Their eyes were wide as they watched him approach. He spoke to Diehls. "They won't be a problem anymore."

Diehls eyed him thoughtfully as he took a deep draw on his cigarette and then dropped it and ground the butt out with the heel of his boot. "*Gut*. Three less that we have to worry about."

Hans nodded. "All right, let's form up and move out."

11:55 a.m.—*Dienerstrasse, near Marienplatz, Old Town, Munich*

After studying the map carefully, Hans determined the most direct route to the English Gardens. If he kept his men marching at a brisk step, they could be there in less than half an hour.

C Company left *Marienplatz* with four of Hans's men out front on point and four more bringing up the rear, and Hans wasn't too surprised when they found the streets pretty deserted. After the earlier battles, people were understandably cautious. Even though it was a beautiful day, most of the windows on the buildings were shuttered. And there were no vehicles—motorized or horse drawn—on the streets. Hans still moved carefully, keeping his platoons in formation, but he wasn't too worried. A and B Companies had passed through here less than an hour ahead of them.

As they continued northward, windows began to open and people began appearing on the balconies. At first, Hans slowed the pace and sent four more men ahead. A balcony or an upper window was a preferred perch for a sniper. But it soon became evident that there was no threat here. The people were coming out to welcome them, like they had in Berlin. They waved flags or handkerchiefs or threw flowers. They were clapping and cheering, shouting their welcome.

Then the doors along the street began to open and people appeared, smiling and waving. At first they stayed close to their doors, but then a young woman in her twenties ran up to Hans. She had fresh red geraniums in her hand and was barefoot. "*Danke, danke*," she cried, thrusting the flowers into his hands. As soon as he took them, she threw her arms around him and kissed him fully on the lips. Then, laughing, she darted away again.

Hans's men erupted into whistles, catcalls, and cheers. Someone behind him yelled, "Hey, Fräulein, come and say thank you to me, too." The citizens were also delighted at her boldness, and soon others came out into the street. At first it was a trickle, then a stream, and then a veritable flood. Suddenly it seemed like every window had someone hanging out of it, and every balcony had people dancing up and down or waving wildly. Flowers, streamers, shredded paper, and wrapped candy started raining down from above. Men and women, grandmas and grandpas, young children, babies in carriages, babies in arms, men in shirtsleeves and without hats—almost unthinkable for this middle-class neighborhood—all ran alongside, calling, shouting, weeping, and laughing. They were waving anything they could lay their hands on—umbrellas, handkerchiefs, scarves, banners, Bavarian and national flags of every size.

Children ran right up to the ranks of the soldiers, grabbing their hands and kissing them or tossing flowers before their feet. Soon there were dozens of young women racing in and out of the ranks and kissing the delighted soldiers.

"Hold your ranks!" Hans shouted, but he was laughing too. No one would have obeyed him even if they had heard him. His men were grinning like thirteen-year-olds who had just gotten their first kiss. Hans knew that his own face was smeared with lipstick.

And then someone started singing *"Deutschland, Deutschland, über Alles."* It quickly spread from person to person. People came to attention. Hans raised his hand and brought the men to a halt. Quickly it swelled until a hundred and then a thousand voices filled the air, echoing off the building in what seemed like orchestrated harmony.

Barely heard in the tumult, a rifle cracked. A soldier three men over from Hans clutched at his chest and stumbled to his knees, eyes confused and white with pain. A moment later, a machine gunner opened up from somewhere above them, and screams erupted, drowning out the words of their beloved national anthem.

Chapter Note

The numbers given here for the opposing forces are accurate, but I could not find any specifics as to where the fighting was other than that there were fierce street battles. So the protection of *Marienplatz*, the attack up *Rosenstrasse*, and moving north toward the English Gardens are not based on actual accounts.

CHAPTER
55

May 4, 1919, 7:10 a.m.—Dienerstrasse, near Marienplatz, Old Town, Munich

Hans turned off the engine of his motorbike and let it roll to a stop. For several moments he just sat there, looking around, letting the memories of the last two days wash over him. Nothing had changed, at least not that he could tell. The street was still filled with rubble—shattered brick and stonework from the field artillery pieces, shards of glass from dozens of shot-out windows, what remained of the barricades hastily thrown up by the Red Army.

The guilt was like a hot iron in his chest. No one was blaming him or Colonel von Schiller. Not officially, at least. But von Schiller had told them in the briefing that when the Communists had taken power, they had expropriated apartments of the middle classes and turned them over to the homeless. And the areas around Old Town center were mostly middle- or upper-middle-class neighborhoods. Why hadn't Hans put that together? What better place for elements of the Red Army to hide than in the apartments of people who had gotten them for nothing?

The other thing he cursed himself for was that he had accepted without question von Schiller's characterization of the Red Army as undisciplined, untrained, working-class incompetents. Maybe some were. Maybe even half or more. But these troops weren't. They had let two companies pass by them without revealing their position. Had they known that Hans's company was the only one left? Was their intelligence that good?

Who knew? But this was clear: one of the greatest signs of battlefield stupidity was underestimating your enemy.

And now twelve of his men were dead. More than twice that number were wounded, several of them seriously. Six civilians, including an eight-year-old boy, had died in the ambush. It had taken them another twenty-four hours to dislodge the enemy, and that was with the full weight of the battalion sent in to rescue C Company. The White Guards couldn't leave *Marienplatz* with fighting that close to them, but they sent up two light Howitzers, a flamethrower, and more heavy machine guns. And even then, the battle had raged through the night.

Sick at heart, Hans put down the kickstand and got off the bike. Just as he straightened and looked around, there was a flicker of movement out of the corner of eye. Instinctively he dropped to a crouch and reached for his pistol. A moment later, when he saw what had moved, he dropped it back in its holster. A little girl had stepped out onto a third-floor balcony and was gravely watching him. He gave her a little wave. She didn't move. It was like she was a statue. A moment later, her mother appeared and snatched her up, holding her close. But when she saw Hans and his uniform, she hesitantly raised a hand and waved. "*Danke schön,*" she called. "God bless you." Then she hurried inside and shut the door behind her.

God bless me for what? For torching one of your buildings? For blowing holes in two more? For bringing war to your doorsteps?

Ignoring the voices in his head, he walked slowly on, taking it all in, letting the sounds of battle and horror and death rush back in at him once again. Mingled with the building rubble and the hundreds of empty shell casings was the evidence of the utter shock that had swept through the crowd when those first shots were fired. Dozens of the miniature Bavarian flags were everywhere on the ground. Here was a woman's purse with dusty footprints on the leather. A man's Homburg hat lay half crushed beneath a brick. And almost everywhere were the ugly smears of blood—dried nearly black now in the sunshine.

Hans saw a little girl's shoe beneath a piece of window frame. He started to pick it up but then shrank back as a wave or horror swept over him. Instinctively, one hand jerked up and touched the spot where the blood had left a dark smear on his tunic two days earlier. Corporal Jürgens had tried diligently to scrub it out but finally gave up and secured him a new one. But that made no difference. It felt like it was still there, crusting up now into a dark reddish-brown stain in the woolen fabric. He had thought he had shielded the girl before any bullets had found her tiny, pitifully frail body. Only when the corpsman had come and pulled Hans off of her did he see that her face and hair were matted with blood, and that it was all over his tunic as well.

He whirled as glass crunched behind him and then relaxed when he saw three young boys come out of an alley. Their eyes were fixed on the ground. Each had a pillowcase. They would call out to each other and then run and pick something up, eagerly show it to the others, and drop it into their bags. Collecting shell casings, Hans guessed. A treasure indeed, for a boy of seven or eight.

Suddenly one of the boys looked up and saw him. For a split second the boy froze in place, and then he gave a low cry and the three of them darted away and disappeared. With that, Hans decided he'd had enough. He had come back so that he would never forget what had happened here. Now, he realized that it was not remembering that he needed. It was forgetting.

He spun on his heel, walked swiftly back to the motorbike, and drove back toward *Marienplatz*. He would stop there for just a moment to look at the statue of Mary and the Glockenspiel tower so he could remember what they had saved, and not what they had lost.

8:05 a.m.—Field hospital, on the grounds of the Maximilianeum

As Hans parked his motorbike in front of the massive tent, he couldn't help but note the irony of where he was. The army had set up the field hospital on the grounds of the Bavarian Parliament Building, which was named for the Emperor Maximilian. This was the building where Kurt Eisner had seized the government last November. And it was not far from here that he been shot down, opening the door for the creation of a Soviet Republic. And now over a thousand people were dead, and many more wounded, and numerous neighborhoods were in shambles.

Hans shook it off, trying to ignore the bone-numbing weariness, but it was too deep in him. Today at 11:00 a.m. he was meeting with Colonel von Schiller, who would ask him yet again to make this his career. And today at 11:00 a.m., he would officially tender his resignation. When Hans told him he was leaving, the colonel would ask him why. He would tell von Schiller it was because of his mechanic's shop. But neither of them would believe it.

"Hey!"

Hans looked up. A motorbike was just turning off the street and driving across the grass toward him. Sergeant Norbert Diehls raised a hand and waved. Hans moved back over and waited for him to park the bike alongside his. As Diehls shut it down and got off, Hans nodded approvingly. "So, Jürgens got you your own bike?"

Bert removed his helmet, plopped it on the seat, and grinned at Hans. "No, this is just a loaner. Actually, I get yours."

Hans couldn't help but laugh. "So you told von Schiller you're staying in?"

"I did. He offered me a commission. Then he'll send me to Officers' Training School in Berlin once we're done here. He says he wants me to be his adjutant eventually."

"Really? He must not have given much credence to what I said about you."

Diehls smiled, and then sobered. "Actually, he told me what you did say. Thank you, Hans."

Hans waved that away. "You're sure this is what you want to do?"

"I am. Does that make you think less of me?'

Surprised, Hans vigorously shook his head. "Not at all. The army needs more men like you. You'll make an excellent officer. Your men like serving under you."

"As do yours."

"Then let's go in and see them."

As they started for the main entrance to the hospital, Bert spoke up again. "By the way, preliminary reports are in on civilian casualties. They think it is around two hundred." Hans nodded grimly as Bert went on. "The poorer neighborhoods were hit especially hard. Ironic, eh? Those are the people the so-called Republic vowed to protect. Jürgens and I drove around a couple of them last night to get a report for the colonel. It was pretty bad. We stopped and talked to one grandmother with a little baby in her arms. I'm not even sure whether it was alive. Someone had tipped over a barrel of potatoes, and she was sorting through them to find any that weren't rotten. In another place we saw kids going through garbage cans. Some of them were barely tall enough to look inside. It was pretty tough to see things like that."

Hans said nothing. He didn't need any more horrific images in his head.

Diehls, seeing that, decided to say nothing more, and together they walked into the hospital.

9:32 a.m.

As they approached their parked motorbikes again, Hans bent over and retrieved a paper sack with something soft inside it from the leather back behind the seat. "Hey, Bert. I've got to drop something off at the nurses' station. I'll see you back at camp."

Diehls nodded. "Remember. Colonel von Schiller, eleven o'clock.

Don't be late. He's got permission from the high brass to go back to Berlin for a week. He leaves this afternoon."

"Got it, I'll be there."

As his friend started the bike and drove away, Hans went back inside. He looked around. There were no signs posted, so he wasn't sure where to go. But a moment later a male orderly approached, and Hans waved him down. "Where would I find the children?"

He pointed. "Go out the west end there. There's another smaller tent just to the north of this one. That's the children's ward."

"Thanks."

At the entrance to the second tent, Hans had to stop for a moment. He took a deep breath, then another. Then, tucking the paper sack beneath his arm, he pulled the flap back and went inside. A nurse in a white uniform saw him and came over. "Can I help you, Lieutenant?"

"Yes, I'm looking for a little girl who was injured the day before yesterday in the *Dienerstrasse* neighborhood."

"Oh, yes. Katya Tobler. Our sweet little Katya. Come. I'll show you." And she started away.

Hans didn't move. The huge rush of relief had made him momentarily dizzy. Then he hurried after the nurse. As they walked down the aisle, Hans was relieved to see that not even half of the beds were occupied. Most of the children seemed okay, though several wore bandages. One boy had his leg in a cast held up in the air by pulley. Hans was about to comment on how good it was to see so many empty beds when he saw another nurse just ahead of them. Standing on the bed beside her was a little girl of four or five. The nurse was removing her nightdress, the front of which was flecked with blood, leaving the little girl only in her underpants.

Hans's feet came to a stop, though he had not willed them to do it. The nurse was tossing the soiled nightdress in a small bin, but the little girl had seen Hans and was watching him gravely. But what had caught his eyes was her rib cage. Every single rib was sharply defined by the tightness of the flesh pulled across it. Her arms and legs looked like sticks. Seeing that he had stopped and was staring at the little girl, the nurse who was guiding him started back toward Hans. He quickly moved forward and caught up with her. "Tuberculosis?" he asked in a low voice.

She nodded. "Yes, and severe malnutrition."

"Where are her parents?"

The nurse, whose name he now saw was Bühler, shook her head. "No one knows."

"Will she . . . ?" He couldn't finish it. He was thinking of Miki, with her robust body and her pudgy little cheeks.

Stricken, the nurse shook her head, and then she started forward again. Less than a minute later, she stopped and pointed straight ahead. "Third bed from the end, on the left," she said. "That's her mother sitting beside her." She smiled at him. "Are you a friend of the family or a relative?"

Hans just shook his head and moved past her. "Thank you," he murmured.

The woman at the bed had seen them coming and got to her feet and hurried toward him, a radiant smile lighting up her face. He noticed her dress was somewhat rumpled and that her hair needed combing, and he guessed that she had been her with her daughter for two straight days now. In the bed, a girl with the top of her head swathed in bandages seemed to be sleeping.

"Lieutenant Eckhardt," she exclaimed as she rushed up to him and gripped his hand. "How wonderful to see you." She turned. "Katya! Katya! Look who's come to see you."

As the girl's eyes fluttered open, the mother pulled him forward to the side of her bed. She turned and bent down over her daughter. "Katya, do you know who this is?"

The girl shook her head, still not quite awake.

"This is the man who saved your life."

"No, no, Frau Tobler," Hans protested. "I just tried to shield her. It was the men in my company who got in front of us and returned fire at the snipers. They saved her." His voice dropped to a husky whisper. "And one of those men died doing that. And two more were wounded."

Tears sprang to the mother's eyes. "I know. I saw it happen. Will the wounded men live?"

"Yes. Actually, they're both here. I just visited them. They're going to be fine."

Hans felt a touch on his trouser leg and turned to see the girl looking up at him now. "I remember," Katya said in a tiny voice. "You were on top of me."

"Yes. Did I crush you?"

There was the tiniest smile. "Kind of."

Her mother retrieved something from her pocket and handed it to Hans. "The doctors found this imbedded in her skull. Fortunately, it didn't penetrate the brain."

Hans held it up so he could see better, and then he gave a low exclamation of amazement. "Do you know what this is, Katya?"

"Mama thinks it's a bullet."

"It's part of a bullet. It's what we call a shell fragment. It probably ricocheted off the pavement. If it had been the full bullet, you would be...." He shook his head and handed it back to her mother. "She is a very lucky young woman," he murmured.

"We know that, and we thank God for it." She was looking at Hans more closely. "It looks like they got the blood out of your tunic."

"Uh ... no. I think they've thrown it away. This is a new one."

The tears welled up again. "Thank you," she said, her voice choked.

Hans retrieved the sack from under his arm. "I brought Katya something. May I?"

"Of course."

He took the chair beside the bed and handed the sack to the girl. She reached in and gave a low cry as she pulled out what was inside. "Oh, look, Mama. It's a toy bear." She held it up and then hugged it to her. "*Danke*," she said, her eyes wide and filled with happiness.

"In America," Hans said, smiling now, "they call this a Teddy bear. It was named for one of their presidents, Teddy Roosevelt."

"Then I shall call it Teddy," she said. "Oh, thank you, Herr Eckhardt."

He touched her hand. "Please, call me Hans." Then he leaned in closer. "Did you know that I once dated a girl named Katya?"

Her eyes grew big. "You did?"

"Yes. And oh my, she was beautiful. She had blonde hair and blue eyes, just like you."

"Did you love her?"

"I liked her very much." He smiled up at her mother. "But I've only loved the woman who is now my wife."

"How very sweet of you to come," Katya's mother said. "Would it be all right if I visited the men who are wounded? Katya can get out of bed tomorrow. We'll go together."

"That would be wonderful."

Tears streamed down her cheeks as she took Katya's hand. "How can we ever repay you?"

Suddenly, catching him completely by surprise, a sob was torn from Hans's throat. "You . . . you just have." Then his shoulders began to shake and he turned away. He couldn't hold it in any longer, and the sobs came one after the other. Frau Tobler stepped forward, weeping openly now too, and put her arms around him. "It's all right," she murmured. "It's all right."

Suddenly he needed her to understand just what this meant to him. "I needed to know that I did at least one thing right the other day," he managed to choke out. "Thank you for letting me come. You have a beautiful daughter."

Frau Tobler shook him gently. "You also saved our neighborhood."

"We destroyed your neighborhood," he cried. "I was just there. We destroyed it."

This time she shook him harder. "You saved us! We had no idea those men were hiding in our buildings. If you had not come, we would have been next."

Hans straightened, pulling free of her, and wiped at his eyes with the back of his hand. "I'm sorry, I . . . I didn't expect that."

She was smiling through her tears now. "Could you give me the names of your two men? Katya and I would very much like to thank them."

Hans nodded and took a pencil and a small notebook from his tunic and wrote their names. He tore the sheet off and handed it to Frau Tobler. Then he looked down at Katya, who now had Teddy perched on her chest. "They will be very happy to see you, Katya, just as I am."

Before she could answer, he had another thought. He wrote quickly on another page and tore it off and handed it to the mother. "I have to go now. I'm leaving for Oberammergau this afternoon to rejoin my wife. But we have a flat here in Munich. As soon as things settle down in the city, we'll be moving here, to the *Milbertshofen* District. We would be delighted if you and your husband would bring Katya and visit us. I would very much like to have my wife meet you all." He looked down at Katya. "Her name is Emilee."

An angelic but impish smile spread over Katya's face. "She must be very beautiful if you love her more than the other Katya."

Hans laughed aloud and then bent down and kissed the girl gently on her bandaged forehead. "Yes, she is," he said. "She is very beautiful." Then he bent down again and whispered. "You keep that bullet safe, Katya. Someday you're going to tell this story to your grandchildren, and they'll think you were the bravest little girl in all the world."

CHAPTER 56

May 4, 1919, 11:17 a.m.—Mars Camp,
Maxvorstadt District, Munich

Well, Eckhardt, I'm sorry to lose you, but I understand. Go home, kiss your wife, start that garage. And if things don't work out, you know where to find me."

"Yes, sir. Thank you, sir." He hesitated and then added, "I would probably be dead by now if it weren't for you."

The colonel shook his head. "I doubt that. You're a survivor, Eckhardt. I'm just glad I was there to give you a hand. Anything else I can do for you?"

"No, sir. I hope it's all right, but Corporal Jürgens said I could use my railway pass one more time today to get home. Then I'll cut it up."

"When is it good through?"

"Through the first of June."

"Then use it until then. The army owes you that much."

"*Danke*. Oh, there is one other thing, sir."

"What's that?"

"If I were to show up at your home this Saturday for that banquet, do you think there might be a place at the table for me?"

Von Schiller threw back his head and roared. "You do have a death wish, don't you, Eckhardt?"

"Yes, sir!" Hans snapped off one last salute, turned on his heel, and marched out.

1:40 p.m.

There was a sharp rap on the door. "Lieutenant!"

"Yes?"

The door opened and Jürgens stuck his head in. "A Corporal Adolf Hitler to see you, sir."

Hans spun around from the duffel bag he was packing. "Really?"

"Yes, sir. I told him you're on a tight schedule. I can send him away if—"

"No, no. Send him in. I have time."

He followed Corporal Jürgens into the hall and met Adolf at the door to the barracks. "Adolf," Hans cried. "This is an unexpected surprise."

They shook hands vigorously. "I know you've only got a minute," Adolf began.

Hans cut him off. "I've got time. Come in."

Once they were seated, Hitler launched in without preamble. "Well, we did it, didn't we?"

"Got rid of the Communists? Yes we did."

"And the Jews. Don't forget that."

"The Jews?"

Adolf gave Hans an incredulous look. "Don't tell me you didn't know those people were Jews."

"What people?"

"Ebert, Scheidemann, Liebknecht, Rosa Luxemburg, Eisner, Levine. All of them are Jews."

"I didn't know that." Hans went on quickly. "So how are things working out in that new assignment of yours? What was it again? Press and News Bureau?"

"Wonderful! In fact, I have already changed jobs again."

"So soon?"

"Yes. I told you about the 'political instruction' the army's doing now to get the soldiers properly oriented." When Hans nodded he rushed on. "Well, in one of those classes, the teacher said something about not all Jews being bad—that some did good. I was so incensed at such muddled thinking that I stood up and set the record straight." There was a wolfish grin. "Two days later I was called in by my commanding officer. I thought I was in trouble. But he was so impressed with what I'd done that he made me a *Bildungsoffizier* and assigned me to a new regiment."

"A what?"

"An educational officer. Our main task is to combat the dangerous ideas of socialism, pacifism, and democracy." He clenched his fist and thumped the desk. "Remember how I told you that it is my strong belief that the way to change the world is to go into politics?"

"I do."

"Well, what is one of the most important prerequisites of a politician?" He didn't wait for an answer. "His oratorical skills. How can you influence people without speaking to them? The spoken word is much more powerful than the written word. But after I was gassed near the end of the war, I was afraid that my throat had been permanently damaged and that I would never be an effective speaker. But I was wrong. In teaching these classes, I have discovered myself to be an excellent orator, with sufficient energy to make myself heard even in large rooms."

Trying not to smile at Hitler's high opinion of himself, Hans nodded. "Wonderful, Adolf."

"I know. I am immensely pleased with myself." Then he abruptly changed the subject. "I must go. I have a class. And you are late too. But there is one more piece of good news."

"What is that?"

"In my new position I have some influence in the army now. So I looked into your situation."

Startled, Hans leaned forward. "What situation?"

"About the shameless way they handled your severance pay."

"What? You talked to them about that?"

He grinned that grin that was meant to be a smile. "I pointed out to the army that the money the government had saved by not paying men their severance pay had been spent paying *Freikorps* men to save them from their own mess. So why not pay you your severance and keep you in the army where you are now?"

"But I'm not in the army now. I quit today. They'll never pay me that."

"Ha!" Adolf cried, jumping to his feet and whipping an envelope from his pocket. He slapped it on the desk in front of Hans. When Hans just stared, he barked, "Open it!"

Hans got the letter opener and slit open the envelope. There was one sheet folded in thirds, some kind of an official form. As he unfolded it, another smaller paper fell out. Hans glanced at it and then jerked forward. He snatched it up and gaped at it.

It was a check from the Ministry of War, made out to Hans Otto Eckhardt for three thousand marks.

"But . . ." Hans was speechless.

Hitler laughed. "You were in the army on the day they wrote the check, weren't you?"

4:39 p.m. — Oberammergau Railway Station, Bavaria

Hans was barely off the train before he heard a shout, saw a blur of movement out of the corner of his eye and dropped his duffel bag just in time to catch Emilee as she hurled herself into his arms. She grabbed his head with both hands and pulled him down for a very long and hard kiss.

When she finally let him go and stepped back, she was a little breathless, and so was he. He gave her a perplexed look. "Excuse me, Frau, but do I know you?"

She slugged him hard and went up and kissed him again. This time he fully cooperated.

As they stood there, clinging to each other, a man in *Lederhosen* slapped Hans on the back. "Good job in Munich, soldier," he said. Others were smiling at him as they passed. By now he wasn't too surprised. At the Munich train station he had been overwhelmed by the number of people who had stopped him. It was quite heartwarming, actually.

Slipping one arm around Emilee, Hans picked up his duffel bag, and they moved out of the way of the other disembarking passengers. Hans looked around. "Where's everyone else?"

Emilee laughed softly, blushing slightly as she did so. "You know your father. Your mother wanted to have a big dinner at the farm, but he said no, a day like today deserves something special. So they're all waiting at the Bright Star Restaurant."

He squeezed her. "Good. I'm glad we're alone. I have some wonderful news to tell you."

"Oh? And I have—"

Hans reached inside his tunic and withdrew the check. He held it up in front of Emilee's face. She reared back for a moment and then turned and stared at him. "Is that what I think it is?"

"Yes. I got my severance pay."

"But how?"

"It's a long story. I'll tell you at the restaurant."

"That's wonderful, Hans. I'm stunned, actually." Then she sobered. "I think we need to pay off that loan your father gave us."

"I knew you would say that." He kissed her again. "I already decided the same thing. But could we wait until tomorrow? Enjoy having almost six thousand marks in the bank for a few hours?"

Emilee laughed merrily, feeling almost as giddy as Hans did. "That's really wonderful, Hans. I mean that. This is great news."

"I know. I can still scarcely believe it."

She took his hand and squeezed it. "Hans?"

"Yes, dear?"

He nodded as a woman thanked him as she walked by.

She jerked on his hand. "Hans!"

He finally looked at her. "What?"

She guided his hand down to rest on her belly. "I have some good news for you, too."

Chapter Notes

As is often the case in times of chaos, estimated figures of casualties in the 1919 Munich Uprising vary from source to source. Most agree that over a thousand of the revolutionaries were killed. Often that was by extremist *Freikorps* units that took their captives out and had them summarily shot. I couldn't find figures of the government losses, so the numbers here are an estimate. The same is true of the civilian deaths.

Shirer tells us that somewhere in the spring or summer of 1919, Hitler spoke up when one of the teachers in his "political course" spoke positively of the Jews. His anti-Semitic diatribe brought him to the attention of authorities and led to his promotion (see *Rise and Fall*, 35).

Hitler's anti-Semitism was pretty virulent by this point in his life. He did believe that all or most of the political leaders were Jewish. While that is not completely true, a surprising number were. Part of this can be accounted for by the great emphasis that Jewish families, then and now, give to education. Because of that, there were many prominent people in Germany in the fields of finance, commerce, manufacturing, education, and government who were of Jewish descent.

CHAPTER
57

June 2, 1919, 3:45 p.m.—EDW Ranch, Monticello,
San Juan County, Utah

M itch?"

"I'm in here. In the tack room." Edie started toward it. The tack room occupied the northwest corner of the barn. When she reached the door, she saw Mitch bent over a saddle, which was on a sawhorse. He had on a leather apron and held a can of neatsfoot oil in one hand and a large oily rag in the other. The saddle, one of her old ones, was glistening as though it were wet. Then Edie gave a low cry. On the other side of the saddle, each twin held a smaller rag and was also rubbing down the saddle. "Mitch!"

"What?"

"They'll have oil all over their clothes."

Abby immediately protested. "Uh-uh, Mama. I be careful."

Benji just looked up and grinned. The front of his shirt already had dark splotches on it.

Mitch frowned and growled at his son. "Uh-oh. *Vati* is in *grossen* trouble."

Benji clapped a hand over his mouth and started to giggle. .

"No, Benji, *Vati* is not in big trouble," Edie sighed. "He's just going to sleep in the barn tonight." She gave Benji an affectionate swat on the bottom. "You two go on up to the house. Change your shirt, Benji. Daddy and I will be up in a minute."

She waited until they raced away and then reached in her apron pocket and pulled out a letter, waving it in front of his face. "This just came in the mail."

Mitch shook his head. "My hands are a mess. Take it inside, and I'll come in when I'm done."

"Whatever you say." She put it back in her apron.

Something in the way she said it made Mitch peer more closely at her. "Who's it from?"

"Never mind," she sniffed. "No big hurry."

He wiped his oily hands on his leather apron and then held one out to her. "All right. Who is it from? You look like the cat who just swallowed the canary."

"It's from Salt Lake City."

He stiffened. "Box B?" He started wiping his hands on his apron more earnestly. Box B almost always meant it was a mission call.

Another sweet smile. "Oh, no. Nothing like that."

"Then who?"

"The return address is 47 East South Temple Street. Isn't that the First Presidency's office?"

Mitch's eyes widened. He took a step closer, still holding out his hand. "Let me see it."

Edie held it away from him. "You can't touch it," she said. "You'll ruin it."

"Then you open it."

"That's more like it," she said. She slowly and deliberately tore off one end and extracted two sheets of paper. Laying the envelope on another sawhorse, she unfolded the letter and turned so she caught the light from the south window. "Oh," she said in surprise.

"*Edie!* Don't you read it first!"

"It's not signed by the First Presidency, Mitch. It's from Brother

LeRoy Mangelsen, the one who called you before." She spread it out on the sawhorse. "Here. Now we can read it together." Mitch moved over beside Edie, where he could read it with her.

> 47 E. South Temple Street
> Salt Lake City, UT
> May 29, 1919
>
> Dear Brother Westland,
> Greetings. I hope this letter finds all well with you and your family. The First Presidency has asked that I convey their best wishes to you as well.
> I am writing this letter at the request of the First Presidency concerning the "special project" the Church is undertaking in behalf of the suffering Saints in Germany.

Mitch nudged Edie. "I told you it wasn't going to be a mission call." She nodded. "And thank heavens for that." They continued reading.

> For several years now, The Church of Jesus Christ of Latter-day Saints has encouraged its members here in America to reach out and bless their fellow brothers and sisters in war-torn Europe. The First Presidency and Quorum of the Twelve are deeply gratified with the response that has come in answer to this request.
> However, our members in Europe, particularly in Germany, are still in desperate circumstances. Therefore the Church is undertaking a special initiative to assist these members in every way possible. Through the office of Senator Reed Smoot, we have learned that there are large quantities of surplus US government commodities that were sent over to support our troops during the war but never used. These are mostly food commodities, but there is some clothing and fuel. All of this is sitting in rail cars in France and Germany.
> Working through Senator Smoot's office, the Church is

petitioning President Woodrow Wilson for permission to buy many if not all of those commodities and distribute them among our needy members in Europe.

Mitch and Edie stopped and looked at each other in wonder but then continued.

We are hopeful that our negotiations will be successful. In the meantime, the First Presidency has asked Senator Smoot to petition the Swiss and German governments to grant Angus J. Cannon, president of the Swiss-German Mission, permission to enter Germany as soon as possible. His purpose will be to visit as many branches and districts of the Church as possible to ascertain firsthand how the Saints are doing, what their most critical needs are, and how we can best assist them.

Senator Smoot will also be asking those governments to grant visas to you and Brother Jacob Reissner so that you can travel with him on that assignment.

"Oh my word," Edie breathed.

Mitch didn't read quite as fast as she did and hadn't gotten that far yet. When he did, he gasped aloud. "So that's it!"

Staring at him with eyes wide, Edie just shook her head in disbelief.

As you might imagine, this is a delicate situation for the Church and the US government. Though your trip is being sponsored by the Church, you will not be official representatives of the Church. You will be going as "Special Humanitarian Emissaries" of our government. You are formally being sent by Washington to negotiate the purchase of US Army commodities in Europe for distribution to Church members in Germany. This distinction is important. Our hope is that the German government will make an exception because we are bringing help to their people. Therefore, while on this assignment, you will be strictly prohibited from doing any proselyting. This is why you did not receive a letter from the First Presidency making this an official Church calling. It is an assignment created to facilitate cooperation between the Church and the US government.

You and Brother Reissner have been chosen for this assignment because you both have high proficiency in the German language; you are both married men with families, which would be expected of emissaries of our government; and you both have German stock in your ancestry. Our hope is that these qualities will convince the German government that you are qualified emissaries on a humanitarian mission.

Our plan is to have you depart from Salt Lake City no later than June 20th. You should plan on being gone for as long as six months. All travel costs will be covered by the Church, but you should bring sufficient funds to cover your personal needs.

You and your wife, along with the Reissners, are invited to an orientation and training meeting on Monday, June 17th, beginning at 9:00 a.m. in the Church Administration Building at the address above.

Please know that you go with our hope and prayers, especially the prayers of our brothers and sisters in Germany. God bless you in this significant and sacred effort.

Sincerely,

LeRoy W. Mangelsen

Edie and Mitch stared at each other for a long moment and then read the letter again, very slowly. When they finished, Edie folded it up and returned it to its envelope. Then she looked up at her husband, her eyes swimming. But she was smiling through the tears. "Are you all right?" she asked.

"I'm . . . Yes. I'm stunned, of course, but yes. I'm thrilled. What an opportunity."

"To take trainloads of food to those people? That will be a miracle."

"And what about you? Are *you* all right?"

"I'm wonderful, Mitch. Absolutely wonderful."

Chapter Notes

Both Scharffs and Anderson talk briefly about the efforts of the Church to purchase surplus supplies from the US government. I could not find much detail of how these negotiations were actually carried out. It is known is that Reed Smoot, who was a member of the Quorum of the Twelve when he was elected to the Senate in 1903, played an instrumental role in negotiating the purchase of war surplus commodities from the US government. We also know that he used his influence from time to time to get visas for our mission presidents and missionaries.

Having worked in the Church Office Building for twenty-five years, I know that when the First Presidency or the Twelve initiate a major project, a large number of resources are marshaled to make it actually happen. These often include paid staff and volunteers in addition to General Authorities.

President Cannon did seek permission to travel through Germany to assess the condition of the Saints. The idea of "Special Humanitarian Emissaries" recruited by a paid staff member in the Office of the First Presidency is, however, my own fictional creation.

CHAPTER
58

June 21, 1919, 5:00 p.m. — Church Administration Building,
South Temple Street, Salt Lake City, Utah

The room was small, hardly qualifying as a conference room, though that was what it said on the door. There were only five people present: Mitch and Edie Westland, Jacob and Adelia Reissner, and Brother LeRoy W. Mangelsen.

As Elder Reissner concluded the opening prayer and sat down by his wife, Brother Mangelsen got slowly to his feet and came to the front. For a long moment he stood there, his eyes searching theirs, and then he began to speak. His voice was soft, and he spoke slowly and thoughtfully.

"Brothers and sisters, before I formally begin, let me just say that I checked in at the office after our last session, and there has still been no word from Germany on visas, and no word from our government, either. So we still don't know when you'll be leaving."

He took a quick breath. "Okay, with that said, let us proceed. We have now come to the end of our training experience together. Thank you so much for making time to be here. I hope it has been significant enough to warrant the time it has taken you away from your families."

Edie tentatively raised a hand. He nodded at her. "Yes, Sister Westland?"

"I just wanted to thank you and the First Presidency for letting me and Adelia—Sister Reissner—be here with our husbands for this experience." She had to swallow quickly before she could go on. "In the weeks and months to come, while my husband is away, it will mean so much to me and my family to have such of clear picture of what they will be doing, and, more importantly, *why* they will be doing it. I have already asked Mitch—Brother Westland—if he will share that vision with our children, if that is permissible."

"Yes," Adelia exclaimed. "Edie speaks for us as well."

Brother Mangelsen smiled, seemingly pleased. "That was our hope, Sister Westland, and yes, you have our permission to share in this experience, except those few things that are confidential."

He reached down and picked up a white notepad. He glanced at it for a moment and then looked up at them. "I am very pleased to announce that in a few minutes, President Charles W. Penrose, Second Counselor in the First Presidency, will be joining us."

All four of them exchanged surprised but pleased looks. *A member of the First Presidency?* Edie thought. *Wow! What will the kids think about that?*

"He will set Brothers Reissner and Westland apart to their assignment and give them both an apostolic blessing." He looked to the two women. "And if you would like, he has offered to give you sisters an apostolic blessing as well."

Adelia and Edie exchanged looks and then reached out and clasped each other's hand for a moment. "I would like that very much," Adelia said.

"Yes," Edie whispered, reeling a little at the thought.

"In the meantime, until he arrives, I would like to give a little context to what you two brethren are about to undertake."

He lifted the pad and began to read.

"In July of 1837, two ordained apostles, Heber C. Kimball and Orson Hyde, along with some other brethren, stepped off a ship in

Liverpool, England, and immediately traveled to Preston, England. By coincidence, the day they arrived in Preston happened to be a parliamentary election day. The first thing they saw as they got down from the stagecoach was a large election banner that contained three simple words: 'Truth Will Prevail.' Heber later wrote in his journal of that moment and said: 'We looked at each other and said with one voice: "Amen and amen."'"

Mangelsen looked up. "In hindsight, it is evident that those words describe the incredibly successful work that followed in England, but also throughout the rest of Europe. Indeed, it could be said that it is a motto that describes the work of the Church. Truth *will* prevail!"

Brother Mangelsen went on. "Up until 1900, almost 92,000 converts from Europe heeded the call to gather to Zion. Thereafter, even though the Church began to encourage them to stay in their homelands, thousands more have come to America."

Brother Mangelsen lowered his notepad. "Think of that for a moment. How many people do you know personally who are first-generation immigrants from Europe?"

Edie was already doing just that. Both of Mitch's parents came from England. Edie's own Oma and Opa Zimmer had come from Germany. She thought of many others of their neighbors and friends who had come from Denmark, Ireland, Wales, and elsewhere.

She stopped as she saw Brother Mangelsen smiling at them. He had been watching them count the people up in their heads. "As one of the Brethren once said," he chuckled, "you can't hardly bump into a tree in Utah without knocking out half a dozen European-born relatives.'"

They laughed. "That's certainly true down in San Juan County," Mitch said.

Brother Mangelsen raised the notepad again. "Now, let's focus on Germany for a moment. The first apostle to visit Germany was Orson

Hyde, who stayed there for ten months while on his way to the Holy Land. That was in 1841, six years before the Saints came to Utah.

"Ten years later, Elder John Taylor arrived in Hamburg and directed a translation of the Book of Mormon into German. The first mission president in Germany was Daniel Carn, who arrived that same year." He smiled. "He set a precedent for other missionaries when he spent time in prison for preaching the gospel.

"By 1906, the Church in Germany had grown to the point that they received their first visit from a President of the Church, President Joseph F. Smith. Since 1900, Germany has been one of the top ten countries in the world for baptisms and number of members."

"Really?" Adelia turned red as she realized she had blurted that out loud.

"Yes, really. At the turn of the century, there were sixteen hundred members in Germany. Now there are an estimated eight thousand!" He laughed at their expressions. "Yes. *Eight thousand!* And that doesn't count the more than six thousand who have emigrated to America since the work there began. And. . . ." He was obviously enjoying himself. "Are you ready for this? If current trends continue, in about eighteen months from now, Germany will not only be the number-one baptizing mission in the world, but it will have more members than anywhere but Utah.

"But those are not just cold, hard facts," he went on. "As President Valentine told you at your reunion, with few exceptions, their faith is strong and their testimonies are unshakeable." He leaned forward, his fists on the table, totally in earnest. "We know that their faith actually increased during the war years. We have a report from a branch president there that most of his members fasted on fast Sunday and gave what they saved to the poor. Can you believe that? In the midst of starvation, they fasted and gave to the poor." He smiled ruefully. "So, how did the branch president decide who to give the food and money to? Everyone in the branch is poor!"

Brother Mangelsen let his eyes move from one face to the other. "How I envy you the experiences you are going to have, brethren. You two, along with President Cannon, will make history. But remember, you are but an instrument in the hands of the Lord. I feel impressed to promise you that if you are faithful, you are going to come away from this experience much more blessed than the people you go to serve." He looked like he was going to say something more but then just shook his head. "And I say that in the name of Jesus Christ. Amen."

As the group murmured their amens, Mangelsen looked at his watch again. "President Penrose should be here any moment. "Sister Westland, would you close with prayer for us?"

Edie wiped quickly at the tears that were streaming down her cheeks. "Oh, Brother Mangelsen," she cried. "That's not fair. I'm not sure I can right now."

He smiled. "I know, but I'm not sure any of us can, either, so do your best."

6:10 p.m.—Temple Square, Salt Lake City, Utah

Mitch held Edie's hand as they strolled along the walkway between the Assembly Hall and the Tabernacle. Several flowering bushes were in bloom, and the flower beds were filled with geraniums, petunias, and a rainbow of other flowers. In the warmth of the summer evening, their aroma filled the air. Mitch and Edie were headed east, moving back toward the Hotel Utah. Mitch was unusually quiet, but Edie sensed that he wasn't looking for conversation at the moment. And she wasn't sure she was, either. It had been an incredible day with an amazing end to it. So she was content to just hold his hand and walk quietly with him.

As they came toward Seagull Monument, Mitch suddenly pointed. There was no one there at the moment. "Want to sit for a while?" he asked.

She nodded.

"If you're hungry, we can head for the hotel and find the Reissners and eat with them."

"In a while. It's such a nice evening, and it's quiet."

They sat down on the rim of the fountain, and she scooted closer until their shoulders were touching. Still Mitch said nothing, and Edie could tell that he was frustrated. So she moved in even closer and took his hand. "Mitch, I know that it seems like this is never going to happen, and for a man who hates having things left undone, that's pretty annoying."

"Annoying doesn't begin to express it," he muttered.

"But six weeks, Mitch. All of this has come about in just six weeks. That's amazing. Now, I understand that in Mitch Westland time, that's about six months. But remember, this isn't like waiting for a calf to be born or for some bull elk to walk into the clearing so you can shoot him. You're waiting for two national governments to act."

"I know, I know."

"And President Penrose said that they're expecting approval of your names any time now."

"I know, Edie," Mitch said, with a touch of petulance. "But what if it's another two months, and then another? I'll go crazy."

"Then I'll just have to lock you in the barn. Tell everybody you've gone looney on me."

"Looney?" He grabbed at her, but she was too quick for him.

Laughing, she danced away from him. He got to his feet, his hands coming up into claws, as they did when he was playing monster with the twins.

"No, Mitch!" Squealing with laughter, Edie whirled to dart away and ran squarely into Jacob Reissner, nearly knocking him down.

"Whoa!" he cried, jumping back.

Edie gasped and went instantly beet red. She saw that Mitch was blushing too.

Jacob managed a smile. "Having a little argument about who gets to throw the pennies in the fountain, are we?" he asked sardonically.

"Uh. . . ." Mitch grinned. "Actually, we were just talking about seeing if you two have had dinner yet."

"Yes, I could see that," he said with a teasing grin.

Adelia stepped up. "No, we haven't. That's why we came looking for you."

"Good," Edie said. "Let's do it. This husband of mine gets grumpy when he's not fed regularly."

But as they headed for the south gate of Temple Square, they stopped. Just coming through the gate in full stride was Brother Mangelsen. He waved and broke into a trot.

"Good news," he said as he came up to them. "The First Presidency has just received word from President Cannon in Switzerland. He now has your visas to enter Germany."

Mitch gave a whoop that turned people's heads from clear across Temple Square. Reissner did a momentary little jig and then asked, "So how soon can we leave?"

"The visas are good for two months of travel anywhere in Germany starting. . . ." He stopped, and the smile returned as he let the silence stretch out.

Mitch shot him a dirty look. "Do you want to go into that fountain and dive for pennies?" he bellowed. "Tell me."

Edie was horrified. Even Brother Mangelsen was a bit shocked. "Starting July first."

In one quick movement, Mitch whirled and swung Edie off her feet. "Did you hear that, Edie? Did you hear that?"

"I did," she said, laughing at his excitement. You would have thought he had just singlehandedly won the World Series.

"And what does that mean for us?" Reissner asked next.

"That's the other good news. The First Presidency cabled Senator Smoot with that information. They just heard back. Now that

President Cannon has Germany's approval, our government has officially approved your departure as soon as you can be ready. The First Presidency wants you there before the first so that President Cannon is not delayed further."

Mitch could barely speak. "Really?" he said over and over. "Really?"

"Yes, really," Mangelsen said. "The question is, how long will it take you and Sister Westland to go back to Monticello and get you packed, Brother Westland?"

Edie laughed, though she was suddenly very close to tears. "He's been packed since the reunion." She turned to him. "If we hurry, we could catch the eight o'clock train to Thompson Springs tonight. That would put us home tomorrow afternoon. That will give you a chance to say goodbye to the children and the ward, and . . ." She had to catch herself. "Then you could be back up to Thompson Springs first thing Thursday."

Mitch was nodding, sobered now by the reality of it all. He turned to Mangelsen. "And I could be back here on Friday."

"Wonderful," Mangelsen exclaimed. "You go back to the hotel and pack; I'll go purchase your tickets.

Reissner took his wife's hand. "I think we'd better head home now too." He looked at Edie. "We'll have to postpone that dinner until we get back, I guess."

Edie managed a smile as she went over and gave Adelia a hug. "And I was hoping we'd have time for a good cry together."

June 29, 1919, 7:05 p.m.—Railway station, Basel, Switzerland

Mitch watched with dismay as the train platform gradually emptied and they were left alone. Reissner, also looking a little discouraged, picked up his bags. "Let's go into the main station. If he got delayed, he'll come in there first."

"*Das ist gut,*" Mitch replied, reaching down for his own bag. "We've been on that train so long, I feel like my legs are sticks of wood."

"*Ja*. It feels good to move around."

"Have you been here before?"

"In Basel? Or the train station?"

"Both."

"Yes. Munich is only about a four-hour train ride from here, so when I was district president there, I would come down from time to time for meetings with President Valentine."

"And you brought your elders out through Switzerland in 1914?"

"That's right. The president was up north with Elder Hyrum Smith, but we didn't dare go north. It meant crossing all—"

"Brother Reissner!"

The shout brought them both around with a jerk. An older man in a business suit was hurrying across the large hall, waving one arm. Reissner waved back, and then to Mitch he said, "I think we are about to meet President Cannon."

Chapter Notes

The Heber C. Kimball quote cited here is found in *Truth Shall Prevail*, xvii.

The stats on emigration from Germany come from *Mormonism in Germany*, 68.

As noted in chapter 57, the assignment of Jacob Reissner and Mitchell Westland, both of whom are fictional characters, is not based on specific historical information. However, President Cannon did obtain permission from the German government to travel throughout the country to assess the members' conditions and needs. There is a slight discrepancy in the accounts of when this travel occurred. However, since we do know that President Cannon sent a wire to the First Presidency on September 2, 1919, with a report on the situation and an urgent request for help, it is likely that he left early in July.

CHAPTER 59

August 30, 1919, 3:35 p.m.—EDW Ranch, Monticello, San Juan County, Utah

Mitch Jr. took off his rain slicker and hat under the overhang of the front porch, shook them off, and came inside the house. Edie, who had stood at the window and watched as he put his horse in the barn, went into the entryway and waited as he hung his things up on the hooks there. "Looks like a real gully buster out there," she said.

He nodded. "And no sign of letting up, either. Those dry washes are dangerous."

"Where's Frank?"

"He and the Adams boys are up on North Cottonwood Creek somewhere."

"The lightning could be real bad today." Edie tried to keep the worry out of her voice.

"Frank knows that. And he knows to stay out of the washes. He'll be all right, Mama."

She sighed but said nothing. To her surprise, her son came over and took her in his arms. "Frank's a good boy, Mom. Since Dad's left, he's really stepped up."

She looked up at him. "Have you told him that?"

"Yes. Before they took the herd up there." He touched her cheek. "He'll be sixteen in February. Dad was riding up on Elk Mountain with Kumen Jones and Lem Redd and facing down Moenkopi Mike by the time he was sixteen."

"I know, but. . . ." Finally, Edie shrugged. "I've got some hot cocoa on the stove."

"Sounds good. Where's June?"

"Up at the house with the twins and your kids. They're making cookies."

Mitch Jr. sat down while she got two cups, filled them with the steaming hot chocolate, and sat down with him. They sipped it quietly for a time. She studied her oldest son as he stared into his cup. Though people said he looked like her, she couldn't see it. . He was so much like his father in temperament that she had to laugh at times. "Do you wish it was you?" she asked softly.

His head came up. "What?"

"In Germany?"

He took another sip and sat back. "Yes and no. I'd love to get to Germany sometime. And what Dad's doing right now is incredibly exciting. Even more than missionary work, in my opinion. But to be gone for years at a time when your family is so young? I don't know how you did it."

"And Dad was gone for only a year," she said. "Some of those early missionaries used to be gone three or four or even five years."

"I was glad I went to England during the war and had a chance to use my German. But—"

They turned as the back door slammed. "Tina? Is that you?" Edie called.

A moment later, her daughter burst into the room, her coat dripping water and her hair soaking wet. Edie shook her head. "I told you it was going to rain. Why didn't you at least take your hat?"

Tina ignored that, unbuttoning her coat and tossing it over a chair.

Then she held up a package wrapped in brown paper and tied with twine. "Look, Mama. It's a package from Daddy." Edie jumped to her feet and took it from her. There were a few spots of water on the paper, but that was all. "Thank you for keeping it dry, Tina. Get a towel and dry your hair."

"Open it, Mama."

She looked at the postmark. "It's dated almost three weeks ago." She carefully unwrapped the paper. "It feels like a book of some kind."

"Hurry, Mama," Tina urged.

Mitch Jr. took out his knife and cut the string, As Edie pulled the paper away, a small card fell out. She picked it up and read it aloud.

15 Aug 1919

Dearest Edie and family,

Sorry I haven't written more. Government still censoring mail, blacking out anything that suggests conditions here are not ideal. Sending this to Switzerland with a member who promises to send it on to you. This says it all. Deeply moving, deeply troubling, deeply inspiring experience. Will try to call when we reach Basel again, hopefully around September 1. All my love, Dad.

As Edie set the card down and picked up the book, Tina gave a little squeal of amazement. "Oh, Mama, it's Daddy's journal."

7:45 p.m

That night, with every member of the family present except Mitch himself, of course, and Frank, who was tending cattle in the wilderness, the Westland family gathered in the living room of the EDW Ranch house. And there, Mitchell Arthur Westland Jr. read the journal that had arrived earlier in the day. At Edie's request, this was to be done without interruption. After that, it would be open for questions and discussion.

JOURNAL OF
MITCHELL ARTHUR WESTLAND. 1919

July 3, 1919. Basel. I arrived in Basel, Switzerland, after a seven-day ocean voyage from New York City to Marseilles, France, and an eleven-hour train ride from Marseilles to Basel. I am in company with Jacob K. Reissner. We have come at the request of the Church and as official emissaries of the US government to assess the needs and the circumstances facing members of The Church of Jesus Christ of Latter-day Saints in Germany.

Prior to our departure, we were told that we had pre-approved visas issued by the German government, which would allow us to travel immediately into Germany with Angus J. Cannon, president of the Swiss-German Mission. However, our visas will not be ready until tomorrow. Because of the urgency of our task, President Cannon left yesterday for Hamburg. We will catch up with him as soon as possible.

July 5. Hamburg. Arrived late last night in Hamburg. Great news on our arrival. President Cannon has been in meetings with US Army personnel. Judge Parker, US Liquidation Commissioner, knows of our mission and has been fully cooperative. The best news is that the army is already moving trainloads of commodities from France to Koblenz, which is near Cologne. This will greatly facilitate the distribution of those commodities once final negotiations are completed.

July 7. Hamburg. Meetings with the Hamburg District. Attendance was astounding considering the distances some traveled and the meagerness of their resources. Some walked for two or three hours. A spirit of jubilation and thanksgiving prevailed. The members were ecstatic to know that Salt Lake City has not forgotten them. We met with several families I knew while laboring here before. NOTE TO EDIE: Your suspicions that I was born without any emotions are now proven false. I have shed many tears already.

Tonight we blocked out a tentative schedule for the rest of the trip. The plan is to visit as many districts as possible. Smaller branches will be visited as time and conditions permit.

July 11. Hannover. We continue to be humbled and amazed at the remarkable faith of our Saints here. In some cases the numbers attending require us to secure larger halls. Our format is simple. Jacob and I speak briefly, and then President Cannon takes the rest of the meeting. He is continually filled with the Spirit, and all are edified. Before and after meetings, he meets with the district and branch presidents and interviews them about their needs and the conditions their members are facing. Jacob and I visit with individual members and families, and where possible we visit them in their homes.

This has been a very humbling experience. And most gratifying. While the people's faces are gaunt and their bodies ravaged by years of food shortages, their spirits burn as brightly as the sun. And their faith in their Savior is unshakable. Reissner and I were able to purchase two loaves of bread from a bakery before visiting one family—a war widow and her four children. When we broke the bread into equal portions and gave it to the children, the oldest boy, who is thirteen, quietly broke his portion into four parts and gave three of them to his younger brothers and sister. I wept at such a tender act of pure love.

July 13. Berlin. We are deeply sobered by signs of the violence and revolution that wracked this great city up until just a few months ago. Many buildings are boarded up. Rubble still blocks some streets. Wilted wreaths mark sites where citizens or soldiers were killed. And still a heavy pall of fear hangs over the city. There is great concern that the bloody struggles with the Communists and Bolsheviks are not over yet.

It is just over two weeks ago now that Germany was forced to sign the Treaty of Versailles, and now the whole nation is in shock. The Allied Forces have set very harsh terms in the treaty in order to punish Germany for their part in the Great War. There is a strong belief here that the Allies are deliberately trying to crush the German spirit and make the nation so weak that they can never again be a threat to Europe.

I am only reporting the feelings we are hearing here in Germany. I'm sure if we were in France or England, we would be hearing a very different story. Yet the reports are that there is much prejudice and anger toward Germany throughout Europe and that they are determined to make Germany pay and to have their pound of flesh, as Shakespeare put it.

According to the members here, the treaty conditions are so harsh, and the way they have been treated as a nation is so humiliating, that a sense of deep outrage is rapidly becoming a festering sore that has to be lanced or it will burst. The German people are a proud people with a strong heritage. In the last fifty years, they have led Europe in many ways with their cultural, scientific, and industrial accomplishments. But basically, the Allies gave Germany two options: sign the treaty or be invaded and destroyed completely. And so they signed.

Local priesthood leaders express two grave concerns. First, under the terms of the treaty, Germany has been forced to give up vast tracts of land. Some of these areas are rich in resources or manufacturing and are critical to Germany's economy. These leaders fear that this, along with the war reparations set by the treaty, will make it impossible for Germany's economy to ever recover. For a people already teetering on the edge of total economic collapse, that is a great concern to them.

Their second and even greater concern is that this growing sense of disillusionment with the government, whom they blame for the whole mess, has already started to encourage the left-wing factions here to regroup and try again. This may lead to a resurgence of the revolutionary chaos that nearly tore Germany apart in the last eight or nine months. They believe that without a strong Germany, Russia and the Eastern Communist bloc countries will spread their influence westward until it engulfs all of Western Europe. That would be a disaster of unthinkable proportions, for the light of freedom in Western Europe would be extinguished. This has enormous implications for us as a church and for our members here.

I'm sorry to have included such a tedious and depressing report on the current political climate here, but these are the forces that are currently shaping Germany's destiny.

July 16. Dresden It is a huge relief to be out of Berlin. It is a beautiful city and the Church is strong there, but the atmosphere there weighed us down even more than we thought.

The German people are amazing. Here in Dresden, when the members learned of our coming, word spread throughout the city, and many non-members joined our meetings. When we arrived at the meeting place, dozens of children were lined up to greet us. They had fresh flowers for us and sang songs.

The spirit here is one of hope, in spite of the challenges mentioned above. There is a great sense of self-reliance among our members. Many of our families have planted small gardens and are growing fresh vegetables, which is a huge blessing. Children in small villages scour the forests for mushrooms and other edible plants. I have learned that dandelion greens provide an edible supplement to a salad. At first I found them quite bitter, but now I think I am acquiring a taste for them. (Tell Frank that I may take over dealing with those pesky dandelions in our lawn when I return.)

It is astonishing how frequently we are invited to eat with the Saints, though their meals are often not even sufficient to meet their own needs. We would refuse, but they are so honored to have us in their homes that we cannot do it. They ply us with food even when there is so little on their tables and even when we protest that we have had enough.

July 23. Mannheim. I am losing weight. In the train station I found a scale—the first that I have seen. I have lost about seventeen pounds since leaving Monticello. I had to cut a new hole in my belt to hold my trousers up. This may cause you dismay, but I am actually quite happy. First of all, as our Abby has so frequently said, "Daddy, you're fat." But secondly, and much more important to me, ever since my arrival I've had this faint sense of guilt. I see these people who are so thin and so gaunt, and I'm an American version of Santa Claus. I am still nowhere near where they are, but I know now more what they are suffering.

We often go without meals, either because we are on the road or because the meals we take with the Saints are so meager. I actually accompanied one of our families a few days ago to stand in line for the distribution of food from the city government. We stood in line for over three hours and got only a few potatoes, two very thin slices of bacon—the first meat the family had seen in three weeks—two pounds of rice, and one cup of milk. This was for a family of four. So I am happy that I am sacrificing with them to some extent. How blessed we are in America, and especially in our red rock country, to have food on our table in abundance each day.

It was not far from Mannheim that Edie's grandmother and grandfather, Franz and Renate Zimmer, lived before meeting the missionaries and coming to America. When I saw that we were coming here, I had hoped to get time enough to go to the little village where they lived, but that did not materialize. We have a full schedule of meetings and appointments, and then we leave for Nuremberg by train this afternoon. Sorry, Oma Zimmer. When our family comes back, we shall return here. Down four more pounds!

August 9. Nuremberg. Word of our coming has spread, and our reception grows even warmer and more welcoming as we continue. Nuremberg has been especially hospitable, and we have stayed here for nearly three weeks, using this as our base as we go out and visit with people. Every day is filled with touching, humbling, heartbreaking, joyful, wonderful experiences, but there is little time to write of them. We leave early each morning and fall into bed late each night. We are now six weeks into our tour.

Brother Reissner is very excited, as Munich is where he served over a year of his mission. President Cannon has given us permission to stay in Munich while he goes on to Basel and writes up a report for Salt Lake City and gets further instruction from them.

There is a member here in Nuremberg who is a banker. He is traveling to Zurich in a few days on business and has offered to take this journal and mail it from there. So this is my last entry. I will buy another journal as soon as possible and continue recording my feelings.

I have written often here of the faith demonstrated by our Church members during the war. It has been truly inspiring. However, recently in some of the branches we visited, we discovered a slight problem that reminds us not all has been in perfect order during these years of isolation from Salt Lake City.

These problems do not stem from wickedness or a contrary spirit on the part of the members, but rather, I think they arose when the American missionaries had to be withdrawn and branches and districts were turned over to local leaders. Most have done remarkably well, even better than we could do. But occasionally, less experienced priesthood leaders, some of whom were new in the Church, brought with them some of the traditions and customs from their previous churches.

One branch president, whose name I will not mention here, decided that the members of his branch who were not paying a full tithing could no longer partake of the sacrament. He said that tithing was the higher law, and therefore they could not partake of the sacrament until they kept it. He also prophesied that after the war, the British would repent of their sins and go to Utah to offer sacrifices on Mt. Zion.

In another case, a branch president who had been converted only about a year before started to introduce new elaborations into the sacrament service. We were quite surprised to find lighted candles on the sacrament table, which was covered with a gilded cloth. Very expensive crystal glassware and silver plates were used for the sacrament. And they had a violinist accompany the passing of the sacrament. The branch president was mortified when President Cannon explained that our sacramental services are to be kept simple and unadorned. He promised to correct it immediately. It was a reminder to us all how important it is to have living apostles and prophets at the head of the Church to keep us from drifting off the track, even when our intentions may be good.

I close with a reaffirmation of my testimony. I know that Jesus Christ is at the head of this Church. But more important to me right now, I know that His sustaining power has blessed the faithful Saints in Germany and has lifted them up in these times of sorrow, suffering, sacrifice, and tribulation. This witness of the richness of His love is such that my testimony shall never again be the same.

Chapter Notes

One of the best sources on the impact the Treaty of Versailles had on post-war Germany is given by Shirer (see *Rise and Fall,* 57–60. See also www .historylearningsite.co.uk/treaty_of_Versailles.htm).

Examples of "doctrinal drift" that occurred during the war years were rare but did occur in a few places. The two noted here are actual examples (see *Mormons and Germany,* 53–54).

CHAPTER
60

Inga?"

Inga's eyes fluttered open and she looked around for a moment, not sure where she was. She heard footsteps coming up the stairs, and then she remembered. She was in Munich, in the flat of her sister and brother-in-law. And she had been taking a nap on Gretl's bed—Gretl having moved in with Bruno during her stay here.

"Inga? Are you awake?" There was a soft knock on the door.

"Yes. Come in. I'm awake."

Paula stepped into the room, beaming happily. "We have company."

"Oh?" Inga sat up quickly. "Are Hans and Emilee here?" She glanced at her watch. "I didn't think they were coming until five."

Paula, obviously enjoying this, shook her head. "It's not Hans. It's not Emilee."

As Inga stood up, Paula gestured toward Gretl's dressing stand with the mirror. "You may want to run a brush through your hair."

Inga stared at her for a moment. "Who is it?"

Backing out of the door, she said, "I'll wait for you downstairs. But do brush your hair."

When Inga came out of the bedroom a minute later, Paula was waiting for her at the bottom of the stairs. Again, Inga shot her a questioning look. Again, Paula just smiled and then took her sister's hand, clasped it tightly, and said, "Are you ready for a real surprise?" And without waiting for an answer, Paula opened the door and stepped into the sitting room, pulling Inga behind her.

The first thing Inga saw was Gretl and Bruno sitting on the two side chairs, and they were grinning like it was Christmas morning. Then she saw that there were two men sitting on the sofa, both dressed in business suits. On seeing her, they both stood up, and then the taller one stepped in front of the other. He was a stranger to her, older, maybe in his fifties, she guessed. He was tall, almost a foot taller than her short little frame. He had thick, dark brown hair that was just starting to grey at the temples. Dark eyebrows emphasized the wide-set blue-green eyes. His face was bronzed by the sun, and his smile was warm and pleasant. He extended his hand. "*Schwester* Eckhardt. What a delight it is to finally get to meet you." He gripped her hand firmly in both of his as he smiled down at her. "I am *Bruder* Mitch Westland."

"I . . . How do you do, Brother Westland?" She was still confused. It was as if he already knew her. "I am pleased to meet you too."

He let go of her hand and stepped aside. The second man was right behind him, and he was smiling even more broadly than the first. He was younger, around thirty she guessed, and—Suddenly Inga's jaw dropped open. "*Kirchenältester* Reissner!"

"*Guten Tag, Schwester* Eckhardt." He didn't extend his hand. Instead, he opened his arms wide. Inga was too shocked to move. Laughing, he stepped forward and swept her up in a huge bear hug. "Oh, *Schwester* Eckhardt," he murmured as he kissed her on both cheeks. "I can't tell you how wonderful it is to see you again."

When he stepped back she was still speechless, though now her eyes were filled with tears. "But . . . What are you doing here?"

"Inga," Paula said, laughing. "It's him. Just accept that."

"But they said we wouldn't get American missionaries for another year or two. How...."

He took her by the hand and led her back to the sofa. Paula followed and sat beside her sister. Mitch took the other chair and sat down. Once they were settled, Reissner gave her a brief explanation of what he and Mitch were doing there.

She started to nod. "So you're here for the meeting with President Cannon on Monday?"

"We are," Reissner said. "And I was so happy when Paula told me that you had come up for it."

Paula spoke up. "They've actually been traveling with President Cannon for the last two months, Inga. But he said they could stay here in Munich while he went to Basel, because he was coming back to speak to our branch Monday night."

"But when did you get here?"

"In Germany? Almost two months ago. Right here? About ten minutes ago." Before Inga could respond, he went on. "Actually, I tried to call you about two months ago."

"You did?"

"I did. I'm not even sure it was the right number. Brother Westland and I were coming up from Basel, and we had a three-hour layover in Munich. We decided to use that time to come and say hello to Paula and Wolfie. But when we got here, we were shocked to find the house had been abandoned and was in shambles. Hateful things were painted on the walls. I was sick to my stomach, thinking something terrible had happened to them and their family."

Inga looked to Paula. "Did you tell them what happened?"

Paula nodded.

"We asked the neighbors about you, but they didn't know. They said you all just disappeared one day. They feared the worst too."

"We didn't tell anyone where we were, in case those men came back looking for Wolfie."

"Anyway," Reissner went on, "by the time we got back to the station, our train was leaving. Knowing we were coming back, I decided I would just ask President Schindler what had happened to you. I called him when we got here, and he gave us your new address."

Inga shook her head. "I can't believe it. I just can't believe it." And then she had another thought. "Have you seen Hans yet?"

"No, but Schwester Groll tells us he's coming here for dinner. And we are invited to stay, too."

Inga reached out and laid a hand on Reissner's arm but turned to look at Mitch. "Did he tell you that he's the one who baptized me?"

"And me?" Paula said.

"And me," Gretl chimed in.

"Oh, yes," Mitch said. "He's told me about all of you. I am happy to finally get to meet you." He looked at Bruno. "Jacob told me that you were just a baby when he left. How old are you now, Bruno?"

"Five and a half. Almost."

"I've got a son who's four."

"And guess what," Reissner said. "The Westlands are considering coming to the Passion Play in twenty-one."

Inga turned quickly. "Then you shall stay in our home. We are just five miles from Oberammergau."

"That would be wonderful," he said. "I would like my family to meet you and all of your family. Several of them speak German."

"That's what Brother Reissner was just telling me," Paula said. "That's wonderful."

"Tell us about your family, Brother Westland," Inga said. "Then I shall tell you about mine."

September 7, 1919, 7:35 p.m.—Munich Branch, LDS Church, Sofallingstrasse 23, Munich

President Cannon had asked the branch president to be the first speaker, but strangely, when President Schindler got to his feet, he stood at the microphone for several moments but said nothing. Then he turned and stepped back, leaning down to talk to the president in a low voice.

Mitch and Jacob were seated on the front row along with Inga Eckhardt, Emilee Eckhardt, and Paula Groll. Both Wolfie and Hans had been invited, but both had declined. Wolfie would stay with the children. Hans was working on a truck that he was repairing. To Mitch's surprise, Emilee had said yes without hesitation.

Mitch had quickly hit it off with Hans and Emilee Eckhardt. He liked Hans's forthright and no-nonsense manner and his quick and often dry sense of humor. Emilee's quiet but pleasant nature reminded him of Edie. She was easy to like.

To everyone's surprise, President Schindler sat down beside Sister Cannon. President Cannon got up and came to the microphone. "I am afraid President Schindler is not following counsel tonight," he said with a wry smile. "He has declined to speak, saying that this is the first time I've ever stood at the pulpit, and he spoke only one week ago."

The people were smiling and nodding. Obviously, though they loved President Schindler, they had come to hear their mission president.

"Actually, I shall call on him later, as well as Brothers Reissner and Westland, but I shall take advantage of this opportunity, because I have news of some importance to share with you."

That brought a little buzz of excitement to the room. He smiled, obviously enjoying himself. "As you know, I, along with Brother Reissner and Brother Westland, have spent the last two months traveling through Germany, meeting with the Saints and feeling of their spirit. It's been a remarkable experience for the three of us, and I want you to hear from them about it as well as me." He reached in his coat pocket and brought out what looked like a couple of envelopes. "But, to be perfectly honest, I am bursting with excitement to share this news with you."

The rustling in the room had completely stopped. "As you know, our purpose in this visit through Germany is to gather information for the First Presidency about the situation and circumstances here. So after earnest prayer and careful contemplation of the last two months, I sent the following wire off to the First Presidency in Salt Lake City before we left." He removed a paper from the first envelope, unfolded it, and read in a slow clear voice:

> Office of the First Presidency
> Salt Lake City, Utah
> Brethren, the eight thousand Saints of this mission are in immediate need of flour, corn meal, condensed milk, fats, dried fruit, beans, peas. Can the Saints at home send such supplies immediately?

He stopped as the reaction went through the group like an electric shock. Then, smiling a delighted little smile, he went on. "On arriving at the station here in Munich, I received the following answer from the First Presidency. And I again quote:"

> President,
> We have arranged through the good offices of Senator Reed Smoot the purchase of US Army commodities in Europe.

He stopped, and then emphasizing every word, he went on.

> I leave the quantity of supplies to be purchased to your judgment. Church will guarantee payment.

Before he had finished those final words, men and women were up on their feet, holding their hands to their hearts and openly weeping.

President Cannon had to stop, for emotion had gotten the better of him. He took out his handkerchief and wiped at his eyes. Behind him, President Schindler's head was bowed, and his shoulders were shaking.

Gradually, people sat down again, still half in shock.

"The other thing I did while at the train station before coming here was to call the United States Army Quartermaster's Office in

Cologne. The three of us met with him and his staff some weeks ago there. When I read to him the First Presidency's cable, he said the following. I shall quote him as best I can remember. 'Mr. Cannon, thank you for your phone call. Be advised that starting tomorrow morning, your request for commodities will start processing, and shipments will follow soon after. Please ask your people to be patient, because this is a very complicated order and it will take time to fill it.'"

He put the envelopes back in his pocket and then looked up and smiled gravely. "Just how large of an order is it?" He waited until there was not a sound and then quietly said, "Fifty thousand pounds of flour. Fifteen thousand pounds of rice. Twenty thousand pounds of dried plums. Five thousand pounds of lard. And twenty thousand cans of condensed milk."

The audience gasped as one. The president swallowed quickly and said, "In addition, the First Presidency is forwarding to our mission's bank account well over two hundred thousand dollars, or about eight hundred thousand marks, which are contributions from members of the Church in America. This is to be used to buy additional foodstuffs, clothing, fuel, and other necessities as we see fit."

The sound of weeping and joy and astonishment was all around them now. President Cannon looked up, tears streaking his own face. "My dear *Brüder* and *Schwestern*, God, our beloved Heavenly Father, has heard your prayers. He has heard the cries of your children. And He has answered. Let us now take this opportunity to bow our heads and thank Him in silent prayer."

Chapter Note

On September 2, 1919, President Angus Cannon sent the cable to Salt Lake City as cited above. Later that same day, he received the reply from President Heber J. Grant as noted (see Swiss-German Mission Manuscript History, 1 December 1919, LDS Church History Library). The quantity of commodities noted here are the actual quantities purchased (see *Mormonism in Germany*, 59; *Mormons and Germany*, 80).

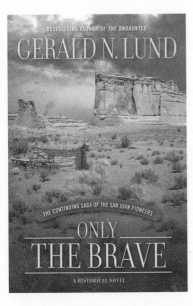